INTO THE FIRE

SUZANNE BROCKMANN

INTO THE FIRE

A NOVEL

BALLANTINE BOOKS • NEW YORK

Copyright © 2008 by Suzanne Brockmann

Published in the United States by Ballantine Books, an imprint of The Random House Publishing Group, a division of Random House, Inc., New York.

BALLANTINE and colophon are registered trademarks of Random House, Inc.

ISBN 978-0-345-50153-0

Printed in the United States of America

For Ed, my own personal dog whisperer.
Just like Gladys said—you're the best thing
that ever happened to me.

ACKNOWLEDGMENTS

Thank *you*, dear reader, for your continued support of my Troubleshooters series, of which this book is the lucky thirteenth installment. (And a heads up, gang, because we're going to try to get the fourteenth book, *Dark of Night*, into your hands early next spring. Watch my website www.SuzanneBrockmann.com for the deets about that!)

Thank you to the wonderful team at Ballantine Books—Jennifer Hershey, Courtney Moran, Kim Hovey, and Kate Blum—and to my agent, Steve Axelrod.

My first-draft readers snapped to it in a particularly short time frame for this book, and gave me some valuable feedback. Huge thanks to Lee Brockmann, Deede Bergeron, Scott Lutz, and Patricia McMahon, aka the Encyclopedia Patricica.

Thanks, as always, to the home team—Ed, Melanie and Jason Gaffney, Eric Ruben, Fred and Lee Brockmann, the amazing Kuhlmans, Apolonia Davalos, and the two greatest Schnauzer puppies in the world—C.K. Dexter-Haven and Lil' Joe. (And Mel, thank you for Aidan, a puppy of the human variety! He makes the world a better place with his sunshine and smiles!)

Mondo thanks to my PayPal goddess, Kathy Lague, who makes my virtual signings possible, and allows me to get hundreds of signed, personalized books into the hands of my readers. If you're reading this in the front of *Into the Fire*, it's probably too late to get a signed copy of *this* book via Internet order and U.S. mail. Sorry 'bout that. But I'll be holding a virtual signing for *Dark of Night* in early 2009. Visit my website in January for details!

Thank you to my good friend and go-to man for research, Navy SEAL Tom Rancich, who never laughs at my silly questions. (Will a handgun that's been submerged in used cooking oil still fire . . . ?) Thank you, too, Tom, for your continued presence on my Internet bulletin board. (Check out the series of video interviews with Tom that I posted on YouTube. Go to www.YouTube.com and search for "Brockmann, Rancich." Tom's a great storyteller. You gotta hear his story of how he met himself . . .)

Thank you to the real-life Gail Deegan and her wonderful husband, Bill Huddleston, for their generous donation to Greater Boston PFLAG. You inspire me! I suspect you would make a truly excellent FBI team leader, Gail, if you ever decide to change careers.

And equal thanks to the real-life Lynn McCrea, who made a matching donation to GB PFLAG and gave her name to Izzy Zanella's crazy downstairs neighbor. (Let me know if he gets too loud!)

Gail and Lynn, you both rock. The money you donated will help fund GB PFLAG's Safe Schools program—thank you, from the bottom of my heart.

Thank you to my team of volunteers, who are standing ready for me to give the signal to hold my next reader weekend: Sue Smallwood, Erika Schutte, Gail Reddin, Dorbert Ogle, Peggy Mitchell, Heather McHugh, Jeanne Mangano, Laura Luke, Beki & Jim Keene, Stephanie Hyacinth, Suzie Bernhardt, and Elizabeth & Lee Benjamin. Any minute, guys, I promise. . . .

Check my website at www.SuzanneBrockmann.com/appearances.htm for information about my next reader event.

As always, any mistakes I've made or liberties I've taken are completely my own.

PART
ONE

SIX MONTHS AGO

CHAPTER ONE

January 2008
Dalton, California

Hannah Whitfield woke up alone in her bed.

Which wasn't that unusual. In fact, this had been her only opportunity to *not* wake up alone for the first time in years—due to the still somewhat unbelievable fact that she'd actually had sex last night.

Hannah swept her hair out of her eyes as she reached to turn on the lamp that sat on her bedside table, trying—not as successfully—to push away her feelings of imminent dread. Her head was pounding and her ankle was on fire so she took a pull from the nearly empty bottle of Johnny W. she'd left next to her bed. Hair of the dog, was the age-old excuse. She knew better, but right now she needed the drumming pain in both her head and her ankle to back the hell off.

Last night had been far from fairy-tale-inducing material, with no impending happily-ever-after in sight. True, she'd wanted to get with this particular man ever since their very first encounter—since he'd knocked her off that Alaskan pier, a hundred years ago.

A hundred years? No. It felt more like a solid thousand since the tall, dark and handsome man with the laughing brown eyes had held out an enormous hand and helped Hannah out of the icy water. It felt like an eternity since either of them had so much as smiled. And maybe it had been. Maybe tragedy had its own rules in the time-space continuum. The year following the death of a murdered wife and best friend passed at the speed of five hundred years in normal, happy, human time, with all of the previous years of laughter and joy instantly fading to ancient-seeming, sepia-toned distant memories.

So, yeah. Last night had been grimly moonbeam- and fairy-dust-free. Once upon a time, Hannah had let herself get laid—except, no, that wasn't quite right. She'd been the layee. It was Vinh Murphy who'd gotten laid—for the first time since Angelina had died.

Last night, like most nights these days, Hannah had been somewhat anesthetized, but she was nowhere near as shit-faced as Murph. They'd had an argument about the same old same old—the keys to his truck. Hannah had swiftly adiosed them when he'd shown up at the cabin at 0100, already wasted. That was his MO—she wouldn't see him for months, and then he'd appear. Usually in the dead of night, flashing his headlights in the driveway, stinking of gin, his brain damn near fried from whatever else he'd ingested in his attempt to forget that his wife—the love of his life, as he called Angelina—was forever gone.

They'd argued—*no, I will not give back your keys*—and Murphy had tripped over the leather ottoman and fallen. He'd hit his head on the arm of the sofa, and Hannah had thought he was down for the night, so after she'd helped him up, she'd dragged him over to her bed. Her intention had been—as always—to let him sleep it off in her room here downstairs, while she pulled herself up the ladder to the mattress in the loft.

But as she'd toppled him onto her bed, her bad ankle had bent the wrong way and the sudden surge of pain had made her lose her balance. She tried to straighten up, but Murphy'd held on to her, the expression in his dark brown eyes far different from anything she'd ever seen there before.

"Hannah," he'd said. "I'm so fucked up." And then he'd kissed her.

Yeah, Murphy had kissed her, and she should have scrambled away, but she hadn't. Instead, she'd pulled up her nightshirt and opened her legs for him and he'd pushed himself inside of her, which, God, had felt so good, even though she knew it was the worst kind of mistake—not just flat-out stupid but incredibly, insanely wrong for too many reasons to count.

And no, sex with Murph hadn't been the romantic, passionate ecstasy she'd dreamed about all those years ago when he'd laughed and pulled her back onto the pier alongside Patrick's boat, but rather a fumbled, clumsy, silent, joyless rutting. Murphy didn't kiss her again. He just kept his eyes shut and his head down as his body strained, as Hannah clung to him, not allowing herself to wish or hope for anything—not even her own physical relief—as he filled her, as she felt his heart pounding alongside of hers. But she came right away because it had been close to forever for her, too, and he was right behind her, shuddering his release.

And then, there they were, mere seconds after it had started. In Hannah's bed with most of their clothes still on. Bonus moron points went to both of them for failing to use protection of any kind.

It was then that Murphy started to cry—which he'd never done in front of her, not even at his toasted worst, not even at Angelina's horror-show of a memorial service. And so Hannah had cried, too, just holding on to him.

He'd finally fallen asleep in her arms, here in her bed, but now he was gone.

A light was on in the living room.

Hannah moved as quietly as she could out of the bedroom, considering she'd misplaced her cane and . . .

"What are you *doing?*" Her shock and volume apparently startled him and he turned, guilt on his grim face, her keys in one giant hand as he held the lock to the gun case in the other. He didn't try to explain—he didn't need to. He just went back to trying the next key.

It was possible Hannah was going to throw up. "What's your plan, Murph?" she asked instead. "You gonna kill yourself—right here in my living room?"

He didn't answer. Or maybe he did, but his back was to her as he fumbled with the key ring. He was still drunk or high or whatever he'd been when he'd first appeared at her door nearly four hours ago.

"Stop," she said, her heart in her throat. He swayed slightly, but he didn't even slow down. "The key's not on there—I don't even have a key." It was a lie. She *did* have a key, even though the weapons weren't hers. They belonged to her uncle—everything in this cabin did. A former Marine and Vietnam vet, Pat had a similar glass-fronted case at his place up in Juneau, and she had the key for that one, too. He trusted her, Pat did. *Semper fi* and *hoo-yah* and all that, even though she'd never actually *been* a Marine.

Murphy had, however. He knew Pat well. And he knew Hannah. Drunk or not, he didn't need to do more than glance at her to know the truth. The key *was* on that ring he was holding.

"Please stop," she said again, begging him this time.

And this time Murphy did. And he turned and looked right at her. "Why?" *How am I going to live without her?* He didn't need to say the words for Hannah to know what he was thinking. God knows he'd said it enough since Angelina had died.

"Jesus, Murph." Hannah felt her voice shake. "I lost her, too. It's time to stop the bullshit. It's time to start dealing—"

He turned to face her again. "Dealing? *You're* gonna to talk to *me* about *dealing,* while you hide away here—"

"I'm not the one who wants to kill myself!"

"Yeah," Murphy said, making sure she understood, speaking carefully so that his words didn't slur together. "Because you're already dead and buried."

Hannah felt herself bristle and the retort was out of her mouth before she could stop it. "Fuck you!"

"Tried that," he said, his eyes filled with such hatred. It took her aback until she realized it was self-loathing that she saw there. "Didn't help." He turned back to the keys, but even as he tried the next one, he sank to his knees, his shoulders shaking as he began to sob.

And all of Hannah's hurt and anger and fear morphed into near-blinding grief. "Vinh," she said as she crossed to him.

"I wanted her," he told her through his tears, his words even more blurred. "Not you."

"I know," she said, as she held on to him, rocking him, her heart breaking for him, and herself, too. "I know that."

"I'm so sorry, Hannah . . ."

"Shhh," she said. "Murph, it's okay. I was trying to help. I thought . . ." She'd thought she could at least give him what he seemed to want—a chance for relief, release. Yeah, right, like it had been all about Murphy and what he'd needed. "God, I'm sorry, too."

JANUARY 2008
SAN DIEGO, CALIFORNIA

The most beautiful woman in the world walked into the bar.

It sounded like the setup to a not-particularly-funny joke. But the bar was the Ladybug Lounge—the SEAL Team Sixteen hangout near Coronado Navy Base—and the woman . . .

She was incredible.

It seemed almost sacrilegious that all movement didn't stop, that the clamor of the place didn't cease, that the room didn't fall into an appropriately reverent hush. Instead, a group of jarheads didn't even look up from their game of pool, the jukebox continued blaring the YouTube-famous treadmill song from OK Go, the crowd at the corner booth burst into raucous laughter, and the bartender blended a new batch of piña coladas with an earsplitting appliance whine.

Instead, Izzy Zanella alone stopped breathing to watch as the most beautiful woman in the world let the door close behind her. His heart damn near stopped, too, as she approached the bar where he was perched on a stool, nursing a beer.

It was true that she wasn't dressed to be noticed in a pair of cutoff shorts and a gray *Colbert Nation* T-shirt, flip-flops on her perfect feet. Her dark hair was pulled back into a casual ponytail, but despite that, with her heart-shaped face and flawlessly smooth skin, her Natalie Portman eyes and that mouth that he knew he'd see tonight in his dreams, she was magic personified. It seemed incredible since Izzy couldn't remember his last girlfriend's chin—she must've had one—but even this woman's chin was freaking perfection.

Which was saying something, because for him to be looking anywhere besides her five-mile-long, suntanned, beach-bunny legs was unbelievable.

Damn. While he'd never passed up a chance to appreciate a nice pair of legs, he was pretty much in the legs-were-legs-were-legs camp.

Not anymore. He'd always thought of himself as a breast man, but now that he'd died and gone to leg heaven, he'd have to rethink that, although she had plenty of C-cup action going on, too.

Izzy could see the string-straps of a bikini—yellow and black—tied around her graceful neck. And for the first time in God knows how long, he found himself praying. *Please, Yahweh, let her be lost on her way to the beach. And let him offer to show her the way so that he could see the rest of that barely there bathing suit . . .*

As she came closer, he saw that her eyes were indeed a rich, dark, mysterious brown. Their gazes locked and . . . She shifted slightly to the right, away from him, putting an empty barstool between them.

Oh. Yeah.

He'd changed out of his BDUs, but he hadn't showered—opting in-stead to beat his teammates over here to the Bug, to get a cold beer inside of himself as quickly as possible—his desperately needed reward after the forty-eight hours of sheer hell that had been described by the senior chief as *an easy training op.* Izzy still wore his olive drab, sweat-stained T-shirt—along with blue-and-white flower-patterned surfer jams that had been among the few clean pieces of laundry in his apartment day before yester-day.

Meaning, they'd *been* clean—day before yesterday. Before that dick-weed Danny Gillman had torn out of the craphole of a parking lot over at the simulated swamp—because God and the senior chief knew that every "easy training op" needed a freaking simulated swamp—and sprayed Izzy and his unzipped sea-bag with *the* stankiest-smelling briny-ass mud known to mankind.

Yeah, thanks to Gillman, the most heartbreakingly beautiful woman in the world didn't want to sit too close to Izzy at the bar.

But she *did* glance at him again, with trepidation on her perfect face.

Wise move, staying upwind like that. Things he should have said—per-haps with a reassuring yet appreciative, warm yet manly smile. But when his heart had stopped—somewhere back when she'd opened the Bug's door—his vocal cords must have gotten gummed up, because all that came out was a great, big, tumbleweed- and cricket-chirping-filled silence.

Izzy accessorized it perfectly with some slack-jawed, openmouthed, glassy-eyed staring.

Of course it could have been worse. He could have stared at her whilst scratching his balls and belching.

She turned away, leaning forward slightly, elbows against the bar to catch the barkeep's eye, which made the bottom of her T-shirt separate from the low-riding waist of her shorts. Skin was revealed. Smooth, perfect, sexy-as-hell skin that proved without a doubt that her bathing suit wasn't a one-piece. Somehow Izzy kept himself in his seat, fighting the urge to fall to his knees and weep with joy.

"Excuse me," she said, in a voice that was surprisingly husky and deep, yet still inspiringly musical.

"We card here," Kevin the bartender told her, his flat rudeness making Izzy bristle.

"No," she said. "I mean, I know. I'm not . . . I don't . . ." She was flustered, but she took a deep breath and started again. "I'm looking for . . . for . . . a friend of mine? He's a SEAL, with Team Sixteen . . . ?"

A *friend* . . .

But then ol' Kev gave her a knowing look, clearly thinking the same thing Izzy was—that she was some ditched ex, looking for one last face-to-face with a guy who'd already left her in the dust—crazy-assed mofo that he had to have been to dump *her*. "You'll have to wait for your *friend* outside. I don't want any trouble in here."

She squared her shoulders, clearly preparing for battle, but Kevin dismissed her by turning away, and then, alleluia, Izzy found his voice. "What's his name?" he asked. "Your friend."

She eyed him warily, and he gave her what he hoped was an "I don't bite—too hard" smile.

"I'm Izzy. I'm with Team Sixteen, too. So I probably know him. Your friend."

"Danny," she said as hope dawned in her eyes, as she looked Izzy over more closely, no doubt realizing that he wasn't just some fashion-challenged homeless man, taking a break from dumpster-diving. "Gillman?"

"Gilligan?" Izzy said in surprise.

And all of the trepidation in her eyes was completely replaced by shining relief. Having her look at him like that almost knocked him over. "You know him?" she asked, way too excited considering this was Gilligan they were talking about.

Did Izzy know Dan Gillman? "Yeah," Iz said. "Me and the fishboy, we're . . . tight." If tight meant locked in mortal combat at every possible opportunity.

And okay, that was an exaggeration. He and Gillman got along just fine out in the real world, while on military ops. Gillman respected Izzy—but he didn't like him, and he didn't particularly want to hang with him during playtime. Out of nearly everyone in Team Sixteen, there was no one who appreciated Izzy *less* during R&R than Dan "Gilligan" Gillman. And that wasn't an exaggeration.

It was also a giant pain in the ass, since Izzy *was* tight with Jenk and Lopez, who were also Gillman's two best friends in the team. More often than not, the four of them hung together. And despite Lopez and Jenk's best efforts, Iz and Gillman had not yet learned how to get along. In fact, over the past year or so, their relationship, as it were, had gotten even more adversarial.

The girl moved closer—a dream come true—slipping onto the stool next to him. "Do you know where Danny is? I kind of need to get in touch with him, like, right away . . . ?"

Up close, she was even more beautiful. She was also younger than Izzy'd first thought. The bartender had been right to try to card her—she wasn't twenty-one. Probably more like twenty. She was wearing quite a bit of makeup, no doubt in an attempt to look older, which pretty much worked. But one thing that she couldn't hide with eyeshadow and lipstick was the fact that she was both worried and enormously upset. And even a little scared.

Ah, Gillman, Gillman, Gillman, you sly dog. For months, the fishboy had been pretending he was pining away over Sophia Ghaffari, an exotically beautiful, yet somewhat mature woman—light-years out of Gillman's league—who worked at Tommy Paoletti's personal security company, Troubleshooters Incorporated. Sure, Danny and Sophia had gone out to dinner a time or two, but nothing had ever come of it. At least not the orgasmatronic fireworks Gillman had been hoping for.

All this time, for months now, Gillman had relentlessly been *Sophia this*-ing and *Sophia that*-ing until even Jay Lopez's eyes had rolled back in his saintly head. And yet, apparently, Gillman had dealt with at least a portion of his despair over the fact that Sophia wouldn't do him by spending some quality time with this extremely healthy member of Colbert Nation.

"I haven't talked to Danny in months," the girl continued, which immediately blew up Izzy's theory. Which was a fairly common occurrence with him and wild speculation, and perfectly fine, because it meant that he'd just move on to salacious theory number two. "I wasn't even sure if he was OCONUS or . . ."

"No, he's Stateside," Izzy said, and got another heavy dose of relief, crossed with a dollop of "you're my hero" from her bottomless eyes. Damn, she had *the* prettiest brown eyes . . .

Okay, focus. What had he just learned here besides the fact that Gillman's relationship with this girl had—allegedly—happened months ago? OCONUS. Whoever she was, she knew at least a little Navy-Speak. So . . .

"Are you Susan?" Izzy asked her.

Back before Sophia had appeared and eclipsed all other women on the planet and possibly on Omicron Ceti III as well, Gillman had dated a Susan. A college student at San Diego State. Lopez, who usually didn't drool over his friends' girlfriends, had described Susan as hhhhhot. But, he'd told Izzy with a sad sigh, she was a total SEAL groupie. Oh, and heads up, all y'all—she was completely insane, to boot.

As Maybe-Susan sat beside Izzy in the Bug, her eyes shifted slightly as she opened her mouth to answer what should have been a simple yes-no question. *Are you Susan?* According to the Body Language of Hot Babes Manual, that slight eye movement was a strong yet unconsciously made signal that an untruth was about to follow.

Gather 'round, kids—it's storytime!

But the bartender interrupted them before she could fabricate her answer. "I'm serious, girlie. I need you outa here. Don't make me call the bouncer."

"Come on, Kev," Izzy said as mildly as he could manage, considering the man was a certified dickhead. "We're just having a conversation. She's looking for Dan Gillman—"

"She's underage—she can look for him outside."

"I'm happy to go outside to talk to her, but I'm not quite done with my beer."

"Yeah, well, 'f I turn back around and she's not gone . . ." The dickhead left the threat unspoken, so of course Izzy had to respond with a silent but very clear *Oh, yeah? And then what?* by taking his good ol' time finishing up his beer.

Meanwhile, M-Susan was looking from him to the Kevster and back. She was still solidly planted on her barstool, clearly intrigued, waiting to see what was going to go down next. Izzy smiled at her, and she smiled back, and his heart did a slow flip in his chest, because damn, he liked a woman with a heavy dose of rebel in her soul.

Too many of the women he'd met were rule-followers. When harshly scolded by the voice of alleged authority, they'd slink away, tails between their legs.

Either that, or they spoke a completely different language from Izzy. Oh, it sounded like American English coming out of their mouths, but nearly every word had an entirely different meaning. And most of the time, his somewhat-sideways sense of humor didn't translate well.

This woman, however, just waited and watched, and—on a certain level—enjoyed. Which may have, in Lopez and Gillman's book, made her completely insane.

But not to Izzy.

He took his time with his last mouthful of beer, waiting to swallow until Kevin did, in fact, turn around. At which point Izzy slowly and carefully put the glass on the bar, all the while holding the dickhead's less-than-happy gaze.

And it was only then, when Kevin didn't do more than stand there and glare—a silent but strongly implied *then I'll go home and bite my pillow*— that Izzy took out his cell phone and lifted his ass offa that barstool. Smiling again at Maybe-Sue, he gestured with his head toward the door. "Step into my office. I'll give Gillman a call."

M-Susan slid off her stool, too, and led the way. Two steps out, though, she slipped on something—maybe a wet patch on the floor. Or maybe her insanity caused her to hallucinate, and she'd tripped over invisible purple poodles. Whatever the case, Izzy caught her arm to keep her from going down.

It was hard to tell what it was, exactly, that stunned him into stupidity—the sensation of her smooth skin beneath his fingers or the sweet smile of gratitude she shot him.

Either way, he didn't feel inclined to let go, and she didn't seem to mind. And when, as they passed the wailing jukebox, she leaned close to ask, "So you're a SEAL, too," Izzy knew with a tingly certainty that, as long as he didn't do anything terrifically assholeish, odds were good that he was going to get some tonight.

"I am," he said. "So, see, maybe you don't need to find Gillman after all."

SEAL groupies were women who would put out—usually in the bar parking lot—merely because a guy had gone through the ball-breaking BUD/S training and wore a trident.

And color Izzy putridly shallow, but right at this moment, considering he filled the criteria quite nicely, he just couldn't see the problem with that. He himself wasn't particularly interested in finding out whether Maybe-Susan had had a puppy growing up, or what classes she was taking this semester, or what she wanted to do when she finished school. As long as they were both consenting adults . . .

"If you can't be, with the one you love, honey, love the one you're

with . . ." Izzy hummed the melody just under his breath as he opened the door and followed the most beautiful woman in the world out of the Bug.

A Lifetime Ago . . .
Summer 1993
Bartlet, Montana

"Hey, you! Scholarship girl!"

Hannah put her head down and kept walking along the gravel road to the mess hall, but the girls from the Sunflower group, led by the insufferable Brianna Parker, ran and quickly caught up.

They surrounded her—eight other fifteen- and sixteen-year-olds, including Bree, who'd been coming to this camp since she was seven, whose father donated liberally to the scholarship fund, which allowed so-called underprivileged girls like Hannah to spend two weeks in the company of Bree and her equally rich-bitch, entitled friends.

It was only day two, and Hannah desperately wanted to go home.

Carolyn Ronston and one of the multitude of Megans moved right in front of Hannah, forcing her to either push past them or stop.

So Hannah stopped, looking around at eight angry faces. One of them, a girl named something ridiculous like Petunia, was in tears. Whatever was up, it wasn't going to be good.

She sighed. Are we happy campers yet?

"Where are you going in such a hurry?" another of the Megans asked—or maybe it was the just plain Meg, who had a note from home that allowed her to break camp rules by wearing makeup to cover her acne. How the gallon of mascara and eyeliner that she wore did that, Hannah wasn't exactly sure.

She didn't need to answer. Bree did it for her. "It's lunchtime," she said. "Careful she doesn't trample you in her haste to stuff her face." She turned to Hannah. "You should really wait and let the paying customers go first."

Carolyn was onboard for that. "They should really make these girls work. I mean, what are they learning here, anyway?"

"Actually," Hannah said, "I've already learned not to write a prizewinning essay ever again." And to keep her Uncle Patrick away from Ms. Julio, the high school guidance counselor. They'd ganged up on her with this totally absurd idea that she needed to spend more time around women and girls—as in two weeks here at Camp Bitchfest. Which also conveniently would get Hannah out of Pat's house just long enough for him to charm Nancy Julio out of her designer jeans and into his bed and then, unceremoniously, dump her.

Which wasn't going to bode well for Hannah's junior and senior years. Because what she was *really* learning here, was that girls—at least the ones she'd met here—didn't play fair or have a strong sense of honor or respect for their peers.

Backstabbing and trash-talking and rumor-spreading and revenge-seeking seemed to be the order of the day.

If Ms. Julio was anything like Brianna or her friends, she was going to react to Pat's dumping her by taking her anger and hurt out on Hannah.

"Give it back," Petunia sobbed now. "You have to give it back."

But first? Hannah was going to have to get through today.

"Give what back?" she asked the smaller girl.

Carolyn got in her face. "Don't play dumb," she said. "We know you took it. Meghan-with-an-H saw you walking in the woods past Tooney's tent."

Tooney was the nickname for Petunia? Really?

"I've walked past a lot of tents today," Hannah admitted. She'd gotten lost, and spent quite some time trying to find her own tent—not that she was going to tell them *that*.

"Just give it back." Carolyn pushed her hard—her hands against Hannah's shoulders, which very well might have knocked her over, had Hannah not seen it coming and braced for it. She brought her own arms up and out, breaking Carolyn's hold on her and causing the older girl to retreat.

But only temporarily.

"I don't know what you're talking about," Hannah insisted. They were drawing a crowd. She could see some of the girls from her cluster—the Daffodils—not that any of them came forward to offer support against the mighty, ultra-popular Sunflowers.

She caught a glimpse of her bunkmate, Lacey, who quickly hid behind a group of other girls—what a surprise.

Yeah. Swell. Hannah was totally on her own.

"As if you really don't know, we're talking about Tooney's bracelet," Bree spat out, in a tone that dripped with *you moron*.

"I didn't take anyone's bracelet," Hannah said.

"Prove it." Carolyn again invaded Hannah's personal space, reaching for the front pocket of Hannah's jeans.

What the hell . . . ? Hannah knocked her hand away. "Get away from me!"

"Empty your pockets!" Carolyn came at her again.

"Get your hands off me!" Hannah couldn't retreat because three or four mouth-breathing Megans were penning her in. She didn't want to hit Carolyn—it was one thing to break a hold, another entirely to plant a right hook in the older girl's face.

She was focused so intently on Carolyn, that she didn't notice when one of the other girls—possibly Meghan-with-an-H—stuck out a foot and tripped Hannah.

She went down into the dust, onto her elbow—ouch—taking off a layer of skin.

Which was when Carolyn kicked her.

She caught Hannah hard in the ribs, knocking the air from her lungs.

Enough was enough.

Gasping for air, Hannah grabbed Carolyn's foot. Twisting, in a move that she'd learned back when *she* was seven from Pat and his Marine buddies, she brought Carolyn down into the dirt with her.

Which surprised the hell out of everyone—especially Carolyn, who wasn't used to her victims fighting back.

And once the fight became a fight and not a one-sided beating, Carolyn did what most bullies did. She ran away.

Hannah scrambled to her feet, panting. She pushed her disheveled hair back from her face as she scanned the group of Sunflowers. "Who's next?" she said and they all took a solid step back.

"Tooney, you total space cadet, is this what you're looking for?"

It was the girl named Angelina. Taller even than Hannah, but with long dark hair, and the body of a twenty-year-old, Angelina wore makeup without a note from home. When Hannah had first arrived, she'd mistaken her for one of the college-age counselors. But one of her Daffodil bunkmates had corrected her.

Angelina, apparently, was the daughter of a rap music producer named BadAss T. She was a Sunflower and even more popular than Brianna, despite the fact that this was only her second year at camp.

Something shiny and gold dangled now off of one of Angelina's well-manicured fingers.

Petunia grabbed it. "Ohmigod! Where did you find it?"

"It was right on your bunk," Angelina informed the smaller girl, then turning to include Bree in her admonishment. "Next time look with your eyes open before calling someone a liar and a thief. My daddy's killed men for less." She turned to the crowd. "What are you looking at? Show's over. Get gone."

Hannah, too, faded back, hoping to slip away now that the attention was off of her. She was almost to the showerhouse door when Angelina caught up to her.

"Yo, Raging Bull, what's the rush?"

Hannah didn't slow down. She opened the heavy door and went into the cool dimness of the bathroom, catching sight of herself in the mirrors over the sink. Most of her hair had fallen out of her ponytail and it hung in strings around her dirty face. Her T-shirt was a mess, too, streaked with dirt where Carolyn had kicked her. And her elbow . . .

It was bleeding and raw. Washing that out was going to hurt, big time. Hannah got right to it, washing her hands first, and then her face, then twisting to get her elbow under the cold water faucet.

"Aren't you even going to thank me?"

Hannah looked up into the mirror, at Angelina, who had followed her inside.

"For what?" Hannah asked.

"Ah, so she *does* have a voice," Angelina said, flipping her long, dark hair over her shoulder. "I thought maybe you were, you know, deaf or something."

"Mute," Hannah corrected her. "It's mute when you can't speak."

"Whatever." She crossed her arms, settling back against the sink. "I saved your ass, girlfriend."

Argh, the soap stung. Hannah gritted her teeth, unwilling to make a sound in front of Miss Sunflower Homegirl 1993. Unless Angelina left, she was going to have to go into one of the toilet stalls to survey the damage done to her side when Carolyn kicked her.

"My ass didn't need saving," Hannah said coolly, when the pain numbed out and she could finally speak. "I was doing just fine by myself."

"Yeah? Where do you think Carolyn went running to? She was getting a counselor. Fighting is a capital offense around here, you know."

Hannah straightened up, reaching for a paper towel to blot her arm. "As opposed to stealing your cluster-mates' jewelry, which is what? A competitive sport?"

"I didn't steal anything," Angelina was affronted. "I found it—"

"Bullshit." Hannah turned to look at her. "We both know you took 'Tooney's' bracelet, so cut the crap. What I can't figure out is why give it back."

Angelina laughed. "Because it's only day two, and I'm already bored out of my mind with Bree and her Valley Girl clones. Because you're different. You're interesting. You fight like you're from the 'hood—"

"Oh, please." Hannah cut her off. "That's more bullshit. You're not from the 'hood any more than I am. Any more than freaking Brianna is. Seriously? BadAss T?"

Angelina was standing there, as if trying to decide what crap to hurl at Hannah next.

She finally laughed. Shrugged. "Most of these girls only listen to country. Toby Keith—kill me now. They're too afraid to admit they've never heard of BadAss T."

"So you just keep on lying to them."

"They like it. When I told them I was working on an album of my own, they practically French-kissed me. Even Bree, who hates that I'm more popular than she is." She looked at Hannah critically. "I think you've still got some dirt by your eyebrow . . ."

Hannah turned back to the mirror. Yeah, she'd definitely missed a spot.

"Did you really write a prizewinning essay?" Angelina asked.

"Yup." Hannah wet the paper towel. She'd won, although she probably would've won even if she'd written five pages of nonsense. She was here because all of her friends at school were boys. Because she lived in a household with four men. Because Ms. Julio had convinced Patrick that two weeks at this camp would make her more well-rounded, which was their way of saying "less of a tomboy," as if there was something wrong with that.

"A brainiac, huh?" Angelina said.

"Yeah," Hannah said, shooting her a look. "I'm a real genius. My prize was this two-week jail sentence." She gave up and just scooped water into her hands, wetting her entire face again.

Angelina waited until Hannah turned the water back off, holding out more paper towels for her. "It's not that bad here. Well, aside from the fact that everyone sucks."

"Maybe I can convince them that my father's a producer, too," Hannah said as she dried her face. "White Chocolate, aka Comb-over Q."

Angelina laughed. "Or we can spread rumors that the essay contest you won was open to all the girls in juvie cellblocks A, B, and C. That'll gain you some respect."

Hannah rolled her eyes as she laughed, too.

"It's gotta be better than the truth," Angelina urged her. She was quiet for a moment, then added, "My mother works for Bree Parker's father. Cleaning his office."

Hannah must have reacted, because Angelina continued, "Yeah. I'm here on scholarship because Mr. Parker wants to screw me. At least he did before he found out I'm his daughter's age. I'm still not exactly sure if his sending me here, two years running, is out of genuine guilt for grabbing my tits when I was fourteen, or if it's some kind of hush-me payoff." She settled back against the sink. "Or maybe I'm his mistress in training. Maybe he's just waiting for me to get old enough to squeeze without jail time. How well do you think *that* truth will go over with Queen Bree?"

Hannah just shook her head. "I'm sorry."

"I made up the whole BadAss T thing last year," Angelina said, "when I saw how Bree and her alleged friends welcomed the other scholarship girls." She paused. "So do you have a partner yet for this afternoon's sailing class?"

Hannah looked at her. "What do *you* think?" At breakfast, Lacey had loudly announced she was partnering with a girl from the Daisy cluster, leaving Hannah odd man out.

"You want to . . . ?" Angelina motioned between the two of them.

"With you." Hannah didn't voice it as a question, but Angelina answered it anyway.

"Yeah."

"I don't have any jewelry worth stealing," Hannah said.

Angelina laughed.

"I wasn't kidding," Hannah said. "I'm not going to partner with a thief."

"I never keep it," Angelina defended herself. "The things I take. Someone always goes home early, and I hide it all in their bunk. We find it and . . . Everyone gets everything back."

"So . . . what?" Hannah said. "You take it because . . . you like it when they start a witch hunt and blame innocent people?"

"I take it," Angelina said, hand on her hip, heavy on the attitude, "because they flaunt it in the faces of the girls who don't have their kind of money. I take it because it gives us something to talk about. And I take it because they expect me to have expensive jewelry, and I can say that it's gone missing, too, okay?"

"Except you don't get yours back," Hannah pointed out.

"Last year that worked out to be kind of a bonus," she admitted. "Everyone figured that Deedee—the girl who went home early—kept my necklace and anklet, on account of, you know, BadAss T's Grammy win? So Bree and her friends all chipped in and bought me a replacement. A diamond pendant."

"So you conned them," Hannah interpreted.

"It was a gift," Angelina argued. "I had no idea they were going to do it. Who am I to turn down something like that?"

"They'll catch on if you do it again this year," Hannah told her.

"They'll only catch on," Angelina countered, crossing her arms, "if you tell them."

"Then they'll catch on," Hannah said. "Because if something else goes missing, I *will* tell them."

And there they stood, staring each other down.

Angelina broke first, laughing. "Yo, Nobody Girl. Don't you get the fact that if you walk into lunch with me, they'll ask you to be a Sunflower?"

Hannah laughed her disgust as she went into one of the stalls to make sure she wasn't bleeding beneath her shirt from Carolyn's kick. "Why, in God's name, would I ever want that?"

"Wow," Angelina said, as if the thought hadn't occurred to her ever before. "Good point."

CHAPTER
TWO

I t was going to be a lovely evening.

The sky had gone into glorious sunset mode after a day that had been unseasonably warm for January. But now the air was cooler and there was a nice breeze. It was perfect weather for riding in his truck with the windows down. And for going back to his apartment to screw his brains out.

Izzy stood in the Ladybug parking lot with an honestly earned tired-on after forty-eight hours of hard physical training. It hadn't all been fun and games, but he damn well preferred it to sitting behind a desk and filling out endless paperwork.

He was good and exhausted, he was beyond hungry, *and* he was more than ready to break his current record-long streak of not getting laid.

"I kind of do," Maybe-Susan told him earnestly, and at first he didn't know what she was talking about, his thoughts had gone in so many different directions, most of them leading to his extremely optimistic dick. But she clarified. "Need to find Danny."

Not the best news, but in the grand scheme of things, it was no real biggie. Izzy would be there, a shoulder to cry on, after Danny blew her off. He searched through the contact list on his cell, landing on Gillman's number. He pushed talk and handed her his phone.

She squinted at it, puzzled until she saw that it was ringing *Gillman, Dan,* at which point she put it to her ear. "You *do* know him. Oh, my God . . ."

She must've gone straight to Gilligan's voicemail, because her recently shored up levels of shining hope took a serious dive south. She abruptly hung up, chewing on her lip, frowning slightly.

She was gorgeous when she frowned, too. She looked like someone, probably some movie star, but Izzy just couldn't place where or when he'd seen her. Probably during some in-flight movie on some recent freaking-endless transatlantic trek.

"You don't want to leave a message?" Izzy asked her.

She met his eyes only briefly as she shook her head. "I need to talk to him. If I leave a message . . ."

"You're afraid he won't call back," Izzy guessed.

"No," she said, certain. "I know he will. I just . . . need to talk to him first. Before . . ."

"Before what?" Izzy asked, but again she just shook her head.

He took the phone from her. Redialed. Left a message, for her. "Gill-man, it's Zanella. Call me when you get this. It's important."

She gave him a smile, but it was significantly more wan than the ones she'd delivered inside the Bug.

Izzy ended the call, then shuffled through his list and dialed Jay Lopez. "I got a friend who might be able to track Gillman down," he told her. Chances were strong that Lopez would either be with Gillman or know where he was.

Lopez picked up on the first ring. "Izzy. Sorry, man. I meant to tell you, I'm not heading over to the Bug tonight."

"You did, I know, I'm cool," Izzy reassured him. "I'm actually looking for Gillman. Is he with you, bro?"

"No, Danny headed out, about two hours ago," Lopez informed Izzy. "He caught a flight to Vegas. Some kind of family emergency."

"What's going on?" Izzy asked. M-Susan was watching him, her eyes again showing some hope mixed in with her anxiety. He shook his head, no, and now that new hope faded some, too, and she was back to lip chewing.

Which looked like fun. *You need any help with that, sweetheart?*

"I don't know," Lopez's voice in Izzy's ear broke into his little fantasy. "He got a phone call from his mother, and then . . . he was gone. Tore out of the parking lot like a bat out of hell."

And didn't Izzy know *that*. So okay. Maybe the mud-in-his-face thing hadn't been entirely intentional.

"Do me a favor, Jay," Iz said now, "and call him. Let him know that . . ." What? He gazed at Maybe-Susan, who was biting a fingernail now, which made her look about twelve. "Just tell him to call me, ASAP."

"Will do."

Izzy hung up his cell phone. "Lopez said Gillman went home, to Vegas, for a few days."

She laughed at that, even as tears filled her eyes. "Of course he did." She immediately steeled herself so that she didn't cry—so much for Izzy being a strong shoulder. In fact, she flat-out turned away from him, surreptitiously wiping her eyes as she pretended to look out toward the setting sun. She breathed and focused—damn, watching her was like watching a home movie of himself as a kid. Never show your fear. Never let 'em know they've won. Deny that you're bleeding, even when your blood is dripping on the kitchen linoleum.

It was as if she were bracing for a catastrophe that was yet to come. Izzy knew that particular feeling well.

"I don't know what went down between you and Gillman," Izzy started. "But—"

She cut him off. "Look, I'm in trouble," she admitted, as she turned back to him, squaring her shoulders and assuming what he was starting to think of as her default fighter's stance. "My wallet, my bag—all my stuff—was . . . stolen."

Okay, so *that* was a lie. Izzy took a mental step back, settling in to hear her out—but more as an audience member instead of someone with an emotional connection—really just ready to enjoy the upcoming dramatic performance.

But then she recanted, choking out what had to be the truth.

"I don't know if it was stolen intentionally—it might have been. But, see, I got ditched. By my asshole of a boyfriend. All my stuff was in the car and he just . . . left me. I was in the bathroom. In a Krispy Kreme. When I came out . . ."

It was that grim little detail—Krispy Kreme—that convinced Izzy. Jesus Christ. The humiliation factor here was so high. No way could she be making this shit up.

She continued, her voice thick with her misery: "I hitched down here from LA because I thought maybe Danny might . . ."

She paused, her eyes averted, and Izzy waited. Of course, maybe she was merely a brilliant actor. A con artist who knew, just from glancing at him, that he would buy her story if she told him she'd been dumped at a Krispy Kreme rather than, say, a Home Depot.

Intermission over, she took a deep breath, and started Act Two, her eyes still fixed on the cracked and potholed tarmac. "I have no money and no place to stay."

And here it came. *Can I borrow some cash? Just a few hundred dollars to tide me over. I'll pay you back . . .*

"Is there any chance," she asked, forcing herself to look up and meet his gaze, "I can stay with you until Danny gets back?"

Whoa.

Izzy was more than merely surprised. He was taken aback. This woman—girl really—was a total stranger. And even more importantly, *he* was a stranger to *her*. A large, strong, dangerous-looking, malodorous stranger.

Yeah, he'd fantasized about her coming home with him and doing the naked Macarena, but he'd imagined that discussion happening in more of a heated moment—*your place or mine?*—after Danny'd told her it was Sophia or the monastery for him, and that he was taking his vows tomorrow. Izzy'd pictured it happening after she'd cried herself dry in his sympathetic arms, and he'd given her some comforting kisses that turned—unexpectedly, natch—to pure fire.

Why that should have made a difference to him was absurd, but it did.

Izzy realized that his stunned silence was stretching on. And on. It no doubt was seeming to last forever for Maybe-Susan, too, who must've truly been at her wits' end to ask if she could come home with him, said total stranger *grande*.

Either that, or she was a freaking idiot—Blanche DuBois reincarnated. *Ah have always relahd on the kahndness of strangahs . . .*

Or she really *was* a con artist, looking to gain access to his apartment, where, while he was sleeping, she would rob him blind. Or she'd take pictures of him in bed with her boyfriend, so they could blackmail him by threatening to post the photos on the Internet.

Note to self: Don't fall asleep tonight.

But before he could make the "Yuh" sound to say *yes, you can sleep on my couch—at least for tonight,* because he really didn't have anything in his apartment worth stealing and lack of sleep was well worth the potential prize of her moving off his couch and into his bed, she upped the ante.

"Rumor has it, I give good head." She smiled, but something shifted in her eyes, just slightly, and the effect was disarming. For someone so young and pretty, she suddenly looked tired—battle-worn—like she was twenty going on fifty.

She took a step toward him, and Izzy took a step back, which was kind of stupid, like what? Did he really think she was going to fellate him right in the middle of the parking lot?

Except, damn, he was depraved, because her offer had gone in through his ears, been processed by his brain, and sent straight to his dick, solidifying the father of all woodies that was lurking behind his zipper. And okay, maybe he was being harder on himself than he had to be, because, to be honest, the kind of Louisville Slugger he was packing was pretty standard MO for him after an adrenaline-filled op—even when that op was just training. He'd had the damn thing—or at least its little brother—before she'd walked into the Bug.

Izzy opened his mouth and "I need a shower" came out, which was a dumbass thing to say, because there was this implication that *after* he showered, she'd . . .

Yeah. Like it was helping him to stand here thinking about that.

"Look, I hate to be a buzzkill," Izzy forced himself to tell her. "But I gotta be honest. It creeps me out when there's this implied exchange of goods and services—yeah, you can stay with me tonight, but in order to surf my couch you've got to . . . you know. Blow me. That's not cool. I mean, yeah, it would be cool in another dimension where God was a fourteen-year-old but . . ." He scratched the back of his head. "I'm not even figuring in the mystery factor. You never did quite tell me your name."

She didn't hesitate this time. "It's Brittney."

"Really," Izzy said.

She looked away. "Of course not. You're friends with Danny. If I tell you who I am, you'll tell him."

"Actually," Izzy said. "Me and Gillman—we're not really friends. I work with him, yeah, but . . . He pretty much hates my guts. So, see, I kinda lied, too." He held out his hand to her. "Let's start over, okay? I'm

Irving Zanella. People call me Izzy, from my initials—I.Z. Izzy, get it? Because, you know, *Irving?* Damn. I'm pretty sure my parents hated me. At the very least they wanted me to die a virgin."

She managed a brief laugh as she shook his hand, and his heart did another flip, because she really floated his boat. And not just because she allegedly gave good head. He liked her. Extremely. Crazy or not. Warnings from Lopez and Gillman be damned. Before this night ended, at the *very* least, Izzy was going to walk away with her phone number. And he was going to call her again.

Probably tomorrow.

He'd invite her to go skydiving. And if he were lucky, he'd be able to keep up.

But maybe—and he still had a shot here—he'd get her into bed with him tonight. But he didn't want it to happen because she was desperate, but rather because she'd discovered that she truly wanted to be there.

"And you are . . . ?" he prompted her.

Her smile faded. "I have no ID. Even if I do tell you, why should you believe me?" She looked searchingly into his eyes, shivering slightly in the breeze off the ocean.

That sassy *Rumor has it, I give good head,* had been an act of desperation—Izzy was at least ninety-eight percent sure of that now. The sun was nearly gone, casting long shadows across the parking lot. The air was cooling fast, and soon it would be dark. She had no money, no jacket, no place to go . . .

"Try me," Izzy told her.

He watched as she thought about trusting him. He watched as she realized that she didn't have much of a choice. And then he saw her surrender.

But he didn't see the massive clusterfuck that was coming when she opened her mouth, not until she uttered words that riveted him to the ragged tarmac.

"I'm Eden," she said. "Gillman."

Holy shit.

Izzy must not have registered any response at all, because she added, "Danny's sister?"

Holy, *holy* shit.

That was who she'd reminded him of—Gilligan, not some movie starlet. Danny, too, was gleamingly good-looking, with his dark hair and brown eyes. In fact, he could see bits of Danny in Eden's eyes, and around her chin and her mouth.

Sweet Jesus, don't think about her mouth and that implied offer she'd made to . . .

"Eden, huh?" he said, because he had to say something. Gillman had two sisters, one of whom was married with kids. But his little sister— Eden—had just graduated—barely—from high school. She was the troublemaker. The problem child. The black sheep of Gillman's otherwise perfect, golden-spoon and trust-fund encrusted family.

"Damn," Izzy said. "Are you even eighteen?"

She was looking at him now with the same trepidation she'd had in her eyes when she'd first glanced in his direction, back in the Bug. "Please don't tell Danny that I—"

"Relax." Izzy took out his cell phone. "Just . . . Look, why don't you give me your parents' phone number in Vegas, so I can—"

Disappointment—and anger—flared in her eyes. "I *knew* it."

"Whoa!" Izzy blocked her route, even though she had limited options. Marching out of that parking lot would leave her alone and cold on a dark street. "Lopez told me your brother went home for a family emergency," he said to Eden. "I'll call and ask for him. I won't say you're with me, I won't speak to your parents. Just Dan. Okay?"

She stared at Izzy.

"Okay?" he said again.

"I can't go back there," she said.

"No one's saying that you should," Izzy pointed out. "But you wanted to talk to Dan, and he's there, so . . ."

She didn't seem convinced.

"Am I right in assuming that you're the family emergency?" he asked.

"I'm always the family emergency," she answered, pissed off. "It's pretty much been a full-time job since I turned twelve."

Izzy laughed. He couldn't help it.

"I've been gone for three months," Eden told him. "I've been e-mailing my mother—she knows I'm safe." She caught herself, shivering again as the breeze kicked up. "Was safe."

"You're safe," Izzy told Gillman's little sister, as his hopes and dreams of nailing her shriveled and died a painful death.

She folded her arms across her chest, sheer attitude in human form. "Probably what happened is Greg, my stepfather, found out about the e-mail. He probably thought he could trace it and find me—which he couldn't. I'm not an idiot. But Mom probably panicked and called Danny because she was afraid when Greg went after me, I'd fight back." She laughed—defiance mixed with despair. "I'm not sure who she's more worried will get hurt—him or me. Probably him."

"If you're eighteen, he can't touch you—if he does, you can press charges," Izzy pointed out.

Eden nodded. "And then there's that. I can press charges." She paused. "Tomorrow."

"You're only seventeen," he said in a burst of disbelief, and she nodded. Flipping great. Not that seventeen wasn't the age of consent in California. It was. But damn, a man had to draw a line somewhere, and his had always been twenty. Okay, depending on extreme circumstances, nineteen and a half.

"Until midnight," she told him, and tears suddenly welled in her eyes. "Happy birthday to me, huh?"

Ditched in a Krispy Kreme by some scumball, a day before her birthday, with her wicked stepfather hot on her heels, ready to lock her in the basement. It was like a master class in the unfairness of life, a bitch-slap from the powers of the universe.

"You must be hungry," Izzy said, and she looked up, having—once again—successfully blinked back her tears. Dang it, this girl was tough.

She nodded. "I haven't slept in a while, either," she admitted.

As she held his gaze, Izzy's heart started its gymnastics routine again, and he had to look away. Gillman's little sister, he reminded himself. Seven-fucking-teen. What the hell was he going to do if the fishboy didn't call back before morning? Viable options swirled through his head, dangerously mixing with the no-longer viable ones he'd been considering mere moments earlier.

He'd open a bottle of wine, and they'd share it out on his deck while they also shared secrets. She'd soon feel comfortable enough around him to let herself weep from the pain of being abandoned, after which they'd have sex, right on his lounge chair.

"I'm kind of at your mercy," Eden told him now.

Shit.

She waited, just watching him.

She was hungry. He could cook her that steak he had in his fridge. After dinner, he'd get her set up on the couch, careful to keep his distance. But he'd awaken in the night, hearing her crying as if her heart were breaking, and he'd go to her and just hold her. And after the storm of tears had passed, he'd make her laugh.

After which she'd kiss him and his head would explode and they'd have sex, right on his couch.

Shit. *Shit.*

"Here's what we'll do," Izzy finally told her. "We'll drive through Mickey D's, get you something fast to eat. I need to go home, take a quick shower, and find something to wear that doesn't smell like ass. I'll grab a sweatshirt that you can borrow, too. Then we'll find someplace for you to stay tonight that isn't with me—maybe Jenk and Lindsey's. They, uh, have a couch that's more comfortable than mine.

"And then, after midnight, if Danny hasn't called by then, we'll call him at your mom's house," Izzy continued. "You'll be eighteen and no one will make you do anything that you don't want to do. Does that sound like a plan?"

Gratitude shone in Eden Gillman's eyes as she nodded. "Thank you."

God *damn*, she was gorgeous and yeah, a little crazy, and more than a little wild. Aside from the too-young thing, she was Izzy's idea of perfection, and the kicker was that he was pretty sure she liked him, too. She thought he was her hero. A flipping knight in shining armor.

He was some hero. Yeah, he was going to call his buddy Jenk and see if he and his wife Lindsey wouldn't mind if Dan Gillman's little sister spent the night, but it didn't have squat to do with the comfort-factor of Izzy's sofa.

No, it was all about the removal of temptation. A total temptation-ectomy, that's what he was looking to perform. Because gallant and brave Sir Izzy was a frakking coward. He was afraid, nay, terrified down to his very scumbag of a soul, that even though this girl *was* Gillman's sister, he would not be able to keep his hands off of her. Especially not when the clock struck twelve and she magically turned into an eighteen-year-old.

Even though, prior to tonight, his line had always been twenty.

"Let's get this show on the road," Izzy said.

And with that, the most beautiful woman in the world crossed the parking lot and climbed into the cab of his truck.

SMALLWOOD, KANSAS

"Loading dock," Decker said, and it was clear he was talking to Dave, not Nash. Dave knew that Deck and Nash could read each other's minds. They didn't need spoken language.

The AmLux Headquarters loading dock was dimly lit, and indeed, the perfect entry point into the building. It wasn't heavily guarded either—a lone sentry, bundled up against the cold, sat at a table near the freight elevators.

The guard's presence was a glitch—albeit a small one—in Troubleshooters Incorporated's red-cell attack plan.

TS Inc. was *the* top personal security firm in the U.S.—no, make that the world. They—and Dave Malkoff, Lawrence Decker, and James Nash were three of the firm's top operatives—provided security to people who needed to venture into some of the most dangerous places on the planet.

They also provided security-testing to "paranoia accounts" like tonight's client, AmLux, whose CEO was convinced that, even though their corporate headquarters was smack in the middle of America's heartland, they were a potential terrorist target.

Which was why Dave had followed Decker and Nash silently around the side of the AmLux building, slipping past a series of ready-and-waiting guards. They were bright-eyed and aware that tonight they would be tested, but not so bright-eyed and aware as to have spotted Dave, Deck, and Nash.

Being *red cell* meant that during tonight's op, the trio of men from TS Inc. would play the part of the terrorists. They were the bad guys, and their job was to break into AmLux, access the corporation's computers—both to steal their "secrets" and to take out their entire system—and then plant a series of bombs that would bring down the building.

Not that they'd actually do any of that, despite Decker's displeasure at being given this assignment in the first place. *Fucking waste of time* were his exact words, and Dave could relate. But the money AmLux was paying for tonight's cakewalk was not insignificant.

So the bombs they'd plant would be pretend, and as for the computers—they'd simply put a very small bug in their system that would read, "You've been compromised!" Dave had recorded the audiotrack for the message, and he'd done his best to sound like the relentlessly cheerful AOL guy who announced the presence of e-mail. He was pretty good at mimicking voices.

And that was probably going to be his sole contribution to this op. Yeah, yeah, when they got to the CEO's office, Dave would break into the computer and plant the bug. But either Decker or Nash could have done it just as easily.

And yet Tommy Paoletti, the commanding officer of Troubleshooters Inc., had assigned all three of them to this job. Theirs was not to question why, but instead to do or mock-die.

Except no way were they going to mock-die, up against this team of total amateurs.

As they now watched from the shadows of the loading dock, the lone guard checked in with the main gate, using his cell phone to do so. "Henderson here." His voice carried clearly over to them. "All clear."

Decker and Nash exchanged another look over the bags of gear they'd silently carried in, and Dave whispered what they were thinking. "No password or code."

No radio, either. But surely this guard had a panic button to alert the rest of his security team to trouble. Without a panic button, anyone trying to break in would be able to walk up to him and take him out before he finished dialing his phone for backup. That was pretty gosh-darn stupid.

"Panic button's over on the wall," Nash pointed out. Tall, dark, and strikingly movie-star handsome to Decker's average height, average hair color, and blandly nondescript face, the two men didn't just look mismatched. They *were* mismatched.

Average-looking Larry Decker had been a chief in the mighty U.S. Navy SEALs. James Nash, however, didn't merely not have a military background—he didn't have a background, period. His entire past had been magically erased from his official file, although Dave suspected that he'd done jail time and hadn't always played for the good guys. Which made him perfect for red-cell type assignments like the one they were currently on.

Personality, background, education—Decker and Nash couldn't have been more different. And yet they were close in a way that Dave—a former CIA loner—had never been close to anyone. The two men were more than friends—they were teammates. And they'd been so for years, having been partners at the clandestine and mysteriously unnamed "Agency" before coming to work for Troubleshooters Incorporated.

"Speed or finesse?" Decker asked Nash now as all three men crouched in the shadows.

Nash just laughed—and moved.

Apparently, speed it was.

"Stay with the gear," Deck ordered Dave. It was a more respectful step up from the "Stay put," Dave would've gotten from the man even just a few short months ago. Deck had gotten injured in a car accident, and Dave—despite his own broken wrist—had carried him through a blizzard to safety. He'd earned Deck's respect that day, but despite that, they still weren't quite friends.

Which was probably as much Dave's fault as Decker's. Although truth be told, Deck had gotten even less chatty and even more grim after his release from the hospital. Dave couldn't remember the last time he'd heard the man laugh.

Out on the loading dock, the security guard didn't see either Decker or Nash coming—Dave barely saw it go down himself. One moment the poor guy was doing the *Times* crossword, the next he was on the concrete floor, his cheek pressed against the dirt and grit, his mouth already gagged as Nash bound his hands behind his back.

Dave winced at Nash's less-than-gentle handling. This was, after all, just an exercise.

Decker, meanwhile, had possession of the guard's cell phone, searching through the list of outgoing calls. "Check-in's every five minutes," he announced as Nash dragged Henderson back toward Dave and the shadows.

Where Nash scared the shit out of the man as he opened his switchblade with the cold sound of metal against metal. "Here's where I slit your throat," he said over the man's alarmed noises.

"Not really," Dave interjected, giving Nash a chiding look.

"Relax, Malkoff. He knew I was kidding." Nash made the knife vanish, instead slapping an "I'm dead," sticker on the guard's forehead. He grabbed the bags of gear and humped them over toward Decker.

The guard was looking up at Dave, lots of white still showing in his eyes. He made noise that sounded like an indignant, *You didn't have to kill me.*

"Yeah, Henderson, we kinda did," Dave told him mildly. "We're ruthless terrorists. If we left you alive, you might have been able to signal for help." So Nash had dragged him back here and "killed" him. Hidden behind the forklift, Henderson's "blood" wouldn't be seen right away from someone just glancing in at the loading dock.

Ruthless terrorists weren't the only ones who knew that, at times, dead was the only guarantee of silence and mission success. Dave didn't want to think about how often they'd all done something similar in a real world situation—only without the cute sticker. And he would be willing to bet that Nash, James Nash, had done it more times than he could count.

"You're dead. If you move," Dave gave Henderson the standard warning, "or raise an alarm, the outcome of this exercise will be compromised. We'll need to reschedule, AmLux will be out tens of thousands of dollars, and you will no longer be employed. Do you understand?"

The guard nodded. He was sullen, but he'd gotten the message.

"Dave." Decker had already overridden the freight elevator's security system, and the monstrous thing was open and ready, the two former partners waiting impatiently inside.

Dave ran to catch up and as the door closed behind them, Nash glanced at his watch. "Three minutes fifteen to check in." Again Nash and Deck exchanged an information-laden look.

"Do we bluff or blow?" Dave asked as the elevator rose, trying not to feel like excess baggage. Why was he here?

Apparently Decker was thinking the exact same thing—except about himself.

"Blow," he said shortly. "Why make it harder for ourselves? They're afraid of terrorists, let's suicide-bomber up."

Prior to 9/11, security teams had assumed that anyone interested in breaking into a facility wouldn't do so unless it was possible for them also to get back out. Suicide bombers, however, needed only to get in.

"Bluff *and* blow." Nash took the guard's cell phone from Deck, handing it to Dave. "Buy us more time, Malkoff. Make 'em think you're Henderson."

The elevator doors opened onto a floor that was dimly lit. As if in unspoken agreement, Nash went left and Decker went right.

Leaving Dave, as usual, standing alone.

He opened Henderson's phone and dialed.

A LIFETIME AGO . . .

JANUARY 2001

FRESNO, CALIFORNIA

Murphy's spirits lifted as he pulled into the apartment parking lot and saw Hannah's familiar little car, with its bumper sticker that announced A WOMAN'S PLACE IS IN THE HOUSE AND SENATE.

He parked near her car, and was up the stairs and . . .

Han opened the door before he rang the bell—she must've been watching for him.

"I'm so sorry about your dad," she said, then, God, she was in his arms—a curious mix of softness and strength. "I wanted to come, but I couldn't get the time off and—"

"I know. It's okay," Murphy told her, closing his eyes as he breathed in the familiar scent of her laundry detergent or shampoo or whatever it was that made Hannah always smell so good—so clean and fresh. "He's been gone a long time, so . . . It was okay, Han."

"I should have been there," she insisted, holding him even more tightly.

He smelled her before he saw her—Angelina—a whiff of exotic perfume in the air or maybe on Hannah, from an earlier embrace. He opened his eyes, still hugging Han, and there she was, lingering in the doorway to Hannah's little living room.

Angelina Esparza, of whom Hannah had so often spoken. Han's best friend for going on eight years now.

Murph's heart didn't stop, and choirs of angels didn't break into heavenly song.

Yeah, the woman was unbelievably gorgeous—dark to Hannah's pale; long, thick, straight dark hair to Han's boyishly short waves. She was curvier than Hannah, too. More buxom, and unafraid to wear formfitting tops with low-cut necklines that featured her extremely, *extremely* impressive cleavage.

Unlike Hannah, she wore jewelry—large hoop earrings, a necklace, bangles on her wrists—and makeup. Not a lot. Just enough to tweak her naturally beautiful features into something truly amazing.

She was watching him as he hugged Hannah, and as their gazes met, she smiled. "You must be the one and only Murphy."

"Which makes you the one and only Angelina."

Her smile broadened. "I guess you've heard a lot about me, too."

Hannah pulled back to look at him, and under the force of her scrutiny, Murph turned his attention back to her.

She was more upset about missing his father's funeral than he'd been about the fact that his father had finally needed a funeral—which seemed wrong. And, of course, being Han, she knew exactly what he was thinking.

"It's okay, Vinh," she said. "That you're all right. It's okay if you're not . . . Whatever you're feeling is absolutely okay."

"It was a relief," he admitted. Man, that sounded awful. He glanced back at Angelina. "My father had Alzheimer's."

"I know," she said quietly. "Hannah told me. I'm so sorry for your loss."

He'd grieved and mourned for the seemingly endless years it had taken the disease to finally steal the part of his father's mind that kept him alive. For most of that time, the old man had had absolutely no idea who Murphy was—his only son. His only child.

Murphy had shared his pain with Hannah, leaning on her more than once through these last few awful years, spending his summers crewing on her uncle Patrick's whale-watching boat in the icy waters of Alaska's Inside Passage.

"It's okay to feel relieved," Hannah told him now, her eyes filled with her compassion and sympathy, "that he's finally at peace."

"Yeah," Murphy said, ruffling her hair. "I know. It's just . . ."

"Weird," she said, understanding. "That he finally gets a eulogy. After all this time . . ."

Murph had told her years ago that it didn't seem fair. His father was gone. His body still moved and needed care, but the man inside wasn't ever coming back. Yet none of his friends had the chance to gather together and remember a life well lived.

At Hannah's urging, he'd written about his father and e-mailed it to all of the old man's Marine buddies. He'd even sent his little essay to family—relatives who still kept their distance because they hadn't approved of Malcolm Murphy's Vietnamese wife.

Most of them didn't respond, although his cousin Nola had reached out to him. "Nola and Ricco were at the funeral," he told Hannah now.

She squeezed his hand. "I'm glad. How are they?"

"Good," he said. "They're good. It was . . . It was nice to see them." He turned to Angelina, because it was time to shake off this too-somber mood he'd brought into Han's apartment with him. "Angelina. I was starting to think you were a figment of Han's crazed imagination."

"Sometimes I think I might be," she said with a smile. It was hard to believe she was only Hannah's age—what were they? Just a year out of college. Little Hannah. Sweet, young Hannah, Patrick's niece—as Murph had trained himself to think of her.

She'd gotten a job as a uniformed beat cop with the Fresno police department—why she hadn't applied for a position up in Juneau, he couldn't figure out. Of course, Angelina was in LA, and these days Murph floated between San Diego and Sacramento.

"Vinh Murphy, Angelina Esparza," Hannah went through the formality. "About time you two met." She turned to Murphy. "You missed dinner. I'm sorry we didn't wait—"

"Don't worry," he said. "*I'm* sorry. Traffic around the airport—"

"It's okay," she said. "You're forgiven. Funeral. Free pass. But if you need food, bwee, you'll have to forage for leftovers in the fridge. Don't you dare drink all the beer before I get back. I gotta grab my bag."

"What?" Murphy said. "Where . . . ?"

"She's got an extra shift," Angelina explained as Hannah vanished into her bedroom. "It's a rookie thing."

"Diaz called in sick," Hannah called from the other room. "And it's not a full shift, just a special assignment. Traffic control after a high school basketball game. I'll be back in a few hours, unless the losing team does something stupid." She came back down the hall, duffle in her hand. "Angel, show him where the leftovers are, will you?" She stopped in front of Murphy. "Sorry to have to run out on you like this."

"Go," he said. "I'll be fine. Angelina can tell me her side of all the stories you've told me about her through the years." He turned to Angelina. "Whose idea was it, really? To put Metamucil into that mean girl's lemonade on the night of the cookout with the boys' camp? What was her name? Brianna something."

"Brianna Parker, the bitch," Hannah and Angelina unisoned, then laughed.

"That was me," Angelina volunteered. "We both had a crush on the same lifeguard. Bobby Contini. I actually thought I had a chance with him."

"You were, after all," Hannah said, "the daughter of the famous BadAss T." Laughing, she shouldered her bag. "I gotta go."

"We'll be here," Angelina said and Hannah shut the door behind her.

And there they were. Still standing in Han's little foyer.

"So," Angelina said. "Let's get you some dinner." She led the way into the kitchen—as if he needed a tour guide—and started getting out a plate and utensils.

"I can do it," Murphy said, opening the refrigerator. "You don't need to. I know where everything is."

"You must visit Hannah a lot." She leaned back against the counter.

"I travel a lot," Murphy told her as he pried open the lid of what looked like some truly excellent meatloaf. "So, yeah. I usually crash on her couch every few weeks or so."

"Très diplomatique." Angelina gave him a golf clap. "Answering my unspoken question—are you sleeping with her—with such tact and grace."

He laughed as he added some mashed potatoes and green beans to his plate. "We're just friends," he said. He put the plate into the microwave and dialed up a few minutes of heat before turning back to Angelina. "Didn't Han tell you that?"

"She did, but . . . She has her secrets," Angelina told him. "I was just wondering if you were one of them."

"She thinks of me like a big brother," he said.

"And when you're crashed on her couch," Angelina asked, "you never lie awake thinking. . . maybe you'd be more comfortable in her bed?"

"Never," Murphy cheerfully lied.

"Do you actually *fit* on the couch?"

"Trust me," he said. "I'm a Marine. I can sleep anywhere."

"Do you have a girlfriend?" Angelina asked.

"Negative," Murphy said as the microwave beeped.

"Boyfriend?"

He shot her a look. "Ditto." He took his plate out, burning his fingers and letting it rattle onto the counter. "Ow!"

Angelina turned on the sink faucet, and he put both hands under the cold water. "You wanna hook up?"

"Come again?" Murphy turned off the water, turned to look at her.

"Hook up," she repeated. "It's what we younguns say when we want to have hot monkey sex."

He laughed. She was too funny. "I know what hook up means, little girl."

"It was kind of a yes/no question," Angelina pointed out, obviously trying hard not to smile back at him. "Big man."

"No," he said. "Thank you. But, no."

He pushed his plate over to the breakfast counter, where Hannah had a pair of bar stools. He slid onto one, but Angelina didn't move—she just leaned against the counter, her smile slipping free as she watched him. Hot damn, she was beyond gorgeous. *Hot monkey sex . . .*

"Hannah told me you . . . sometimes say outrageous things," Murphy told her.

Her smile broadened, and her perfect white teeth flashed as her eyes sparkled. "Oh, come on. *That* wasn't particularly outrageous. It *is* the twenty-first century. Women *are* allowed to make the first move."

The meatloaf tasted even better than it smelled. "What would you have done if I'd've said yes?"

"Total win/win situation here," she said. "You say no, I find out you really are this pillar of honor that Han made you out to be. You say yes, I get to have sex with a guy I've pretty much wanted to do since Hannah first described him."

Murphy laughed. "Right."

She laughed, too. "I'm serious."

He got up, took a beer out of the fridge. "Hannah said you rarely were. You know, serious."

"Hannah said the very same thing about you, hot stuff," Angelina countered. She didn't back away as he opened the bottle and tossed the cap into the garbage. She smelled incredibly good.

"She also said I'd probably fall in love with you at first sight." He took a slug as he went back to his seat.

"How's that going?" she asked.

He shook his head in mock dismay. "Sadly, she was wrong."

"Most guys need to see me naked," Angelina pointed out. "She probably meant you'd fall in love with me at the first sight of me naked. With that in mind, the offer of hot monkey sex stands." She glanced at her watch. "For the next . . . ten minutes."

"Ten minutes," he said on a laugh. "Does that include the actual *having* of the hot monkey sex, or is that just my window of opportunity to change my mind?"

"One would hope," she said sternly, "that true hot monkey sex would take the better part of an hour."

Murphy laughed again. "While I appreciate the repeated offer, I don't need to see you naked," he said. "The reason I didn't fall in love with you at first sight is because I've been in love with you for, wow, it must be four years now. Pretty much since Hannah told me about you. The magnificent Angelina." He toasted her with his beer. "Even more magnificent in the flesh."

"And yet," she pointed out, "you say no to hot monkey sex."

"It's a pure and chaste kind of love," he told her, digging in to the potatoes.

"Spoken like a true pillar of honor."

"Assuming pillars can speak."

Angelina slid onto the stool next to him. "I know you were . . . only joking, but . . ." Up close, her eyes were almost unbearably dark brown—the kind of eyes into which a man could lose himself forever. She was speaking softly, practically whispering and he found himself leaning closer. "That's exactly what it feels like. Like I've known you forever and . . . Like I've loved you for even longer. I'm going to marry you, Vinh." She reached up and touched him, her fingers cool on the back of his neck. "I've been waiting for you, all my life."

She was serious. Everything up to this point had been flirtatious, outrageous fun. But now she was serious, and, with his heart beating double-time, Murphy didn't feel the need to mock her about the fact that *all her life* was a mere twenty-three years. She was *serious,* and she leaned in and kissed him and—

Murphy awoke with a start and for a moment, he didn't know where he was.

A cabin.

He was on the hard wooden floor of a cabin. Weak morning light filtered in through a window, illuminating the rustic beams that supported the roof. He could see the stone chimney of a fireplace. The light from that window reflected on the gleaming glass of a gun case, keys in its lock.

It was Patrick's cabin—although Murphy wasn't sure if he was in Dalton or Juneau.

What he *did* know was that he wasn't alone. Angelina was nestled, warm and solid against him, curled up tightly. They must've had too much to drink. She would laugh when he told her he'd dreamed, so vividly, about the night they'd met, about their first kiss—so sweet and hot and . . .

Angelina stirred. "Murph?"

But it wasn't Angelina, it was Hannah and . . .

No. God, *no.*

But try as he might to stay here in this place where Angelina could well be in the next room, his memories of the past few years came crashing down around him.

Angelina was dead.

Dead and gone.

He was in Dalton, where Hannah was living these days after her own hellish tragedy. He'd come here, not to see her, but to get one of Patrick's handguns. To put it in his mouth and . . .

The brightening dawn sparkled and danced on the glass of that gun case, taunting him.

End it. Now.

Jesus Christ, what had he been thinking? Hadn't he already damaged Hannah enough for one night? For one *lifetime* . . .

Murphy scrambled to his feet—his head a near-solid block of pain. Somehow Hannah had fallen back to sleep.

Somehow? She wasn't sleeping, she'd passed out—just like he had—courtesy of her drug of choice, which was whatever top-shelf booze she found in Pat's voluminous liquor cabinet.

Staggering only slightly, Murphy put a pillow from the sofa beneath her head and she didn't even stir.

"I'm so sorry," he told her, even though she couldn't possibly hear him.

He took a blanket from the couch and spread it over her, then went out the door.

CHAPTER
THREE

E den Gillman was crying as if her heart was breaking.

She was trying to be quiet, but her muffled sobs woke Izzy from the restless state of semi-sleep that he'd finally fallen into.

He lay there in the darkness of his bedroom, listening to her, knowing that the dead last thing he should do was get out of bed and go into the living room, where she was sleeping on his sofa.

Yeah, genius that he was, he'd had it all figured out. Gillman's little sister could have a sleepover at Jenk and Lindsey's. It was the perfect solution to the dilemma created by his relentless hard-on for this girl.

Girl, girl, girl. Yeah, it was well after midnight, but now, instead of being a seventeen-year-old girl, she was an *eighteen*-year-old girl.

His fatal error had been in underestimating the effect of a double cheeseburger on a girl—girl!—who hadn't eaten or slept in close to forty-eight hours.

He'd only taken three minutes in the shower. Okay, maybe four and a half. But when Izzy'd come out the bathroom, fully dressed and ready to load Eden back into his truck—his plan was to make that phone call to Jenk and Lindsey from the safety of the road—she'd been completely unconscious, on his couch.

He paced back and forth in front of the damn thing, once, twice, thirty times, but she didn't arouse. In sleep, she was much as she was while awake—angelically ferocious. She was curled tightly into herself, hugging the sweatshirt he'd given her as if it were a lifeline.

He tried calling Gillman's cell again, but again, the dickhead didn't pick up.

Izzy had fixed himself dinner then, cooking that steak he'd had marinating in the fridge, hoping the smell of food would wake Eden.

It hadn't.

He'd washed up. Hell, he'd cleaned his entire kitchen. He even scrubbed the freaking floor.

Zero movement from the couch.

He called Mark Jenkins then, aware that it was getting late and that Jenk—like Izzy—had also been out on the training op. Like Izzy, he had to be tired, too. Jenk's wife Lindsey had answered the phone and it was beyond obvious that they were already in bed.

Not necessarily sleeping.

"No, Zanella," Lindsey said in lieu of a traditional greeting, like *hello* or even *what-the-fuck do you want?* "Whatever you're calling for . . . Thank you, but no."

"Really?" Izzy asked her. "Because I have this lottery ticket and I think I just won twenty million dollars that I'd love to share with you, but if you don't w—"

"This is the sound," Lindsey said, "of me not laughing. If there's a point to this phone call, get to it quick, Z-man, so that I can tell you that I love you, say no, and then hang up the phone."

"Gilligan's little sister, Eden, came into the Bug, looking for him," Izzy got to it. "Her boyfriend ditched her in a Krispy Kreme in LA. She's got nothing. No money, no clothes—"

"No *clothes*?" That caught Lindsey's attention.

"Besides what she's got on," Izzy explained. "She's not, like, naked." Christ, don't think about Eden Gillman naked. . . . Shit, too late. He cleared his throat. "I was hoping she could sleep on your couch tonight. I don't think it's appropriate for her to stay here with me."

Silence.

"Linds? You still there?"

"Who are you and what have you done with Izzy Zanella?" she finally said.

"Go on," he said. "Mock me. The one time I'm being serious and trying to do the right thing." He lowered his voice in case his talking on the phone had awakened Eden. "She's gorgeous and she's funny and she's too young and she's too young and sweet Jesus, she's too freaking *young*, okay? Oh, yeah, and here's a recipe for disaster: She's Gillman's sister. And I like her. Too much. So can I please, *please* bring her over so that she can sleep on your couch instead of mine?"

"Wow," she said. "Of course you can."

"Bless you."

Izzy could hear the murmur of Jenk's voice in the background, no doubt wondering WTF Lindsey was doing, *of-course-you-can*-ing Izzy when any and all responses to a request made when they were already in bed should have been a resounding *no*.

"Hang on," Lindsey told Izzy, then covered the mouthpiece of the phone as she no doubt explained the sitch to her adorable yet height-challenged husband.

"Remind him of that time I saved his life," Izzy suggested, but then Jenkins himself came onto the phone.

"Eden *Gillman?*" he asked.

"Yup," Izzy said.

"She's alone with you, in your apartment."

"She is."

"Are you out of your freaking mind?"

"That's the point," Izzy said. "I'm not. Hence this SOS. You gonna help me out here, man, or are you going to leave me with my dick in this extremely uncomfortable vise?" Although, he suspected that there was no such thing as a *comfortable* vise when one's dick was involved.

Jenk sighed heavily. "Bring her over," he said.

"Thank you," Izzy said.

"Can you just . . . maybe take your time getting here?" Jenkins asked.

"No problem. Eden's out cold on my couch." Izzy checked his watch. "I'll let her sleep for another hour. That work for you, Romeo?"

"See you then," Jenk said, and hung up the phone.

Apparently, it worked for him. Lucky little bastard.

But an hour came and went, and Eden didn't wake up.

When Izzy tried to talk to her, she just burrowed her way deeper into the couch.

Part of his problem came from his unwillingness to touch her. Yeah, sure, he could have gathered her up and carried her to his truck—but first he'd have to touch her. And he couldn't bring himself to do that with her shirt all up and twisted around her and . . .

Nipple! Holy shit!

Izzy quickly put a blanket over Eden and her lovely wandering nipple, paced the room a few hundred more times and then called Jenk and Lindsey back. "She won't wake up."

"Is she all right?" Jenkins asked, no doubt speaking softly because Lindsey had fallen asleep.

"Yeah, I think she's just exhausted," Izzy said, before it occurred to him to say, *I don't know. Do you think you can get Lopez to come over to check her out?*

Even though all Navy SEALs had some degree of medical training, Jay Lopez was a hospital corpsman. And once Lopez was here—albeit under false pretenses—Izzy would no longer be alone in his apartment with Eden Freakin' Gillman.

"I know this is asking a lot," Izzy said instead, "but could you and Lindsey maybe come over? You can have my bed. I'll go back to your place and crash on your—"

"Zanella." Jenk cut him off. "Just go into your bedroom and close the door. Go to sleep. If you're even half as tired as I am—"

"Yeah, see, that's just it," Izzy said. "I'm not. I didn't spend the last hour perfecting my technique of Palm Tree in High Wind from page seventy-five of the Kama Sutra, with my incredibly sexy wife."

"Go to sleep," Jenk said again. "If Eden wakes up—which she probably won't before morning—call us then, okay? If you need to. Which you won't, because she won't wake up, all right?"

"What happened to *are you out of your freaking mind?*" Izzy asked. "Gillman's gonna—"

"I'll tell him you went above and beyond, trying to find a place for her to stay that wasn't your apartment," Jenk promised. "He'll be cool with that. I'll make sure of it. He'll thank you."

Gillman would thank him—as a trio of pigs singing "Lean on Me" in perfect harmony flew past Izzy's apartment window.

He hung up the phone and called Lopez. Who didn't answer. "Fuck you," Izzy left a cheery message on his voice mail. "I know you're awake, Jay-Lo. It's barely 2100 hours. Danny's sister Eden is here and I fucking need a fucking chaperone. Call me back, douchebag."

But Lopez never called, so Izzy finally went to bed because Jenk was right and Eden didn't wake up.

But she was awake now. With her big brown eyes and her gorgeous legs and that errant nipple. Crying in his living room.

Izzy's alarm clock said it was just after oh three hundred as he swung his legs out of bed. Just to go to the bathroom. He moved quietly out of his room and down the hall. He quietly took a leak and quietly flushed—and realized that there was no such thing as a quiet flush.

Sure enough, when he came back out of the bathroom, Eden was silent.

Izzy stood there for a moment, in the doorway to the living room. He should have gone back into his room and shut and locked the door. Instead, he proved that his older brothers were right. He *was* unbelievably stupid. He spoke into the darkness, asking her, "You all right?"

"I'm fine," she said, a small voice from the shadows.

Fine? "I . . . kinda don't believe you," Izzy told her.

"Well, duh," she said, shifting to sit up on his couch. "Because I'm lying. I mean, God, nobody's *really* fine. *Are you all right? I'm fine.* It's like going to church and saying the responses to the prayer. It's automatic—and meaningless. A stupid ritual."

"I, uh, pretty much meant it," Izzy pointed out. "You know, when I asked. You."

"No," she said. "Okay? No, I'm *not* all right. What could possibly be *all right* about my stupid boyfriend ditching me, and me being stupid enough to wait there, at that *stupid* doughnut shop, *praying* that he'd come back, even though I knew he was gone for good."

A-ha. Eden had reached the anger phase of her heartbreak. Over the coming days and weeks it would cycle around—despair, sorrow, pointless what-if-ing, self-recrimination, emptiness, equally pointless hope-for-a-reconciliation, and yes, scalding anger. Shake well and repeat. Over and over.

"I *knew* he was a total asshole," Eden continued, her voice shaking, "and I must be one, too, because I love him. Loved him. I don't love him anymore, how could I still love him after what he did?" The self-recrimination mixed with sorrow and body-slammed the anger to the mat, and she started to cry again. Big time, with body-shaking sobs. But the anger wasn't gone without a fight. "I hate him, God, I hate him—I should hate him, right?"

"Well, yeah," Izzy said, because she seemed to want a response.

"I must be a total idiot, because he played me, right from the start, because I *still* can't believe he left me there like that, like, something must've happened, he must be hurt or bleeding or dead because he *said* that he *loved* me. He said I was the one, only I know he's not dead because some girls who work for Richie came into the Krispy Kreme and they told me Jerry was working for him again, too, even though he promised me that he wouldn't go back, and they said he already has a new girlfriend, so apparently I *wasn't* the one. And all I could think was *thank God he's not dead.* I'm *such* an idiot . . ."

Jerry was, no doubt, Eden's douchebag of a former boyfriend. Richie was . . . apparently some local LA lowlife?

During Eden's tirade, Izzy had gone back into the bathroom to get a spare role of toilet paper because the box of tissues on the back of his toilet had been empty for about three years. He stood there now, right in front of her, holding that TP ineffectually, able to see her a little more clearly in the light from the streetlamp that shone in through the front window. Tough-as-nails Eden Gillman had buried her face in her hands and was crying her heart out.

"Hey," he said, at a loss as to what to say, what to do. He set the roll of TP on the arm of the couch as he crouched down next to her. "He's an asshole. Jerry is. You have every right to feel betrayed and hurt. And upset. And sad. He definitely played you, Eden, and that's definitely . . . sad. But don't put that on yourself. That's his shit. He's the idiot. Yeah, you missed the clues—if there even were any. Some guys are skilled and . . . It takes a while to, you know, recognize exactly who deserves your, you know, time."

Listen to him. Izzy Zanella, counselor for hot teen girls. Jesus save him. This was one of those nights that made him wish he kept a scrapbook. This would be a ten-pager, for sure. Scumbag that he was, he'd devote an entire special section to that nipple that was now securely covered by the blanket.

Christ, he had to give himself double scumbag points for thinking about that while she sat there, sobbing away.

He focused. "You know, it's good to cry," he told her because she was fighting her tears again, trying to force herself to stop, pulling a length of paper from the roll and using it to wipe her shiny face and blow her runny nose. "Everyone needs to do it every now and then. Get all the hurt and shit out of your system. Just . . . go for it. Flush Jerry and Richie and all their crap away."

She turned to look at him, with big, dark, wounded eyes in a face that was pale in the dimness. "Do you cry?" she asked.

"Well, no," Izzy said. "Because I'm a guy and . . . Yo, Powderpuff, don't be such a pushover, believing everything that comes out of everyone's mouth. Of course I cry. I'm human, and humans cry. That's the way it works. Anyone who tells you that they don't cry is a liar. We get the big brains, and the emotional shit comes standard. And yeah, okay, maybe I try to work it so that I don't cry in public—I know you're on *that* train with me. But you're not in public right now. You're in my living room, which is private."

A little too private, especially considering he was wearing only a pair of boxer shorts.

And yeah, now she'd noted that factoid, too, her eyes widening slightly as she took in the scar on his chest as well. It was ragged and still angry-looking—even after all this time. It was a real chick-repellent, which was why, more often than not, he kept his T-shirt on.

"That must've hurt," she said, which surprised him. Most people looked but then looked away. Pretended it wasn't there. Nothing to see, move it along . . .

Izzy nodded, trying not to feel self-conscious as she continued to look at him. "Yeah."

"What happened?"

"I tried to stop a bullet with my chest, only my superpowers weren't working, so I kinda got shot. Hurt like a mother, if you want to know the truth. Did I cry? Hell, no. Not one tear. But I cried a shitload when I found out a friend of mine died, in that same . . . event. So . . ."

Eden met his eyes in the dimness, and Jesus H. Christ, there was that spark again. Izzy tried to look away. And failed. "He was a good man. Frank," he told her quietly. "He deserved to be mourned, so yes, I cried."

"Jerry doesn't deserve it," Eden told him vehemently, as her tears started up again. "He deserves . . . He's never touching me again. Never."

"Good plan."

She pulled off another length of toilet paper and forcefully blew her nose. "I hate that I can't stop crying about him."

"You're not crying about him," Izzy told her. "You're crying for you. For . . . lost innocence."

She rolled her eyes. "Lost innocence? Get real. I lost my innocence when I was fourteen. Theresa Franklin's older brother took me for a ride in his car. Of course, I didn't exactly say no, so . . ."

Holy shit. "I'm not talking sex," Izzy said. "I'm talking about . . . you know, love. You said Jerry told you that you were the one. And you know, maybe, in that moment when he said it? Maybe he meant it. But you believe in something different. Something bigger and . . . better. Something that I think most people don't believe exists. They give up on it, you know? After they've lived through too many Jerries of their own."

She was listening to him, watching him with those luminous, tear-filled eyes, and he was unable to stop himself from reaching out and pushing her sleep-tangled hair from her face.

"But see, here's the thing," he told her, gently using his fingers to comb out her hair. "It does exist. I've seen it, Eden. It's rare, but it's out there. So, I'm a believer, too. People like you and me, though? We've got to learn to stay away from the people who don't believe in it, so they don't rip our hearts in two."

She closed her eyes, and the tears that welled there ran unchecked down her cheeks, and Izzy shifted closer.

He caught himself and shifted back, because, damn, that was a bad idea. He forced himself to pull his hand back, too. "It takes work. Constant training," he said, desperately searching for a way to lighten things up, as she opened her eyes and pulled more toilet paper from the roll to wipe her face. "Because even when you get the real deal, you don't just float along, like, on some perfect, golden river. Like, you know, *All you need is love,*" he sang. "Works in theory. But in reality, if the guy you love isn't Gandhi or Jesus?" He sang again: "*All you need is love and a hefty bank account and maybe even a partial lobotomy, yat da dah-dat dah . . .*"

That got him a watery smile. "You have a good voice."

"I also play a mean guitar," he told her. "But, shh, don't tell your brother. He doesn't know."

"Why not?" she asked, blowing her nose again.

Izzy shrugged. "No one I work with knows. It's just . . . It was the path I didn't take. I haven't taken my guitar out of the closet in years."

"That's too bad," Eden said.

"Yeah," Izzy agreed. "But I don't have much time, and . . ." He shrugged again.

And there they sat, just looking at each other.

"That felt nice," Eden finally said. "What you were doing. If I somehow made you think I wanted you to stop—"

"Actually," Izzy told her, "I wanted me to stop, because, um, I kind of like you, and the last thing you need is—"

"I like you, too," she whispered, and oh damn, the look in her eyes was unmistakable.

"You're probably . . . feeling vulnerable." Izzy couldn't seem to work the muscles in his body that would allow him to push himself to his feet and walk away, but at least his mouth was functional. "And lonely and really, *really* . . ."

She kissed him.

She just leaned forward and pressed her mouth to his.

She was both salty and sweet, soft and firm, and Izzy had to clench every cell in his body to keep from kissing her back the way he wanted to.

He could have been anybody—anyone besides Jerry, that is. Izzy tried to focus on that. Yeah, maybe Eden liked him, but this was entirely about payback. She wanted to screw Jerry, figuratively—by screwing, literally, someone who *wasn't* Jerry.

He doubted it was that clear-cut-and-dried inside of Eden's own head. It was, no doubt, mixed with a need for an exorcism of sorts. By using Izzy, she would drive the ghost of Jerry away.

Or maybe this girl who'd had her first sexual encounter when she was freaking fourteen simply didn't know how to be friends with a guy without getting naked.

No doubt about it, it was past time to stand up, to walk away. Time to lock himself in his bedroom. To call Jenkins and scream, *Help me, for the love of God, someone help me!*

Instead, Izzy sat there, on the carpet in front of his couch, and let himself get kissed. He heard himself groan as Eden licked his lips, as she deepened the kiss, her sweet tongue inside of his mouth, and then she was in his arms, in his lap, wrapping herself around him, and God damn, he was so fucked. He knew what this was about, he knew it wasn't real, and he knew that he shouldn't be doing it for so many reasons, yet he ignited anyway, kissing her back hungrily, filling his hands with the softness of the skin beneath her shirt.

Game over. He'd lost—so to speak. Of course, on the other hand, it was also true that he'd really, really, *really* won.

"Please," she breathed between soul-sucking kisses, her body soft and supple against him, as his exploring fingers found that perfect nipple he'd glimpsed earlier. "Please . . ."

It was more than clear what she was after—with her legs wrapped around his waist, she was rubbing herself against the hard length of him, reaching—sweet Jay-sus—between them to grab his dick—right through his shorts—and press him more precisely where she wanted him.

She moved to unfasten her shorts, and Izzy had enough brain cells still firing to recognize what a terrible, horrible, no-good idea *that* was. Dry humping Gillman's little sister was one thing. Full penetration sex would send him to an entirely different, much deeper level of hell.

So he rolled her up and onto the couch, pinning her onto her back as he moved between her legs, as he kissed her and kissed her and kissed her. With reluctance, he let go of that nipple he'd found and reached between them, sliding his hand up the paradise-perfect smoothness of her thigh, up the leg of her shorts. He hooked his fingers beneath the edge of her bathing suit and . . .

Money.

No, what he'd found was better than any paycheck he'd ever received.

She was mindblowingly soft and wet and she'd gasped, too, inside of his mouth, at the contact, then shifted to push his fingers more deeply within her.

She wasn't done trying to take off her shorts, though. "Let me—"

"Shhh," Izzy said, capturing her mouth again as he continued to explore. His reach and movement were both limited, but . . . Yeah, *there* it was. Ah, God, he wanted in. And she wanted him, too, but . . . Not him. She didn't really want *him*.

She was trying to guide his dick along the same route his hand had taken—which wasn't going to work, but damn, he liked that she was willing to try. And yeah, if she kept touching him like that, even through his shorts, he was going to . . .

He shifted his hand, only slightly, but his move made for a bull's-eye, and Eden exploded. She just went right over the edge.

And Izzy went, too. Right in his boxers. *Gahhhhhhd.* . . .

He lay there then, on top of her, catching his breath, as she tried to catch hers, as well.

But then he realized that her ragged breathing wasn't going to end anytime soon. She was crying again.

No doubt because payback sex never really worked to make anyone feel better. It was designed to hurt the payee, but the payer usually got slammed in the process.

As for the payer's partner . . . ?

He was the one who usually walked away unscathed. Yet Izzy was lying there, wondering how the fuck had he let this get so totally out of control, and feeling not just uncomfortably damp, but extremely scathed.

Beating a hasty retreat to the bathroom seemed like a smart option— but it meant deserting Eden, who had gone full circle and was back to despair.

So Izzy lifted himself off of her and gathered her into his arms so that she was spooned against him, there on the couch. "It's okay," he reassured her. "It's going to be okay . . ."

Although, for the life of him, he couldn't figure out how.

SMALLWOOD, KANSAS

Dave woke up early, the morning after the AmLux invasion. He hadn't brought workout gear because the hotel out here in this timewarp back to 1981 didn't have a health club. Truth was, it barely had beds. It *did* have what the proprietor called a continental breakfast starting at 0600—provided "continental" meant stale pastries and coffee that smelled as if it had been brewed with insecticide.

He beat the hotel staff to the alcove where the food was being served, waiting while two very slow-moving elderly women unwrapped what looked like bagels and croissants. Looked like but were not—a fact Dave had learned the hard way during yesterday's morning meal. They were, in fact, faux versions—food-like, but not quite food. The bread that granny one and granny two put out for toast was slightly more real, so Dave popped two slices into the toaster.

He was standing there, caught up in making a massive decision—peanut butter or strawberry jam—when Nash came through the hotel's front doors.

"Hey," Dave called to him, and Nash stopped short, clearly surprised and a little put-off at seeing him there.

"Hey." Nash glanced at the elevators, as if gauging his escape, but then came toward Dave—or maybe just toward the coffee. "You're up early."

"My room doesn't have a bed," Dave informed the taller man, who poured himself a cup. "It has a bowl that's bed-shaped. My back's already spasming, so . . ."

"I hear you," Nash said. He looked tired, and even slightly pale, his jacket still zipped up tight despite the hotel lobby's heat. And yet he still managed to look like a movie star. "I don't sleep well without Tess."

It was more likely that Nash didn't sleep, *period* without Tess Bailey, his fiancée.

"Is there something going on that I need to know about?" Dave asked.

Nash didn't stop reaching for a lid for his coffee cup. He didn't telegraph anything at all. No guilt, no nothing. His smile was completely natural as he glanced at Dave. "That's the problem with you former CIA types. You see spooks and monsters in every shadow."

Dave took the plunge and spread strawberry jam on his toast. "Yeah, well, I saw you leaving the hotel last night around 0200."

Nash laughed with a flash of his perfect, white teeth. "See what I mean? I got up at sunrise, Malkoff. I went to take a walk because I couldn't sleep. I don't know who you thought you saw, but it wasn't me."

With his coffee in his hand, Nash turned toward the elevator.

And Dave realized that he'd just been conned by a master. He reached out and caught Nash by the arm—the arm that he'd kept close to his body throughout their entire conversation, elbow pressed against his side . . .

"Ow—Christ!"

Sure enough, Dave's hand came away smeared with Nash's blood.

As one of the breakfast grannies toddled out of the kitchen, Dave grabbed Nash by the jacket and hustled him over to the elevator. It wasn't until they were safely inside, the door closed behind them that Dave dared to look at Nash. "Maybe we should try this again. Is there something going on that I need to know about?"

Nash let his head thump back against the grimy, once-elegant wall, no longer trying to hide from Dave the fact that he was in some serious pain. "No," he said quietly. "There's something going on that you *can't* know about. Decker can't either."

"How about Tess?" Dave couldn't peel Nash's jacket back from him—not here. The elevator probably still had security cameras in place.

Nash shook his head. "Especially not Tess. I'm okay. Really. It's just a ding."

"Just a ding." Dave had once heard Nash describe a stab wound from a KA-BAR knife as "just a ding."

"Yeah." The elevator opened on the third floor—Nash's floor—and Dave helped him out and over to his room, taking his cup of coffee from him. Nash's key card was smeared with blood, and he wiped it on his pants before pushing it into the slot. "I'm here, I'm okay, and now I need you to walk away."

"I'm sure you think you're okay," Dave agreed. "But either I come in with you, or I go get Deck."

Nash no doubt would have stood there and argued, but another of the hotel's patrons came out of his room at the end of the hall, briefcase in hand, ready to start his day here in the land of corn.

Dave pushed Nash inside a room that was a mirror opposite of his own, but identical in every other way. Desk by the window. Absurdly uncomfortable plaid easy-chair with atrociously matching ottoman. Big mirror on the wall across from a king-sized bed-bowl—that was still neatly made up.

So okay, not identical in *every* other way . . .

The door closed with a thunk behind them, as Nash looked from Dave to the bed and back. "Busted," he said.

"Yeah," Dave said wryly as he put Nash's coffee cup down on the desk. "You didn't sleep in here last night. *That's* my big clue that something's going on. First aid kit?"

It wasn't *just a ding*, because Nash gave in, far too quickly. "In the front zipper section of my duffle," he directed Dave as he winced his way out of his jacket.

"Dear God," Dave said. The entire side of Nash's shirt was bright red with blood.

"Relax," Nash said. "The bullet was spent."

Bullet? "You were *shot*?" Dave clarified.

Nash unbuttoned his shirt as he went into the bathroom, leaning toward the mirror to examine what looked like an angry entry wound, just above his right hip. "It hurts," he announced, "but it's just a .22."

"Oh, good." Dave brought him that first aid kit. "Because if it were a .45, you'd probably be dead. What the hell happened, James?"

Nash met his eyes in the mirror as he thoroughly washed his hands. With his dark hair tousled and his leading-man chin sporting GQ-quality stubble, even with fatigue and pain lining his face, he looked like he should have been on some Hollywood producer's short list of candidates to play the next James Bond. "Nothing happened. I was in my room all night."

Dave gazed steadily at this man—this very, very dangerous man—that he couldn't quite call friend. "I know you don't like me—"

"I like you fine," Nash told him as he fished through the kit, finding and opening a pill bottle—antibiotics. He took one out, washing it down with tequila from a bottle that was sitting out on the bathroom counter. He dug back in the kit, then unwrapped what looked like a medical version of pliers. "I used to not like you, but you kinda grew on me. Especially after you saved Decker's life."

"Ah," Dave said, as Nash shifted to sit on the sink counter, so he could clearly see his bullet wound in the mirror. Was he really intending to remove that bullet himself? Although Nash was right about it being spent.

Fortunately, Nash had been at the very far end of the range of the handgun that this bullet had been fired from, which was why it hadn't blasted a hole through him. Instead, most of its energy "spent," it had lodged in the fleshy part of his side. It was close to the surface and would be easy to remove.

Relatively easy to remove—compared to a bullet that *wasn't* spent.

Significantly harder, compared to a splinter.

"I didn't realize we'd, um, moved into a new phase in our relationship," Dave continued. "I mean, you don't really know me, so—"

"I know you well enough," Nash told him. "Enough to know that you wish you were me. Or Decker. Probably Decker more than me, right?"

There was no point in answering that. Nash was just baiting him, trying to make Dave be the one who was flustered and defensive.

Except Dave wasn't the one with a *bullet wound* after being—mysteriously—out all night.

Nash winced as he pulled back the raw flesh from around that entry
wound, trying to widen the angry-looking hole, and succeeding only in
making it bleed more. "If you were Decker, you'd sweep Sophia off her
feet."

Keep Sophia out of this. Dave clenched his teeth around the words.
No point in responding to the fact that Nash had leaped on Dave's button
with both feet. At the same time, he glanced at his watch. It was nearly
0630, which was a personal record. He'd actually gone almost twenty minutes without thinking about the ethereally beautiful blond woman who
thought of Dave as her best friend.

Yeah, Dave and Sophia were tight—in a purely platonic way. Tight
enough so that Sophia had often used him as a sounding board, to discuss
the fact that she was hung up on Lawrence Decker, who relentlessly kept
her at arm's length.

But Nash wasn't done with his attempt to piss Dave off. "Or maybe
you'd settle for being me. You could give Tess to Decker and *then* sweep
Sophia off her feet."

In the world according to Nash, Decker had a thing for Nash's fiancée. And yes, there was a time when Dave, too, had suspected Deck had
feelings for Tess, but that was long past. These days, Decker seemed to be
made of stone. If he felt anything for anyone, he hid it well. And as for
Nash . . .

"Believe me," Dave told Nash evenly, "I have no desire to be you."

"Really," Nash countered. "With Sophia in your bed, and Decker as
your new best friend . . . ? You'd all live happily ever after. Well, except for
Tess, who for some reason really does love me. Arrrgh." He'd tried and
failed to get the bullet with that tool, and let loose a string of curses.

"And yet," Dave pointed out as he took the surgical instrument from
Nash—it would be much easier for him to get the bullet out from this
angle, "when you're not home with Tess, you stay out all night—doing
something dangerous that gets you shot."

"And yet, I do," Nash agreed, as Dave clenched his teeth and went for
it. *"Holy Mary, Mother of God!"*

The bullet clattered in the sink, and, cursing a blue streak, Nash swiftly washed out the wound with antiseptic soap that Dave knew had to sting like hell. He then pressed a clean hand towel against his side to stanch the fresh flow of blood, his face tight and pale.

Dave washed his hands off in the tub, scrubbing his nails clean. "You need stitches. Old buddy old pal."

"Yeah," Nash agreed, moving to sit on the closed commode—another sign that he was in worse pain than he was letting on. He grabbed the tequila bottle, took another long slug. "But I'm good. I can—"

"That was a statement," Dave pointed out. "Not a question or a request. Either I can help you with the stitches or Decker can."

"Then go get him," Nash said hotly, even as Dave unwrapped a sterile needle and thread. "Because I am not going to have you holding this over me for the rest of my life. But when you do go get him? Be ready for him to die. What he doesn't know is keeping him alive. Do you understand?"

"No," Dave said as he crouched next to Nash and began stitching him up, as he wasn't particularly careful to not make it hurt.

"Ouch! *Ow! Shit!*"

"I *don't* understand. Not at all," Dave said. "You've got plenty of friends—"

"Who can't fix this," Nash told him through clenched teeth. "They can't, but they'll try, and then they'll die, too."

"Too?" Dave asked, as he tied off the thread.

Nash just shook his head, his face clenched with pain that was only partly from the wound in his side. He closed his eyes as Dave bandaged him, far more gently this time. "Dave. Please. I'm asking you to . . . Christ, I'm asking you to help me, okay?"

"No, you're not." Bandage secure, Dave washed his hands again. "In fact, you're asking me to *not* help you." He took the bottle from Nash's hands. "And speaking of *not helping*—"

"Careful, I feel myself slipping back to actively not liking you."

Dave put the bottle on the counter and pulled Nash up and into the other room. Still holding tightly to the bigger man, he yanked the cover from the bed, and knocked some of the multitude of pillows to the floor. "Our flight home's not until noon. I'll take your key and come back and wake you at nine-thirty."

"Thank you," Nash said, as he sank back into the bed. "Malkoff . . ."

"This never happened. I wasn't here. You didn't go anywhere. I got it," Dave reassured him. "But if you ever change your mind . . ."

Nash shook his head and closed his eyes.

Dave let himself out of the room, closing the door tightly behind him.

DALTON, CALIFORNIA

Hannah woke up on the living room floor, a pillow from the couch beneath her head, the fleece blanket she used when she read late into the night draped over her.

The house was still. Empty.

She sat up fast and the blood rushed out of her head, which was already feeling fragile from all the Johnny Walker she'd had last night—even before Murphy had arrived.

But falling over was not an option, and Hannah pushed herself to her feet. *God.* The sunlight streaming in the window was too bright and cheery, and she squinted against the sensation of knives to her brain as she looked out at the driveway.

Murphy'd either found his keys or he'd hot-wired his truck. Either way it was gone—and he was, too.

Apprehensive, Hannah turned to her uncle's gun case, her head throbbing and her bad ankle shaky and weaker than usual. The glass door was locked, and she moved toward it as quickly as she could, counting . . .

They were all there. She counted again. Three hunting rifles and two sidearms. One big-ass shotgun to complete the collection.

Murph hadn't taken a weapon with him when he'd left—which didn't mean he still didn't intend to hurt himself. A man could do a lot of damage behind the wheel of a pickup truck.

He hadn't left a note, but that was his MO. He'd appear and disappear. It was nothing new.

The sex, however, had been shockingly new. But it was a mistake that they'd both acknowledged and apologized for. It wouldn't happen again.

Yeah, it wouldn't happen again, because *this* time? Hannah seriously doubted that Vinh Murphy was ever coming back.

Last night, Hannah had lost him as a friend—as absolutely as she'd lost Angelina to a gunman's bullet all those years ago.

She didn't have a phone that she could use, let alone a cell—not that it would work up here—so she couldn't even text message him. With no Internet access, e-mail wasn't an option, either. Unless she went into Dalton, the nearest little town—twenty-five miles away and *little* was a generous description—to use the computer at the public library . . .

Head throbbing so badly it was making her eyes water—yeah, that was why tears were running down her face—Hannah stripped the sheets from her bed and stuffed them into her washing machine.

The last of the Johnny Walker was still open on her bedside table. Instead of putting the top back on, she took the bottle with her into the bathroom and poured it down the sink.

And then she climbed into the shower, to get cleaned up for one of her rare forays back to civilization.

SAN DIEGO, CALIFORNIA

Bang, bang, bang, bang.

Eden woke up with a start, and then a flood of alarm as she realized someone's arms—someone significantly bigger than Jerry—were wrapped tightly around her.

She fought to get free, and whoever he was released her almost immediately and she rolled off the edge of the bed and onto the floor.

Couch—it was a couch that she'd been sleeping on, pressed tightly up against the SEAL whose nickname was Izzy. She remembered it now.

All of it.

Dear Lord.

He loomed over her, concern on his face as he tried to help her up.

Whoa, he was jacked. Standing next to him, her dirtwad of an ex-boyfriend, Jerry, would have looked anemic. Even Danny would look skinny, which was saying something. Izzy was built kind of like the Rock, hard muscled and lean, only bigger. His bare chest was marked by a scar that looked even more angry in the daylight. *I tried to stop a bullet with my chest, only my superpowers weren't working, so I kinda got shot.*

God. Eden couldn't imagine being able to joke about something like that. Yet Izzy had a joke or a flip comment about nearly everything.

And while he wasn't handsome, not by a long shot, not like Jerry or

even her brother, both of whom were prettier than she was, there was something about Irving Zanella's quick smile. There was something, too, that
gleamed in his dark eyes—amusement or intelligence or probably both—
that made him good-looking. Charismatic. That was the word for him.

He had crazy charisma.

He was also crazy attracted to her. Eden had been around the block
enough times to recognize *that* look in a man's eyes. Not that there weren't
other obvious signals for her to read. Izzy was wearing only boxer shorts,
after all. He realized it, too, and quickly sat down on the couch.

"Good morning," he said, his voice thick from sleep.

"Hi." Great, she was blushing as she tried to rearrange her shirt and
her shorts. Her bathing suit top was completely twisted, the two triangles
of fabric practically beneath her arms. She turned slightly away from him
and . . .

Bang bang bang!

They both jumped—Izzy to his feet again.

"Zanella! Open the door! I know you're home—I know Eden's in
there, too!"

Oh crap, it was her brother. Eden turned to Izzy. "You spoke to
Danny?"

"I didn't," he said. "I swear, I . . . Oh, fuck me." He met her eyes
briefly. "I'm sorry, I . . . This *is* my fault. I called both Jenk and Lopez last
night. I didn't want to be alone with you, because . . . well, hello. Look
what we did." He shook his head. "What *I* did. It was all my fault. I took advantage of you, you know that, right?"

"Zanella! I swear to God, I'm going to kick down this door!"

"Hold on, asshole," Izzy shouted. "I'll be right there." He looked back
at Eden. "You ready for this?" he asked her. "Because if you're not, I'll stall
him. You can go into the bathroom—shower if you want. I'll go out with
Danny and get bagels or something for breakfast. Bring 'em back . . ."

Eden looked into his eyes as the buzzer rang again. He was serious.
"You didn't take advantage of me," she told him, as she once again started
to cry. God, God, was she *ever* going to stop? She reached for the roll of toilet paper he'd so gallantly brought her last night. "*I* took advantage of *you*.
I thought it would help, but . . ."

"Yeah, well," he said as he headed for his bedroom. "In case you
didn't notice, I'm more than a few years older than you. I've been around

long enough to know what was going on inside your head—and to know that what we did last night absolutely *wasn't* going to help."

He peeled off his boxers before he'd even gotten out of her line of sight and . . . Wow. Nice . . . tattoo. Eden quickly turned around, afraid that he'd catch her staring, suddenly aware that up to this point, nearly all of the men in her life had been mere boys.

"I'm the bad guy here," Izzy said, coming back out, wearing a pair of cargo shorts, yanking a T-shirt down over his messy hair. "Okay?"

Eden opened her mouth to argue, but outside, the last of Danny's patience evaporated. *Bang bang bang!*

"I just want to get this over with," she told Izzy. "If that's okay with you."

Izzy nodded, forcing a smile that softened the hard planes and angles of his face and made him look both younger and almost handsome. Almost. "It's your call," he told her. "But . . . maybe you should go into the bathroom while I get the door. I'll make sure he's alone, while you get, you know, cleaned up."

Crap, she hadn't even thought that Danny might not have come here alone. Her mother was the last person on earth she wanted to see right now. No, strike that. Greg, her wicked stepfather, won *that* honor. "Thanks," she said, heading for the bathroom.

"Hey, Eden."

She stopped and looked back at Izzy.

"Jerry's a tool," he told her. "Totally. I know, because I'm . . . kinda one, too. It's that old takes-one-to-know-one thing." He paused, looking down at the floor, and when he looked back up, his eyes were serious, yet somehow softer, too. "You can do way better than the both of us."

Izzy turned toward the front door before she could respond, and she ran into the bathroom as he let her brother inside. She locked the bathroom door behind her, heart pounding, uncertain as to exactly what her response to Izzy should have been.

You can do better was classic asshole guy-speak. In her experience, it meant *last night was so great that I could imagine us hooking up again, and yeah, even making it something of a regular thing, but I'm afraid that'll make you read more into it than there is, so even though I want to do you again, I'm going to end it now while we're both clear that what we shared was just a one-night stand.*

Message received. Loud and clear.

One glance at herself in the bathroom mirror, and Eden knew why Izzy had sent her in here.

She was disheveled, with her hair all crazy around her face, and she hadn't quite managed to cover her boobs completely with her bathing suit top.

And her eyes were filled nearly to overflowing with tears.

"I *can* do better," she said into the mirror, but the bedraggled and mournful-looking girl looking back at her didn't seem convinced.

There was only one way to tame her hair when it got like this.

Eden turned on Izzy's shower, stripped out of the clothes she'd worn now for going on three days straight and stepped under the still-cold spray.

This all still seemed surreal, like she'd go back out into the living room to discover that Jerry had come looking for her. He'd be there with Danny, and he'd get down on his knees and beg her to forgive him.

"Screw you and anyone who looks like you," Eden practiced saying as the water blasted down on her head. Because some things, although eventually forgiven, should never be forgotten.

Like coming out of that ladies' room to find both the doughnut shop and the parking lot empty. At first she'd been bewildered. The usually busy street had been deserted, too, not even the taillights of Jerry's ancient Mustang fading in the distance, the traffic light on the corner switching from green to red and back again, as if regulating a parade of ghost cars.

She'd stood there, with her cell phone still in her purse—which was on the floor of the front seat of Jerry's car—and the truth had crashed down around her. Jerry had somehow found out about that night that Richie'd come over. He'd probably gone to Richie to confront him—and had ended up believing whatever bullshit Richie had told him. Jerry hadn't even bothered to get Eden's side of the story—not that he'd believe her. He'd simply ditched her. At a Krispy Kreme.

Eden hadn't cried at the time—she'd been too numb.

And then she'd gotten scared. Maybe Jerry hadn't believed Richie. Maybe he'd got into a fight with the older man and gotten jumped by Richie's squad of thugs. Maybe Jerry was injured or, God no, dead.

She'd gone inside and sat at a table by the window until long after dawn, praying that Jerry would come back for her, with his quicksilver smile and his infectious laughter, saying, "TCB, baby. TCB."

For as long as she'd known him, Jerry was always taking care of business, looking to get rich quick, which in the past had meant working for people who skated around the letter of the law. But after last month's close call with the police, he'd promised Eden to stay on the straight and narrow. To stay away from Richie for good.

With his extreme hottie-factor, Eden had thought Jerry had a serious chance of becoming a movie star. That was why she'd followed him from Vegas to LA in the first place—with the intention of learning how to be his makeup artist.

They were going to get an apartment of their own—not just housesit for Jerry's brother, who was in Iraq. They were maybe even going to get married.

Except Jerry's promises had been nothing more than lies. *You're the one, you're my sweet garden of Eden . . .*

She helped herself to some of Izzy's shampoo, lathering up her hair. It smelled good. Like he did. Well, not so much like he'd smelled when she'd first met him, in the bar. But last night, when he'd sat with her, stroking her hair, his hand so gentle . . .

You can do better.

Donnell and Jessilyn—two girls who worked the street off and on for Richie—had come into the Krispy Kreme in the morning, still dressed from the evening before. They told her that Jerry wasn't dead—and Eden had actually been relieved. But then they'd told her that he was back on Richie's payroll, hanging out at his gated estate, with—and this one had really hurt—his brand new girlfriend Tiffany.

Jerry already had a new girlfriend named Tiffany.

Eden had known then that he wasn't ever coming back. He'd chosen Richie and his so-called easy money over her. But she didn't cry—no way would she give Jerry the satisfaction of hearing that she'd broken down in the Krispy Kreme. It was bad enough that he'd find out she'd still been waiting there, hours after he'd left her.

While they were talking, Donnell had gotten a phone call from a client who needed an emergency massage—yeah, right—down in Laguna Beach. It was on the way to San Diego, so Eden had hitched a ride, borrowing Donnell's cell phone to make a few long-distance calls of her own, putting into place a plan B she'd been considering back before Jerry first bounced into her life.

It had taken her the entire rest of the day to hitch a ride from Laguna—using her thumb this time—out to Coronado. Then she'd walked to the Ladybug Lounge, where she knew her brother Danny often went after hours.

Not that she thought he'd be happy to see her or anything.

As Eden turned off the shower and stepped out of the tub, she could hear the rumble of male voices from the living room. Danny—staccato, higher pitched with anger. Izzy—lower and slower, then suddenly crazy loud: "Show your sister some respect, asshole! You get the *fuck* out of here if you're going to talk about her like that!"

Oh, God. Self-proclaimed tool that Izzy was, he was also one of the nicest guys she'd ever met. He was certainly the nicest guy that she'd ever slept with. And now, because of her, he was going to mix it up with her brother. Who, for all his Boy Scout attitude, for all of his honors and medals and awards, didn't fight fair.

Eden pulled her clothes on over her still-damp body, and jerked open the bathroom door.

Sure enough, Danny and Izzy were facing off across his coffee table, bristling at each other like a pair of dogs, ready to go for each other's throats.

"Don't you dare!" she said.

They both turned and looked at her and she realized that she proba-bly wouldn't have recognized her brother if they'd passed on the street.

His hair was longer than he'd ever worn it, and he had a full mustache and a scruffy beard. Which meant he'd probably been spending a lot of time recently in the mountains between Afghanistan and Pakistan. The fact that he hadn't shaved upon his return to CONUS meant he was prob-ably scheduled—soon—to go back.

Her chest clenched and her anger deflated because the truth was that, despite the fact that they'd never gotten along, she loved and admired her older brother. Unfortunately, he couldn't say the same about her.

And sure enough, as Danny gazed back at her, he radiated impatience and disgust and frustration, letting her know that, once again, she had completely screwed up his day.

No, make that his week, month, probably even year.

"Eden. Jesus Christ. Do you have any idea how worried everyone has been?"

"Hi, Danny," she said, chin high, voice steady. And the Oscar goes to Eden Gillman. "Nice to see you, too."

CHAPTER
FOUR

Hannah was drunk.

Murphy could tell, from the way she was sitting at her kitchen table. And if her posture hadn't given it away, the array of empty beer bottles in front of her certainly would've provided the necessary clue.

"Hey," she said, turning to greet him.

"Hey."

"Angelina borrowed my car and went to the grocery store," Hannah told him. "She's going to make dinner. I was kind of out of everything." She laughed. "Except beer. Which I'm also now out of."

"Ah," Murphy said.

"It's okay." Hannah kicked a chair back from the table for him with one of her big clunky boots. She still dressed like she lived in Alaska—cargo pants with legs that zipped off into shorts, boots, tank top. "She told me what happened last night—not like it's a big surprise."

"It kind of was to me," he admitted as he sat down. "I didn't come here, expecting . . ." He shook his head. "She's, um, really something. I just . . . um . . ."

"It's okay, you know that? Right?" Hannah said.

"Is it?" Murphy asked.

She nodded. "Absolutely." But she was unable to hold his gaze, and started peeling the label from her beer bottle. "I love you, man. You know that. I'm happy that . . . you're happy. I am."

"It's not like we're getting married," Murphy pointed out. "It's just . . . She's great, and . . ."

"You wanted to do her," Hannah finished for him. "You and the entire male population of California. Do you know besides the two years she went to camp in Montana, she's never traveled out of state? I've been trying, for years, to get her to come to Juneau."

"I'll get her to come," Murph said.

Hannah looked at him. "Heh-heh," she said à la Beavis and Butthead, and he cracked up.

"Mind out of the gutter, Whitfield. God." It was possible that he was blushing. "That's not what I meant."

"I know. I was just kidding." She turned to face him. "Honestly, bwee, I know she comes on strong, but she's . . . She really hasn't been with that many guys. Don't mess with her if you're not serious. Except you've already messed with her, so . . ."

"Actually, I haven't," Murphy said. "I mean, yeah, we kissed last night, but . . . I would never . . . In your apartment . . . ?"

"Really?" Hannah said.

Murph nodded. "Han. Come on. How long have you known me?"

Hannah laughed and finished off her beer. "She made it sound as if . . ." She put her bottle down. "Do you know she once got the girls at camp to give her a necklace with a diamond pendant? It's not stealing, she told me, if you get them to give it to you." She laughed again. "Freaking amazing."

Murphy wasn't sure what she was trying to tell him. "If you don't want me to see her—"

"You'll have to blindfold yourself, because she's pulling up right now."

Sure enough, Murphy, too, could hear the unmistakable sound of Hannah's car's near-death-rattle.

"That's not what I meant," he said. "And you know it."

"Yeah," Hannah said. "But who am I to tell you what to do?"

"You're my best friend," he told her. "Say the word, and I'll walk away."

"From the first woman in, like, fifty years that you've been even remotely interested in?" she countered.

"Fifty years is kind of an exaggeration," Murphy pointed out. He was barely thirty.

"She's completely into you," Hannah told him. "Totally, absolutely into you. And from what she told me, the attraction is mutual."

"She's an extremely beautiful woman," Murphy agreed.

"And she's intelligent and fun to be with," Hannah added.

"I just always thought," Murphy started, but then stopped.

"That the perfect little blond Republican chick from West Wing—"

"Ainsley," Murphy supplied the name.

"Right. That she's going to knock on your door wearing an apron and nothing else?" Hannah scoffed at him. "Don't be a fool. Perfection is relative, by the way."

Murphy shook his head. "I don't see you going out with that guy Mike."

Hannah rolled her eyes. "Oh, good, let's make this be about me."

"I'm just saying."

"One of the many—might I add another *many*—reasons I haven't gone out with Mike," Hannah told him tartly, "is because I happen to be in love with someone else." She looked aghast, as if she'd just let slip a state secret. "Just forget it, Murph—"

But Murphy had to push. "Diaz?" Last night, Angelina had told him she thought Hannah might be interested in one of the younger cops she worked with.

Hannah looked surprised. "Who? No." She laughed. "Can I just say *Ew*? I mean, nice guy, but . . . Ew."

"So, who?"

She rolled her eyes and gave him a rather obvious lie. "This . . . guy from college. So just . . . don't ask."

Murphy didn't believe her, and selected the least likely candidate from all of her college friends. "You mean Bennie, Bernie—what was his name?"

Hannah laughed. "Yeah. It's Bernie. Okay? I'm pathetically in love with a guy who thought lighting his farts was more entertaining than watching the Aurora Borealis. Woe is me."

Murphy laughed, too, pushing all of her empty beer bottles into a line on the table. "That is pretty woeful," he agreed.

She got serious. "Let it go," she said quietly.

He nodded. And changed the subject only marginally. "How come I didn't know about this?" he asked.

"Because I don't share everything with you," she told him.

"Yes, you do."

"No," she said. "I don't. For example, I didn't tell you that I've got, like, a period from hell. Like, change my pad every hour, with menstrual cramps that make me want to curl up on the floor in a fetal position."

"Point and match," Murphy said.

"It's why I'm drinking all this beer," she pushed it. "It actually helps the cramps. Not so much with the massive bleeding though."

"Great," he said. "I get it. Thanks."

She leaned across the table, toward him. "Murph, do you like her?"

She was talking about Angelina.

"I do," he admitted. "Very much. I just . . . I don't want to screw things up between us, you know? You and me. I mean, if it doesn't work out . . ."

"What if it does?" Hannah said, her eyes such a striking mix of green and blue as she gazed at him with such conviction. "What if all you need to do to be wildly happy is just take that chance, that risk?"

And Murphy did it. He took that chance, and he leaned forward, his hand under Hannah's chin and . . .

He kissed her.

Her mouth was soft and so sweet and she tasted not of beer, but of Johnny Walker and then, God, he was pulling her down, on top of him, rolling over, her legs wrapped around him and he fumbled with his pants and then—

Murphy opened his eyes and found himself staring up at the overcast grayness of the morning sky. He was in the back of his truck and the air was cold, but he'd burrowed beneath some old blankets that he'd thrown back there.

A dream. It was only a dream. About Hannah, not Angelina, which was different, but still made him cry.

It hadn't happened that way—the way that he'd dreamed it. He hadn't kissed Hannah, not ever. Not once in all of the years he'd known her, in all the years they'd been friends.

Not until earlier tonight.

Murphy searched beneath the blankets for the bottle of Bacardi 151 that he kept for precisely this type of emergency—when he found himself excessively cognizant.

He fumbled in his jacket, too, for the pill bottle he carried there, shaking two of the little rounded tablets into his hand. He washed them down with the rum, and sure enough, in a very short amount of time, his world faded back to black.

January 2008
San Diego, California

There was a woman standing in the Troubleshooters office waiting room.

She was either military or law enforcement—Decker guessed it right away, first from her short hairstyle and then from her posture. *Former* military or law enforcement, he quickly realized. She was leaning on a cane.

Her manner of standing also screamed *I don't want to be here*, which was often the case with clients, particularly when they first walked in.

This woman was younger than most people who sought help from Troubleshooters Incorporated—maybe in her late twenties—and tall. About as tall as Deck was, which made her tall for a woman, but not particularly tall for a man. She was solidly built, too, but not as solid as he was. He, however, wasn't built quite as poetically—a fact that was apparent despite this woman's efforts to keep her inspiring curves concealed. She was wearing a loose T-shirt and cargo pants, running shoes on her feet.

Not that she was doing much running these days. Not with that cane.

Tracy, the firm's receptionist, had gone out to dinner with some of the other women in the office, and she'd left a sign on her desk saying *Back At 1830*. It was Thursday—the one night a week they kept evening hours.

As Decker approached the young woman, she was looking at her watch, checking to see what time it was, and apparently didn't hear him coming.

So he spoke up. "May I help you?"

She turned away without answering, leaning heavily on her cane as she headed for the door.

Okay, so that was odd. "Are you looking for Tracy?" Decker tried. And again, nothing. She didn't even look up.

In fact, she would've just walked out the door, if Dave Malkoff hadn't picked that exact moment to rush in and nearly knock her over, dumping his Coffee Coolatta down the front of her shirt.

"Shit! Sorry! *Sorry!*" he said, catching her and taking the situation securely from bad to worse, as he attempted to wipe his coffee slushee from her chest. "I didn't see you there and—"

"Dave," Decker said sharply.

"Oh! God!" Dave realized what he was doing and went from embarrassed to mortified. "I'm so, *so* sorry . . ."

She had come to life. "I'm sorry," she said over him, shaking clumps of frozen coffee from her sneaker, even as she folded one arm across her upper body in self-defense. "My fault. I'm not moving too quickly these days. Do you work here?"

Dave was on the verge of blushing himself into spontaneous combustion. He, too, had been slimed profusely, and he tried to wipe his hands even as he surveyed the damage done not just to the two of them, but also to the floor and even the walls. "I do," he said, with the additional grimace of a man who knew he was going to be using a mop in the very near future. But then he focused his full attention back on the client. "I'm *really* sorry—"

"It's all right," she cut him off. "Do you know where I can find Lawrence Decker?"

And now, as Deck watched, Dave ricocheted into an even weirder dimension, because there Decker was, standing right there, behind her, in the waiting room. Which was where this young woman had come from. He looked at Deck questioningly, even as he answered her. "You haven't met Decker . . . ?"

He pointed, and she turned, looking at Decker, and Dave kept on talking. "Do you want to get cleaned up? We have a locker room in the back. I'll scrounge up a T-shirt and maybe some shorts that—"

"I'm Hannah Whitfield." She spoke right over Dave, holding out her hand to Decker, but then pulling it back as she realized she was sticky. "I'm sorry, is there maybe someplace I can get cleaned up?"

Deck looked over her shoulder at Dave, who'd stopped talking and was looking as perplexed as Deck was feeling. They were both jet-lagged from the flight home from the AmLux job, true, but this was just plain bizarre.

Hannah turned to look at Dave, too. "I'm sorry," she said. "Were you still speaking?"

And Decker got it. Big eureka. Hannah Whitfield was deaf. She lip-read, but if someone spoke to her when her back was turned—the way he had when he'd first spotted her by the receptionist desk—she would have no clue that he was talking to her. Or that he was even there.

Decker moved to stand next to Dave, because how freaking hard did *that* have to be—standing between the two of them, unsure who was going to speak next, looking back and forth as if she were playing monkey in the middle.

"Thanks," she said. "Most people don't . . ." She was actually embarrassed. And sincerely grateful. "Thanks."

And now Dave had it figured out, too. "Oh," he said.

"Yeah," she said. "I'm . . . kind of hearing impaired."

"We've got a locker room in the back," Decker told her again, and yeah, she was definitely watching his mouth move, which was extremely odd. It gave off a hint of sex, or at least a whiff of potential sexual attraction. Which was doubly strange since he'd short-circuited that part of his brain years ago.

Hannah Whitfield wasn't particularly pretty, but then again, she wasn't not, with those steady eyes that were a curious mix of blue and green, and the winsome freckles that spilled across her cheeks and nose. And of course, Decker had always appreciated women who wore their hair short. He loved the vulnerable gracefulness of a slender female neck.

"I've got a clean T-shirt in my locker." Dave, too, spoke clearly and slowly.

"Thanks, but I just need to rinse my hands," she said.

"It's down this way." Decker turned to face her, walking backward as he led her past the individual offices. "Can I get you anything? A coffee or . . . ?"

"No, thanks," she said. "If I get thirsty, I'll just suck on my shirt."

Decker laughed—she did, too, but just briefly. Whatever had brought her here was a source of tension. He could relate. These days, working here was a source of tension, too.

"I'm so sorry," Dave said, from behind her.

"Dave says he's sorry," Deck told her, stopping in front of the ladies' room door. "Take your time. We'll be in the conference room directly across the hall." He pointed.

"Thanks," she said, with another smile that made him realize he was standing there smiling foolishly at her.

As the door closed behind her Dave said, "Tess Bailey."

Tess? What? Where?

Dave no doubt caught Deck's massive confusion, because he paused on his way into the men's. "Hannah reminds me of Tess," he explained. "It's more than just the short hair and freckles. It's something about her manner. Like, she's bullshit-free. What you see is what you get. A lot like Tess."

Tess Bailey was TS Inc.'s top com-spesh—computer specialist. She was also Jimmy Nash's fiancée. She'd gone out to dinner with some of the other women in the office, clearly upset with Nash when he'd insisted on leaving immediately for an assignment in Arizona, without taking any downtime after the AmLux job.

"I don't really see it," Decker lied.

"That's right, you weren't at the wedding," Dave said and for one crazy second, Deck thought he'd finally lost his mind.

Tess and Nash hadn't even set a date for their wedding yet. Had they? Jesus, Deck hadn't been socializing with anyone at all lately, going from assignment to assignment himself, without so much as a fifteen-minute stop at the local watering hole, just to grab a beer.

Still, Nash was his second in command, and a good friend. No way would Decker miss his wedding.

"Murphy's wedding," Dave supplied the missing info.

Murphy's?

"No," Deck said. "I wasn't there." He'd been in Kazbekistan on a security detail. What the hell did former Troubleshooters operative Vinh Murphy's wedding have to do with—

"That's where I met Hannah before," Dave told him. "I knew she looked familiar. She was a friend of, um, you know, Angelina's."

Angelina Murphy. Gunned down in the street during what was supposed to be an easy Troubleshooters assignment, protecting a Hollywood producer.

Deck had been the team leader of that goatfuck. Murphy had been badly injured and in intensive care himself, when Decker had gone to the hospital to break the news to him that his beloved wife hadn't survived her brain surgery.

Jesus, that look in Murphy's eyes when he'd realized Angelina was dead—it still haunted Decker's dreams. Part of Murph had died along with her. And part of Decker had died that day, too. Even now, after all these years, his stomach clenched and his blood ran cold through his veins, just thinking about it. Any thaw that he might've imagined from Hannah's sweet smile was instantly gone.

"I remember thinking then that Hannah reminded me of Tess," Dave prattled on. "They even wore a similar style dress and—"

"Get cleaned up," Decker ordered tersely, "and meet me in the conference room."

Why Hannah Whitfield—friend of Murphy's murdered wife Angelina—had come here today, Deck couldn't begin to guess. But one thing he knew for sure? Whatever it was that brought her here, it was going to make his evening truly suck.

It was extremely odd—sitting here in Greene's Grill, having dinner with Lindsey Jenkins, Tess Bailey, and Tracy Shapiro.

Although, it was hard to say exactly what was most odd. Being back in San Diego after so many months away, or having a meal with someone who wasn't Dave Malkoff.

Sophia had stayed closely in touch with Lindsey while she was gone. The tiny Asian American woman was, without a doubt, the closest female friend that Sophia had ever had. A former detective with the LAPD, Lindsey's petite stature was deceptive. She was one of Troubleshooters' most skilled operators, and she could take a much bigger man to the mat, every time.

She was married to a Navy SEAL named Mark who was, in Sophia's opinion, Lindsey's perfect match. Which didn't mean that Sophia wasn't envious of her friend's happiness. She was. But it was a good kind of envy. It was inspirational. It helped Sophia define what she wanted in a relationship, which was a change from her standard, which was knowing what she *didn't* want.

The two women had talked on the phone nearly every day, even when their time zones were wildly out of sync.

But Sophia's contact with Tracy, the Troubleshooters' receptionist, had primarily been when she'd called in to the office. Tracy was usually too busy to say more than a quick hello before connecting her to the boss or his second in command. And Sophia's contact with Tess Bailey had been even less frequent.

She considered Tess, Troubleshooters' top computer specialist, to be more of a casual acquaintance. They'd been through hell together, years earlier, but hadn't quite been able to translate that into an honest friendship when back in the real world.

As a matter of fact, Sophia's dinner tonight was supposed to be only with Tracy and Lindsey. But Tess's fiancé, Jim Nash, had insisted that he personally handle a problem with a client in Arizona, and despite having been out on a red cell assignment for the past three days, he was catching an immediate flight to Tucson.

Nash had kissed Tess hello and good-bye, and she grimly prepared to spend the evening in her office, attempting to catch up on paperwork.

Sophia had looked at Lindsey, who'd nodded her agreement. They couldn't *not* invite Tess to come out with them.

So here Tess was—albeit quiet and moody.

Not that being quiet was a bad thing, with talkative Tracy at the table.

Tracy and Lindsey had obviously been spending time together over the past few months. In fact—miracle of miracles—some of Lindsey's tomboy was rubbing off.

Clotheshorse Tracy was actually wearing a T-shirt and jeans. And yes, okay, the jeans were from Lucky, and the T-shirt was silk, but still. And the sandals she wore on her feet, showing off her brightly painted toenails, had only the tiniest nub of a heel.

She looked good. Happy and relaxed. And still as completely enamored of her job as Troubleshooters' Lieutenant Uhura—as she herself referred to her position. *Hailing frequencies open, Captain!*

It wasn't that long ago that nearly all of the operatives and support staff had rolled their eyes at Tracy's ineptness. Now they weren't sure exactly what they'd do without her.

She was upbeat and chatty and bright.

And okay, maybe—at times—a little *too* chatty, but there were certainly worse things.

And Sophia could relate. She could do a mean mindless babble herself when she was feeling off-balance or ill at ease.

"So I'm in the coffee room—thank you," Tracy said, as the waiter brought their salads, "and there's like, a guy under the table, plugging something in to the outlet down there by the wall. And I look down, and he's on his hands and knees, you know, backing out, and it's like, hello! It was, you know, the faded jeans thing . . . ?"

"Oh, yeah," Lindsey said. "Levi Strauss is my God."

Sophia laughed her agreement. Most of the men in the Troubleshooters offices—both in San Diego and in Florida—were particularly talented when it came to wearing faded blue jeans.

Tracy continued, "And I'm thinking *That's not Decker,* who ranks, like, top three greatest butts in the universe—" She cut herself off. "That's just a fact. I'm not trying to, you know . . ." She shook her head, her blue eyes earnest as she leaned over and reassured Sophia, "I know you have dibs on him."

Sophia laughed. "Dibs?" She shot a look at Lindsey, who was shaking her head in a silent *Not me, I didn't say a word* . . . "I don't have dibs on anyone. I don't . . . dib."

Tess, whose fiancé was Decker's XO and best friend, seemed fascinated by the little dish of dressing that had come on her salad's side.

"Then maybe he has dibs on you. Whatever." Tracy was determined to finish up her story. "So it's not Deck, and I can tell it's not Sam or Jim—not enough leg length—or even the new guy, Ric—" She interrupted herself to ask Sophia, "Have you met Ric?"

"In Florida," Sophia said. "Yes."

"Be still. My heart," Tracy said, hand on her chest.

"Have you met Ric's wife?" Tess came alive to ask tartly.

"Yeah, yeah," Tracy brushed the thought away. "Annie. She's very nice. No one's doing any shoplifting here. I'm just looking, respectfully, from a distance. Isn't this girls' night out? Isn't that why we didn't invite any of the guys to dinner? So that we could talk about them?"

"I suck at being a girl," Lindsey admitted around a mouthful of arugula. "Aside from the blue jean appreciation thing."

"So it's not Ric and it's not even Tom," Tracy continued with her story. "And I'm taking my sweet time getting my coffee, because there's no one else there, and Mr. Blue Jeans can't see me, so I can ogle away without getting caught, only who am I ogling?" She looked from Lindsey to Tess to Sophia, with a huge *eureka* in her eyes. "Dave. Malkoff. Yes, that's right, ladies. David Malkoff has been quietly getting back into shape and he is now officially eye candy." She speared a grape-tomato with her fork. "And I have a theory about that. I think he got in shape because he had a crush on Paulette."

"The new UPS driver," Tess told Sophia.

"Although he only went out with her twice," Tracy reported.

"Dave went *out* with the UPS driver?" A UPS driver named *Paulette*? Sophia looked at Lindsey for confirmation. Dave hadn't mentioned anyone named Paulette to her, not even in passing. And she'd spoken to him on the phone possibly more often than she'd talked to Lindsey.

"Maybe it was three times," Tracy mused. "I think she might've dumped him. It's hard to imagine it happening the other way around."

"I don't know," Tess said. "You know that old saying: Still waters run deep? Dave's pretty deep."

"Maybe you're right," Tracy said. "Come to think of it . . . It wouldn't surprise me at all if a guy like Dave was totally, mindblowingly great in bed. Ooh, we should give him a makeover. There's a nice-looking man under that Jerry Garcia hair. With the right cut, and T-shirts that actually fit him instead of—"

"This conversation is making me a little uncomfortable," Sophia said, her words softened by her inability to keep a straight face. She could just picture Dave, out shopping with Tracy. Dear God, as Dave would say. "He's my best friend."

"He needs to lose the dorky reading glasses," Tracy proclaimed. "He looks like my Great-Uncle Ivan, which is *not* a good thing. He should get regular glasses—progressive lenses. They would actually bring balance to him. He's got that long face—"

"Has it occurred to you that Dave uses his appearance to blend in?" Sophia asked. "Because he *wants* to be ignored?"

Tracy blinked at her, then smiled. "Then someone needs to tell him not to wear those jeans anymore."

Sophia put down her fork. Tracy wasn't kidding—at least not entirely. The receptionist actually found Dave attractive.

"Sophia'll tell him." There was laughter dancing in Lindsey's dark eyes as she turned to Sophia. "You can also ask him for us: Is he great in bed and did he heartlessly dump Paulette the UPS lady after getting into her pants. Inquiring minds need to know."

Of course, Tracy found most men attractive. She liked men. All men. Genuinely. In all shapes and sizes. It made kind of odd sense that, after noticing the UPS driver noticing Dave, Tracy should notice him, too.

And maybe it wouldn't be a bad thing for Tracy to take him under her generous wing. Dave could use a good haircut.

What he couldn't use, however, was a broken heart. And Sophia just couldn't see a potential relationship with beautiful, vibrant, vaguely super-ficial Tracy ending any other way.

"At the very least," Tracy told Sophia, "ask him to do a slow turn for you so you can check out his buns." She smiled. "From a respectful dis-tance, of course."

Sophia had to laugh. "If you want to know the truth, I think Dave would appreciate the fact that we've spent the entire salad course of our dinner discussing his backside." She couldn't quite believe it herself. "So after you discovered those were Dave's jeans . . ." she started.

Tracy lifted one perfectly shaped eyebrow. "Are you suggesting there could be something between me and Dave Malkoff?" She shook her head. "I'm trying to move beyond *Looks great in jeans* as the sole attribute I look for in a new boyfriend."

"But Dave has brains," Tess pointed out.

"Says the woman who's engaged to a man who looks like a movie star," Lindsey teased.

"I wouldn't be marrying Jimmy if he weren't as smart as he is handsome," Tess defended herself.

"Have you set a date?" Sophia asked, and Tess's smile instantly became stiff. Shoot. Stupid question.

Tess shook her head and forced another smile. "Not yet."

Lindsey saved the day by changing the subject. "Speaking of new boyfriends, Trace," she said, as the waiter took away their salad plates. "How'd it go with the new guy?"

Tracy had a new guy? "I've missed a lot by being away," Sophia said. Tracy and some new guy, Tess and Nash's latest failure to yet again set a date for their wedding, Dave and the UPS lady . . .

Sophia had seen her—Paulette—this morning. She was pretty, with dark hair, and a lushly generous bosom, sparkling eyes, and a musical laugh. She looked kind of like Tracy, as a matter of fact. And she pretty much made Sophia feel like a pale, washed out, silent, and repressed wilting daffodil.

"His name's Michael," Tracy announced, "and he's a first-grade teacher in Spring Valley. I met him at the rock climbing gym. He's adorable and . . . We're incredibly compatible. We love the same movies, the same bands, the same food. It's like we're twins separated at birth, except that would be icky, since I kind of, um, invited him back to my place. Last night."

Lindsey was surprised. "You just met this guy!"

"I've known him for longer than you knew Mark when you and he first, you know," Tracy defended herself. "Got busy."

"Yeah," Lindsey said. "That was stupid, too."

Tess raised her hand. "Vice president of that club."

"I mean, not in hindsight," Lindsey added, "because it all worked out, but . . . I was lucky."

"I was lucky, too," Sophia said, "when I met Dimitri."

All three women turned to look at her in surprise.

"My husband," Sophia told Tracy.

"I know," she said. "You just . . ." She glanced at Lindsey and Tess. "You never talk about him. Ever."

"He was perfect," Sophia said. "A lot like you described Michael. At first, I didn't believe he was for real. And he wasn't. Not totally. He didn't really like red wine, or . . . Well. It took him a while to admit that he didn't love everything I loved. But he wasn't lying about being in love with me, which was pretty instantaneous when we first met. For both of us. So . . . it can happen. And I'm glad, now, that I didn't wait a single minute."

Tracy, Lindsey and Tess were silent.

Way to kill a dinner conversation—by talking about her dead husband.

The waiter, of course, delivered their meals, placing heaping plates of food in front of them.

"Bon appétit," he said.

But there they sat. Not eating.

Lindsey reached across the table and took Sophia's hand. "I can't imagine what it must have been like for you to lose him."

"It was a nightmare," Sophia said. Literally. She took a deep breath. "I think this is why I don't talk about him because it's . . . too hard to process, you know? I know you worry about Mark, when he goes to Afghanistan or Iraq . . ." She looked across the table at Tess, who clearly worried about Jim Nash *all* of the time.

"We're grown-ups," Lindsey said. "We can deal."

"You should be able to talk about him," Tracy spoke up. "Just because he's gone now . . . It doesn't mean he didn't exist, that you don't think about him, that he isn't still important to you." She reached over and took Sophia's other hand. "You can talk about Dimitri with me. Any time."

"How did you meet him?" Tess asked quietly.

Sophia looked from Tess to Lindsey to Tracy. They sat there, watching her, waiting patiently, their dinners forgotten. They truly wanted to know.

She swallowed past the lump in her throat. "It was my birthday," she said. "And I took a trip to Greece . . ."

Dave Malkoff realized that he'd spoken the magic word that never failed to ratchet Decker up to puckerfactor five thousand.

Murphy.

"You should probably know," Dave told Decker as he came out of the men's and into the conference room, after pulling on a less sugar-coated T-shirt, "that at the wedding? Hannah got up and sang with the band." Which explained why she spoke so clearly. She hadn't been born deaf. She'd had her hearing up until just a few years ago. "If I remember correctly, she was a cop. Somewhere up near Fresno, I think."

Deck shook his head. "Shit."

"It's possible," Dave said, "that she's here looking for employment. If you want, I can talk to her. I'll tell her you had an appointment—"

"No."

"You don't owe her anything."

"Yeah," Decker said, "but I do owe Murphy."

"Sorry that took so long." Hannah came into the room, her hair damp. "I had some whipped cream in my . . ." She pointed to her curls as she looked around the room, at the big conference table, the plush chairs. She sat down on the very edge of the one closest to the door. "This really isn't necessary. I'm only here to see if you've heard from Vinh Murphy lately. See if he'd . . . maybe come by here. I'm, um, a friend of his and . . ."

"We know," Dave told her. "I remember you from the wedding."

Hannah looked at him. "Oh, I'm sorry, I . . ." She shook her head.

He helped her out. Most people tended not to remember him, which had been a huge asset when he'd worked for the CIA. It wasn't quite as useful when in conversation with attractive women. "Dave Malkoff." He wrote his name out for her on the notepad that Deck had put on the table for that very purpose. "We talked about how you'd introduced Murph to Angelina . . . which is something you probably told everybody at the reception, so . . . you wouldn't necessarily remember telling it to me."

"I did tell that story a lot that day," Hannah agreed. "It's . . . nice to see you again," she rather obviously lied.

"I haven't seen Murphy in years." Dave got to the point. "Zero contact with Murphy," he wrote it down for her. He looked at Deck.

"Same here," Decker said. "Nothing—not since he left the hospital."

Hannah didn't look disappointed—just resigned. "Does he still keep a weapons locker here?"

"He does." Deck nodded. "Yes."

"Would he be able to access it without anyone knowing?" she asked. "I mean, could he have come here and gotten his gear . . . ?"

"Unlikely," Decker told her, writing that down and underlining it for emphasis. "Both the main and secondary locks—and the access codes to the security system—they're changed regularly. He'd have to get past all those levels of security in order to access his locker."

"Of course, this *is* Murphy we're talking about," Dave pointed out.

"Someone would know he'd been in there," Decker countered. "Which isn't an impossibility. Murphy had—has—plenty of friends here."

"That was my next question," Hannah said. "Can we check with the rest of your staff?" She fished in her pocket for a piece of paper. "I made a list of the people he's talked about," she explained, flattening the paper out on the table in front of her. She read aloud. "Decker—that's you, someone named Nash, Tess, Dave." She looked up at him, nodding, "Lindsey, Diego, James, Tom, Cosmo, Sophia . . ."

Decker waited until she looked back up at him to say, "The Tom on your list is Tom Paoletti. He's Troubleshooters' CEO—and CO. Commanding Officer. He's out of town this week, along with his second in command, Alyssa Locke and *her* XO, Sam, or I'd take you in to meet them. You know, Murph was one of the first operatives Tom hired, right after he opened for business. Murphy and then Dave."

Dave nodded. "I didn't work with Murphy all that often," he told Hannah. "But the few times I did . . . He had a joie de vivre that was . . ." Irrepressible, he was going to say. Instead he cleared his throat and pointed to her list. "James Nash is on your list three times." He wrote on the pad, *James = Nash = Diego—same person.* "Not that he's Latino or anything. He's just . . . pretentious."

"I heard that," Nash said from the hall. He leaned into the room as Hannah used her teeth to uncap a pen she'd taken from her pocket, making notes on her list.

Of course, *she* hadn't heard *him*, so Decker tapped the table in front of her to get her attention. "Nash," he said, pointing behind her at the man. She turned to look at him, her eyes widening slightly as women's eyes often did when they first looked at Nash.

Deck spoke to him. "I thought you left."

"Flight got cancelled," he reported. "Next one's not until ten-thirty. What's up? Did I hear you talking about Vinh Murphy?"

Decker quickly filled him in.

Dave knew Nash's side had to be hurting like hell, but he hid it completely—God forbid Decker find out that he'd been shot while out doing God knows what. The man's luck was holding, because he was on his way to an assignment which would keep him away from Tess for another three days. At which point his injury would be healed enough to be able to pass it off as something less alarming than a bullet wound.

Although, knowing Tess, it was likely she wouldn't be fooled.

"Have *you* heard anything from Murph lately?" Deck asked Nash now.

"I haven't," Nash reported, with an apologetic smile to Hannah. "I'm sorry."

"Will you check with Tess?" Decker asked as Nash, too, took a seat at the table.

"I'll text her, right now." Nash got out his cell phone.

"She's having dinner with Lindsey," Decker pointed out. "Check with her, as well."

"Sophia's with them, too," Dave said.

Decker nodded. "That's right. She's, um, also here today. She's primarily support staff," he told Hannah, "but she and Murph were friends."

Sophia was, indeed, "um, also here today." Dave, for one, had not missed the fact that her car was out in the office parking lot. She spent the bulk of her time out of the office, visiting various clients, racking up frequent flyer miles. Slim and blond and elegantly, regally, *fabulously* attractive, a savvy businessperson and top-notch deal negotiator, Sophia acted as the public face of Troubleshooters Incorporated.

She'd done some training as a field operative, and had even gone out on some real missions, but she'd realized—she'd told Dave over one of their frequent lunches at his desk—that it didn't make sense not to take advantage of her strengths. She'd never be more than average as an operative, but let her walk into a business meeting?

She would totally kick ass.

Plus, her stepping into that role freed up Tom and Alyssa, allowing both Troubleshooters' CO and XO to take advantage of *their* strengths.

It was a win-win.

Except it meant, more often than not these days, that Sophia was away from the San Diego office.

And now Dave ate his lunch alone.

As did Decker most days.

The two of them could've started a "The Office Just Isn't the Same Without Sophia" support group—although Dave suspected that they didn't quite share the same emotions regarding her absence. Decker appeared to experience some relief when she wasn't around. Dave just flat-out missed her.

Of course, she called often, because she missed Dave, too. He was, after all, her good pal.

Yeah, she missed their lunches—sitting around talking about her relentless crush on . . . Who else?

Decker.

Life could really suck.

Except who was Dave to complain? He still had his hearing. And he still had Sophia for a friend, as screwed up as that relationship might be.

"Neither Tess, Lindsey, nor Sophia have seen Murphy since, uh, he left town," Nash reported, having just text messaged them at dinner. "Tracy never met him. When they get back from dinner, we'll show her his picture. That way if he does show up . . ."

Dave read Hannah's list upside-down. "Cosmo Richter's still active duty," he said. "He's a Navy SEAL with Sixteen—Tom's old team. He hasn't worked with us since . . ." Angelina died. He used Nash's euphemism instead. "Since Murphy left town."

"But Richter's got a key," Decker said. "And access to the alarm codes. Quite a few of Tommy's SEALs do. We'll follow up on that."

"Can we check Murph's locker and see if he's been here?" Hannah asked.

Deck sat back in his chair. "Why do you think he has? When did *you* see him last?"

She didn't answer right away as she looked around the table from Deck to Nash to Dave. And then she dropped one hell of a bomb. "He was at my cabin last night," she admitted.

CHAPTER
FIVE

"Get your things," Gillman told his sister, his voice tight, "and let's go."

As Izzy watched, Eden lifted her chin even higher. With the last of her makeup scrubbed from her face, she looked her age. Younger. Damn, what had he done?

"I'm not going back to Vegas," she told her brother.

"Yeah, you are," he said. "So get your things—"

"I have no things," Eden told him, and even though she was trying desperately hard, she couldn't keep her voice from shaking. "Everything's gone. Congratulations. You were right about Jerry. Go on and say it—*I told you so.* He's an asshole and a moron, and I'm an idiot for trusting him."

"He ditched her," Izzy told Gillman, *sotto voce*, because there was a time and place for *I told you so*, and this was so not it. "All her stuff was in his car."

Gillman turned and gave Izzy a *fuck-you* look, but directed his words to his sister. "I see you picked a new president for your fan club. Why am I not surprised? You always gravitate directly to the total assholes."

So much for Jenk's promise that Gillman would thank him. Although, to be fair, it was Lopez who'd let slip the news to the fishboy that Eden was here at Izzy's. Jenkins was probably still home in bed, resting up after throwing his gorgeous wife a bang before she left for work.

It was times like this that Izzy was genuinely envious of Jenk. When he'd gotten married, they'd all made noise like, *Oh, now you're not going to be able to go out and have any fun.* Yeah. Truth was, the little bastard was having way more fun than Izzy, Gillman, and Lopez put together.

And right now? Whatever Jenk really was doing, even if he was cleaning his toilet, he was having tons more fun than Izzy.

Eden no doubt realized that, because she shot Izzy an apologetic look. "Danny, he let me stay here last night because I didn't have—"

"Yeah, Zanella's a real prince," Gillman said. "He's always doing favors for me."

"I'm pretty sure the favor was for me."

"For the record," Izzy started, but Gilligan cut him off.

"You're not part of this discussion."

"Yeah, I am," Izzy said. "I'm standing right here—you're in my living room, and you're discussing *me*. The favor was completely for Eden, asswipe."

"Yeah, and what kind of favor did *you* get in return, douchebag? Did you know that she's only seventeen?"

"Didn't *you* know that today's her birthday? Some brother." Izzy looked at Eden. "Happy birthday, by the way."

She looked miserable, but her eyes were dry. He knew with a certainty that the dead last thing she would ever do was cry in front of Danny.

Izzy had an older brother, too. He actually had a whole pack of 'em.

"I'm so sorry about this," she told Izzy quietly.

"So what's your plan if you're not going back home?" Gillman asked Eden, still heavy on the adversarial. "You going to move in here?"

"Yeah, right, Dan," she said, sparking with anger. "I'm going to move in here, just to piss you off." She forced herself to take a deep breath. She also squared her shoulders and said, "I know this is the last thing you want to hear but . . . I need to borrow some money."

"You got that right," Gillman said. "It's one of the many things I don't want to hear."

"I'll pay you back," she said. "I will. I mean, not right away, but—"

"And I'm supposed to believe you're not going to turn around and just give this as-yet-undisclosed sum to Jerry because . . ." Gillman let his voice trail off.

"I spoke to Dad," Eden said quietly, and for some reason that shut

Gilligan up. "If I can get the money for a plane ticket to Germany, he'll let me stay with him for a while."

Silence. Great big, fat, honking silence. Izzy looked down at his bare feet, because looking at Gillman suddenly felt too intimate. For some reason—and Izzy would've bet big money it had everything to do with the D-A-D-word—Gillman could not control the vast array of emotions that flitted, now, across his matinee-idol face.

Of course, maybe Izzy also looked away, because—shit—*Germany*. So much for his fantasy that he'd be able to call up Eden a coupla times a year—just a friend, touching base, going out for a casual lunch or coffee, letting time pass during which she'd not only get over this Jerry wonk, but she'd also turn twenty.

But now . . . His going to flipping Germany for lunch would not be perceived by anyone as *casual*.

"Dad's in Germany?" Gilligan finally asked his sister.

"Yeah," Eden said. "Ramstein."

Gillman laughed. "Jesus, Eed, if you want to go to Germany, why don't you do it the way everyone else does?" he asked. "By enlisting in the Army."

"Okay." Eden sat down on the couch, crossing her million-dollar legs beneath her. "Go for it, Danny. Lecture me for the four billionth time on why I should enlist. If I sit through it—again—without bitching and moaning, will you lend me the money for the airfare?"

"How else are you going to get to college, if you don't enlist?" her brother said. "With your grades—"

Eden looked over at Izzy. "Danny seems to think that the Army or college are my only two choices, and that I won't get into college *without* joining the Army, so there's really only *one* choice. Like there's not an entire *world* out there—"

"There *is* a third choice," Gillman said sharply. "The women's penitentiary."

"Or I could be a porn star," Eden said just as hotly. "Don't leave that off the list, Captain Perfect."

"Why the hell would you want anything to do with him?" Gilligan exploded. "For the love of God, Eden, Dad's a total shit. You don't remember—how could you? You were just a baby when he left, but he's . . . Even if he said you could stay with him, he'll probably change his mind when you get there. He does that. And then what'll you do?"

"Then I'll be a *German* porn star," Eden said.

Izzy laughed—he couldn't help himself.

Gillman savagely turned to him, a finger of warning damn near stuck up Izzy's nose. "Stay out of this, asshole. You're not helping."

"It's hard to tell what's pissing you off more." Izzy just couldn't keep his mouth shut, probably because of the finger-in-his-face thing. "The fact that Eden's willing to take a chance on your father, or the fact that he seems open to letting her come stay. Are you worried about her, or are you just jealous?"

"Fuck you!"

"Fuck you," Izzy countered evenly. "I assume, since you didn't answer my question, that I can put you down as big-time jealous. Which means being a *total shit* is probably hereditary."

Gillman smiled, but his eyes were arctic cold. "You're her new fuck-buddy. Why don't *you* give her the money she needs to go to Germany?"

Eden spoke up. "Maybe the reason he's willing to let me stay with him is because I didn't threaten to kill him before he left. Dad," she clarified as they both turned to look at her.

Izzy then looked at Gillman. "I thought you were, like, twelve when he split." Twelve, but apparently with the balls of a thirty-year-old . . .

But Gillman had clearly had enough. "Go to Germany," he told his sister. "I'll pay for your ticket, but that's it then. No more. When Dad kicks you out, don't even *think* about calling me to come bail you out."

"Thank you," Eden said.

"I'm so going to regret this . . ."

"She's going to need a passport," Izzy pointed out.

"Crap! My passport was in my purse," Eden told them, turning to Izzy with a great big *what do I do now* on her face.

"I'll get it back for you," Izzy found himself promising. "Just give me Jerry's cell number. I'll take care of it. I'll get your other stuff, too." And he'd enjoy doing it.

"You're certainly in a hurry to see her go OCONUS," Gilligan scoffed.

"Just trying to help," Izzy said, "is all."

Eden was looking at him, with those dark brown eyes that made him think of last night's encounter. Almighty Jesus save him. "Thank you," she said again. "It's 702—"

Izzy took out his cell phone and plugged the number in. He turned to Gillman. "I'll call you when I've got her passport back."

"Let's get the fuck out of here," Gillman told Eden.

"You're welcome," Izzy told him.

Eden was looking around.

"Your flip-flops are in the bathroom," Izzy said. "You wore them in there. You can take, um, my hairbrush with you if you want."

Her smile was wan. "Thanks. I'll just use it here and . . ."

She vanished down the hall, closing the bathroom door behind her.

The silence was a *leetle* awkward.

Izzy knew what *he* was thinking about. He could only guess what color the noise was that was playing inside of Gilligan's head.

He cleared his throat delicately. "You know, Dan, maybe you should think about going with her," Izzy suggested. "To Germany. See your father, too."

Gillman laughed his scorn. "Yeah, that's a *great* idea."

"I'm just trying—"

"Don't." Gillman cut him off. "Just shut the fuck up, Zanella, all right? Just because you screwed my sister, that doesn't make us friends."

"I didn't—"

"She's not real particular about who she gets with. Obviously. You might want to get checked for STDs."

Izzy had had enough of Gillman's sanctimonious bullshit. "Did you ever get ditched in a Krispy Kreme? You ever been abandoned, huh, Captain Perfect?" He used Eden's nickname for him, which really was quite perfect, indeed. "Do you have *any* idea what your sister is feeling right now? She was in love with this jerk-off, and yeah, maybe that wasn't the smartest thing she's ever done, falling for him in the first place, but it happened. And if she and I *did* hook up last night—and whether we did or not is none of your business, gutterboy—*if* we did, it was more about payback and breaking ties and feeling lost and alone and being fucking *abandoned* so just back the hell off and give Eden some space. God damn it, Dan, she's finally doing something smart—she's putting half the fucking globe between herself and this prick, even though a part of her is probably wondering if maybe she shouldn't go try to patch things up—because she *loves* him. Instead, she's looking out for herself, she's starting over. And no, it's not going to be easy, and no, she's not perfect—and Jesus H. Christ, it must've been a nightmare growing up in *your* house, with you around—is it any fucking wonder that she doesn't want to join the Army and live by your rules, in your world? And the *least* you could do is go to Germany with her to make sure your father isn't really the suckhole you thought he was back when you were twelve!"

Izzy stopped to draw in a breath and realized that Eden had come out of the bathroom. She was just standing there wide-eyed, her hair back in a ponytail again, watching him lose his shit.

Verbally, that is. If he'd really lost his shit, he'd be driving Gillman to the hospital right about now.

Izzy's living room seemed to echo with the sudden silence—talk about awkward to the nth. He had no idea where in the midst of his tirade Eden had come in.

Gillman's body language was so clenched, he was practically folded in on himself. Arms crossed, shoulders hunched, teeth ground together, jaw muscle jumping.

Eden didn't even look at her brother, she just stood there, gazing at Izzy.

"Sorry," he said. "I just . . . Sorry."

She didn't move. She just stared.

"Good luck," he tried instead. "In Germany."

"Thanks," she said, finally looking away, as if she were suddenly shy.

But then Izzy realized that she was glancing at her brother, making sure she had his attention. Because then she marched over to Izzy and gave him a hug.

Damn, she was soft in his arms, and he could smell his shampoo in her still-damp hair. It was beyond weird, as if he'd somehow marked her as his.

"Thank you for . . . everything," she told him softly, as she stood up on her toes, her mouth against his ear.

Izzy turned his head to answer her, intending, again, to wish her luck, and she kissed him.

He knew it was for show—for Gillman's benefit and discomfort—as was the hug. But he closed his eyes and kissed her back, this funny, fresh, vibrant, sad, partly broken girl.

Ah, God, he didn't want this to end . . .

But it finally did—because Gillman stomped his way out of Izzy's apartment.

Eden pulled back, and Izzy let her slip out of his arms.

"See ya," she said, her bravado manufactured but securely in place, as she headed for the door.

"Call me if you're ever back in town," Izzy said. He couldn't help himself.

She stopped with her hand on the doorknob and looked back at him. "You can do better," she told him, giving him one last heartbreaking smile. And with that, the most beautiful woman in the world closed the door behind her.

Leaving his life for good.

Or at least until she turned nineteen and a half . . .

Izzy flipped open his cell phone and dialed Jerry's number, moving to the window, so that he could watch Eden following Gillman out to his truck.

He was bumped straight to voice mail. Which would probably make things easier for everyone. "Jer!" he said, after the beep. "You don't know me, dude, and I gotta be honest with you, you really don't *want* to know me. So listen up—here's what's going to go down . . ."

"Is Murphy all right?" the earnest man named Dave asked.

All three of the Troubleshooters operatives—Dave, Decker, and Nash—were watching Hannah intently across the conference table.

"He hasn't been back here?" Hannah asked. "At all? Not since . . ."

"Not since Angelina died," Decker—the quiet one—told her. He'd been the team leader on the op in which she'd been killed—Hannah knew that. She couldn't imagine living with the mountains of guilt and responsibility he must've felt. Sure, it wasn't really his fault. And yes, the man who'd murdered Angelina had been stopped. The son of a bitch had been shot when he'd attempted to kill again. Decker had been part of the team who'd taken him down, keeping him from harming anyone else, making him pay for what he'd done.

Still . . .

Hannah suspected not a day went by that Lawrence Decker didn't think about Murphy, about Angelina.

"How often do you see Murph?" he asked her now.

"He stops in every few months or so. I have access to a cabin, in the mountains. Near Yosemite," Hannah told them. "It's pretty remote, so . . . He comes by every now and then, and he doesn't stay long. And he's . . . not doing very well. I can't remember the last time I saw him when he wasn't intoxicated."

It was clear that this wasn't what Decker had hoped to hear, but she wasn't going to lie to the man.

"The cabin's my uncle's," she told him, told Dave. The other man, the gleamingly handsome one that Murphy had referred to as James, Diego, and also Nash, had gotten up and left the room. "He owns a bunch of weapons. Hunting rifles and . . . Murph tried to break into the gun case last night."

"Tried?" Dave asked. With his reading glasses and his Green Day T-shirt and his long hair worn pulled back from his tired-looking face, he looked like an escapee from Caltech, when in fact Murphy had talked about him with respect and even reverence in his voice. Lionhearted, Murphy had called the man.

"He was, um, pretty out of it," Hannah admitted. "He even had my keys, and . . ." She shook her head.

Nash came back into the room, already talking. Hannah caught only a few words. "Murphy" and "locker."

She looked sharply at Decker, hoping he'd realize. . .

He did. "Murphy's gear is all still here," he told her, writing it down for her, too.

She exhaled, hard. "Thank God. Can you change the lock?"

Decker and Dave exchanged a look.

"We could," Dave said. "But . . . it's Murphy's stuff. If he comes back for it . . ."

"But at least you'll know," she pointed out. "This way, he'll have to go through one of you."

"What are you afraid he's going to do?" Decker asked.

Hannah shook her head. Murphy had been talking crazy for months. It was hard to know, though, if it was grief and anger mixing badly with alcohol and drugs, or something else entirely . . ."He blames the Freedom Network and Tim Ebersole," she told them. "For Angelina's death."

Murphy had talked—more than once—about going after the white supremacist group's founder and leader, Tim Ebersole. He wanted to erase Ebersole from the face of the earth. One time he'd even asked Hannah to help take him out.

Murphy had told her that he'd never be allowed inside the Freedom Network compound because he wasn't white. Hannah, however, could walk right in. That same night he'd driven her down to the Dalton town library, where he'd used the computers there to register her as a Freedom Network member. It was the first step, he'd told her, in infiltrating their organization.

"He gets drunk and . . . He wants someone to pay for his pain." She could relate. She stood up now. "I appreciate your giving me this much of your time."

Dave stood, too. "I'll walk you out."

Hannah shook both Decker and Nash's hands.

"If Murphy comes by," Dave asked once they were out in the hall, "or if we find out he's been in touch with someone here at Troubleshooters, how can we reach you?"

"E-mail's best," she told him, digging in her pocket for the piece of paper upon which she'd written her e-mail address. She'd have to go to the library to access her e-mail account—at least until she did what Pat had been urging her to do ever since the accident. Set up a satellite dish and bring Internet access to the cabin.

"Thanks," Dave said as she handed the slip of paper to him, giving her his card in return. "My home number's on the back. If Murphy shows up again . . . I'd love to speak to him. It doesn't matter what time it is. If you could call me . . ."

"I don't have a phone," Hannah said. "Not one that I can use." Pat had also been trying to talk her into getting one of those TTY things, but she just wasn't motivated. There was no one that she wanted to talk to. At least not until now.

"If you had a cell," Dave suggested, "you could text message me."

"Not much cell service where I am," she said. "It's pretty remote. But I'll look into it."

They were back in the lobby, puddles of his coffee still on the floor.

"Sorry about before," he said.

"It's okay," she said, even though it was going to be a long, sticky ride home. Hannah turned toward the door, but he stopped her, a hand on her arm. She turned back.

"This feels kind of impolite . . ." His eyes were apologetic. "But . . . How did you lose your hearing?"

"Car accident," she told him, impressed that he'd had the nerve to ask. Most people didn't. Still, she gave him the Cliffs Notes version. "On the job. High-speed chase." Of a DUI perp who'd hit and run—and killed a six-year-old girl. "My leg got mangled, it got infected and . . . It was one of those super strains—resistant to antibiotics. I was pretty much dead, but one of my doctors tried an older drug that was known to be ototoxic. It took my hearing, but saved my life."

"Wow," Dave said. "You're amazingly lucky."

Lucky? To live in a world of total, suffocating silence?

Right. Kind of the way Murphy was lucky to have lived through the attack that had killed Angelina.

But Dave was serious. He was standing there, looking at her as if he truly believed she was . . .

Lucky.

"You know, when I was overseas with Murphy," he told her, "he kept something that he called his 'worst-case scenario' bag." He was carrying a note pad and he thoughtfully wrote the phrase out for her, making sure she understood. "You know, weapons, a little C4 . . . ? He hid it away, in case he was ever left high and dry. I'm not sure he'd do the same thing here in the States, but . . ."

"Last night he was either too out of it to remember where he put it," Hannah concluded, "or he doesn't have one in California."

"Or," Dave said, "he didn't really want to get that weapon out of your uncle's gun case."

"Or," Hannah countered, "he wanted to use it right then and there."

On himself. She didn't have to finish the sentence. She could see Dave's understanding in the sadness in his eyes.

"If Murphy really wants a weapon," he told her, "he won't just try. He'll get one. You and I . . . we're the ones who can try. To stop him. But . . ." He shook his head. "Ultimately? It's up to Murphy."

"Nice seeing you, Dave," Hannah said, leaning heavily onto her cane as she pulled open the door and went out into the coolness of the early evening.

PART
TWO

PRESENT DAY

CHAPTER
SIX

I t was a Wednesday in early July—the day that Murphy reappeared in
Hannah's yard.

It was half past noon, and as she straightened up from weeding
the green beans in her garden, she jumped, startled to find him standing
there, just a few feet away from her.

"Sorry," he said as she gaped. "I didn't mean to sneak up on you."

She almost didn't recognize him in the sunlight. She shaded her eyes
against the glare from the too-blue sky and . . .

It was definitely Murph, a bright red gym bag at his feet. He must've
walked up the hill, and quite possibly all the way out here from Dalton.
His truck was nowhere in sight.

He'd lost quite a bit of weight in the months since she'd last seen him,
but that only meant he was extra-large instead of extra-extra. His leanness
was apparent mostly in his face. His cheekbones stood out, accentuated by
cheeks that were no longer boyishly soft.

She'd always thought he was a good-looking man, with his cafe-au-lait
skin and dark brown eyes—eyes that revealed his part-Vietnamese heritage
with their exotically graceful shape. His mouth and nose came directly
from his African-American father, fitting his face perfectly, especially those
full lips that—once upon a time—had been quick to curl up in a smile.

Murph had been out of the Marines for years, but he still wore his hair
regulation short. Wavy and black, Hannah knew firsthand that it was soft
to the touch.

Yeah, she'd always thought he was handsome, but now other people would agree.

Further scrutiny revealed that his clothes — jeans and a black T-shirt — were clean. He was wearing sunglasses but he took them off so she could see his eyes. They were clear. He was sober.

For now, anyway.

He was also waiting for her to say something. Anything. So Hannah pulled off her work gloves and, wiping the sweat from her forehead with her arm, she stepped over the chicken-wire fence she'd built to keep the rabbits at bay. "You must be Dalton's new Avon lady."

Murphy laughed. It was a terrible joke, but he actually laughed, even though it was over too soon. "Hannah," he started.

She held her hand out to him. Cut him off. "It's good to see you, Vinh."

He took her hand, engulfing it in both of his, and as she looked up at him, she saw his remorse, his regrets, his apology, his embarrassment. He opened his mouth, but she looked away. "Don't," she said. "Let's just . . . let the past be the past. Shit happens, you know? Especially when Johnny W.'s involved. He's a sonuvabitch."

Murphy squeezed her hand, waiting until she looked back up at him. "I wasn't sure I'd be welcome," he said.

Her heart clenched. "You're always welcome here," she told him. "Always."

He was scrutinizing her as carefully as she'd looked at him, taking in her recent haircut, no doubt noting the toned muscles in her shoulders and arms, the way her cargo pants hung loose around her trim waist. Yeah, she'd spent the past few months getting back in shape, too, storing her cane in the bathroom closet. She still limped when she got tired, and her ankle hurt like a bitch when she tried to run, but . . .

"So where've you been?" she asked him, pulling her hand free, walking backward so she could watch him as they headed toward the cabin.

"Juneau," he said. At least that's what she thought he'd said. But . . .

"Excuse me?"

"I went up to Juneau, Alaska," he told her. "This time of year . . . I thought you'd be up there, helping Patrick find whales to show to the tourists."

She stopped short. "No, Pat's getting married. Didn't I tell you?" She had, but apparently it had been one of those nights Murphy had wiped from his memory. "He's selling his boat and . . . He's in Arizona with his fiancée, Debbie. So I'm here in California all summer again." Like last year. "Hence the garden." She still didn't quite believe what he'd just told her. "You really went to Juneau. To look for *me*?"

"Yeah." Murphy nodded.

"That's one freaking expensive apology, bwee," Hannah told him. "I mean, shit, Murph, flowers would've worked. You know, with a note— *sorry about accidentally having sex with you and then crying about it like a little girl.*"

He laughed again. Twice in one visit—a miracle. "I thought we weren't going to talk about that."

"We weren't," she told him, "but then you went to *Juneau* and . . . It wasn't *that* horrific, you know. The sex. I actually came, which isn't exactly my MO. It's doubly great, because now I can cross *have an orgasm with someone besides myself* off this decade's to-do list. I was toying with making the date a personal annual holiday, but—"

"Hannah, God, I'm so sorry." Great, instead of making him laugh, she'd pushed him into apology mode. She really didn't mind talking about what had happened but she absolutely didn't want him to beat himself up over it, turning their conversation into a raging blamefest.

"It didn't mean anything," Hannah reassured him. "It just . . . happened."

Murphy shook his head. "It meant a lot," he argued. "And it never *would* have happened if Angelina was still alive. It meant she was gone. It meant that, on some level, I was acknowledging that she was gone."

He was gritting his teeth, the muscle jumping in the side of his jaw.

If Hannah were braver, she would have touched him, just a hand on his arm. Instead, because now, forevermore, she wouldn't be able to touch this man without remembering the feeling of his body inside of her, she tucked her hands safely away, wrapping her arms around herself. She gently told him, "She *is* gone."

"I know," Murph said. "I knew it that night and . . . I'm sorry about . . . I wasn't thinking about anyone but myself. I was, um, in a truly dark place."

Hannah nodded. "No shit."

Murphy looked out over the garden, his eyes tracking a butterfly that flitted across the verdant lushness that she'd coaxed from the soil.

"So where are you now, Murph?" she asked.

He smiled, very slightly. "I'm not here to steal one of Patrick's rifles, if that's what you're asking."

That was good to know. She waited, sure he had more to say. And he did.

"I'm taking life one day at a time," Murphy told her. "Just . . . moment to moment. I'm still alive, you know? Maybe it's random that . . . I lived and she didn't. But it happened, and . . . I'm here."

Hannah's heart was in her throat. "You're here," she said around it. "And I'm happy to have your company. You're welcome to stay for as long as you like."

Murphy briefly met her eyes as he nodded. "I was hoping I could crash in your loft for . . . I don't know, maybe a month or two? If that's okay with you."

"Of course," she told this man who'd married her best friend back when Hannah hadn't truly understood the meaning of the word *tragedy,* "it's very okay with me."

SAN DIEGO, CALIFORNIA

The apartment was trashed.

The sofa and draperies had been slashed, other furniture smashed and overturned. Drawers and cabinets had been emptied onto the floor, bookshelves tipped.

It wasn't a burglary, even though someone had taken pains to make it appear so. The TV and stereo equipment were piled in the middle of the room, as if ready to be carried out, along with Tess's computer equipment, a blender, and . . . Two pairs of Jimmy Nash's shoes . . . ?

"They're Italian. Gucci," Tracy said from where she was trying to jam the stuffing back into the sofa, as she saw Decker frowning at them. "Figure seven hundred dollars a pair."

"Jesus. Really?" He blinked at the Troubleshooters' receptionist, who had thrown a sweatshirt on over pajamas. Her pants were covered with little cartoon pictures of dogs in sunglasses surfboarding, and her feet were bare. "What are you doing here?"

"I live in the building," she said. "Remember? I helped Tess and Jim find this apartment."

Something stirred in the back of Decker's memory. Nash, with his arm around Tess, her eyes sparkling as she smiled up at him. *We're looking for a new place. Something that's ours this time . . .*

"But you weren't at the housewarming party." Decker also remembered that.

"Yeah, I was," Tracy told him. "I came late, you left early. Your loss—we got a poker game going that went on until dawn."

"I think I probably lost less by leaving early," he told her.

"Maybe," she said, "but you missed the fun."

Fun. Huh.

Her hair was back in a ponytail, and there were remnants of a hastily removed mudpack on her astonishingly pretty face—a face she now twisted into a grimace. "I know, I know, I missed a spot. I was kind of in a hurry to get down here. When Tess called, she sounded out of it. I think she hit her head pretty hard. You know, when they knocked her down?"

Decker's stomach lurched. "She's hurt?"

"She walked in on them doing this." Tracy gestured to the vandalism around them. "You think these jerks were going to say *excuse me?*" Her indignation faded quickly to solemnity. "She's lucky they ran away. Really, it could have been so much worse."

Decker couldn't breathe. "Is she . . . ?"

"In the kitchen," Tracy said. "With Dave."

"Excuse me." He headed for the kitchen, but Tracy stopped him. She actually body-blocked him.

"Deck, wait. Where's Jim?"

He shook his head. "I have no idea."

"Great," Tracy said with a sigh. "I was afraid of that. Tess told me that Jimmy told *her* that he was going out on assignment—with you."

As Dave swept up the kitchen floor, Tess sat at her kitchen table, holding an icepack to the back of her head, toying with several pieces of what had once been a little porcelain cow.

Every dish and glass in her kitchen had been smashed, the rest of her apartment was destroyed, she had a welt on the back of her head the size of an egg, yet it was the destruction of one little cow that made tears fill her eyes.

"It was a present from Jimmy," Tess told Dave. "It's stupid, I know. This could have been so much worse. If they'd had guns, or if Jim had come home to find them instead of me . . . They'd be dead right now. He would've . . ."

Dave cleared his throat. "Tess."

"I know," she said, pushing the pieces of cow away from her. "They wouldn't've been here—the men who did this—if Jimmy hadn't been out of town. This is . . . some sort of message to him. I know that. I'm not stupid."

Understatement of the year. Tess Bailey was unbelievably intelligent. She was Troubleshooters' top computer specialist and a true techno-geek. But she wasn't just book smart, she came equipped with plenty of midwestern farmgirl common sense, too.

And with her freckles and short, curly hair, with her sweet, round face, she looked far more like a soccer mom than a kickass field operative. And the least likely woman in the world to be James Nash's fiancée.

"No one thinks you're stupid," Dave reassured her.

Decker was standing in the doorway that led to the living room. Tess hadn't seen him yet, and as he met Dave's eyes, he briefly shook his head.

Perfect. James Nash was AWOL. Again.

"Do you have any idea why someone would want to deliver this kind of message to James?" Dave quietly asked Tess, since it seemed clear that Decker wasn't ready yet to announce his presence.

She laughed her despair. "Like he ever talks to me?" Her eyes filled with tears again, and she bent her head over that broken cow. When she spoke again, her voice was low. "Something's been wrong for a really long time. He disappears. He's just . . . gone. At first I thought maybe it was . . . someone else. Another woman. I mean, this fidelity thing is still pretty new for him. But when I asked him about it . . ." She had to stop.

Good old pointblank Tess. Falling in love with her must've been the most terrifying thing that James Nash had ever done in his long, complicated life.

"He denied it," she said. "But he wouldn't tell me where he goes or . . . He said, *You gotta do what you gotta do,* as if I were going to walk out the door." She laughed again, again disparagingly. "I almost did, but . . . He wouldn't look at me. Like, he was waiting for me to leave so he could cry. So I didn't. Leave. I told him that I trusted him to keep the promise he made me. And things got . . . a little better. For a while. But now . . . He's drinking again."

"I know," Dave said.

She looked up at him, surprise in her eyes. "Thanks so much for telling me."

"I knew you knew," he said. "And, for the record? The way he can just stop, whenever he wants . . . ? I don't think he's an alcoholic. I just think he's trying to drown out the noise in his head."

"I don't think I would mind so much," Tess admitted, "if when he drank he'd at least talk to me. But no. When he drinks, he shuts down even more. All he'll say is how much he loves me. Apparently, I'm everything to him. Not that you'd know it through his actions." She shook her head in disgust. "I think he stays away because he gets hurt, doing whatever he's doing. Whatever's going on, it's dangerous, but he won't tell me *any*thing. He just . . . shows up, with all of his stupid *dings*. Sometimes I could swear he's been stitching up his own bullet wounds."

Dave didn't look up, sifting through the rubble to pick up an unbroken plate. Oops, no. It, too, was cracked.

"Is it possible," Tess asked, "that he and Decker are still working for the Agency?"

Dave shook his head no, as he straightened back up. "Yeah, I suppose there's a very slim chance, but . . . My guess would be that if someone from James's past is coming back to smack him with something like this"—he gestured to the mess—"it dates from . . . before his years with the Agency."

"Possibly from his time in prison," Tess said. "I know about that. You don't have to tiptoe around it. It's just . . . I also know that some of his Agency assignments were . . . pretty unkosher."

Dave glanced again at Decker, who visibly steeled himself and stepped into the kitchen.

"If he's still working for the Agency," Decker said, "he hasn't talked about it with me."

Tess turned toward him with such hope on her face, it nearly broke

Dave's heart. "Where's . . ." Jimmy. She didn't even bother to ask. She knew just from looking at Deck that Nash wasn't with him. Disappointment and then something that looked a lot like grief filled her eyes.

"He had to stay an extra day," Decker started, but she cut him off.

"Oh, please," she said. "Don't lie. For God's sake, Deck. Don't disrespect me that way." She stood up. Raised her voice. "Tracy, can you give me a lift to the airport a little earlier than we'd planned?"

Tracy appeared in the doorway behind Decker, her eyes wide. "Of course."

"I was supposed to catch a flight to Florida, tomorrow—today now— at noon. I'm scheduled to spend a few weeks in the Sarasota office, getting their computer system up to speed." Tess sounded as if absolutely nothing was wrong. The giveaway was the tears that she couldn't keep from escaping. But she just steadfastly kept wiping them from her eyes. "I was going to change my plans, get this mess cleaned up, but . . . I'm thinking now that I should let Jim receive his message. I'll see if I can't get an earlier flight. If not—I'll probably be safer at the airport than I am here."

"I'm sorry, Tess," Decker said, his voice gruff.

"Yeah." Tess scooped the broken cow off the table and threw it into the trash on her way out of the room. "I am, too."

Chapter Seven

Several Weeks Later
Monday, July 28, 2008
San Diego, California

Bang bang bang! Someone—guess who—hammered on his door, as Izzy was making himself dinner.

True, the "making" involved little more than heating some leftover pasta and meat sauce in the microwave and throwing together a salad, but he was hungry and he was tired, and he was looking forward—thank you, Tivo—to catching up on two months of new episodes of *South Park.*

Bang bang bang bang!

Okay this proved it. His downstairs neighbor was insane. Certain that the two men who'd recently moved into the apartment across the courtyard were part of a terrorist sleeper cell, Mrs. McCrea had taken to spying on them—which was fine with Izzy, although he could think of about four million other far more productive hobbies for the elderly woman. What *wasn't* fine, however, was the way she relentlessly tried to enlist Izzy's aid in her campaign.

They keep their curtains down all day, Mrs. McC., because they know if they didn't, all of their crazy neighbors would be looking in their windows hadn't convinced her of anything.

She was solidly in the *if they're not doing anything wrong, then they should have nothing to hide* camp.

Bang bang ba—

"I met 'em in the parking lot, Mrs. McC. Matt and Ryan." Izzy yanked the door open mid-bang. "They're—Whoa!"

It wasn't Lynn McCrea standing there, it was Dan Gillman, wearing his usual expression of *Hey, look, I stepped in shit again—it must be Zanella's fault.* Marky-Mark Jenkins and Jay Lopez were right behind him.

"What are you—" doing here, he was intending to ask, when Gilligan just pulled back and, *wham,* punched Izzy in the face.

Ow! "Gillman, what the fuck!" Izzy said from his new position on the floor. "God damn, I think you broke my nose!"

"You said you weren't going to hit him," Jenkins chided Gillman.

"Jesus H. Christ!" Blood poured down Izzy's T-shirt.

"I lied." Gillman was flexing and opening his hand as if he'd hurt himself with that suckerpunch. It would serve the bastard right to find out he'd broken his hand and be put off active duty for the next few months.

Lopez crouched next to Izzy, his body language making it clear that, first and foremost, he was there to keep Izzy from leaping to his feet and doing unto Gillman. But he was also obviously there to further torment him by touching the areas around his nose and his eye sockets, making sure the bones in his face were intact.

"Ow!" Izzy said. "*Ow!*"

"Nothing's broken," Lopez announced, handing Izzy the dish towel that had been hanging on the refrigerator door handle—Jenkins had thrown it to him from the kitchen. "Head back to stop the bleeding."

Jenk brought him ice in a ziplock baggie. "Back of your neck," he advised.

"Fuck that." Izzy put it directly on his face, using the towel to stanch the flow from his nostrils. He glared up at Gillman as best he could. "I repeat my question. What. The fuck?"

"I just got back from Germany," Gillman told him. "I brought Eden home with me."

Eden.

Izzy pushed himself to his feet, pretending that this breaking news from Gillman hadn't, in fact, made his nose stop hurting. Just in case Gillman wanted him to be in pain. "So this is, what?" he asked. "A preemptive strike? Your sister's back in town, so—"

"She's pregnant," Gillman cut him off.

Whoa.

Really?

Izzy looked to Jenkins and Lopez for confirmation and they both nodded.

"She's six months along," Gillman announced, hostility radiating from him, and Izzy suddenly understood his anger. Six *months* . . .

"You think that *I* . . ." He laughed, which was probably not the smartest thing to do, under the circumstances.

Both Jenkie and Jay-Lo moved to hold Gillman back.

"Dude," Izzy said, juggling the ice and the blood-soaked towel along with Gillman's scathing hatred. "We had this conversation six months ago. It's none of your business what happened between your sister and me that night. But I will tell you this, I did *not* get her pregnant."

"That's not what she says," Gillman nearly spit at him.

"She claims you're the father, Iz." Jenkins was mega-unhappy. "This is partly my fault. I mean, you called me that night and . . ."

"*Eden* says that *I'm* the father?" Izzy repeated because it just did not make sense.

"She says it wasn't her ex-boyfriend," Jenk told him. "What's his name. Apparently he shoots blanks."

"Jerry. She says Jerry's sterile from the treatment of some kind of child-hood cancer," Lopez explained.

And you believe her . . . ? Izzy looked at Gillman, who apparently did believe his sister this time. Or maybe he didn't, but he just wanted someone whose ass he could immediately kick. Namely Irving Zanella.

"Where is she?" Izzy asked as Gillman's cell phone rang. Lopez stayed close as Gillman answered it, moving with him into the kitchen.

"Las Vegas," Jenk answered.

Ah, damn. *I'm not going back to Vegas* . . .

Jenk lowered his voice. "What the *hell*, Zanella?"

Izzy just shook his head. "I gotta go see her."

"You *think*?"

"She's really six months pregnant?" Izzy asked.

Jenkins nodded. "She was staying with their father—who's apparently not dead. I don't know why I thought—" He caught Izzy's look of impatience. "He's regular Army, stationed at—"

"Ramstein. I know," Izzy said. The bleeding was slowing—shit, no it wasn't. He adjusted the towel and applied more pressure.

"Shortly after she got to Germany, he went TDY to Iraq. It was supposed to be for a month," Jenk told him. "But it was extended and he just got back, day before yesterday. He walks into his apartment, and there's Eden. Preggers. He freaks, calls Gillman's mom, who calls Gillman. Who went over, got her, brought her home."

"He see his dad while he was there?" Izzy asked.

Jenk shook his head. "He didn't mention it."

"He hates his father," Izzy said.

"Not as much as he hates you." Jenk shook his head, disappointment in his eyes, which hurt more than Izzy would've believed. Jenk actually thought Izzy had . . . But he couldn't set him straight. He wouldn't—not until he'd talked to Eden. "You've really got to learn to keep your pants zipped, bro."

"I prefer a button-fly," Izzy pointed out.

"Why do you do that?" Jenkins asked. "Like you don't have trouble enough, without dumping a bucket of your crap on top of everything?" He exhaled his exasperation. "You better go wash up and grab your bag. We're roadtripping to Vegas. And this time, Zanella? What happens in Vegas is, no doubt, going to follow you home and fuck up the entire rest of your miserable life."

Dave immediately knew what this was about as he went into the conference room and sat down between Sophia and Tracy, the Troubleshooters receptionist.

Tracy had no clue as to what was going on, chattering on as always, as everyone found seats around the big table—talking about a new restaurant that had opened down the street. "It's Greek, but not greasy Greek, you know, like, heavy on the goat? Their salads are amazing, and they have this . . . well, it's like hummus, but it's made from eggplant? It's *so* good."

She was talking to Decker, who looked shell-shocked as he sat on her other side—no doubt because he knew this meeting was at least partly his fault.

They were all there—everyone who had been part of the original assignment in which Angelina Murphy had been killed. Everyone except for PJ, who was still in Iraq.

Dave, Decker, Sophia, Lindsey, and Nash—who looked as if he'd been hit by a truck. He was sitting as far as humanly possible from Decker, across the table and next to Tess, who had flown back from Florida and was looking pretty grim. Which wasn't easy for her to do with her freckles and Sunday-school-teacher face. Still, somehow she pulled it off.

Even SEAL Chief Cosmo Richter was here today, no doubt at Tom Paoletti's request. Three and a half years ago he'd taken leave from the Navy when his mother had fallen and broken both wrists. Looking to earn some extra cash to help pay her medical bills, he'd taken what was supposed to be an easy assignment with Troubleshooters Incorporated, protecting Jane Chadwick, a Hollywood movie producer who had been targeted by the neo-Nazi Freedom Network, because the bio-pic she was making outed a gay WWII military hero whose father had been a beloved leader of the KKK.

First the death threats had come via e-mail. Then someone started shooting—and Murphy had been injured and his wife had been killed.

With the exception of Tracy, everyone sitting around this table had been part of the team assigned to protect the movie producer. And with the exception of Tracy, everyone sitting around this table had been irrevocably changed by the tragedy of Angelina's death.

Some, however, had been changed more than others.

Tom Paoletti came into the conference room, followed by Alyssa Locke, his second in command, and a woman Dave had never seen before. She was in her late forties and had what he thought of as hippie hair. Long and dark and streaked with silver—she was going gray naturally. Tom pulled out a chair for her, directly to the left of his seat, and she sat down, thanking him with a smile that lit her still-pretty face.

As Dave watched, she folded her hands calmly in front of her. And then, as Tom and Alyssa both settled in, taking these few moments before the meeting started to deal with some of their relentless paperwork, the woman calmly looked around the table.

She studied each of them, one by one, and when she saw that Dave was looking back at her, she held his gaze, her mouth lifting slightly at one corner—as if they were sharing a joke.

He couldn't quite tell what color her eyes were behind her glasses—blue or maybe green. Either way, they were filled with a mix of amusement, compassion, warmth, and understanding.

She knew that he'd figured out why she was here—but it was no joke.

Every operative in this room was about to get his or her head shrunk. Whether they wanted to or not.

Beside him, Sophia was surprisingly serene, especially considering the turmoil last Friday. But then again, Dave knew that she'd been going to therapy—willingly—for nearly a year now. This wasn't terrifying new territory for her.

But for the rest of them . . . The idea of sitting down and talking about their feelings?

Dear God.

Dave had called Sophia over the weekend. She'd left early on Friday, and he wanted to make sure she was okay. He'd wanted to talk to her about what had happened that morning, out in the parking lot.

Instead, they'd spent the entire phone call discussing Ken Burns's documentary on World War II.

Dear God, indeed.

Today, even their mighty leader Tom looked far less easygoing than usual, his face showing signs of strain. But he also had the determined expression of a man with resolve. He'd made up his mind—there would be no talking him out of this one.

Not that someone wouldn't try.

Dave glanced down the table at Decker, who, yes, had also figured out their mystery guest's secret identity.

Deck wouldn't meet Dave's gaze—no doubt because he was well aware that this was mostly his fault.

Yeah, this meeting was a direct ramification of what would forevermore be known as the Friday Morning Parking Lot Brawl. Which Dave, at least, had seen coming for well over six months now.

Larry Decker had been tied in an emotional knot *before* Hannah Whitfield showed up in the Troubleshooters San Diego office six months ago, looking for Vinh Murphy. After her visit, however, Deck got wound up even more tightly.

And James Nash's ongoing crazy-ass behavior hadn't helped things any. Tension in the entire office had spiked to an all-time high.

Decker got super terse. He normally wasn't any kind of a chatterbox, but Dave hadn't heard him utter more than a few sentences in as many months. Never one for socializing, Deck had stopped even pretending to hang with the team after hours.

He stayed late, came in early—and showed up on every weekend, too. He worked as if work were as necessary to him as the air that he breathed.

Dave suspected that it was.

He'd seen it happen before, to men and women alike. It was not uncommon, in this business, to try to grab tightly to what little you thought you could control. And to believe that, if you just worked longer hours, everything would be all right.

Except the lives you save don't make up for the ones you've lost. But you can't stop hoping that somehow, someway, if you just keep trying, you'll reach a magical point of absolution—and with it will come sweet relief.

But there was no mathematical formula, no secret recipe, no guarantees. The only guarantee was death—dark, and sudden, and permanent. Too many good men and women sought relief by walking into a bullet. It didn't matter whether they pulled the trigger themselves or let some perp do the dirty work. The end result was the same.

The pain would end, sure. But it was, absolutely, the coward's way out.

Still, Dave had been worried about Decker for months, but everyone he spoke to seemed to think that Deck was just being Deck. The current spate of al Qaeda Internet chatter had him on edge—it had everyone ramped up. Decker wanted to get out there and *do* something—just like the rest of them.

But then, three days ago—last Friday—it had become crystal clear that Decker was starting to fray.

They'd all pulled into the Troubleshooters parking lot at the same time that morning. Dave, Decker, Nash, and the always-lovely Sophia, who was back in town after another several-month stint away. They got out of their cars and trucks, ready to start another day of work, greeting each other as they unloaded briefcases filled with files and various bags of gear and equipment.

One thing about the personal security industry—one rarely traveled light.

Decker was surprised to see Nash. "I thought you were heading for Sarasota," he said as he lifted a duffle out of the back of his truck.

Just last year, Tom Paoletti had opened up a Troubleshooters office in Florida. Tess had been down there for several weeks running—ever since the break-in at the apartment she shared with Nash.

According to the office scuttlebutt, she and Nash had patched things up—intending to take a weekend vacation out on Sarasota's Siesta Key, which had one of the best beaches in the world.

But now Nash shook his head. "Change in plans." It was the pointed way he didn't meet Dave's eyes that telegraphed the fact that he had a reason for not wanting to see Tess today—or even this week. Dave would've bet big bucks that somewhere, beneath Nash's natty clothes, there lurked another bandage. Either that, or the man was about to depart for another mysterious non-Troubleshooters assignment that would result in placement of said bandage beneath his natty clothing.

Decker slammed shut the tailgate of his truck and turned to look at Nash in disbelief. "You're fucking kidding me."

It was his uncensored use of the f-word in front of Sophia that was Dave's first clue that Deck was about to blow.

But then Dave didn't hear Nash's response to Decker's question, because another truck pulled into the lot, braking to a stop and sending a cloud of dust into the air. "Sophia! Hey!"

It was Sophia's pet Navy SEAL, Danny Gillman. Apparently the youngster hadn't paid close enough attention to the memo she'd sent out nearly a year ago, which started with those oh-so-damning words, *Dear Danny, I think it's important for you to know that my feelings are those of friendship . . .*

Gillman didn't bother to park, he just left his truck right in the middle of the lot as he jumped out. He looked upset. "Soph, please, can I talk to you for a sec? Please?"

Great. No doubt Danny had reached a place where he was willing, publicly, to beg.

Dave was standing close enough to Sophia to hear her sigh. It was just a little one, but it was not a happy sound. Still, she greeted the SEAL pleasantly enough as she crossed toward him. "What's up, Dan?"

Dave went with her. "How's it going, Gillman?"

"I've got this thing—" Gillman looked at Sophia "—with my father—" back to Dave "—that I wanted to talk to Sophia about," the younger man said. "Privately, if that's okay with you."

Sophia put her hand on Dave's arm. "It's okay," she told him, but then several yards away, Decker snarled at Nash.

"I am *not* going to let you fuck this up!" Deck actually pushed the taller man. Hard.

Gillman's mouth dropped open. Decker rarely lost his temper and it *was* pretty shocking when he did. This, however, was turning into a full-scale meltdown of epic proportions.

Because Nash pushed Deck—equally hard—in response. "Back off!"

"Guys!" Sophia couldn't believe what she was seeing either. But neither one of them so much as glanced at her.

"You treat Tess like shit." Deck didn't back off. In fact, he got further up into Nash's face. "She's the best thing that ever happened to you and you treat her—"

"I'm doing the best I can!" Nash came back at the same high volume.

"Guys!" Sophia got louder, too.

And Decker actually aimed some of his anger at her. "This doesn't concern you."

She flinched, as surely as if he'd reached out—*tock*—and smacked her across the face. But she was tough and she came right back with, "It most certainly does concern me—and it would even if all we were was co-workers, not friends. If you've got a problem with Nash, you've got to sit down and *talk*—"

"Yeah, because talking really helps," Decker said. He got back in Nash's face. "You get on that plane and you go have your weekend with Tess or I will *fuck* you *up!*"

"Go ahead," Nash said, all but begging Deck to hit him in the face. "Do your best. Because I'm not going."

"What is *wrong* with you?" Decker was livid.

"Why don't *you* go to Sarasota," Nash shot back. "She's gotta be sick of me by now. It's your big chance. Oh, wait, you don't take chances. You just bury yourself in paperwork and let your entire life pass you by!"

"Is that what you're doing when you tell Tess you're with me, all those nights that you're not?" Decker pushed Nash again, harder this time. "Taking *chances?*"

"Nah, that's just me hooking up with some old girlfriend," Nash taunted him. "Yeah, Tess is sweet, but variety *is* the spice of life."

It was obvious to Dave that Nash was lying, but Decker lost it. He swung.

And it was the damnedest thing Dave had ever seen, because Nash just went still. He didn't move to defend himself. He just . . . stood there, waiting to get hit.

And Decker obliged him, repeatedly, knocking him down to the ground and pulling him up to knock him down again.

"Stop it!" Sophia shouted. "Stop it, *stop* it!"

Gillman, foolish boy, jumped into it, trying to yank Decker off of Nash, and getting flipped, hard, onto his back for his effort.

"*Do* something," Sophia implored Dave as Gillman lay there, the wind blasted out of him.

What, like, get hit, too? "Maybe this *is* their way of talking," Dave suggested.

The look she shot him was so black, for a moment, he thought Sophia might just take a swing at him and turn this ass-kicking into a free-for-all.

With the tension they were all feeling, maybe that would be a good thing. Tracy Shapiro had pulled into the parking lot now, too. Dave could see the receptionist's wide eyes through the windshield of her little car, as she took in the chaos.

Sophia, meanwhile, was ready to throw herself into the fracas.

Dave grabbed her. "Best thing to do is just stay—*oof!*" She'd actually elbowed him in the stomach, breaking free to dash over and catch Decker around the waist. She just wrapped her arms around him and hung on for dear life. "Don't do this," she told him. "Please, *please*, Deck, stop!"

Apparently, she, too, was willing to beg.

Of course, now Dave *had* to get into it. He'd never forgive himself if, as he stood here with his thumb up his butt, Sophia got hurt.

So he did the only thing he could do, and put himself directly between Decker and Nash, bracing himself for Deck's fury. "Guys! That's enough!"

And just like that, it was over. Although, Dave knew that Decker's surrender had nothing to do with him, and everything to do with Sophia.

Decker let her pull him back, away from Dave and away from Nash, who was on the tarmac, bleeding.

Sophia just held on to Decker as he caught his breath, his chest heaving, his knuckles raw. Her eyes were tightly closed, one arm around Deck's waist, the other up so that the palm of her hand lay across his heart, her face pressed against the broad expanse of his back.

The sudden silence was deafening.

Nash let his head loll back against the blacktop, turning to spit out a clot of blood. He was going to have one hell of a black eye, and his lip was split, yet he still managed to twist his mouth up into a rueful smile. Beaten and bleeding, he was still more attractive than Dave would ever be, even at his cleaned and shined up best.

Bastard.

"Look at you," Nash said quietly to Decker. "Telling *me* not to fuck it up? You're the master of the fuck-up. At least I had it right for a while. But you? You're too much of a coward to even *try*. You *must* still be in love with Tess, you stupid fool, to flat-out ignore the best thing that ever happened to *you*."

Gillman had climbed to his feet, and realization was dawning in his eyes as he looked at Sophia, who was still holding tightly to Decker. Yeah, that's right, Navy-Boy. Sophia had never given Deck her *Let's Be Friends* memo. Sophia, for years and years and *years* now, wanted something else entirely from Larry Decker—who was, indeed, a coward extraordinaire for failing to deliver.

And there they all stood, with Nash's words ringing in the silence.

Dave watched Decker—because it was now or never. If he didn't turn around, if he didn't surrender into Sophia's embrace, if he didn't kiss the shit out of her and tell her he was sorry for being so afraid . . .

Decker moved, but it was to pull free from Sophia's arms. "I'm sorry," he told her although it wasn't quite clear exactly what he was apologizing for. He looked down at Nash. "I'm not in love with Tess," he told this man who was allegedly his good friend. "But that's the really fucked up part of this, Jimmy. I know that you are. I *know* it."

Sophia stood there, her arms now wrapped around herself. She'd gotten so quiet and seemed significantly smaller than she had when she'd dared to wrestle Decker back from Nash. She met Dave's gaze, just briefly, and he knew she'd been thinking the same thing he had. *Now. Or never.*

Apparently, it was going to be never.

Decker didn't want her arms around him. He didn't want her support. He didn't want her.

How she kept from crying, Dave couldn't imagine. He himself was struggling not to weep from the injustice of it all.

As if completely unaware that he'd damaged Sophia even more than Nash, Deck picked up the bag he'd dropped when the altercation began. He had a newspaper stuck in one of the side pockets, and he took it out now, and handed it to Dave on his way past. "Page three," he said, and went inside.

Tracy had parked by now and as she dashed over to them, Dave handed the paper off to her as he looked at Sophia, afraid to get closer, uncertain how to approach her, but unwilling to let her fend for herself.

Yet she seemed to shake herself off and even turned to help Gillman pull Nash to his feet.

"I'm okay," she said, in response to something Nash said, too low for Dave to hear. "I think I'm . . . just going to go home, though . . ."

"Dave." Tracy'd opened the newspaper and she held it out so that he could see and . . .

There it was. The straw that had broken Decker's back.

It was—no big surprise—a straw named Murphy.

Freedom Network Leader Dead read the headline. Dave took the paper from Tracy and quickly skimmed the article, holding it out so that Sophia, Nash, and even Gillman could read it, too.

A body discovered in the mountains east of Sacramento had been identified as Tim Ebersole, the founder of the neo-Nazi Freedom Network. An autopsy revealed the cause of death to be foul play—rifle shot to the head—with the murder occurring approximately four months ago. Out of the office, on something that sounded like a cross between a vision quest and a sabbatical, Ebersole had only recently been reported as missing by the Freedom Network elders, who discovered the body in a cabin in a remote part of their newest compound, in California.

Gail Deegan, the FBI team leader in charge of the investigation, was quoted as saying that the killer was believed to be someone with extensive training as a sharpshooter or sniper, possibly with a military background.

Someone exactly like Vinh Murphy.

And, in fact, *Vinh Murphy* were among the first words out of Tom Paoletti's mouth as he started their Monday morning meeting, after introducing the hippie-haired woman on his left as Dr. Josephine Heissman.

"Our agenda today is two-fold," their boss told them. "Both segments having to do with our old friend Vinh Murphy." He cleared his throat. "I think we're all aware that Freedom Network leader Tim Ebersole's body was found last Thursday."

There were nods, all around.

"I got a call from Jules Cassidy over the weekend." Tom turned to tell the doctor, "He's high level FBI. He was the Bureau's team leader for the Jane Chadwick death threat investigation, back in '05. We were hired to provide security for both Chadwick and her movie set while they were filming *American Hero,* so we worked closely with Cassidy. He's a good man. An outstanding agent."

She nodded.

Tom went on, looking around the table: "When Cassidy called me on Sunday, he let me know that the FBI team investigating Tim Ebersole's death would like to bring Murphy in for questioning. Apparently Murph was in the habit of writing e-mails to Tim Ebersole, telling him to watch his back, that he was coming after him, that he blamed him for his wife's death."

"Oh, Murphy," Sophia put voice to what they were all thinking.

"I told Cassidy we'd locate Murph," Tom continued, "and convince him to surrender himself to the authorities. They just want to ask him some questions, give him a chance to provide an alibi. The sooner he goes in, the better."

"And of course it's also better if he goes in voluntarily," Tom's XO Alyssa Locke added.

Decker looked down the table at Dave, his expression grim. "You still have Hannah Whitfield's e-mail address?"

"I e-mailed her last Friday," Dave told him, told Tom and the rest of the team, too. "Last time I checked—" he looked at his watch—"about a half hour ago, she still hadn't responded." He pushed himself to his feet. "I'll start tracking her IP address."

"We're not quite done here," Tom pointed out, which was his easygoing way of ordering Dave to sit.

It didn't make it any less of an order, so Dave put his butt back into his seat.

"In addition to finding Murphy," Tom said, clearing his throat, "we're also going to be . . . talking about Murphy." He nodded to Tracy, who began passing out blue report folders. "Dr. Heissman comes highly recommended. I'm not going to go into detail here regarding her credentials—that's included in the file you're receiving, you can read it at your leisure."

Decker spoke up, his voice tight. "Excuse me, sir. How exactly does our *talking* about Murphy help him?"

Tom looked at him steadily. "It doesn't help him, Chief," he said quietly. "It helps us."

Decker pushed his blue report folder back to Tracy. "I'm assuming this is voluntary."

Tom nodded. "It is." He cleared his throat again. "However. Anyone who chooses not to participate also won't be participating in any overseas assignments until further notice."

Decker sat back in his chair, clearly stunned.

"In other words," Dave clarified, "if we don't talk to Dr. Heissman, we'll get stuck playing red cell for the paranoia accounts, here in the States, until our hair turns gray." He turned to the doctor as he realized what he'd just said. "No offense. Your hair is really . . ." He cleared his throat. "Quite striking. And . . . Lovely."

"None taken," she said easily. "And thank you."

"Next time you beat the shit out of me?" Nash leaned forward and said down the table, to Decker. "Don't do it in the parking lot."

Decker just shook his head. "With all due respect, sir," he started to say to Tom.

But Sophia cut him off. "This was my idea," she announced. "It's supposed to help, not make things harder."

"Swing and a miss," Decker shot back. He looked from Tom to the doctor and back. "So when do we start? Can we start right now? I'd like to go first, get this voluntary requirement over with."

DALTON, CALIFORNIA

Hannah had installed a satellite dish.

With it, she could use a phone to send and receive text messages. She also had Internet access.

Not that she ever bothered to check her e-mail.

Still, Murphy was impressed. She'd done way more over the past few months than rehab her ankle to the point where she no longer needed a cane.

She'd clearly already worked on improving her lip reading—although that was a skill she'd always possessed.

Murphy couldn't read lips if his life depended on it.

Hannah had gotten a number of books on American Sign Language, and there were brochures on her desk for Dogs for the Deaf and a letter from her health insurance company about something called a cochlear implant that she'd be eligible for, but only after an extensive waiting period. It was proof that she was actively returning to the land of the living.

He'd said some harsh things to her that night—the last time he'd been back here . . . Or . . . Was it the last time, or had there been a visit in between then and now?

He honestly couldn't remember. So much of the past six months was a fog, a blur, a blending of days into nights into weeks.

And yet that one night, six months ago, had moments that he remembered vividly. Hannah's stricken face as he'd tried to unlock Patrick's weapons case. As he'd flung hurtful words at her: *You're already dead and buried . . .*

The sex, however, wasn't imprinted in his brain in such glorious high definition. Of that part of the night, he remembered only vague bits and pieces.

Hannah's cool fingers in his hair.

The sweetness of her mouth—he'd purposely not kissed her more than that once because she'd tasted too good.

The freakish sensation of a woman's body beneath him—soft and warm and welcoming—a body that wasn't Angelina's.

God, he'd wanted to die.

Murphy watched Hannah now, as he sat, pretending to read in the shade out on the cabin porch. She was in her garden, straw hat on her head, pulling weeds. Tall and strong. Invincible. Unkillable, she'd called herself once, years ago, after she'd stopped a convenience store holdup in progress. Both the store owner and the perp had been wounded, but she'd miraculously walked away unharmed. *That* time.

"I don't know what I would've done if you'd died," Murphy said, knowing full well that she couldn't hear him.

Hannah had been rushed to the hospital not quite two weeks after Murphy had gotten out. Eight short days after Angelina's god-awful memorial service.

The worst of Hannah's life-threatening infection was over before he'd even found out she had been injured in a car accident in the first place. He'd been off bingeing, trying to erase his own pain, ignoring the repeated phone calls from Patrick, not realizing Hannah's uncle was calling to tell Murphy that she lay at death's door . . .

As Murph now watched, she rinsed her hands in a bucket that she'd filled with water from the garden hose.

It was weird, being with Hannah without music blasting in the background. She and Angelina, both, had believed that life not only should have a soundtrack, but that it should be played with the volume cranked.

But things could change in a heartbeat. Now Hannah's world was silent, and Angelina was gone.

The truth of that no longer stabbed him like a bayonet to the heart. No, it was more of a constant ache these days. He no longer woke up surprised to discover that, for a few short hours while he'd slept, he'd returned to a world where Angelina laughed and danced and breathed.

Because now, even though Murphy still dreamed about his wife, he knew, even in his dreams, that she was gone.

She was gone—but he was still here. And Hannah was here, too.

As Murphy watched, she came onto the porch, dripping with perspiration, grabbing the sweating glass of iced tea he'd made for himself, and nearly draining it.

"Hey," he said, tapping her leg with his foot to get her attention. "That's mine."

She smiled as she flopped back onto the porch swing. "Consider it a vegetable tax. The day you weed, I won't drink your iced tea. So if you want to keeping eating my tomatoes—" She cut herself off and laughed. "Even I can tell that that must've sounded really wrong."

After just a few weeks together, they'd fallen into an easy routine. Whoever woke up first in the morning started a pot of coffee. They'd grab a quick breakfast, then hike down to the pond and go for a swim.

That kind of PT was easier on Hannah's ankle, but not on Murphy, who'd never counted speed-swimming as one of his strengths. He'd finally pulled out Patrick's old fishing dinghy and rowed alongside of Hannah. Or he would run the trail around the pond while she did laps.

Lunch was catch as catch can, every man for himself.

Afternoons were for the occasional chore, but mostly for lazing around, reading or cloud watching.

They took turns making dinner. Eating was a mostly silent affair—Hannah sometimes even brought a book with her to the table, which was fine with Murphy.

Evenings were quiet, too. With no television, there was no mindless noise. Just the sounds of the falling night. They'd play a game—backgammon or Carcassonne—before settling in for more quiet reading.

Around eleven, Hannah would put down her book and stretch. That was Murphy's cue to sign *good night* and climb the ladder to the loft.

The next day, they'd do it all over again.

One day at a time.

"What's for dinner?" Hannah asked now. It was Murph's turn to cook tonight.

"I don't know," he said. "There's ground beef in the freezer. We could either go tacos or spaghetti and meatballs."

"Oh, man, I love your meatballs," Hannah said, then laughed. "Is it just me, bwee, or does everything I say come across as sexual innuendo?"

"It's not just you," Murphy reassured her. "I've been . . . choosing my words more carefully, too."

Hannah finished off his iced tea, putting the glass back on the little side table with a clunk before she started untying the laces of her boots. "It gets in the way, doesn't it? That night. But it shouldn't."

Typical Hannah—going pointblank with the awkward topic of conversation.

He waited until she was done kicking her boots to the porch, and pulling her socks off, too.

"Yeah, I don't know," Murphy said when he finally got eye contact. "It doesn't quite seem right that there shouldn't be consequences." He spelled out the words, forming the ASL letters with his hand, making sure she understood.

"Can I be honest with you?" she asked, and he laughed. Even more honest than she usually was?

"Go large."

"I thought the consequences would be that you'd never come back," Hannah admitted. "I suppose anything that *isn't* that, is acceptable to me."

Murphy had been afraid that the consequences were that he'd gotten her pregnant.

It was weird, but he'd been a little disappointed at first that he hadn't. Like, that would have been a viable solution to how he was going to spend the rest of his life. Caring for and raising a child . . . But he'd quickly realized how unfair that would be to Hannah—who hadn't yet met the love of *her* life.

Although, her chances of finding him—that one person in a billion— were slim to none while she was hiding her ass out here in Nowhereville.

"You should know," Hannah told him now, her eyes a serious mix of green and blue as she held his gaze, "that in hindsight? I don't regret what happened that night. If I could do it over again? I'd do exactly what I did. It was part of the grieving process, Murph. It was something you needed to do in order to get to this new place in your life that you . . . seem to have gotten to."

Murphy shook his head, breaking the connection, looking out at the garden instead. Conversations with Hannah had always been intense, but now, with her need to keep her eyes glued to his face when he spoke . . . It felt extra-intimate. Which was maybe why he felt compelled to answer her honestly. "I don't think that was the turning point." Again, he spelled out the phrase. "I don't know if I'll ever reach a turning point."

"You will," she said. "You'll meet someone, and . . . You won't have to think, *oh, shit, sex is going to be this huge deal.* You won't have to worry about hating her forever, and screwing up your relationship because . . . Well, it's been handled."

"I didn't hate you forever," he said.

"You hated me for six months," Hannah pointed out, and he turned to look at her again. She was serious. "Which was pretty close to forever, for me."

And there they sat, just gazing at each other.

I'm so sorry. Murphy signed it. It was one of the first things he'd learned.

"Hey," she said. "You came back. For which I am extremely grateful. You're my best friend, Murph." She laughed, rolling her eyes. "Right now, you're my only friend. I've pretty much pushed everyone else away. And maybe that's what really happened that night. Maybe I was trying to run you off for good."

"You were trying to help," he corrected her.

"Two twisted birds with one large stone," she said. "It can be a dark, crazy place inside my head at times. Especially when Johnny W. comes to the party." She smiled. "I know you've noticed that I've rescinded his open-house invitation."

Murphy nodded. He'd been here going on two weeks now, and not only had he noticed that Hannah hadn't taken a drink once, but that Patrick's liquor cabinet was filled with canned goods. She was keeping the cabin dry.

He carefully folded down the top corner of the page of his book, marking his place. "The person I really hated was myself," he admitted. "The damage done that night was . . . Man, I hated that I hurt you."

"Well, you can cross me off your list of worries," Hannah said. "I came through the ordeal just fine. In fact, it kind of . . . pushed me to do some things I'd been putting off. And as for the sex . . ." She shrugged. "Yeah, we're friends, but I'd be lying if I told you I'd never wondered what it would be like. You and me. I think it's human nature, you know? You're male, I'm female. You've got tab A, I've got slot B—hmmm, I wonder what *that* would be like? It definitely crossed my mind a time or two, and . . . now I know."

Murphy had to laugh. "I thought only guys thought like that."

"Nope," Hannah said. "Dude, I'd wanted to get with you for years."

Murphy laughed. And everyone had always thought that, between the two best friends, Angelina had been the outrageous one.

"And I'm not expecting you to say something similar back," Hannah told him. "That's always so awkward. You know, like you're fifteen and the first guy you French kiss goes *I love you*, and then looks at you like, *well?* And you're like, *Um, Billy? I really just wanted to see what the fuss was all about.* Of course, you end up saying *I love you, too*, because you're too much of a coward. Don't be a coward, okay?"

Murphy just shook his head and laughed as she took his empty glass and headed into the coolness of the cabin.

He followed her, but he knew better than to answer while her back was to him. Which, right now, was completely intentional. She did that every now and then. He was starting to think of it as her own version of a hit and run.

But the truth was, he'd definitely thought about sex with Hannah. In fact, he'd thought about it a lot, before she'd introduced him to Angelina.

After that, he'd thought about it only occasionally. But it was along the same *never gonna happen* fantasy lines as his occasional thoughts of sex with Jennifer Garner or Charisma Carpenter.

Except it *had* happened. And he'd be lying if he said he hadn't spent a significant amount of time these past few weeks, thinking about it happening again.

Problem was, he wanted to do it again, but at the same time, he desperately, absolutely didn't.

And if Murphy were Hannah, he'd just announce this odd paradox of feelings. He'd say, *It's like my body is done with the grieving, but my heart and mind are still miles behind.* He had no idea what he'd feel, how he'd react, and he *would not* put Hannah through that again.

She was rummaging in the open refrigerator, her back still pointedly toward him, so Murphy sat down at her laptop computer and jumped online and . . . Holy God.

"Han."

Of course she didn't hear him.

He took one of the crumpled balls of paper they kept around for exactly this reason, and launched it into the corner of the room that was the kitchen. It bounced off the freezer door, and she looked up.

Come here, Murphy signed. *Look.*

She closed the fridge door and came, leaning down to look over his shoulder at the computer screen.

Her e-mail inbox had nearly a dozen new messages. All from dmalkoff at tsinc dot com.

Need your help, read several of the subject headers. The others said *Hannah, are you there?* and *Trying to contact you* and *STILL trying to contact you . . .*

Murphy turned to look at her. "You know Dave Malkoff from Troubleshooters?" he asked.

"Um," she said.

CHAPTER
EIGHT

Welcome to Las Vegas.

If Izzy squinted his eyes and tried really hard, he could pretend that this was just another road trip with the guys.

He never brought more than two hundred dollars with him when he came to the City of Sin—and that included the money he'd spend on his share of a hotel room and all his meals, to boot. He knew himself well enough to limit, financially, the amount of fun he had.

Still, he usually ended up coming home with at least as much in his pocket, if not actually more.

Vegas was, to him, a shiny, lucky, happy-fun-place.

But today his pockets were nearly empty and here in Lopez's hybrid car—it was not for nothing that Lopez's first name was Jesus—it was grim to the nth degree. Although, the grimosity that enshrouded them wasn't just because Izzy and Gillman were sharing the barely-there backseat.

Just outside of Barstow, Jenkins had gotten a call from his wife Lindsey, who worked for Tommy Paoletti's Troubleshooters.

"Whoa, shit," he'd said into his cell phone. "No, I hadn't heard. That's . . . He's really dead?"

"Who's dead?" Gillman sat forward to ask.

"Hang on, Linds," Jenkins told his wife, turning to announce to the entire car, "Timothy Ebersole, the leader of the Freedom Network, was found with a bullet in his head."

No way.

"That's old news," Gillman scoffed. "I read about it last Friday."

"And you didn't throw a party?" Izzy asked. At Gillman's dark look, he added, "What? We all want to do a happy dance because the mother-fucker's dead. Why pretend we don't?"

Tim Ebersole had believed in Amerika, the land of the free white Christian male and the not-so-free everyone else. He believed wholeheart-edly in white supremacy, a national tax-supported religion, and control through hatred and division. Although he'd never quite made it onto the watch-list, he was believed to be a bubba—a terrorist of the homegrown variety. He'd written and distributed countless instruction booklets on how to create explosives from fertilizer and other handy household items. And his website spewed more than just bullshit. The Freedom Network site often posted personal information—addresses and phone numbers—of people whom they hated. People, including children, that they were tar-geting—although they never told their followers to wreak vengeance in so many words.

Still. All it took was one crazy with a gun.

"He *was* kinda like Hitler, lite," Jenk pointed out before going back to his phone call with Lindsey.

"Timmy E. was a Holocaust denier," Izzy said. "Shit, I love saying that. *Was.* And that was when he wasn't extolling the virtues of the Nazis' Final Solution. I mean, Holy Heil, Timbo, you can't have it both ways. You know, if he could've, he would've kicked Lopez back to Mexico, for-get about the fact that he was born in the United States. Citizen, smiti-zen."

Lopez glanced at him in the rearview mirror. "My father's from Puerto Rico. My mother is, too, but she was born in Queens."

"No shit, florecita," Izzy said. "But to little Timmy Ebersole, you speak Spanish so you must be a fucking Mexican. Go fart your refried beans south of the border, mojado."

"Jesus, Zanella." Gilligan was disgusted.

"*I'm* not saying that." Izzy was beyond sick of having to explain him-self to this asshole. "That's what Ebersole would've said. Before he got his ass killed. And again, I'll say *yay.* Although, frankly, I wish he'd been struck dead by a bolt of lightning. I realize God works in mysterious ways, but IMO, this wasn't a time for him to be subtle."

"I don't know how long we'll be in Vegas," Jenk said into his phone.

"But you know, Lopez is here, so if I need to fly back . . ." He paused. "I'll ask, but . . ." He sighed. "Thanks, Linds, I know. You, too. I'm really sorry about . . . Yeah. I love you."

"We love you, too, Lindsey," Izzy said in his best Cookie-Monster voice, but Jenk had already hung up. "Ow!" Gillman had whacked him in the chest with his fist, and Izzy rubbed himself now, indignantly. "What the fuck, Dan? We've got hours to go. What, do you want to ride in silence?"

"Yes," Gilligan said. "Yes, I want to ride in silence."

"Well, tough shit," Izzy said, "because I don't. Last time I checked, this wasn't a monarchy and you weren't king of anything but your own dick."

"Guys," Jenkins said.

"Yeah, well, who slept with whose sister and got her pregnant?" Gillman came back.

"Guys," Jenkins tried again.

"Well," Izzy said, ignoring Jenk as completely as Gillman did. "Let's see. I don't *have* a sister, so *that* wouldn't be me, although . . . Jenkins does and she's married with kids so . . ." He drew the word out and then gasped, as if he'd just figured it out, and announced, all in a rush, "Jenkins' brother-in-law slept with Jenkins' sister and got her pregnant."

Gillman hit him again.

"Ow! Mom, Danny hit me. Twice."

Jenk was shaking his head in disgust. "Zanella, are you *trying* to piss Dan off?"

Anything to keep from thinking about Eden. Waiting there in Vegas. Although no way could she be as spectacular as Izzy remembered. She was, after all, six months pregnant. Except, there were currently a rash of pregnancies among the wives of quite a few SEALs in Team Sixteen. Meg Nilsson was pregnant again. As was the senior chief's wife, Teri.

Izzy had always found Teri Wolchonok attractive, but now? She was unbe*liev*ably hot. It didn't take much for him to picture Eden in the same kind of loose-fitting dress that Teri had worn to Tommy Paoletti's latest cookout. With Eden's hair down around her shoulders, and the breeze pressing that dress against the swell of her belly and full breasts, all round and ripe and radiant and soft and . . .

He realized that Jenk was looking at him. Uh, what was the question? Was he trying to piss off Gilligan?

"Maybe a little," Izzy confessed. "Maybe we should have a bonding sing-along. *The road is lo-ong, with many a winding turn . . . ?*"

"Shut *up*, Zanella," Gillman spat.

"Not an Osmond Brothers fan? How about a little Carole King? *When you're down and troubled, and you need a helping hand . . .*"

Lopez looked at him again in the rearview. He put an edge into his normally soft-spoken voice. "Stop. Both of you."

That shut Izzy up. Although it might be mildly entertaining to see if they couldn't actually get Jay-Lo to shout at them.

Danny appeared willing to go for it. "I'm not the one who—"

Lopez cut him off. "Dan. Take a deep breath and think, okay? Izzy's got to be totally freaking out. I think he's doing pretty well, considering. Try to step back from the fact that this is your sister—"

"I can't," Gilligan said bitterly. "Believe me, I've tried to step back from the fact that she's my sister for years."

Izzy shook his head in disgust. "And no doubt Eden's well aware of that. Did you try to *step back* from her when she was fourteen, when she got in way over her head with a guy who was older and should've known better? There's a word for what happened to her, by the way. It's called statutory rape."

Gillman stared at him.

"Where were you then, Dan?" Izzy pushed him.

Gillman came back to life. "Talk about older and should've known better!"

"We're not talking about me, but if we were, I'd cop to every mistake I've ever made, and yeah, I've made a shitload—including that night with Eden," Izzy said, staring Gillman down. "But we were talking about you. Where were *you?*"

Gillman looked away first. He was gone, was the answer and Izzy knew it. Gilligan had escaped into the Navy, leaving his kid sister behind to fend for herself.

"And what the fuck were you doing," Izzy said, more gently now, "bringing her back to your mother's place in Vegas?"

"Where else was I going to take her?" Gillman asked. "She can't exactly bunk with me on base."

"Yeah, but *Vegas?*"

Eden had said that their stepfather was raging crazy.

Which was one of the reasons why Izzy was so anxious to see her. To make sure she wasn't being held against her will. Although what he'd do if she was, he wasn't quite sure.

"So you'll cop to your mistakes," Gillman said, his hostility level rising again, "but are you going to take responsibility for them?"

Jesus H. Christ on a pogo stick. "May I state for the record," Izzy said, "that if, by some miracle of impregnation via wishful thinking, I *did* manage to knock up your sister, I *will* take full responsibility."

"So you're saying you didn't touch her," Gillman said.

Izzy sighed. That silence thing was starting to seem like a good idea. "I'm saying, yes, if I'm the father, I will take responsibility."

"Which means what? That you'll marry her?"

"Yeah," Izzy said. "All right? I'll marry your fucking sister." Okay, that came out wrong, and Gillman once again was on the verge of hitting him.

Lopez raised his voice. "Stop. Being. Assholes." It wasn't quite a shout, but it was damn close.

"Lindsey wanted me to ask you guys a favor," Jenkins broke the stunned silence that followed. "Do you remember Vinh Murphy? Former Marine who used to work for Tommy at Troubleshooters?"

"Big guy," Lopez said, back to using his inside voice. "Nice guy. Part Vietnamese. Part African American. Looks kinda like Tiger Woods, but super-sized."

"He's the one whose wife was killed by that nutjob shooter," Izzy remembered. "Angelina." He'd only met Vinh Murphy a few times, and had never met the man's wife, but he would never forget her name. That had been bad, bad shit that went down that day. The news of her death had rippled like a shockwave throughout the entire SpecWar community.

"That's him," Jenk said. "He's wanted for questioning. FBI thinks he might have something to do with Tim Ebersole's death. Apparently, Murphy blamed the Freedom Network for Angelina's murder."

There was silence in the car for several long moments.

Danny, ironically, broke it. "Does Lindsey think Murphy did it?" he asked. "You know, shot Ebersole?"

Jenk shook his head. "She doesn't know. She hasn't seen the guy in years. He's pretty much gone dark—nobody knows where he is. Tommy's looking to find him before the FBI does, and Lindsey says he needs all the help he can get. That's the favor. This is not a paying gig," he added. "They're all going off the clock for this one. Linds knows we've got a few days free so . . ."

"I'm in," Izzy said.

"Anything to get away from Eden, huh?" Gillman snarked.

Izzy looked at him in renewed disbelief. "I'm the one who asked to go see her, dickhead."

"I'm in, and Danny is, too," Lopez said quietly. "Because if I were Murphy? I would've gone after that motherfucker Ebersole years ago. I would have put him down like a rabid dog."

Damn, Lopez. Tell us how you really feel.

"If they find proof that Murph did this," Lopez continued, "or even if they don't? They're going to put out a BOLO and they're going to label Murphy armed and dangerous, and some frightened rookie is going to shoot him on sight, because he's big and he's black and yeah, he's probably carrying. So let's find him before that happens, okay?" He looked at Izzy and Gillman in the rearview. "That work for you guys?"

"Yeah," Izzy said.

Gillman nodded, too.

And with Murphy and Angelina on all of their minds, they did manage to ride in silence for the last few hours.

Izzy even managed to sleep, waking only as Lopez pointed the car toward the glitter of the casinos and the main strip. But then, at Gilligan's instruction, he turned onto a tired looking street, lined with tired looking houses, circa 1969.

Izzy couldn't keep from singing, but he kept it quiet. *"Here's the story, of a man named Brady . . ."*

It was totally Brady-Bunch-land, except Greg and Peter had become heroin addicts, Bobby gambled and chain-smoked, Marcia was in jail for killing her abusive fifth husband, and Cindy moonlighted as a call-girl when Jan got too drunk to work as a pole dancer.

Izzy first thought they were taking a shortcut, but then Lopez pulled up in front of a house that had one of its front windows covered by a big sheet of plywood. Shards of broken glass glittered on the parched dirt out front.

"God damn it, Eden," Gillman swore, getting out of the car and running toward the house. Jenk was on his heels.

Izzy followed more slowly. *This* was where Gillman's parents lived? Lopez was right behind him, and Izzy turned to say, sotto voce, "I thought Gilligan came from some serious money."

"That's what he wants people to think," Lopez said just as quietly. "Business was bad for years, and then they lost everything in Katrina. Their entire store in New Orleans was destroyed, all the inventory gone . . . They didn't have the right kind of insurance. They couldn't even go bankrupt, what with the changes in bankruptcy laws. That's why Danny's been living on base. He's helping his mom pay off the debt and he's chipping in rent on this palace, making sure his little brother has a roof over his head."

"Shit," Izzy said, stopping short on the pitted concrete path that led to the sagging front screen door. "I didn't know."

"Well, yeah, man." Lopez's eyes were somber. "You never talk to him. You just talk *at* him."

Ouch.

"His current stepfather's useless," Lopez continued. "In fact, he's worse than useless, the way he's always picking fights with Eden. And now . . ." He shook his head. "None of them have health insurance. Danny's been applying for credit cards, pretty much nonstop since he got back from Germany. He figures that's the only way he's going to be able to pay Eden's hospital bills. You know, labor and delivery. God forbid she or the baby have any complications."

Damn.

"I didn't get her pregnant, Jay," Izzy told his friend. "I didn't. Please don't tell anyone this—especially not Gillman, it's none of his business—because we kinda did get to third base. But that was it, I swear. Eden was . . . It was payback. Her ex treated her like shit, and I was handy and . . . I tried saying no, but . . ." He squinted in the heat and glare of the afternoon as he looked up from the sparkle of that broken glass in the dirt, down the row of ugly-ass houses, with dead weeds and cars up on blocks littering the yards. He forced himself to meet Lopez's patient gaze and confessed, "I didn't try very hard. I really liked her, man. Wait 'til you meet her, she's . . . Spectacular. Even now, I'm feeling a little light-headed at the idea of walking in there and seeing her again."

Lopez nodded slowly. Alleluia, he actually believed Izzy. "Dan's going to want you to do a paternity test. Cut him some slack, okay? Don't fight him on that."

"I won't," Izzy promised. "I'm happy to do whatever needs to be done." He looked again at the glass in the yard, at the boarded up window. Clearly someone—Eden—had tried to exit the house via unconventional methods. "Including letting Eden crash at my place until she figures out what she's going to do, where she's going to go."

"That might not be such a good idea," Lopez warned.

"Maybe not," Izzy said. "But at least I can't get her *more* pregnant, right?"

Lopez just looked at him.

"That was a joke," Izzy said.

"Maybe it's time to stop joking, Zanella," Lopez told him, and turned and went into the house.

Izzy took a deep breath, and followed.

San Diego, California

"Please sit down."

"I'd really rather stand."

Dr. Heissman sighed and tapped the end of her pen on the desk in front of her as Decker closed the door to Tommy's office behind him. "Do we really need to turn every little thing into a power struggle—"

"No," Decker said, perhaps more forcefully than he'd intended. "I'd really rather stand because yesterday I got ripshit drunk, fell down the stairs and bruised my coccyx. So if it's all right with you, ma'am, I'll stand."

She gazed at him—giving him a long, measuring look from behind those glasses. "Does that happen often? The ripshit drunk part."

"Nope," he said. "Never. Well. Obviously not. But almost never."

She nodded, glancing down at what he had to assume was his file, there on the desk. He could only guess what was in there.

Dr. Heissman was using Tom Paoletti's office for her interviews or sessions or whatever the hell this was supposed to be. It felt strange being in there with the door closed, without the CO leaning back in that very chair she was sitting in. But Tom had had a meeting in Hong Kong that couldn't be rescheduled. Until he returned on Saturday, it made sense for her to take advantage of the privacy. After that? Who knew? With luck she wouldn't be around much longer than that.

She cleared her throat delicately as she looked back up at Decker. She reminded him of Emily, and it was disconcerting—both the reminder and the realization that he was still able to be reminded of Em, so many years after she'd moved out. "Your friends are terribly worried about you."

She'd surprised him with that one, and he laughed. "Yeah, well, I'm terribly worried about them, too. Particularly Murphy. So if we can't move this along . . . ? I'd like to get to work looking for him."

She sat back, her elbows on the armrests of Tom's chair, fingers laced in front of her as she looked up at him.

It wasn't so much that she looked like Em, because she didn't. In fact, there was nothing of Emily's girlish cuteness in this woman's strong face. But in her take-charge attitude? In the way she dressed, in colorful, flowing clothes that hinted of Wiccan influence, in the steady intelligence of her gaze . . . Yeah, she and Em were both plankholders in the Modern American Women's Take-No-Shit club.

"What do you want to talk about first?" Dr. Heissman asked him. "The fight you got into with James Nash, or Angelina's death?"

Jesus.

"Those are my only choices? Don't you want to hear about my crappy childhood or—"

"The Khobar towers bombing?" she interjected.

"Oh, good," Decker said. "I was afraid you were going to make this too easy."

She laughed and then stood up. Back in the conference room, he'd thought that she was tall, but now he could see that he had at least a couple of inches on her. "Can you lean? Because I can sit on the edge of the desk, if you want to lean over here, by the window."

"I appreciate the effort, Doctor, but trust me, you're not going to make me comfortable."

"Please call me Jo."

"Like we're friends, huh?" he said, moving to the window. Looking out of it would give him something to do.

"No," she said, perching on the edge of the desk, "like we're colleagues, working together toward a common goal. How long have you known Murphy?"

"Since 2004," he said. "I knew him before that, but I didn't know him well."

"But in 2004—a year before Angelina died—you got to know him well."

"Yes, ma'am. He was a good man. A strong operative. Good attitude, highly skilled. I was always pleased to have him as part of my team, regardless of the op."

"He was injured back in 2004, when he was part of your team, on assignment in Kazbekistan," she pointed out. "Can you tell me about that?"

"Car bomb," he said. "Other than that—nope, can't tell you about it. The mission was classified."

She smiled. "I have clearance," she said. "The details are in your file."

"Then you don't need me to tell you about it, do you?" he countered.

"Let me rephrase," she said. "How did you feel when Murphy was injured by a car bomb in Kazbekistan?"

Blue. Behind her trendy, square-shaped glasses, her eyes were blue.

Decker looked out the window. His own office was two doors down the hall, facing the same view of the park across the street. Pretty much any time of day, children were out there, playing on a colorful climbing gym that was decked out as a pirate ship. Tommy's wife, Kelly, sometimes brought their son, Charlie, to play, and Tommy often joined them.

Decker had watched them once, from his office window, as his boss let Charlie chase him around and around, over and even under the pirate ship, as Kelly laughed.

Tommy made a great pirate.

He glanced at Dr. Heissman, who was sitting there, patiently waiting for him to answer her question. *How did you feel . . . ?*

Mad as hell. And as if he were spiraling out of control.

"It was a trying day," he finally said. "Murph's injury wasn't the only . . . problem I was dealing with at that time."

"You managed to get him onto a helicopter, out of the country, to a hospital with far more advanced technology," she said.

"Yes," Decker said. "We did."

"As a result, doctors were able to save his leg."

"That's correct." And, as a result, Murphy was back at work, mere months later. Where he rejoined Decker's team, which was assigned to protect a Hollywood movie producer who was receiving death threats . . .

The shrink—Jo—was gazing at him. "Isn't that something to be proud of? Saving his leg?"

This time Decker held her gaze. "I did my job. It was part of my job as team leader."

"To protect and care for your team members," she clarified.

"Yes, ma'am."

She swung one foot a little, just gazing at him, so he turned back to the window.

"You ever *what if*?" she asked.

He turned. "Excuse me?"

"What if you hadn't been able to get him out? What if Vinh Murphy had lost his leg that day?"

Decker shook his head. Jesus. "I never . . . *what if.* No."

"What if you hadn't been able to get him out, and he'd died?" she pressed. "Because the description of the conditions in Kazabek at that time are horrific."

"I never *what if,*" Decker repeated.

"I think it's highly likely that he *would* have died if you hadn't gotten him out, don't you agree?"

Jesus. "Yeah," Decker said. He knew exactly what she was driving at. So he gave it to her. "He would have died. I don't doubt that. And *what if* he'd died? Angelina would be alive today. But Murphy didn't die, and *she* did. We can stand here what if-ing until the sun goes down, and it won't change a thing."

"Would you have preferred that outcome?" she asked. "That Murphy die instead of his wife?"

Jesus. "I know for a fact that *he* would've preferred it," he said. "I'm sorry, is there a point to this?"

"But would *you* have preferred it?"

"She didn't volunteer to be put in danger," Decker told her. "Murphy knew—we all know—the potential consequences of our chosen profession. So yes, okay? It would have been better if Murphy had died. But I forgot to bring my crystal ball on that earlier op."

"Would you say that, when Murphy was injured by that car bomb, you did the best you could, given the circumstances that you found yourself in?"

"Yes, ma'am."

"It might be good if you actually said it every now and then," the doctor gently said. *"I did the best I could."*

"I did the best I could." Decker was determined to play whatever games she wanted to play, but as the words left his mouth, something tightened in his chest.

They stood for a long moment, in silence.

She broke it. "How do you feel—right now?"

He forced a laugh around that tightness. "Like this is bullshit."

"You ever talk about any of this with anyone?" she asked. "A girl-friend—"

"No."

"No, you haven't—"

"No girlfriend," he clarified. "But if you write me a prescription, I'll go out to the CVS and pick one up, right away."

She laughed. "You're funnier than your file implies."

"Tell me what I need to say or do to get your clearance to go on over-seas missions."

The doctor—Jo—shook her head. "That's not the way it works."

The tightness continued to bear down on him. It was making him vaguely nauseated, and he desperately needed air. He needed to get out of here, but he planted himself, determined to see this through. "I'm cooper-ating."

"Are you?"

"Yes."

"Or are you just telling me what you think I want to hear." She made it a statement, not a question.

"It doesn't serve me," Decker told her tightly, "to dwell on past mis-takes. I like to focus instead on making sure they don't happen again."

"I'm assuming we're talking now about the Hollywood assignment," she said, "where . . . mistakes were made?"

"Shit, yeah," he exhaled. "And because of it, Angelina's dead." His voice actually cracked, damn it.

But the shrink didn't leap all over it, all over him. Instead, she just sat there, on Tommy Paoletti's desk, looking at him with those gentle eyes in that warrior goddess face, giving him a moment to regain his equilibrium.

And somehow, that made him even angrier than he would've been if she had jumped down his throat.

"You want to know how I *felt* when Angelina died?" he asked as the tightness in his chest moved up into his neck and his face as well. He practically had to squeeze the words out. "I felt bad. I felt so goddamn bad, I wanted to die, too. I thought about killing myself—about killing Murphy and then killing myself. It was only for a half a second, but yeah, I actually considered it."

He'd shocked her. Shit, he'd shocked himself.

"So you blame yourself for Angelina's death."

"I was team leader," Decker said quietly now. "The mistakes made were mine." Jesus, the tightness had turned into a solid block of sorrow, so profoundly heavy, it was as if an enormous monster were crouched on his chest.

"You mentioned mistakes before, too," the doctor said, just as quietly. "Exactly what mistakes—"

He cut her off, turning abruptly, heading for the door. "I have to go now."

She slid off the desk, but she obviously knew better than to try to stop him. "I'm going to recommend to Tom that you and I set up a regular time to talk—"

"Do whatever you need to do," he said curtly as he went out the door.

DALTON, CALIFORNIA

Murphy was sitting there, in front of Hannah's laptop computer in the main room of the cabin, waiting for her to explain why Dave Malkoff, from Troubleshooters Incorporated, had sent her nearly a dozen e-mails over the past few days.

"I went there," she told him as she pulled another chair from the dining table over to the desk. "To the Troubleshooters office. I thought you were going to . . . do something crazy, so . . ." She scanned the subject headers as she sat down next to him. *Hoping this is still your e-mail address* was the first one sent—last Friday morning. She reached for the mouse and clicked it open.

> *Hannah,*
>> *Have you heard from Murphy lately?*
> *—Dave Malkoff (from Troubleshooters Inc.)*

Murph tapped her arm, and she looked over at him. He'd shaved this morning, as he'd done every morning for the past two weeks, and his lean cheeks were smooth. He smelled good, too. Unlike Hannah, he always showered and changed out of his workout gear well before lunchtime. She sometimes stayed grunged up until dinner, because what the hell.

But now she was aware both of the bead of sweat that was lazing its way down past her ear, and the fact that her tank top was soaked. She couldn't smell herself, but that didn't mean that she didn't reek. It just meant that she'd gotten used to her own stench.

Personal toxic fumes aside, it was a little disarming to be sitting quite this close to Murphy, particularly after that conversation they'd just had on the porch.

Dude, I'd wanted to get with you for years.

"You went all the way to San Diego?" Murphy asked her.

"Yeah." She opened the next e-mail. *Re: Hoping this is still your e-mail address.* It was dated Saturday morning. Murphy tapped her arm again, but she shook her head. She was reading.

> *Hannah,*
>> *I didn't manage to convey just how important it is that I get in touch with Vinh Murphy, as soon as possible. It's quite important. Hoping you can help me,*
> *Dave (from TS Inc)*

"Dave Malkoff wants to talk to you," Hannah said, even though he was sitting right there and reading the e-mail, too.

But Murphy was directly in front of the keyboard, and he opened a memo window and typed, "How did you get down to San Diego?"

He had such large fingers, it seemed almost unbelievable that he could manipulate the small-sized keyboard, but the words appeared on the screen almost as fast as she could read them.

"I drove," Hannah answered. E-mails three, four, and five were variations on the same theme. Dave was looking for Murphy. Did she know where he was?

"Are you allowed to drive?" he typed.

"Probably not," she said. "My license expired—I haven't tried to renew it."

"If your L expired, the answer would be a NO, not PROLY NOT," he typed.

"Too bad I'm no longer a police officer," she told him, "so I can't arrest myself."

"Ha ha," he wrote.

Yeah, she was a real comedienne.

Sunday's e-mail from Dave was a little different.

Hannah,
    In case you haven't heard—Tim Ebersole of the Freedom Network is dead.

"Holy God," Hannah said.

Dave had included a link to a *New York Times* article, and Murphy bogarted the mouse in order to click on it as quickly as possible.

The news article appeared on the screen, and they both leaned forward, shoulder to shoulder, to read it.

Ebersole had been found in a remote part of the Freedom Network's compound, in the mountains east of Sacramento. Shot in the head. The murder weapon was believed to be a sniper rifle. The killer was believed to have military training. An investigation was under way.

"Now we know why Crazy Dave's been looking for me," Murphy typed.

"I'll let him know that you've been here with me," Hannah said through her relief, reaching to regain control of the mouse, clicking back to Dave's e-mail so that she could hit reply.

But Murphy covered her hand with his own. She looked at him, in surprise, but he was shaking his head. "I don't want you to . . ."

"What?" It looked as if he'd just said "life for me."

He typed the words. "I don't want you to lie for me."

Lie? Hannah still didn't get it. "You've been here for two weeks—"

Murphy typed: "TE was killed four months ago."

Oh, *shit*. She must've been reading too fast. She went back to the article and . . . Yeah, there it was.

Holy God.

And there they sat. In silence. As Hannah's heart thumped unsteadily in her chest. All of the relief that she'd felt—that Ebersole had gotten his just desserts without Murphy having to spend the rest of his life in prison—had morphed into fear.

Holy God . . .

Then Murphy reached over and sent the article to the printer. Apparently, he wanted a hard copy. His fingers flew over the keyboard again. "It's okay if you ask me."

She looked at him, looked into his eyes, searching for answers. If they were there, she couldn't see them.

"It's okay," he told her, also signing it. He typed again, "I know what you're thinking. I'm thinking it, too."

"I'm not sure what to ask you," Hannah admitted. "Did you do it, Murph? Or maybe I should ask, How did you manage to get away?"

Murphy laughed, but his smile quickly morphed into a grimace. And he wouldn't meet her eyes.

"I don't know," he typed, as the muscle jumped in his jaw.

"Don't know what?" Hannah asked, her heart in her throat.

"Don't know if I did it," he typed, "and if I did, I don't know how I got away."

Las Vegas, Nevada

"God damn it, Eden!"

Danny was back. Eden heard him coming into the house, even from the confines of the tiny bathroom where she'd been locked for the past few hours.

There was no window, no chance of escape.

Her wicked stepfather, Greg, had manhandled her in here after she'd thrown a chair through the bedroom window, hoping to attract the attention of the neighbors — let them know that she was being held against her will.

Not that she necessarily had anywhere else to go.

She now sat on the floor, trying not to cry, rubbing her stomach as Pinkie did somersaults inside of her.

It had all gone down, of course, while her mother was at work and her little brother Ben was at school.

"What the hell happened here?"

She could hear Danny's voice, and the lower rumble of Greg's as he no doubt expounded on what a *reasonable* idea it was for Eden to give up her baby for adoption — that there were people who would make a generous donation toward her college fund, *and* pay all of her hospital bills as well as her expenses for the next three months, in return for a healthy, white infant.

All she had to do was sign her name, and in three months she'd have her life back.

But the life she wanted back was the one she'd started to make for herself in Germany, while her father was away. A life that included this baby. Her baby.

But Greg had stood there, with a pen in his hand, and she'd laughed in his face and asked him what exactly was his percentage in this baby-selling deal. How many tens of thousands of dollars would *he* walk away with?

He didn't deny it. He'd just gotten angry and threatened to cut off all food and water until she signed the papers.

And even though Eden knew that his threat would last only until her mother came home, she'd panicked. And she'd launched that chair out of the window. Greg had slapped her hard across the face, and she'd scratched him, drawing blood.

No doubt he was now telling Danny that *she'd* attacked *him*. But there were other voices out there, too. Not her mother or Ben, but . . .

"You locked her *where?*"

Dear God, was it possible . . . ?

"Unlock this door *now*, or I'm calling 911 —" the voice got louder "—because you're gonna need an ambulance after I beat the living shit out of you!"

Eden awkwardly pushed herself up to her feet.

The heavy-duty deadbolt that Greg had put on the door rattled and clicked and the door swung open and . . .

Izzy Zanella was indeed standing in the hallway, looking in at her.

He was bigger and wider than she remembered, but dressed almost identically to the way she'd left him, all those months ago. T-shirt and cargo shorts. Boots on his feet. His hair was longer and his tan was darker, as if he'd recently spent a lot of time outside.

He looked unbelievably good—strong and solid and beyond pissed at Greg for locking her in here.

"Hey," he said, as if he'd run into her at the mall.

"Hey," she said, her heart doing a sudden nosedive as she realized that he hadn't come to save her. He'd come because she'd told her brother that this baby she was carrying was Izzy's. The pissed-off she was reading on him probably wasn't entirely directed toward her wicked stepfather.

She honestly hadn't expected him to show up here—to come all the way to Las Vegas. She'd expected him to deny it. To insist on a paternity test. To tell Danny that Eden was lying.

To buy her a little more time to figure out what she was going to do.

"You got a suitcase or something?" Izzy said now. "Because I'm thinking that while we're talking? You should probably pack."

His words didn't make sense. This was where he was supposed to accuse her of lying. And he wanted her to . . ."Pack?" she echoed stupidly.

He held out his hand to her. And he made a face that she realized was an attempt at a smile. Beneath it though, he was really, *really* angry.

But not at her.

"Come on, sweetheart," he said. "Let's go pack your things. I'm getting you and Izzy Junior the hell out of this shithole."

Eden couldn't help herself. She started to cry.

CHAPTER
NINE

E den had done one heck of a job on the window. Izzy stood in the bedroom that she'd been sharing with the youngest of the Gillman siblings, checking out the damage as she hurriedly threw her clothes into a duffle.

Her tears had lasted all of ten seconds—she was as tough as he remembered—and she'd left her bathroom prison with her head held high.

He was the one who had almost been undone.

The still-angry-looking hand-sized mark on her face had blinded him with anger—as if locking a pregnant woman in a tiny bathroom, with no place to sit comfortably or lie down, with no food for hours, wasn't bad enough.

"I don't expect more from you than a ride to San Diego," she told him now, as she zipped her bag. "I just want you to know."

Izzy turned to look at her. She'd put her hair back into a ponytail, and with her face scrubbed clean of any makeup, she looked about twelve. Except for the pregnancy thing. She was wearing running shorts and a T-shirt that was stretched tightly across her expanded abdomen.

Holy shit, there was a baby growing in there.

"Most women expect child support from their baby-daddy," he pointed out.

She made a face. Lowered her voice as she glanced toward the door that was ajar. "We both know that you're not the father, so just . . . don't."

"Why did you tell Dan that I was?"

Eden sighed heavily and sat down on the edge of the bed. There were dark circles beneath her eyes—it was clear she was exhausted. "I was trying to stall for time. I figured you knew it wasn't you, so . . . I really didn't think you'd come all this way."

"Danny nearly broke my nose," Izzy told her, and her aghast dismay made him laugh. "I'm fine," he added. "But really, Eden, what did you think he was going to do? Buy me a cigar?"

She shook her head. "I didn't . . . I just . . . I'm so sorry." She lowered her voice even more. "I didn't want him going after Jerry."

And . . . great. Six months in Germany apparently hadn't done the trick in curing her of her misguided affection for this dickweed. "So . . . Jerry's the father."

"No," Eden told him wearily. "Jerry's sterile. But he knows the father. And he'd figure it out. And he'd tell Danny, and then Danny would end up dead."

Izzy sat down next to her. "Dangerous guy, huh?"

"Extremely." She exhaled loudly. "I'm worried about more than Danny, okay? *I'm* afraid of this guy. I don't want anything to do with him, and I *really* don't want him to know he's got any connection to my baby. He's a pig—I don't want him in my life."

She held onto her extended stomach as if she were cradling the baby that was swimming around inside of her.

"So . . . what are your plans?" he asked.

Eden gave him a look. "Why do people always say that when what they really want to know is whether or not I'm going to keep the baby? And yes, I'm keeping him."

"Papa don't preach," Izzy sang. "My apologies for being pedestrian. I was just . . . we have a thing in the teams—*never assume.* I was actually trying to be polite. So *him.* He's a boy, huh?"

Eden smiled at his change of subject and it lit her up.

"He's a boy," she verified.

"He got a name?"

Eden nodded, but then shook her head. "Just a nickname, really. I call him Pinkie."

"What?" Izzy pretended to nearly fall off the bed. "Are you kidding? Do you *want* him to be gay?"

She laughed. "I don't care about that. I just want him to be healthy."

"Okay," Izzy said, "because Pinkie isn't just gay, he's, like, the kid everyone beats up in the cafeteria. Which is *very* unhealthy for him. Believe me, I'm a veteran expert when it comes to bad names for children."

As she kept on laughing, some of the despair in her eyes faded. "It's just his *in utero* name. It was actually . . . well, see, at first I thought he was a girl. But then, at the ultrasound . . . Penis! It was kind of a surprise. It was pretty funny, too. The technician just kind of shouted it. Like that. *Penis!*"

"People are always shouting that at me, too," Izzy said, and Eden laughed again. "So me and Pink already have something in common."

As she met his eyes, there it was—that freaking electric shock. She felt it, too, because she immediately looked away, her laughter quickly fading.

"So," Izzy said, because this seemed as good a time as any. "Wanna get married?"

She exhaled and rolled her eyes.

"I'm serious," he said.

She looked at him sharply, and it was a classic Gillman *Zanella, are you out of your fucking mind?*

It was entirely possible that he was. And yet, this seemed like the perfect temporary solution.

"Danny already thinks the baby's mine," he told her with a shrug. "This keeps Richie from killing him, right?"

Izzy could tell from her silence and from the look on her face, that she was stunned that he'd figured it out. Or maybe she was stunned that, after all this time, he remembered the name of Jerry's lowlife, scum-sucking boss.

He could see her weighing her options. She was considering whether she should try to lie her way out of this. *Richie? What are you, kidding? It's not Richie's baby.*

Maybe impending motherhood had mellowed her, or maybe she already simply knew Izzy well enough, even after six months spent on opposite sides of the world. She opted instead to throw herself on his mercy. "Please don't tell Danny."

"I won't," he promised.

And now she was worried for another reason. "It's not what you're thinking—me, with Richie. It wasn't—"

"I'm not thinking anything," Izzy said. "Except maybe that you and Pinkie could use some health insurance and a place to stay for a while.

And maybe a misleading last name on the birth certificate for the Pinkman. Like, you know. Zanella."

She didn't say a word. She just sat there, looking at him, tears welling in her eyes.

"It would only be a temporary, short-term thing," he reassured her. "Just until you get back on your feet. And you're not the only one who benefits," he pointed out as he took her hand from her lap, interlacing their fingers. Her nails were short and bitten—damn, she was young. "I get a double win. Danny no longer punches me in the face. And I get to piss him off by becoming his brother-in-law."

She laughed, but it was decidedly low energy.

"Look," Izzy told her. "I'm gone a lot. And the apartment's big enough so that even when I am around . . . You can have your own space. And if you want to, you know, pull your weight, you could do the laundry every now and then. That kind of thing. We could take turns cooking. You one night, Pinkie the next, then me . . ."

"Pinkie has to cook?" she said.

"Boy's gonna be gay, he should learn his way around the kitchen." Izzy smiled back at her. "Under your supervision, of course."

It was then that Gillman knocked on the door. It couldn't have been anyone else out there—his impatience was evident in each sharp rap.

"Congratulate me, fishboy," Izzy said as the door swung open, as he gazed into Eden's still-anxious eyes. "Your beautiful sister and I are getting married and having us a baby."

SOUTH OF SACRAMENTO, CALIFORNIA

Sacramento was going to be plenty familiar.

Murphy braced himself for that.

All it meant was that he'd been there before—plenty of times, in fact.

He had friends in the area—one a former Marine buddy. Years ago he wouldn't have thought twice about crashing at Paul's place when he was in town. But he honestly didn't know if he'd seen Paul and his partner Steve over the past six months.

Hannah'd text-messaged them, asking when they'd last seen Murph, but hadn't yet received a reply.

Murphy also had a low-rent motel on his list of frequently visited loca-tions—for when he didn't want to sleep on Paul's lumpy couch.

Favorite restaurants, favorite bars—these were all places that he and Hannah needed to check in their quest to find out whether or not he'd been in Sacramento during the last week of March, when Freedom Net-work führer Tim Ebersole had been sent, express, to hell.

Murphy's hands tightened on the steering wheel of Patrick's ancient VW Rabbit as they headed north.

He would think he'd have at least a sliver of memory, if he had, in-deed, shot and killed Ebersole.

The weight of the sniper rifle in his hands.

The unmistakable scrape of the slide as it chambered the round.

The stalk—waiting, possibly even for days, for his target to move into range.

Ebersole's hatred-inducing face, through the scope.

The recoil—and the rush of satisfaction that had surely come . . .

Murphy wasn't exactly certain what he was hoping he and Hannah would find when they arrived in Sacramento—a lack of evidence that would send them searching elsewhere for an alibi, or hard evidence that he had, indeed, been there, that he might well be the man the FBI was looking for.

"You're going to have to set these so they don't ring," Hannah said from the front seat, where she was looking at the disposable cell phones they'd picked up as they'd passed through Fresno. They'd gotten them so that they wouldn't have to use their own phones, so that they'd be truly anonymous even when making calls. "I think I've done it, but you'll need to check 'em."

She set them in the little car's cup holder.

She'd loaded the trunk and the backseat of the Rabbit with camping gear. Sleeping bags. Air mattresses because, as Hannah had pointed out, "I'm not twenty-two anymore."

No, she was an ancient twenty-nine.

They didn't discuss it in so many words, but it was very clear that they both knew they weren't going to stop at any motels. They also weren't going to buy gas or any additional supplies with anything other than cash.

This little trip they were taking was completely under the radar—as-suming that, living in isolation at Patrick's cabin, they'd been on anyone's radar to start with.

Hannah hadn't responded to any of Dave Malkoff's e-mails. She had, however, packed up her laptop. Sacramento had plenty of coffeeshops with free wireless. Not that they'd necessarily e-mail Dave from there, either, though.

Because all it would take was one e-mail, and Dave—or Tess Bailey, who was Troubleshooters' computer specialist—would be able to track them.

At this point, the best Tess could do was to trace a three-month-old e-mail that Hannah had said she'd sent to Dave from the Dalton public library in early March.

But Murphy had no doubt that, if Dave really, truly wanted to find them, he would. Even though the cabin was a solid twenty-five miles from that library, it was only a matter of time before Dave and the rest of his Troubleshooters team pulled up the cabin's dusty drive. Which was another reason he and Hannah had bugged out.

Dave had made clear his mission, in the last of his many e-mails. He wanted Murphy to turn himself in, to answer the FBI's questions.

It didn't, however, make a hell of a lot of sense to do that until Murphy's answers were more than *I don't know* and *I can't remember.*

Hannah took out a battered spiral notebook and clicked open a pen. "This is going to suck," she said, "but we've got to talk about where you've been over the past few months. See if we can't fill in some of your blanks. It's probably best to work backward, starting with what we *do* know. First, that Ebersole was believed to be killed on or around March fifteenth." She wrote that date on the top of the page, underlining it twice.

Murphy glanced at her. "Before I came, you know, back, I was in . . . well, it wasn't really rehab," he said. "But it was a program that . . . helped. I checked myself in on my birthday actually. April twenty-fourth."

Hannah was surprised. "You were in for two and a half months?"

"I was there for a month as a participant," he told her now. "The rest of the time I was sort of semi-staff. I pretty much stayed until they kicked me loose."

Hannah wrote down *April 24th through July 9th*, which was the day he'd returned to Dalton, over two weeks ago. "I don't mean to pry, but . . ."

"It's called Fresh Start. It's in San Diego," he told her. "And yeah, they'll have a record of my being there."

She nodded. "Was it . . ." She stopped herself. "If you don't want to talk about this, you don't have to, but . . . I've never heard of it and . . ."

"It's okay. I don't mind. It's a new program, put in place by a veterans' rights organization," he told her. "They focus on grief counseling, as well as overcoming substance abuse and PTSD." She frowned, and he spelled the acronym for her before she could say *what?*

"While you're there," he continued, "you kind of take it slow and . . . I guess learn to live again. It's all done through private funding, and it's non-faith-based, so you don't have to feel browbeaten into drinking the Kool-Aid. I mean, there're church services if you want to go but . . . I actually found the Eastern Philosophy classes useful." *Zen* he spelled for her. And *Buddhism*—except he never did know where to put that H. She nodded, though.

"Long story short, the program helped," he said again.

"I'm glad," Hannah said. "It's really nice to have you back. You know, you. Not crazy-angry you."

Murphy glanced away from the road and over at her again. "I may not be crazy-angry, but I'm pretty sure I'm not me anymore, Han."

"Maybe, maybe not," Hannah said. "But you're still my best friend, whoever you are." She looked back at her notebook. "So. April twenty-fourth, you were in San Diego, checking in to this program. Let's work backward. Where were you on April twenty-third?"

San Diego, California

About an hour ago, Decker had come flying out of Tom's office—where Jo Heissman was holding court—like his ass was on fire.

He went into his office and shut the door—something he rarely ever did.

So Dave waited.

And waited. But the door stayed tightly shut. And then Dave couldn't wait any longer. So he knocked.

"Yeah." Deck's voice didn't sound as if he were curled weeping, in a fetal position in the corner, so Dave opened the door a crack and peered in.

Deck was standing behind his desk, leaning over his computer monitor, reviewing the police report on Tim Ebersole's murder. Dave recognized it—he'd gone through it in detail himself.

"I tracked the IP address of the computer Tess used to send me that March fourth e-mail, asking again if we'd seen Murphy," Dave told his team leader now. "Hannah. *Hannah* used. Sorry. I don't know why I keep doing that."

Decker didn't respond. Other than to straighten up, completely expressionless, and prompt him. "And?"

"Hannah sent it at 1423 hours, from the public library in Dalton, California," Dave said. "I've checked public records, but there's no property registered to anyone named Whitfield, not in Dalton or any of the other towns in the vicinity. But I remember Hannah saying she was staying at a cabin owned by an uncle—it could well be her mother's brother. I'm trying to dig up her mother's maiden name, but I think it would be quicker just to go up there, flash her picture around. Murphy's, too. See if anyone's seen either of them."

Decker nodded. "Do it." He turned back to his computer.

"I'm, uh, going to take Sophia," Dave told him, and Deck looked up. "And Lindsey. Mark Jenkins and some of his friends—SEALs—volunteered to help with the search. We're going to meet them up there, first thing in the morning."

Another nod. "I'll tell Tom. Let them know we appreciate it."

"I will." Dave stood there, just looking at Decker, who was obviously waiting for him to leave and close the door behind him. "I'm, uh, scheduled to talk to Dr. Heissman in a few minutes."

Decker sighed.

"It occurred to me," Dave muscled on, "that I'm probably going to reveal information that you probably don't want me to tell her."

"Dave," Deck said. "I'm already having a really bad day."

"I'm sorry, sir," Dave told him. "But . . . I respect you more than anyone I've ever worked with. In all phases of my career. And yes, there have been times that I've avoided you, due to . . . personal differences. Okay, I'm just going to say it. Due to your callous treatment of Sophia. But that never had anything to do with your abilities and skills as a team leader. When we're out there, you make hard decisions look easy—and I know they're anything but. But."

He took a deep breath. "Over the past few years, since Angelina was killed in particular, although I believe it started before that, I've watched you cut yourself off from everyone you care about. On Friday, when you blew up at Nash, all I could think was, *Decker's only noticing this now?* Something's up with Nash, something that has him running scared. He's been trying, for awhile, to push Tess away, and the first time you call him on it, you do it with your fists?"

Dave shook his head. "I'm standing here, looking at you, and, sir, I see someone who's in serious trouble. And I've been thinking and thinking about it, and I figure, well, I can't lose you as a friend, because you and I were never more than colleagues. So I'm going to go in there, and I'm going to be honest with Dr. Heissman and I'm going to tell her things that I know you don't want me to say, things that absolutely violate your privacy. Because maybe if she knows, she can help you."

Decker was silent, just staring at a spot on the wall, several feet to the left of Dave's knees. As the silence stretched on, his gaze finally flickered up and over. He met Dave's eyes, but only briefly. "Are you done?"

Dave nodded. "Yes, sir."

"Then you should let me get back to work," Deck said quietly.

"Yes, sir." Dave wasn't sure what he'd expected Decker's response to his little speech to be, but it wasn't this calm acceptance.

"Thank you for the warning," Decker said as Dave let himself out the door.

LAS VEGAS, NEVADA

Eden's brother was crazy.

He was certifiably insane.

He'd grabbed Izzy and pulled him out of her bedroom and down the hall, through the living room and into the front yard. Where he hit Izzy in the face.

"Stop it!" Eden was right behind them. "Danny! Oh, my God!"

"Damn, Gillman, I thought this was what you wanted," Izzy was in the dirt, scrabbling away from Danny, scrambling back up to his feet. He wasn't fighting back—just trying to stay out of range of Danny's fists and feet.

"What I *wanted*," Danny said through clenched teeth as he went after Izzy again, "was for you not to get her pregnant in the first place!"

He feinted left and went right, but Izzy was faster and danced out of reach.

"What I *wanted*," Danny said, "was for you not to disrespect me. I *wanted* you to have both the common sense and code of fucking honor to stay away from a seventeen-year-old!"

"For the record," Izzy pointed out, still remaining purely on the defensive, "she was eighteen. And what happened that night had nothing to do with you. Trust me, Dan-O. No one was thinking of you."

"That's bullshit." Dan swung again and missed. "Everything Eden ever does is payback. You'll find that out—sooner or later. Probably sooner."

"Stop," Eden said again, moving toward them and nearly getting clobbered by her brother.

"Damn it, Dan, be careful, she's right behind you," Izzy said. "Eden, get *back*!"

Danny turned his rage on Eden. "Get away from me! I'm so goddamn tired of your shit!"

He didn't hit her. Eden had been hit often enough before to know that her brother hadn't hit her. But his swift turn to face her provided a body block and a very solid hipcheck. She went down, knocked onto her hands and knees in the dirt.

It was an accident, but Izzy didn't realize that, and he launched himself at Danny. "You *son* of a *bitch*!"

"Zanella, don't!"

It happened so fast—one second Danny was standing there, and the next he was curled in a ball, retching into the dust.

"You hit her *ever* again," Izzy spat through clenched teeth, "I'll fucking kill you!"

"Zanella!" Two of Danny's other friends were there—one short, the other Hispanic. Eden hadn't noticed them until they started making all kinds of noise, but Izzy ignored them. He was already done with Danny.

He pushed aside the dark-haired man who'd come to try to help Eden. "Are you all right?" There was real concern in Izzy's eyes as he crouched beside her, helping her to sit.

"I'm okay." Her knee was red and sore, but she hadn't quite skinned it. And she was definitely better off than Danny. "He didn't do that on purpose," she defended her brother—who was, as he'd said, so goddamn tired of her shit. Tears welled in her eyes.

Izzy somehow knew exactly what she was thinking, because as he pushed her hair back from her face with a hand that was almost unbearably gentle, he said, "I'm not. Tired. I actually kinda like your shit. Let's go find us an Elvis impersonator to get this thing done."

Eden actually found herself laughing as she looked into his eyes. But then, she started to cry. "I can't marry you," she said. "It wouldn't be fair."

"What, the cooking thing?" He tried to make it into a joke. "Okay, you win, Pinkie doesn't have to take a turn."

"It wouldn't be fair to *you*," she said. "Please don't think I don't appreciate it, because I do. I just . . . You want to rescue me because . . . You're a hero and that's what heroes do. But tomorrow . . ." She didn't want him waking up and regretting his impetuous decision.

Again, he knew exactly what she was thinking. "Okay," he said. "So we'll wait. We'll be engaged for a coupla nights. Just long enough to sleep on it, you know?" He straightened up, helping her to her feet. "Hey Jenk, will you do me a huge-large and drive me and Eden into town? I'm going to rent a car—I think we need to put some space between me and Gilligan for a while."

Jenk—the shorter man with the lighter hair—seemed down with that as he approached. "Lindsey just called. The Troubleshooters gang traced a friend of Murphy's to Dalton, California. It's near Camp Nelson, east of Fresno? She seems to think tracking this friend is our best lead to finding Murph. The plan is to head in that direction. We're going to meet up at the local Day's Inn—it's about three hundred miles from here." He glanced at Eden and even held out his hand. "Hi, I'm Mark Jenkins. Um, congratulations?"

"Thanks?" As Eden shook Mark's hand, Izzy laughed, probably because she'd answered him with the exact same tentative inflection.

"Sorry." Mark was chagrined. "I meant, congratulations. Definitely." He turned back to Izzy. "Maybe you want to, uh, stay in Vegas for a few days?"

"No, actually," Izzy said. "We're going to wait a coupla days to get married—" he looked at Eden for confirmation "—Right?"

She just shook her head as Mark went to get the car keys from the gleamingly handsome dark-haired man—Lopez—who had helped Danny into the shade.

"Troubleshooters gang?" Eden brought her focus back to Izzy.

He smiled. "Not that kind of gang," he said. "Trust me, I wouldn't let you near anything that so much as smells of danger. I'll explain what's up, when we're outa here."

Trust me. Funny thing was, she did trust him.

"I'll get your bag," Izzy said. "Why don't you go ahead and wait in the car?"

But Mark was already back with the keys. "I think I should get her bag," he volunteered.

Which was a good idea, since Greg was standing on the front stoop, tall and angular and disapproving. When he saw that Eden was looking at him, he called out, "If you leave now, missy, you're never coming back. You're on your own."

He made it sound so dire—like a curse or an evil spell that she would bear forever, and she felt herself tense.

But then Izzy draped his arm around her shoulders. "If you leave now, missy," he quietly imitated Greg with pitch-perfect accuracy, "you'll never have to hear another jackass call you *missy* again." He was solid and warm against her.

And Eden knew without a doubt that if she took him up on his offer, if she married this funny, generous man, Greg's spell would be broken.

"Tell Mom I'm getting married in a few days," she called so that Greg, even with his bad ear, could hear her. "Tell her and Ben that I love them, okay? And that I'll call when I know when and where."

Greg didn't respond. He just stood there with his prune-face twisted in disapproval.

"Yes, I will," Izzy said loudly. "That's what you say, dickweed, when the woman you assaulted and imprisoned—the woman who apparently has chosen *not* to press charges against you—politely asks you to give a message to her mother and brother. *Yes. I. Will.*"

"I will," Greg finally grudgingly responded.

And when Izzy helped her into the backseat of a very nice little car that still smelled new, when he and Mark climbed into the front, when they pulled away from the curb, Eden didn't look back.

SOUTH OF SACRAMENTO, CALIFORNIA

"I remember being in Juneau," Murphy said, turning his head slightly so that Hannah could read his lips even as he watched the road. "I mean, I was also there a few weeks ago, but this was . . . Before my birthday. Must've been early April because I got a job cleaning up, you know, prep for tourist season. They wouldn't have started the cruise-ship-shine much before that." He sighed. "But I don't remember exactly when—or how—I got there."

"That shouldn't be hard to find out." Hannah made a note on her pad. There were only two ways in to the coastal capital of Alaska. Via plane or boat. "Do you know when you started working? How many weeks you were employed?"

"It was day labor," Murphy said. "Off the books."

"Who hired you?" she asked. Even if there was no paper trail, they could maybe jog someone's less cloudy memory. "Frank Kinderman? Or—"

"I didn't know him," Murphy said. "My boss. And I seriously doubt he'd know me from Adam."

Okay, so that wasn't good. "Where'd you stay?" Hannah tried a new tack.

"Pat's cabin. I broke in."

Her uncle's Juneau cabin was in the middle of nowhere, similar to his place in Dalton. With no neighbors close enough to notice smoke from the chimney.

"You must've hung out with—"

He cut her off. "I didn't. Not that I know of. I remember sitting at the bar in DocWater's, and Sparky and Don came in. They walked right past me. They didn't recognize me, Han. I worked, I got paid, and I drank myself un-conscious. And then, one day, I worked, got paid, and I went to the airport. One of the local air services has some kind of vagabond fare. Last-minute cheap seats. I hopped a flight to . . . Seattle, I think. And I'm sorry, I'm trying to remember, but . . . I have no clue how I got to Juneau. I'm also pulling a total blank on where I was before I arrived." He glanced at her. "But I'm pretty sure I went north looking for you. I mean, what else is in Juneau?"

"So then you probably didn't head up there until April," she deduced. He knew she'd never willingly gone to Juneau before the spring.

"That's assuming I knew what month it was," Murphy said. "Which . . . I'm not sure we can assume."

Hannah looked down at her notebook. "Maybe we should try working from the other end. We know where you were, early in the morning on January eighth." In her bed, having sex with her. Yeah. They both knew that. "Where did you go after you left my cabin?" She looked over at him.

Impatience and frustration lined his face. "I don't know, Hannah. I barely even remember that night. I should, considering it was the first time, in years, that . . ." He met her eyes only briefly, then was back to frowning at the road. "I don't know."

"You were somewhere," she said. "Someone saw you. Someone knows."

"Unless I was already hiding in a blind, inside the Freedom Network compound, waiting for Ebersole to . . ." He cut that thought off, too. "Look, I know you don't understand how I could have lost track of so much time—"

"Actually," Hannah said. "It doesn't surprise me. You used to come to see me, remember? Well, except for that six months after we did the big nasty. But before that? You came to visit. And sometimes you made absolutely no sense. Non sequitur city. Of course, when you had a serious swerve on, it made it harder for me to read your lips."

"God, I'm sorry," he said, and she reached over and gave him a skull duster with her notebook. "Ow."

"We're done with the apologies," she reminded him. "Another reason I know how out of it you were is . . . well . . . I got a letter from you. In early March. It was, um . . . Kinda incoherent."

Murphy looked at her. "You got a letter," he repeated. "In *March*. You want to be a little more specific with that date?"

"March fourth," she told him.

"You got a letter, from me?" he said again. "Just a few weeks before Ebersole was killed. And you don't mention it until *now*?"

"You have any recollection of sending me a letter?" she asked.

"None."

"It was postmarked Sacramento," Hannah told him. "It kind of scared me, so I, uh, went looking for you."

"In March," he clarified.

She nodded.

"You went to Sacramento."

"I did," she said. "I actually, uh, gained access to the Freedom Network compound there. Well, it's not really in Sacramento. It's east, in the mountains—"

"You were *in the compound*? In *March*, when Ebersole was *killed* . . . ?" Murphy went all the way from the left lane over to an exit, on the right. He got off the highway and pulled into a deserted gas station and braked to a stop. "Hannah, what the hell?" He looked at her searchingly. "Jesus," he said. "I asked you to help me kill Ebersole. In that letter. Didn't I?"

"Kind of," Hannah admitted. "Like I said, it was pretty incoherent."

"I want to read it," he said. He didn't even bother to ask if she'd saved it. He knew her that well.

"No, you don't," she told him. Part of it was written to Angelina, part of it to Hannah, part of it to Tim Ebersole himself.

"Where is it?"

"It's hidden."

"Hidden hidden?" he asked. "Or FBI investigation hidden?"

"The latter," she said. She'd put it in a box in the bedroom closet. It was buried among four hundred and some odd letters that her Uncle Wayne, whom she'd never met, had written to his mother, from his soul-crushing tours in Vietnam. He'd died in the Tet offensive, long before she was born.

"When we get back," Murphy said, "we're going to burn it."

"Murph. It kinda points to temporary insanity."

His eyes were grim. "It kinda also points to conspiracy." He spelled out the word for her, his fingers jerky with his anger. "Or you being an accomplice." He spelled that, too, but with only one C. "Or even . . ." He shook his head. "Did you find me? In Sacramento?"

"No," she admitted. "And I also didn't kill Tim Ebersole."

He believed her. But despite his challenges when it came to spelling, he was a very smart man, and he knew, as surely as she did, that the FBI investigators were going to compile a list of visitors to the Freedom Network compound, during the approximate time of Ebersole's death.

And Hannah's name was going to be on that list.

Which was going to raise some giant red flags, particularly since they were already looking for Murphy.

Just to ask him questions.

Right.

"I spent a week up there," Hannah told Murphy. "Looking for you. After getting that letter . . . I was pretty worried."

"Oh, God." He closed his eyes. "Please let me say I'm sorry." He forced himself to look at her, and no doubt about it, he was anguished. "Jesus, Hannah, it was bad enough when I . . ." He couldn't bring himself to say it.

But Hannah knew. It was bad enough when his transgressions had merely been limited to his using her for sex and then trying to kill himself in her living room.

"But this . . ." There were tears in his eyes. "And you just . . . welcome me back into your life, like it's all okay."

"But it *is* okay." Damn it, now she was tearing up, too. "That letter . . . You were asking for help. Not to kill Ebersole. Just to . . ." She couldn't look at him so she looked out the passenger window. "You said you needed me. And maybe that was just part of the crazy talk, but . . . If you need me, bwee, I'm there. Whether it's Sacramento or San Diego or . . . or . . . *London* or, shit, the tenth level of hell. I'm there. You know, *you* were the one who had the problem with us having sex, Murph. Not me. If it were up to me, we'd still both be using each other shamelessly. Twice a day. And three times on Sundays."

God damn it. Sometimes she said way too much.

Hannah sat there, in the passenger seat of Uncle Pat's battered little car, as Murphy sat, frozen like a statue, behind the wheel. And neither of them said anything for quite a few moments.

But then he reached over and touched her. Just a finger beneath her chin, turning her head so that she'd look at him.

"You always say things that are . . . kind of major," he told her, "and then you don't look at me, so . . ."

"I'm embarrassed," she admitted.

"You don't think it would . . . change things?" he asked. "You know, aside from the obvious fact that we'd . . . both probably sleep a whole lot better on Sunday nights?" He thought about that. "Well, probably every night, but definitely on Sundays."

"Sleep is good," Hannah said, as she searched the darkness of his eyes. Were they truly discussing this . . . ?

"I've already lost too much," he told her. "I don't think I can risk . . ."

She nodded, swallowing her disappointment. "I don't want you to disappear for another six months, so . . . It's probably not worth the experiment."

This time Murphy looked away. "Han, if I killed Tim Ebersole . . . I'm going to prison and it'll be for way longer than six months."

"If you killed Ebersole," she said, "you'll plead temporary insanity. If you don't remember doing it—Murph, you were very much out of your mind."

"Maybe," he said, "but what if I'm not sorry? Now that I'm supposedly back in my right mind. What if I'm glad that he's dead?"

"You're not the only one," she told him. "So drive. Let's get to Sacramento. We know you were there in early March when you sent that letter. Let's see if we can't find someone who knows where you went after that."

CHAPTER
TEN

Sophia put her overnight bag into the back of Dave's car and climbed into the front seat. "How'd it go with Dr. Heissman?"

Dave glanced at her only briefly as he navigated his way out of her condo complex parking lot. "It didn't," he reported, adding, "She cancelled," before Sophia could express her disappointment. "Postponed, really. Tom thought she should come up to Dalton with the team, so we rescheduled for tomorrow." He glanced at her again, his smile wry. "Lucky me. I was ready to do it, so of course, now I have to wait."

"She seems nice," Sophia pointed out, as she settled in for the long trip north. It seemed like forever since she and Dave had spent more than just a few minutes together. Sure, they spoke on the phone almost every day, but it just wasn't the same. She'd missed him, missed the easiness of their friendship.

And sitting in his cluttered car was a lot like sitting across from him at his cluttered desk, in his crowded office. The clutter wasn't from garbage—old doughnut bags or empty soda cans—but rather things he thought he'd need. Maps, a roll of quarters, an ancient ice scraper, a windshield shade, his iPod, a spare pair of hiking boots, a cooler with bottles of water, a stack of library books, a floppy sunhat, a crank-powered radio, a box of power bars, a portable GPS device, a NASA-approved heat-retaining blanket, a first aid kit, a handful of MREs, binoculars, night vision glasses, a digital camera, a bathing suit, a jacket and tie . . .

Sophia was pretty sure clean underwear and socks were in there, too, somewhere.

"I'm sure she *is* nice," Dave agreed evenly. "But whether she's nice or mean isn't the issue. I was thinking about it, on the drive over here. You know, what's everyone so afraid of? And I think it's her psych degree that makes her so terrifying. What if we talk to her, and she goes, *Yep, you're totally bonkers. Certifiably nuts. Bring in the men with the white coats.*"

Sophia had to laugh. "She's not going to say that."

"Probably not," Dave said. "But she might. Best case scenario, she'll tell us what we already know—that we're exhausted and that we have stress and anger management issues. Which will create more stress and anger that we won't be able to manage. And no matter what happens, we're afraid that, once we walk out of her office, we won't be able to look at ourselves in our bathroom mirrors anymore and fool ourselves into thinking we're okay."

"Wouldn't you rather actually *be* okay?" Sophia asked. "Which is not to say that I don't think you're already okay, because I do."

Dave grinned at her. "Nice save."

When he smiled, the fatigue that lined his face eased, making him look younger. The new haircut helped in that department, too. Except it wasn't new. "I can't believe," she said, "that you didn't tell me four months ago that you finally cut your hair."

Dave reached up and ran his hand through his casually messy shock of thick, dark hair, almost as if he still needed to remind himself that it was no longer shoulder-blade length and tied back from his face. "It just . . . never came up," he said as he braked to a stop at a red light.

Sophia turned in her seat to get a better look at him. "You look great, by the way. A lot less like you time-warped in from Woodstock. More like you time-warped in from 1980. It's very Sid Vicious."

"I can't help it—my hair grows ridiculously fast," Dave defended himself. "Not cutting it was much easier. You know, Tracy has to cut it every two weeks."

"*Tracy* cuts it," Sophia repeated, and he rolled his eyes.

"Yeah," he said as the light turned green and he accelerated through the intersection. "And okay, yeah, *that's* why I didn't tell you. Because I knew you'd start with the Tracy thing again."

Months ago, she'd told him about a conversation that she'd had with Tracy, in which the Troubleshooters gorgeous young receptionist had expressed appreciation of . . . certain of Dave's physical attributes. He'd blushed and muttered something about his cousin having had a heart attack, so he'd started working out again to avoid a similar trip to the hospital.

"She thinks you're cute," Sophia reminded him, "and now she cuts your hair. Every two weeks. And you don't think she wants to—"

"There was a point," Dave interrupted, "where I was aware that, yes, I could've been a rebound. You know, when what's-his-name, the school teacher, dumped her. But Tracy and I have very little in common. It would've been purely about sex and frankly, I've never done that."

"Never?" Sophia asked. Dave had once admitted to her that he'd never had a serious girlfriend. In high school and college, he'd been too geeky and shy. And after he'd joined the CIA, he hadn't had time for a romantic relationship. He'd gotten his masters and then a doctorate degree in his spare time, but Sophia had always suspected that *too geeky and shy* remained the real reason that he'd always been so relentlessly alone.

But she'd also always assumed that, after being sent out on dangerous overseas assignments, he'd had his share of 007-like dalliances with the equally dangerous women he'd met. Although now, as she thought about it, that seemed absurd.

Dave was silent, keeping his eyes on the road.

Except, the flipside of that thought—that Dave could still be a virgin—was equally absurd. Wasn't it?

"So . . . do you . . . pay for sex?" she asked, and the look he shot her was so incredulous that she had to laugh. "Sorry. It's just . . ." If he didn't pay for sex, and he didn't have casual sex, and he'd never had a serious girlfriend . . .

He was mortified, no doubt because he knew exactly where her thoughts had gone.

"It's not a big deal," she told him, and he finally glanced over at her.

"Right," he said. "Sex is always a huge deal, and you know it."

"Yeah," Sophia said. "Sorry."

"I'm not, you know, a . . . You know. What you were thinking," he said, his eyes back on the road, his fingers tight around the steering wheel.

"I wasn't thinking anything."

"Yes, you certainly were, and I'm *not*."

"Okay," she said.

He was silent, glaring at the road, the muscle jumping in the side of his jaw.

What a great way to start a five-hour drive.

He finally glanced at her, chagrin in his eyes. "Is that really what people think when they look at me?" he asked. "That I'm like that guy in that movie—a forty-year-old virgin?"

"You're only thirty-eight," she said, and he shot her another look, this one humorously dark. "Besides, Steve Carell's pretty hot. If people are comparing you to him—"

"Nice try," he said. "But they're not comparing me to Steve Carell. They're comparing me to some loser he played—"

"Just a few months ago, everyone in the office was speculating on your hot and heavy affair with Paulette," she interrupted.

He blinked at her. "Paulette?"

"The UPS driver," she reminded him. "With the big, um . . . voluptuousness?"

"I know who she is. She moonlights as a personal trainer," he said. "We made a trade. She helped me set up a workout schedule, and I helped her and her partner install a security system in their home." He looked at Sophia. "Her lesbian partner?"

Ah. "Well, okay," Sophia said. "But there was still . . . rampant speculation."

"Not anymore," Dave said. "About a week ago she brought in pictures of her and Denise's commitment ceremony."

"Well, before people knew, they weren't thinking, *There goes Dave the virgin with his lesbian friend.*"

Dave stared at the road. "Tell me honestly, Soph, that you're not thinking it right now. *Dave the virgin.*"

She sighed. "You said you weren't, so—"

"You don't believe me."

"What does it matter?" she said. "I don't understand why you think that if you were—I said *if*—that it would make you some kind of loser. You're *not* a loser."

"Oh," Dave said. "What a *good* segue you've just handed me, because in fact, I *am*. I'm very *much* a loser, thank you. I was also a virgin for an embarrassingly long time—there, I've said it. And it wasn't because I was being noble or a romantic. I *didn't* want to pay for it, and the women I was attracted to weren't interested in me." He laughed his disgust. "So that *never* I told you before? It was pretty sanctimonious, considering that I would've said yes to Tracy's rebound when I was twenty. Or thirty. Or thirty-three.

"And in the end, I *did* end up paying for it, although at the time I failed to see the price. I was so in love with her and—" He broke off, swearing sharply.

"I'm so sorry," Sophia said.

"Me, too," he told her, forcing a smile. "If I could, I'd go back in time and I'd stay far, far away from her, even though doing that would probably make me, yes, still a virgin at age thirty-eight." He winced. "Did I really just say that out loud?"

Oh, Dave . . . "If you were a woman, you'd be considered virtuous."

"But I'm not a woman, therefore I am a loser."

"Stop saying that."

"But it's true," he said with absolute certainty. "She not only left me for dead and robbed me blind, she also gave me gonorrhea. But the worst was when she turned up dead, with my DNA all over her." He glanced at her again, as if to gauge her shock. "A lot of people thought I killed her. Some of them still think I did. I ended up having to leave the CIA because of it. I'm lucky I didn't go to prison."

Dave's leaving the CIA had led him to work for Troubleshooters Incorporated, which had led him to be in Kazbekistan, where he'd helped save Sophia's life all those years ago. . . .

"What was her name?" Sophia asked now.

"Her real name, or the one she gave me when she was pretending to fall in love with me, too?"

Oh, Dave.

"It was Anise," he answered her quietly. "She told me her name was Kathy, but it was really Anise. She wasn't a good person, Soph, so don't go thinking *there but for the grace of God*, all right? Her life wasn't in danger—at least not when she first met me. She didn't need help, she didn't need . . ." He shook his head. "Love couldn't save her—nothing could. She conned men for a living. She charmed them, she had sex with them, and then she robbed them, and she targeted me while I was in Paris, undercover, and when she found out—somehow—I still don't know how. But she somehow found out that I worked for the CIA, and she tried to sell me to the highest bidder, which nearly killed me, and did kill her. End of story. Except somewhere in there I lost my virginity and caught gonorrhea. Which sucks, by the way. It feels like you're peeing razor-sharp shards of your shattered heart."

"It's not as painful for women," she told him. "I used to pray that I'd get it again." Because it meant that Padsha Bashir, the Kazbekistani warlord who'd killed her husband and taken her as one of his many wives, wouldn't touch her—or pass her around to his friends—until the antibiotics had cleaned her up.

Dave, of course, had taken note of that *again*. "Whoo-hoo," he said with absolutely no inflection. "We can start our own STD club. Go us."

"It was a lifetime ago," she said.

"Yeah," Dave agreed. "That's kind of the way I look at it, too. It all happened in my other life. BTS. Before Troubleshooters."

"Before Decker," she added softly.

Dave glanced at her again. "You . . . want to talk about that?"

"Nope," she said. Absolutely not. In an attempt to lighten things up, she said, "Too bad you don't do rebound sex, because I could help you lose your virginity, which, by the way, I've reinstated for you, since the gonorrhea definitely canceled out the sex."

The look he shot her was both alarmed and horrified. There was not much amusement in there. In fact, she could see exactly none in his eyes.

"Sorry," she said. "Bad joke. It's just . . . We're like some awful setup for a road movie. A *thirty-eight-year-old virgin and a former hooker-with-a-heart-of-gold set out on a life-changing journey, discovering they have a common bond in the various STDs they've been exposed to in the past.*"

"You were never a hooker." Dave was always quick to defend her— even when her self-deprecating words were merely an attempt at a bad joke. "You did what you had to do to survive."

Sophia didn't bother to argue, because on one level, he was right. She *had* survived. She'd done more than survive, because after being horribly, hideously battered by life, she'd actually recovered enough to want an intimate relationship again. Sure, she'd been in love with Larry Decker for years—but it was only because on some level she'd known he would always safely keep his distance. She'd instinctively known that she would have to make the first move when *she* was finally ready. She'd have to grab him, the way she did in the parking lot last Friday.

Except, when she'd finally grabbed Decker, he'd gently disengaged and walked away. Probably because *he* hadn't yet recovered from *her* hideous past. Probably because he never would.

"Do you ever wonder what the exact number is?" Sophia asked. "You know, of the men I've had sex with? I was in Bashir's palace for forty-one days. I didn't work every single day"—it had helped to think of it as work—"but sometimes, when he had guests, I would . . . Three, maybe four times a day . . . I was American and blond, so . . . I was pretty popular. Of course, it wasn't always sex they wanted." She knew that Dave knew about the cutting—he'd seen her multitude of fading scars. "I figure it was somewhere between seventy-five and a hundred and ten."

The muscle was jumping in Dave's jaw.

"I wouldn't want to have sex with someone who'd had that many partners in that short a time span," Sophia admitted. "It's creepy."

"It might be if you're Wilt Chamberlain," Dave told her. "You know, if the sex was by choice. But it wasn't."

She started to make her usual argument—she never fought back, she always submitted and did what she was told—but he cut her off.

"That number doesn't have anything to do with partners. It's the number of times that violent crimes were committed against you. And if you're asking me if I think Decker is freaked out by that, I'd have to say yeah. He struggles with it. I do, too."

"But *you* don't run away from me," she pointed out. "Except, maybe you'd run, too, if you really thought I wanted to get intimate with you."

He laughed—a fast bark of sound. "Sophia, if I thought, for even half a second, that you truly wanted to have rebound sex with me, if I honestly thought that would make you feel better about the way Decker's been avoiding you, I would pull this car over to the side of the road right now. *Right* now."

He was serious.

"You don't do rebound sex," she reminded him.

"Yeah, well, I would do anything for you," Dave told her. "Anything. Including lose my recently reinstated virginity—which I'm not so sure I'm completely happy about. The reinstatement, that is."

He *was* serious. And as he stopped the car at another traffic light, he turned to look at her. "I would never run away from you," he told her. "The problem is with Decker, not with you, Soph, okay? There's nothing wrong with you. Yes, you've been a victim, you've lived through some pretty intense stuff, but you've obviously moved on. If he hasn't . . ."

The driver in the car behind them leaned on his horn. The light had turned green. But Dave just sat there, looking at her. He had hazel eyes— a mix of brown and green—with ridiculously long lashes.

"That's on him," he continued. "You're one in a billion, Sophia. Decker's a fool."

"Thank you," Sophia whispered, as the car went around them with a blaring doppler effect of noise.

He smiled as he waved his hands over her. "Presto-change-o!" He clapped, sharply, twice. "There. I've reinstated *your* virginity. If you could do it for me, I can do it for you."

"Dave, I was married." Talk about a lifetime ago . . . She met his eyes and knew he was thinking the same thing she was. They'd never talked about Dimitri, about how violently her husband had died at Padsha Bashir's hand. And yet, she knew that—somehow—Dave knew. Maybe not every gruesome detail, but he knew enough.

"That was your first life," he told her now, as he put the car in gear and finally drove. "The nightmare with Bashir was your second, and this one's your third. We're both starting fresh. So okay. In *this* version of the movie, the thirty-eight-year-old virgin and the ho no mo' hit the road—"

Sophia laughed. "Ho no more? Nice."

"Thank you. Thank you very much. They hit the road on a journey of self-discovery and unexpected surprises, as they attempt to locate and help an old friend—" He broke off. "I always thought Murphy would come to you. For, I don't know, help or . . . If anyone could talk to him—really understand what it had been like for him to lose Angelina . . ."

"I don't know if I could have done it," Sophia confessed. "Even if he had come to me. I still . . ." She cut herself off. Even after years of therapy, she hadn't yet talked to anyone about the details of Dimitri's death. *I was standing beside him,* she'd told her therapist, reciting only the cold hard facts. *And Bashir swung his sword . . . And just like that, Dimitri was dead.* "I still struggle with it."

"Of course you do," Dave said quietly. "It's never going to be easy. Just maybe someday a little easier. For Murphy, too," he added. "Provided he doesn't spend the rest of his life in jail."

DALTON, CALIFORNIA

"You got *two* rooms . . . ?" Eden was genuinely surprised.

"Yeah." Izzy carried her duffle bag up the stairs, looking at the numbers on the motel keys: 218 and 222. He'd purposely requested that the two rooms not be right next to each other. "I thought that would be best."

He unlocked 218's door, opening it to reveal a standard motel setup. Two double beds, a TV, built-in dresser, little table with chairs, sink outside the bathroom, big mirror above it. It was small but clean—not that there was another choice here in Dalton. This was definitely a one-motel town.

Eden silently followed him in as he put her bag on the dresser. She'd slept away the entire drive from Vegas. She'd just instantly shut down as soon as she'd climbed into the rental car. Apparently needing copious amounts of sleep was a pregnant woman thing.

Although, ironically, her swollen belly made her look less like a woman and more like a little girl. Her lack of makeup wasn't helping. Izzy didn't have to work to imagine the muttering and whispering of gossip when he brought this girl back to San Diego. Zanella and his child bride.

He didn't particularly care what people said, but Dan Gillman, his new b-i-l, would hate it.

And it was possible that Eden would hate it, too.

"I thought maybe we could take the next couple of days and get to know each other better," Izzy told her. "Before sharing a . . . room."

He could see worry in her eyes. "Can you really afford two?"

"We're good," he reassured her. "I've got some money saved. Not a lot, but . . . Enough. And okay, I'm just going to say it. Please don't be offended, but when we get married, I'm not going to give you access to my bank accounts."

She shook her head. "I'm not offended. I didn't expect—"

"You're going to need to trust that I'll be able to pay our bills," he said. "We'll work out a weekly budget for things like food and . . . of course, you'll need clothes as you continue to . . . expand."

"I won't," she told him earnestly. "I have a lot of hand-me-downs from a neighbor in Germany. I'm all set."

Izzy nodded. Damn, she was tense—both unsure of what she'd gotten herself into, *and* afraid that he'd change his mind and leave her once again adrift. He should've just squelched her protest while they were in Vegas, and just gone and married her. She would be feeling a hell of a lot more secure right now.

"We've got a lot to talk about," he said, trying to keep it all matter-of-fact, even though, inwardly, he, too, was wondering what the Jesus God he was doing. "I think we should be really up front about what we both expect from this . . . arrangement." He made himself say the word. "This marriage. Things like, if you're home all day, you could maybe do the laundry, or keep the apartment clean. If you're feeling up to it."

"I will," she promised. "I can also grocery shop." She did a quick one-eighty. "But I don't need to, if, you know, you don't want to let me use your truck." She shook her head. "Forget it. I'm sorry. Just . . . tell me what you want and I'll—"

"I'm fine with it," Izzy interrupted her. "It's just a truck—it's not like I'm in love with it or anything. You have a driver's license, right?"

"Not exactly," she said.

He laughed. "Any reason why you can't get one? Like, warrants out for your arrest? Or maybe a suspension for going a hundred and seventy on the Five?"

Eden shook her head. "No, I just never got around to getting one. I know how to drive. I just need to pass the test."

"We'll put that on our to-do list," Izzy said. "That way, when I'm OCONUS, you'll be able to drive Pinkie downtown, to get his first tattoo."

Finally—a smile. But it faded too fast, particularly when he said, "We should also talk about sex. As in not having it for a while," he added. "I mean, yeah, if it turns out that we really do both like each other, sure, I could see sex being a . . . part of this relationship, but . . ." He cleared his throat. "I don't want you to feel like it's a requirement, because it's not."

Eden nodded, but he could see in her eyes that she didn't believe him.

Probably because he was still standing there, in her room, taking up all that space—and talking about sex. God damn, but he was an idiot.

So he cleared his throat again and backed up to the door. "Look, I'll let you get settled in. How about I come back at 1800—six o'clock—and we go out to dinner? We could, you know, go out on a date."

Her nervousness was apparently contagious. He hadn't delivered such a pathetic and kerflummoxed-sounding invitation to dinner since high school. And here he was, talking to his freaking fiancée, for Christ's sake. What did he think this girl was going to say, no?

And he'd apparently surprised her again. "You mean, like, get dressed up?"

"If you want," Izzy said. Mr. Smooth. "Yeah."

She was silent.

"We don't have to," he quickly backpedaled. "I just thought—"

Eden burst into tears.

"I'm sorry." Izzy literally backed up and bumped the door. "I didn't mean to—"

"No," she said, and he realized that she was laughing, too. "Please, don't think . . . I'd love to. Have dinner with you. My hormones are just . . . Lately I've been crying a lot. It's awful, and . . ." She grabbed a tissue from the bathroom sink and loudly blew her nose. "Sorry."

"Well, okay," Izzy said. Holy shit. "Then I'll see you at six."

Eden nodded. "Thank you," she said. "For everything." Her eyes flooded with tears again. "I just want you to know that I'm . . . aware of how lucky I am." Her voice shook, but she soldiered on. "I still can't quite believe you're doing this. I didn't expect it and . . . We don't need to talk about anything. Just tell me what you want me to do, and I'll do it."

Rumor has it, I give good head . . .

Oh, of all the things in the world *not* to be thinking . . .

Except Izzy realized with a flash of heat, that she was thinking it, too. He'd gotten them two rooms to make her feel more comfortable, and instead had ratcheted up her stress levels. Because sex was the only thing she felt certain that she could give him. It was—in her eyes—the only way she could guarantee that he wouldn't change his mind.

"It was your idea to wait a few days," he reminded her. "If it were up to me, we would've gotten married this afternoon. And I still would've gotten us two rooms tonight."

Eden was standing there, struggling to comprehend.

"Yeah," Izzy said, "I don't really get it myself. I like you, and I'm in a position to help. And yeah, everyone makes a big deal about getting married, but it's just a piece of paper. A contract. I sign a lease every year for my apartment. This is just another contract, except you're going to sign it, too. We'll also sign a prenup, and . . . If you want, we can make sure I get something—a reward—for being Mr. Nice. Like, if I win the lottery while we're married, the money is mine. But if you win, we split it, fifty-fifty, okay?"

"If I win the lottery," she repeated, her skepticism in her eyes.

"Or if you write your memoir and sell it for a quarter of a million dollars," he said. *"Pinkie and Izzy and Me."*

Eden laughed at that. "So half of mine is yours and none of yours is mine." She sounded a little less worried. "Okay, but . . . I'm not exactly planning to write a memoir any time soon."

"Or if you go out for a hike and discover oil," he said. "Or you find old Mrs. Flurgenbloomen's lost cockapoo Pointdexter and get a twenty-thousand-dollar reward. You buy an old book at a yard sale and it turns out to have belonged to George Washington and—"

"Okay," she said, laughing. "I get it."

"The possibilities are endless."

"They sound more like impossibilities to me," she said.

"Pinkie is the cutest baby in the history of the world, and the *National Voice* wants to pay you two million dollars for his pictures," Izzy continued. "Or he's, like, bat-boy . . ."

"That's not funny." She narrowed her eyes at him as she tried not to laugh.

"I have a similar idea for how we handle sex," he said, and yeah, that was totally her hot topic. Her body language rocketed to defcon two. "Say we give it a coupla days and decide we're going to leave sex out of our marriage. For whatever reason, it doesn't matter why." He pushed it, hoping for a reaction. "But if we're not having sex—together? Then I can have it with other people, but you can't. As long as you're married to me, it's me or no one. I won't have you stepping out on me, especially when I'm out of the country."

Her chin went up. "I would never do that."

"Good," Izzy said. "Because if you did, I would divorce your ass so fast you wouldn't know what hit you."

Her stance changed completely from what had once been impending flight to full fight. Atta girl. He gave himself a pat on the back while he was at it—for flipping the issue of sex upside down.

"You sign that marriage contract," he continued, "and you're agreeing not to get it on with anyone else, until after the marriage is dissolved."

As opposed to her signing on to become his sex slave, which would've been nice for a while, but eventually would've messed up his head. His big one, with the brain in it, that is.

"Fair enough," Eden finally said, apparently deciding not to fight him on this. "The rules apply to me, but not to you. I can live with that."

"Great," Izzy said, swallowing his disappointment. What did he think? She was going to say, *No way am I even potentially sharing you with someone else. Of course we're going to have sex—great sex. Not because of any sense of obligation on my part, but because I find you alarmingly attractive and I'm already halfway in love with you* . . .

Right.

"Why don't you unpack or . . . whatever," he continued. "Maybe put on a little makeup so that you at least look, you know, eighteen. And we'll sit down to dinner and talk about . . . all the other things we need to talk about."

He didn't wait to hear her response. He just opened the door, and made his escape.

THE MOUNTAINS EAST OF SACRAMENTO, CALIFORNIA

Hannah had been inside the Sacramento-area Freedom Network compound.

Murphy couldn't shake the image of her driving inside and having the gate clang shut behind her, locking her in with hundreds of Tim Ebersole's true believers—people who would have torn her to pieces had they known who she really was, and why she was there.

She had gone in because she was looking for him. Because of some letter he'd written her in the throes of grief-stricken alcohol-and-drug-induced madness.

Murph finished up his cold dinner—a couple of cans of tuna and a chunk of bread—sitting on the slightly damp leaves that littered the forest floor outside of their blind.

They were down to checking out the camping areas outside the Freedom Network compound because they'd had no other leads. They'd come out here to see if they couldn't trigger any memories. And see if it was even possible for Murphy to have gotten inside.

They'd set up this home camp a good mile from the electric fence that protected the compound's perimeter. Murphy'd constructed the blind—a hiding place that blended in with the brush and a fallen tree—because Freedom Network security teams frequently left the compound and patrolled the surrounding area. They often traveled up to five miles out from their fence.

Hannah had told him that she knew this for a fact—because she'd gone in there and applied for a job as a member of one of those security teams.

"I was on their membership roster," she'd reminded him, as they spent most of the day coming up cold in their search for someone, anyone who would be able to provide information as to Murphy's exact whereabouts last March. "I saw on their website that they were hiring, so . . ."

She'd told the Freedom Network, via e-mail, that she would be driving up from Southern California for the interview, and would appreciate a place to stay. Her contact, security chief Craig Reed, had informed her that there were guest quarters in the compound that she would be welcome to use.

And so she'd walked straight into the mouth of hell.

"Han."

She didn't hear him, of course. She was sitting several yards from him, finishing up her own meal, turned almost completely away.

Murphy picked up a stick and tossed it in front of her, and she spun, weapon drawn, scanning for the threat.

"Whoa," he said, hands up. "That was me."

She exhaled hard as she glared at him, then holstered the sidearm that she'd taken from Patrick's gun case—along with its twin, which was currently tucked under his own arm. "Don't do that."

"Then don't sit with your back to me."

He could see that she was beyond tired—they both were. But he knew her ankle was hurting her, too.

Finding absolutely no clues in Sacramento—including their discovery that their friends Steve and Paul were not at home—had added frustration and disappointment to their fatigue. Add in that freaky conversation they'd had in the car, where Hannah had admitted to wanting to get busy with him again . . .

It was not a good combo.

"We should get some rest now, head out toward the compound after midnight," Murphy told her. Their plan was to see if the compound had a "back door" as Hannah believed.

While inside, she had lip-read a conversation between two guards. She was convinced, from what she'd "overheard," that a segment of the fence wasn't electrified so that Freedom Network leaders could leave the compound without having their movements tracked by the FBI, who were keeping the front gate under surveillance.

Hannah now nodded and glanced at the blind. It was just large enough for both of their sleeping bags to fit, side by side. With no room between them.

As it was, Murphy had made it larger than he usually would've. In fact, any larger, and he might as well have installed a neon sign on top flashing "Hiding Place."

Still, for two people who preferred to keep their distance on account of having once had sex . . . It was going to seem incredibly tight.

"Can I just say something?" Hannah said.

And Murphy braced himself.

"Will you please relax?" she complained. "I'm not going to force myself on you, okay? Jeez, Murph. Ever since I said what I said, in the car? It's like you're terrified I'm going to jump you."

"I think I could probably take you," he said as he gathered up their trash, "so I'm not real worried."

She was not amused by his attempt at humor. "Yeah, well, you're acting all . . . weird and shit. So just stop."

Murphy felt his patience fray. "You know, Han, I generally find that I act *weird and shit* when I'm just a few miles away from the site of a murder that I may have committed."

"While you were temporarily insane," she pointed out.

"Whoo-fucking-hoo," he came back. "Hope I don't snap again and kill someone else."

She was contrite. "I just . . . What I'm trying to say is that I'm sorry if I made it worse."

And great. Now he felt guilty for making *her* feel bad. He kicked her boot and she looked back at him.

"None of this is easy," Murphy told her. "And even though it's sometimes harder because you're with me? Most of the time, your being here makes it . . . bearable."

Well, that shut her up.

She was sitting there, in the rapidly fading light, gazing at him with those eyes that were so different from Angelina's. Different, yet similar when it came to spark and life.

He tried to imagine Angelina adjusting to a life of silence. But he couldn't do it. The same way he couldn't imagine Angelina doing anything other than turning and running, if she were to meet him for the very first time, as he was now, today.

Damaged, beyond recognition.

His wife's world had been filled with music and laughter, with light and success. True, she'd spent part of her childhood in darkness, losing her brother to gang violence, but that was then, and she had very much been a woman who'd lived for *now*. She'd told him—many times—that she loved the sound of his laughter, the sparkle in his eyes, the way that he could—as she put it—get the party started, just by walking into the room.

But now when he looked into a mirror, he saw the despair and heartache, the sorrow and pain that dulled his eyes, his face, his entire being. And he knew, had she met him today, Angelina would have kept her distance.

But not Hannah—who could still laugh, even though she couldn't hear the sound of her own voice. Not Hannah, who remained his best friend, loyal to the bone, despite how much he'd changed. Hannah, who'd walked into the hell of the Freedom Network compound, all alone.

For him.

"I think," Murphy admitted, stopping for a moment to clear his throat, "if you weren't here, I'd've turned myself in by now. Just, what the hell, you know? I'll go to jail for the rest of my life. Because who the hell cares?"

"I do," she said, without hesitation, just as he'd known she would.

"Yeah." He twisted his mouth into what he hoped was a smile.

"You should care, too," she said.

It was his turn to be silent then.

"I miss her most at times like this," Hannah said. "Angelina. When there's this awkwardness between us that wouldn't be here if she hadn't died."

Murphy just sat there.

"I get angry at her sometimes, too," Hannah said. "Like, God, she should have fought harder—"

"That's not fair," he said.

"I know," she said. "I do. I saw the autopsy. I just . . ."

The bullet that had entered Angelina's brain had done so much damage. Even if she had survived the series of surgeries, she wouldn't have been the same person. She would have been irrevocably changed.

Kind of the way Murphy had been.

"I'm not going to let you go to jail for something you didn't do," Hannah said, then. "I'm going to care enough for both of us, okay?"

"Will you care a little bit more about yourself while you're at it?" Murphy said. He was still freaked out that she'd gone into the compound.

As usual, she accurately followed his train of thought.

"I was fine," Hannah reassured him. "Except, you know, for the part where I had to have sex with Tim Ebersole. He smelled kinda bad." She laughed at the look he shot her. "Bwee, I'm kidding."

It was Murphy's turn to not be amused. "He was known for doing that, you know. It was part of the new member initiation. Sex with the women."

"I know," Hannah said. "Not big on women's rights, our boy Tim."

"I'm surprised they'd even consider hiring you as security," Murphy said.

"Yeah, well," Hannah said. "When you signed me up as a Freedom Network member, you did it as H. Whitfield. I filled out my job app as Han. They weren't too happy when I showed up packing a vagina, but I got the sense they were desperate for manpower, so they did interview me. Briefly. It was hard to say what exactly made me most unhirable—being a woman or being deaf or hobbling around with a cane. Whatever it was, was okay with me, because it gave me more time to wander the compound."

Words to make his blood run cold.

"I was fine," she said again, probably because his expression was stony. "When everything was said and done, they offered me a job on the serving staff. See, I pretended that I couldn't read lips without wearing glasses—I made like I'd just broken them—and the entire interview had to be done by questions written on a notepad, with me peering at them, holding the pad, like, four inches from my face." She grinned. "It was pretty funny."

"If your 'glasses' were 'broken,' " Murphy asked, somehow having no trouble containing his laughter, probably because of how *funny* it *wasn't*, "how did you manage to drive out of there the next day?"

"Um," Hannah said, which was never a good sound.

"You didn't," he answered for her. "How long did you stay in there?"

"Just three days," she said, a tad defensively. "Until Reed and one of his men took a trip into Sacramento. They dropped me—and my car—at one of those eyeglasses-in-an-hour places."

"*Just* three days," he repeated.

"I was treated very well," she told him, gesturing to herself. "White woman. Hello."

"Woman," he pointed out. "Hello."

"I didn't see Tim Ebersole at all while I was there," Hannah reported. "It was all Craig Reed—who is one scary bastard, might I add. I was never in danger," she quickly said, "but my Craziometer got pinned to sociopath whenever he walked into the room. It wouldn't surprise me one bit if he took over as grand poobah or chief dipshit or whatever the official position was that Ebersole held. Provided ability-to-be-a-psycho is a job requirement."

Great. So much for his hope that, without Ebersole, the Freedom Network would lose its momentum and disappear into forgotten oblivion.

They sat in silence as the light continued to fade.

"So what do you want to talk about now," Hannah said. "I hear Mel Brooks is bringing *Blazing Saddles* to Broadway."

Murphy laughed. Yeah, they were definitely stalling. Anything to keep from crawling into that blind together . . .

"Seriously," she said, "we got one more biggie to discuss before we lose the light—which has to do with us losing the light. We need to figure out how we're going to communicate when we're out there tonight. As talented as I am, I can't read your lips in the dark."

DALTON, CALIFORNIA

Eden followed the hostess into the Italian restaurant, aware of Izzy right behind her, aware of all the eyes on them.

Him, really. Dressed in his naval uniform, with a chest covered with colorful ribbons, his hair military short, he cut an imposing figure. He was tall and solid and yes, even handsome in the candlelight. Especially when he smiled, as he did after they sat and the woman handed them both menus.

Eden opened hers and—dear Lord. A plate of spaghetti was nearly twenty dollars. Lasagna even more. She'd been craving a hamburger all day, but the closest thing to it on the menu was filet mignon for—cough, choke—thirty bucks. She closed the heavy leather folder, and Izzy looked up at her.

"That was fast," he said. "Is that a pregnancy thing—that kind of, boom, decision making, or—"

A waiter appeared next to the table. "May I take your drink order?"

"I think the lady's hungry," Izzy told him, "so we're ready to just order it all. Unless . . . are there specials?"

"Yes, sir. Would you like to hear them?"

"Absolutely."

Izzy sat back in his seat, giving his full attention to the little man who began describing some kind of Alaskan fish that was cooked in a paper bag for twenty-nine dollars.

"I'm having that," Izzy interrupted him. "You don't need to go on." He looked across the table at Eden. "Unless you want to hear—"

"No, thank you," she said. "I'm just . . . going to have the minestrone soup." For—yikes—eight ninety-five. But it was the cheapest thing on the entire menu.

"That sounds good," Izzy said. "I'll start with that, too. Oh, and a Sam Summer Ale for me, a glass of your finest milk for my lovely fiancée."

"And your main course, madam?"

Both the waiter and Izzy were looking at her, so she shook her head. "Just the soup," she said. "Is fine."

The waiter turned away, but Izzy stopped him. "Hold up there, Jack. She'll also have the steak, pasta on the side."

Eden leaned across the table, her voice low. "Izzy . . ."

"Shhh," he said, taking her hand, waiting until the waiter left. Then he smiled at her. "I know this place is pricy, but think of this as forty dates rolled into one, okay? If we're getting married in just a few days, we've got to work fast. What's your favorite color?"

Eden shook her head. "Yellow. What does that have to do with—"

"I like red," he said. "Yellow is too school bus, and I never really liked school. No doubt due to the repeatedly getting beaten up thing. Favorite song?"

"We should have gone to Denny's," she said.

"I don't know that one," he countered. "Me, I got this shameful, secret love for Karen Carpenter. *Long ago, and oh so far away . . .*"

She pulled her hand away. "Or Taco Bell."

Izzy stopped pretending to misunderstand. "Yeah, and I'm going to look Pinkie in the eye and tell him I gave his mother an engagement ring in a Taco Bell? It's bad enough that it's Manbearpig."

"It's . . . what?" She couldn't have heard him right, could she have?

He tapped on the table, and she realized he'd put a little box there, right by her bread plate. It was fuzzy and purple and definitely the kind of box that held a ring.

The same kind of box that Richie had waved at her—*Jerry left this in my car*—that night she'd taken the chain off the door and let him in.

She swallowed hard, aware of Izzy sitting across from her, watching her.

"You didn't have to do this," she said.

"I know," he said, "but I wanted to. Kind of like I wanted to eat dinner here instead of Taco Bell or Denny's."

Eden closed her eyes.

"Don't cry," he said, laughing. "Holy jeebus, you weren't kidding about the crying thing, were you? Come on, sweetheart, really, it's just dinner."

In Germany, she'd been able to feed herself for a week with five dollars. True, she'd supplemented her groceries by helping the butcher clean his delivery van in return for scraps for her "dog."

"Dinner and a ring," she pointed out as she wiped her eyes with the soft linen napkin.

"Babe, it's a ring in that it's round. Really, you haven't seen it yet.

You might not like it. In fact, if you *do* like it, I'm going to be a little worried."

She looked directly into the amusement that danced in his eyes and felt the same surge of panic that had hit her back in the motel room, when she'd realized they wouldn't be sharing a room and a bed. *Please, dear God, don't let him change his mind* mixed crazily with *please, dear God, don't let him ruin his life this way.*

She opened her mouth and "I've never been given a ring for not having sex before" came out.

Izzy didn't look away, didn't so much as falter. In fact, his smile broadened. "This *has* been a crazy day. And who knows what the future'll bring. Well, besides Pinkie, who's not exactly on the express train, is he? You should probably try not to scream when you open that. Thank you." He glanced up as the waiter brought his beer and her glass of milk.

She waited until the man was gone, then reached for the ring box, and . . .

She laughed—she couldn't help it. But it was okay, because Izzy was laughing, too. "It's a real diamond, but . . . Think of it as a placeholder," he said. "Until we get to a town that has a real jewelry store."

The diamond—a relatively big one—was in the very center of the ring, but the setting was a dog or maybe a bear's head—it was hard to tell which. But the animal held the gem in its snarling mouth, lips back, teeth bared.

It looked an awful lot like a roasted pig holding an apple. But the gold was worn in places—the ears were mere nubs—which also gave it a kind of scary-human-monster vibe.

"Dalton *does* have a pawn shop," Izzy said. "This was the only thing they had with a diamond. So . . . lucky you."

"I don't need a diamond," Eden told him, trying not to cry. "Really, Izzy, I . . ." There was something engraved on the inside of the ring. "Tutto E Possibile," she read aloud. "What does that mean?"

"Anything," Izzy said, "is possible."

Eden was quiet, tears welling again in her eyes as she sat looking at the ring Izzy'd found in Davio's Pawn and Paycheck Advance. She put it on her finger and held it out toward the candle to look at it in the light. "It *is* Manbearpig," she said with a tremulous smile. "Someone call Al Gore. And you *should* be afraid, because I do love it."

Izzy laughed his surprise. "A fellow South Park fan," he said. "Be still my triple-lutzing heart."

"Anything is possible." She nodded, still blinking back her tears. "I really love that it says that."

"Yeah," he said. "Me, too." The fact that those words had been engraved inside the ring had made buying it a no-brainer.

A tear escaped, which both pissed her off and made her laugh. "This is going to get old fast," she said, "isn't it?"

"No," he said. "It's . . . charming. And it's nice that you like the ring. Weird, but nice."

And there they sat, gazing at each other in the candlelight. Damn, she was pretty. And with makeup on, she looked closer to her real age, which was good. Particularly since she was wearing some kind of sundress type thing that featured her super-sized bosom. Featured and flaunted it.

She tugged the top north, probably because his gaze had drifted south. And she was looking at him now as if she couldn't quite figure him out.

Izzy cleared his throat. "Finding you a doctor'll be a priority when we get back to San Diego. That and getting your driver's license."

She narrowed her eyes at him. "I still haven't figured out what you get out of any of this. Aside from a share in my nonexistent future lottery winnings."

Izzy shrugged. "I told you. I get to help you. And I get to help your brother. And to torment him at the same time. It's all good."

"What if you meet someone?" Eden leaned forward to ask, which gave him quite the scenic view. Which probably was not unintentional. This time, though, he kept his eyes on her face. "Like, next Monday, you're just walking down the street and, bang! It's love at first sight. Only now you're married."

"If that happens," Izzy said, "I'll introduce her to you. I'll explain what's going on, you'll verify, and she'll fall completely in love with me because I'm such a terrific guy."

"But what if—"

"Eden," he said. "Stop worrying. You're worried that I'm going to change my mind, and you're worried that I'm not. That's a little nuts."

She sat there in silence, just looking at him. "I would understand it," she said quietly, "if we were going to have sex. I understand sex."

And there it was. Right out on the table. As Izzy stared back into her unswerving gaze, he was suddenly back in his apartment, in the middle of the night, with this girl's legs wrapped around him and her tongue in his mouth.

"Do you?" he asked. "Because I'm not sure that you do."

She laughed at that, pointing with both hands to her belly. "Pregnant," she said.

"That kind of proves *my* point," Izzy said. "Not yours. I mean, you and Richie weren't trying for this, am I right?"

That shut her up.

"Can I ask you something?" he said, but he didn't give her a chance to answer. "Why keep this baby?"

She looked up at him, but stayed silent.

"Knowing who the baby's father is," he continued. "Did you . . . Do you love this guy?" True, she'd told him that Richie was dangerous, but love wasn't always sane.

Now she was shaking her head. "I don't," she said. "I didn't. It wasn't—"

Izzy didn't need her excuses. He'd made his share of stupid mistakes. It happened, end of story. But . . . "So why keep the baby?" he asked again.

She played with the ring he'd given her, twisting it around and around her finger. "I don't know," she finally said. "While I was in Germany, I made an appointment to, like, end the pregnancy? But I woke up that morning and . . . I don't know," she said again. "Maybe it's because no one has ever depended on me the way Pinkie does. I know it's going to be hard, raising a baby all by myself. I just . . . Suddenly I didn't feel so alone, and I just . . . couldn't. I know it sounds crazy—"

"It doesn't," Izzy said. "I get it." He did. He was sitting here right now because *he* just couldn't. Leave Eden in Vegas.

The waiter brought their soup, and Eden met his gaze across the table. No way would this thimble-sized cup have been enough to make an entire meal, and she knew it, too.

"Thank you," she said, tears back in her eyes. She swore like a sailor, under her breath.

He had to smile. "You're welcome."

"*She Will Be Loved*," she told him. "My favorite song. Favorite band, too. Maroon 5."

Izzy nodded. "They're cool."

"Not as cool as Karen Carpenter," she said, unable to keep from laughing.

"Zing," Izzy said, and as they sat there, smiling at each other and eating their soup, he knew that just about everything he'd told himself up to this point was a lie.

He wasn't marrying Eden Gillman merely because he wanted to help her. Although he did. He wanted to help Danny, too—possibly out of guilt that he'd been blind for so long to the financial woes that plagued the fishboy. But helping Eden and her brother were down toward the bottom of his list of reasons why he was doing this.

Because first and foremost, Izzy was marrying Eden Gillman because he wanted her to keep on smiling at him, the way she was smiling at him right now.

He wanted to be her hero.

Even the appealing idea of getting it on with her was secondary in his quest to see her eyes lit up and her crazy-beautiful smile aimed directly at him.

And how fucked up was that?

CHAPTER
ELEVEN

TUESDAY, JULY 29TH
SAN DIEGO, CALIFORNIA

"So you heard the gunshots from the car."

"That's right. There were five of them." Decker brought his mug of coffee back to the table, carefully lowering himself into one of the conference room chairs, keeping the table between Dr. Heissman and himself.

"How's your . . . coccyx?" she asked, then snickered, but then laughed—at herself. "Sorry. But it's such an obscene-sounding little word."

Decker didn't want to smile, but he found himself doing just that. "It's a little better today. Thanks."

"I do appreciate your coming in this early in the morning to do this." She flipped through the pages of the file that lay open on the table in front of her. Dressed down for travel, she wore jeans and a sleeveless top, sandals on her feet, but looked no less the warrior queen. It wasn't just the shape of her face, it was the way she sat, as if surveying her kingdom. And her subjects. "On the chance that we do find Vinh Murphy today, I'd like to have as much information as possible."

That was probably psycho-bullshit, meant to make him feel as if the spotlight weren't shining in his eyes, but Decker nodded. Still, he knew that the doctor had sat down with Tom and his wife Kelly last night. They'd both been on the scene when Angelina had been shot.

As had Sophia.

The doctor was planning to meet with her later today, up in Dalton, where the search for Murphy's friend Hannah was ongoing. Hannah was, they all believed, their best bet at finding Murph.

When Tom had called last night to set up this early A.M. session, Decker had been certain that the focus of his discussion with the doctor was going to be all about Sophia. In fact, Deck had expected Jo Heissman to come knocking on his door immediately after talking to Dave.

"You were there, when the shooting occurred—just by chance," she prompted Decker now.

But apparently she really *did* want to talk about Angelina's murder.

So Deck told her the story. He'd told it many times in the hours after the shooting—to the local police, to the FBI, to Nash and Tess, to everyone at TS Inc. who was struggling to understand what had happened to Murphy and his wife. "I was in the car with Jane Chadwick—our client and the shooter's real target—and yes, it was just by chance that we both were there. Jane was having an episode of cabin fever. To protect her against the death threats, we'd secured her inside of her home and she was feeling, rightly, confined. She insisted on driving out to Malibu where Tom and Kelly were vacationing in a house on the beach. I was riding along with her—I'd done all I could to talk her out of going in the first place. Although, to be honest, it wasn't until shots were fired that I truly believed the threat was real."

"How did that feel?" Dr. Heissman asked. "To be proven wrong about something as important as that?"

And this information about how Decker felt was going to help her help Murphy . . . *how?*

"We were all shaken by it," he told her. "We were all surprised. In hindsight, it was clear that we should have taken more precautions."

"Who's we?"

"Me, Tom, the FBI team leader. Jane. Everyone."

"Including Murphy?" she asked.

"Yes. But we—I—should have reinforced procedure. Murphy and Angelina were followed up to Malibu—they went there for dinner, it was a social occasion. If I'd reminded the entire team to take extra precautions 24/7, Murph might've spotted the tail and . . ." Decker cleared his throat. "The night would've ended differently."

She consulted her notes. "According to Tom, Angelina's murder was premeditated."

"That's right," Decker agreed. Angelina hadn't been mistaken for Jane, even though the two women had had similar build and coloring. The killer, John Bordette, had followed the Murphys not because he'd expected them to lead him to his real target, Jane, but because he'd intended to shoot *Angelina* that evening. If the motherfucker hadn't tailed them to Malibu, he would have followed them somewhere else. Bordette had shot and killed Angelina to get their attention. So that they'd take him seriously.

It still made Decker's stomach churn with anger.

And guilt. Because until Murph and Angelina's blood had spilled on that Malibu driveway, he *hadn't* taken the threat seriously.

"So you're in the car with Jane," the doctor nudged him. "You hear the shots . . ."

"Jane was driving, so I reached over with my foot and hit the gas pedal," Decker told her, working to keep his voice even and measured. "My immediate goal was to get the client out of there. But she saw the blood and the bodies, and she jammed on the brake and ran from the car—toward them. I think she thought it was Cosmo, her boyfriend—husband now—who'd been shot. I followed her. Of course, by this time, the shooter was long gone."

"You knew this at that moment?" she asked, her head tipped to one side.

"No," he said. "At that moment, we had no real idea where Bordette was, or even how many shooters were out there."

"And yet you ran into his potential kill zone."

"My job was to protect Jane."

"With your life?"

"If necessary," Decker said. "We secured Jane, called for medical assistance for both Murphy and his wife, secured the area, then located the shooter's position. Former position. He *was* gone."

"When you first saw the bodies on the driveway," Dr. Heissman asked, "who did you think had been shot?"

"I saw right away that it was Murphy and Angelina," Decker told her. "But I didn't know that there weren't any additional casualties. Tom's wife, Kelly, was pregnant at the time . . . I was afraid that she'd been hit, too," he said, because he knew the next question was going to be *how did you feel*. He threw her a little extra touchie-feelie emotional pain. "I was afraid for the baby. It was like a . . . horrendous nightmare."

Too much?

Possibly, because she smiled at him. But her eyes were sympathetic as she looked up from her notes.

Decker waited for it. A question about or mention of Sophia. *Sophia Ghaffari was there, too, wasn't she? Can you describe the way your heart nearly stopped when you saw her, covered with what turned out to be Murphy and Angelina's blood?*

But it didn't come. She didn't say anything other than "You're doing great."

So he asked, "Great enough to be greenlit to go overseas?"

Dr. Heissman sat back in her seat as she studied him. "What exactly happens when you go overseas?"

"I get to keep bad people from killing good people," he said. "And sometimes I get to kill the bad people, which is something I'm very good at doing."

"And you don't maybe think that has something to do with your . . . current nihilistic behavior?"

Decker smiled. "Nihilistic. Is that your diagnosis?"

"Officially?" she asked. "No. But it's certainly a symptom of post traumatic stress disorder, which is the diagnosis I'm leaning more and more toward."

"Jesus," Decker said. "Here we go."

"You disagree?"

"Oh, yeah."

"What would you call it?" she asked.

"I'd call it nothing," he answered. "I'd call it normal. I'd call it skillfully doing a difficult job that's fucking got to be done to keep the world safe for democracy. Excuse me."

"Honest language doesn't offend me. In fact, I'd prefer that you didn't try to censor yourself. Let's go back to the driveway."

Oh, let's not. Let's never go there again. At least not voluntarily. God knows Deck went there often enough in his dreams.

"What were the extent of Murphy and Angelina's injuries?" the shrink asked.

"I'm sure Kelly Paoletti was able to tell you, with far more accuracy," Decker replied. Tommy's wife was a doctor.

"As a former SEAL, you've had *some* medical training. You must've had some sort of initial reaction to their condition, when you first arrived at the scene."

"I was sure Angelina was dead," he said flatly. "When I first saw her. Murphy was . . ." The man had been critically injured himself, yet he was trying to get to his wife, trying to put back the pieces of her skull that had been blown away.

Angelina! No! Angelina! Murph's anguished voice still echoed in Decker's head.

Jesus.

"In critical condition," he finished the sentence he'd started. "But still conscious. Tommy and Cosmo both were telling him that Angelina was going to be okay, but we all knew she wasn't going to make it."

"Tom told me that he'd hoped she would."

Decker nodded. "Kelly believes in miracles. So Tommy pretends he does, too."

"And you don't?"

"Fishes and loaves, maybe on a sunny day. Lazarus raised from the dead? No."

"That must've been hard," Dr. Heissman said. "Feeling as if you were lying to Vinh Murphy."

"We kept him alive and relatively calm until the paramedics came," Decker said. "We did what we had to do."

"Do you mean that?" she asked. "Or is it just lip service?"

She was almost unbearably astute, holding his gaze with a challenge in her eyes. *I dare you to be honest . . .*

"It's lip service," he agreed.

She didn't celebrate her victory at all. She just pushed harder, but gently, her voice softer. "What do you think would've happened if you had been honest with Murphy about his wife's condition?"

"I think he would've stopped fighting," Decker said. "I think he would've let himself die."

"Which you now believe would've been a better option for him."

"Regardless of what I believe now, the fact is we didn't give him that choice."

"Was Murphy really in a place where he could make—literally—a life-and-death decision?" she leaned forward to ask.

Decker stared into her eyes. How the hell had she gotten him to actually talk about this? She'd done it yesterday, too. She asked, he dodged or told her what he thought she wanted to hear, and then, suddenly, before he knew it, he was putting voice to things he usually didn't even dare let himself *think* about.

"Was he in a place where he could've made *any* kind of decision?" she persisted. "As team leader, surely you've allowed your team members to make command decisions from time to time. But at *that* time, in *that* moment, would you have allowed Murphy to decide, say, the best way to approach the place from whence the shooter had fired those five shots?"

"Of course not."

"You did what you had to do," she repeated his own words. "It's not lip service, Lawrence."

Maybe not. But he *had* known about the anguish that was roaring Murphy's way. He knew, too, what it felt like to want to die, but to be unwilling or maybe just unable to take his own life. But somehow, for now, he managed to break the spell this woman had cast over him, and he didn't admit to any of that.

"Thank you for that insight," he said instead, trying his best to sound appreciative and sincere. "That was . . . helpful."

But she didn't respond. She just gazed at him. It was all he could do not to squirm.

"Is there anything else I can help you with this morning?" Decker finally asked.

She smiled at that. "Are you planning to come out there? To Dalton?"

"No," he said. "I have work to do, here."

She lifted an eyebrow.

"If I were Murphy," Decker told her quietly, "I wouldn't want anything to do with me. He was . . . relatively close to Dave. I'll let Dave handle . . . the situation."

"Dave." She checked her notes. "Malkoff. With the pretty eyes. Right. I haven't had a chance to meet with him yet."

What? "Didn't you speak to him yesterday afternoon?"

"No," she said, "I had to reschedule that session. I'll be talking to him later today."

"Ah." And *that* explained the lack of probing questions about Sophia.

Dr. Heissman looked up at him. "So . . . what are you afraid Dave is going to tell me?"

"I'm not afraid," Decker said, laughing because the only other option was to cry, and he sure as hell wasn't going to do that. "What's my tell?" He was definitely telegraphing something. Either that, or she could somehow magically read him, despite all of his years working to make sure he gave nothing away with his facial expression or body language.

"You're a poker player, huh?" she said.

"Occasionally. What was my tell?"

"Your energy level changed," she told him. "Just slightly."

"Guess I won't be playing poker with you."

"I've worked with a large number of military and agency operatives," she said, "none of whom come skipping in to our meetings, eager to open up and talk, none of whom have what you call a *tell*. But I've learned to read when you're being evasive, or when you're presenting half-truths, or, such as with your question about Dave, when you've been thrown off balance—even if it was just for a fraction of a second."

"I'm usually pretty good at that kind of thing, too," Decker admitted. "But I'm not as good as you."

"Take that statement, for example," she said with a smile. "It's an attempt to redirect. To steer our conversation away from the danger zone. In this case, Dave, and whatever it is that you're afraid he's going to tell me."

Decker laughed as he pushed himself out of his chair, as he headed for the conference room door. This session was over. He had work to do. "Again, I'm not afraid he's going to tell you. I *know* he is."

"So why not just tell me yourself?"

Decker turned, with his hand on the doorknob. She'd turned, too, swiveling her chair to face him. She had delicate ankles for someone so tall. Her feet were narrow and graceful, too, with toenails she'd painted a bright shade of red.

She sat there, patiently waiting for him to finish staring at her.

"He's going to tell you about me and . . . Sophia Ghaffari," Decker finally said.

Dr. Heissman nodded. "I have a note in my file that you and Sophia have . . . something of a history."

Something of. "Dave's going to tell you about an . . . incident that happened, something that we never told anyone. Tommy didn't even get the full story. It was kept private among the team that went to Kazbekistan a few years back."

"Was this the same op where Murphy injured his leg?"

"Yes, ma'am."

She sifted through her notes. "Where you first met Sophia." She looked up at him. "Met and rescued her."

Rescued. Right.

"Just say it," the doctor urged him. "What is Dave going to tell me?"

"That I raped her."

The mountains east of Sacramento, California

Murphy touched Hannah, his fingers warm against her arm.

"This is where I would've set up," he said, after she'd turned to look at him in the growing morning light. He pointed to a particularly dense cluster of brush that had a relatively unrestricted view of the outpost cabin where Tim Ebersole's body had been found.

They'd scaled the perimeter fences—there were three of them—shortly after midnight, after an uncomfortable nap in too close quarters.

Hannah had been right. There was an entire segment of the electric fence that was current-free. Their first clue in finding it had been the sentries posted nearby. She and Murph had watched and waited until first one and then—jackpot—the other had fallen asleep. At which point they'd made the impromptu decision to go in.

Murphy had given her a boost, helping her up the first of the three fences—a rather dauntingly high chain-link affair, with barbed wire at the top. She'd carefully swung herself over and tried to land as silently as possible—no easy task since she was also trying to keep her weight off her bad ankle.

The second fence was the electric one—it consisted of a series of wire strung from metal pole to metal pole. Warning signs posted both nearby and on the first fence declared it capable of delivering a lethal shock.

Murphy had pissed her off by his carelessness in testing that fence. He'd reached out to verify that the thing was indeed touchable by, how else? Touching it. She'd gritted her teeth in the darkness, silently cursing him for his recklessness.

But when he hadn't recoiled with mega-volts of electricity surging through him, he'd lifted the bottom wires and they'd slid beneath.

Then came another chain-link fence and another boost from Murphy, another landing—ow—this one far closer to the snoozing guards. Hannah had no real clue as to whether or not she'd succeeded in being noiseless. There was no movement from the guards, though, so that was good. And then Murph was right behind her, touching her lightly on the back, and together they'd faded into forest.

He'd stopped her, though, almost immediately, squeezing her hand twice.

Back at their camp, they'd set up a rudimentary communications system through touch. One squeeze meant yes, two meant no. A touch to Hannah's ear meant it was safe for her to talk softly.

They'd reviewed some hand signals, too—much easier to see in low light. Stop, get down, quiet, go back, quick, someone's coming. That, with the little bit of ASL that they both understood, allowed for basic quick communications. If Murphy had anything complicated to say, they'd decided, he would spell out words with ASL letters. It wasn't exactly efficient, but it was better than nothing.

Maybe.

Because in the middle of the dense forest, inside the Freedom Network compound, Murphy had squeezed her hand twice, telling her *no*.

No what?

It probably wasn't any darker here than it had been on the other side of the fences, but it sure seemed that way.

Murphy put his finger on her lips—a classic signal for "shh!" And then he brought her hand to his mouth and panted, three quick breaths. He brought his hand back to her mouth, covered it, and used it to shake her own head, no.

And Hannah understood. She was breathing too loudly. Oh, God. She'd had no idea. She tried to slow herself down, tried to breathe through her nose. Inhale. Exhale. But her heart was pounding. Being in here was scaring the crap out of her.

She moved Murphy's hand to her ear, hoping he'd recognize her question, and sure enough, he squeezed her hand once. Yes, she could speak.

"Tell me when it's better," she whispered, willing herself to breathe slowly, steadily. Silently.

Calm. Stay calm. No one was going to see them. Murphy would act as her ears, and they would stay well out of sight. Breathe . . .

He finally squeezed her arm. Once.

"This sucks," she whispered.

He squeezed.

"If you hear someone coming," Hannah whispered, "don't rely on hand signals. Grab me and hold on, okay? So I don't misunderstand."

Murphy squeezed once and let her go.

And with that, they were on their way.

It took them a while, since they had to watch for booby traps. There weren't a lot of them, but they were out there, so they had to move slowly and carefully.

Another time waster had been their lengthy argument about which way they should go, Murphy spelling out his opinion in ASL letters, some of which she had to identify by touching his hand, which seemed too intimate and even faintly, disturbingly erotic.

But as dawn lit the sky, they'd finally found the cabin where Ebersole's body had been discovered. It was still festooned with drooping yellow crime scene tape.

It was also annoyingly close to the part of the fence that they'd jumped. They'd taken a circuitous route—made only slightly less annoying by the fact that neither of them could say "I told you so." They'd both been spectacularly wrong with their choices.

Of course, finding it at all without maps or directions or a GPS device was a huge triumph.

As was finding that it was completely deserted.

They sat and watched for quite some time, to be certain there was no one there. And then they'd done a search pattern, in circles, outward from it—to make doubly sure there were no Freedom Network patrols—other than the napping boys at the gate—camping nearby.

Despite the definite lack of immediate danger, Hannah was crazy on edge.

Murphy touched her and regardless of the fact that he'd had his hands all over her nearly all night, she practically shot up into the nearby trees. But he was only trying to get her attention. It wasn't a warning that someone was coming.

"You all right?" He let her read his lips, touching her ear to let her know it was safe for her to talk, too.

She shook her head yes, then no. "I keep straining to listen," she said.

"Which freaks me out and is making me jumpy as hell. I'm also pissed as shit that we didn't find this cabin before now." The delay meant they were going to have to hide here in the compound until nightfall, because there'd be no sneaking past those guards and back over that fence in broad daylight. "I'm also scared that you're not going to hear 'em coming, or that you won't be able to warn me. That's why I'm glued to your side by the way. It's not your incredible sex appeal. It's fear that I'll be stupidly clomping along and I won't notice that you're trying to tell me to zip it."

"You were in here all by yourself three months ago," he pointed out.

"That was different," Hannah said. "I was alone. If I got caught . . ." It was no big deal. "I had a story."

"A story."

She nodded. "I was going to pretend to be a Tim Ebersole groupie," she said. "You know, all breathless and big-eyed and hoping to meet him." She fanned herself with both hands. *"I'm sorry to be such a pain, but I was only trying to get a glimpse of him. I really wasn't going to bother him. Hey, is it okay if I take that pebble home with me? Because he probably walked along this path and stepped on it and . . . are you* sure *I can't see him for just a few minutes . . . ?"*

The look Murphy gave her was a mix of horror and disbelief. "What if they took you to him?"

"Chill, bwee," Hannah said. "I was ready for that, too. *I hope it's okay that Reverend Tim takes a few extra minutes to lay hands on me and heal me? I just* cannot *shake this current outbreak of herpes."*

Murph laughed, but he was clearly exasperated and not at all comfortable with the fact that Hannah had put herself at risk.

"I knew I could sell it if I had to," she told him. "You, my extremely non-Wonderbread friend, are not going to be able to get away with that. And right under *don't get caught*, add another rule: Don't touch anything." Man, they should've thought to bring gloves. "Last thing we want is your prints at this crime scene. Try not to shed any hair, while you're at it. Leave no fibers or DNA behind."

He nodded and she followed him over to the area he'd pointed out. It *was* a good location for an assassin's sniper blind. It was back far enough from the building, but close enough so that a shooter would have options.

The best thing about it, though, at least in Hannah's mind, was that the ground around it was only mildly trampled. As the authorities had searched for the point from which the killer had fired the murder weapon, they'd obviously done only a cursory check before rejecting this particular spot.

There was another good location, but it was much farther back, where—sure enough—there was a marker flag on a tree.

Murphy touched her again, and when she met his eyes, he shook his head *no,* and she nodded. No kidding. He was a decent enough marksman—within a certain range. Add in years without practice plus copious amounts of alcohol . . . No way could he have made that shot from way back there.

"You didn't kill him," she said, mostly to see how it would feel coming out of her mouth. It felt . . . not as absolute as she would have wished.

The muscle jumped in his jaw, and his mouth was tight—Murphy, too, was not convinced. "Maybe I shot from up there," he pointed to the area he'd first selected, "and planted the shell casing back here. Will the forensic evidence be able to show exactly where the bullet was fired from?"

"I believe yes, usually," Hannah said. "But we can check that." She hadn't been in touch with Norma and K.C. over at the state forensics lab in years, but they'd once been friends. She'd let lots of friendships slip away over the past few years. "What I don't know for sure is what extensive decomposition does to forensic evidence. Four months is a long time for a body to lie around." She suspected that even the FBI's forensic team was going to be challenged by that. "Whatever they found up by that tree— probably a shell casing—is going to be deemed major evidence."

"Even though it could have been planted there," Murphy said.

"Criminal investigations use KISS thinking. Keep it simple, stupid," Hannah said. "Why would the killer move the shell casing? If he's going to find it and touch it, why not sanitize the area—take it with him? Or her. Let's not be sexist."

Murphy shook his head. Unhappiness was radiating from him as he looked back toward that first site he'd identified.

"Why would *you* move the shell casing?" she asked.

He met her eyes. "I don't know," he admitted. "It just . . . feels like something I would've done."

Leaving a shell casing behind could, indeed, be a message. Usually a two-word memo: *Fuck you.*

Or it could be a taunt. *Even with this casing as evidence, you won't catch me.*

Or it could be the sign of an amateur. *What shell casing?* Except, considering the shooter had killed Ebersole with a single shot to the head, they could probably cross any amateurs off the murder suspects list.

"I don't believe you were capable of this," Hannah finally said. "I'm not talking about killing Ebersole, that's . . . a different conversation entirely. I'm talking about pulling this off without getting caught. If you came in here, so drunk and drugged up that you don't remember where you were or what you were doing . . . How could you *not* have been caught and hung from the nearest tree?"

"I don't know," he said again, his frustration evident in the way his words were clipped and short. "I just . . . I hoped I'd come out here and . . . know that I hadn't been here before, but . . . I think I might've been here, Han."

Oh, God. "Are you starting to remember—"

"I don't remember shit," Murphy said. "It's just a feeling. It's . . . familiar."

She looked around at the trees and the leaves and needles that covered the soft loam. Years ago, they'd spent a lot of time camping, both in the mountains near Dalton, as well as outside Seattle, and up in Alaska. Angelina, Murphy, Hannah, and their mutual friend Mike, whom Angelina and Murphy had both thought was Hannah's boyfriend. Truth was, Mike had a crazy crush on Murphy. Which kind of made three of them, didn't it? Still, they'd had fun, and Mike, an enthusiastic hunter, had taught them all a thing or two about wildlife, both in the Sierra Nevadas and the Pacific Northwest.

Hannah took a deep breath, inhaling the rich, damp scent of the earth. "It's familiar to me, too," she told Murphy. Familiar yet alien, the same way everything was in this strange world she now lived in, a world with the mute button permanently engaged. "Remember the time Mike took us on that hike, and it took longer than we thought to get to the place where he wanted to make camp?"

Murphy nodded. He remembered.

Angelina, even more of a city girl than Hannah, had mocked them endlessly about it. For years. Hannah didn't doubt that she'd be mocking them still, if her life hadn't been tragically cut short.

The hike had been grueling, and halfway there it had started to rain, which had really slowed them down. It had been dark when they finally stopped, and they'd made camp and crawled into their tents, exhausted, wet and hungry, unable to start a fire in the deluge. The next day, Hannah awoke to the sound of Angelina laughing. In the early morning fog, the patch of forest upon which they'd set up camp looked exactly the same as the one they'd left, the day before.

Angelina first merrily accused Mike of leading them in a circle. Then, when he'd convinced her that he hadn't, she made Hannah take her photo as she stood next to a tree that looked exactly the same as every other tree in that part of California. She'd teased Mike mercilessly, telling him it was worth all of the past day's Herculean effort to get a chance to see that particular tree.

Mike, meanwhile, insisted that there *was* a spectacular waterfall somewhere out there in the mist, but they never managed to find it in the relentless rain. They had finally given up and gone back home.

They never had seen that waterfall. Several months later, Mike had drifted out of their lives. Last Hannah had heard—at Angelina's memorial service—his reserve unit had been called up and sent to Iraq.

But Hannah still had that picture of Angelina hugging that tree. It was framed and on the mantel in Patrick's house in Juneau.

"I'm not even going to ask you whether this cabin seems familiar," she told Murphy now, and he turned and focused his attention on the building where Tim Ebersole had shut himself away in a seclusion so private that his own followers hadn't realized he was dead for a full quarter of a year.

It was relatively new construction, one of those partially-prefab deals with a vaguely arts and crafts feel that had popped up all over the place, over the past few years. They were the little-cabin-in-the-woods versions of the McMansion—in that they had a generic feel to them. A real *seen one, seen 'em all* vibe.

And she—and Murphy both—had seen plenty.

She tried not to limp as she went up the stairs and onto the little front porch, peering into the window. Sure enough, the ceiling had exposed beams and a river-rock fireplace, bookshelves that were built in.

"You'd think *some*one would've been in contact with Timmy during his retreat," she said, her face close to the glass. She took care not to touch it. Murphy wasn't the only one who had to be careful about leaving prints. "Or at least have noticed he didn't pick up his groceries."

She turned, expecting Murphy to be right behind her, but he wasn't. He was gone. "Murph?" She wasn't sure whether to shout or whisper, so she whispered.

He appeared immediately, just as she stepped back and realized that the cabin's front door was open.

Relief hit her dizzyingly. "Damn it," she said. "Don't *do* that."

"Sorry," he said. "I thought you saw me go in. The door was unlocked. I . . ." He demonstrated how he'd turned the knob, by covering it with the bottom of his T-shirt.

But now her heart was pounding so hard, she had to bend over, put her hands on her knees. Jesus. "When I said I needed you to stay close," she said, "I wasn't freaking kidding."

He crouched down next to her, concern in his eyes. "Are you going to faint?" He put his arms around her. "Maybe you should sit."

"I'm not going to faint," she said, slapping at his hand. Still, he'd helped her down so that she was sitting on the cabin's porch, and—just for a moment—she rested her head against her knees.

He rummaged in his pack for his bottle of water, opening it and handing it to her. She took a sip.

"Okay?" he asked.

With his hand warm on her shoulder, she was definitely more okay. And simultaneously less okay. He'd been touching her all night, and she still couldn't decide if she liked it or hated it.

Hannah handed him back his bottle. "Everything's different," she told him, "when you can't hear. Sometimes I even feel as if my balance is off. It's not just scary, Murph. I should have been more clear before. You're my ears out here. If you walk away from me, I'm in this awful, vulnerable place where . . . A squadron of choppers could be coming, up over the hill, and I'd probably feel the vibration, but . . . not soon enough. It's terrifying. Okay? I'm *terrified* when you're out of sight. Do you need me to say it again?"

Murph shook his head, no. "I'm sorry," he said. "I . . . forget. You were talking, and you're . . . you, and I forget."

"Well, I'm not me," she said testily. "If you're not you, then I'm *really* not me, because I can't do the things I used to do, and God, I hate that I'm such a coward."

"You're not," he said.

"Hello, I'm freaking sitting here shaking!"

"Yeah, well, we both know that's really because I'm irresistible."

Hannah laughed her surprise. "That's a dangerous thing to joke about, bwee."

"Yeah, well, I don't have a whole hell of a lot else in my bag of funny these days."

"So . . . you think it's *funny* that I'm attracted to you."

"I think it's funny," he countered, "that I'm attracted to you."

"Wow," she said, turning away. "Talk about damning with faint praise."

"You know what I mean," he said, after he pulled her chin up so that she had to look at him. "After all those years of . . . I don't know, training myself not to think about you that way. You're Hannah. I'm not supposed to want to get naked with you." His grip on her changed somehow into something softer, something more like a caress, his thumb against her cheek. "Plus, here we are, in, like, the least appropriate place on the planet. I mean . . ." He looked around. "Could we *be* any more exposed? Not to mention the fact that this is a murder scene—as far as romantic ambience goes, it's about a negative twenty." He met her gaze again, and held it. "Yet here we are. I've spent the whole night touching you, but not the way I really want to touch you and . . . I've got this total rocket in my pocket with your name on it, Han. Maybe I'm sick and twisted for finding that funny, but I do."

Hannah's heart was in her throat. He'd looked at her like that, with uncensored heat in his eyes that night that he'd . . . That they'd . . . "Deathwish, anyone?" she whispered.

Murphy smiled—a brief curving of his lips. "Could be," he agreed. "Or maybe the idea of me getting it on with you here in the compound is just such a spectacularly fine *screw you* to Ebersole and the entire Freedom Network . . ."

"Kind of like dancing on his grave," Hannah said. "Only better."

He was going to kiss her. She could see it in his eyes. He was thinking about it. He wanted to . . .

But instead he broke contact, moving back slightly, shaking his head. "I would never put you in that kind of danger."

"Whoa," she said. "What is that? That's so lame. Don't you dare use *me* as an excuse to suddenly dial this down. You want to nail me, do it. I'm ready to go. If you honestly don't, then don't. But don't keep your pants on and pretend it's for *my* sake."

Murphy forced a laugh as he pulled himself to his feet. "Well, jeez, Han. Don't hold back. Tell me what you're really thinking."

Hannah stood up, too. "Life is too short," she said. "If we both think we can find comfort in sex, why *not* go for it? I've been thinking about it all night, too, Murph. You touching me and . . . We're both totally on the same page. Neither one of us is looking for some fairy-tale happy ending. I'm just so tired of being alone. And I know that's where you're coming from, too. And as far as our friendship goes? I've been thinking about that, too—it's already screwed up to the point of weirdness. Maybe if we set aside a couple weeks and just lock ourselves in a room somewhere . . . We'll either be okay afterward, or we won't. If we *are* okay and we go back to being friends, then we can look at each other every now and then and smile. It'll be way better than the way we look at each other now, loaded down with all this guilt and embarrassment and . . . longing. And if we're *not* okay, well, is it really going to be all that worse than the not-okay we are right now?"

A few years ago, Hannah might've made note of the moment immediately following her rant by thinking something like *the silence was deafening.* Murphy's body language was tight, tense. And he was looking out at the forest as if he were keeping watch.

"Great," Hannah said, when it became obvious that he wasn't going to respond anytime in the near future. "You wait here, right in the doorway. I'll go inside and . . ." What? "See if you wrote in lipstick on the bathroom mirror *Murphy was here.*"

He surprised her by shifting and blocking her path, and she had to tip her head back to look at him. "When I said, you know, *don't hold back,* I was being sarcastic. You really didn't need to keep going."

"I know," she said. "I'm not stupid."

"Angelina always used to say that. *Life is short.*"

Hannah pushed past him. She knew that, too. "Angelina was right."

San Diego, California

The doctor blinked at Decker's use of the R-word. Just once.

Well, that he could see. He'd turned to the door and closed his eyes, leaning his forehead against it. Even just thinking about it made him sick. Saying it aloud, to a stranger . . .

"You raped Sophia," she repeated.

"Pretty much, yeah." His voice, bouncing against the hardwood of the door, sounded loud in his own ears.

"Define *pretty much*," she said.

"We're out of time." Decker made himself straighten up, open his eyes, turn slightly—but not enough so that he had to look her in the eye. "You have to go."

"This," she said, "I can stay for. Define *pretty much*."

Jesus. "It wasn't forced," he told her, managing to drag his gaze over to her feet, with their gleaming red toenails. "She was . . . the aggressor. But she was afraid for her life, and I knew that. And I had sex with her anyway." He forced himself to look up at her face. "Which fits my definition of rape."

She didn't look shocked or horrified or angry or . . . anything other than compassionate. Kind. She didn't just trick people into thinking she cared.

She actually cared.

"Without knowing the details," Dr. Heissman told him carefully, "going just on what you've told me and information I have in my notes stating that she's been, uh, pursuing you romantically, I'm guessing that Sophia might see the entire . . . encounter in a slightly different light."

"You have a *note* that Sophia's been . . . pursuing me?" he asked. "Who told you that?"

"Tom, for one," she said. "And FYI, I'm not violating his confidence. He gave me permission to talk openly about any information he gave me."

"Tom's got it wrong." Tom didn't know the details either.

"He's not the only one who mentioned it," she said. "Trust me, it's only in badly written soap operas from the 1980s that women pursue a romantic relationship with their rapist."

"The details," Decker said hoarsely, "are that she tried using sex to overpower me, and I let her. Try. It didn't work. I ended up beating the crap out of her after she shot me. At me. She missed."

"I suspect," the doctor said quietly, "that there are more details than that."

"It was oral sex," he told her flatly. "I ejaculated."

This time, she didn't so much as blink. "Most men would be making excuses," she commented. "Trying to explain why they did what they did. You seem intent on making sure I understand that you're the villain here."

"I shouldn't have to fucking make excuses," he said in a burst of anger. "I should have paid attention to what she was telling me. She was afraid for her life and . . ." He'd just let Sophia unfasten his pants. "I can't look at her without remembering."

As soon as the words left his mouth, he wished he could take them back. But this woman had done it again—she'd made him say something he hadn't even realized was true.

Dr. Heissman tapped her pen on her notepad. "How was it, exactly, that Sophia came to work for Troubleshooters?"

"We got her out of K-stan," he said, "and I hooked her up with Tommy. He was recruiting and . . . She had skills, he hired her."

"So *you* got her this job. Working with you." She laughed. "I'm sorry, but that's pretty crazy. I usually don't use that word, because it's kind of un-PC, but . . . In this case, it seems to fit."

"We don't work together that often," he said. "And when we do . . . We're both professionals."

Dr. Heissman exhaled hard. "Except you can't look at her without re-membering that you did something of which you're obviously deeply ashamed. Is this meant to be penitence or punishment or—"

"I have to go," Decker said. "Dave can give you the rest of the details."

She stood up. "He can't tell me how you feel."

"No," Decker agreed, "he can't. But he can tell you how *he* feels. Be sure to ask him about that."

And with that, he escaped out the door.

THE MOUNTAINS EAST OF SACRAMENTO, CALIFORNIA

The door to the Freedom Network cabin wasn't just unlocked—it didn't even have a lock.

Hannah used the toe of her boot to push it open and . . . Man-oh-man. The place still reeked of the unmistakable putridly sweet smell of de-caying human flesh.

Someone had done their best to clean up. The wood floor was stained where the body had lain, but it had been scrubbed. There had been an at-tempt at maggot removal, but dozens of big black flies still buzzed against the windows, searching for a way out. There were nowhere near as many of them, Hannah knew, as there surely had been when the body was first discovered.

That didn't make them any more pleasant. Those flies had fed on Tim Ebersole. His rotting body had nourished them and given them life.

Yeesh. Somehow that made them even more hideous, like they were carriers of his evil.

Hannah glanced back at Murphy, who'd positioned himself in the open door. He could see her and she could see him—and he could see and hear if anyone was approaching along the dirt road.

I'm not stupid, she'd told him. But if she wasn't, well, then, she was pretty seriously messed up. Because if Murphy had so much as kissed her, she would've had sex with him, right there on the porch. Forget about her fear—not for her own safety, but for his. Forget about everything but immediate gratification.

And here she'd thought she'd long outgrown her need for that.

Apparently not.

As Hannah wandered around the little two-room structure, she breathed through her fingers. The odor wasn't quite a bandanna-worthy stench, but rather merely a vaguely unpleasant smell. After several days without a shower, her hands weren't particularly squeaky clean, but they still smelled better than the inside air.

Her hand smelled like Murphy's hair, she realized. At some point last night, she must've had her fingers in it.

The cabin's living area contained a kitchen that was tucked into one corner. Back behind that was a single bedroom, a tiny bathroom, and a door leading out into the backyard.

Not that there was a backyard, per se. Several wooden steps led down and out into more of the same dense forest, with far less of a clearing than was out front.

"No lock on the back door, either," she announced.

Keeping Murphy in her peripheral vision, Hannah went into the kitchen area, trying to focus on the task at hand, rather than the fact that the smell had been significantly less strong back by the bedroom. Where there was a bed with what looked from the doorway to be a clean, new spread atop it.

If, like Hannah, Murphy hadn't had sex since that terrible night six months ago, they could probably do the deed in ninety seconds—which, although quick, would be a two hundred percent increase in time spent getting it on. Add another ten seconds for her to kick off her boots and peel off her jeans . . .

The refrigerator had been cleaned out, the door left ajar. Several of the cabinets held canned and dry goods—in fact there looked to be enough here to feed one person for at least six months. So maybe that was why no one noticed Ebersole hadn't picked up his groceries. He may not have had a grocery delivery.

Another cabinet held glasses and mugs. Another held a sturdy-looking collection of glass plates and bowls, all neatly stacked and . . . Huh.

Hannah had been using her bandanna to keep her prints off the cabinet door pulls, and now she kept it over her hand as she lifted the top plate off the stack. She turned it over and . . . sure enough.

The plate's price tag was still on the bottom. It was crisp and easy to read—it had cost a dollar ninety-nine from the local Wal-Mart. It was hard to get those stupid little tags off. Most people just washed the dishes with them on, which took care of the ink and most of the paper, but left behind an annoyingly sticky little spot of glue.

Hannah carefully went through the plates, and the bowls, the salad plates, too. They all had price tags that she would've sworn had never been touched by water.

And sure, okay, maybe someone from the Freedom Network had replaced all the dishes in this kitchen. Maybe they were intending to sell the old ones on eBay. *Own a plate that Tim Ebersole used right before he shit the bed.* Or the floor, in this case.

But maybe . . .

Hannah looked at the empty bookshelves, the department store display room feel to the furniture that had been pushed against one wall, no doubt by the floor scrubber. "Murph," she said as she got her digital camera out of her pack.

He turned from his post at the door, moving so he could both keep an eye on the road that led into the cabin, and let Hannah see his face.

"What exactly are you looking for?" he asked her.

"I'm not sure. Do you know how long Ebersole was here?" she asked as she took photos of the tags on the plates, of the rest of the room. "Before he died? Did that article mention when his retreat started?"

"I don't think so."

"I'm getting a major model-home vibe," she told him. "All of the plates still have their price tags."

She could see he didn't get it.

"As if no one ever really lived here," she tried to explain. She used her bandanna to open all of the kitchen drawers. Silverware, large utensils and knives, potholders . . . "Like, okay, there's no junk drawer."

Murphy scratched his head, waiting until she looked back up at him. "Isn't that the purpose of a retreat? To get away from all the junk? To simplify?" He spelled out the word.

She had to give him that. "But why are the tags still on the plates?"

"Because Ebersole was a guy and didn't give a shit?" he suggested.

"So . . . you're saying he just never used his dishes?"

"Maybe he only ate microwavable meals," he said. "The ones that come in little trays."

And that was another explanation that she hadn't considered. Except . . . "Didn't he have some kind of weird thing against microwaves?" They were part of Ebersole's long list of things that were "unnatural," including women who worked or thought for themselves. "There isn't one here."

"Someone probably took it away before the FBI made the scene," he said. "Along with all of his kiddie porn and Madonna CDs."

Hannah laughed. For years, Ebersole had waged a public war against Madonna, calling her the anti-Christ. She took a moment to visualize him here in this kitchen, dancing to "Like a Virgin" while his Lean Cuisine dinner cooked in his satanic microwave, as the generator that powered this place hummed.

"Or maybe he liked using paper plates," Murph said. "God knows there was a time in my life when I would've eaten out of my hand to not have to wash a dish."

"I'm going all the way into the bedroom," Hannah announced.

"I'm right here," Murphy reassured her. "Someone comes, I grab you and we're out the back door in zero point five seconds."

Bandanna around her right hand, her left holding onto her camera as a reminder not to touch anything, Hannah went in.

The room was small, and filled almost entirely by that king-sized bed. And the smell of death and decay was indeed significantly less strong. Which allowed her to catch a whiff both of new carpet and sawdust.

There was a dresser in the corner, but it was as empty as the closet. There weren't even any hangers on the clothes pole. Which didn't mean anything. Hannah knew that. She took a picture of it anyway.

The bathroom was more of the same. Nothing in the medicine cabinet. A lonely roll of toilet paper under the sink.

Towels neatly folded in the closet. *New* towels. Their tags had been torn off, but there was a little trim of paper—card stock—trapped by the edging stitches. That paper definitely would've melted away in a washing machine.

Hannah brought one out to show Murphy. "They're all like this," she said.

"Which proves . . . what?" he asked.

"That the Freedom Network is lying about . . . something," she said. As soon as the words were out of her mouth, she realized how stupid she sounded. These were people who published hateful lies about gays and immigrants on their website. These were people who insisted reports of the numbers of Jews killed in the Holocaust were grossly exaggerated.

"Great," Murphy said. "With that in our arsenal, along with my *I couldn't have been the killer because I never would have picked that spot to shoot from* defense, I've got that *not guilty* verdict completely in the bag."

"Sorry," Hannah said. She stuck her camera into the front pocket of her jeans as she rolled the towel up, as tightly as she could.

"You're taking that?" Murphy tapped her arm and asked.

"It means something," she said, as she squeezed it into her pack. "I just have to figure out what."

"It means," Murphy said, "that it was there for show. That there were other towels that Ebersole used while he was here."

"Or it means that he wasn't here before he was killed," she said. "This cabin is new. You can smell it back there. You want to go into the bedroom and take a whiff?"

And grab a quickie while we're at it? Hannah didn't say it, but she knew *he* knew she was thinking about sex. She could see it reflected back at her, in his eyes.

"Han," he started.

"Forget it," she said. "Look, the Freedom Network built this place— recently—all the way out here on the edge of their property for a reason. They went to a lot of trouble to get water out here and—"

"Yeah," Murph said. "So that Ebersole could use it for his personal retreat." His frustration showed on his face.

"Or so that they could use the remote location to cover up the fact that he was never going to use it at all," Hannah argued as she followed him out the door and down the porch stairs. "We're about as far as possible from the compound's main living area—"

"What if I wasn't drunk?" he interrupted her. "What if I don't remember killing Ebersole not because I was drunk, but because I've blocked it out? What if I didn't even bother to hide in a blind, what if I just walked up to this window and blew him away?"

He was serious. And as he spoke, Hannah could see Murphy doing it, like the hero of some Western movie coming to avenge Angelina's death.

Appearing out of the misty forest, all six feet five inches of him, moving precisely, intently, his powerful stride accentuating his determination as he approached the cabin in classic Hollywood slow motion, rifle held loosely in one enormous hand. His face would be hard and his eyes would glitter as he climbed the porch steps, as he looked in the window, as he shouldered that weapon and . . .

Hannah could remember—clearly—what a gunshot sounded like, but this movie playing in her head took place in her new, silent world. She could see the recoil, though, and the hot shell casing being ejected from the rifle, spinning through the air and bouncing on the rough boards of this very porch.

She could picture Murphy, his expression unchanging as he looked through the window at Ebersole's lifeless body, as he turned to scoop up the shell casing, unmindful of its heat, and head back down those stairs. In that same slow motion, she could imagine him striding effortlessly back into the forest, not even bothering to turn his head as he tossed the casing into that clump of trees as he went past . . .

"This was a waste of time," he said now. "I'm sorry I dragged you here. And I'm twice as sorry about—"

"Nobody dragged anyone," she said, purposely looking away from him so as not to hear the rest of his apology, "so just . . . settle down. Maybe we should try an entirely new approach."

"Such as?"

"Hypnosis," she said, adding, "What?" at his disbelieving look. "You've got some missing *months*, bwee. You were somewhere, doing something all that time. Let's see what you say when you're hypnotized. What's the worst that could happen? You'll quack like a duck, and tell us nothing. It's worth a try."

Murphy took her arm and squeezed.

"I'm glad—" *you agree*, she was about to say, but then she realized Murphy wasn't letting go.

Someone was coming.

His mouth moved, but her brain had seized.

"Truck?" she repeated. Was that what he'd told her? That a *truck* was coming along the road? Or had he merely sworn? *Fuck.*

He didn't answer, or maybe he did, but she couldn't see his face as he dragged her back, back, back with him into the brush. He pushed her down into the soft, loamy earth then stretched out beside her, covering them both with a layer of leaves.

Hannah felt his arm around her, and he squeezed her three times. Not truck—trucks. Plural.

As in three of them.

CHAPTER
TWELVE

"Did you know Danny Gillman was going to be here?" Sophia asked Dave sotto voce, as they got themselves coffee at the breakfast buffet in the restaurant attached to the Dalton motel.

Dave shook his head as Sophia checked out the quivering mass of scrambled eggs and the small mountain of bacon with an expression of semi-horror. "I didn't." It made sense, though. Gillman was a friend of Troubleshooter Lindsey Jenkins's husband.

Mark Jenkins generally traveled in a pack with three other SEAL enlisted men. Gillman, Lopez and—oh, joy—Izzy Zanella. SEALs tended to take up a lot of space—both physically and cosmically—and Zanella, in particular, was extremely emotionally large.

As for Gillman, he not only had been persistent to the point of obnoxiousness in his pursuit of Sophia, he'd once nearly gotten her killed, which had pissed off Dave royally. And okay, yeah. Threatening to kick the shit out of a Navy SEAL—probably not the smartest thing Dave had ever done.

Particularly since Gillman obviously carried a grudge about that, in addition to his ten-ton torch for Sophia.

Thank God for Jay Lopez, who, compared to his wild and woolly friends, was like a Buddhist Zen master.

Lindsey, Jenk, Lopez, and Gillman were together at a table, finishing up their breakfast. Izzy and a very pretty, very young girl that Dave didn't recognize were sitting clear across the room.

As Lindsey saw that Dave and Sophia had come into the restaurant, she got up and approached them.

"You guys just get in?" she asked.

"Last night," Sophia said. "Late."

Lindsey nodded. "Same here. Sorry about Gillman. I didn't know you would be coming out here and—"

"I'm fine with it," Sophia told her friend. "Danny and I are friends."

"If only someone would tell Danny that," Dave muttered. "Oh, wait. Someone did."

Sophia ignored him, gesturing to the food in the warming trays. "Is that edible?"

"A total cholesterol deathtrap," Lindsey said. "But surprisingly tasty. If you dig to the bottom, the eggs are nice and hot."

Sophia looked around, searching for any sign of the serving staff. "Do you think if I ask nicely, someone will make me a veggie egg-white omelet?"

"The cook's name is Billy," Lindsey said. "He's maybe nineteen. Don't ask too nicely or he'll put himself on the plate as a garnish."

"Talking about youngsters, who's Zanella's flavor of the week?" Dave asked. Maybe that was where he'd gone wrong in his nonexistent sex life. He would never have considered bringing a date on a search operation.

"Easy on the disrespect," Lindsey said. "If you're not careful, you'll walk into a double whammy. She's Eden Gillman. Danny's little sister. And Izzy's fiancée."

"Seriously?" Sophia was amused. "Izzy's marrying Danny's . . ." And then she was stunned into silence, as the young woman in question pushed herself out of her chair.

"Whoa," Dave said.

The girl was pregnant.

"Yeah," Lindsey said. "Eden just got back from an extended trip to Germany, and kinda . . . took everyone by surprise."

"And the baby's . . . Izzy's?" Sophia asked.

"Apparently so," Lindsey said. "Their plan is to get married in Vegas, some time this week."

"Wow," Sophia said. "Is Danny . . . ?"

"Head-exploding angry?" Lindsey finished for her. "Pretty much." She looked at Dave. "Speaking of plans, kimosabe, you got one for today's game of Where's Murphy?"

He laughed. "I'm not team leader."

"But you knew Murph best," Lindsey pointed out.

"Yeah, right," Dave scoffed. "You just don't want to have to be in charge, so you can sneak off with your husband and—"

"Absolutely," Lindsey said. "Considering this is one of his rare days off." She lowered her voice. "We're stockpiling alone-time because we're pretty sure he's going back to Iraq in five days—" she looked at her watch "—twelve hours and forty-three minutes."

Dave glanced at Sophia, who was unable to hide her smile. "You walked right into that one," she told him. "Excuse me."

She'd spotted the cook. Dave turned slightly, so that he could watch Sophia as she spoke to the young man.

"The good news," Lindsey said, "is that Tess called. She and Nash are on their way. Tess'll be team leader—she's always up for that. You'll just be in charge in the interim."

"What's their ETA?"

"They'll be here soon," she reassured him.

Dave could tell from the way Lindsey was smiling that she was bull-shitting him. "How soon?"

She shrugged. "A few hours?"

"Be more specific."

"Maybe . . . five?"

"That's not *soon!*"

"Five hours," Lindsey told him sternly, "is a very short amount of time, compared to the hundreds—possibly thousands—of hours that Mark'll spend in Iraq."

"Oh, enough," Dave said. "I'll be the interim team leader, already. Just . . . spare me the guilt trip."

"So what's your plan?" Lindsey said again, cheerful once more.

"We get our butts out there," he told her crossly, "and we start asking people if they know Hannah, and if they've seen Murphy around lately. A town like this, he's going to stand out." Over near the kitchen, Sophia laughed and threw her arms around the cook, and Dave paused, distracted. Apparently, she really loved veggie egg-white omelets. She kissed the boy on the cheek, then headed back toward Dave and Lindsey, still laughing. "Everyone'll take a street. We'll work in pairs. You and Mark, Izzy and his child bride, Lopez and Gillman. Sophia and I will head over to the town library. We know Hannah sent e-mail from—"

"I found her," Sophia announced.

"No way," Lindsey said.

"Billy's friend Beau recently helped his father install a satellite dish for Hannah Whitfield, up at her uncle's cabin on Warson's Gate Road," Sophia told them, her obvious pleasure practically spilling off of her. She was so happy, it was hard not to smile, too. "Billy says it's the only cabin on the left after the turnoff from Calico Ridge."

"Well, shoot, that was easy." Lindsey turned to Dave. "What now, boss?"

Dave gritted his teeth. Waiting five hours for Tess to arrive was clearly not an option. "We go pay Hannah a call."

THE MOUNTAINS EAST OF SACRAMENTO

Murphy put his hand on the back of Hannah's head and pushed her down, so that she was facing him, nose to nose, looking directly into his eyes.

He put his finger on his lips. Shhh.

"Good thing you didn't let me talk you into going into the bedroom," she said silently but very clearly.

No shit. Although, as he lost himself for a fraction of a second in Hannah's eyes, he saw a definite echo there of his own errant thoughts. In the space of a heartbeat, he'd imagined her pushing him back onto that bed, straddling him, her fingers strong and sure as she unfastened his jeans . . .

He'd imagined it, and he knew Hannah had, too.

"They don't know we're here," he told her, trying to pretend that, in the fertile corners of his imagination he wasn't buried, deep and hard, inside of her. Jesus, what was wrong with him?

Hannah was not convinced that they were safely hidden—he could see doubt mixed with the heat in her eyes. "I'm not going to let them hurt you," she told him, slipping her handgun from its holster.

Typical Hannah—now that the threat had moved from maybe to definitely, she'd pushed past her fear and was ready to kick ass.

"Seriously." He spoke silently, really just moving his lips. "If they were coming to intercept intruders—us—the approach would've been high speed."

The three SUVs that were pulling up in front of the cabin had been moving at a purposeful but not frantic pace.

Murphy risked a peek through the brush. In front of the cabin, men were getting out of the SUVs. Jesus. A lot of men. Four per vehicle, twelve total.

All twelve were guards, heavily armed, but only four were operators, with serious paramilitary training. The others were all flash and no substance—brandishing their automatic weapons as if extras in a low-budget TV show.

It was particularly comical to watch them unhook some sort of trailer-tank from the back of one of the SUVs—it was possibly a water tank—as they juggled their weapons. They unloaded cargo, too—canisters of what looked like kerosene.

The four who were true operators didn't fetch and carry. They stood and scanned the surrounding forest.

One of them, a height-challenged individual with a swastika tattooed on his neck, seemed to look directly at Murphy and Hannah.

Beside him, Han froze—which was exactly the right thing to do. It was instinctive to duck for cover, but someone who was trained would spot the sudden furtive movement.

Nazi Neck looked through them or past them—it didn't matter which—then turned away.

And Murphy let himself start to breathe again.

Hannah looked at him and silently mouthed a word that he didn't understand.

She leaned closer and spoke directly into his ear, her breath warm against him. *Bonfire.*

Indeed. He nodded. He, too, believed that this cabin where Tim Ebersole had died was about to be torched. Funny, he'd've thought the Freedom Network would try to make this place into a pilgrimage destination. The white supremacist Graceland.

Unless maybe Hannah had been right and there was something in that cabin—evidence of some kind—that the FBI had missed.

As Murph watched, two more men came out of one of the SUVs, bringing the total to fourteen. Neither of these newcomers were carrying weapons, and one was clearly some kind of prisoner. The dead giveaway being the bag over the dude's head.

And he was most likely a man, judging from his height and build. He was dressed in a black robe with a rope-like belt tied simply around his waist, his feet bare. The morning sun caught and glistened off the metal of the cuffs that secured his hands behind his back.

Cah-chick. Cah-chicka-chick.

Hannah was taking pictures. She'd put her weapon on the ground in front of her, and had taken out her camera.

The sound seemed thunderously loud to Murphy, and he caught Hannah's eyes even as he grabbed her arm and squeezed twice. *No.*

"The man with the beard is Craig Reed," she told him silently, touching her chin so he'd understand *beard.*

Hannah had told him that Reed was the Freedom Network's head of security—and the man she believed would take over Ebersole's now-vacant leadership position.

As Murphy watched, Reed—who was leading the prisoner toward the cabin—pulled the bag off the man's head.

Whoever he was, he was completely bald—but his hairlessness wasn't a gift from mother nature. He'd recently had his head shaved. He had that extremely pale, never-seen-the-light-of-day semi-glow to his dome.

Whoever he was, he was shoved down into the dirt, onto his knees, and he bowed his head in submission.

Reed gave orders to the worker-guards, but Murphy was too far away to hear more than the murmur of his voice. As several of the men carried the kerosene into the cabin, and one unfastened the prisoner's handcuffs, Murph nudged Hannah, looking at her camera and nodding. "Get more photos," he told her and she nodded.

Cah-chick. Cah-chicka-chicka-chicka-chick. Cah-chick.

If he couldn't hear them talking, they couldn't hear the camera.

He hoped.

Hannah nudged him back. "Are they gonna kill this guy?" she asked, as she continued to snap pictures. "Like, burn him alive?"

The guard who'd taken off the handcuffs helped the black-robed man to his feet. Dude wasn't fighting, despite the fact that his hands were now free. Head still bowed, he submissively went up the wooden steps of the porch, and into the house.

"What," Hannah said, putting her camera down, "the hell? Is he drugged?"

Murphy shook his head. He had no clue.

Hannah nudged him and as he looked into her eyes, he knew exactly what she was thinking and feeling.

The idea of hiding here and watching a man die didn't sit well with him either. But God knows they were outmanned and outgunned.

The guard who had brought the prisoner into the cabin came back out, joining his comrades.

He hadn't been in there long enough to tie up or gag the black-robed man.

Murphy did a quick head count of the guards. Ten, eleven, twelve. Plus the man Hannah had identified as Craig Reed . . .

They were all standing out front expectantly.

No one was guarding the back door. Which, like the one in the front, didn't have a lock.

Hannah looked ready to elbow crawl back behind the cabin, ready to go in there to get that prisoner out. "Maybe the guard knocked him unconscious," she breathed, and yeah, that was a possibility. It didn't take much time at all to shut out someone's lights with a swift blow to the head.

Still, there was something extra-funky happening here, with two of the guards uncoiling a hose that was attached to that water tank, with another powering up the cabin's generator with a roar.

Craig gave a command, and a quick burst of water shot out of the hose and into the trees, as if they were testing their fire-safety equipment.

It was then Murphy realized that the cabin was already burning, flames licking up around the window that wasn't boarded up, smoke starting to pour out the slightly open front door.

And still Reed and the guards waited and watched.

"We can't just sit here," Hannah said, as in the clearing in front of the cabin, Nazi Neck shifted impatiently, too, saying something to Reed.

As Murphy put his hand on Hannah's arm—"Wait . . ."—Reed no doubt said something similar to his subordinate.

It was then the bald-headed man burst out of the cabin—as naked as the day he was born. His head wasn't the only thing he'd shaved. Dude was completely hairless and cavefish pale.

"Holy God." *Cah-chicka-chicka-chick.*

The men with the hose sprayed him down—maybe as a precaution, maybe to cool any burns he'd received, maybe as part of whatever freaky ritual this was.

Cah-chick. Cah-chick. Hannah took more pictures.

Craig Reed held out another robe—a white one this time—for the hairless dude.

Yeah, it was definitely some kind of ritual they were watching here. Black robe, fire, white robe . . . Possibly a new member initiation?

"I've heard of walking on coals," Hannah breathed, "but this seems a little extreme."

The cabin was burning in earnest now, with all of the guards—not just the ones manning the water tank—focused on keeping the nearby trees from being engulfed in the flames. Murphy tapped Hannah, motioning for her to fade back with him.

They had to move—he could feel the heat from the fire. They didn't have a choice. And yeah, okay, they hadn't witnessed an execution as he'd first feared. Which meant that even though they were in minutely less danger, they were still in danger.

Which was why, about three hundred yards from the burning cabin, when Hannah breathed, "Oh, *shit!*" he didn't soundly curse himself for his hastily made command decision to retreat.

He saw right away that she had tripped a booby trap, and he grabbed her and rolled, bracing himself for the explosion of a claymore mine, of the spray of shrapnel that would tear them into pieces.

But it didn't come and it didn't come, and he realized, as back by the cabin a siren started to wail, that the tripwire had been connected to some kind of electronic surveillance device.

That siren was some kind of intruder alert. In minutes, this entire compound was going to be swarming with angry neo-Nazis with guns.

He dragged Hannah to her feet and started to run.

DALTON, CALIFORNIA

"I'm sorry to bother you, ma'am, but my car broke down." Eden practiced saying it as she walked up the dirt and gravel drive that led to Hannah Whitfield's cabin.

Actually, it was Hannah's uncle's cabin, which was one of the reasons everyone had gotten into such a cramp about trying to find it. They didn't know the uncle's last name.

But it had taken Sophia all of four seconds to wrangle Billy-the-cook into submission. He'd delivered up the apparently not-so-secret location of Hannah's uncle's cabin without blinking.

Of course, it didn't hurt that Sophia looked as if she could have played an elf princess in *Lord of the Rings,* long blond hair and porcelain complexion and all. Billy gave off a heavy Jerry vibe—good-looking, but completely useless for anything besides a beer run. It was more than obvious that, like Jerry, he, too, was a captive to his own wayward and far too optimistic penis.

But Sophia was one of those women who cast a spell on everyone male, wherever she went. Eden's own brother was one of her altar boys. And the nerdly guy in charge named Dave practically peed in circles around her—as if he actually stood a chance.

Even Izzy had a moment of eye glaze when Sophia shook his hand and said hello. But she'd turned and greeted Eden just as warmly. Her congratulations seemed honest and heartfelt, which was refreshing, here in the land of the frozen smile.

And even though, when standing next to her, Eden had felt large and clumsy, she knew from the wistfulness in Sophia's eyes that she had something Sophia didn't. Something Sophia wanted, but wasn't sure she'd ever have, yet at the same time, didn't begrudge Eden for having.

As in Pinkie, sleeping now, inside Eden's belly.

And, okay, yeah, maybe she was just telling herself that so as not to feel threatened by Sophia's petite perfection.

Eden stopped halfway up the driveway to shake a pebble out of her sandal. She couldn't imagine living off the grid, but if she ever did, it would be in a place like this, in a sunlit clearing, high in the mountains, with a garden growing.

And a super big-ass satellite dish.

She could feel Izzy watching as she went up onto the front porch. He'd purposely positioned himself at the front of the cabin, so as not to be far from her.

Danny was out there, too—no doubt expecting her to somehow mess this up.

The entire team was strategically positioned, hiding in the woods around the cabin, watching all of the various windows and doors. They were afraid this Murphy guy they were looking for was going to make a run for it, and they wanted to be able to stop him.

Eden had volunteered to approach the front door pretending that her car had broken down, since both Murphy and his girlfriend Hannah had never laid eyes on her before. The idea was to draw Murphy out of the cabin and onto the driveway, at which point the team would close in, surrounding him, and Grumpy Dave, the team leader, would step out of the bushes.

She looked around the porch as she knocked on the door. There was a swing and some comfortable-looking wooden rocking chairs, lots of plants in festively colored ceramic pots. A pair of work boots, covered with mud, had been kicked off and pushed out of the way. One was on its side.

Hannah Whitfield had big feet. Either that, or this guy Murphy had tiny ones.

Eden opened the screen and knocked on the door itself this time. "Hello? Is anyone home?"

It was kind of stupid for her to shout, because Hannah was profoundly deaf, which was kind of freaky. Although, if Eden truly were a stranded motorist, she wouldn't know that Hannah was deaf, so it made sense for her to call out a greeting.

Eden peeked through the window into what looked to be the main room of the cabin. It was dark and rustic looking, with a leather sofa. Very manly. She couldn't tell if there was actually a moose head on the wall, but it wouldn't surprise her one bit if there was.

There was no one inside—at least that she could tell. There looked to be a bedroom in the back, plus a ladder leading up to some kind of loft space.

It was tiny and pretty cute. Living here would be kind of like living in the playhouse her father had built, for Danny, before he'd left for good. Eden had done that for a while—she'd moved into the playhouse, the summer she was twelve—just to see how long it would take for her mother to notice she was gone.

The game kind of lost its shine the start of week number three.

Eden opened the screen again and tried the doorknob, then tried not to gasp as she realized Izzy had appeared, standing right behind her.

"It's locked," she said.

He nodded, running his hand along the top of the door frame. "Car's gone. She's probably out."

"That's assuming she has a car," Eden pointed out.

"She definitely does," he told her as he now searched beneath all of the plant pots. "A subcompact—you can tell by the tire tracks. Bingo." He smiled triumphantly as he pulled a key out from beneath one of the chairs' rockers.

It was impossible to not smile back at him. "Kind of an obvious hiding place," she said.

"Most people go with obvious." He unlocked the door, knocking again as he opened it. "Anyone here?"

"Heads up," Eden said. "Grumpy Dave at six o'clock."

Izzy glanced behind him, his grin broadening. "Grumpy Dave," he said. "I like it. He's gonna *Zanella* me. Wait for it . . ."

"Zanella," Dave called. "What are you—"

Izzy waggled his eyebrows at her, and went inside.

"Doing?" Dave huffed his exasperation. "She's probably out, getting groceries. We didn't need to break in."

"The key was right there," Eden told him. "She practically left the door unlocked."

The look he gave her was a standard *oh, my God, a talking monkey.*

See, Dave was a little afraid of her. She'd met guys like him before— the kind who got deeply mired inside their own heads when it came to sex. It was pretty obvious, despite his being high priest to his goddess Sophia, that Grumpy Dave found Eden attractive. It was also obvious that he didn't think his attraction was even remotely appropriate, probably on account of their age difference, but who could be sure? A guy like him probably had about four billion rules.

Whatever the case, his strategy, to this point, had been to ignore Eden and pretty much pray she do the same to him.

The end result of *that* was his current look of shock that she'd spoken to him. In proper English.

She smiled at him—a simple *you've got a penis and not only do I know it, but I'm actually thinking about it right . . . this . . . second* smile—and yep. He took so many steps back, he practically fell off the porch.

Izzy rescued Dave, saving him from having to respond, by coming back to the screen.

But now Eden was the one who was a little freaked out, because while he was inside, her fiancé had morphed into someone serious. Someone who suddenly seemed much older and harder than he'd been just moments earlier.

"Murphy's definitely been staying here," he told Dave. "His gear's up in the loft."

"You're sure it's his?"

"Unless Hannah's got another extra-large friend who randomly writes the word *Murphy* on his boots and equipment. But feel free to come on in and check it out yourself, G.D."

Dave cursed, because he so obviously didn't want to invade Hannah and Murphy's privacy, but then he went into the cabin.

Eden followed.

Okay, so she'd been wrong about the moose head. There was nothing dead on any of the walls. The few pictures that were hanging were actually real art. Modern paintings with bold colors and shapes and fascinating brushstrokes. It smelled good in there, too, kind of like Christmas in July. It was cozy, with brightly colored fleece throws, an old-fashioned writing desk tucked in the corner near the kitchen, and that leather sofa that looked perfect for an afternoon nap.

She tried not to yawn.

"You see a computer anywhere?"

She looked up to find that Izzy was speaking to her. "No," she said, doing a quick scan, "but there's a cable modem thingy here by the desk."

"Hmm," Izzy said as he came to look at the uncluttered surface. "Hannah's not out shopping," he called up to Dave, who'd gone up the ladder and into the loft. "You ever take your laptop shopping?" he asked Eden.

"No laptop," she said. "But if I had one? Definitely not."

Dave came down the ladder fireman style, sliding, with his feet on the outside, hands slowing his descent on the rungs. It was quite the he-man move, but it wasn't done to impress. The man was in a hurry, his cell phone tucked between his shoulder and his ear. "Out," he said to Izzy, then turned to include her. "Please. Sophia says there's a car coming up the hill. It might be them."

THE MOUNTAINS EAST OF SACRAMENTO, CALIFORNIA

Hannah ran.

Bushes and branches slapped and whipped her, but she tried to push it faster and harder, despite the fact that her ankle was screaming with pain. She'd already walked farther last night than she had in the years since the accident, and she'd been trying to conceal her limp long before dawn.

She'd thought that she'd managed to keep it hidden from Murphy, but apparently not.

He was half-carrying her now, supporting her weight by hooking her arm up and around his shoulders, his arm around her waist.

But God, she was slowing him down.

"Leave me," she gasped, which was a stupid thing to say, because she would never leave him were their roles reversed.

Sure enough, he didn't bother to respond. He just kept running.

They were heading toward the fences, and Hannah knew that if they didn't get there soon, before reinforcements arrived, they were screwed. They'd be trapped here, inside the compound. They'd be hunted and eventually captured. Because even if they could stay hidden, they'd run out of food.

They had to get out, and they had to do it now.

Hannah knew they were getting close to the compound's back door—she could feel the vibration of the siren, wailing through a loudspeaker that was positioned somewhere up in the trees.

Indeed, Murphy slowed, pushing them both down so that they were concealed as they made their approach.

Despite being compromised, they still had an element of surprise on their side. No one—including the two guards who, yes, were standing at high alert, their weapons aimed out at the surrounding forest—knew exactly who had tripped that wire. It could have been one person, or an army.

"I'll distract them," she told Murphy. "You circle from behind."

He nodded. "Don't get too close—they're already scared."

Scared plus automatic weapons equaled trigger-happy.

"Go," she said.

He nodded, looking hard into her eyes, reaching up to touch the side of her face. "Be careful," he said.

And he kissed her. Hard.

Hannah wasn't ready for it. He crushed his mouth against hers, amidst a burst of noise in her head. It was over so quickly, she didn't have time to properly kiss him back.

"Murph," she said, but he was gone.

Talk about a distraction . . .

Hannah focused and counted to five, giving Murphy a little more time to get into position as she dug her camera back out of her pocket, then . . .

"Hey!" she shouted, stepping out from the brush and into the road that led directly to the fence and the two guards. "Can I get your picture? I'm a reporter from the *Sacramento Bee*, and . . ." She snapped their picture, and pretended only then to realize that both weapons were raised and aimed at her. "Oh, my goodness, haven't they told you yet? They've opened the front gates and let the media in. The sirens are wailing in celebration—the FBI caught the man who murdered Tim Ebersole!"

With their attention completely on Hannah, neither guard saw Murphy as he came from the side and tackled them, taking them both to the ground.

Hannah ran toward them, but before she could get there, the battle was over. Murph had them both disarmed and unconscious.

He grabbed her and gave her a boost up that first fence. She was quickly over it and landing—shit, that hurt! Her ankle didn't hold her and she tried to roll as she hit the ground, instead belly flopping and getting a mouthful of dried leaves. But then Murphy was there, dragging her over to the mock-electric fence, where they both scrambled beneath the wires.

Hannah's pants got caught on the barbed wire of the third fence, but again, Murphy was there, pulling her free. She landed—this time succeeding in rolling. But the damage to her ankle had already been done.

Somehow Murphy knew, pulling her up and damn near carrying her as, once again, they began to run.

DALTON, CALIFORNIA

Izzy crouched close to Eden as they hid in the brush that surrounded Hannah's little house in the big woods, waiting for the approaching car that—hopefully—contained both Hannah and Murphy.

"This feels kind of like hide-and-seek," she whispered. "For grown-ups."

He laughed. Or he would have, if she hadn't added, "Whoops," and then kept herself from losing her balance with a hand high on his thigh.

A hand she then kept there.

Not that Izzy didn't want her to touch him. In fact, he wanted her to touch him a little too much.

Especially when she looked at him the way she was right now, with heat in her deep brown eyes.

Although to be honest, that *I know you want to do me* smile he'd seen Eden deliver to Dave Malkoff just a few minutes ago had thrown him a little. It didn't seem to fit with everything he'd learned about her over the past few days.

Or maybe it did. She was surprisingly insecure. Despite the ring she wore on her finger, despite the fact that he introduced her to everyone as "my fiancée," despite all of Izzy's reassurances that he wasn't going to run away, she was afraid that he was going to ditch her in a Krispy Kreme.

It all boiled down to his refusal to bring sex into the equation.

And the really stupid thing? He was starting to think it might be a good idea to calm Eden down a bit by throwing her a boner. If she really believed that sex would guarantee his sticking around, then maybe he should just let the girl give him a BJ. Just a little one. What harm would it do?

It would be a tough job, but he'd endure it. For her sake.

Right.

"So what's with you hitting on Dave?" he asked, because why the fuck not ask it.

It got her to remove the hand. She also adiosed the eye contact. "I wasn't hitting on . . . anyone."

"Then what was it?" Izzy said. "That look you gave him? An emotional game of chicken? Or some kind of power grab . . . ?"

Eden was silent for a moment, but then she said, "I didn't know you were there."

What? Izzy laughed. "Like it would've been okay if I hadn't've seen it?"

"Maybe you should just give me a list of rules—what I can and can't do." She was serious—and really worried.

"I'm just trying to understand," Izzy said. "I'm not saying don't do it. I just want to know why. Is it automatic? You're occupying the same square footage as someone with a dick, so you crank up the sex without even thinking about it? Is it—"

"He disapproves," Eden said hotly. "Of me. Okay? I was just giving him a reason to."

So it was a *fuck you*. And *that* Izzy understood.

"There's gonna be a lot of people out there who disapprove of you," Izzy pointed out. "And of me, too—even after we get married. The fact that you're so young is going to bring out the snark in people. We both better start thickening our skin toward it, starting now."

She looked up at him apprehensively. "You still want to get married?"

He looked at her. "You honestly think I'd change my mind because you gave Dave a *look*?"

"I don't know," she admitted. "I don't get you, at all."

No doubt because he didn't shove his dick in her mouth, first chance he got.

"You know, Dave's a good guy," Izzy said, trying to tease her out of the anxious place she'd dug herself into. "I know he comes across as a little uptight, but . . . You want to marry him instead of me, just say the word."

She didn't realize he was kidding at first, her head jerking up as she gazed at him wide-eyed. But then she laughed, albeit still a little nervously. "I don't want to marry Dave. Don't be a jerk."

"Sorry," he countered. "That's going to be too big of a challenge."

"No, it's not." She looked up at him and met his gaze, all of her attitude stripped away. All that was left was Eden, uncertain and a little scared. "I want to marry *you*," she whispered.

Want to? It was more like *have to*. Still, it was nice to know that, to Eden, he was the lesser of most evils.

"I like you," she said. "You're funny and . . . sweet and . . . I really do like you."

And Izzy couldn't help it. Her mouth was right there, her full lips slightly parted. So he kissed her, and Lordy, she was delicious.

It was a kiss for the record books, tender and soft, just his lips against hers, the sweetness and warmth of her breath mingling with his, the very tip of her tongue shyly tasting him. Ah, God. He opened his mouth to her and that was a mistake, because it was as if he'd hit the switch for the green light on the jump deck. Shy no more, she sucked his tongue into her mouth, because this was what she thought he wanted, and damn, she went directly for his package, too, grabbing him through his cargo shorts, like he was some kind of bargain at a department store sale, that she had to hold on to with all of her might, or risk losing.

And yeah, okay, it wasn't as if he hated it. In fact, he really, really didn't hate it.

Last person who'd grabbed his dick—not including himself, which he did kinda regularly—was Silverman, whose intention had been merely to save Izzy's ass by pulling him into an extracting helo, in northern Afghanistan.

Of course Silverman couldn't just let it go—figuratively, that is. Literally, he let it go pretty damn fast once Izzy was securely on board. Of course, then he had to discuss what had happened, telling everyone that he'd grabbed Izzy by the "handle."

It wasn't the first time it had happened and it wasn't going to be the last. The hard-on was standard equipment for just about all of them while getting shot at by the Taliban, and the way Izzy looked at it was that it was nice it was useful for a change.

But the main point was, Izzy couldn't remember the last time he'd had sex. Real, full-penetration, rock-his-socks intercourse. God knows he'd gotten it on with some frequency over the past few years, but the women he'd "dated" all blended together in one homogenous, generic blur.

The most memorable, stand-out, take-notice event had been that hand job Eden had given him on his couch all those months ago. The one where he'd shot right in his boxers.

Kinda like he was on the verge of doing right now.

Izzy grabbed her wrist and took back his tongue and . . . Whoa.

Her basketball-taut abdomen was pressed against him, and . . .

It rippled again.

Eden was breathing as hard as he was, and she definitely misunderstood what he wanted, because she was ready to plant her face in his lap.

He stopped her, his hand on her stomach where, again, he felt her baby move.

"That's surreal," he said. He'd never felt anything like that, and he was fascinated.

Yeah, he'd grown up with a pack of older brothers, some of whom knocked up their wives and/or girlfriends while Izzy was still in high school. There was always a lot of commotion and noise made over feeling the baby kick, but as a fifteen-year-old, no way was he going to lay hands on one of his sisters-in-law. Not even Martin's wife Mandee, who'd worked for years as an exotic dancer, and used to sunbathe topless when she knew damn well she and Izzy were home alone.

Maybe *especially* not Mandee, who, come to think of it, was probably one of the reasons Izzy found pregnant women so unbelievably hot.

Eden meanwhile was fixated on his stopping her from giving him head. "Is it too weird?" she asked. "Is that what the problem is? Me being pregnant?"

"It's pretty weird," he agreed, as beneath his hand, Pinkie did the cha-cha. "Damn! What does this feel like on your end?"

She shook her head, refusing to be distracted. "I don't get you."

"Because I don't believe that every kiss needs to lead to sex?" Izzy asked, "or because I'm squirrelly about getting sucked off not just while your brother could be in earshot, but while I'm supposed to be paying attention to an approaching car?"

Which he'd totally missed. It was now parked in front of the cabin, surrounded by Dave and Sophia and . . . everyone was out there, except Eden and himself. Terrific.

A tall woman got out from behind the wheel. She looked nothing like the pictures of Hannah that Dave had passed around. She was significantly older, with streaks of white in her long, dark hair. Ergo, it was safe to assume she was not Hannah.

"*You* kissed *me*," Eden was saying, which as far as comebacks went, was kind of juvenile. Very eighteen-year-old, and quite beneath her.

"So what?" Izzy countered, which, yeah, was just as stupidly high school. Clearly, they brought out the best in each other. "I *kissed* you. I didn't say, *Hey, Eden, yank my crank.*"

"You don't find me attractive," she accused, which made him laugh in her incredibly attractive face.

Tears bloomed in her eyes, which, of course, made him feel like a rat bastard.

"I don't get why you kissed me," she said, "if you didn't want—"

"I kissed you," he said, "because you said you liked me and it didn't sound like it was your typical *fuck me* bullshit. You know, it could've been a moment. You say I *like you*, we kiss, we pull back, there's a little eye contact, a little smile, maybe an honest connection. Which, okay, eventually leads—much farther down the road—to you smoking my pole as I try to lick you all over, which is something I *very* much want to experience, FYI."

"So why wait?" she asked, her hand back on his thigh and traveling north, fast.

Izzy caught her wrist again. "Because I want to be different from Jerry and Richie and old what's-her-name's brother, the statutory rapist, back when you were fourteen. Okay? Because I don't know how else to show you that I respect you."

Because—crazy as he was—he wanted her to fall in love with him.

She was silent then for several long moments. "Maybe you shouldn't." She met his eyes only briefly. "Respect me. No one else does."

"Yeah, but you respect yourself," Izzy pointed out. "That's one of the things I liked about you, right from the start."

"Yeah, right," she scoffed. "Sitting in the Krispy Kreme all night long, waiting for my loser boyfriend to come back."

"It took you a while," Izzy agreed. "But you finally got it in gear and showed yourself the respect you deserved. You walked out, and you didn't look back. That was huge. Just keep doing more of that."

"Like marrying a total stranger for his health insurance?"

"People get married for a lot of different reasons," Izzy pointed out. "Besides, we're hardly strangers. We're united by the powerful love we share for South Park."

She laughed, but her smile faded far too quickly. "I feel like we're characters in a Jane Austen movie, about to enter a marriage of convenience. I'm dooming you to a passionless existence. Which is stupid, because I could—"

"I'm pretty sure the main characters in most of Jane Austen's *books* married for love," Izzy said.

"Yeah, well, we're the horrible secondary ones who are miserable. I'll call you Mr. Zanella," Eden decided. *"Mr. Zanella, shall I pour your tea since it appears that, once again, we are not going to have sex this year."*

Her British accent was pretty good—very Merchant Ivory, mixed with a little Winston Churchill.

"Look," Izzy said, "I just want to . . . give us both some time."

"Well, I'm ready," Eden said, although it would have helped if she'd looked less as if she were bracing for a category five hurricane. "I'll sign whatever prenup you want me to sign. If you're sure that marrying me isn't going to ruin your life, then let's go to Vegas—today—and just do it."

The sound of laughter from the driveway caught Izzy's attention, and he realized that while he and Eden were talking, someone else had gotten out of the car. It was a woman, and her back was to him as she spoke to Lindsey and Jenk.

Oh, damn.

Izzy didn't need to see her face to recognize Tracy Shapiro, the Troubleshooters receptionist. He'd know her from any angle, from any approach.

Because he remembered now. The last time he'd had real, full-penetration, rock-his-socks intercourse had been well over a year ago.

With gorgeous, grown-up Tracy Shapiro.

Who didn't get his jokes or speak his language.

Izzy looked at Eden, who'd wrapped tape around the band of the atrocious diamond ring he'd given her so she could wear it proudly on her finger, for all the world to see. She'd followed his gaze out to the driveway and she looked at him now, questioningly. "Who's *she?*"

"She's no one," he said.

Eden didn't buy it. Her female sixth sense had been activated—accurately. "She must have a name."

"Tracy," he told her.

"She's way out of your league."

"Been there done that," Izzy said.

Eden shot him a look. "You're so full of crap."

"Honestly?" Izzy said. "I'm not. Her ex, who wasn't her ex at the time, cheated on her, so she came a'knockin' on my door. Apparently there's a sign tattooed on my forehead in invisible ink that only spurned young ladies can see. *Revenge Sex R Us.*"

Eden exhaled what might've been a laugh, or possibly disbelief. "Did you offer to marry her, too?"

"No," Izzy admitted. "I most certainly did not. She kinda wanted a relationship and . . . That woulda sucked, on account of me knowing absolutely nothing about shoes or handbags." He frowned. "I'm not sure who she slept with to get over *me*. Probably an entire battalion, because, well, damn. Once you go Zanella, everyone else pales in comparison. That's another reason why I want to take it slow, you know, you and me. You should probably check with your doctor, get the whole sex-with-Zanella thing an official go-ahead."

Eden was laughing in earnest now. "In other words, she dumped you," she interpreted.

Izzy pushed her hair back behind her ear. "Seriously? It was pretty mutual. We didn't have that love of South Park as a foundation. That and she must not have gotten the memo—you know, the one that said I was funny and sweet."

"Seriously?" Eden said. "*That* was you being serious?"

He nodded, loving her smile. This time, when it faded, it didn't expose uncovered anxiety or fear. Just Eden, content to sit here in the woods and gaze into his eyes.

"I'm sorry I ruined the moment," she said quietly. "Before."

"That's okay," Izzy said. "Because I think maybe we're having one right now." He leaned forward and kissed her, just a gentle brush of his lips against hers.

Eden didn't move. She just closed her eyes and let him kiss her, as his heart pinwheeled wildly in his chest.

It was *quite* the moment, perfect in just about every way.

Except for the way it ended.

"Jesus Christ, Zanella! Can't you keep your hands off my sister for ten goddamn minutes?"

Eden rolled her eyes at Izzy. "Danny, shut. Up."

Out on the driveway, Tracy and the older woman had gotten back into their car and were pulling away.

"Dave's convinced that Hannah found out that the FBI was looking to talk to Murphy, and fled," Gillman said, heavy on the surl. "Apparently, because he sent her the heads-up e-mails himself. Some frickin' genius." He laughed derisively. "It's unlikely they're going to show up here any time this decade, so we're heading back to the motel." He stomped away. "I thought you'd appreciate not having to walk twenty-five miles."

Izzy took Eden's hand and helped her up.

She smiled into his eyes. "I think I finally get it," she said. "You know, what you want."

"Well, good," he said.

She stood on her toes and kissed him the very same way he'd kissed her mere moments ago. Sweetly. Tenderly. "I can do this," she told him.

"Then let's go to Vegas," Izzy said, since they were finally both on the same take-it-slowly page. "Looks like I've got the rest of the day free, so . . . Let's do this thing."

Chapter
Thirteen

"We should get you some ice for your ankle," Murphy said.

"I'm all right," Hannah said, probably for the fourteenth time since they'd scrambled into the Rabbit and hit the road. "We need to keep moving."

They'd run directly for the car, abandoning the camping gear that they'd left back in the blind. They'd made sure, before leaving it there last night, that everything was sanitized—with no marks or labels to identify it as belonging to Murphy or Hannah.

The two-hour marathon back to the parking area where they'd left the car had been grueling, but Hannah hadn't complained once. In fact, whenever Murphy had tried to slow the pace, she'd tossed him one of those *I'm all right's* and kicked it up a gear.

She was lying—Murphy had been there a time or two himself. *I'm all right* became a mantra. Hannah was using it as a chant not just to reassure him, but as an attempt to talk herself into believing it, too.

They'd finally hit the trail that led to the parking lot where they'd left the Rabbit, slowing and approaching more cautiously when they realized there were other people—hikers—sitting on the open tailgate of a truck. There were a half a dozen other cars in the lot now, too—a lot that had been empty when they pulled in, late yesterday afternoon.

But the hikers seemed like hikers—mostly college age young men and women—probably waiting for the rest of their group to arrive.

Murphy'd looked at Hannah, who'd nodded, but unfastened the Velcro snap of her shoulder holster, making her sidearm easier to grab.

Trying their best to look more like a romantic couple coming back from a dawn foray down the trail, than two people—one of them injured and limping—running for their lives, they crossed the parking lot. Murphy helped Hannah into the front seat of the Rabbit, then quickly climbed in himself.

The car started on the first turn of the key, and, with his eyes on the hikers—none of whom had moved other than to look over at them curiously—he pulled out of the lot. Slowly and steadily. Not racing, not running, not attracting any attention.

Now, ahead of them along the still-narrow back road, was a ramshackle general store with crudely lettered signs for everything from gas to coffee to beer. Hannah couldn't see it from her spot down on the passenger-side front floor, but she must've felt his hesitation. There was absolutely no one on the road behind them . . .

"Don't you dare stop," she said.

Murphy glanced down at her—her pain made her freckles seem to stand out, her face pale, her eyes all but burning as she narrowed them to stare back at him.

"Getting us the hell out of here will do far more for my ankle than any ice," she told him. "Trust me, ice or no, it's going to hurt like a bitch until it stops. That's the way it works."

Murphy nodded. "We'll stop when we hit Folsom."

He went back into fourth gear, driving as fast as this POS could go, pointing them directly toward Sacramento. His strategy was to lose themselves in the bustle and crowds of the city. Each mile west took them into a more populated area, which was a good thing.

He had no doubt that Craig Reed had the entire Freedom Network already actively hunting them. Including members who lived outside the compound, in the surrounding area. Every vehicle they passed was a potential threat.

Which was why Hannah had moved to sit down on the floor, out of sight from any other cars.

They'd be looking for two people—a man and a woman. Not a single man.

And if she'd merely reclined her seat in order to not be seen, she wouldn't be able to read Murphy's lips. As it was, when he spoke, he had to tuck his chin into his chest and watch the road through his eyebrows.

"Why would they have surveillance equipment in the middle of the forest, but not around the cabin?" Hannah asked about the booby-trap they'd tripped, as she valiantly tried to distract herself from the pain of her ankle by taking out her digital camera and shuffling through the pictures she'd taken in the compound. "Or at the fence?"

Where there had been guards, but, indeed, no surveillance cameras. They'd made note of that before they'd gone into the compound, late last night.

"Because whoever uses both the cabin—and the fence as a back door—they don't want any videotaped evidence," Murphy suggested.

"And *what* was with Mr. Shave My Pubes?" She looked up at Murphy, then frowned. "Did he even have eyebrows . . . ?" She looked back at the camera's view screen, searching the photos . . . "Yep. He kept his eyebrows. *Bold* aesthetic choice."

Murphy laughed as he checked the rearview. No one was following them. There were only a few other cars on the road, and they'd left them in the dust long ago.

"That was *freaky*." Hannah shifted, trying to get comfortable, and obviously failing. She was still sweating. They both had been soaked with perspiration when they'd gotten into the car, but Murphy had long since started to cool down. "You know, I've been thinking about it. That was no run-of-the-mill new member initiation. Nuh-uh. That was some kind of major-ass voodoo ceremony."

"I think you got some action shots," Murphy agreed, "of the Freedom Network's newly appointed leader."

"And his cute little hairless male parts," Hannah informed him. "You know, he kind of looks familiar." She glanced at Murphy. "I'm talking about his face. I think maybe I met him while I was in the compound. It's hard to tell, though, without his hair." She shifted again, wincing.

No doubt about it, she was hurting. Bad. "What do you take for pain?" Murphy asked her.

"Johnny Walker and oxycontin," she said, "but not anymore. That shit's addictive." She looked back down at her camera. "And here I thought the new FN leader was going to be psycho of the hour, Craig Reed."

"You didn't answer my question," he pointed out.

"I did, too."

"What do you take for pain, *now*?"

"An over-the-counter anti-inflammatory. Advil. Aleve. As long as it starts with an A and doesn't really help me, that's what I can take. You have any idea who Mr. Clean could be?" Hannah looked up at him.

"No." Murphy shook his head as he checked the rearview again. There were cars behind him now, back quite a bit though. Still, he made note of makes, models, and colors.

"I'm going to be all right," she said quietly. "The ice'll help. We going to Steve and Paul's?"

He looked down, into her eyes. "Yeah."

"You sure you want to get them involved?"

"I'm pretty sure," Murphy told her, "that they're still not home."

"So . . ." Hannah said, "that's gonna be weird. Staying there without them. You have a key?"

He shook his head.

"So we're breaking in."

Murphy nodded and they rode in silence for several miles, before Hannah finally said it: "You kissed me."

He nodded again. He'd been sitting here, hanging on to the steering wheel, driving like a bat out of hell. And more afraid of the fact that she was inevitably going to bring *that* up than he was of the Freedom Network's wrath.

"I did," he agreed, because what was he going to do? Deny it? *That wasn't really a kiss—I tripped and accidentally hit your mouth with mine?* Or maybe throw her the classic, *I didn't mean to—it was a mistake.* No. He'd kissed her. He'd kissed her, and he'd meant to, and yeah, it probably was a mistake, but what, in these past few years of his wretched life *hadn't* been?

"I wish you'd given me more warning," Hannah was saying. "It was . . . kind of awkward. I didn't get a chance to, you know, get a proper lip lock. Which would've made it a little nicer. FYI, I'm usually a better kisser than that. When I, you know, get some kind of warning."

Murphy's entering the Fresh Start program down in San Diego probably hadn't been a mistake, but everything else . . . ? The past few days in particular had been a royal blunder. Crashing around in the Freedom

Network compound? What had they found out? That Murphy might've done it. Oh, and that the dishes and towels were brand new in the cabin where Tim Ebersole had died—a cabin that was now a pile of ashes.

He glanced down to find Hannah watching him, uncertainty in her eyes, probably because he hadn't responded. "I should have just turned myself in to the FBI," he told her.

"For kissing me?"

"Don't be cute, Hannah." He knew that she couldn't hear the sharpness in his tone, but she sure as hell could read the tightness of his mouth, the grim he knew was in his eyes. "You know what I mean."

A rush of emotion filled her face, and she wrapped her arm around the calf of his leg and hugged him, her head down, against his knee. "Don't give up, bwee," she said. "Okay? You're not doing this alone."

And Murphy couldn't help himself. He put his hand on her head, his fingers in her hair. It was messy but so soft, almost baby-fine.

So different from Angelina's hair.

Angelina, who was gone.

"I think we should find a hypnotist," Hannah said, still holding on to him. "I know you think it's crazy, but even if you—"

Murphy lifted her head so that she was forced to look up at him, so he could interrupt her.

"I'm going to kiss you again," he said. "When we get to Steve and Paul's. Is that enough of a warning?"

Hannah nodded, her eyes more blue than green in the morning light. "I'm pretty sure they have ice in their freezer," she said. "We don't have to stop in Folsom."

Murphy nodded. And drove.

DALTON, CALIFORNIA

"I really hoped he'd be there," Sophia said. This was ridiculous. She shouldn't feel so nervous. She'd been going to therapy religiously, once a week, for over a year. Talking helped. She knew that. She believed in it.

Dr. Heissman smiled, obviously trying to put her at ease. "What would you have said to him—Murphy? If he'd been at his friend's cabin?"

"I don't know," Sophia admitted. "Probably nothing. Probably just . . . that I'm here and I want to help—" She cut herself off. "But I can't help. There's no help. I can't go back in time and make it not happen. Angelina's murder. And that's all you want at first, you know? You just . . . run through all of the minutes leading up to . . . You run them over and over in your head, trying to figure out where, exactly, you could've blinked or stood up or said something different, and kept the violence from happening."

"I know you lost your husband," the doctor started.

"Lost?" Sophia said. Like she'd *misplaced* Dimitri? His blood had sprayed her as— She took a deep breath and steadied her voice. "I thought we were talking about Murphy."

"We are."

Dr. Heissman was sitting in one of the chairs by the window in the motel room—Sophia sat in the other. She'd opened the curtains, and they had a glorious view of the ill-kept parking lot.

Sophia's rolling carry-on bag was open on the bed. The plan was to check out and head back to San Diego after lunch. At least that was Dave and Sophia's plan. But they were already running late.

"We're discussing how your personal experience gives you greater insight into what Murphy might be going through," the doctor continued, in her oh-so-reasonable voice that matched the matter-of-fact calmness of her eyes. "And maybe brings you back, a little too uncomfortably close, to that very experience."

Sophia gazed back at Dr. Heissman for many long seconds, but the other woman just waited.

"You're right," Sophia said, because she got the very solid impression that if she didn't say something, they'd sit here like this, forever. Besides, Dr. Heissman *was* right. "It does."

Dr. Heissman laughed and immediately apologized. "I'm sorry, I'm just so used to what I think of as squeezing water from a stone syndrome. SpecWar operators are not big on admitting to what they perceive to be a weakness. Even though awareness of vulnerability ultimately leads to strength. Either from directly dealing with the issue or learning to work around it."

"I've spent a lot of time," Sophia told her, "dealing with the violence that . . . impacted my life. I was going to say *touched*, but that's not the word for it. Slammed. Battered. Invaded. Those are better choices. Yet

there are . . . certain details I've never told anyone. And I seriously doubt
I'm going to choose to tell *you* in this session today. No offense."

"None taken."

"I was there when Angelina was shot," Sophia said. "Which I'm sure
you already know. Seeing the blood on the driveway . . ." There had been
so much blood. She'd gotten it all over her clothes, on her hands, and even
her face.

After the ambulance had sped both Murphy and Angelina to the hospital, after Sophia had answered questions and given her statement to all
of the various FBI agents and law enforcement officials, she'd sat, numb
and exhausted, on the back deck of that Malibu beach house, just watching the darkness of the ocean.

The FBI team leader had finally come and sat down next to her, his
concern for her evident in his kind brown eyes. *Is there someone I can call
who can come and drive you home?*

She'd shaken her head. *My husband's dead.*

He must've been used to people in shock saying crazy things, because
he didn't so much as blink. *I know. I'm so sorry for your loss,* he'd said, and
he'd touched her, squeezing her hand. *You know what I bet you could
really use? A shower. Why don't we find you a bathroom so that you can do
that, and while you're in there, I'll see if I can't scrounge up some clean
clothes for you to wear.*

A familiar voice interrupted them. *I've got a spare T-shirt and shorts in
my car.*

Sophia had looked up to see Dave Malkoff standing there, tears in his
eyes as he held out his hand to her. *Hey, Soph. Tough night, huh?* He'd
nodded to the FBI agent. *Thanks, Cassidy. I'll see that she gets cleaned up
and . . . I'll get her home. She's safe with me.*

Dave had stayed with her that night, and the next few nights after,
sleeping on her sofa. He'd somehow known that the nightmares of Dimitri's death would come rushing back, and with it the irrational, smother-
ing fear of being alone.

"Let's start at the beginning," Dr. Heissman said now to Sophia.

The beginning. *One of the first times I talked to Murphy—really talked
to him—he told me he was engaged to be married. He positively sparkled
when he talked about Angelina. God, he loved her so much . . .*

"It was a dinner party," Sophia told her instead, because when Dr.

Heissman said beginning, she meant the beginning of the evening that Angelina was shot. "Casual. Pizza." Surely the doctor knew this already. "Kelly—my boss's wife—called me, last minute. Murphy and Angelina were bringing the pictures they took on their honeymoon. There was also a blind date element—well, not really a *blind* date. I'd met the man before—his name was Cosmo—when he came into the office. He was one of Tommy's SEALs. It was pretty clear, though, when I got there, that Kelly was trying to set us up and . . ." She shook her head. "She meant well, but it was a little awkward. I wouldn't have come if I'd known. Murphy knew that and . . ." She trailed off, remembering.

Angelina had been too much of a walking party to be aware, but Murphy had taken note of Sophia's discomfort immediately.

He'd pulled her aside, moments after he and Angelina had arrived. *You okay?*

I think I'm most disturbed by the realization that now, whenever someone invites me over, I'm going to have to worry that they're trying to set me up with some friend.

Murphy'd hugged and noogied her, his knuckles against the top of her head. *Angel and I will never do that. I'm making a promise to you right now. I meet George Clooney on the street, he wants to come over for dinner—I'm absolutely* not *calling you.*

Sophia had laughed—Murphy could always make her laugh—but she'd also gotten tense because Tom and Cosmo had come in from the deck. And Murphy had whispered, *Say the word, and I'll help you play the stomach flu card. You know, "Sophia thinks she might be coming down with that bug everyone's getting. Me and Angelina'll drive her home."*

Sophia had wanted, so badly, to say *Yes, please. Get me out of here.*

She'd wanted to go home. Instead, she'd smiled at Murphy and said *I'll be fine.*

Sophia now looked up at Dr. Heissman, who was just sitting quietly, watching her.

"Sorry," Sophia said.

"Remembering one of those minutes that might've changed everything?" Dr. Heissman asked, with a perception that was uncanny.

"Murph saw that I was uncomfortable and offered to drive me home," she said. "So yes, it might've. Or it would have ended Angelina's life that much sooner. The shooter was believed to have followed Murphy up to

Tom and Kelly's. He may already have been in position." She needed a sip of water—her throat was so dry. "We'll never know, because I stayed."

"You stayed," the doctor echoed.

"Which is why Murphy cut all ties with me, because maybe, if I'd said yes . . ." She shook her head as she put her bottle of water back on the table. "He blames me. He blames everyone. I know exactly what that feels like. Because, see, mostly he blames himself. Although he has no clue what it's like to *really* be responsible for . . ." She stopped. Took another sip of water.

Even though she hadn't finished her sentence, she knew she'd opened a door.

Sure enough, Dr. Heissman came inside. "You feel responsible for your husband's death." She said it as a statement, not as a question.

"I *am* responsible," Sophia squared her shoulders and told her. "I trusted business partners I shouldn't have. I walked us into what was supposed to be a lunch meeting with the man who killed him. *Lunch.* With a man I knew was dangerous. What was I thinking? And yet, to this day, I cannot talk to a friend who tried to convince us to leave Kazabek after the coup. Our world was dissolving around us. I remember she said those words to me and I laughed at the melodrama, because I just didn't believe it. But she was right. And I still sometimes think, why didn't she try harder? Why didn't she insist we leave, too? It's absurd, I know it. It's juvenile. It's not even *close* to her fault. And yet, I don't answer her e-mails. I . . . can't face her. As Murphy can't face me, because I didn't ask him to drive me home."

"Maybe you should," Dr. Heissman said slowly, "talk to this friend who has reached out to you. You could ask her forgiveness—for not listening."

Sophia shook her head. "That's not what I said."

"Isn't it?"

"I'm the one who can't forgive *her.*"

"Those were the *words* you said," she agreed. "That's your reasoning for why you didn't try to reach out to Murphy. But what I *heard* was that, after all this time, you can't forgive yourself for your husband's death."

Sophia laughed her surprise. "Why *I* didn't try to reach out . . . ?"

"Did you look for Murphy? After he left the hospital? After Angelina's memorial service?"

"No," Sophia admitted.

"You just . . . made up excuses for why he'd never come talk to you?"

Made up? Sophia was silent, because she couldn't deny it.

"Did anyone at Troubleshooters reach out to Murphy?" the doctor asked, not unkindly.

Sophia nodded. "Dave did. He was always trying to find Murph. Always." Thank God for Dave.

"It's okay that you didn't," Dr. Heissman said, leaning forward slightly, "reach out to Murphy. You know that, right? Having lost—" She stopped herself. "Having a spouse die violently, in front of you, and then being witness, again, to another violent crime in which your friend's wife was killed . . . ? You're certainly allowed to keep your distance from Murphy's pain. I just think you should be honest—with yourself—about why you do the things you do."

Sophia nodded again as tears flooded her eyes. "I lied," she whispered, blinking them back. "When we started the session. I was glad Murph wasn't there. I'm so afraid to see him."

"And yet you came all this way, to be present, in case he was here," Dr. Heissman pointed out. "That makes you pretty courageous."

Sophia just shook her head. "I'm not."

"Maybe," the doctor suggested, "Murphy can be the person you talk to. Maybe you can tell him the things you haven't been able to tell anyone else—about Dimitri's death. Maybe he can help you forgive yourself. It really doesn't matter, Sophia, if you're truly responsible or if you just think you are. Either way, you deserve to forgive yourself, and to stop punishing yourself. Do you know why most people hang on to anger and blame after a loved one is violently murdered?" She answered her own question. "It keeps us feeling connected to our loved ones. Because with forgiveness comes release. When we finally start to let go of the anger, it can feel scary and even wrong—as if we're losing that final piece of our loved ones—until we realize that we already have the ultimate connection. We loved them. We love them still. We carry them always in our hearts."

"I wish I could tell Dimitri that I'm sorry," Sophia whispered.

"Did he love you?" Dr. Heissman asked.

Sophia nodded. "Very much."

"Then I'm pretty sure," Dr. Heissman said, "that he knows."

They sat for a moment in silence, then the doctor spoke again. "This may seem like too much all at once, but . . . I really need to ask you some questions about an incident that happened several years ago. With Lawrence Decker? In Kazbekistan. It must've been just a few weeks after your husband died."

Sophia sat very still. "Did he talk to you about . . . what happened?"

"He brought it up," the doctor said. "Yes."

She could only imagine what he'd said. "Deck still blames himself," Sophia told her. "I see it in his eyes. He thinks it was this terrible, awful thing. And maybe it was, for him. But for me?" She shook her head. "At that time, after what I'd lived through—Dimitri's murder and . . . For me, it was just another day, another meaningless blow job. By that point, I'd used sex, for so long, just to stay alive . . . I used Decker's attraction to me to try to distract him—so that I could kill him. At the time, neither of us realized that we were both on the same side. And I *would* have killed him, I tried—because I thought it was him or me. If *I* could forgive myself for that, why can't *he*?"

Dr. Heissman just sat, quietly, listening.

Sophia leaned forward. "You know what's *really* stupid?"

The doctor shook her head.

"I barely remember it. The sex. I remember that he managed to follow me back to this abandoned hotel where I was hiding. I remember talking to him, and being afraid. I remember crying so that he'd put his arms around me. And I know what I did. I know that I kissed him, and I unfastened his pants and . . . But I really don't remember it. I remember him hitting me—knocking me down to get the gun out of my hand after I fired it. And I remember waiting then, for him to kill me. But he didn't. Instead, he . . ."

Sophia couldn't say it. Her throat tightened and she couldn't get the words out. And the tears that she'd successfully fought while talking about Dimitri overflowed her eyes and spilled down her cheeks.

Dr. Heissman just waited. Patient. Respectful.

Decker had paid her. Five dollars, American. He'd tossed the slightly tattered scrip onto the floor, next to her. Like she was some low-rent whore.

"He paid me for the sex," Sophia whispered, "and he left."

SACRAMENTO, CALIFORNIA

They parked around the corner.

It wasn't so much that Murphy was afraid the police would come investigate if a neighbor noticed a strange car in Steve and Paul's driveway. They owned a repair garage with three huge bays, which meant there were always a half dozen or so strange cars parked there.

It was more of an escape option—which was just as ridiculous because they hadn't been followed. Murphy had made damn certain of that.

Still, he positioned the car on the street, beneath one of Steve and Paul's living room windows. Of course, the apartment was on the second story, which would make an escape out that window problematic. More so for Hannah who definitely needed to restrict her jumping for a while.

She was silent as she got out of the car, as she shouldered the bag of clothes they'd left locked in the back during their foray into the woods.

Murphy lifted the strap off her shoulder, taking it from her as he gave her a look. She wasn't fooling him. Her ankle was hurting her badly, and he knew it.

She was trying not to limp, but enough of that bullcrap—he didn't ask, he just looped her arm around his shoulders, held her around the waist, and supported most of her weight.

They headed down the back alley, toward the wooden stairs leading up to Steve and Paul's kitchen door, with Hannah trying not to reveal just how much her ankle hurt, and Murphy trying not to think about his right hand, which had accidentally slipped up beneath the edge of Hannah's T-shirt. He tried not to think about the smoothness of her skin, the soft curve of her waist.

They made it to the stairs, which were easier for Hannah to navigate on her own, holding the railing with her left hand and bracing her right against the side of the building. Murphy let her go first, ready to catch her if she faltered.

"Still smells like french fries," she said, and it did. Steve had always been something of a mad scientist, and he and Paul had a business converting cars to run on bio-fuel. They lived above their garage, and the entire area smelled, indeed, like cooking oil. They collected vats of used oil from restaurants and used it to power their cars.

The super-size-me odor didn't permeate the apartment though, thank God, even though they had a plastic container for collecting used oil under their kitchen sink as well. Hannah jimmied the lock and opened the door like a pro.

"Not bad for a cop," he said.

"Former cop," she reminded him.

"Being a cop's like being a Marine," Murphy said. "There's no such thing as former."

It was cool and dim inside with the shades already pulled down.

He closed the door behind him, putting on the chain—like that would help—and dropped their bag on the kitchen floor.

"Anyone home?" Hannah called, looking to Murph to see if there was a response.

He shook his head. The place was as silent as a tomb.

It would've taken him forty-five quick seconds to thoroughly check out the apartment, but that would've meant leaving Hannah alone in the kitchen, and he wasn't making that mistake again. Instead, he looped her arm, again, around his shoulders, this time being more careful—pulling her T-shirt down before he held her at the waist.

Together they slowly went through the place. It was clear that Paul had made an effort to tidy up before leaving. And it was definitely Paul's work. Steve was one of those guys who filled whatever space was available, and left a trail of clutter behind him.

But right now, their bed was neatly made.

No one was home. Not even their cat. The litter box sat empty in the master bathroom. Hannah saw it, too, and briefly met Murphy's eyes.

They must've dropped Hercules at a friend's.

"How did you know they wouldn't be back?" Hannah finally spoke, as they went down the hall to the back rooms, one of which was Steve's office. "I thought you didn't get through when you called."

Steve obviously hadn't let Paul anywhere near the little room where he kept his desk and computer. It looked as if a bomb had gone off, with papers and files cluttering every available surface, and piles of books everywhere else, many of which had grown too high and tipped over.

"I didn't," Murphy said. "There was an article, I must've read it online. About some conference . . ."

"The Grassroots Alternative Energy Symposium?" Hannah said, and he looked at her in surprise.

She gestured with her chin to the corkboard that hung on the office wall. Where, sure enough, there was a flyer about a conference being held in Boston—featuring a special appearance by one Dr. Steven Downes.

"Damn," he said. "I thought losing your hearing had made you psychic."

She probably didn't hear him, because she'd leaned closer to the flyer, to look at the little picture of Steve's smiling face. "Go, Steve," she said. "Do you think they drove the stank-mobile all the way to Massachusetts?"

Murphy was certain of it. He nodded as she turned to look back at him, which was disconcerting, considering how close they were standing. According to the flyer, the conference ran until next Wednesday, which gave them some breathing room. He pushed open the last door, at the end of the hall and . . . Whoa.

"Speaking of stank," Hannah was saying, "I could use a shower and hey, what happened to the chaos room?"

The room where Steve and Paul had, for over a decade, jammed all of their excess clutter had been transformed into a guest bedroom, neat and cozy. It was like something out of a trendy furniture company catalogue, down to the gleaming white bedspread and the interesting artwork on the walls.

"I bet," Hannah said, "right about now you're regretting that you came and crashed with me at the cabin instead of coming here. My shitty little loft, versus this . . . ?"

Murphy waited for her to glance up at him so he could respond. "I didn't come to the cabin for the loft."

And there they stood, in the doorway of that perfect room, with that perfect bed looming there in his peripheral vision as he gazed down into Hannah's face, Hannah's eyes.

"I didn't come for this, either," he said, then tried to explain, glancing over at that bed that was waiting for them to fall upon it. He gestured between the two of them. "This—"

She cut him off. "I know."

"But, God, maybe I'm just lying to myself because—"

She stood on her toes and kissed him.

And Murphy closed his eyes and kissed her back. She was salty and sweet, coffee and sweat, soft and hard—these lips that had always been so quick to curve up into a smile, this mouth that he knew so well.

She wrapped herself around him, her arms holding him close, her body soft against him, her fingers in his hair as he held her just as tightly as he kissed her, again and again and again.

Hannah, whom he'd met back when she was still in college. They'd worked together for a few months, that first glorious, brilliant summer with its endlessly long days, on Patrick's whale watching boat. She was really still just a kid back then, but she was funny and smart and fun to be with, and he hung with her even when they both weren't working.

It wasn't about sex. And okay, sex had definitely crossed his mind a time or two hundred because, hey, he was human, but it wasn't *about* sex.

And it became a thing. A tradition. A habit. Wherever he was, whatever he was doing, even if he couldn't take the entire summer, he'd take a couple weeks and head for Juneau.

To hang with his pal Patrick. But really, to hang with Hannah.

Whom he'd kissed for the first time, in all the years that they'd been friends, that awful night six months ago. He'd kissed her, and then he'd cold-fucked her, and even though it had to have been soul-crushingly awful it must've felt too good, because he'd blocked most of it out. God forbid he feel good or laugh.

Or live.

But, Jesus, blood was rushing through his veins right now. His heart was damn near pounding out of his chest.

Murphy tugged her now, toward the bed, but she stopped him, pulling her mouth free.

"Clean and slow," she said breathlessly, her hand on his chest to stop him from kissing her again.

He shook his head, not understanding.

"Look at this room," Hannah said, amusement dancing in her eyes. "Do you really want to mud up that perfect bed?"

And they would make mud, Murphy knew. They were both covered with dust and grime. That plus the way they were already making each other sweat . . .

And he got it. Clean. And *slow* . . .

"I don't know if I can do slow," he confessed. He used to be good at it—a million years ago. But right now? Highly unlikely.

"It's just a wish list." She hobbled around him to the hall bathroom. "It's not like I'm going to send you back into the kitchen if you don't bring me exactly what I order."

He followed her, lingering in the doorway as she turned on the water and made sure there was soap and shampoo in the shower stall. "My wish list is kind of . . . fast and now."

"If you shower in the master bathroom," Hannah told him as she sat on the john to take off her boots, trying not to wince as she freed her ankle, "*now* will be in about three minutes. I'll meet you back in the chaos room."

"It's not the chaos room anymore," Murphy pointed out.

"Don't count on it," she said and shut the door in his face.

DALTON, CALIFORNIA

"Eden. May I talk to you for a minute?"

She was standing and crying at the open trunk of the rental car, pretending to be organizing the clothes in her bag, but now she quickly wiped her eyes before turning around.

It was one of Izzy's friends—Jay Lopez—standing there. His sudden expression of sheer dismay at the sight of her no-doubt still-teary eyes and red nose would've been funny under normal circumstances. Provided she had room for funny in today's range of emotions, which ran the gamut from frightened to sad. Oh, and then even sadder, with her mother's such obvious lies.

Ben can't come either. He's got soccer practice this afternoon, and then a . . . a big math test to study for tomorrow.

Why don't you just say it, Mom? Greg won't let you or Ben come to the wedding, and, once again, you're just going to let him win.

"You okay?" Lopez asked, obviously praying that she'd *I'm fine* him.

So she nodded and gave him pregnancy excuse B. "Crazy hormones." It was only half a lie.

He nodded, too. "Danny told me you're going back to Vegas," he said in his gentle, almost apologetic voice. He had only the slightest hint of an accent. "To get married. Today. You probably don't know this, but . . . Izzy really has to go to San Diego first."

And wasn't *this* exactly what she needed? Eden twisted the ring on her finger, around and around. There was definitely more coming, so she lifted her chin and waited for it.

"He needs to request permission from our commanding officer," Lopez told her, still apologetic—yeah, right. "To get married."

Eden nodded. "He told me about that." Apparently, several years ago, Izzy had received six months of punishment duty, for what he'd called *a UA incident.* Which translated to "unauthorized absence," which was the Navy's version of going AWOL. He'd gotten into serious trouble and was lucky, in fact, that he hadn't been given a dishonorable discharge.

But two months into his punishment, Izzy'd cut a deal with both his CO—his commanding officer—and the team's senior chief. He was allowed to return to Team Sixteen on the condition that he follow all rules and regs to the T. *And* that he get permission from the CO before he did anything out of the realm of everyday and ordinary.

"Izzy told me getting permission would be no problem," Eden told Lopez now. "That it was just a formality. Because I'm pregnant. He said it would be fine if he spoke to the CO first thing, after we got back."

Izzy didn't want to make Eden drive all the way to San Diego, then back to Vegas, then back again.

Lopez was nodding his agreement. "It would, indeed, be a formality. If the baby was his." He shrugged. "I kinda know it's not."

"He," Eden said. "The baby is a *he* not an *it.*"

"Excuse me," Lopez said. He did sincere extremely well. "*He's* not. Zanella's." He held her gaze. "I know this, Eden."

If this guy thought he could intimidate her with a stare-down, he had another think coming.

Eden let him think he won—but then slid her own gaze down his nicely put together upper body, lingering on the fly of his pants. She even tipped her head slightly as she looked—a small detail, sure, but extremely effective in reducing most men to penises with a human appendage, working brain optional. "You know this . . . because you were there that night? Maybe hiding in the closet? Hoping to make it a three-way? I really don't know Izzy that well, but if this is something you guys regularly do . . . I've never really been into that, but since you're kind of hot . . . I'll definitely think about it."

She returned her gaze to his face, but he was already looking away, staring down at the broken macadam and dirt of the driveway, smiling slightly and shaking his head.

His smile faded though, as he looked back up at her—with absolutely nothing she'd expected in his eyes. No heat. No embarrassment. Just . . .

Pity?

"Izzy's a good friend of mine," he said quietly. "I care about him—very much. I know things seem really . . . scary and uncertain right now, and he's providing what seems like a quick fix, which I also know must be impossible for you to resist—"

"There you are." And there came Izzy, loping across the parking lot, looking from Eden to Lopez and back as he tossed his duffle into the trunk. "What's up, kids?"

Lopez opened his mouth, but Eden spoke first. "Jay was just expressing his regrets. About not being able to come with. You know, to the wedding?"

Silence.

Izzy finally broke it by laughing, but it wasn't because he found anything particularly funny. "Okay, I *so* don't buy that." He again looked from Eden to Lopez, and he got large. "What the *fuck* were you saying to her, dickhead?"

Lopez didn't back down. "I'm just being your friend, man."

"By making Eden cry?"

"He didn't," Eden tried to tell Izzy. "I was . . . crying about . . ." He wasn't paying her any attention—she was talking to herself. " . . . something else. Something stupid. Something you obviously don't care about."

"I lied, okay," Izzy told Lopez. "When I told you . . . what I told you. Yesterday? I *lied*. This baby's mine."

And there they stood, practically toe to toe, staring each other down.

This time, Lopez blinked first. And backed away. "I hope you know what you're doing."

"I'm getting married," Izzy said quietly. "Trust me, this is not something that you do without at least a little thought."

"There *are* other solutions," Lopez said, just as quietly. "Welfare programs that Eden could go into that would pay for—"

"Danny would never agree to that," Eden said.

"Danny would have nothing to say about it," Lopez pointed out. "He's not responsible for—"

"Jay," Izzy said, "come on, bro, just let it go."

Lopez nodded, but then shook his head. "At least take the time to talk to the counselors at the navy base, sign a prenup. And man, you've *got* to talk to the senior chief."

Across the parking lot, Miss Been-There-Done-That—aka Tracy Nice-Shoes—came clickety-clicking out of the motel lobby, along with Lindsey and Mark Jenkins. She caught sight of Izzy and stopped seriously short. It was as if, boom, she'd hit an invisible wall at the very sight of him. And at the sight of Eden.

Izzy didn't notice. He was too busy delivering a look of total disbelief to Lopez. *"Talk to the senior chief* is how you let it go?"

No, Miss Shoes, Eden wasn't fat, she was pregnant. She shifted so that she was more in profile as, across the parking lot, Tracy all but pointed in her direction. Mark leaned closer, no doubt explaining to Tracy who Eden was, and where she and Izzy were going.

"Why are you in such a rush?" Lopez asked earnestly. "You barely know this girl." He dissolved into a barrage of Spanish that Izzy just shook his head throughout.

"I'm sorry, she's . . . I'm sorry, man. Look, I know her well enough," Izzy countered. "I do."

Across the parking lot, Tracy abruptly spun on her expensive heels and walked—quickly—back into the motel. Lindsey shot her husband a classic *well done, Mr. Insensitive* look and chased after her.

"And the rush," Izzy added, "is that the *girl* needs prenatal care."

"And after that?" Lopez asked. "After the baby's born and the hospital bills are covered? What then?"

Izzy glanced at Eden. "We'll play it by ear."

"I gotta be honest," Lopez said. "I know you don't want to hear this, but to me, marriage is a holy sacrament. It's supposed to be forever, Iz. To enter into it on the . . . the three-month lease plan—it's an insult to the institution. It's an insult to God."

"Says the man who recommends we sign a prenup," Izzy told Eden, as Mark Jenkins crossed the parking lot to join them.

"You're supposed to be in love," Lopez implored him. "*Both* of you, Zanella. How is this *not* going to end badly?"

Jenkins realized what he'd walked into. "Are you seriously trying to talk Zanella out of marrying Eden?" he asked Lopez, laughing his surprise. "Dude, Danny's going to crap ballistic missiles."

Lopez turned to Eden as if to say something more, but Izzy blocked him.

He opened the door to the front of the car, motioning for her to get in. "Time to go."

Eden acquiesced as Lopez just stood there, shaking his head.

As Izzy closed the car door, Jenk lowered his voice, but Eden could still hear him. "Did you know Tracy's here?"

"Yeah," Izzy said. "I, um . . . Yes, I know."

Jenk's voice got a little louder. "And you didn't even bother to *talk* to her? *Hey, how are you, Trace? Things are crazy with me ever since I found out I knocked up a sixteen-year-old.*"

"Eden's not sixteen," Izzy said.

"Newsflash, Z! She *was* sixteen only *two years ago!*"

"Get the fuck out of my face!"

"You couldn't've at least had the common decency to *mention* it to Tracy?" Jenkins asked. "She had to find out from me, and I messed it up, because I was sure you'd done the right thing and talked to her."

"I haven't *seen* her in months," Izzy said. "Why would I go looking for her now? Dude, I haven't even told my brothers yet. Or maybe you expected me to touch base with every random woman I've—"

"Random?" Jenk pushed Izzy, and the car rocked as he bumped into it. "Fuck you, douchebag—she's a friend of mine, and you know it. *That's* why you should've talked to her."

Izzy pushed Jenkins back. "Fuck *you*—you're just jealous because I had a taste of something you never tapped."

Lopez said something in Spanish that sounded like a plea to God for strength.

But Jenkins just laughed as he walked away, pulling Lopez with him. "Zanella, you're *such* an asshole."

"That *was* a pretty assholeish thing to say," Eden pointed out as Izzy got into the car and turned the key. He jammed the car into gear, his movements jerky.

When he turned to look at her, it was clear some of his anger was aimed at her. "For the record," he said. "I'm not into three-ways—at least not with another guy."

Oh, *crap*. "You speak Spanish?"

He pulled out of the driveway a little too fast. "Did you really tell Jay Lopez—"

"I'm sorry," she said. "He was . . . Just . . ." She closed her eyes. "This is going to sound crazy . . ."

"I know he didn't hit on you," Izzy said. "Not Lopez. No chance. So if you're thinking about lying, babe, spare yourself the effort."

"He was nice," she said. "Okay? That's what I was going to say. He was just so . . . nice."

"So you ask him if he wants to have a three-way?" His voice went up an octave. "That's what you say to someone you think is *nice?*"

"*Too* nice." Eden fought the tears that sprang to her eyes. "I'm sorry," she said. "I just . . . I open my mouth and it just . . . It comes out."

Izzy was silent then, just driving, his eyes on the road in front of them.

"Please don't be mad at me," she finally broke the silence by whispering.

He glanced at her. "Is that what happened with Richie?" he asked. "You tried to play hardball and put him in his place, and he took it as a real invitation?"

"I thought it didn't matter to you—how it happened."

"It doesn't," he said, but then added, "I'm just concerned, because, if that *is* what happened, you haven't seemed to learn your lesson."

"My lesson," she asked. "My *lesson?*"

"I've been watching you, Eed," Izzy said, "and you can't seem to have a simple conversation with a man without bringing sex into the equation. And cranking the volume to eleven. First with Dave and now—"

"I'm sorry," Eden cut him off. "I'm still back at *lesson*. So what you're saying is, if I mouthed off to Richie and he forced himself on me, that would be *my* fault?"

"That's not what I said!"

Her voice shook. "Yeah, I'm pretty sure you just told me that I should learn to keep my mouth shut and my eyes averted to avoid being raped in the future."

Izzy turned the wheel sharply, pulling into a side street and breaking to a stop. "Please tell me that's not how it happened. That he raped you."

Oh, crap, she was screwing this up. Izzy was going to take her to Vegas—and dump her back at her mother's house. "That's not how it happened," she said obediently.

But it was obvious he didn't believe her. He just sat there, looking at her. Waiting. Angry and apprehensive.

"He sent Jerry to Palm Springs," Eden told him quietly, looking down at her lap, praying she could get through this without crying, praying he would believe her. Her own mother hadn't. "To pick something up—probably drugs. I was home alone. In Jerry's brother's apartment. And he came over—Richie. To drop off this stuff that Jerry supposedly left in his van. He wasn't sure what it was, right? This was what he told me when I opened the door—but he thought it was really important to Jerry. And it was so obviously, you know, a ring box. Like the one you gave me? Only it was wrapped, so I couldn't open it to see what was inside. He had these flowers, too. Roses. An armful. And a bottle of wine.

"And he goes, *I'm not really sure what's up, but Jer's on his way back and he asked me to bring this over and open the wine, let it breathe.* And I was so sure this was it—that Jerry was going to ask me to marry him, and . . . I was stupid. I took the chain off the door and . . . I let Richie in. I never did before. He came knocking a lot when Jerry wasn't home, but I never let him in. I didn't pretend that I liked him—he knew I didn't. He knew that I didn't want Jerry to work for him.

"But now he's in the kitchen, and he's opening the wine, and he gets out three glasses—you know, 'cause Jerry's coming home? And I'm putting the flowers into water, and I only had my back to him for a few seconds and . . ." She shook her head. "I don't remember drinking the wine. But I must've.

"Next thing I know, it's morning, and I'm in bed and I'm naked and I'm . . ." She cleared her throat, because damn it, her voice was starting to wobble. "I'm bruised. Sore. In . . . sexual places. And, God, I was so sick. I barely made it to the bathroom before I threw up. The headache was . . . I've never felt anything like it."

"Rohypnol," Izzy said. "The date rape drug. God *damn* it."

Eden nodded. "That was my guess, too. The good news is that I don't remember any of it." She looked away, because the darkness in his eyes was just too hard to face. "At first I thought I was just hung over, you know? But Jerry wasn't home and . . . the kitchen was clean. No flowers, no ring box. Just two wine glasses in the dish drain. Two—not three. When I saw that, I knew."

"And you didn't . . . ?"

"No. I did it all wrong. Totally. I didn't know I could get a blood test." Eden had done her share of research well after the fact, and had discovered that traces of the drug would've still been in her bloodstream—but only that next morning. "Although, I couldn't go to the police—they would've sent me back to Las Vegas, you know? I knew about the morning-after pill, but . . . I had no cash."

Fifty-three cents. That was all she'd found in the apartment, even after searching through pockets and under the couch cushions. It wasn't even enough to ride the bus.

"I knew I couldn't afford either the visit to the clinic or the prescription," she continued. "And the only free clinic I could walk to refused to treat me because I was under eighteen. I needed a note from one of my parents."

"God *damn* it," he said again.

"So I went home," Eden told Izzy. "And I crossed my fingers."

She rubbed her belly, but it was more to soothe herself than Pinkie, who was sleeping. "I was afraid of him," she continued softly. "Richie. And I was probably even more afraid that if it came down to a he-said-she-said, Jerry wouldn't believe me. So I pretended that I didn't remember anything about that night—no recollection whatsoever of Richie coming over. I just played it like it didn't happen, and just kept leaning on Jerry to find another job. He told me he did, but . . . He lied. And Richie finally told Jerry that I'd called *him* that night. He said *I* came on to him and . . . Jerry believed him. And he left me at that Krispy Kreme."

Izzy was holding on to the steering wheel with both hands. "I don't get how you could want to have this guy's baby."

"I'm not," Eden told him. "I'm having *my* baby. Maybe not being able to remember it—the sex . . . See, even though I know what happened, what Richie did, it feels like there was me, and then . . . there was me and Pinkie."

"Immaculate conception, huh?" Izzy said.

"I *do* remember that next morning," she told him. "Not so much with the immaculate. The whole thing was so obviously meant to put me in my place. Or maybe to make me leave LA."

Which, in the long run, had worked.

He touched her, then, pushing her hair behind her ear, his fingers gentle. But Eden couldn't look at him.

"Can I kill him?" Izzy said. "Because I really, *really* want to kill him."

She did turn to him then, suddenly aware that she'd been holding her breath. "You believe me?"

"Nothing dramatic," Izzy said. "No conversation beforehand. None of that *This is for Eden* avenger movie-dialogue shit. Just a fast double-pop and out go his lights."

"You're kidding, right?" she said. "Sometimes I can't tell when you're kidding and when you're—"

"I'm dead fucking serious." He was. He was even angrier than he'd been when he'd found her locked in the bathroom. "You don't want me to kill him, how about if I beat him," Izzy suggested, "within an inch of his miserable life? Rearrange his face, a few teeth on the sidewalk, break a knee or an elbow . . . ?"

"*This* was why I couldn't tell Danny."

"Both," he decided. "I'd like to break 'em both."

"Unless," she argued, raising her voice, "he has his posse break *your* knees and elbows first. Please, Izzy, I don't want you to kill anyone—what's done is done. I'm gone—I don't want to go back there, and I really don't want *you* to go back there, because you'll drag me with you. Please, *please,* if you want to help make it better just . . . tell me you believe me!"

"I believe you," he said, no hesitation. "I'm just . . ." Now he paused, and looked at her, hard. "Why do I get the feeling there's something more—that you're not telling me?"

Because there *was* something more that she wasn't telling him. Something that she'd hoped she'd never have to tell him—she'd just pray he never found out.

"Ah, fuck me," Izzy said. "I'm right. What else did he do to you?"

Eden shook her head. "It's bad."

"Just tell me," he said.

So Eden opened her mouth. "Richie told me that there's a video," she admitted. "From that night."

Izzy nodded. "A video."

"I haven't seen it," she said. "For all I know, he was bluffing, but . . ." She braced herself and just said it. "He said he was going to put it on the Internet."

Izzy was silent for several long moments. "That's it?" he finally said.

"He said I walk around and I talk—I act like I'm drunk. Like I'm having . . . fun."

"Rohypnol can do that," Izzy said.

Eden couldn't help it, she started to cry. "What if your friends find out? What if they see it?"

He touched her again, his hand warm against her head as he stroked her hair.

"Some of them will think I'm a sucker and a loser," Izzy told her, "and some of them will think I'm the luckiest bastard on the planet. Which is no different than the current consensus. Who the fuck cares what they think?"

Eden searched through her handbag for a Kleenex, but finally gave up and just wiped her nose on her sleeve. "What if *you* see it and think I'm lying?" she whispered.

"Why would you lie?" he asked her just as quietly. "When I asked you to marry me, it didn't have anything to do with the past. As far as I'm concerned, it's all about the future. You want to look me in the eye right now and say, *whoops, sorry, Iz, I got a little carried away and made up all that shit about Richie and the roofies—*"

"I didn't," she said hotly.

"I'm not saying I don't believe you," Izzy told her. "I'm saying that it doesn't matter. I mean, yeah, it matters that this guy did this to you. That matters a fuckload. And it also matters—from here on in—that you're honest with me. That we're honest with each other. Okay?"

Eden nodded.

But he wasn't done. "If you really don't want me to kill Richie, I won't. But can I just state for the record that if there is a video, it's evidence of a crime."

"And what do we do with this *evidence?*" she asked. "Go to the police, and have them watch it while I sit there, in the room—"

"No," Izzy said. "Of course not. It just . . . feels wrong to let him get away with this."

"He-said-she-said," Eden told him. "Who's going to believe me? Jerry—who supposedly loved me—didn't even want to *hear* my side."

"Jerry's a tool," Izzy said. "I thought we established that months ago."

"You said you were, too," she reminded him.

"I am," he agreed. "I'm also a jackass, a jerk and . . . an asshole, I believe is what Jenkins just called me. Oh, my God. What if *your* friends find out?"

Eden actually laughed. Rolled her eyes.

"No, no," he said. "I say, *What if your friends find out?* and you say, *Who the fuck cares what they think?* Let's try it again. What if your friends find out?"

"Who the fuck cares what they think?" Eden obediently countered.

"Spoken like a true Zanella," he said, and put the car back in gear. "Let's take this show to Vegas and make it so."

CHAPTER
FOURTEEN

Murphy sat in Steve and Paul's tastefully decorated master bathroom, towel around his waist.

He'd been sitting there for way more than three minutes. Probably more like sixty-three.

His original intention had been to wait just a little while, until it became a little less obvious that he'd broken down and cried while he was in the shower.

He should have just gone with the soap-in-the-eyes explanation. But he knew that Hannah would know that he was lying, which would totally ruin the mood.

She wouldn't understand why he'd cried—and he wasn't sure he could explain. But she'd think it was about Angelina, and, yeah, in a way it was. In a way, everything he did, every breath he took was about Angelina. But this . . .

He'd cried not because he'd wanted Angelina, but rather because he wanted Hannah. He *wanted* Han—with a sharpness and desperate immediacy that no longer existed when he thought about his wife.

He'd cried, not because it felt wrong, but because it didn't.

It was weird. With Han being Angel's best friend, it should've felt like the worst of betrayals.

But it didn't.

He would've thought that looking at Hannah, spending time with her, would've been a wound-opening reminder of what they'd both lost.

But it wasn't.

Instead, it was . . . what it was.

Life. Unfair and painful at times. But always moving forward, always shifting, changing, with time's relentless passage smoothing down the jagged parts until it no longer hurt quite so much just to breathe.

Murphy stood and adjusted his towel. He opened the bathroom door and . . .

The house was dead silent.

He crossed through Steve and Paul's freakishly neat bedroom and into the hall. He went down to the right, past the bathroom, where the door to the guest room—the former chaos room—was ajar.

He gently pushed it open.

Hannah was in the bed, asleep, her breathing slow and steady.

She'd taken off the spread and hung it carefully on the back of a chair. The bedclothes beneath it were white, too, and she lay on her side beneath the covers, pristine sheet clutched to her chest as she faced the door—no doubt so that she could see him if he came in.

She wasn't particularly pretty—at least not in delicate-flower mode. Her nose was too big, her face too round, her shoulders too broad, her mouth too wide, her laughter too loud.

Her eyes were uncommonly beautiful, though. They sparkled with humor and flashed with anger—and held such warmth and passion. With them closed, she looked almost childlike and sweet, dark lashes against her soft cheeks.

But the freckles? Completely ridiculous on a woman who could kick most people's asses. And yet, somehow? Adorable.

She had them on her arms and shoulders, too—she'd always complained about the copious amounts of sunblock she'd had to use. Where the sun kissed her skin, she freckled and burned.

She currently had her classic summer farmer's tan—which meant most of the freckles on her arms were below a clearly marked T-shirt sleeve line. But she had some on her shoulders, too, from the super-hot days she'd worn a tank top or her bathing suit. It was all contrasted sharply by the paleness of the rest of her skin.

No doubt about it, she was naked beneath that sheet.

Jesus, he was a fool.

He shouldn't have kissed her. Or he shouldn't have *stopped* kissing her. He should have just climbed into the shower with her. Or he shouldn't have brought her here at all. He should have driven her back to Dalton and then gone and turned himself in.

But trying to figure out what he should have done an hour or more ago wasn't going to help him. What was he going to do now, was the question he should be answering.

Climbing into bed with Hannah was no longer an option.

Which meant he should probably start by getting dressed.

Han had dragged their duffle into the room—the bag into which they'd both thrown several changes of clothes. It was over by the door, and he went to it, to find a clean pair of boxers and a T-shirt, some shorts and socks.

He didn't move quickly, but somehow, in moving, he woke Hannah.

"Murph," she said quietly, and he turned.

Her eyes were open—such a powerful mix of blue and green amidst all that white. Blue and green and sadness and remorse.

"I'm so sorry," she said. "I wasn't thinking."

She was apologizing to *him*?

She sighed. "I should've—"

"No." He shook his head, straightening up and crossing to the bed. "You didn't do anything wrong."

"Except give you too much time to think."

"Nah," he said, "that wasn't it."

She gave him a disbelieving look that was pure Hannah. That, combined with the fact that he knew she was naked under that sheet was doubly disconcerting. She was *Hannah*, and for so many years he wouldn't allow himself to want her, but goddamn, now he could and he did.

"Don't bullshit me, bwee," she told him. "We know each other better than that."

"I'm not. I'm . . . here, right?"

"To get your clothes," she pointed out.

"Only because you were sleeping."

"I'm not sleeping now," she said.

Now.

She realized what she'd said and immediately backpedaled. "That wasn't meant to be . . . I wasn't trying to . . ." She closed her eyes. "Can we just go back to me saying I'm sorry? I'm just . . . really sorry. Just go, okay? Let's not beat a dead horse. Wake me up whenever you're ready to go out." She turned away.

God, but he hated when she did that. And God, her shoulders and back were lovely—all that smooth skin.

Murphy sat down on the edge of the bed and tapped her arm.

She turned her head to look at him.

"Please don't turn your back on me when we're having a conversation," he said.

She blinked at him. "The conversation was over."

"Because you turned your back on me," Murphy argued. "It's beyond passive aggressive. It's rude—and you're better than that."

"Rude?" Her temper sparked and she pushed herself up on one elbow, her other hand holding the sheet to her chest. "What am I supposed to do, Murph? What's *not* rude? Wait until *you* decide that the conversation is over?"

"You could say, *I'd like to end the conversation.* That gives *me* an option to say, *well, I've got something else to add.*"

"I'd like to end this conversation," she said from between clenched teeth.

"I've got something else to add," he shot back.

Hannah looked at him, widening her eyes as she shook her head slightly, her expression a very impatient *go on.*

Problem was, he wasn't quite sure exactly how to say this . . .

"I just wanted to, um," he cleared his throat, "point out that I'm, you know, clean. Now. And yeah, it's now—a different now. But it's definitely . . . now?"

Hannah was silent. She just looked at him. And looked at him. Finally, she said, "Was that, like, a really *lame* way of saying that you still want to have sex with me?"

"I didn't think it was *that* lame," Murphy defended himself.

"So . . . Your answer would be *yes*?"

"Yes." He nodded.

She narrowed her eyes and got defensive. "It's not because you're feeling sorry for me, is it? Because if—"

"No," he said. "Jesus, Han, if I'm feeling sorry for anyone here, it's me. Because I blew it. You were right—I got too much inside my head. I took too long—and I . . . made you feel bad again. Not to mention totally killing the mood."

Hannah sat up, letting the covers fall away from her bare breasts. She'd fallen asleep with wet hair, and it stood straight up, charmingly, in places. Not that Murphy was looking at her hair.

"Mood back?" she asked.

She was beautiful—and self-conscious, despite the snappy comeback. Murph dragged his gaze back up to her eyes. "Miraculously jump-started," he agreed as he reached for her.

She melted into his arms as he lost the towel and slipped into bed beside her. She was smooth and cool beneath his hands, against his body, her hands sliding down his back, her legs intertwined with his as he kissed her, as she kissed him.

And he understood completely why *clean* had been on her wish list.

Along with *slow*, which he was pretty sure he was going to fail to deliver. Particularly when she opened her legs, cradling him exactly where he wanted to be. And especially when she reached between them to find him and guide him . . .

"Han," he said, pulling away from her kisses to look down at her.

She held his gaze as she shifted her hips, pushing him even more deeply inside of her.

"Hahhh," he said. "Cahhh."

She laughed up at him, as she moved beneath him—no small feat, considering he was so much taller and broader than she was. "I have no clue what you just said."

"Condom," he managed, trying to speak clearly, which was stupid because, Jesus, the last thing he wanted was to stop what they were doing. "Do we need one?"

She was on the pill—she'd told him that when he'd wondered what she was taking, every day at breakfast. It was to regulate her periods, which maybe wasn't the same thing as birth control. But, "We're good," she told him now.

Good was such a massive understatement. It was so beyond good, it hurt, and Murphy had to close his eyes and even put his head down to hide his face. He had to have been crushing her, but she clung to him, pulling him even closer, straining, her fingers in his hair, her thighs taut against him.

Slow. She wanted slow, but he couldn't remember what the word meant, as he moved on top of her, inside of her. There was only Hannah and pleasure—which, right now, were one and the same thing.

"Murph," she breathed into his ear. "God . . . Don't . . . stop . . ."

Stop was somewhere out there with *slow*—not in his current two-word vocabulary—but he knew enough to recognize that *stop* combined with *don't* was a good thing, that he could quit worrying about what he wasn't doing and focus on what he was, and just . . . feel.

Just be.

Just feel . . . good . . .

Not angry, not sorrowful, not hopeless, not lost.

And, dear sweet Jesus, not, not, *not* alone.

"Hannah," he said, even though he knew she couldn't hear him, couldn't possibly read his lips, with his mouth against her throat. "God, I need you so much . . ."

She came, almost as if she'd heard him, as if she knew from the tightness in his voice that he was seconds from his own release.

And Murphy remembered, with a sudden sharp clarity. Hannah.

Beneath him, just like this, her legs locked around him, coming completely undone. It was as sexy now as it had been then, and he surrendered the last of his tenuous control, letting himself crash into her even as she unraveled, and . . . *God.*

It was unbelievably good.

As they lay there, together, gasping for air, Murphy could feel Hannah's heart beating. He could feel his, too. Pounding. Triple time.

He was okay.

He was.

Or he would've been—if Hannah hadn't started to cry.

Las Vegas, Nevada

The Happy Ending Wedding Chapel rented wedding gowns.

They also had locker rooms where the brides and grooms could shower off the dirt from the road before they took this monumental step toward the rest of their lives.

Or toward the rest of their next three months.

Lopez's words rang in Izzy's head as he made sure his rows of ribbons were neatly lined up on the left breast of his dress uniform.

He'd forgotten to pack socks, but that was no big. It wasn't as if he'd never gone sockless before.

You're supposed to be in love. Both of you.

"That's crazy," Izzy answered Lopez now, as he stared at himself in the mirror. "I'm not in love with her."

Are you sure about that, man? Because you weren't in love with Tracy, and all she did was whisper the word relationship *and you were running for the next county. Why should this girl be different?*

That was a no-brainer. Eden was pregnant.

So are 750,000 unwed fifteen- to nineteen-year-olds across America. You're not marrying them, dickweed.

"You're making that number up," Izzy scoffed.

I read it online. While I was researching the myriad of programs available for single mothers in the state of California alone. You want to spend time with this girl, Zanella? You don't have to marry her. Help get her into a program. Then, you know, date her.

"You're not here," Izzy told the imaginary Lopez in his head. Which meant that Izzy was the one who made that stupid number up. And he damn well knew exactly what *he* meant when he used the word *date.*

You really think, with her living in your one-bedroom apartment, that you're going to be able to keep your hands offa her? Talk about deluded . . .

"Shut the fuck up," Izzy said.

"Excuse me, sir?"

Oops. The little bald man in the tuxedo—the guy who'd taken Izzy's credit card after he'd ordered the deluxe package: wedding, gown rental, photo of the happy couple and custom prenup—had beamed himself into the locker room, inches from Izzy's elbow. There was no other way Izzy wouldn't have heard him come in.

Either that, or this wedding thing was far more distracting than he'd thought.

"Sorry, I wasn't talking to you," Izzy told him.

The man delicately cleared his throat. He had a fake English accent that didn't work well with his Elmer Fudd face. "Sir, if you'll just—"

"Whoa. Stop. I'm not an officer."

The man blinked at him through his impossibly thick eyeglasses. "I'm sorry, sir—"

"I'm enlisted," Izzy explained.

"I address all of the gentlemen who come to this establishment as *sir*," Fudd told him, pushing his glasses up his nose for punctuation. "The lady awaits you. Sir. If you'll step this way . . . ?"

Izzy made sure the locker where he'd stashed his street clothes was secure, then followed Elmer out into the hallway.

What are you *doing*? What are you *doing*? Their feet on the gleamingly polished floor tapped out a rhythm that bounced around inside Izzy's head, along with a hundred fragmented lyrics from a hundred different songs.

Going to the chapel . . .

Won't you marry me, Bill . . .

Marry me and I'll be there, be there . . .

I'm getting married in the morning. Ding dong the bells are gonna chime . . .

I'm not talking 'bout moving in . . .

Okay, where the fuck did *that* come from? The let's-screw-because-it's-1976 soft-rock masterpiece from England Dan and John Ford Coley didn't fit with the rest of the soundtrack in his head. *There's a cold wind blowing the stars around . . .* The song was doubly preposterous—astronomy-wise. No wind—no matter how cold—could actually blow stars around, although, clearly, some guys would tell a girl anything to get some. And that included pretending to be from England.

Dude was from, like, Texas. He went on to be a country singer in the 1980s and what was Izzy doing thinking about England freaking Dan Seals when he was about to walk into a room and marry a girl who, in eighteen short years, had managed to piss off her stepfather, cut herself off from her mother, alienate her older brother, survive Hurricane Katrina and the FEMA debacle, run away from home a half dozen or so times, hook up with an asshole who thought working for a drug lord was a good career choice, and get pregnant as the result of being tranked by that same evil drug lord. Oh, and maybe even have a sex video released onto the Internet.

It was quite the résumé.

Of course, Eden had also graduated from high school against all odds, managed to support herself for six months in Germany, and didn't hold Pinkie responsible for his sperm donor's odious sins.

And her smile . . .

Her smile made Izzy want to be her hero.

It was stupid. And he knew it. Which made him doubly stupid.

A girl with a history like Eden's didn't believe in heroes. Which was why she was still waiting for him to give her the signal that it was finally okay for them to have sex, so she could start paying him back for his kindness.

And when he dug down, way down deep inside, he knew that this marriage ceremony was his golden ticket. It was just a silly ritual—Lopez's holy sacrament be damned. And okay, if there was a hell, he was probably going there for thinking that. But silly or holy, there was definitely a switch in Izzy's head that was going to be flipped when he married this girl today.

He could pretend that it wouldn't happen, that he was going to take her home to his apartment—that was his plan, to drive back to San Diego tonight—and *not* have sex with her.

But way down deep, he knew that being married was going to do it. It would make it okay. And he would rationalize that she wanted to—and who was he to deprive her of their newly wedded bliss?

Only then? She would know that she had been right—that Izzy was just like every other man she'd ever met—that beneath his kindness, that at the bottom of his generosity lay his throbbing, engorged motivation. And the trust they were slowly building between them would go back to zero. Or maybe negative twenty.

But she would dutifully climb into bed with him every night, and rock his world.

Because she felt that she had to.

Elmer Fudd opened the door to one of the rooms off the hallway with a flourish.

"Eden, look, we've got to—" Izzy walked in and stopped.

Eden wasn't in there.

Fudd perceived a need for more of his faux-English-accented yapping. "This way, sir. The groom waits at the altar while the bride processes in."

While there was a red carpet laid out down the aisle between rows of chairs, they had no guests. Zero. Not Danny, which was not unexpected. But not even Eden's mother and little brother, which was beyond sad. "Isn't it going to seem kind of, well, pathetic . . . ? To process in an empty room, without—"

Fudd interrupted, taking him by the arm and leading him toward the altar. "Brides *like* to process, sir."

"Yeah, but here's the thing, Elmer." Izzy took back his elbow. "I've kind of gotta talk to her first."

"May I remind you, sir, that your payment was nonrefundable."

Izzy headed back toward the hall. "Where is she?"

"We've already spent considerable time drawing up the prenuptial agreement," Fudd continued, following. "And of course, there's the rental of the gown."

And there, indeed, was the gown—with Eden inside of it. She was coming down the hall, toward them, with someone who had to be Mrs. Fudd carrying her train.

Still, Eden was the one who stopped short. "You look amazing," she told Izzy.

"It's the uniform," he said. "It makes everyone . . . look . . ." Talk about amazing. Her hair was up, pulled almost severely back, with just a few strands to soften the effect. It accentuated the perfection of Eden's face, and made her big brown eyes seem even larger.

She smiled at him almost shyly. "I wore makeup," she said. "Since you said . . ."

"You look beautiful," Izzy told her.

The dress itself somehow managed to draw attention away from her pregnant belly. Somehow? It was all thanks to the plunging neckline, which framed her shoulders, her delicate collarbone, her graceful neck, and the full, smooth tops of her breasts.

"I feel like a princess," she said. "Marrying a prince."

"I'm no prince, Eed," he told her.

"Well, I'm not a princess either, so . . ."

"Smile, sir." Elmer Fudd conjured a camera out of thin air, and Izzy automatically stepped closer to Eden. She took his elbow, the softness of her breast grazing his arm, and the camera flashed.

"Wait," Eden said. "Nipple check—no, it's okay—I'm good."

What? Izzy looked down and . . . Yeah, the dress was definitely a costume malfunction waiting to happen. God help him.

"Can we get an extra picture to send to my mother?" she asked.

Her mother.

Eden had told Izzy that her mother wasn't able to stand up to her stepfather and, because of that, even though they lived a mere ten minutes away from the wedding chapel, she and Eden's little brother Ben would not attend. When Izzy had made noise about how spineless that was, she hadn't defended her mother. But she told him that it wasn't as if she were surprised. "It's always been that way," she'd matter-of-factly said and changed the subject.

But now she was looking at him as if the ultimate wedding gift would be this extra photograph, of Eden and Izzy—with Eden in her rented fairy-princess dress. For her spineless mother.

"Unless it's too expensive," she quickly added, because he hadn't said yes fast enough. "I can always make a photocopy at Kinko's."

They'd stopped at a jewelers when they'd gotten into town, and Eden had picked out the plainest, simplest, least expensive, slender gold band for her wedding ring. She'd also refused to trade Manbearpig for a real engagement ring, agreeing only under severe pressure to let him buy her a ring guard so it would stay on her finger without all that sticky tape.

And she'd already picked out the location of their wedding dinner—a restaurant that served an all-you-can-eat buffet for $5.95. It had, she'd told him earnestly, a really great salad bar, too.

"An extra photo's not too expensive," Izzy told Eden now.

"Are you sure?" she asked—she was surely picking up how totally freaked out he was.

"Yes," he said, even though he was sure of only one thing—that he was completely screwed. He was going to do this, because no way could he blindside her by changing his mind at this late hour. He was going to do this, he was going to take her home—and he was going to lose her.

Elmer was at his elbow again. "Shall we, sir?"

"You're supposed to wait down there." Eden gestured into the room with her bouquet of fake flowers. "I'm supposed to process, although I have to warn you, I can't move too fast. I don't think popping a boob is what they mean by 'making an entrance.'"

Izzy laughed despite himself. "It certainly puts the *yes* in process."

Eden laughed, too, but her smile faded into an expression far more serious and extremely sincere. "Thank you," she said again, reaching out to squeeze his hand. "For all of this. It's really . . . lovely."

Izzy let Elmer pull him back, as Mrs. Fudd hit a remote control and music started to play. It was the standard wedding fanfare—thundering and majestic organ music—with Bugs Bunny singing the classic made-up words. *Here comes the bride, all dressed in white.*

Out in the hall, Eden started to laugh. "Did you pick this music?" she asked.

Izzy nodded. He'd figured, since they were going with a traditional white gown . . .

Eden grinned at him, and gave him a thumbs-up before pulling her veil down over her face and, chastely holding her bouquet atop her prominent baby bump, she processed quite ceremoniously down the red carpet.

SACRAMENTO, CALIFORNIA

Steve and Paul had the crappiest selection of tea.

It was all Sleepytime and Peaceful Slumber. Where was the Triple Caffeine Punch-in-the-Face or Heart Palpitation Rage Inducer?

Hannah settled on a plain old green/black mix, heating a mug of water in the microwave before she realized the tea was decaffeinated.

Which was just swell.

She brewed it and sipped it anyway, looking around the cozy room. Farmhouse-style wood-slab table, rustic Mexican tile on the floor, refrigerator covered in magnets and photographs, pots and pans hanging from the ceiling. Despite the transformation of the chaos room, nothing had changed in this kitchen in years.

In fact, the last time she'd been here was with Angelina. Before the wedding. Murphy was out of the country, on some Troubleshooter assignment, and she and Angel had come to Sacramento for a Mary J. Blige concert.

Paul had found out they were in town, and talked them into coming over for dinner and to see Steve's latest version of the stank-mobile, which was fascinating, sure, but nauseating to ride in for more than ten minutes.

But they'd taken the obligatory spin around the block, and then come up here for a beer while Steve showered off the day's grease—which had an oniony bouquet, having no doubt deep-fried Vidalia rings at some local restaurant in its previous life.

They'd sat right at this kitchen table and she and Paul had entertained Angelina with Murphy stories while he cooked dinner. Remember the time when Murph lit his tent on fire, but didn't know it? Remember the time Murph entered the open mic night at the Alaskan bar—and got a standing O for being able to burp the entire alphabet? Remember when that asshole Bernie broke his leg while hiking up to Mendenhall glacier, and Murph carried him all the way back—fifteen miles—to the cars? Remember when Murph decided he needed to go on a vision quest, because so many tourists thought he was an Inuit shaman—which was totally Pat's fault, because he was the one who'd told them that? Remember when Murph convinced Paul that Hannah was studying to be an opera singer and Paul got her a gig singing the "Star Spangled Banner" at a minor league baseball game—and *she'd* gotten a standing ovation?

Remember when Murphy laughed all the time?

All the time.

God, how Hannah had adored him—even though he saw her only as a friend. Even as he prepared for his wedding to *her* best friend.

Remember how badly she'd wanted him to kiss her the way he'd kissed Angelina, to hold her, to make love to *her*?

Be careful what you wish for.

Despite the fact that Hannah had started to cry, she and Murphy hadn't talked at all after they'd had sex. And she had to be honest with herself—what they'd done in that bed was have sex, not make love. Still, Murph had held her close afterward, gently stroking her hair, until they'd both fallen asleep.

Hannah'd woken up first. She'd taken another shower, and when she came out, Murph was already out of bed and in the master bathroom.

Where he still was now.

Hannah ran water in the kitchen sink, washing out her mug and setting it in the drying rack. God, her ankle hurt like a bitch. Cleverly, she'd chosen sex over icing it and would no doubt pay for it.

For the rest of her life.

Because, God, all she could think about was how stupid she had been, to get out of that bed. If she hadn't, they might still be there right now, doing it again, and keeping the harsh reality of the world at bay.

There was a towel hanging off the refrigerator door, and Hannah grabbed it to dry her hands—and came face-to-face with a photo.

It was one of many—most were of Steve's nieces and nephews with an occasional beefcake shot of former Marine Paul without his shirt—stuck to the fridge.

But Hannah was in this one, her smile only slightly stiff as she stood next to Murphy. Who had his arm around Angelina.

Murphy touched Hannah's shoulder and she jumped about a mile— he'd come into the kitchen and was standing right behind her.

Jeez-us.

"You scared me."

"Sorry." He signed it as well as said it.

And there they stood. Considerably less at ease than they'd been before his dingle had tangoed in her cha-cha. As Hannah's grandma would have said. Although she never would have used all three ridiculous euphemisms in the same sentence.

"You want some tea?" she asked, exactly as Murph, too, spoke. "I found a hypnotist who's willing to see me today."

"No, thank you," he added, as she asked, "When?"

"Three o'clock."

"That late?" she asked, and he pointed to the clock on the microwave. It was almost 2:30 now.

"We slept for a while," he said.

"I was tired," she said.

"Me, too."

"Oh, my God," Hannah said, "we're in the freaking twilight zone. Can we please just look each other in the eye and acknowledge that what we had was really great sex?" But then she had to ask. "That *was* great sex, wasn't it?"

He nodded, laughing a little, a fleeting ghost of Murphy from the past. "Yeah, it was, you know, pretty solidly in the *great* column for me, too." But he still couldn't meet her eyes more than briefly, instead glancing over at the fridge.

And that photo of Angelina.

"I would trade all the great sex in the world," Hannah told him, "every second of it—to have her walk in that door."

"I know," Murphy said with another smile that, God, made him look so sad. "But . . ." He finally held her gaze. "She's not coming back, Han."

Hannah nodded, blinking back a rush of tears, turning away to hide it. Or maybe she was trying to hide all of the other emotions that surely shone in her eyes. How could she miss Angelina so much—while so desperately wanting Murphy to touch her again?

He tapped her arm to get her attention, but immediately took his hand away. "Nobody betrayed anybody this morning," he said. "I don't feel that way, so you shouldn't either. And Angelina? If she feels anything at all, she's probably glad we've still got each other, that we don't have to be alone."

Murphy reached out and touched the edge of that photograph as he leaned forward to really look at it, and Hannah braced herself. But he didn't look upset. He didn't look anything. He just . . . was.

"This was taken right before we left for the honeymoon," he realized.

Hannah nodded. She remembered. She'd made the arrangements for a car and driver to take Murphy and Angelina to the airport immediately after the reception. She knew going in that she wouldn't be able to do it herself, because her plan for the day was to drink until she dropped.

Celebrating. Yee-hah.

Murphy leaned in to look even more closely at the picture. "You're, like, totally shit-faced."

He was looking at *her*? "Yeah, well, so were you, bwee."

But Murphy shook his head. "No," he said. "I wasn't. I didn't want to lose the day, you know? I wanted to be able to remember it. Angel and I got a bottle of nonalcoholic champagne—which really sucked, so we each had a half a glass of the real deal—to toast with. But that was it. We were both present and accounted for." He gazed back at the picture. "Look at me. I have no idea what's coming."

"It's better that way, don't you think?" Hannah said.

"I guess." He touched the photo again, as if smoothing down his own slightly rumpled shirt. "If you'd asked this me about the future, I would've talked about saving up to buy a house, about approaching Tommy at Troubleshooters about an idea he had to open another office. I was pushing for

Seattle—Ang and I figured we'd be able to talk you into moving up there. She really wanted to live near you. I did, too." He nodded at her surprise, glancing at the picture again. "We talked about kids, too. Did we want two or maybe three or . . ." He exhaled hard. "Then everything changed in a heartbeat. Back then I would've been sure we'd've had a baby by now. Maybe a condo. A solid job with people I admire and respect . . . Instead?" He laughed again. "I have nothing."

Hannah nodded. Nothing. Right. "We should get going. We don't want to be late."

Murphy caught her arm. "That came out wrong."

"It's okay," she said.

"No, it's not—"

Her temper sparked and she pushed him, hard, both hands against his chest, which was about as effective as trying to knock over a brick wall. "Fuck you, Murphy! Where do you get off on deciding what's okay for me and what's not? I'm telling you: It's. Okay. I have *no* misconceptions about what we just did—what it means." Nothing. It meant nothing.

"It came out wrong," he said again. "What I meant was—"

Hannah turned away. "You don't need to explain."

Murphy grabbed her and spun her to face him. "Don't turn your back on me!"

He was mad at *her*? "This conversation is *over*." She jammed her eyes shut, which was childish, but no way was she going to stand patiently as he made excuses. "I don't *want* you to explain." She struggled to get free—but he was holding her too tightly. "Let *go* of me! Or, God, bend me over the kitchen table and give it to me again! *That's* what I want from you—not your bullshit excuses, and certainly not some lame-ass make-me-feel-better lies!"

"Hannah—"

She kissed him, hard, on the mouth, reaching between them to find him, already heavy, nearly completely hard. "You want to make me feel better?" she breathed as she kissed him again, as he kissed her back as if he, too, couldn't bear to stand here, so close, without touching her. As if he wanted her again, as much as she wanted him. Blood roared through her veins, as she unbuckled his belt and unbuttoned his pants, reaching into his boxers to touch him, stroke him. "Then come on. Make me feel better. God, it felt so good, Murph, and I just want to feel good. I just want—"

He roughly spun her around, her back to his front, pushing her forcefully down. Her hands smacked the bare surface of the kitchen table as she caught herself, as he jerked her pants down her legs.

Hannah didn't have time to kick off her boots. With her jeans around her ankles, she could barely spread her knees, but that didn't stop Murphy from ramming himself, hard, inside of her.

"Yes," she gasped, "God, yes . . ."

She surrendered her full body weight to the table, trying to open herself without hurting her goddamn ankle, wanting more, *more* even as he thrust himself, long and thick, inside of her again and again and again and again.

"Please," she breathed, not sure exactly what she was asking for, but desperate to get it.

And Murphy wrapped his arms around her, holding her up off the table, so that her body molded against his, so he could penetrate her even more deeply—yes! He cupped her breast with one hand as, with the other, he reached to touch her. *Yessss* . . .

She could feel his breath, hot and fast, against the side of her face, and she tipped her head back to touch her cheek to his. He'd shaved during his second shower, just minutes ago, and his face was sleek and smooth. She felt his arms tighten around her, felt the vibration in his body as he shouted words or sounds she couldn't hear, but it was okay, because she knew that he was coming. She knew she'd made him feel unbelievably good, even if just for this brief moment in time.

And Hannah let go. The noise in her head became music as the world disappeared in an explosion of light and sensation—of pleasure so intense that she, too, felt herself cry out.

But it ended too soon.

It ended, and there they were, breathing hard, collapsed across the kitchen table, with Murphy supporting himself on an elbow and a hand as he kept himself from completely crushing her.

Hannah kept her eyes closed and just breathed. In and out. Breathe. Don't cry again, like a total idiot. Just breathe.

Murphy finally moved, pushing himself off of the table, pulling out from inside of her.

She let him help her up, finally opening her eyes. She could tell from the way his hand was still on her arm that he was waiting for eye contact, so she gave it to him.

"Your ankle okay?" he asked, his eyes warm with concern and chagrin and too many other emotions she didn't want to attempt to identify.

"It's fine," she told him, focusing on pulling up her jeans, so that he couldn't say anything more.

Still, he held on to her, as if helping to steady her. And sure enough, when she glanced at him, he said, "Han—"

"That made me feel better," she told Murphy as, yes, she turned her back on him as she headed for the bathroom to get cleaned up, raising her voice so that he could hear her as she limped away. "If there's ever any doubt in your mind, just do more of that, okay?"

CHAPTER
FIFTEEN

"Let's talk about Murphy, about the day Angelina was shot."

"I wasn't there," Dave told Dr. Heissman. "I didn't arrive at the scene until long after the ambulance was gone."

He'd wanted to have this meeting over coffee, in the motel restaurant, but she'd insisted that they talk somewhere more private. Dave knew that the privacy was intended to make him feel comfortable. Emotionally secure. He could weep uncontrollably if need be, sobbing out the pitiful story of his pathetic existence.

Never gonna happen, Doc.

But here they sat, in Sophia's motel room, in two absurdly uncomfortable chairs over by the window.

Sophia's suitcase was on the bed, zipped up and ready to go. The room smelled like her, plus Dave could see her through that grimy window, sitting in the shade at the edge of the parking lot, legs curled beneath her, reading a book.

Way to make him super-comfortable, Dr. H.

Or not, he realized suddenly. It was far more likely that she'd chosen to talk here because she knew he would find it unsettling.

Crafty.

"That must've been difficult," Dr. Heissman told him, with her wise-woman sincerity ringing in her carefully modulated voice. "*Not* being there. Hearing about it and wondering, if you *had* been there, would that have made a difference."

"I didn't wonder that," Dave told her. And he hadn't. At least not actively. "Besides, I wasn't exactly invited."

She nodded and made a note on her pad.

Great.

"I don't have a problem with not being invited to social occasions," Dave told her. "Let's not waste our time going there."

The doctor looked up at him, her eyes brightly attentive through the lenses of her glasses. "Sophia was invited," she pointed out, "by Kelly Paoletti, who was trying to set her up with one of Tom's friends."

Dave sat and looked at her, and she just gazed back at him.

"If that was a question," he finally said, "I missed the part that was, you know, the question?"

She laughed. She really did have a lovely, sweet smile. "Have Tom or Kelly ever tried to set *you* up with one of their friends?"

"Navy SEALs aren't exactly my type." Speaking of Navy SEALs, out the window, across the parking lot, Danny-the-relentless-asshole Gillman had been unable to leave Sophia alone with her book. He stood talking to her now, with that stupidly macho yet typical-SEAL, deck-of-the-SWCC-boat, legs-spread stance.

"Have they ever tried to set you up with one of their non-SEAL friends," Dr. Heissman clarified.

"No," he said as he dragged his gaze back to the doctor. "They haven't. Why don't you ask me what you really want to ask me—although how it pertains to Vinh Murphy, I don't have a clue."

She tapped the eraser end of her pencil against her pad as she gazed at him. "What is it that you think I want to ask you?"

"Why don't you ask it, and we'll see if I'm right?" Across the parking lot, Dan Gillman sat down in the grass, next to Sophia, as she nodded, listening to him talk. Gillman's tall, dark, and handsome was a perfect complement to Sophia's delicate china-doll beauty. Anyone passing by would remark, *What an outrageously attractive young couple*. Dave felt his blood pressure start to rise.

"You're used to being right, aren't you, Dave?"

"I'd prefer it if you called me Dr. Malkoff," he said. "Dr. Heissman."

She smiled with what looked like genuine amusement as she tapped her pad again. "I'd expected this kind of . . . vaguely hostile evasiveness from Lawrence Decker," she said, "but not from you."

Dave laughed and started to applaud. "You *are* crafty. Way to twist me even tighter. Compare me to Decker. *Very* nice."

"Is that really what you think this is?" she leaned forward to ask, her notepad and pencil momentarily forgotten. "Me trying to twist you up?"

"Absolutely," he said. "I've done interrogations, and you're obviously a pro. Not as good as I am, but . . . Top notch, ma'am."

"I assure you, this is not an interrogation," Dr. Heissman said. She gestured to the room around them. "Certainly not an enhanced one. No waterboard."

"Not funny." Outside, Sophia laughed at something Danny said.

"You're right, torture's extremely not funny. I apologize. Let me try again: This conversation we're having is not meant to bring you pain."

"And yet . . ." Dave said.

"Why don't you like being compared to Decker?" she asked, jumping right back into it.

"Was that what you were doing?" he countered. "Comparing me to Deck? Or not-so-gently reminding me that I'm perceived to be almost his total opposite?"

"Decker's a mess," she told him.

Dave sat back in his seat, surprised. "Are you really allowed to tell me that?"

"It's not an official diagnosis," she said. "It's an observation. Do you disagree?"

"No. In fact, I came here today to give you information that I know he'd never tell you himself," Dave said. "I happen to believe he's a *complete* mess, and very much in need of help."

"Then I would think you'd appreciate being perceived as 'almost his total opposite,' " she said, quoting his own words. "Assuming that's true."

"It is," Dave said. "Along with the fact that his being a complete mess adds to his allure." Outside the window, Danny leaned over and kissed Sophia—chastely, on the cheek. That was new.

"Not to your boss," the doctor said, as Sophia smiled up at Dan, who stood and bade her farewell. That was new, too.

Sophia returned to her book, as Dan went to Lopez's little hybrid and pretended to clear trash from the backseat. He was really just looking for a reason to linger there in the parking lot, so he could sneak looks at Sophia.

Who really did look quite lovely, with her blond hair shining in the dappled afternoon sunlight.

"I'm talking about . . . among women," Dave said.

"Ah," Dr. Heissman said. "Women. And . . . *women* don't find you alluring?"

Enough. "No," Dave answered. "She doesn't. *She* being Sophia. Let's cut the crap. It's not like you don't know. I'm . . . infatuated with Sophia, who finds me about as alluring as a ham sandwich."

"Hah," Dr. Heissman said. "It only took me twelve minutes to break you."

Dave looked at her.

"I'm kidding," she said. "That was another inappropriate interrogation joke. If you were me, Dave, what would you write on my notepad right now?"

"Patient has a firm grasp of reality," he answered.

"Maybe a little too firm," she said. "Reality can be fluid. It can change."

"The way it changed for Murphy," he asked, "when Angelina died?" Those three words, *when Angelina died* still made his throat feel tight, made the backs of his eyelids ache.

"That's terrifying, isn't it?" she agreed quietly. "How quickly tragedy can strike? Especially for a man of science like yourself. You know what you know, and you know that you're right, except a madman pulls the trigger on a rifle and, boom, your reality is instantly altered. But if it can happen with tragedy, with bad things, doesn't it make sense that it can also happen with good?"

He sat there, silent.

"But when something like Angelina's murder happens," the doctor told him, "it's human nature to assume a bunker mentality. Let's shore up our defenses and put up our guard so that when something like this happens again—when, not if—we won't be blindsided. Problem is, we become so risk averse, we cut ourselves off from the potentially dangerous things that could bring great happiness and joy. We stop taking chances, and without those sometimes risky chances, there's no way we can win big. Our best case scenario becomes losing not *too* badly. *At least no one died* becomes our mantra. Yes, we're trapped here in this prison that we've made, where we can't possibly be happy, but at least we're not devastated by our loss and our grief."

"You think I don't take chances," Dave said.

"Do you?"

"With my career?" he countered. "All the time."

"With your personal life," she said.

Dave was silent, and she added, not unkindly, "Do you even have a personal life?"

"Of course I do," he said, a tad defensively. "I have parents. I visit them, every year. I . . . read. Quite a lot. I . . . ."

She sat there, waiting for him to continue.

"It's personal," he said. "That's why it's called a personal life."

"Girlfriend?" she asked.

He shot her a look.

"Maybe if you took more chances," she said, "your suitcase would be on that bed, next to Sophia's."

"I doubt it," Dave said testily. "I'm not enough of a mess."

"I'm not so sure about that," Dr. Heissman said. She took a file from the briefcase that was sitting on the floor beside her chair. She opened it, glanced through it, then said, "Let's talk a bit about Anise Turiano, aka Kathy Grogan."

Oh, *Christ* . . .

"No," Dave said flatly. "I'm here to talk to you about Decker. About an incident that happened, with Sophia, while they both were under a great deal of stress in—"

"Kazbekistan," she finished for him. "I know all about it."

"From Sophia?" Dave said. "Because Decker's version of the story is different." He corrected himself. "The facts are the same. It's the interpretations of those facts that are miles apart. Decker calls it rape, Sophia calls it just another blow job."

Dr. Heissman still held what had to be Dave's Personal Hell file on her lap, but she'd closed it.

So Dave kept going. "Sophia thought Decker was a mercenary who would tie her up and drag her back to some very bad men who wanted to cut off her head. Decker thought Sophia was an agent for those same bad people, and that her knowledge of his presence would put his entire team—myself included—into serious danger. Sophia did what she did, and Decker, possibly to see if she'd reveal any helpful information, let her. But what she revealed was that she was terrified enough to try to kill him.

"As an impartial third party—" He broke off because of the look she gave him. "I *was* impartial at the time. I remember Deck coming back to the house where the team was staying and I'd never seen him that upset—and it wasn't because he'd almost just died. But okay. Obviously, everything worked out. Everyone's true identity was revealed, apologies were made. Decker not only finds Sophia again, but he saves her life, and she turns around and helps save ours.

"Years pass, during which he loans her a substantial sum of money and he helps her get a job at Troubleshooters. Sophia works hard to heal from the traumas of the past. She's amazing, by the way. And I'm not the only one who believes that. But somewhere down the line, she fancies herself in love with Decker—who can barely look at her without flinching.

"It's not because he thinks that *she* thinks he took advantage of her or raped her or whatever he wants to call it to compound his guilt. She's made it very clear that she forgave him completely—*and* that she forgave herself, too.

"No," Dave continued. "In my opinion, the bottom line is that Decker let himself get, well, *serviced* by a woman that he thought was a prostitute. I believe that's really what his guilt is about. It doesn't matter who Sophia really was. It doesn't even matter to Deck that her goal at that moment was to kill him. He can't see past the fact that he didn't stop a whore—his perception in the moment, true or not—from unzipping his pants.

"He had a moment of weakness and he made an extremely human mistake. You accused me earlier of wanting always to be right. That's absolutely correct. But when I'm wrong—the few times it's happened—and yes, that was a joke, Doctor. When I'm wrong, I tend to be exceedingly wrong, and it's happened far more than a few times, but, here's the thing? I admit it and move on.

"Decker hasn't been able to do that. He's a good man. An honorable man, with extremely high morals and principles—who now knows the truth about himself. That when push came to shove, he went for the cheap sex. And Sophia's his constant reminder. His hair shirt, if you will. For some completely screwed up reason, he doesn't *want* to forgive himself. He wants to wallow in his sins."

Dave signaled that he was finished by crossing his arms and sitting back in his chair, but Dr. Heissman didn't say anything. She just looked at him.

"It must be hard for you," she said when she finally spoke. "Loving Decker so much."

Dave laughed. "Oh, please," he said.

"I'm not suggesting that you're gay," she countered. "There are all types of love besides the romantic, sexual kind, and you know it. What I probably should have said was *It must be hard for you, loving them both so much.* Wanting them to be happy."

He nodded. "Yes," he admitted. "That's been very hard."

"What about you, Dave?" the doctor asked. "When do you get to be happy?"

Interesting question. Dave looked out the window at Sophia, who turned the page in her book. But then she looked up, as if startled.

A car had pulled into the parking lot and the driver practically stood on the brakes. It finished squealing to a stop and a woman got out from behind the wheel and slammed the door shut.

"I am done," she shouted, loudly enough for Dave and Dr. Heissman to hear her through the window. "I am *done* with your *bullshit!*"

It was Tess Bailey. Dave had never seen her so apoplectic.

Who was she shouting at?

One guess. And yes, James Nash opened the passenger side door of the car and got out. Whatever he said to her over the roof of the car was too soft for Dave to hear, but his body language was an odd mix of apprehension and resignation.

"Excuse me," Dave said to Dr. Heissman. "I think I better . . ."

She nodded, slipping his file back into her briefcase. "Go. I'm right behind you."

SACRAMENTO, CALIFORNIA

Hannah was silent as they left Steve and Paul's apartment, locking the kitchen door behind them.

She was wearing the daypack that she used as a modified handbag, and she secured it on both shoulders as she prepared to hobble her way down the stairs. Her ankle was sore—Murphy knew it. He also knew that she wouldn't complain.

He'd written her a note while she was in the bathroom, trying to explain what he meant by that ill-thought-out *I have nothing*.

Things not to say to a new lover. Especially not one who was an old friend.

He'd handed the note to her, but she'd folded it and jammed it into the zipper pocket of her daypack—an obvious equivalent of her turning her back to him—which pissed him off. But the truth was that even if she had her hearing, he couldn't force her to listen.

So here they were, heading to some hypnotist, with a farfetched hope of unlocking his memories, when in truth he would have preferred going back to bed.

And not just because he was still exhausted. After years without any sex at all, it was suddenly all he wanted, although he definitely preferred it without the tears. It was a little ironic. Han was still in the *I would give anything if . . .* phase of her grieving for Angelina, and *he* had been the one who'd ended up comforting *her* after they'd made love that first time.

As far as what had just happened in the kitchen . . . Murph's brain was still in something of a jumble about that. Although, God knows how he was going to be able to sit and share a meal with Steve and Paul at that table ever again. At least not without smiling.

Of course, now that he was thinking about it, Steve and Paul both smiled a lot in their kitchen. And yeah, now he *really* wasn't going to be able to sit at that table and—

"You coming?" Hannah said, impatience in her voice.

Heh-heh.

The snicker in his head stopped him cold. It had been so long since he'd paid any attention to sexual innuendos—even middle-school-stupid ones.

Hannah, meanwhile, had paused halfway down the stairs, looking back at him over her shoulder, unwilling to put too much space between them.

"Will you please read the note?" he said, as long as he had eye contact. "Please."

She rolled her eyes in frustration, but sat down on the step in order to shrug off her pack and—

Boom!

Gunshot! Jesus, no!

The wood shingle siding of the building splintered—exactly where Hannah had been standing a heartbeat ago. If she hadn't sat down, she would be dead. Or dying.

Yet she looked up, only mildly perplexed and completely unaware—doing exactly as he'd requested, about to dig through her pack for the freaking note he'd written.

"Hannah! No!" Murphy shouted, thundering down the stairs toward her.

Her eyes widened as—

Boom!

Murphy grabbed her and pulled, aware that—God, no!—now there was blood. He couldn't tell where she was hit or how bad it was as he dragged her back up the stairs.

Boom!

Something slapped his leg, but he barely felt it as he kicked open the kitchen door and pushed Hannah inside, kicking it shut again.

He grabbed the phone off the wall and dialed 911, then let it go as he dropped to his knees next to Hannah.

She was conscious and alert and saying something to him, but he couldn't hear her over the roaring in his ears, over the sound of someone screaming.

Her blood was everywhere, on his hands, on her face and he had to find the bullet wound and stop the bleeding, oh Jesus oh God—

Hannah slapped him. Hard. A cracking blow right in the face. And he realized, when it abruptly stopped, that the screaming voice had been his.

"I'm okay," Hannah told him. She had her gun drawn, which was damn good, because although he was mostly back, he was shaking so hard he couldn't've held his own weapon. "How many gunshots?"

"Three." God *damn*, he was going to throw up. "You're bleeding."

"I'm fine," she said. "Just nicked." She twisted slightly, showing him just a flash of her upper left arm. Her shirt was crimson with her blood, so much blood, and he did vomit, right there, on the kitchen floor, in front of the dishwasher. "Vinh, stay with me, bwee. We're all right—we're both all right. How many shooters? What kind of weapon? Could you tell?"

"Just one, a rifle," he said, wiping his mouth with the towel that hung on the refrigerator door. "Maybe. I need to see your arm. I need to . . . make sure . . ."

"You have to focus and listen, Murph," Hannah interrupted him. "Have there been more gunshots?"

He shook his head.

"Are they coming in after us?" she asked. "Up the stairs?"

"I don't think so."

"Could you hear if they tried to come up the front stairs, through the garage?"

Murphy could hear sirens wailing in the distance, coming closer. And closer. He heard a car, tires squealing as it pulled away. "They're leaving. The police are coming."

"Shit," Hannah said. "We have to get out of here, too."

"No," Murphy said, and she looked at him, incredulously. "Han, I called them." He pointed and she looked at the phone hanging off the hook, dangling from the springy, elastic cord. "I *need* to see your arm."

She knew quite well that there'd probably been a half dozen other 911 calls—telling the police there were shots fired in the area. He hadn't needed to stay on the call for the 911 dispatcher to locate him. Not while calling from a landline.

"That's it then?" Hannah asked. "It's over? You're just going to let them take you in? Because if you think—"

He tried shouting at her. "I need to see your arm *now!*"

She turned, heavy on the resentment, finally allowing him to look and—

"That's not a nick, Hannah." He turned her head so that she could see him and said it again. "*Nicks* don't have entry and exit wounds. We're going to the hospital."

She touched the side of his face. "Murph—"

He grabbed her wrist. "Don't fucking argue with me!"

Whatever wildness she saw in his eyes made her back down. She nodded. "All right." But then she kissed him, hard, right on the mouth, vomit-breath and all, and held him tightly for just a moment. "Murphy, God, I'm not ready for this to end." Still, she held out her weapon to him then, moving painfully, unfastened her holster, giving that to him, too. "You better hide this. Yours, too. Under the sink . . ."

As the sirens abruptly silenced, as the police cars pulled into the driveway at the bottom of the stairs, Murphy opened Paul's holding-container of used cooking oil that was under the kitchen sink, and dropped both his and Hannah's holstered weapons in. They disappeared immediately in the murk.

"Police!" one of the officers shouted as Murphy resealed the container.

"Up here!" he shouted back. "Second floor apartment! I made the 911 call. Shots were fired—I've got a retired police officer down—our hands are empty and up! We need medical assistance and an ambulance, right away!"

DALTON, CALIFORNIA

Sophia stood up as Dave came flying out of the motel room where he'd been having a session with Dr. Heissman.

His hair was a mess and he looked about as worn out and weary as she'd ever seen him, but he didn't hesitate. He just ran right up to where Tess Bailey and Jimmy Nash were faced off, across the top of Tess's car.

Their noisy entrance—tires squealing, gravel spraying—had caught the attention of every SEAL still in the area, too. Sophia saw Mark Jenkins on the second floor balcony outside his motel room. He ducked back inside, obviously to give Lindsey a shout. And sure enough, she came running, too, but she slowed as she came down the stairs, where she was joined by Tracy Shapiro.

Jay Lopez was over by Danny Gillman—the pair were staying back, but both were on high alert.

And okay, yes, it was true that Jim Nash was something of a wildcard, but there was no way he'd ever raise a hand to Tess. Never. Sophia could take that fact to the bank and cash it.

Visually, they were an unlikely-looking couple. Nash had a James Bond vibe. Movie star handsome, with a love-child-of-Elvis-and-Pierce-Brosnan face, he exuded danger and intrigue.

Tess, not so much.

Intellectually, though, they were an astonishing match. It was hard to tell which of them was smarter. But emotionally, they were back to dissonance. Tess belonged to the pointblank, straight-shooting, all-cards-on-the-table school, while Nash was a walking enigma.

"Guys." Dave was the only one brave enough to march right up to them. Even Dr. Heissman hung back.

"If you can't trust me," Nash said. "Then maybe—"

Tess cut him off, her voice loud and clear. "Save your breath," she said. "I said I *don't* want to hear it!"

Dave tried again, looking from Nash to Tess and back. "How about we take this inside?"

Nash ignored him, speaking directly to Tess. "I'm not making excuses."

Someone's cell phone started ringing from inside the car—probably Tess's. Nobody moved to answer it.

"Dr. Heissman is here," Dave said. "You can go inside and cool off and sit down with her and—"

"I'm simply stating that I can't tell you what you want to know," Nash continued to implore Tess. "If you don't like it—" He broke off, shaking his head.

"I'll get some coffee," Dave said, as the cell phone abruptly stopped.

"No," Tess ignored Dave, too. "Don't stop there. This I *do* want to hear. If I don't like it, *what*?"

Dave persisted. "Give me your keys. I'll park your car while you—"

"*What*, Jimmy?"

"I thought you were done with my bullshit," Nash said.

"Apparently not," she shot back. "If I don't like it, then *what*?"

"Please," Dave begged. He turned to Nash, taking the taller man's arm. "James . . ."

Nash shook him off. "Then you should just . . . do it. Be done with me," he told Tess. His voice broke, and Sophia's heart twisted. "For christ's sake, Tess, just . . . leave already."

The silence that followed was terrible. Tess looked as if he'd stabbed her in the heart. No one spoke, and even Dave knew better than to try to intervene. In fact, he looked as if he might start to cry.

His cell phone started to ring a jaunty little tune, but he silenced it in his pocket—he didn't even take it out to see who might be calling.

As they all watched, horrified, Tess got into her car. She closed the door and turned the key, but since the engine was already running, it made an awful squealing sound.

"Tess, don't go," Sophia called, unable to stay silent.

Dave, too, couldn't not speak. "You're a fucking idiot," he told Nash, his words even more shocking since he so rarely used that kind of language. But his voice was more sad than angry. "You could've asked me for help."

Nash shook his head. "No," he said. "I couldn't."

But then, instead of driving away, Tess climbed back out from behind the steering wheel. She was crying, but she stood tall. "No," she said to Nash, over the top of her car.

He didn't understand. He had his cell phone out, as if someone were calling *him* now. He checked it and laughed—a short burst of exasperation or despair, Sophia wasn't sure which—but then put it back into his pocket. "No . . . what?"

"No," she said. "I'm not leaving you. You want me to go. That's what you're doing, isn't it? You *want* me to leave you. And I'm saying *no*. No, Jimmy, I'm saying *hell no*! I won't do it."

Nash laughed. "That's crazy. I—"

"It suddenly all makes sense," Tess told him, her eyes blazing. "All the bullshit. You've been *trying* to make me leave you. There's something going on that you can't tell me. Something has you scared. You've been trying to cross my line, to make me say *that's it. I'm done.* But you know what? Look behind you, Jim, because that's where my line is. It moves with you. Do what you will, do what you have to—I'm not going anywhere. I'm staying right here."

Nash was laughing, but Sophia got a sense that it was to keep himself from breaking down and crying.

"I was trying not to hurt you," he said. "You're right, I was . . . It was easier if you left me. I didn't want to have to tell you this, but . . . There's . . . someone else."

Tess stood there, frozen, uncomprehending. Or maybe it was Sophia reflecting her own confusion on the dark-haired woman. Someone else? As in another woman? It didn't make sense. Nash's love for Tess was of epic proportions. Any fool with eyes in his head could see that.

Dave broke the silence. "He's lying," he said flatly.

Nash shot him a vicious look. "Shut up, Dave."

"Why are you lying?" Dave asked. His voice was low, but Sophia could hear him. "Please let me help you."

Nash grabbed Dave by the shirt, pulling him close and speaking right into his ear. Sophia couldn't hear what he said, no one could but Dave. Who turned and looked directly at Sophia, more raw emotion than she'd ever seen in his eyes before Nash pushed him roughly away.

It was then that Tess spoke, her voice ringing, loud and clear. "I don't believe you." Head high, she was glaring at Nash.

"Yeah, well, it's true."

"Introduce me," Tess shot back.

Nash didn't understand.

"Introduce me," Tess said again, crossing her arms. "To her. What's her name? Who is she? I want to meet her."

Nash made a sound that was a cross between laughter and death by choking.

She gestured to her car. "Let's go. Right now. Come on, Jimmy. We'll just drop in on her, say hi."

"No," he managed to spit out.

"Then I'm with Dave. You're lying. And I'm not leaving you." Her voice shook.

Sophia had never seen Nash this upset. He was breathing hard and the expression on his face was terrible. He was moments—she was sure—from total meltdown.

Dave tried again, looking over at Dr. Heissman for help. She stepped forward, clearing her throat. "I think Dave's idea that we come inside and sit down—"

Nash savagely cut her off, his hand out, one finger up, as if warning her not to come closer. "*You* stay the fuck away from me. I don't need your *help*."

"That kind of language isn't necessary." Dave was somehow channeling Decker. All trepidation and uncertainty were gone, and he seemed almost taller and broader. And absolute. "We all agreed to talk to Dr. Heissman. If it's not going to be now, it's going to be later. You can make this worse, James, or you can—"

"I changed my mind," Nash said, his voice harsh, loud. "I'm not talking to her." He spat at her. "Fuck you."

Dr. Heissman didn't so much as flinch, but Tess was aghast. "Jimmy!"

He turned back to her. "And *fuck* you, too, for making this so hard. I'm done, okay? *I'm* done."

He turned and walked away, with long, hurried strides that put him nearly around the side of the motel before anyone could speak, move, breathe.

Tess broke this new, awful silence. "I love you," she called after him, anguish in her voice.

Nash didn't stop, didn't turn around. He just kept walking.

Dave was ready to follow him and try to beat some sense into him. Sophia could see it.

But Tracy had her phone out and open, and she crossed the parking lot now, holding it out toward Dave. "Decker's been trying to reach you," she told him. "The FBI just called. They located Murphy. He's at a hospital in Sacramento, in the ER—with a gunshot wound."

CHAPTER
SIXTEEN

Murphy had been shot, too.

One of the emergency room nurses had noticed that he'd started leaving behind a sneaker-print of blood, and he was now up on the bed next to Hannah's.

They'd been moved into a more private room a few minutes ago—it came with a door that closed. And an armed police guard outside that door. Murphy'd noticed that, too. He nodded when Hannah'd met his gaze.

No doubt the police on the scene had entered their names into the system, and his had come up red-flagged. *Wanted for questioning by the FBI . . .*

"You okay?" Murphy asked her for the twentieth time.

Hannah nodded. Again. "I'm not the one who didn't know I was shot," she pointed out.

"I honestly didn't feel it," he told her, wincing as the doctor cut open the leg of his jeans. "I do now."

It wasn't that much of a surprise that he hadn't felt it—and it wasn't a bullet, it was a ricochet—a piece of wood from the stairs, lodged in his muscular calf. He hadn't felt much of anything because he'd gone a little crazy in the moment.

Hannah could only imagine the awful sense of déjà vu Murphy must've been having. The blood from the bullet that had passed neatly through the fleshy part of her arm had sprayed her face and gotten in her hair. She must've looked as if she'd taken a hit directly to the head.

The way Angelina had.

Murphy's face was still a little red where Hannah had slapped him. She'd needed his ears—needed him to stop shouting. She'd needed him in the here and now, not flung back to that terrible evening, all those years ago.

He'd thrown up again, after they'd gotten to the hospital. And he'd even cried a little, too, holding Hannah so close, she almost had trouble breathing.

Or maybe she was the one who held him that tightly—she wasn't quite sure.

The police had been willing to wait to ask most of their questions— they'd gotten Hannah into an ambulance within moments of their arrival at Steve and Paul's apartment. Murphy'd insisted that he ride with her.

Was the shooting gang related?

That was the question of the hour, asked not just by the police but by the hospital personnel as well. Their concern was understandable. If there was some kind of gangland fatwa going down, they wanted to know about it before it came bursting in through the hospital's automatic doors.

Problem was, it was Murphy whom they looked at sideways, as if, had there actually been gang violence, he was either the target or to blame.

He'd rolled his eyes and shrugged it off, but Hannah was offended for him.

"We'll let the anesthesia take hold before I go digging around in there," the doctor announced before vanishing out the door.

Leaving them alone for the first time since the police burst through Steve and Paul's kitchen door.

"I don't get it," Hannah said. "Why would the Freedom Network follow us?"

Murphy shook his head. "God, I'm sorry, Han," he said. "I thought I made sure they weren't. Following us. I was careful, but . . ."

"It wasn't your fault," she told him.

"Apparently not careful enough," he finished, misery on his face. "I almost got you killed."

"But you didn't," she said. "Instead you saved my life. Let's focus on why they followed us. Not how they did it or whose fault it is that they found us—shit! GPS, Murph. If you didn't see anyone . . ."

"There was no one behind us," Murphy told her again. "No cars. No one to see." He realized what she'd said. "But a GPS tracking device? How . . . ?"

"That crowd in the parking lot."

He stared at her. "The hikers?"

Hannah nodded. "Maybe they weren't really hikers." And if one of them had attached a portable GPS device . . .

Murphy just shook his head in disbelief.

"There was enough time," Hannah persisted. Even moving at highest possible speed, it had taken them close to two hours to get from the fence back to the car. "We set off the alarm back in the compound, everyone's on high alert, right? So Craig Reed sends his Freedom Network minions out to all the parking lots near the popular hiking trails outside the compound—not to stop us—we're armed and dangerous—just to monitor us—to be able to follow us. We fit the description given by the guards who saw us—so the minions-slash-fake-hikers call in to the mothership and let Reed know that the GPS they attached to the white Volkswagen Rabbit with Alaskan plates in lot six is live and running."

"Why?" Murphy said, clearly not buying it. "Those miniature GPS things cost money. We're out of there—we're gone. Why the hell come after us and try to kill us?"

"Maybe it was only meant to be a warning," Hannah theorized. "Shots fired across our figurative bow."

"No," Murphy was positive. "That first shot? Han, you sat down and . . . If you hadn't, that bullet would've been square in your face. I saw where it hit." He looked green, as if he were going to get sick again.

"I'm okay," she reminded him. But, God. She hadn't realized that. If Murphy hadn't written that note—that she *still* hadn't read, because her pathetic, mixed-up feelings—including jealousy of her dead best friend, way to go—were extremely low priority at this point. "So why do they want us dead?"

"Maybe they know something we don't know," Murphy said grimly.

"Such as?"

"Maybe they have proof that I killed Tim Ebersole," he told her. "And now? They probably think you helped me do it, too."

SAN DIEGO, CALIFORNIA

Eden was quiet as she followed Izzy up the stairs to his apartment.

She'd slept most of the long ride home from Las Vegas. Izzy'd turned on the radio—the rental car got XM satellite, which was sweet—and had cruised, flipping back and forth between the sounds of the sixties and the seventies.

They'd actually played *The Night Chicago Died*, which had made him want to wake up Eden, to share it with her. But she was so freaking young, she'd probably never heard the song before and upon listening would stare at him as if he were out of his mind. And he'd have to explain that he only knew it himself because his oldest brother was fifteen years his senior, and it was the song's off-the-chart dork-factor that made it great and . . . nevermind.

And then they'd both sit there, uncomfortably, listening—nah-neh-*nah*, nah-neh-*nah*, neh-neh-*nah*-nah—thinking, *Holy shit, what have I done?*

Instead, he'd let her sleep.

And tried not to think about anything at all.

Knock three times on the ceiling if you want me . . .

Come and get your love . . .

If I fell in love with you, would you promise to be true . . . ?

Baby, baby, try to find, hey hey hey, a little time and I'll make you happy . . .

I don't know where, but she sends me there . . .

Wild thing, you make my heart sing . . .

Baby baby, feels like maybe, things will be alright . . .

Izzy now fumbled the key into the lock as Eden looked around the neatly manicured courtyard.

"It's so quiet here," she whispered.

"The complex has strict rules and restrictions about noise at night," Izzy told her, which was a stupid-ass thing to come out of his mouth. Rules and restrictions? Since when did he aspire to be the world's hall monitor? He pushed the door open and stepped back to let her go in first.

But, "I understand," she said as she went past him. Her hair was still up, and despite the too-large tent of a hand-me-down maternity dress that she was wearing, she managed to look beautiful. She smelled really good, too.

Too good.

Izzy turned on as many lights as he could after he closed the door behind him. Yup, the place was a total cluttered craphole.

But Eden didn't seem to notice. She just stood there, in the middle of his living room, looking as nervous as he felt.

"This is . . . weirder than I thought it would be," she said.

"Yeah," he agreed. "Sorry about the mess."

She glanced around her, then, at his various piles of laundry, at the pizza boxes, the empty bottles of beer, his dive suit dangling from the dining area ceiling fan like a hanging victim, his guitar, which he'd taken to playing again, these past six months, the box of rock-climbing gear that he'd dumped onto the floor in his search—last month—for the right size clip, and, of course, a virtual mountain range of video games.

"If you want," she said, "I'll clean the apartment first thing in the morning."

"We'll clean it up in the morning," he said.

Eden nodded. "Of course. You can show me where everything goes."

That wasn't why he'd said we. What was it with this girl? She was either submissive to the point of creepiness or talking about three-ways with his super-religious friend.

"Do you want something to drink?" he asked, going into the kitchen, flipping on all of those lights, too. Please Jesus, let him have beer in the fridge. He opened it and . . . jackpot. He found his bottle opener and damn! She was right behind him—she'd followed him in.

"If I'm going to live here," she said, unable to hold his gaze for more than a few short seconds, because she was currently in her where's-my-burka mode, "you shouldn't be getting me . . . things."

"Please help yourself," Izzy said. "There's soda in the fridge, although . . ." He opened it and checked again. "Nothing without caffeine." He'd noticed over the past few days that she was staying away from it.

"That's okay. I've really been trying to stick with milk and water," she told him, opening cabinets until she found his glasswear, most of it beer pints with the logo from the Ladybug Lounge. She took one, went to the tap and filled it, then took a sip.

"We'll go to the grocery store tomorrow," he told her. "I'm pretty sure the milk in the fridge is from last October."

Her smile was a ghost of its usual brilliance. "I appreciate the warning."

The kitchen was a mess, too. The dinner he'd never eaten because Gillman punched him in the face was still in the microwave. Damn, when he opened that, it was going to smell like rotting ass. The past two days had surely taken their toll. Best to wait until Eden wasn't in the room. Pregnant women and bad smells were not a good combo. He knew that one from experience.

Izzy finished half his beer in one long pull, aware that she was watching him. Expectantly. As if awaiting further instructions. His gorgeous new Stepford bride. *Rumor has it I give good head.*

Fuck that. "Stop," he said, much too loudly, and she actually flinched.

But instead of dropping to her knees in total submission, she got defensive. "I'm not doing anything," she said, but she was obviously working to keep from sounding too hostile.

So he pushed it. "Yeah, you are," he said. "You're . . ." What? Too hot? Too pretty? Too wearing his wedding ring? "Just . . . stop, okay?"

"I'm looking at you," she said, unable to disguise her annoyance. "I'm thinking. I'm drinking water. Which of those is the big problem for you?"

"You're waiting for . . . something," he accused her. "You're freaking me out."

"You're freaking *me* out," she shot back. "And if I *am* waiting? Maybe it's for you to turn back into Izzy instead of this . . . angry, too-polite stranger." She put her glass down on the counter and wrapped her arms around herself, as if she were cold. Or maybe as if she were trying to rein herself in. "You know, if you're having seconds thoughts, we can get it undone. What's it called? Annulled."

"Sweetheart, I'm not having second thoughts," Izzy admitted. "I'm having twenty-second thoughts."

Again she flinched as if he'd smacked her. "And you're mad at *me?*" she asked, all pretense of patience and obedience kicked out the window as she let fly with what she was really thinking. "What kind of idiot are you? If you didn't want to get married . . . If I'm going to live with someone who's mad at me for no good reason, I might as well go back and stay with my mother and Greg!"

"I'm not mad at you," Izzy told her just as heatedly. "I'm mad at me."

"Yeah, well, big diff," she said, heavy on the attitude. "Either way? Right now? You're not much fun to be around."

"Fun?" He couldn't believe it. "You thought fucking up my life would be *fun*?"

Okay, so that was much too harsh, and indeed, she took a solid step back, bumping the counter. "No! I just . . ." She was stricken, but before he could backpedal and apologize, she got her mad back on. "God, you *are* an idiot! It was *your idea*. And *I'm* an idiot, too, because I actually thought it wouldn't be awful. Guess I'm *wrong* again." She exhaled her disgust. "I thought you were different. Everyone wants me to be ashamed or . . . remorseful. To walk around apologetic and . . . and . . . mournful because I made some terrible mistake and got knocked up. But I'm not going to do that. I'm *not* ashamed. I married you because it was okay with you when I laughed. Because I thought you were funny and . . . Because this is my life that I'm living—right now—and if I've got to spend the next three months with someone, I thought that it wouldn't suck too badly if it was you."

"Oh, *that's* nice," he said.

She started to cry—and was obviously furious at herself for it. "And if I looked like I was waiting? You were right. I was." Her sadness overcame her anger and she crumbled. "I was waiting for you to turn back into your real self and put your arms around me and tell me that you know I'm scared, but it's okay because everything's going to be all right."

Way to be a total, solid piece of shit. Izzy's own anger instantly evaporated and he reached for her, wrapped his arms around her, breathing in the sweet scent of her hair. "I'm so sorry," he said. "I'm completely fucking this up."

"I'm sorry, too," she sobbed. "I was waiting for you to tell me what to do. I know what you want, at least I think I do, but I don't know how to give it to you. I don't know how to be that person."

"What?" He tried to understand. "What person?"

"When we were up by the cabin," she said. "You told me . . . And I thought I could be who you wanted me to be. I thought I could do it, and then you'd be happy, but I suck at it and now I've fucked up your life—"

"Whoa, Eden, no, you didn't. I didn't mean that."

"Yes, you did."

"No, I didn't," he said. "Look around you at this kitchen. My life is already fucked up, and your being here is a definite improvement and I don't want you to change who you are. I want you to be yourself."

"No, you don't."

"Yeah, I *definitely* do."

"Trust me, you don't. You should just take me back to Las Vegas."

"I'm not going to do that," he said. "You just . . . You've gotta cut me some slack, because I'm . . . scared, too. It was like it was a game until we hit the chapel. But it's not a game, it's real and . . . Eden, I want to do right by you. Only I've got this . . . devil whispering in my ear, saying that . . . God *damn* it."

"What?" she asked, lifting her head to look up at him. Even with tears streaking her face, with watery eyes and a red nose, she took his breath away.

"That the ring on your finger makes you mine," Izzy admitted softly. "Damn, Eden, I want you so bad. *You*, not this fake submissive robot you that you're pretending to be. I want the real you. The one who kinda scares my friends."

He didn't lower his head to kiss her—at least he didn't think he did, but suddenly her lips were against his, soft and sweet and impossibly tender.

She must've stood on her toes to kiss him, because she pulled back to look into his eyes, her fingers soft in his hair. "I think maybe everything's going to be okay," she whispered, tears back in her eyes.

And shit, he wished that were true. But it wasn't that easy.

He tried to explain. "Eden, I didn't marry you just because I want to make love to you. I married you for a lot of reasons. But the making love thing is one of them, and God damn it, I'm gonna do it, aren't I, and I'm afraid it's really going to ruin things between us."

"I think it'll make things easier," she whispered, as she wiped her face and eyes with the heel of her hand. "We won't have to try to out-martyr each other over who gets to sleep on the couch."

Izzy laughed his disbelief. "Now *there's* a butt-crack-stupid reason to have sex."

"We're married," she pointed out. "You said it yourself—it's not a game. It's real. So . . . let's be married. Let's have a wedding night."

"It feels wrong," he persisted, "like you owe me. Like, I was nice to you so now you're thanking me by having sex with me."

"Talk about butt-crack-stupid . . ." She kissed him again, which was freaking distracting—and probably her intention.

This time he was the one who pulled back. "Eed," he said. "You want to pay me back? For helping you out? Tell me *thank you*. And tell me that you want to keep sex out of this . . . arrangement we've got going here."

She was looking at him as if he were speaking Farsi. "But we're married," she said again. "And I agreed that while we were married, I wouldn't have sex with anyone else. So, if I'm not having it with anyone else, and I'm also not having it with you, then it kind of follows that I'm just . . . not having it. This is probably a good place in this conversation to point out that the last time I had anything close to sex was six months ago, out there," she pointed toward his living room, "on that sofa. If you want to know what I really want—"

He tried to cut her off because he knew what was coming, and there was a good chance it would make his head explode. "Eden—"

"You," she said, her hands in his hair again, her basketball stomach pressed against him. "I want you inside of me. I want you to make me come."

Yep. *Boom.*

With the very small part of his mouth that was left, Izzy tried again to explain. "The whole sex thing just . . . it feels like . . . payment to me and—"

"You making *me* come is . . . me paying you back?" She laughed, all their angry words apparently forgotten. "That's some great deal we made. Remind me to do business with you more often."

"Don't be a smartass," he said, but he let her tug him toward the bedroom. "You know damn well I'll be right with you—and probably leading the charge."

"So don't," she said. "If you're really afraid that sex will feel too much like me paying you back, then just . . . don't come." She knew damn well that *that* was never going to happen. Amusement sparkled in her eyes. "You can be like my living sex toy. You can just lie back and close your eyes and, you know, do math problems while I entertain myself."

Izzy had to laugh, but it was definitely edged with hysteria. "Sweetheart," he said, "I struggle not to unload just from thinking about you, okay? If we get naked . . ."

Which, of course, was exactly what she was doing right now, her underwear following her dress onto his bedroom floor.

"If?" she asked, standing on her toes to kiss him again, but again her mouth was soft—she let him kiss her instead of coming on too fast and furious.

Damn, she was beautiful, all ripe and round and smooth, soft skin that slid like silk beneath his fingers.

"It doesn't bother you?" she whispered. "Me being . . . I look so—"

"Sexy," he finished for her, skimming his hands across her belly, her breasts. "You're unbelievably sexy."

She was pregnant with someone else's baby. Izzy tried that thought on for size, hoping it would slow him down, or put him off, or maybe make him feel something other than this overwhelming desire to take off his clothes as well.

But it didn't. He didn't care. Pinkie was Eden's baby—that's all that mattered to him, too.

She smiled because she knew she'd won when he brushed aside her hands and finished unbuttoning his shirt himself. She pushed him back so he was sitting on his bed, and she pulled off his shoes and socks, kneeling before him like some kind of super-erotic variation of slave and master, which, as far as sex fantasies went, was one of his all-time favorites. The whole *pregnant* naked slave girl thing sent it soaring into all-time first place. Of course, maybe it was the fact that the beautiful naked woman on her knees before him was Eden Gillman that was giving the experience its future Greatest Hits status.

"If it'll help you stay in control," she said, looking up at him with her gorgeous laughter-filled eyes, "while we're doing it, you can call me Mrs. Zanella."

Izzy laughed his horror. "Now there's an instant soft-on. Mrs. Zanella is my mother."

"It's me, now, too," she pointed out, reaching for his belt buckle since he'd stalled out before unfastening it. He had to give the girl credit for knowing what she wanted and going for it with a single-minded determination. "Eden Zanella. Mrs. Irving Zanella—which sounds like I should be seventy years old and having lunch at the country club with all of the other doctors' wives."

Ah, God. Izzy surrendered, sinking back on the bed and closing his eyes as she freed him from his pants.

"Hello, you," she said and he laughed.

"Are you seriously talking to my—*Ah, God* . . ."

But she didn't answer, because she'd finally gotten what he'd wanted—and yeah, what he'd actually married her to get, guilt free.

Rumor has it I give good head.

Although, he was still working on the "free" part of that guilt.

And yeah, the rumor was definitely true, although, really, Izzy suspected there was no such thing as a *bad* blow job. Maybe something involving teeth and/or the relentless repeated playing of *Achy Breaky Heart*, although under certain circumstances, even *that* probably couldn't be defined as truly awful.

"*Don't tell my heart, my achy breaky heart, I just don't think it'd understand,*" he sang, just to test his theory, pushing himself up on his elbows, because really, for him, watching what was going down, so to speak, played heavily into the mind-blowing pleasure.

Eden lifted her head to smile at him. "What are you singing?"

"Nothing," he said.

"You have such a great voice." She touched him with hands that were almost as soft as her mouth. "I liked listening to you sing in the car."

"I thought you were sleeping," Izzy said.

"I was," she said. "But then I woke up and . . . I was afraid if I said something you'd stop."

She was right. He would've.

"It was nice," Eden murmured. "You know the words to everything."

"Come here," Izzy told her. "I want to touch you, too."

"You sure? I kind of like it down here," she said, taking him into her mouth even as she maintained eye contact. She smiled, no doubt at the Yippee-it's-Christmas-morning expression on his face.

"I thought my job was to make you come," he said when he could focus his eyes again. "And can I just point out that what you just did is not something you should do again, unless you want to save the you-wanting-me-inside-you thing for later in the evening."

"Really?" Eden said. "*This*?"

"Yuh . . ." Izzy said, and damn, it wasn't just what she was doing with her mouth—not just once but again and again and again and *again*. It was the entire Möbius strip–like endless connection, complete with that amazing eye contact—the fact that she was so obviously getting off on watching him while he was getting off on watching *her* watching him, watching her, watching him . . . "Eden, *ah, God* . . ."

She didn't move back. Instead, she took him more completely into her mouth as sheer pleasure ripped through him, thoroughly displacing all of his blazing guilt and making his heart pound damn near out of his chest. It felt so-ho-ho good, and the image of her perfect face, her eyelashes long and dark against the softness of her cheeks was burned into his brain as he came. And came.

And came.

Only then, after he'd barely regained control of eyes that had rolled back in his head, did she join him on the bed, laughing softly.

"No fair," he said, when he could finally speak.

"Would you believe me," Eden said, propping her head up on one elbow as she smiled down at him, "if I told you I used to fantasize about doing that while I was in Germany?"

Izzy laughed. "Not a chance."

"It's true," she said, her eyes closing halfway as he touched and then kissed her breasts. She was still completely, sexily aroused and he was . . . useless. Well, partially useless. "That morning after we . . . You know. Danny was at the door, and you changed out of your boxers and . . . I caught a look at Mr. Big."

"No," Izzy said, pulling sharply back to look at her. "Nuh-uh. No *way* are you *naming* my dick."

"Too late." She caught her lower lip between her teeth as she smiled at him, her eyes actually twinkling.

"No it's not," he said, trying to look imposing and stern—which was impossible to do when she was laughing and bare breasted.

"*You* can call him whatever *you* want," she told him, "and I'll—"

"Great," he interrupted. Him? Oh, no. No no. "I'm going to get a little boring here and call *it* 'my penis.' Not Mr. Penis, not mister anything. No *him*, no, thank you. With the understanding that I do appreciate the ego-stroking behind the whole *big* thing. I mean, you're the mastermind behind *Pinkie*, so it could've gone in an entirely different direction. But here's the deal, Mrs. Zanella, I have an absolute no-name policy for body parts."

Mrs. Zanella.

They both froze, nose to nose, eye to eye. His hand was filled with the decadent softness of her breast, her nipple taut against his palm. That was his wife's nipple, his wife's breast.

His wife.

For the next three months.

"Everything's going to be all right," Eden whispered again, kissing him softly, and he nodded, even though he didn't believe it.

She smiled then and reached down to wrap her fingers around that which she undoubtedly still thought of as Mr. Big. Izzy could see the silly nickname in her eyes, clear as day. And while he could stop her from saying it, he couldn't stop her from thinking it. And she knew it. No—she knew that *he* knew she knew it.

Which made it twice as much fun for her.

"Whoa," she said, at his obvious response to her touch. "I didn't think old guys could—"

Izzy kissed his wife. And, assuming that twenty-nine could be considered old, he showed her exactly what old guys could do.

SAN DIEGO, CALIFORNIA

Vinh Murphy was in Sacramento.

Decker didn't quite know how to process that information. Murph had been on the dark side of the moon for so many years, Decker had subconsciously started to think of him as dead and gone.

But he wasn't. He was very much alive. At the Methodist Hospital.

His gunshot wound was superficial. As was Hannah Whitfield's injury. Just as they'd suspected, he'd been in the former police officer's company when the shots were fired. She was with him right now.

Jules Cassidy, a high level agent with the FBI, had given Decker a courtesy call, letting him know that Murphy had finally surfaced. It was highly irregular, but due to his long-standing relationship with Troubleshooters, Cassidy was willing to wait to take Murph into custody until after Dave and his team made the scene—provided they could get to Sacramento, ASAP.

Of course, there was an armed guard at Murphy's hospital room door—to keep him and Hannah from walking away in the interim.

Hannah—who reminded both Deck and Dave of Tess Bailey.

The direct line to Decker's desk rang, and he looked at the phone's flashing light for a moment. Dave had told him—about an hour ago, when they'd last spoken—that Jim Nash had had another meltdown.

And maybe *another* wasn't fair, since the meltdown in the Troubleshooters' parking lot had been Decker's.

Regardless, Nash had lost it, telling Tess that there was another woman in his life. That he was "done."

Something's up with Nash, and you're only noticing it now? Dave's accusation echoed in Deck's head.

No doubt about it, something was definitely up with Nash. And Decker *had* been buried too deeply in his own pile of shit to notice.

And now Tess was a casualty. He could only imagine what she was feeling.

Dave insisted that Nash was lying about this other woman he'd mentioned, but over the past few years, Decker had distanced himself so much from his former Agency partner, he honestly didn't know.

The growing distance, he'd told himself, was a natural thing. It happened all the time when one of a pair of friends got into a serious romantic relationship. And at first he'd worried significantly less about Nash's crazy tendencies. He actually remembered thinking, *He's got Tess now— she'll take care of him.*

But apparently Tess wasn't enough.

Dave wanted Decker to give Tess a message that echoed Dave's words. *No way would Nash ever . . .*

But yes, way, Nash would.

He was completely capable of screwing around. He'd never been faithful to any woman, ever—not before Tess. And all he'd have to do was walk into a room—any room—and women would start lining up to go home with him. So Nash certainly had the means, if not the motive.

And Decker wasn't going to lie to make Tess feel better now, when it was clear that, before this was over, Nash was going to rip her heart in two.

The really messed up part was that Nash was trashing his own heart in the process, because Tess truly was the love of his pathetic life.

Decker braced himself and picked up the phone. "Yeah."

"Decker?" The voice on the other end was female. It was Tracy, the Troubleshooters receptionist, who had a reputation for being not quite the sharpest shovel in the shed. Which was bullshit—she was plenty smart.

But every now and then she pulled something like this, which kept alive her reputation as a ditz.

"Honey, when you call my direct line," Decker said, "you're going to get me and only me."

"Of course," Tracy said. "I just . . . You sounded . . . Are you all right?"

Funny you should ask . . . "What's the status?" he asked.

"I'm sorry," she said. "Yes. Dave asked me to call and update you. He and Lindsey and Jenk and . . ." He could hear paper rustling as she checked her notes. "And Danny Gillman and Jay Lopez. They're about an hour outside of Sacramento."

"Wasn't there a fourth SEAL?" he asked.

"Irving Zanella," she said. "He went to Las Vegas to marry his pregnant teenage girlfriend—who also happens to be Danny's sister and what kind of name is Eden, anyway?" She stopped. Took a deep breath. "I'm sorry. Everyone knew about it but me and . . . I haven't seen him in months so . . . I'm sorry."

"You used to date him," Decker remembered.

"We never dated," Tracy said. "We just . . . collided once and . . . I'm not, you know, jealous or anything. I'm just . . . It was a surprise. Besides, the girl's, like, twelve." She laughed her disgust. "As if *that's* going to last. Not that I'm wishing him misfortune or—"

"Was there anything else?" Deck asked.

"Yes," she said, immediately snapping back to business. "Dr. Heissman. I should have mentioned—she's going up to Sacramento, too."

"She didn't stay to . . ." Talk to Tess.

"No," Tracy said. "Tess didn't think that was a good idea, considering she was kind of the target of Jimmy's, um . . . freak-out, I guess is a good description."

"Dr. Heissman was?" Decker asked. He hadn't heard that part of the story.

"Deck, it was weird," Tracy said. "I've never seen Jimmy like that. He actually said . . ." She lowered her voice even more. "F-you."

"To Jo Heissman?" Jesus. Dave hadn't told him that either.

"It was like he just . . . I don't know," Tracy said. "He was possessed. And he's gone. Just like . . . *gone.* Tess has been looking for him, but . . ."

"She's not going to find him," Decker told her grimly. "Until he wants to be found." Fuckin' Nash . . .

"If he shows up back in San Diego," Tracy said, "will you please give me a call? I'm going to stay here in Dalton, with Tess. Sophia's with us, too. Tess doesn't want to leave without Jimmy, and we don't want to leave her here alone. We'll get a room and . . . Wait and see if he turns up."

"Thank you," Decker said. Fuckin' Nash. "Please, uh, thank Sophia for me, too."

"I will. And it's not a problem," Tracy said. "Tess is a friend."

"Is there anything else?"

Tracy paused, her sudden silence ominous.

"Christ," Decker said. "What else?"

"No," Tracy quickly said. "Nothing bad. I just . . . I wanted to make sure you're really all right."

Decker said nothing.

But that was okay, because Tracy had regained her expert-level control over the conversational ball. "I don't think anyone actually expected that we'd find Murphy, well, besides Dave who's . . . Dave." She paused. "It seems as if this is really hard for everyone—seeing Murphy again or . . . even just having to *think* about him and Angelina's death and—"

"I'm fine," Decker said.

"Are you?" she asked quietly. "Because I've been watching everyone leaning on everyone else and I've never seen you lean on *any*one. Maybe Jimmy Nash a little, but . . . Right now he's *adding* to your stress levels and . . ."

Decker looked out his window at the playground. Tom's wife Kelly usually brought little Charlie over there to play, right around this time of day, but today she was going to the airport in LA, to meet his plane from Hong Kong. She was flying up to Sacramento with him.

Normally Tom would have gone on his own, but Kelly knew just how hard this was for him. Because it was hard for her, too. She'd been there when Murphy and Angelina were shot. She'd invited them to dinner. Maybe if she hadn't done that . . .

But she and Tom had each other, as Tracy had pointed out, to lean on.

"I'm fine," Decker said again.

"I'm not," she confessed. "I'm a wreck, and I never even met the guy. You were *team* leader and—"

"I'll call if I hear from Nash," he told her.

"You're not alone," Tracy insisted. "I just wanted to make sure you remembered that. You've got a lot of friends who're dying to give their support—and to *get* some support from you, too. It goes both ways."

Message received. "Tell Tess . . ." Decker hesitated. He still wasn't about to offer support in the form of a lie. "That I'm here if she needs me. And please ask Dave to keep me updated."

"I will," Tracy said. "And Deck?" She didn't wait for him to respond. "I know we're not really friends, but if you ever want to, um, talk? *I'm* here if *you* need *me*, okay?"

Decker was silent again.

"Oh, my God," she said. "Did that sound like a sexual invitation, because it wasn't supposed to be, only you just got really quiet—quieter—and I kind of played it back in my head, and I can see how you might interpret it as being inappropriate or—"

"I didn't," he lied. "I was just . . . overwhelmed by your generosity. I appreciate your reaching out to me, but I meant it when I said I'm fine."

"Sophia's my friend," Tracy continued to babble. "I would never—"

Jesus. "Go back to Tess," Decker ordered her, and hung up the phone.

He then sat in his office, at his desk, surrounded by silence and stillness. He was the only one in the building—everyone else was either on assignment overseas or rushing off to help Murph.

Tom, however, had asked him to stay behind—to "hold down the fort," but really, it had been because he'd thought Decker's seeing Murphy would be too hard.

For Murphy.

"I'm fine," Decker said again, more forcefully this time, his voice echoing throughout the empty office. He picked up the phone and dialed Nash's cell, even though he was certain that the son of a bitch wouldn't answer. Still, it was the first step in tracking him down, and Decker was nothing if not methodical.

And he *would* find Nash. It might take a while, but he'd find him.

He had no doubt about that.

It was what he was going to do once he found him that was questionable. Although kicking Nash's ass straight to hell was very high on Decker's list of possibilities.

Chapter
Seventeen

E ven though Izzy was sleeping, Eden went into the bathroom to cry.
She was such a dork.

She'd told herself that, this time, she would do it. This time, she would have sex like a man.

Men didn't cry after sex. They didn't do a postcoitus analysis, trying to glean the meaning behind every touch, every kiss, every sigh. They got revved up, they had only as much foreplay as mandatory, they shot their wad, and then they got up and made a sandwich.

Or fell into a complete, restful, triumphant sleep, the way Izzy had done.

No need for unnecessary conversation. And certainly no need for emotional proclamations.

I love you.

God.

What was wrong with her, that she was unable to have sex without falling hopelessly in love?

Sex was sex. It felt good. It was fun.

And one penis wasn't really all that different from all the others. Izzy was just a nicely built, kind of funny, very generous man, who, like all other men on the planet, was a total slave to his genitals. And okay, maybe there were *some* differences, because he happened to be hung like a porn star. Not that she'd seen a lot of porn, but she had seen some and if anyone ever wanted to make a musical version of *Star Whores*, with his voice and equipment, Izzy could've starred.

Eden splashed water onto her face, both laughing and crying now—God, she was a total hormonal mess.

Because the stupid thing was? It wasn't Mr. Big that she'd fallen in love with. It wasn't even the fact that Izzy was an amazing lover—and, for the record, that and being well endowed didn't always go hand in hand. But bottom line? None of that mattered.

What mattered was the way he'd laughed with her. It was his smile and the light in his eyes.

It was the way he was so careful to give her control, making sure she was on top, letting her decide how fast and how far to move. He'd realized that this was a first for her—having sex while pregnant. And while all of her doctors had reassured her that sex well into the third trimester was perfectly fine, it *was* a little weird, especially after going for so long without. But she hadn't had to tell Izzy that—he already knew. He'd reassured her. *It's all right, sweetheart. We've got about a billion possible alternatives from the Creative Option Box, and I'm already a very happy camper. So if you don't want to . . .*

But she did. And they had. And he was so gentle and careful and sweet.

It was that—and the way he'd touched her, watching her as she'd moved atop him, his smile so fierce and hot.

It was the catch in his voice, calling out her name as he'd come that second time. He'd sent her flying, too, which didn't always happen—at least it hadn't with Jerry.

God, it had felt *so* good.

Except the giddy euphoria that came with knowing that she held such power over Izzy had vanished like the crash following a sugar shock. She'd gone from high to desperately low in record time, finally escaping into the privacy of his somewhat grimy bathroom when he fell asleep.

And here she was, replaying it all in her head, trying to figure out how, in God's name, she'd managed to mess it up again.

She'd purposely gone down on Izzy right at the start—it was a power play, meant to prove that she was in charge.

It was also a test. Some guys—Jerry for one—rolled over and went to sleep immediately after—without a single thought about her needs.

It was also a kind of a twisted turn-on. Eden both loved and hated this crazy power she had over men. It was a thrill to know that they found her irresistible—even Izzy, who'd fought his attraction to her for so many days. Especially Izzy. It was a definite kick to see the submissive vulnerability of a man who'd finally surrendered—flat on his back. Especially someone as big and commanding as Izzy Zanella.

And yet it was deeply disappointing, too, because at the very same time, as soon as sex entered the equation, she knew that she was replaceable. Exchangeable.

What was it that he'd said about that woman Tracy?

Been there done that.

He could now say the same about Eden.

And yes, she could also say that about him. But she couldn't help but notice that, out of the pair of them, *he* wasn't the one who was crying in the bathroom.

Although, really, what had she thought was going to happen? Had she honestly believed that Izzy was going to experience the wonder of all that was Eden, and fall madly and stupendously in love with her?

Speaking of stupendous, the really stupid thing was, even if he had? Even if he'd proclaimed loudly that he wanted to be with her and only her until the very end of time?

Eden wouldn't've believed him.

If there was one thing she'd learned since she'd gotten into the back of John Franklin's car, it was that "I love you" really meant "I want to do you again in the very near future." And lust often faded as fast as a post-blow-job hard-on.

A soft knock on the door made her freeze. It was, of course, Izzy. He'd apparently come out of his sex-induced coma and found her missing from his bed.

"You okay in there?" he asked through the door.

"I'm great," she lied.

He was silent for a moment, as if deciding whether or not he was going to push her on that, because even to her own ears she sounded ridiculously far from great. "I'm going to make a sandwich," he finally said. "You hungry?"

"No, thank you," she replied.

He was silent then—but she didn't hear him go into the kitchen. It was as if he were still standing there, outside the door, listening to her standing silently in the bathroom, as she, in turn, listened for him to leave so she could blow her freaking runny nose.

"You coming out anytime soon?" he finally asked. "I kinda have to . . ."

Perfect. Wonderful. Eden quickly blew her nose with toilet paper, then wrapped one of his towels around her.

"Please?" he continued. "I'm also worried that I might've somehow hurt you—"

She jerked open the door, far more pissed at him than she had the right to be. "You didn't," she told him. "I'm pregnant. I cry. Get used to it."

"Are you sure you're okay?" The concern that was practically radiating from him was enough to make her well up all over again—because he wasn't really concerned for her. He was concerned for himself. He was happy to screw her, but only if it was guilt-free. After all he'd actually gone and married her to get some. Yes, his goal was to help her, but he himself had admitted that he'd also done it because he wanted her.

What she *should* have said now was, *I'm fine—I just need a little space because wow, that was really great sex and I didn't expect it, and I'm a little thrown by how much I like you.*

Instead, what came out of her mouth was, "I have an excruciating backache. I don't *think* it was anything that you did."

He looked horrified. And she immediately felt like the bitch that she was.

"I know that it's not," she tried to reassure him, but it was too late. "I've had it pretty much all day."

And now he looked stunned—as if she'd hit him in the face with a two-by-four. "You have an *excruciating* backache," he reiterated, "that hurts enough to make you cry and you don't think that *maybe* that was something you should have told me *before* we had sex?"

"I did tell you. In the car."

He stared at her.

"We stopped at that gas station," she reminded him, even though she knew that she was only making things worse, but he was standing there, completely naked and totally delicious and she could've been back in bed with him right this very moment, but no, she had to have sex like a stupid girl and then go and cry about it. "Because I said I wanted to—"

"Stretch your legs," Izzy finished for her.

"Because my back was hurting," she told him.

"You didn't say that." He was getting mad. "And you certainly didn't say it was *excruciating.*"

"I did say it," she argued, even though she didn't remember exactly what she'd said. "And yeah, okay, I probably didn't use that word, but even if I had, it wouldn't have mattered. You didn't want to hear it. You had your agenda."

"My agenda," he sputtered. "*My* agenda? Remember me—I'm the one who wanted to take things slowly. I'm the one who wanted to wait."

"No, you didn't," she countered. "We both knew exactly what you meant, back at the cabin when you said *let's go to Vegas.*"

Izzy's bullshit meter was usually dead-on accurate, but right now it was obviously out of order. Apparently sex screwed with his head.

He wasn't the only one. Eden was standing there, making him feel awful, when all she really wanted was for him to pull her into his arms, so that she could pretend that she was loved.

She couldn't help it, she started to cry in earnest, which upset Izzy even more.

"All right," he said, "let's get some clothes on. I'm taking you to the hospital."

Was he an idiot? "Where they'll tell me what? I'm pregnant? Pregnant women get backaches. It's part of the deal. The baby leans on a nerve or something, and it sucks, okay?" She pushed past him, heading into the bedroom. "I shouldn't have told you."

He reached for her. He was really just going for her arm, to slow her down, but she saw his sudden movement out of the corner of her eye, and she reacted instinctively and ducked.

Izzy instantly backed off, both hands out where she could clearly see them, but positioned low in a completely nonaggressive stance.

"I will never, ever hit you, Eden," he said quietly. Absolutely.

Her hero.

Whom she'd just purposely made to feel like crap.

Talk about payback.

"I'm so sorry," she managed to say. "I know that. I didn't . . . It wasn't . . ." She couldn't look at him. "My back. It doesn't hurt that much. It's not excruciating. I don't know why I said that. It aches a little. Pretty much constantly. I'm used to it, though. It's not . . ." She shook her head.

"Will it help if I rub it?" Izzy asked in that same quiet voice.

"I don't know," she admitted, just as softly. No one had ever offered to rub it before.

Izzy held out his hand to her. "Why don't we try," he said.

And from the pocket of his pants on the bedroom floor, his cell phone loudly rang.

SACRAMENTO, CALIFORNIA

A few hours after the doctor removed a chunk of wood from Murphy's leg and patched him up, Dave Malkoff knocked on the hospital room door.

He didn't wait for permission before coming in—the knock was merely a formality. And Dave would probably be, Murphy knew, the last person to do even that much. Suspects being taken into custody for questioning didn't have a whole hell of a lot of privacy rights.

Murphy looked at the clock on the wall. "Took you long enough," he said.

Dave nodded to Hannah as he scrutinized the both of them, taking in the severity—or lack thereof—of their injuries. "Are you all right?"

"Peachy," Murphy said. He hadn't seen Dave since Angelina's memorial service. He hadn't *talked* to the man since . . . Wow, last time they'd had a conversation must've been sometime that week before Angelina was shot and killed.

Sometime between then and now, Dave had cut his Frank Zappa hair and bought a shirt that didn't advertise one of his favorite rock bands. The man had gone heavy grunge immediately after leaving the cheap-dark-suit-and-tie world of the CIA, but now he appeared to have swung back to a more moderate fashion statement. Jeans with a button-down shirt. An honest-to-God sports jacket to hide the fact that he was carrying concealed—instead of that ridiculous windbreaker he used to wear.

"It's good to see you, Murph," Dave said, and his voice actually cracked with his sincerity.

Just a few months ago, Murphy would have said something like, *You'll forgive me if I don't pretend to have fond memories of working with you at Troubleshooters* . . . Instead he simply said, "It's good to see you, too, man," as he reached out to shake Dave's hand.

Because it *was* good to see him. He'd always liked Dave. And Angelina's death wasn't the fault of anyone over at Troubleshooters. The two men responsible for that—John Bordette, who'd pulled the trigger and pumped lead into her brain, and Tim Ebersole, who'd allegedly been "only kidding" on the Freedom Network website, when he'd issued a fatwa on that movie producer who'd been the real target, inciting Bordette to pick up his gun—were both dead.

The handshake turned into a slightly awkward hug, made even more strange by Dave's actually getting misty-eyed, and then hugging Murphy again, longer and harder.

And Murphy realized, with a sudden sharp shock of awareness, that his and Hannah's were not the only lives that had been permanently damaged by Angelina's murder. There had been a ripple effect from the tragedy. And his friends, like Dave, had lost more than Angelina. They'd lost Murphy, too.

"I'm sorry I didn't . . ." Murphy said. "Stay in touch. I just . . . Man, I . . . I couldn't . . ."

"I know," Dave said, finally pulling back. "It's okay. I knew that . . . When you were ready, I knew that you'd . . ." He actually had to wipe his eyes, laughing at himself as he did so. "Not that you're actually ready for this, huh? You obviously heard about Ebersole, so you know why I'm here."

"Yeah." There was no reason to lie—not about this, anyway. "I've been trying to piece together where I was when he was killed," Murphy admitted. "We're pretty sure I was here in Sacramento on March fourth. We've also got me up in Alaska by the end of April. It's a little murky, though, in the middle there." Which was embarrassing to admit, but Dave nodded as if it were no big deal.

Then handed him back some equally honest information. "I wasn't sure if you'd, um, need to go into detox," he told Murphy. "Tom's got a psychologist on staff these days and she's, uh, waiting in the lobby, ready to help if necessary."

"Wow."

"A what?" Hannah didn't understand, and Murphy fumbled the spelling, settling on the far easier *shrink*.

"Yeah," Dave said. "I'm glad you're, um, okay. You *are* okay . . . ?"

Murph nodded. "Yeah. I'm . . . Very sober."

"I'm glad," Dave said again, his words heartfelt.

"Is she by any chance a hypnotist?" Hannah asked. "Because that's about where we were. About to dive into the unconventional end of the pool, hoping to find a clue."

Dave turned to her. "It's nice to see you, too, Hannah."

"We need more time," she told him intently, skipping over any and all small talk, refusing, even now, to concede defeat. "If you could give us a week—"

Dave laughed.

"A day," Hannah negotiated. "Twenty-four hours—"

"Can't do it," Dave said apologetically, turning to include Murphy. "It's something of a miracle that the FBI's held off this long—taking you in for questioning . . ." He shook his head.

"Twelve hours. We just need a *little* more time," Hannah persisted, ready, as always, to bring it to the mat for Murphy. God, she was fierce, and for a moment, he was back in Steve and Paul's apartment, pushing her down across the kitchen table, losing himself in her strength and passion, giving himself up to a need that was so raw, so powerful, so absolute.

It had been exactly as he'd imagined sex with Hannah would be—passionate and terrifying. Mindblowingly so.

"You need more time to find a *clue*," Dave repeated the word Hannah had used earlier. "Getting shot at's not a major clue?"

"We don't know who was shooting at us," Hannah said, which wasn't exactly a lie. They didn't know for sure it was the Freedom Network.

Dave sighed and looked at Murphy.

"Dave's kind of not an idiot," Murphy told Hannah.

"There was a disturbance out at the Freedom Network compound early this morning," Dave told them both. "Sirens went off and ten vehicles left via the compound gate in a cloud of dust. The FBI surveillance team couldn't follow all of them, and of course the tailed cars went out on an innocent grocery run. Sat-images haven't come back yet, but the experts are guessing they'll find that the other cars trolled the hiking trail parking areas." He paused. "You guys do any hiking recently?"

Hannah met Murphy's eyes, and he knew exactly what she was thinking. *GPS device* . . .

But then she turned back to Dave. "Are you working for the FBI now?" she asked and Dave sighed again. "Because I thought you were here to talk Murph into turning himself in—which is really just a formality, considering we're already in lock-down."

Dave nodded. "You know how it works. It's what's down on paper, after the fact. Did he willingly cooperate upon finding out he was wanted for questioning? If so, he might catch a break at a future date." He turned to Murphy. "So yes, I'm here to inform you that the FBI would very much like to ask you questions regarding your whereabouts at the time of Tim Ebersole's death, at which point you should probably say, *Thanks, Dave. Of course I'm willing to cooperate immediately and disclose all information I have regarding the current ongoing investigation because I have nothing to hide.* A lot of important people pulled a lot of strings to make this happen for you. Tom Paoletti's on his way here, from Hong Kong. Jules Cassidy is coming, too, and he *does* work for the FBI. He's a good friend and ally, and he'll probably get some serious crap from his boss for not sending a subordinate instead. As for me, I'm not just here to act as liaison. I'm also here to help. If you let me."

"Of course I'm willing to cooperate," Murphy echoed. "I just . . ." He looked at Hannah who was watching him intently, no doubt working hard to follow the conversation.

Hannah, who would willingly march into hell for him. Who'd come damn close to dying just a few short hours ago.

Because of him.

"I could definitely use your help," he told Dave. "I need someone to get Hannah to safety. After she talks to the FBI, another *of course.*"

"What?" She either didn't understand or couldn't believe what he'd just said.

"Her uncle's in Arizona," Murphy ignored her. "Phoenix. Patrick O'Keefe. He's a former Marine. Can you get her there for me?"

"Absolutely," Dave said. "But—"

Hannah cut him off. "I'm not going anywhere. You *need* me."

"No, I do not," Murphy said emphatically, and now the look in her eyes was the same as when he'd inadvertently implied that she was nothing to him. God, now as then, how could she have thought that was what he'd meant?

But maybe it was good that she did.

Because she was all he had left, and he wasn't going to lose her, too— even if that meant he had to lose her as a friend.

As a lover.

They were lovers now, God help him.

"I don't need your help, and I don't need you," he said, because he *was not* going to bury Hannah, too. "You've done enough. And I thank you. For everything. For . . . all of it. But it's over now."

He could see from her eyes that she knew he was talking about the sex. It was also kind of clear that Dave caught that subtext, too. He looked as if he'd rather be anywhere else in the world right now, and tried to become invisible.

As for Hannah, Murphy knew that she'd found his words cold. *Thanks for getting me off* . . .

"You know as well as I do," he told her, "that it's likely the FBI will arrest me. Shit, I'd arrest me. Plus, I'm kind of obviously a flight risk . . ."

"You do need me," she insisted. "They're going to be looking to prove you did it. You need someone to prove you didn't. That you *weren't* there."

"What if I was, Han," Murphy said quietly. "What if I killed him? God knows I *wanted* to . . ."

"Then we'll fight it in court," she responded in true Hannah-fashion, with plenty of fire in her eyes. "Temporary insanity." She turned to Dave. "I have a letter that Murphy sent me—"

"No," Murphy said, but Hannah didn't hear him.

"—back in Dalton," she continued, "at the cabin—"

Murphy got down off the bed, to get in her face. "No way," he said again. Jesus, was she serious? "You're *not* going back there."

"Whoa, Murph," Dave said. "Are you sure you should be out of bed?"

Murphy ignored him just as completely as he ignored the pull of the stitches in his leg. "Hannah. Think about it. The Freedom Network surely has the plate number of the car—"

"Which is registered in Alaska," she pointed out. "If they're using Patrick's Rabbit to track us, then they're heading for his place in Juneau— they probably don't even know about Dalton. I'm getting that letter, Murph." She paused. "Assuming I'm not arrested first, as your accomplice."

"Which you will be, immediately after you show them the letter," he lit into her.

"What letter?" Dave asked.

"Don't say anything more," Murphy ordered Hannah, and wonder of wonders, she actually shut her mouth. He turned to Dave. "I need to talk to Hannah privately."

Dave looked from Murphy to Hannah and back. And nodded. "Five minutes," he said, but then paused. "FYI, the FBI hasn't connected you to the early morning incident at the Freedom Network compound. It hasn't occurred to them that you're crazy enough to have gone over that fence."

"Thank you," Murph said.

Dave nodded and left the room.

Hannah spoke first, reaching for Murphy, her fingers cold against his arms. "I just want to get it, Vinh. I'll take it to a lawyer before—"

He interrupted her. "I want you safe," he said, and if she didn't have that bandage on her arm, he would have shaken her by the shoulders. As it was, he just took her hands. "Hannah, for God's sake, promise me you won't go back to Dalton."

"I can't do that," she said, bringing his hand to her face and pressing it against the softness of her cheek. "I can't."

"If anything happens to you—"

"You mean, like kinda the way this—right now—is happening to you?" she countered hotly.

He broke free from her grip, because, God, if he didn't, he'd put his arms around her and start crying like a baby.

"I mean like you, on the floor, with your brains coming out a hole in your head," he said through clenched teeth. "*This* is nothing—being questioned, going to jail for something I probably did—something I would have done if I could've, something that, God, I hope I did!"

It was stupid—him raising his voice to a deaf woman.

But she damn near shouted back at him, her eyes blazing: "Even if you did it, that wasn't really you! Six months ago, when you came to the cabin, trying to break into the gun case? You would *never* quit that way! You would never even *think* about taking your own life—never!"

Her conviction rang in the room, but Murphy just shook his head.

"Maybe not the man I used to be," he admitted quietly. "But the man I am now *still* thinks about it."

She didn't have a snappy response to that—but her eyes did fill with tears. Which broke his heart.

What had he done to deserve her love? And she loved him. Murphy knew that absolutely, with another stroke of clarity that illuminated the truth.

That bullshit she'd given him about them hooking up because they were both lonely was just that. Bullshit. She loved him, and God help him, she'd probably loved him right from the start. Right from that first day, as he'd pulled her from the icy water alongside the pier.

I'm Hannah, Patrick's niece.

Oh, good, he'd said, trying not to stare as her T-shirt clung to her body. Amazing how someone could be both freezing cold and steaming hot. *Way to impress my former CO. By drowning his niece.*

I know how to swim, she'd said, laughing. She pulled off her soaking wet T-shirt, which nearly made him panic until he realized that that was her bathing suit she was wearing beneath it. *I should have known you were one of Pat's Marines. You're Vinh Murphy, right?*

Yeah, he'd told her. *Are there a lot of us?*

Visiting, yes, she'd informed him. *Working here, no. In fact, you're in the one-and-only category for that. You must be pretty special.*

I am, he'd said as he smiled down at her. *And yeah, I know you're probably thinking it, and you're right. It's kind of obvious, just from looking at me that I'm part leprechaun.*

Hannah had laughed, which had made her eyes sparkle. . . .

And okay, wait. Maybe *he* was the one who'd loved her from the first.

As friends—except, yeah, that was what he'd always told himself. He loved little Hannah Whitfield as a friend. He'd repeated it often enough to himself until it became true. And then he was hit by Hurricane Angelina, and he'd fallen, hard and fast and so-less-complicatedly in love with her.

And Hannah hadn't said a word. She hadn't spoken up. She'd just let it happen, let him marry her best friend.

"Why didn't you fight for me?" Murphy asked her now.

She didn't understand. "I *am* fighting for you," she told him. "I'm trying to—"

"It doesn't matter." None of it mattered anymore. So he pushed it, trying to push her away, because, Jesus, what *did* matter was Hannah not being part of the body count, when this snafu finally sorted itself out.

If it ever did.

"Han, I've changed. You keep saying *temporary insanity,* and I just don't see the temporary. If you put me in a room with Tim Ebersole, I would kill him. I wouldn't need a weapon—I'd just tear him apart with my bare hands. I'd do it without hesitation—knowing I'd go to jail for life for doing it. Because I just don't care what happens to me. I've tried to care because I know you do, but . . . I honestly don't."

She was shaking her head, and he knew she was going to give him more of that *I'll care enough for both of us* crap, so he twisted the knife he'd already stuck into her.

"I shouldn't have slept with you," he told her. "I knew it was a mistake. I knew you'd end up hurt. I know you love me, Han, and I should've just kept my distance the way I've done all these years, but . . . I just didn't care enough to do the right thing. That's who I am now. I just don't care about anything. Please don't go to jail for me. And please, God, don't die for me."

Hannah opened her mouth to argue, as usual, but there was a knock on the door, and Dave came back in. He was followed by Jules Cassidy, the same FBI agent who'd helped track down Angelina's killer, all those years ago. It was a lucky break for Murphy, because Cassidy not only knew Murphy, he also knew the history of the case.

Cassidy greeted Murphy and Hannah both, explaining that while Hannah would be interviewed here in this room about the shooting incident, he and Murphy would go to a different location, away from the hospital.

Which would have been extremely uncool—leaving Hannah unprotected like that—except that Dave was there.

"Stay with Hannah, all right?" Murphy asked his old friend. "Get her on a flight to Arizona."

"Consider it done." Dave shook his hand.

"This way, Vinh," Cassidy gently directed him, and Murphy realized that it was probably going to be a long time—if ever—before he saw Hannah again. But he knew he couldn't look at her.

If he did, she would see just how desperately he did care. Not about himself—that much was true. He didn't care about himself.

But he cared, very much, about her.

"Murph," Hannah said and he stopped, but he didn't look back at her. Her voice was rough with anger and hurt. But it was filled with her certainty. "You're full of shit, and we both know it."

"Not this time," Murphy said. He looked at Dave. "Tell her that for me." And he followed Cassidy into the hall.

SAN DIEGO, CALIFORNIA

"Fuck me!" Izzy snapped his phone shut.

This had Gilligan's fingerprints all over it.

A pre-dawn phone call from the senior chief. Three words. "Get over here." Five more added on top of Izzy's "But . . ."

"Move your ass, Zanella. *Now.*"

News of his nuptials had apparently spread—thanks so much, Danny-bo-banny—and the senior was going to ream him a new one for playing fast and loose with the rules of their agreement.

That was no big surprise. Izzy had never been one of Senior Chief Wolchonok's favorite people—and things had gotten worse after his little unauthorized absence incident a few years back.

Izzy'd done two months punishment duty behind a desk in freakin' Hawaii for that goatfuck. It had been excruciating—cooped up inside, doing paperwork so that other guys could dive and jump and swim and practice blowing shit up. It was supposed to have lasted six months, but because of the shortage of troops and the escalating hostilities in Iraq, he'd cut a deal with Commander Koehl and the senior chief, and he'd gone to Afghanistan with SEAL Team Sixteen.

The deal had put a leash on him. It was also open-ended. And the senior had let him know, every day since then, that if he so much as failed to fart according to rules and regulations, Izzy would find himself back behind a desk.

And so he'd behaved.

Most of the time.

"I've got to go to the base," Izzy told Eden now, as he searched the bedroom floor for his boxers.

"This late?" She was incredulous.

"Sweetheart, we get the call, we go," Izzy said, putting his uniform pants back on. "That's how it works in the Teams."

"Oh, my God. Are they sending you to Iraq?"

"I doubt it," he said, shaking out his shirt and jacket. "I think this has more to do with us getting married, than—"

"Are we in trouble?"

"You're not," he reassured her. His night of roller-coaster-worthy highs and lows, however, was about to take a serious nosedive.

"What if they *are* sending you to Iraq?"

Izzy looked up because there was real fear in Eden's voice. She was seriously frightened.

"My father went on a two week TDY and ended up gone for six months," she reminded him.

Damn. It wasn't as if it couldn't happen. And wouldn't that be just their luck? He had no clue what Eden's crying-in-the-bathroom, pain-in-her-back thing was about. He'd barely managed to talk her down from whatever ledge she was on. If he left now . . . Not to mention the PITA-factor of his not being around to help her find a doctor and just be there when Pinkie made his debut . . .

"Okay," he said as he tied his shoes. "Let's worst-case-scenario it—while keeping in mind that best case has me back in a few hours. Don't lose sight of that, okay?"

She nodded, eyes glued to his face.

"Worst case," he said. "I kiss you good-bye and immediately go wheels up. That means we get on a plane and leave."

"I know that," she said, impatient.

"I won't be able to tell you where I'm going," Izzy said. "You know that, too?"

She nodded again.

"I'll leave my truck in the team parking lot," he continued. "The keys'll be in the commander's office. You'll be able to pick it up. Well. *After* you get your driver's license and *shit!*" He'd just remembered. "The rental car. Will you check online—my laptop's on the kitchen table—and get the phone number for the nearest Avis rental office? If I'm not back by noon, call them and ask them to come pick it up. I'm sure there'll be an extra charge, but fuck it. They'll just add it to my credit card. Better that than having to pay for an extra day. I'm pretty sure you'll have to be here, though, to give them the keys."

She nodded as he dug in his pocket for cash. Damnit, he only had about fifty dollars. He gave it all to Eden, pressing it into her hand. "My ATM card is in the top drawer of my dresser," he said. "The PIN number—"

"I don't want to know it." She cut him off. "You said—"

Izzy kissed her, swift and hard, on the mouth. "3292," he told her anyway. "F-A-Y-A. It's kinda my war cry. *Fuck all y'all.*"

She didn't laugh. She didn't so much as smile. She was sitting on his bed clutching both the money he'd given her and her towel. Neither of those items was doing a particularly good job of covering her, but she either didn't mind or didn't notice. She looked shell-shocked.

Welcome to life as a Navy wife.

"Team Sixteen has a wives' support group," Izzy told Eden. "I'll make sure someone gets in touch with you. They'll help you find a doctor and . . . They'll help you with everything, okay?"

She nodded, but he couldn't tell if she'd really heard him.

"Eed, this is worst case, remember?"

She gave him eye contact at that, which was good. She nodded again.

"I gotta go," Izzy told her. "Oh, key to the apartment. There's a drawer in the kitchen—it's got shit like batteries and keys in it. Spare key's on a Family Guy key ring. I think it's a picture of Stewie . . ." Was she listening? He honest to God couldn't tell. "I'll go get it."

"Stay alert," she said as he went into the kitchen. "Please?"

That was refreshing. Izzy had been a SEAL for quite a few years, and had been "Be careful-ed" damn near to death by various long-forgotten girlfriends. But aside from the fact that SEALs tended to be men who didn't have "be careful" on their daily "to do" list, it was also a superstition among Team Sixteen that being too careful could actually get you body-bagged.

Of course, Eden's brother was a SEAL. Apparently, she'd paid attention to what Danny had told her in the past. Which was nice—family members sometimes didn't get it at all.

"I always do," Izzy promised her now to, indeed, stay alert as he dangled the key from his finger, coming back into the bedroom. "And really, Eed, I'm probably going to be back in a few hours."

She nodded and even forced a smile as she took the key from him. "I'll be here," she said.

"Good." He kissed her again. But okay, *he* was now a little freaked out about the potential for a worst case scenario. And truly? The worst case Izzy had come up with wasn't the absolute worst case.

Which was that he could very well die out there. It was true, he could also be hit by a bus in downtown San Diego, so he usually didn't give his chances of being KIA all too much thought. But he was thinking it now.

So he kissed Eden again, longer, slower, deeper. Just in case it was the last time. And then he crouched down and pushed aside her towel, so he could kiss her belly, too. "Later, Pinkman."

As he got back to his feet, Eden caught his hand. "Izzy . . ." As she stood up, too, her towel fell off of her, forgotten.

Eee-doggies. "Baby, I've really got to go."

She nodded. "I just . . . In case you *are* gone for a while . . ." She took a deep breath. "I don't expect you to be faithful to me. This marriage is . . . it's you doing me a favor. I know that. You don't love me and I . . . I don't love you and it's . . . It's not real. But you've been so . . . great. So nice. So . . . You should feel free to . . . You know."

"Fuck other women?" Izzy finished for her.

She flinched at the harshness of his language, but quickly recovered. Far more quickly than he had from her words. *I don't love you . . .*

She nodded. Yes. She also realized she'd lost the towel, and wrapped it back around herself.

"Wow," he said. "That's . . . Um . . ."

"I mean, we should be honest about what this is," she told him, oddly unable to meet his gaze. "And if you were here, and we were, you know, sleeping together, then I would prefer it if you didn't . . . You know, for . . . for Pinkie's sake. But when you're away, for so long . . . You shouldn't have to . . . You should, you know . . ."

"Feel free to fuck away," he filled in for her again.

"Just . . ." Eden actually achieved eye contact. For someone who cried all the time, her eyes were remarkably dry. "Be safe. Use a condom?"

Izzy managed to nod. He was the idiot who was having to blink a lot. She obviously cared about him—and therefore wanted him to have lots of sex with other women while he was on the other side of the world. Yippee.

"I have to go," he said again.

And he walked out the door.

CHAPTER
EIGHTEEN

Eden managed not to cry—at least until the door closed firmly behind her husband.

She found an Izzy-sized T-shirt on the floor and slipped it on as she went to the window. She watched him through her tears as he climbed behind the wheel of his truck.

It was the same one he'd used to drive her home from the Ladybug Lounge, a lifetime ago. Apparently, he was not one of those guys like Jerry and Richie, who needed a new car every few months.

Izzy's face was tight and grim as he backed out of his parking spot, as if he were already thousands of miles away.

Eden watched his taillights until they disappeared, well aware that it might be months before he returned. Yeah, the way things were going in Iraq, it could well be *years* . . .

No, Eden, I will not have sex with any other women, even if we are forced to be apart for years and years. The truth is, sweetheart, after making love to you, I cannot imagine wanting even to touch another woman for the entire rest of my life. So, no. I will not agree to your ridiculous suggestion, especially since you so obviously made it with a heart filled with your deep and abiding love for me. You see, I know this about you, baby, because I, too, love you, deeply, endlessly . . .

File that one under things Izzy hadn't said before leaving.

And the truly foolish part was that, because he was such a nice guy, if she'd said, *Hey, it's really important to me that you stay faithful while you're away. Even though this marriage isn't a conventional one, I think maybe we've got something here that's worth taking kind of seriously. So please, while you're gone, will you wear your wedding band . . . ?*

If she'd said that, he would've said *yes.*

Instead, she'd given him permission to have sex with other women as a kind of a test. Which they'd both failed, since he'd seemed pretty cool with the idea.

Yeah, like, what guy wouldn't be?

Eden was exhausted and queasy, but she went into the kitchen, where his laptop computer was, indeed, out on the table, just as Izzy had said.

She'd promised she'd find the phone number for the nearest Avis rental car return and came up with a location several blocks away. The website said the place had a drop box for the keys of cars dropped off while the office was closed. It would take two minutes for her to drive the car over there, and about fifteen to walk back.

She mapquested the directions and printed them out.

And then, because the sun wasn't up yet, and she didn't want to walk back in the dark, she checked her e-mail. It had been weeks since she'd last been online.

She had an e-mail from Anya in Germany. *Everyone misses you. Frau Schutte asks me daily for an update . . .*

She had one from Brittney, too. Britt—who had allegedly been Eden's friend back in high school, in Vegas. Britt—who had a little brother Ben's age. Britt—who still stayed in touch with Jerry, because she'd always had a crush on the jerk. Subject header: *Omigod, are you really MARRIED?*

> *Kyle told me that Ben told him that you were marrying some soldier named Irving that you met in Germany. Irving?!?! Is that TRUE? And that you've got to get married because you're having a BABY?!?!*
>
> *You barely even broke up with Jerry, and you're hooking up with an IRVING who gets you preggo—you total slut!*

That winking smiley face was the cyber-equivalent of Britt's sweet-tea-serving mother saying, "Bless your heart" to pretend it softened her judgmental insults.

*Have you talked to Jerry since you've been back? He's still
FURIOUS with you, and I don't blame him. Really, Eden, how
could you? You told me you hated Richie. I didn't believe Jerry until
I saw it with my own eyes.*

PS You might want to google yourself.

PSS dont do it while your mother or IRVING's in the room

bff, Britt

Best friends forever. Right.

With an impending sense of doom and dread—*I saw it with my own
eyes*—Eden went to Google and typed in her name. *Eden Gillman.*

Her MySpace and FaceBook pages both came up, along with Brittney's MySpace page.

There was an obituary for a John Gillman, and what looked like a
whole list of medical publications for a Dr. Erika Gillman.

She sifted through several pages of additional hits. An article on one of
Danny's recent triathlon wins, several other mentions of him in a publica-
tion about Navy SEALs called *The Blast* . . .

She went back to Brittney's e-mail, about to reply with a brief *Not sure
what you mean about googling myself* . . . when one of those all-caps IRV-
INGs caught her eye.

Irving.

Eden clicked back to Google and typed in *Eden Zanella* and . . .

The very first hit was a site called GirlsWhoLoveToShag dot-com. It
was a free Internet video site—a porn equivalent of YouTube, where users
could post and share their homemade sex tapes.

Stomach churning, Eden followed the link and . . .

The name of the video—posted just last night—was *Eden Zanella's A
Lying Ho.*

It was her. It was definitely her. The video's quality was crisp and clear.
She was sitting on the couch in Jerry's brother's apartment—completely
naked. She was lolling back, but her eyes were open. She looked a little
drunk—not drugged.

"Smile for the camera, baby." God's-gift-to-women handsome, his hair in dreadlocks, white teeth gleaming, Richie came into the shot as Eden did indeed smile.

The camera was at a kind of weird angle, as if it were low to the floor. Richie, too, was naked, his variety of tatts practically covering his muscular upper body, his dark brown skin gleaming, and he sat down next to her on the sofa. "Come on, baby," he said. "I got what you want right here."

He pulled her up, facing him, so that she was straddling his lap and—

That was why the camera was positioned down there.

Eden squinted at the computer screen, looking through her eyelashes, but that didn't make the video any less horrifying.

She was compliant. She didn't fight, didn't argue. She didn't do anything but seemingly willingly have sex with the bastard.

Eden hit the stop button, forcing herself to breathe. Crap, she was dizzy. She dropped her head between her knees.

It was okay. It was going to be okay. She'd told Izzy what had happened, told him that Richie had made a video. He seemed to be fairly well educated about the effects of rohypnol. He'd definitely be pissed when he saw this—who wouldn't be. He'd want to kill Richie—and Jerry. This was Jerry's handiwork, posting this here, of that Eden had no doubt.

She'd change her name. What was it that Izzy had called her that very first time they'd met, all those months ago? Susan. She'd become Susan Zanella. She'd cut and color her hair.

Eden sat back up, to back-button that awful video off the computer screen when . . .

Oh, no.

There were two other video links. *Eden Zanella's A Lying Ho, The Sequel* and *Eden Zanella's Still A Lying Ho.*

Eden clicked on the sequel, which started with Richie grinning into the camera. "This bitch wants me—anytime, anywhere, anyhow."

It cut to a shot of Jerry's kitchen. Eden was standing at the sink, washing dishes—or trying to, anyway. She was washing the same plastic bowl, over and over. It frequently slipped out of her hands.

The good news was that she had clothes on—a skirt and a tank top that she would never have worn together. Never. Someone—no doubt Richie—had dressed her in those clothes.

The camera panned around her so that there was a close-up of her face. Again, she looked a little drunk, her eyes a little strange, a little glazed. But open.

"Say hi Richie," he said, still off-camera.

"Hi, Richie," she said and—oh, God—smiled.

In the next shot, she was bent over the kitchen counter, her head down and her skirt up—revealing that she was wearing nothing underneath. Richie came from behind the camera, grinning and giving a thumbs-up right into the lens and then . . .

Eden grimly back-buttoned, clicking on the third link.

This video started with her opening her apartment door. Again, she was dressed, again in clothes that she'd never wear—at least not in public. A white tank top with no bra, and a pair of terry-cloth running shorts that had shrunk in the wash and were uncomfortable.

The video cut, oddly, jerkily, as if the camera position had been moved a few inches to the right.

But she still stood there, in the open doorway, leaning against the door.

"Come on in," she said.

Another jerky cut, and she said, "I'm so hot for you," and then laughed.

Another cut, and the door opened to reveal that she was wearing an entirely different outfit—jeans and a T-shirt.

Then the door opened again, and she was wearing her pink and black dress.

And Eden realized that each of these shots of her in different clothes had a different date stamp. Somehow Richie had altered the date on the camera to make it look as if he'd shot the footage over the course of eight different days.

The eight different outfits came off in a montage of cuts that made it look as if she were in a hurry to get naked. Her clumsiness played into the illusion. And then she *was* naked, and Richie was nailing her—against the wall by the apartment door, on the kitchen table, on the living room floor, in the shower, in the bed she'd shared with Jerry. And over it all was an uneven soundtrack of her voice, some of it soft and hard to hear, some of it very loud. "Oh, yes, oh, God, oh, Richie, oh, Richie, oh *Richie* . . ."

Somehow he'd gotten her to say that, and spliced it all together, but if she were Izzy, seeing that . . . ?

He'd never believe her. Why would he, when what seemed to be the truth was right in front of his eyes?

The scene cut to Richie, solemn, speaking into the camera. "I know this looks like I've betrayed you, Jer, but your girlfriend's been grabbing for me, every chance she gets. I been, like, fighting her off for months now. I wanted to see how far she'd go and . . . I made this video for you, for your own good, so that you know. Your girl's a ho."

Cut to Eden, close up, saying, "Jerry doesn't have to know." Her speech was slurred—dozshn't—but the words were coming out of her mouth.

No wonder Jerry had ditched her in the Krispy Kreme.

And Izzy, when he saw this? He was going to do the same.

Eden rushed over to the kitchen sink and threw up.

SACRAMENTO, CALIFORNIA

Decker pulled into the Sacramento Residence Inn shortly before 0230.

This was crazy. He knew it.

And yet he'd found himself driving north, his phone conversations with Tracy and then with Tess playing over and over in his head.

You stay the fuck away from me, Nash had said to Jo Heissman. *I don't need your help . . .*

It made sense that Nash would naturally be mental-health-care-averse, but his hatred of Dr. Heissman seemed extreme. It seemed . . .

Personal.

So Decker had gone into Tracy's reception desk, to find that blue folder that held the doctor's background information.

And then, after reading it, he'd used his computer to dig even deeper.

Dr. Josephine Heissman. Age forty-eight.

Graduated Boston University in 1982, with a liberal arts degree. Married Michael Quincy in 1983, immediately had two kids and was a stay-at-home mom, but for only a few years. Went back into the working world in 1988—as a secretary—when she and Quincy divorced. Took him to court again in 1990 for being a deadbeat dad, but shortly after he was killed in a car accident so she probably never saw even a penny of support.

Despite that, she managed to go back to school and get her masters and PhD in developmental psychology from Boston College. Her daughter attended Harvard and graduated with high honors. Her son currently attended a graduate program at MIT.

Nowhere in that blue folder with its detailed bio and four-page list of publications was the fact that she'd also worked, for nearly five years, for the clandestine government organization known only as the Agency.

Uncluttered with an alphabet nickname, it was where Decker and Nash had worked before signing on with Tommy's Troubleshooters.

They'd left when Doug Brendon, the newly appointed director of the Agency, put into place some politically partisan policies. Brendon's also-newly-appointed support staff also came damn close to burning Decker— leaving him high and dry in a situation where he'd very nearly wound up dead.

Nash had been convinced the accidental almost-burn had come about because Decker had obstinately put bumper stickers supporting the opposition political party on his truck. Decker refused to think that. The new Agency director couldn't be *that* much of a fascist.

Still, after some of the dust settled, he and Nash had handed in their resignations.

Not at all oddly enough, regardless of their years of exemplary service, there was no attempt made to make them stay.

It had been ages since Decker had so much as spoken to anyone from the Agency. He now had reason to believe, however, that that was not the case for Nash.

Fuck you, he'd snarled at Jo Heissman. Tess had told Decker that for one, brief, awful moment, she'd been afraid that Nash was going to attack the doctor.

Something was definitely wrong. And since Nash still wasn't answering his phone, that meant only Dr. Heissman was currently available to answer Decker's questions.

She was in hotel suite 408. Fourth building, first floor.

Decker parked near the entrance. The door was locked, with one of those electronic locks that allowed only keycard-carrying hotel guests to enter. He got out his B&E kit and in a matter of seconds did just that— broke and entered. He made sure that the door clicked securely closed behind him.

The corridor was carpeted and smelled faintly of wet dog—an aroma

"I'm sorry, ma'am. Not until you answer some questions—"

"You do understand this falls under the category of erratic behavior. I have every intention of reporting this to Tom Paoletti."

Decker felt his polite bone break. It just snapped, and he got in her face, manners discarded. "Terrific," he said as he invaded her personal space. "Let's get a dialog with Tommy going, shall we? Let's talk about your years—was it five?—with the Agency."

She laughed her anger, held her ground. "I should have known. After James Nash's performance this afternoon—"

Decker's temper flared even more brightly. "*Perform*ance?"

"It seemed that way to me," she said. "Yes. It was purposely done in public. He was alone in the car with Tess for hours before his outburst." She managed to move away from him gracefully, without seeming as if she were retreating, by striding to the door. "Time to go, Mr. Decker. Your coming here like this is completely inappropriate—"

"I have an idea," Decker said. "You let me search your room, right now, and if I don't find anything that ties you to Brendon or his Agency, well, then I don't kill you."

"What, no threat of rape?" It was a low blow, and she knew it, and she took a deep breath. "I'm sorry. Look, I'm *not* going to let you search my room, so—"

"So you *do* have something to hide."

She was back to being pissed. "What a surprise. You're one of those troglodytes who believes that privacy is a luxury. *What's the big deal about losing a basic constitutional right. If you don't have anything to hide you shouldn't be worried*, huh? Well, screw you, buster. I don't have anything to hide, but I'm not going to let you search my room, because I still cherish my right to privacy. Do you *seriously* think that I managed to keep the fact that I worked with the Agency from Tom Paoletti? That's the reason he hired me! He thought I would have insight into what's going on with you and Jim Nash." She picked up the phone, brandishing it at him more as if it were a weapon than a communication device. "Call him and ask."

"I will," Decker said. "Count on it. In the morning."

"You don't want to wake *him* up, but you think nothing of breaking into *my* room . . ."

"He's on a flight from Hong Kong," Decker told her. "I have no problem waking him."

that was, for him, more nostalgic than offensive. Once upon a time,
had a dog.

Hell, once upon a time, he'd had an entire life. A live-in girlfri
who would have made him see reason if he'd told her his crazy-ass plai
drive more than seven hours from San Diego to Sacramento to wake
near total stranger in the middle of the night and accuse her of . . .

What? Decker wasn't even sure.

These days, as Agency scandal after Agency scandal made the news
Deck himself kept his years of employment with the organization off of his
own résumé.

Of course, there was another reason why someone like Dr. Heissman
wouldn't mention an Agency connection—and that was if she were still
working for Doug Brendon.

Decker stopped in front of the door marked 408 and knocked.

Loudly.

He knocked for quite a long time, then—knowing full well that it was
a mistake—got his B&E kit back out and gained access to Heissman's suite
as quickly as he'd gotten into the building.

It was dark in there, the kitchen area lit by a dim glow from the microwave clock. There was a sofa, several chairs and a TV set up by some
windows, and a door that was tightly shut, no doubt leading to the bedroom.

No wonder she hadn't heard him.

Deck started turning on lights—in the kitchen and in the living room
alcove. He made sure he got them all, so that the place was blazing. At
which point, he went to the bedroom door and, once again, knocked.

This time she heard him.

She opened the door, clearly thinking that the knocking had come
from the outer door. Her hair was pulled back severely from her face, in a
single braid down her back, and she was pulling a bathrobe on over what
looked like a pink silk nightgown.

As Decker's mind did a quick boggle—she didn't seem the type to own
anything pink—she quickly covered herself, securing the belt around her
waist with an extremely businesslike square knot.

Deck found his voice. "I'm sorry to bother you, ma'am," he said. "But
I have some questions that couldn't wait."

"So you just . . . broke into my room?" She was not happy. "How dare
you? Get out."

But she didn't care. She pointed to the door again. "Just get out before I call hotel security."

Decker laughed. "Was that supposed to be a threat?"

"It very much was one, yes. Perhaps not as violent and offensive as your threatening to kill me was—as if I thought for a moment that you'd actually—"

"You worked for the Agency. You're aware of what its operatives are capable of." Decker planted himself on the sofa, feigning a casualness that he didn't come close to feeling. In truth, he could feel himself shaking. "I'll have my coffee black, thanks."

He'd rendered her speechless, but it was only temporary. "If you think for one *second* that I'm making you *coffee* . . ."

"Why don't you start by telling me who you worked for at the Agency," he said, "and for how long, and—the question of the hour, drumroll, please—if you're still working there now?"

Hands on hips that were, beneath that terry-cloth robe, covered by a pink nightie—he still couldn't get over that—she glared at him. "Why don't you answer that last question yourself?"

"I'm pretty sure you know," Decker told her. "But, okay, I'll say it. No, *I'm* no longer working for those motherfuckers. Your turn."

"And what? You're just going to take my word for it . . . ?" She let her voice trail off.

"I want to see if you're ballsy enough to lie," he said. "We've had enough conversations—I can tell when you're lying."

And there it was, on her face. A flicker of something—uncertainty? Possibly.

And sure enough, she tried to redirect. "Well, I've had enough conversations with you to know you're capable of pulling one past me. Why should I believe you?"

"Because Doug Brendon forced me out," Decker told her, "and I almost died in the process. And if you worked there when your background information indicates that you did—you damn well know it."

"Almost died," she pointed out. "The Agency that I'm familiar with doesn't do *almost.* Unless they—and you—want the world to think you're not working for them anymore . . ."

It *was* a classic Agency move. Pretend to cut ties, and then coerce former operatives into completing one more assignment. And then one more, and then another and another and another. With proper leverage to guarantee cooperation, of course.

Decker was almost completely convinced that this had to be what was going on with Nash. Because if Nash *was* still working for Brendon's Agency, he wasn't doing it by choice, that was for goddamn sure.

"For all Tom and I know," Dr. Heissman pointed out—nice strategy to imply that she and Tom were on the same team, opposing Decker, *"you've* continued to work for them for the past four years."

Enough of this bullshit. "Well, *I* know I haven't," Decker said.

"And I know *I* haven't," she countered.

"Which is what you would say if you still worked for Brendon."

"Ditto to what you just said," she shot back. "And around and around we merrily go."

And there they indeed were, staring at each other, neither one backing down.

"What am I going to find out when I talk to Tommy?" Decker asked her, trying a different tack. "That you're doing extensive research on the effects of trauma on field operatives, for some fictional paper you're working on? That you agreed to shrink all of our heads at a special discounted rate in order to have access to more subjects for your study?"

He'd hit a truth there—he could see it in her eyes. "The paper's quite real," she started, but again, he cut her off.

"What are they looking for—the Agency?" Decker asked. "More shit to use to hold Nash's feet to the fire? Or are they gunning for me now?" God knows he'd given Dr. Heissman all that she needed, to provide the Agency with plenty of blackmail material on himself. Jesus, he'd blow his own brains out before he'd let himself get entangled back in one of Brendon's razor-sharp snares—and the idea of doing so was so starkly absolute, and oddly, crazily enticing that for a moment, he couldn't breathe. But she was talking, so he had to focus.

"I don't know," she said tartly, "seeing as how I'm no longer working for them?"

His hands were shaking again, because now he couldn't help but think about Nash, possibly caught in a similar trap, only with way more—Tess—to lose. And as much as he'd said otherwise, he honestly couldn't tell if Jo Heissman was telling the truth. "But you *were* still working there after Nash and I left," Decker persisted. "You seriously expect me to believe that no one—*no* one—discussed either one of us?"

She didn't answer, so he pushed it harder. "Come on, Doctor," he said. "You said *I want to help you.* Well, here I am. I'm asking you to help me." His voice shook. "So for fuck's sake, help me!"

She was trying—and succeeding—at keeping her composure. She was cool and aloof. "This was not what I meant."

"You want to know how I *feel?*" Decker rocketed off the couch, unable to sit still a moment longer, and this time she retreated, so the crazy must've been radiating off of him in waves. "I'm sick about Murphy. Jesus, he's finally surfaced and I'm scared shitless that I won't be able to help him, that I *haven't* helped him, that he's already too far gone, that he *did* kill Ebersole, and, Christ, I'm glad that the motherfucker's dead, but I'm sick that I didn't think to do it for him. And I'm fucking sick about Nash, too, about not seeing that this bullshit was going on, about assuming that his having Tess would be enough—because it was easier for me to stay away from them, because—shit, *shit!*—I wanted it! I wanted what he found with her. And Jesus, I'm sick because if Tess couldn't fix Nash, there's no goddamn hope for me, so I might as well just eat a bullet tonight!"

To his complete and total horror, he found that somewhere in his rant, he'd started to cry. He bolted for the door, but now—damn it—she actually blocked him from leaving. He was afraid to touch her, afraid he'd hurt her. "Get out of my way!"

"Okay," Jo said, hands out, as if she were calming a mad dog. "It's okay. Why don't you sit down, and I'll make that coffee?"

Decker had to get out of there. He couldn't stop his tears and he would not cry in front of her, in front of *any*one. So he picked her up and moved her aside, only now she held onto him in an embrace, her arms tightly around him, and the shock of the sudden contact blew out a door that he'd thought was already wide open, but in fact had only been ajar, because now, Jesus, he was actually sobbing, and he couldn't stop, couldn't . . .

"It's okay," she said again, her voice soothing, her body solid and warm against him. "You're safe with me, Lawrence. You're safe here. You can say what you feel, and still be safe. You don't have to run away."

God help him, it had been so long since he'd been touched, let alone embraced like this, but then he thought of Sophia in the Troubleshooters' parking lot, holding him from behind, her arms around him, her hand over his heart, and he was so screwed up, because he *knew* what she'd wanted from him for so many years, but he couldn't forgive himself enough to give it to her, he just couldn't, and it was stupid as shit, because the gentleness of the voice in his ear made him think about his mother, whom he hadn't thought about in years, whom he suddenly missed with such a sharp, twisting ache and could he *be* any more pathetic, crying like a baby and missing his mommy?

He remembered the way Murphy had cried in the hospital, that awful day Decker had gone with Tommy to tell him that Angelina had died—the hoarse, keening sound of the man's grief still echoed in his head, sweeping through him with a desolate, freezing loneliness, and he didn't want to be here, he couldn't stay here, not like this, so he kissed her, this woman who was holding him in her arms, and all of the pain turned instantly to need, hot and strong, and just like that his tears shut off, because Jesus God, her mouth was sweet—

But she pulled away from him and he realized with a jolt of shock that it was Jo Heissman's mouth that his tongue had just been in. Her hair had partly come undone from her braid and her blue eyes were enormous as she caught her breath and adjusted her robe and said, "Okay, that's okay, because, you know, sex is just another form of running away, another way to hide, to avoid talking—"

"I should go," Decker somehow managed to say, because now he was completely freaked out on top of being mortified. He wasn't even remotely attracted to Jo Heissman.

But she moved, again, in front of the door, and he found himself acutely aware of the fullness of her breasts beneath her bathrobe. No doubt about it, she was nicely put together for a woman of their age.

"I know for a fact that the majority of men in your occupation," she told him, pushing her hair back behind her ear, no doubt in an attempt to look more professional, "use sex as a form of emotional release. A surrogate to expressing themselves through words or even tears, so you should know that I absolutely don't take what just happened personally. It was pretty classic avoidance and . . . I need to make it absolutely clear, though, even as I insist that you stay, that nothing of a sexual nature can or will happen between us. But I urge you to sit down so we can talk about some of the things you said. If you want, we can start with your concerns about Jim Nash. I think you're absolutely right—that Nash is under some kind of severe pressure, probably from the Agency."

She was no fool, of that Decker was certain. She knew the magic words that would keep him here, despite his being mortified and completely unmanned. He'd wiped his face, but he knew his eyes were red and the fact that he'd actually broken down and wept was as palpable as if there were another person in the room with them.

But she gestured toward the sofa where he'd been sitting mere moments earlier. "I *can* help you," she said. "I will. Please."

It felt like an out-of-body experience, as if Deck were floating above himself, watching from afar. But he nodded and he got his feet to move and then he sat.

SAN DIEGO, CALIFORNIA

The SpecWar Group Sixteen parking lot was almost completely deserted, which was a good portent—at least in terms of his not being sent overseas within the next twenty minutes. Izzy parked next to the senior chief's truck and went into the equally empty building, his dress shoes clicking on the floor despite his attempt to walk quietly.

Light was blazing from the senior chief's office and as Izzy headed toward it, the expression *moth to the flame* came to mind.

The senior chief was sitting behind his desk and scowling. If he were surprised to see Izzy in full uniform, he didn't show it. He didn't so much as blink. He just affixed Izzy with his *you-are-toast* dead-eye stare.

"Senior." Izzy greeted him.

Despite looking like a hired killer who used to box and had received one too many nose-breaking, face-smashing blows, Senior Chief Stan Wolchonok had a heart and a soul. He had to—he was married to one of the prettiest, sweetest, most kick-ass helo pilots in the United States Coast Guard. His wife, Teri, used to be an officer in the Naval Reserve, but she'd made a lateral and somewhat downward move in order to marry Stan, who was career Navy enlisted.

It was not the kind of thing a highly skilled woman would do for a man who was a total bastard.

So despite the fact that the senior frequently acted like a total bastard, Izzy knew he wasn't one.

He'd also heard rumors that the senior and his wife had been trying to have a baby for quite some time now. Teri'd had a couple of miscarriages before her latest so-far successful pregnancy, which couldn't have been easy for either of them.

And, perfect. Here came Izzy, instantly married with a wife who was effortlessly pregnant. Way to rub it in Stan's face.

Izzy cleared his throat as Stan just sat and glared at him. "May I—"

"No," Stan said, before Izzy even said the word *sit*.

So Izzy assumed parade rest. This was going to be one of *those* kinds of meetings. The kind where he stood silently and got yelled at.

"Have at me, Senior," he said. "I know I broke the rules of our agreement, but she's six months pregnant. The idea of driving her all the way to San Diego and then all the way back to Vegas—"

"Jay Lopez called me," the senior said. "He told me what's going on. I assume since you're back that you already married the girl."

"Yes, Senior Chief. A few hours ago." *Lopez* had called the senior chief, not Gilligan. "And her name's Eden."

As Stan looked steadily up at Izzy, it was obvious that the senior was aware that his phone call had interrupted Izzy's wedding night. And maybe Izzy was imagining it, but there seemed to be a flicker of chagrin in the older man's eyes.

And when he spoke, his words surprised the hell out of Izzy.

"Call me on your cell phone," he ordered. "And tell me again exactly what you told me before—about not being able to get to San Diego to request the CO's permission, on account of your fiancée's health."

Izzy stood there, stupidly, staring at Stan.

"I want to go home," Stan said, each word distinct, as if he were talking to a moron. "Where my wife is in my bed. I have fought for you, Zanella. I championed you when Commander Koehl wanted to kick your ass back to Little Creek. *He's too fucking smart for his own good, sir,* I said. *If we keep him challenged, I know he'll do us proud. Beneath all the bullshit, Zanella's a very intelligent young man and an exceptionally excellent operator.* Don't prove me wrong by making me sit here a minute longer than I have to."

Izzy was beyond surprised and well into stunned territory. "Senior, I thought you hated me."

"Zanella, shut the fuck up and call me."

Izzy got out his cell phone, and with a thumb that felt clumsy, he dialed the senior's cell number.

"Wolchonok," the man answered. The signal, of course, took its time and caused a delay. The speaker at Izzy's ear echoed, "Wolchonok."

"Senior," Izzy said, because he knew, with a flash of insight, exactly what Stan wanted him to do. "I realize this is short notice, but I'm calling to request permission to get married this evening. My fiancée is six months pregnant. I was unaware of her condition until very recently, otherwise I would have approached Commander Koehl and made this request sooner. I realize there's going to be a ton of paperwork to sign, and also request that permission be granted to delay that until after the wedding. I'm available to come in to your office to sign the forms immediately upon arrival from Las Vegas."

"Son, are you sure you don't want to talk to a counselor," Stan said, "or at least ascertain that the child is, in fact, yours?"

"The baby's mine, Senior," Izzy said, past the lump that had appeared in his throat at that completely uncharacteristic and unexpected *son.*

"Lopez says otherwise."

"Despite popular belief, Lopez is, on occasion, wrong."

"This girl—Eden—is very young. Lopez said you told him—"

"The baby's mine," Izzy said again.

"Then take a paternity test, to confirm—"

"I don't need to. I'm taking responsibility. I had a . . . sexual encounter with the young lady six months ago, she's currently six months pregnant . . . With all due respect, Senior, I'm down with that math."

"Lopez told me Eden is the sister of one of your teammates," the senior chief said. "Is that going to create a problem for—"

"No, Senior. It will not."

"It better not." Stan paused, then asked, "Do you love her?"

Izzy met the senior chief's steady gaze across that big desk, as the man's voice echoed in his ear. *Do you love her?*

As the silence dragged on, the senior chief added, "It's a simple yes/no question, son."

So Izzy answered him. "Yes, Senior," he said. "She's . . ." He nodded. "Yes."

God help him.

"Permission granted," Stan said and snapped his cell phone shut. "I'll make it right with the CO. In the meantime . . ." He pushed a stack of papers and a pen toward Izzy and gestured with his chin toward the chair in front of his desk. "Sit. Read and sign."

"Thank you, Senior," Izzy said. It was amazing. All of the forms had been filled out. It was all completely ready for him and . . . There were more than just the standard forms needed for changing his marital status. The senior chief had prepared all the additional paperwork, too. The forms Izzy needed to make Eden the beneficiary of his life insurance, forms that would allow her to get medical care, the form in which Izzy was to list the person or persons who would notify Eden in the event of his death . . .

Damn.

It was a standard military form. Everyone—officer and enlisted—had to fill one out. He'd just never thought of it before in terms of having someone who depended on him. Someone who might actually be upset if he were dead.

Of course, if Eden didn't particularly care if he slept with every available woman in Europe and the Middle East . . . Maybe his death wouldn't be that big a deal.

The senior chief saw what had stopped him.

"You can take that one home if you want," he said. "Just bring it back soon. First thing tomorrow."

Izzy glanced up at Stan. "Is that a hint that we might be going wheels up?"

The senior didn't blink. "No," he said. "It's a hint that we're definitely going wheels up. Before the end of the week."

Hence the necessary expedition of his paperwork.

Izzy finished signing everything and stood up. "Senior Chief, I really don't know what to—"

"No need for speeches, Zanella," Stan said, standing too. "You're welcome. Now, let's both go home to our wives."

CHAPTER
NINETEEN

H annah wasn't questioned at all about her visit, last March, to the Freedom Network compound.

As she sat in the hospital room and the questions didn't come, and then *still* didn't come, she realized it was entirely likely that Craig Reed had refused to give the FBI access to a list of compound visitors. Probably because it would identify all of those people as being card-carrying members of the vitriolic hatemongering organization, and most of them wouldn't want that information going public.

It was also possible that Reed feared the FBI would be able to use that information for other purposes, such as monitoring the movement and location of Freedom Network leaders.

So the good news was that the FBI didn't know that Hannah had visited the compound last March, and at this point, she wasn't about to volunteer that fact.

She was, however, questioned extensively by both the police and FBI—right there in the hospital room—about the shooting at Steve and Paul's place. She was able to tell the interrogators the time of the incident and little else. She saw no one, didn't hear any of the shots and only felt the impact of one.

Did she know of anyone who would wish to harm her?

As a former police officer, she could probably come up with a four-page list, yes.

Where was she prior to the attack?

In her friends Steve and Paul's apartment, taking a nap.

And before that?

Driving around the Sacramento area. Murphy and his murdered wife Angelina used to visit friends in this part of the state rather often. Murphy was seeking closure, but rewind a bit to that wish-to-harm question, because Hannah knew that, as a gay couple, Steve and Paul had been targeted more than once.

Before they'd moved to California, they'd lived in the Florida panhandle, where drive-by gun blasts to their house had been, sadly, a common occurrence. As far as Hannah knew, nothing like this had happened since they'd moved to Sacramento, but she'd read on-line about an organization called the Watchmen on the Walls, an Eastern European immigrant-based homophobic group who'd recently set up shop in the area. Between the Watchmen and the Freedom Network, that part of California was becoming quite the place for haters.

The police and FBI might want to round up the usual suspects from both groups, because the bullets fired may well have been meant for Steve and Paul, Hannah had theorized, inwardly apologizing to her friends for using their sexual orientation as a handy excuse.

Notes were made and heads nodded before she got the next question: What was Hannah's relationship with Murphy?

Longtime friends. She'd introduced him to his now-dead wife.

There was no need to mention that they were friends with benefits. Murphy had made it clear before he'd left that that was over, anyway. Which was probably for the best. *I know you love me . . .*

Hannah pushed the thought away and focused on the questions being asked.

Had Murphy ever spoken to her about Tim Ebersole?

She wasn't comfortable discussing conversations held in private, conversations in which she allowed a grieving friend to vent. Whatever his intentions had been, Tim Ebersole's ugly words on his website had resulted in Angelina's death. Cause and effect. Murphy, in his grief, had every right to be angry—not just with the Freedom Network, but also with the movie producer who was their official target. Hell, he'd had the right to rail against Hitler, too, since the controversial, true-life movie being made, the one Ebersole had been protesting, was set during World War Two.

Talk about cause and effect.

So Murphy *did* express anger against Tim Ebersole?

Murphy was angry with everyone in the entire world. Are you also looking at him as a suspect in last week's murder of that shopkeeper in Calcutta? Because Murphy was angry with him, too. He was angry with *you.* He was *angry.* He was allowed to be. His wife, whom he loved, was dead.

To Hannah's surprise, the questions ended there.

She was free to go, as soon as she received her official discharge from the hospital.

However, Murphy—who'd been taken off-site to be questioned—was going to be detained longer, for an undetermined amount of time. The police detective and FBI agent both gently suggested Hannah not expect to see him soon—and she knew from experience that it was probable that Murph was going to be arrested and charged.

Which meant she absolutely had to go and get that letter that he'd sent her back in March.

The police and FBI left her room, and, after sitting there for about half a minute, Hannah got out of bed.

God, that hurt. Forget about her arm, it was nothing compared to the three-ring-circus of pain in her ankle.

The nurse had given her a painkiller, which Hannah had promptly stuck deep inside of the pillowcase, only pretending to swallow. Now was not the time to be drowsy. Or to dance with the prescription drug devil. She'd weaned herself off of painkillers once already. She was not looking to do *that* again.

She hobbled across the room and peeked out the door into the hallway.

The police guard was gone.

And Dave Malkoff was down at the end of the hall, talking to the police detectives, his back to her.

One of the nurses who'd been in just moments earlier to take her blood pressure had told Hannah that the doctor wouldn't be in to sign the hospital discharge papers until midmorning at best. That would, she'd cheerfully suggested, give Hannah a little time to send one of her friends out to pick up something for her to wear, to replace the bloodstained T-shirt she'd traded for a hospital gown. Hannah should try to get some rest—which was hard, the nurse knew, with everyone traipsing in and out all the time. But they wouldn't be bringing the breakfast trays around for another few hours, so. . . .

Hannah gently closed the door and then, using the pillows and blankets from the hospital bed Murphy'd been in before they'd taken him away, she formed a human-seeming lump under the covers of her bed. It was an old camp trick, and when the light was low . . .

She adjusted the blinds and turned off as many of the lights as she could, pulled on her jeans and boots, grabbed her daypack and opened the door to the hallway again.

Dave's back was still to her.

Dave—who'd promised Murphy he'd put Hannah on the next flight to Arizona.

Hannah slipped out the door and around a corner, heading for a different exit—discharge papers and Murphy's apathetic death wish be damned.

SAN DIEGO, CALIFORNIA

The rental car was gone.

Izzy stood for a moment in the apartment complex parking lot, looking at the empty spot where he'd parked the damn thing, mere hours earlier.

Maybe Avis's midnight to six a.m. shift was super efficient.

Or . . . Maybe he was a freaking idiot.

He took the stairs two at a time, unlocked his door and . . .

"Eden?"

The place was silent. The lights that he'd left blazing, turned on when he and Eden had first come home, were all off. Nothing but the dawn's early light, gleaming through the windows, lit the place as Izzy checked the bedroom.

Eden was not there.

She wasn't in the kitchen either. Or the bathroom.

He knew it was stupid, but he even checked the closets.

It was then that he realized that the bag with her clothes was gone, too.

With his heart doing an express elevator ride all the way down to his large intestine, he checked the top drawer of his dresser . . .

His ATM card was still there.

His relief was short-lived.

His fucking ATM card was still there, sure, but Eden was gone.

She hadn't cleaned out his bank account—she'd *only* stolen the rental car.

And the fifty bucks he'd handed her.

And his motherfucking heart.

Disappointment and anger competed in an attempt to choke him as he stood, alone in his apartment.

There had to be a note. Somewhere. Surely she'd at least left him a note.

Izzy could still smell traces of her perfume in the kitchen—where she'd actually cleaned up the mess in the microwave. The sink was scoured, dishes in the dishwasher, counters clear.

It didn't make sense.

Why would she do that?

His bed had been made, too, and the towels neatly arranged in the bathroom.

He went back into the kitchen, where his laptop was out on the table. She hadn't taken that. As far as he could tell, she hadn't taken anything.

Except the rental car . . .

Which he'd asked her to help him with, by finding the nearest rental location—by looking it up online.

He pulled his computer toward him, pushing the screen down almost flat, so he could see it better and . . .

There it was.

Eden's note.

She'd written it on his computer. It filled the screen in an unsent e-mail.

Izzy, I am so, so sorry. I couldn't find a pen or pencil. I hope you find this. I returned the rental car for you at the Sweetwater Road location. There was a drop box for the keys. I borrowed the money you gave me. I'll pay you back, but it might take me awhile. I had

no idea it would be this bad. I hope you'll believe me, but I know
you won't, so I couldn't stay. I'll call you when I figure out what
I'm going to do, and then we can do whatever it takes to annul the
marriage. If it costs money, of course I will pay you back for that,
too. Again, I am deeply sorry.
Sincerely, Eden

What. The fuck?

As Izzy printed out a hard copy of Eden's note, he realized that she'd left her freemail account open. He clicked shut the e-mail she'd left unsent for him, and a recently received e-mail from someone named Britt appeared on the screen. He quickly scanned it—oh, fuck. He clicked on the web browser, where a list of all his laptop's recently visited URLs appeared and . . .

Oh, *fuck.*

Bracing himself, he highlighted GirlsWhoLoveToShag dot-com slash edenzanella and . . .

"Oh, Eed, no," he breathed as the first of what looked like three different homemade sex videos began to play.

DALTON, CALIFORNIA

Hannah put the car that she'd borrowed from Steve and Paul's driveway in a little overgrown pull-off at the bottom of the hill. She backed it in, ready for an easy getaway, which made her feel a little foolish.

But Murphy wasn't going to be happy with her for coming back to Dalton. Maybe if she told him she'd been ridiculously careful, he'd forgive her that much sooner.

And she *was* being ridiculously careful—now, anyway.

Going back to Steve and Paul's had involved some risk, but Hannah had needed a car. Plus, she'd wanted to recover those handguns Murph had submerged in her friends' to-be-recycled kitchen cooking oil.

She was carrying them now, still slippery and coated in grease, in ziplock baggies, in her daypack.

She'd gone into Steve and Paul's apartment via the front stairs from the garage. She'd moved quickly, swiping a clean T-shirt to wear in place of her hospital gown, as well as the keys for this nondescript little not-yet-converted Toyota on her way back out.

As she'd driven away, she'd checked constantly to see if she were being followed. She'd also pulled over at a convenience store to search the vehicle for GPS tracking devices and had found none.

Once back in the car, she hadn't stopped again. She'd driven straight here to Dalton, along roads that were mostly empty, as the night became dawn.

She was going to get that letter and then . . . What? Bring it back to Dave, she supposed, to show it to both a lawyer and to that in-house head-shrinker who had joined the Troubleshooters team.

And ultimately turn it over as evidence, to the FBI.

So, careful or not, it was probable that Murphy was never going to forgive her for that.

I just didn't care enough to do the right thing. That's who I am now. I just don't care about anything . . .

Bullshit.

It was possible that Murphy didn't care about himself, but he cared about her. Hannah knew it. She had it in his own hand, in that note he'd written her.

The note that, because she'd sat down on those stairs to attempt to read it, had saved her life.

Han, he'd scribbled, his penmanship god-awful as always. His handwriting and spelling were that of a slightly dyslexic seventh-grader. His words, however, were something else entirely.

When I said what I said, I meant that I don't have any of the things I thought I'd have, back when that picture was taken. Those things—Angelina, my career, our plans for a home—they're gone. Out of all the things that I had, and things that I thought I'd have by now, I have none. That's what I meant to say. But I don't have nothing, because I have you. Without you, I would have quit a long time ago. Without you, I'd be nothing. I look in the mirror and most of the time I don't recognize my own face. But I'm me again, Han, as much as I'll ever be, when I'm with you. And the really crazy thing is how much you still care about me, how totally you disregard just how different I am, how you can still find me

inside this stranger I've become. And I love you for that. More
than words can say. You made me feel good, too, Han. For the first
time in forever. So don't give up on me. Not yet, okay?

But between the time he'd written that note and the time the FBI had
taken him from the hospital, *Murphy* had quit. *Don't give up on me . . . ?*
He'd gone and given up on himself.

And all that implied "thanks for the sex" bullshit he'd hit her with
back at the hospital had been just that—bullshit. He was actually trying to
hurt her so that she'd . . . what? Run away crying like a little girl?

I know you love me . . . In truth, he had *no* idea.

At any rate, here she was again, demoted from lover and back to playing the role of best friend. Which she was going to do, whether or not Murphy wanted her to.

Hannah climbed the back trail up to Patrick's cabin, acutely aware
that if someone had come here before her, she wouldn't hear them. They
could be hidden in the woods around her. She wouldn't hear the gunshots
that killed her, even if the first one missed.

A bird flew up from the brush in front of her and she dropped to the
ground and rolled to cover, heart pounding. God *damn* it.

She lay there, knowing that she was breathing too loudly, straining to
hear something, anything instead of this freaking nothing. And she knew
that the longer she lay here, the harder it would be to get back up. She had
to do what she'd done at Steve and Paul's. Just keep moving.

Hannah brushed herself off with shaking hands and headed back up
the trail, trying to be as small a target as possible, cursing Murphy. It was
his fault—he'd gotten her all paranoid.

As if the Freedom Network didn't have better things to do than track
her down. If they hadn't bothered to stake out Steve and Paul's apartment—which they hadn't—there was no way they could have tracked her
here. Certainly not through Patrick's car with its out-of-state plates, now
being held in some Sacramento police station lot.

Besides, she hadn't helped Murphy kill Ebersole. If Murphy *had* done
it, and the Freedom Network had proof? They would go after him, not
Hannah.

It was a good theory, albeit slightly flawed.

Murphy had said that the first shot fired outside of Steve and Paul's had been at Hannah. Which meant they'd either pegged her as a co-conspirator or . . .

Or the Freedom Network had a different reason entirely for wanting her and Murphy dead.

That was ridiculous, since it went against the KISS or *keep it simple, stupid* model of investigative reasoning.

Didn't it?

As Hannah climbed the trail, approaching the clearing where her cabin stood, she realized that the KISS method applied, perhaps even more aptly, to a different conclusion.

Just because she and Murphy were intensely aware that he may, indeed, have gone into the Freedom Network compound last March and fatally shot Tim Ebersole, the Freedom Network didn't necessarily know that. Hannah hadn't, after all, been wearing her *My lover shot Tim Ebersole and all I got was this stupid T-shirt* T-shirt.

The only thing Hannah and Murphy could be one hundred percent KISS certain that the Freedom Network knew, was that two outsiders had trespassed onto the Sacramento West compound early yesterday morning. The Freedom Network also knew that those outsiders had tripped an alarm near the location of one of their freak-show ceremonies, and then temporarily taken out two guards as they'd escaped over the back fence.

And in doing so, had created a situation of high alert.

What was it Dave had said? *Ten* Freedom Network vehicles had left the compound in a rush.

So going with that assumption—that the Freedom Network *hadn't* recognized Murphy as Tim Ebersole's shooter—why else then would Craig Reed expend so much energy and expense to chase them down and attempt to kill them?

And there the true KISS-simple answer was—in the camera that Hannah still carried in her daypack.

Not only had Hannah and Murphy seen something that they weren't supposed to see, they'd taken photos of it.

Except, okay. It was possible that the Freedom Network didn't know about the photo part for certain, although Hannah *had* distracted the guards at the electric fence by pretending to be a journalist, waving her camera.

If the ceremony that they'd seen, and the photos they'd taken, *were* something that the Freedom Network would kill them over, well, her current step-one should be to get those pictures to the FBI.

Which was bound to be a little awkward. *Hey, you know the way you questioned me for several hours and I absolutely failed to mention the fact that Murph and I broke into the Freedom Network compound two nights ago?*

And didn't it figure that Hannah hadn't had this epiphany until now, when there wasn't a handy-dandy FBI agent nearby? But she'd been so focused on ending the interview and getting Murphy's letter. She'd been focused on the still-likely possibility that Murphy had killed Tim Ebersole. She'd assumed that revenge was the motive behind the shooting outside of Steve and Paul's apartment.

So okay. She'd blown her chance at an easy hand-off of her camera. Which meant her current priority had to be downloading the pictures onto her computer, and e-mailing copies to everyone she knew—including their FBI brother or sister.

The next step would be to take her camera, with copies of the photos, back to Dave and the FBI, along with Murphy's letter.

Except, shit. She'd taken her laptop to Sacramento. It was in the trunk of Pat's VW Rabbit, in that police parking lot, two hours north.

But . . . all was not lost, because Murphy's laptop was up with the rest of his gear, in the cabin's loft. She'd get it set up and start downloading the pictures while she dug through the boxes in the closet and found his letter. She'd be on her way back to Sacramento well inside of an hour.

Hannah slowed her pace as she approached the back of the cabin. Movement caught her eye out by her garden, but it was only a butterfly.

Her plan was to keep within the cover of the trees and brush, circling around to the front and . . .

Shit. Someone had been here, hiding in the underbrush. Recently. There were scuff marks and even a footprint made by someone with a very large-sized boot. Large, but not quite as large as Murphy's. And okay, that print wasn't two-minutes-ago fresh, as she'd first heartstoppingly thought. It was definitely starting to decay.

Hannah forced herself to breathe because Dave Malkoff had said he'd been in Dalton, looking for Murphy. He'd brought a team with him, and no doubt some of them had been up here, staking the place out, hoping that wherever she and Murph had gone, they'd soon return. It was entirely possible that these footprints belonged to the good guys.

But it would be foolish to assume that without further observation.

Nothing moved up by the cabin, and the driveway was empty.

Which, of course, didn't mean a thing. If she were waiting for someone to come home so that she could kill them, she wouldn't park her car near the house, either.

Trying to move as silently as possible, Hannah got one of the bagged handguns from her pack. She wasn't even sure if the thing would fire, coated as it was with grease and french fry oil, but it would, at the least, be an effective visual aid.

Praying she was being silent, she crept through the brush, moving closer to the front of the house and . . .

A car was coming.

Hannah felt the vibration and saw the light reflecting off the windshield mere seconds before the vehicle—a midsize sedan—pulled up the driveway, and she flattened, weapon held at ready.

The driver was an elderly woman with white hair, as was the person sitting beside her in the front passenger seat. Neither were what Hannah would have expected from a Freedom Network strike force, but she'd learned through experience as a police officer that nothing was impossible.

The passenger turned as if to speak to someone in the backseat. And the driver put down her window. The car's back door opened and a young woman got out. Dark hair, medium height, very pretty.

And heavily pregnant.

Whoever she was, she pulled a duffle bag out behind her, shaking her head to something the driver had asked. As Hannah watched, she lugged the bag right up the stairs to the cabin's porch. Without hesitation, she reached under the rocking chair, where Hannah hid the spare key. She pulled open the screen and unlocked the door. Waving to the sedan's driver, who'd clearly waited to make sure she got safely inside—as if this wasn't already weird enough—she dragged her duffle into the house, the screen slapping shut behind her.

And the twin grannies in the sedan drove away.

What the hell?

The pregnant woman was much too young to be one of Patrick's girl-friends—wasn't she?

But whoever she was, she'd clearly been here before.

Hannah stayed down, prone in the brush, for a good long time, just watching the cabin, wishing that she could hear whether or not there was a conversation going on inside, wondering if this angelic-looking girl was part of a team sent to kill her and Murphy.

SACRAMENTO, CALIFORNIA

"I'm sorry, sir." Danny Gillman had the enlisted man's talent of making *sir* sound like an insult, even over the phone. "Hannah's gone. She put pil-lows in her bed to make it look like she was there, but . . . You had Jay and me guarding an empty room."

Subtext: It was Dave's fault.

And it was. He should have known better.

And okay, in his defense, he'd checked with the nurses' station, where he'd been told that Hannah had been given pain meds that would, indeed, make her want to sleep. So he'd assigned Gillman and Lopez the task of guarding her door while he went downtown to check on Murphy.

"Okay," Dave said, running his hands through his hair in exaspera-tion. "Okay. How long of a lead does she have on us?"

Gillman made a disgusted noise into his end of the phone. "You should have a better idea of that than we do. She left on your watch."

Which was . . . Dave looked at the clock on the wall of the FBI recep-tion area . . . At best, two and a half hours ago. "Unbelievable."

"Yup," Gillman said. "She could be anywhere by now."

"She went to Dalton," Dave told the smug bastard. He had no doubt whatsoever that Hannah would be able to get her hands on a car. If she wasn't in Dalton already, she'd be there soon.

It didn't take a genius to figure out that the mysterious letter of which Murphy and Hannah had spoken contained evidence of Murph's unsta-ble state of mind on or around the time of Tim Ebersole's murder.

An FBI agent was coming down the hall, his shoes clicking on the tile. It was Jules Cassidy, and he was clearly coming to talk to Dave.

Gillman was not convinced. "You know for a fact—"

"Hang tight," Dave said. "I'm going to call you back." He cut the connection and quickly dialed Sophia's number, holding up one finger to Cassidy. "I'm sorry, sir, one minute, please."

Sophia answered on the first ring, speaking softly as if she didn't want to be overheard. "Still no sign of Nash."

"Are you still in Dalton?"

"Yes, we are," she said. "Well, Tess and I are. Tracy had to go back to San Diego for some crazy thing called *work*."

"Put Tess on the phone," Dave ordered.

"She's taking a nap," Sophia informed him. "She didn't sleep at all last night and . . . We're going to check out at noon—"

"Wake her," Dave said. "Now. I need you both to go over to Hannah's. Is Tess armed?" He answered his own question. "It doesn't matter, there's a gun rack in the cabin. Have Hannah unlock it—I have reason to believe she's on her way over there. Arm yourselves, help her find what she came to find, and get out, all right? Murphy thinks the Freedom Network is going to go there, looking for them. On the off chance he's right, I want you in and out."

The FBI agent sighed. "I probably shouldn't have heard any of that," he said as Sophia asked, "Is Hannah going to cooperate?"

"Heard what?" Dave said to Cassidy, turning away slightly to tell Sophia, "Yes, but be careful. She's not expecting you, she's deaf, and she's on edge." He lowered his voice even more. "I'd also bet my next paycheck that she's already armed, so be extra cautious in your approach."

"Got it," Sophia said.

"Call me when you connect with her, okay? And text message Nash. Tell him where you're going, what you're doing, and why. Tell him you need backup, because it's going to be two hours—at least—before I get there."

"Wow," Sophia said. "You know, that was an *awesome* imitation of a team leader—"

"Ha," Dave said, "Ha. Be safe, Soph, okay?" Hanging up he turned to Cassidy.

Who'd clearly heard it all and wasn't happy. "Hannah Whitfield's gone AWOL?" he asked, obviously to confirm he'd heard correctly.

"You got it," Dave said.

"Shit," he said.

"Yeah."

"Murphy's going to be pissed," Cassidy said, as if Dave hadn't figured that one out for himself. The FBI agent laughed his exasperation and disgust as he ran his hands down his face. "This complicates an already complicated situation." He sighed again. "You're going to hate this. You ready?"

Wonderful. "No," Dave admitted. "But go on. Hit me."

"We don't have enough evidence to hold Murphy," Cassidy told him, "because the Freedom Network's been uncooperative. We have reason to believe they're conducting their own investigation, *and* that they have security camera footage that clearly identifies Ebersole's killer. Their intention is not to find him and turn him over to the authorities, but rather to execute him on contact to avenge Ebersole's death."

He took a deep breath. "Gail Deegan, the local agent in charge of this investigation, thinks Murphy did it. Personally, I'm not so sure. But I do think *Murphy* thinks he might've done it. And I think it's entirely possible, after yesterday's shooting, that the Freedom Network thinks Murphy did it. I've been trying to convince Murphy to go in for a series of psychiatric evaluations, during which time he'll be in FBI custody."

And thereby protected from being executed by the Freedom Network. Dave nodded. "What does he have to do to . . . ?"

"It involves a voluntary commitment in a mental health facility," Cassidy said, "which includes a four-day minimum lockdown."

Dave was already shaking his head. "He's never going to agree to that."

"Yup," Cassidy agreed. "Certainly not now that Hannah's AWOL. Thanks so much for that."

"I can't not tell him," Dave said.

"I knew you were going to say that." Cassidy was resigned. "You *do* understand that when he walks out our door, he's a target. And if he's the man they're looking for? They're going to go for him, Dave. I have no doubt of that."

Dave nodded. "Well, it'll be over my dead body," he told the FBI agent.

Who laughed, but not because he found Dave funny. "And somehow I knew you were going to say that, too."

Dalton, California

"Hands where I can see 'em. Now. *Now!*"

Eden opened her eyes to find herself staring into the barrel of a very deadly looking gun. Her hands were under the fleece blanket she'd burrowed beneath as she'd settled in for a nap on the sofa. She struggled to pull them free.

"Don't shoot me, I'm pregnant," she shouted back, which was pretty stupid. "I'm unarmed," she added as she put her hands in the air, which was really what mattered.

It was a hell of a way to wake up, damn near wetting her pants, immediately bursting into tears.

But crap, she'd never seen the business end of a weapon at this proximity. Danny used to hunt, and he'd instilled in her a deep and abiding respect for firearms. You never, *never* aimed a weapon at another person, unless you were willing to use it—and live with the consequences.

Richie had had a handgun not unlike this one, which was one of the reasons Eden had urged Jerry to break ties with him. She'd hated it when he waved it around.

"How many are you?" It was a woman who was holding this gun in Eden's face. Short dark hair, dead-serious eyes that were a mix of blue and green, slightly round cheeks—it was the same woman who was in some of the photos that were on the fireplace mantel and magneted to the refrigerator door. The woman who lived here in this cabin. Hannah Something.

Eden didn't understand the question. How many . . . ? Hannah was deaf, not blind, wasn't she? Hadn't someone said she could read lips?

"Are you here alone?" Hannah all but snarled at her. "That's a yes/no question. Shake or nod your head!"

And Eden got it. "Yes," she answered, nodding emphatically. "It's just me. I'm alone. I didn't think you were coming back right away, so I let myself in. Please, *please*, point that thing away from me!"

With that, the gun, thank God, was out of her face. Hannah, however, did not make it disappear altogether, handling it—unlike Richie—the way Danny always had, as if she knew how to use it.

She was bigger than she looked in the pictures. Taller and more solid, and way more unfriendly for someone who seemed so photogenic. In all the photos, she'd had such a warm, wide, welcoming smile.

Right now, her mouth was a grim line. "Are you with the Freedom Network?" Hannah demanded.

"The who? *No!*"

"Then who the hell are you?"

Of course, she had every right to be angry. Eden *had* broken into her home . . .

"I'm so sorry," she said, wiping her eyes. "I'm Eden. Gillman. I was here just yesterday with some people who were looking for you. You're supposed to be out of town, helping someone named Murphy. I didn't think you'd—"

"Who?" she demanded.

"Murphy?" Eden repeated.

"No, who was looking for us?" She didn't talk like a deaf person, like that character, Joey, on *West Wing,* so maybe she wasn't Hannah. "Give me names."

"Dave," Eden said. "Malkoff. And . . . and . . . Lindsey." What *was* her last name? "Jenkins. And their company. Troubleshooters."

Recognition mingled with relief in the woman's eyes. But there was disbelief there, too. "*You're* one of the Troubleshooters?"

"You *are* Hannah, right?" Eden asked, and the woman nodded. "Should I write this down? Do you understand me? Should I talk more slowly?"

"No," Hannah said. "You're doing fine. Although I didn't get your name. Eve?"

"Eden," she repeated. There was a pad and paper right on a coffee table, probably exactly for this purpose, and she wrote it out for Hannah. *Eden Gillman.* It was probably best to leave Izzy out of this.

The older woman nodded. "Thanks. And yes, I'm Hannah. Do you really work for Troubleshooters?"

"No," Eden said, shaking her head to be even more clear. "My husband—ex-husband—well, he's not my husband, he's a friend. *Was* a friend. He's a SEAL and he and his friends were helping Dave find Murphy."

"Okay," Hannah said. "Most of that before *helping Dave find Murphy?* I didn't get it."

"It's a long story," Eden told her, unable to keep her eyes from tearing up. If Izzy wasn't on his way overseas, he was surely back at his apartment by now. He'd probably found those videos and had already called his lawyer about that annulment. "I didn't think you were going to be back here for a while, so I came because I needed a place to stay while I figured out what I'm going to do. I was going to clean up before I left and . . . lock the door and . . . It was wrong, and I'm sorry, but I was desperate."

Hannah's eyes were not unkind as Eden forced herself not to cry. "How far along are you?"

"Six months. I'm due September second."

"Okay, that's good at least." Hannah carried the gun over to the kitchen and put it on the counter next to the sink. She limped as if she'd twisted her ankle, and as soon as she reached the counter, she leaned on it to keep her weight off her left foot.

Dave had told Izzy, who'd told Eden, that Hannah had been in a really bad car accident, and that the infection in her leg had somehow made her deaf. Eden didn't really get how that could have happened, so it was possible she'd missed something in there.

Hannah quickly washed her hands before turning back to Eden, drying off with the hand towel that had been hanging on the oven door handle. "I was a little afraid I was going to have to add delivering a baby to my *to do* list. You look like you're going to pop any second."

Eden rolled her eyes as she laughed her despair. "I know. What I'm going to look like in September, God only knows." She shifted her feet onto the floor. Lord, she was so tired. "I'll go. I honestly didn't mean to—"

Hannah interrupted. "Who dropped you off? Those ladies in that car . . . ?"

She'd been *watching*? "I was hitchhiking and they picked me up," Eden told her. Sarah and Mary. She'd had to listen to their lectures on the dangers of accepting rides from strangers, for four solid hours. In return, they'd dropped her at the cabin door. "I think they might've been nuns." She took a deep breath. "I know it's a huge imposition, but if I could just sleep on your couch for a little while . . ."

But Hannah was shaking her head. "Sorry," she said. "It's not safe. I'm pretty sure the Freedom Network wants to kill Murph and me." She pulled back the sleeve of her T-shirt and there was a bandage on her arm. "They shot at us in Sacramento."

Eden couldn't believe it. "Shot at you? Why?"

"Long story," Hannah said. "I'll tell you after we're out of here. I'll give you a lift into Dalton, my car's at the bottom of the hill—but until we leave, I need you to be my ears. Sit by the door and let me know if anyone drives past or, God forbid, pulls in. Can you do that?"

Eden nodded. A lift into Dalton. Great.

Hannah dug through a pack that she'd been wearing over one shoulder and took out a cell phone. It was one of those disposable kinds that she'd probably picked up at a drugstore. "I also need you to call Dave Malkoff and tell him where we are, give him this phone number. I think he's probably looking for me, and the sooner he stops freaking, the better. For all of us. Please tell him we'll call him again, when we're done here. We can coordinate where to meet." She held out the phone to Eden. "If you want, you can come along. But I'm not sure how safe it is, and I'm pretty sure we'll end up going to Sacramento. But maybe that's better for you than Dalton."

Eden nodded as she took the phone, her heart still sinking. Dave was going to ask why she wasn't with Izzy and . . . "I don't know Dave's number."

"Then call the Troubleshooters office," Hannah told her, "and get it."

This was, quite possibly, a test. If Eden truly were who she'd said she was, she'd know the location of the Troubleshooters office. As Hannah watched, leaning against the kitchen counter, right next to that handgun, Eden dialed 411.

"What city please?"

"San Diego, California," she told the automated operator, and Hannah nodded. And slipping her weapon into a ziplock baggie, which was kind of odd, she tucked it into her pocket, then limped up the ladder into the loft.

CHAPTER TWENTY

Murphy couldn't believe it.

"As soon as Sophia and Tess have contact with Hannah, they're going to call me," Dave tried to reassure him.

"What the hell, Dave?" He was microseconds from losing it. "That's supposed to make me feel better? That Tess and Sophia could be caught in the next crossfire, too?"

"Lindsey and Mark Jenkins are in the parking lot," Dave told him. "A couple more of their friends–SEALs–are on their way. As soon as they get here—"

"No," Murphy said. "Nope. I am *not* doing this." He looked at Jules Cassidy. "Am I done here?"

"You are." The FBI agent wasn't particularly happy about telling him that.

Murphy bee-lined for the elevators, and when the doors didn't open quickly enough, he pushed open the door to the stairs. It hit the wall with a crash.

Dave was right behind him, reaching for him. "Murph—"

"Get your hands off me!" Murphy kept moving, batting the other man's hand away and great. He'd gone and hurt Dave's feelings. Well, too bad. It was better than Dave or, God, Lindsey ending up dead. God help him, he would not survive another friend getting killed because of him. He would rather die himself, first.

Hurt feelings or no, Dave refused to back down, rattling down the stairs, after him. "We'll go to Dalton, we'll find Hannah—"

"*We* won't do jackshit," Murphy informed him. "*I* will find Hannah, *I* will get her to safety, and you and your team will stay far the hell away from me, do you understand?"

Dave shook his head as he followed Murphy out of the stairwell, into the lobby, into the parking lot. "Sorry. Can't do it."

Lindsey, part Japanese- part Korean-American, was leaning against her car—an unremarkable white subcompact—with her husband. Back in Murphy's other lifetime, when he worked for Troubleshooters, before Angelina's murder, before Lindsey had met her husband, she and Murph had been friends. At maybe one half of his size, she'd often asked him to help her hone her hand-to-hand skills. And he'd often had to resort to sitting on her as the only way to keep her from kicking his ass.

She straightened up as she saw him coming, trepidation in her eyes, clearly unsure as to how happy he'd be to see her again, after all this time. Or maybe it was the fact that he was barreling down upon her, like a freight train, that made her look so uncertain.

"I need to borrow your car," he told her, to hell with the fact that they hadn't so much as said hi to each other in years.

She glanced at her husband, Mark, who was not all that much taller than she was, but far more powerfully built. A SEAL, Dave had said.

"We're here to help," Mark told Murphy, instinctively knowing not to greet him with an outstretched hand. "Get in, and we'll take you wherever you want to go."

"We're waiting for Gillman and Lopez," Dave reminded them. "And damnit. I forgot all about Dr. Heissman. Linds, will you call her for me?"

"I'm on it." Lindsey got out her cell phone.

"The guys'll catch up," Mark said easily. "I'll call and tell Jay that Gillman's gotta drive—"

"No," Murph interrupted. "You misunderstand. I don't want a ride. I want to *borrow* your *car*. You hand me the keys, you stand here, you wave good-bye."

"No way," Lindsey said. "Absolutely not." She turned to Dave. "I'm going straight to the doctor's voice mail. Should I leave a message?"

"Please," he said. "Ask her to call me."

"Why not let us ride shotgun?" Mark asked, easygoing and super-reasonable, good cop to Lindsey's bad.

"Because I don't want you to live through what I did—scrambling on the tarmac, searching through the blood and brains for the missing pieces of your wife's skull," Murphy told him, his voice tight.

"Oh, great, Murph, thanks." Exasperation and disgust rang in Lindsey's voice as she pocketed her phone. "Mark's going to Iraq, probably within the week. Way to distract him while he's over there."

The SEAL was pretty tough. His freckles stood out on his face, as he went slightly pale at Murphy's grim words, but he didn't back down. "I'm sorry for your loss," he told Murphy. "I'm sorry for what you had to endure, but it's my experience that working in a team—"

"Fine," Murphy said, giving up and looking around at the rows of parked motor vehicles. "Don't lend me your car. I'll hotwire one."

"From the FBI headquarters parking lot?" Dave asked, disbelief and amusement in his voice.

"You find this funny?" There was an older model Chevy Impala, the window open a crack, a few cars over from Lindsey's. Murphy checked the plates. California. Good.

"Of course not," Dave said. "Murph, come on. This is insane."

The key to not getting immediately picked up for stealing a car lay in buying extra time by switching license plates. All Murphy needed was a few hours, so he didn't have to do too much switching around—three cars should do it. He checked the bolts that held the Impala's plate in place, but they were too tight for him to turn just using his fingers. "Linds, you got a tool kit?"

"To help you steal a car?" Lindsey asked. "I don't think so."

Dave rubbed his forehead as if he had a terrible headache. "You're not stealing a car, okay? Can we just all take a deep breath—"

Murphy put his fingers into the space created by the partly open window, to see if he couldn't work the glass down. Push came to shove, he could break it . . . But then he saw that the door was unlocked, so he opened it. That was easy.

Dave tried a different approach. "Do you really want to go to jail for stealing a—"

"I don't give a shit what happens to me." Murphy looked up from

where he'd crouched to examine the casing around the base of the steering column. He'd be able to pop that off, no problem, connect a few
wires . . . "Don't you get it? I thought I made that clear *before* you let Hannah go off on her own—"

"Well, way to go." Dave lost his temper, too. "Way to let me know in
advance that your new girlfriend has a WonderWoman complex! I
would've taken precautions if you'd given me a warning. Although you
know what? She probably would've gotten past me anyway. She's as crazy
as you are! *Damn* it, all she had to do was *ask* me and—"

Murphy exploded. "Yeah, like she's going to ask for help from the
company that helped kill her best friend!"

The expression on Dave's face—guilt, remorse, anguish—was one
Murphy recognized. He'd seen it often enough in his own mirror.

"I just want Hannah to be safe," Murphy said, more softly now. "That's
all I want. I'll go to jail forever if I have to, just as long as I know she's safe.
And you're right. You couldn't have stopped her. I'm sorry that I—"

"No," Dave said. "You have every right."

Lindsey was there, then, with the keys to her car. "Take it," she said,
holding the key ring out to Murphy. "Just . . . call me and let me know if
you need help. Oh, and if we don't catch up, letting me know where you
leave it would be nice, too."

As Murphy hugged her, hard, he met her husband's somber gaze over
the top of her head. No doubt Murphy's harsh words about blood and
brains were still echoing in his mind.

Good.

"Don't follow me," Murphy told him, told all of them. "Don't come
near me. It's not safe."

Decker woke up, drooling into a throw pillow on Dr. Heissman's hotel
room sofa.

He'd actually fallen asleep. The fact that he now had to wipe off the
entire lower half of his face was testament to just how soundly he'd been
out.

Light was coming in beneath the heavy curtains that covered the windows and the sharp aroma of something burning filled the room. It was the
coffee pot, in the kitchen corner of the suite. Sometime between now and

late last night, when the doctor had made a half-pot of the stuff, it had boiled itself dry.

Decker took the glass pot from the heater and filled it with cold water—which of course, shattered the damn thing, right there in the sink. Heckuva way to start the morning.

Except it was hardly even morning anymore. He stared at the clock on the microwave. Had he really slept that long?

He checked his watch. Apparently so.

Last thing he remembered was talking with Jo about his "misguided" idea that a relationship could "fix" someone who was broken, i.e., Decker, although they both pretended they were talking about Nash and Tess.

Last night, he'd told Dr. Heissman things he'd never told anyone before—how relieved he'd been when Nash seemed to settle in to their new job at Troubleshooters, and to his new life with Tess. It was as if Nash had been given a chance to start over, start fresh—and he'd embraced it enthusiastically, with a joie de vivre that Decker had never witnessed before.

Thinking back, Decker couldn't remember when that honeymoon period, so to speak, had ended. He'd purposely drifted away from Nash, not wanting to feel like a third wheel. And okay, yes. A truth had been outed in his rant that Jo Heissman had not missed. *I wanted what Nash had found . . .*

Last night he'd admitted to Dr. Heissman that, before Nash first hooked up with Tess, Deck had had a little fantasy going. One that included him coming home from a mission to find Tess waiting there, with her warm smile and . . . Yes, he'd imagined definite possibilities—that Nash had stomped on with both feet. Not out of malice, but out of ignorance. Decker had, after all, played the maybe-Tess-could-be-his-girlfriend card extremely close to his chest.

So after Nash and Tess got together, Decker had kept his distance. Not because he loved Tess—he didn't—but because he *could* have loved her.

And because, yes, he wanted what Nash had appeared to have found.

And then Angelina had died, leaving him even more isolated.

It was then that the doctor had laughed and asked him if there were any disasters that had happened in the course of his lifetime that he *didn't* feel responsible for . . .

And somewhere in there, in one of the moments of silence that grew longer and more frequent, he'd fallen asleep.

The suite was now quiet. Empty.

Decker stuck his head in the bedroom, but the doctor wasn't in there, the bathroom door open, the room dark. Her suitcase—small, with wheels—was open on the low dresser, beside another TV.

Decker didn't hesitate. He flipped the light switch and carefully went through her bag. Her pink nightgown was on top, and it slipped through his fingers, as soft to the touch as he'd imagined. Slippers, robe, a plastic baggie with travel-size toiletries. The clothes she'd been wearing yesterday, neatly rolled up. A hooded sweatshirt that said *MIT*. A romance novel about . . . vampires? Huh. He would have expected nonfiction. Something dry and scholarly, perhaps trying to prove a connection between ADD and spec ops warriors.

But vampire lovers . . . ? Of course, he'd been surprised by the pink nightie, too.

And, after he'd had his little meltdown, he'd also been surprised by the way Jo Heissman had opened up, so seemingly candidly, about her years with the Agency.

"I left shortly after you and Nash did," she had told Decker as he'd sat on the sofa, still numb and emotionally exhausted. "It was within a month." She smiled. "Douglas Brendon didn't like me very much either."

"How come I never met you at HQ?" Decker managed to ask.

"The Psych department kept a low profile," she told him. "Although I did run into Nash once, in the basement hall."

Which was why Nash had pulled her aside, after that meeting where Tommy'd introduced her to the team. Deck had heard him ask her, "Have we met?" At the time, she'd denied it.

"I didn't think he'd remember me," the doctor said now. "We really just . . . crossed paths. Of course, I knew who *he* was. Before Doug Brendon took over and changed procedures," she explained, "certain key staff members in the psych department regularly convened to review the profiles and evaluations of those operatives given high stress assignments— such as Nash. And yourself."

"You've seen my Agency psych file?" Decker couldn't believe it. Or, Jesus, maybe he could. Still, he couldn't just take her word for it. "So you know about the little, uh—" he cleared his throat delicately "—impotence problem?"

She smiled. "I don't recall any reference to that, no. And as a symptom of stress, it would have been a topic of discussion. However, I do believe we spent quite some time on your insomnia. John—Dr. Westley—felt your failure to sleep was tied to your self-imposed celibacy, which was a subject of intense fascination to him. Probably because, as a field operative, you could have gone into Support, snapped your fingers, and had a half a dozen attractive women vying to go home with you. His finger snaps didn't get quite the same results."

"Yeah," Decker said. "Because he was married."

"Divorced," she corrected him, "although perhaps he didn't share that with you. Dr. Westley was impressed—we all were—with your moral compass. Whether it was the right choice or not, you felt strongly about your decision to refrain from intimate relationships with your coworkers, and you stuck with it. Even though it apparently cost you your potential relationship with Tess Bailey." She paused. "What else can I tell you to convince you that—"

"I'm convinced," Decker said. "At least that you've seen my file, and talked about me with John Westley. How about Nash? You review his file with Westley, too?"

"Not in detail, no."

Decker nodded. "Well, that's convenient."

"He wasn't one of Westley's cases," Dr. Heissman told him.

"Yeah, he was. He told me—"

"Did he?" she asked. "Or did you just assume?"

Decker was silent. It was entirely possible that he'd assumed . . .

"That hallway in the basement? Where I saw Jim Nash?" she said. "It led to a highly classified, high-security-clearance section of the building. He was alone, and he went through the door, so he must have had the code to unlock it." She got up to pour herself another cup of coffee from the pot she'd made. "You were aware, of course, that there was a sector within the Agency that performed primarily black ops. Your file was flagged as approached, but black op status was denied. Do you want to know why?"

Black ops were operations or missions that were so top secret, so covert, that there were no records kept, no paper trail. Early in his Agency career, Decker *had* been approached, very much in a sideways manner, about the possibility of his accepting a black op assignment. He'd gotten as far as a psych eval, but then all talk stopped. "I'll bite," he said. "Why?"

"According to your file," Dr. Heissman said as she sat back down across from him, tucking her legs up underneath her, "you were considered too much of a straight arrow to be considered for such an assignment. Again with the moral compass. I believe the phrase *too grounded in a fact-based reality* was used to describe you."

"Too *what?*" Had she really meant what he'd thought she'd meant . . . ?

"They didn't believe they could successfully manipulate and therefore control you," she translated.

"And you're saying Nash was . . ."

"A ghost," she finished for him. "That was our little psych department nickname for the black sector operatives. It would explain why his file never appeared in our bimonthly meetings."

Decker nodded. "But you don't know for sure."

"I saw him go through that door."

"What were *you* doing down there?" Decker asked.

"It was toward the end of my tenure with the Agency," Dr. Heissman told him. "Doug Brendon had just been appointed new director, and I was naively hopeful he would bring about some desperately needed changes and, well . . . He changed things, all right. At that time, though, he was interviewing everyone in the department, because his goal was to expand the black ops sector. I was told by my supervisor that I was up for a particularly important promotion, and she gave me what she called the correct answers to all the questions Brendon was intending to ask in the interview—questions about how the department should be run, questions about basic procedures—such as required downtime between difficult assignments—procedures that were put in place years ago to keep our operatives healthy . . ." She shook her head. "I wouldn't do it. I went into the interview and answered his questions with truth, not this . . . cockeyed truthiness he wanted to hear. He didn't want our input, he wanted yes-men and -women. Needless to say, I wasn't given the promotion, so I never made it past that locked door. And shortly after, I tendered my resignation." She smiled. "I suspect there's now a note in *my* Agency file that says, *too grounded in a fact-based reality.*"

They'd sat for several long moments, in silence, and then she'd leaned forward and said, "I'm sorry I don't have more definite information about Nash to share with you, but I'm pretty sure, as it stands, I've broken the law forward and backward and upside down by telling you all that I have."

He'd nodded. "I appreciate that."

"We're on the same side," she'd told him.

Decker had nodded again, even though now, in the harsh light of day, he still wasn't convinced of that.

He'd just unzipped the side pocket of the doctor's bag when he heard the keycard in the door. He quickly zipped it shut and was in the bathroom, toilet seat up and taking a leak before she got the door open.

"Hello?" she called.

"I'll be out in a sec," he called back, taking time to wash his hands and try to smooth down the sorry mess that was his hair. He finally gave up and stuck his head under the faucet, and used his fingers as a comb.

"I brought you coffee," she said, when he finally emerged.

She was wearing a dark pair of pants and a colorful, flowing blouse that made him think of photographs of women from the sixties. Kent State. Haight-Ashbury. Woodstock. It worked with her hair, loose from its braid in full earth-mother splendor, and with the bright red toenail polish revealed through the leather straps of her sandals.

She was holding out a hotcup with a lid, and he managed to take it from her without their hands touching.

"So, did you go through my bag?" she asked while he was trying to pull back the plastic opening in the lid.

Of course her direct question made him burn his fingers. It took all he had not to react. Still, he answered her honestly. Why the hell not? "Most of it. Yeah."

She nodded, not at all perturbed. "It was a gamble, but I was starving, and I was pretty sure that an opportunity to violate my right to privacy would trump your need to run away, as far and as fast as possible." She smiled. "Provided you woke up. When I left the room, you were sleeping extremely ferociously. Do you still have trouble sleeping?"

Decker took a sip of coffee and it burned all the way down. "Shouldn't you put out your sign? *The Doctor is In.*"

"Darn," she said. "I almost made it through an entire month without a single *Peanuts* joke."

"I really have to go," he said.

To his surprise, she acquiesced. "All right." But then she said, "My ride has been temporarily sidetracked. Can I trouble you for a lift over to FBI headquarters?"

DALTON, CALIFORNIA

Murphy's laptop was ancient. Hannah tried not to be overwhelmed by her frustration as she coaxed it to connect with her camera.

It was, after all, a miracle that he still had his laptop at all. He'd lost his truck during the months she was coming to think of as the Time of Darkness. Someone had rolled him and he'd woken up without his keys, his truck never to be seen again.

But he'd had his laptop in long-term storage in Juneau and had retrieved it during the trip he'd taken there after going through the Fresh Start program.

Because the cabin in Dalton was small, he hadn't bothered to set it up in the living room. Instead, he'd kept it in the loft. But as Hannah climbed the ladder, she saw that he'd taken his computer out of both his duffle and its case. It was open, out next to the mattress that lay directly on the floor because the ceiling was so low up there, it didn't make sense to set up a real bed.

Murph's laptop was plugged into the loft's single outlet, and powered up. His screensaver—a series of photos that were clearly of Alaska—presented a continuous slide show.

Mendenhall glacier.

Juneau's harbor, taken from the windows of the Hanger—Murphy's favorite place to break for lunch. It was summer—cruise ships were docked at the deep-water port.

The breathtaking view of the mountains, from the deck of the *California Dreamin'*, Pat's boat.

Hannah, jubilant, as four different whales simultaneously breached off the stern side of the boat.

God, she looked impossibly young in that picture, but she still remembered the day that photo had been taken. She and Murph had gone out that night, to see Rory Stitt in concert over at the high school, and she'd been so certain that Murphy was finally going to kiss her after they'd stopped for a beer at the Triangle on their way home.

Instead, he'd told her about his stepmother moving his father into a nursing home, because the old man didn't recognize her anymore, and had held her at gunpoint—this strange woman he'd found in his house—until the police came.

The elder-care facility was a nice enough place, clean and bright, and Murphy said his dad seemed puzzled but happy to be there. Still, the lockdown security had made Murph's skin crawl. He understood—it wouldn't do to have one of the patients go walkabout—but it still seemed oppressive, particularly for a man who'd spent most of his life out-of-doors.

And the way his stepmother vanished from the old man's life had shaken Murphy, too. She'd disappeared completely, as if her husband of seven years was already buried and gone. Still, Murphy couldn't blame her. It was as if, to Murphy's father, she'd never existed. When he asked for his wife, it was Murphy's mother he was looking for, Murphy's mother he spoke of with love and affection.

Murphy, too, often went unrecognized by his dad. It wasn't uncommon for the old man, lost in his memories of Vietnam, to accuse Murphy of being an agent for the Viet Cong. The racial slurs that had come out of the mouth of a man who'd been known for his acceptance and tolerance were shocking.

Murph had come the closest Hannah had ever seen to crying when he'd told her about that. Yet in true Murphy style, he'd bright-sided it. It had given him new insight, he'd said, into this man who, despite his battlefield prejudices, had fallen desperately in love with a Vietnamese girl and, after her untimely death, had lovingly raised their only child.

So, there had been no kissing that night, although several days later, via phone, when Hannah had dissected the nonprivate parts of their conversation, Angelina was convinced that Murphy'd been looking for some "comfort with a capital s-e-x." Why else get all touchy-feely?

One of these days, Angelina had counseled, Hannah was simply going to have to risk everything, throw caution to the wind, and jump that yummy Vinh Murphy. Go big or stay home.

Of course, Angelina had said that before she'd met Murph. Before he came to Hannah's apartment the night of his father's funeral, took one look at Angelina and jumped *her*.

Or so she'd said, when she'd told Hannah about it. Hannah had found out later, after she'd wrapped Murphy up, put a bow on him and virtually given him to her best friend—because she'd thought that that was what

Murphy'd wanted—that Angelina had been the one to jump *him*. And the jump, so to speak, had been incomplete, thanks to Murphy's code of honor.

Angelina's code of honor had been slightly different.

It's not stealing if they give it to you.

Hannah had forgiven her friend, assuming—incorrectly—that Angelina would eventually tire of Murphy. And then, when it became clear that the pair truly were a match made in heaven, Hannah had danced at their wedding, glad for their happiness, unaware of the tragedy that was yet to come.

Hannah unplugged the laptop and—God, it was heavy—lugged it down the ladder. She put it on the desk, dug through the drawer that held a collection of computer cables, found the one that would allow her to download the pictures from her camera, connected everything together, and . . .

Got the hourglass of doom.

"Shit."

Eden Gillman, who looked like an escapee from a Lifetime movie about teen pregnancy—Hollywood-attractive even while exhausted and bedraggled—brought over the notepad, upon which she'd written *What's the problem?*

"I have no idea," Hannah answered. "I need to download these pictures . . ." She pointed to the camera.

Want me to try? I'm pretty good with computers.

"Please." Hannah relinquished the chair. "Did you reach Dave?"

Eden reached for the pen, but Hannah stopped her. "I can lip-read. If I have a question, I'll ask."

The girl nodded. She *was* extremely pretty—obviously too pretty for her own good, which, okay, wasn't fair but was probably true. She had long, straight dark hair that, even worn back in a ponytail, was sleek and beautiful. She was wearing makeup that made her look at least old enough to vote, but in truth, she could have been anywhere from fourteen to twenty.

"I left a message," she told Hannah, as she worked the mouse, "because Dave didn't pick up. Here's one of the problems. It's going so slowly because there're too many files and programs open. We need to close— Whoa, is that you?"

Hannah looked at the computer screen, where there were, indeed, what looked like a dozen photos of her, thumbnailed in a picture file that Murphy had named *Juneau*. Some of them were landscapes, sure, but most were of Hannah, laughing on Pat's boat.

Eden leaned forward to look closer. "These are amazing. Whoever took these is an excellent photographer." She moved the mouse, scrolling down and Hannah realized there weren't just a dozen, there were closer to a hundred.

"They're Murphy's," Hannah told her.

She'd had no idea he'd taken so many photos over the years. She knew he had a camera, but he wasn't one of those people who always interrupted the flow of the moment to make everyone pose. Instead, he snapped candid pictures.

Eden spoke, but Hannah missed it—intent on looking at one of the rare shots where Murphy was also in the frame. In this one, he was tickling her, and she was trying to escape. "Excuse me?" She looked at Eden.

"He's completely in love with you," the girl said. "I mean, he's gotta either be your boyfriend or your stalker."

"He was married to my best friend."

"Really? That's kind of creepy. I mean, he's got everything but the altar and the candles."

"These were taken a long time ago," Hannah told her.

"Yeah, well, he was looking at them the last time he used his computer," Eden pointed out. "So you should probably tell your friend—"

She'd clearly missed Hannah's use of the past tense. "She's dead."

"Oh, my God." Eden briefly closed her eyes, then looked at Hannah in sincere apology. "I'm so sorry. I knew that. I wasn't thinking—"

"Just . . . do whatever you need to do to download the pictures from the camera," Hannah said.

"Already doing it," Eden said, and sure enough, there were the pictures from the compound, in a neat little file on Murphy's laptop screen. She leaned closer. "*What* is *this*?" She enlarged the photo of the naked guy bursting out of the burning house. "Oh, *yuck*. Please tell me that's not Murphy."

"Murphy has hair," Hannah reassured her. "Plus he usually wears pants."

Eden leaned even closer to the computer screen. "Oh, my God," she said. "Is he . . . ?"

"A victim of a tragic Nair accident?" Hannah finished for her. "Either that, or he's the new leader of the Freedom Network, participating in some weird initiation ceremony."

Eden looked at her sharply. "Are you serious?"

"There's a good chance these pictures are why Freedom Network shooters put a bullet hole in my arm yesterday," Hannah said.

Eden flipped through them. "Black robe to white robe," she said. "Kinda cliché, isn't it? Although we should probably be glad there wasn't a human sacrifice." She looked at Hannah with trepidation. "There *wasn't* a human sacrifice . . . ?"

"No. But when they took Naked Guy here into the cabin, we had a few minutes of pretty intense oh-my-God. We thought maybe *he* was going to be the sacrifice."

Using the mouse, Eden clicked through the pictures, and seeing, in rapid succession, Naked Guy's exit from the burning house was both humorous and bizarre. Eden ran it backward and then forward, rubbing her expanded belly with her left hand. "It's like he's being born," she mused. "Symbolically. Which would explain the lack of body hair. Which you've got to assume was intentional. I mean, he's got his eyebrows, so it's not some weird no-hair medical condition. What I don't get is, why the fire? If I were trying to symbolize birth, it would be from darkness to light, from wet to dry—not leaping from a burning building."

"Rising from the ashes," Hannah realized. "It's not a birth, it's a rebirth." Was it possible?

She'd had a feeling that she'd seen the Naked Guy before, but until this moment, it hadn't occurred to her that he could be . . .

Tim Ebersole . . . ?

Hannah had seen pictures of the Freedom Network leader, but never without the beard and his thick, dark head of hair. She pulled the computer closer to her, took the mouse out of Eden's hand, excited by the possibility. Murphy couldn't be found guilty of murder if Ebersole were still alive. "We need to find a picture of Tim Ebersole without his beard."

Eden still hadn't put two and two together. "The dead guy?"

"The guy most in need of a rebirth." Hannah typed in the URL for the Freedom Network's website. She'd visited the site often enough and had learned to brace herself for the ugliness of its home page. Ebersole was known to be camera-shy, but there was definitely a picture of the man on his bio page and . . .

Huh. It was gone.

Hannah quickly surfed through the site and . . .

Someone had pulled all of the photos of Tim Ebersole. There wasn't even one included in the article about the national day of mourning, called for by Craig Reed and the other FN leaders.

She jumped to Google, and went to the latest newspaper articles about Ebersole's death. The picture at the *New York Times* website was blurry, and in it Ebersole had his trademark heavy beard.

Eden tapped her on the arm. "I'm pretty sure there are computer programs that'll compare faces or bone structure or—" She turned her head, a sudden sharp movement. "I hear something." She stood up, moving toward the front windows, but then turned to look back at Hannah, alarm in her eyes. "A car's coming!"

Time went into slow motion, as all of Hannah's options clicked clearly into place.

Grab the camera—she'd already done that when the word *car* was still on Eden's lips.

Grab her pack.

Grab a weapon—Hannah was still carrying the grease-coated handguns, but she still didn't know if they were little more than a threatening prop. Two quick strides brought her to the gun case, her keys already in her hand. She grabbed the lightest weight rifle and ammo, some extra for the handguns, jamming it into her pack.

Grab the girl. "Get back from the windows!"

Option A: Go out the back, hope whoever was coming for her was unaware of the trail, unaware of her car parked at the base of the hillside.

But with her bad ankle, weighed down further by a heavily pregnant young woman, they weren't exactly going to fly down that trail. And being caught in the open by people who quite probably wanted to kill her?

Not good.

Which left Option B: Lock the windows and doors and hunker down. Call for help.

"Lock the front door," she ordered Eden, while she went to the back, but God, it was too late, a man was already coming inside.

And the world switched from slow-mo to strobe, like some cheap action movie without a budget for special effects.

He was tall, he was dark, but even backlit the way he was, Hannah knew that he wasn't Murphy, and she dropped the unloaded rifle and pulled out the handgun, aiming it at him through the ziplock baggie, shouting, "Freeze!"

But he didn't freeze.

Maybe his world was as silent as hers, or maybe she hadn't been loud enough, or maybe he couldn't tell that she had a weapon inside of this baggie, so she squeezed the trigger, pumping a bullet into the frame of the door, just to the left of his head.

At least that was where she'd intended to aim it, but he fell to the floor like a stone.

Chapter
Twenty-one

Tess was trying her hardest not to be distracted, but Sophia knew it was a struggle.

They'd both expected *some* kind of response from Nash, to the text message Sophia had sent about needing backup.

Of course, it was entirely possible he was already in Mexico— apparently that was where he went when he ran away from life. It was also possible, wherever he was, that he was too drunk to hear his cell phone ringing.

Maybe it's time to move on. Sophia and Tracy, both, had gently made that suggestion to Tess last night.

But that's what Jim wants me to do, she'd argued. *He's here. I know he's still here. He's waiting for me to leave, to give up, to quit. He needs to see me walk away. But I'm not going to. I won't do it . . .*

Now, Sophia was driving Tess's car, and before she pulled onto the dirt and gravel drive that led to Hannah Whitfield's cabin, she braked to a stop. "Ready?" she asked the other woman, who had far more experience as a field operator.

Tess checked her sidearm and nodded.

At the start of the half-hour ride out here from the Dalton motel, they'd discussed the best way to approach Hannah's cabin. They knew that if she believed the Freedom Network was hunting her she'd be leery of all visitors.

But they'd agreed that a completely overt approach would work best. Sure, Hannah might see their car, get spooked and run. On the other hand, if they crept up on her through the woods, she could well open fire. Dave had said she was most likely armed.

So Tess had written a sign with a black Sharpie on the back of their motel invoice: WE ARE MURPHY'S FRIENDS.

Sophia had to rev the car's engine to make it up the steep driveway, and gravel spun beneath the tires. She pulled to a stop in front of the cabin, turning off the car as Tess got out, holding the sign up, with two obviously weapon-free hands.

The cabin looked much as it had when Sophia was here yesterday, the door tightly shut. It was silent and still, no birds chirping, nothing moving.

But then, from inside the cabin, someone started shrieking— "Freeze!" "No!"—and the unmistakable sound of a gunshot exploded, echoing in the morning heat.

Eden had thought it was Izzy—that shadowy shape of a man coming through the cabin's back door—and when she'd seen Hannah raise her gun, she'd screamed. "No!"

It was useless, futile—screaming at someone who couldn't hear her, and as Eden had watched in horror, the gun went off and the man slumped, lifeless, to the ground.

Hannah had killed him. She'd killed Izzy, except whoever was lying there dead wasn't Izzy after all. His hair was darker and he wasn't as tall or as wide, but he was definitely dead, lying in a growing pool of blood.

Hannah was on her knees next to him—was this Murphy?—saying, "No, God, no," as Eden sobbed both her relief and her fear, then, "Get me a towel! Eden! Now!"

What did Hannah think? That a towel was going to help a bullet wound to the head? Oh, crap, she was going to throw up.

"Do it!" Hannah shouted, and she was still holding that gun, so Eden forced back the bile that was rising in her throat and scrambled for the kitchen, just as the front door—that she hadn't yet had a chance to lock— burst open.

Hannah didn't hear it, but she felt it, and saw it—in the sudden shift of Jim Nash's still slightly glazed eyes.

She hadn't shot him—Jim Nash, from Troubleshooters.

He wasn't dead as she'd first believed, because no way could anyone have survived a pointblank gunshot to the head, except as Hannah had dropped to her knees beside him, he'd stirred, and God, opened his eyes, and she'd realized that a golf-ball-sized chunk of wood had been ripped from the rough-hewn walls by the force of her bullet, hit him in the head and knocked him out.

He had one hell of a gash, and it was bleeding profusely, as head wounds often did, but he tried to sit up, which was when his gaze shifted left, over her shoulder.

Whoever'd been approaching in that car had come through the door, and Hannah turned, bringing her gun hand up into firing position. Except Nash then moved, and with more force than she would ever have believed possible from a man who mere moments earlier had been unconscious, he threw himself on top of her, on top of her weapon, bringing it down and knocking it out of her hand where it skittered, still in its plastic bag, across the floor.

A petite woman, with the kind of Glinda-the-good-witch coloring and complexion that Hannah had dreamed of having, back when she was five and still had Cinderella aspirations, stopped the weapon with one tiny foot.

"We're friends," she said, looking directly at Hannah and speaking clearly. "Of Murphy's. From Troubleshooters. I'm Sophia and this is Tess. You've clearly already met Jim Nash. Dave Malkoff sent us to help you."

And Hannah sagged with relief.

"I'm all right," were the first words out of Jim Nash's mouth, as Sophia closed the cabin door behind her.

Tess just shook her head in disbelief. "This is what you call backup?" she asked. She was livid. No doubt she'd first thought, as Sophia had, that Hannah had shot Nash, that he was bleeding to death, or even already dead. "This is how you *help*?"

She had every right to be angry, but there were other far more pressing questions to be answered first. Such as, what on earth was Eden Gillman doing there? "Is Izzy here?" Sophia asked the girl.

But Eden, delivering a kitchen towel to Hannah, who used it to stanch the flow of Nash's blood, shook her head, no. She was clearly shaken by what could well have been a catastrophe. But there was no time now to *what if.* Or even try to figure out why Eden was here without her fiancé. No, Izzy was her husband now. The girl was wearing a slender gold wedding band on her left hand.

"Eden, sit down before you faint," Sophia ordered. "Jim, do you need help getting cleaned up, or . . ."

"I'm fine," he said, which was such a bald-faced lie, it was all she could do not to laugh in his battered, blood-splattered face.

"Then go wash up," she told him, turning to Tess. "Someone needs to—"

"Stand guard," Tess finished for her. "I'm on it." She went out the front door without looking back, closing it tightly behind her.

The impending conversation between Tess and Nash was most likely going to get noisy. But both operatives were professionals, and Sophia knew it wouldn't happen until later.

Sophia held out a hand to help Hannah up from the floor. "Did you get what you came back here for?" she asked her. "Dave said something about . . . a letter?"

"Yeah, not yet." Hannah limped over to the kitchen sink to wash Nash's blood from her still-shaking hands.

Dave had told Sophia that Hannah Whitfield reminded him of Tess, and she could definitely see why. Hannah was taller than Tess—and more buxom—but they had similar coloring. Dark hair, fair complexion, similarly shaped faces with wide, generous mouths that, in better times, would be equally quick to quirk into a warm smile.

There were similarities, too, in the clothes they chose to wear. They both dressed for efficiency and comfort, although Hannah leaned more toward the Lieutenant Starbuck end of the spectrum with her clunky boots, cargo pants, and T-shirt.

They had the same no-nonsense attitude, and probably the same inability to see themselves accurately, as the enormously attractive women that they were.

Sophia waited until Hannah turned back around to say, "Well, find it, fast, so we can get out of here." She took out her cell phone—she'd promised Dave she'd call him upon contact with Hannah.

"There's something else I have to do," Hannah told her. "There are photos I need to e-mail to the FBI, ASAP." She glanced at Eden, who was sitting, silent and pale at the dining table, holding what looked like a disposable cell phone to her ear, as if she were listening to voice mail messages. "We got them downloaded to the computer, but I still need to . . . You wouldn't happen to know if there's a clear, mug-shot quality photo of Tim Ebersole anywhere online, would you? I checked the Freedom Network website, but they've pulled all their photos of him. Which is kind of weird."

"I'm not sure," Sophia admitted. "But I'd bet Dave would know. What's going on?"

"This is going to sound crazy," Hannah said, "and maybe this is just wishful thinking on my part, but . . . I think it might be possible that Murphy didn't kill Tim Ebersole. I think it's possible that Ebersole's still alive. That Murphy and I saw him yesterday morning."

Sophia stood there, about to dial Dave, uncertain of what to say. Nash had come out from the bathroom to listen, towel wadded up and pressed against the side of his head. She met his skeptical eyes briefly before looking back at Hannah. "I'm pretty sure Ebersole's remains were carefully identified. Using a number of scientific tests. Dental records, DNA . . ."

"I know," Hannah said. "I'm probably wrong. But . . . tests *can* be manipulated. And we have these photos. I just want to see a recent picture of Ebersole. Preferably without a beard."

"Photos can be manipulated, too," Sophia pointed out. "Even if you do have a photo of him, who's to say it wasn't taken before he died."

"I am," Hannah said, defensively. "I took these pictures. Yesterday morning."

"I believe you," Sophia soothed her. "It's just . . . with photographs so easy to doctor, the FBI may require slightly more substantial proof. If your goal is to free Murphy—"

"Murphy's free," Eden announced from her seat at the table.

Hannah, of course, didn't hear her, so Sophia repeated her words for the deaf woman.

"What? When?" Hannah looked at Eden, who was holding up the disposable cell phone.

"Dave called back, a few minutes ago, probably during all the screaming," she announced. "He said to tell you that Murphy's coming here—and he's mad as hell that you put yourself in danger. Oh, and also?" She laughed, but it was on the verge of hysterical. "Dave says that Sophia and Tess are on their way."

NORTH OF DALTON, CALIFORNIA

Murphy's disposable cell phone rang, and he looked at it, to see who was calling.

Which was kind of stupid, since only two people had this number. Dave. And Hannah.

It was Hannah's disposable cell number flashing on the cheap little screen, so he answered it. Not that he'd be able to talk directly to her, which was just peachy keen. Just what he wanted—to have *this* conversation through an intermediary.

"Yeah," he said, as he tucked the damned thing under his chin.

"Murph. It's Sophia. Ghaffari?"

As if he'd forgotten her, or had more than one friend name Sophia.

She didn't give him time to respond. Or maybe she did, and he simply didn't use it quickly enough. "I'm here, at the cabin in Dalton, with Nash and Tess. We've got Hannah. She's safe. I've got you on speaker, so she can talk to you directly."

"Did she find what she went there for?" Murphy asked, waiting as Sophia communicated his words to Hannah.

"I did," Hannah answered herself.

"Soph, don't tell Hannah what I'm saying," Murphy said. "I'm talking to you right now, okay? I want you to burn it. Just take a match and—"

"Murph," Sophia started, her tone conciliatory.

"It's a letter that I wrote, asking Hannah to help me kill Ebersole. I don't remember writing it, so she thinks it's proof of temporary insanity, but I think it's what they'll use to tie her to me as an accomplice to murder, so burn—"

"What if the Freedom Network's not after us because they think you killed Tim Ebersole?" Hannah spoke over him, probably able to tell from Sophia's expression what he was saying. "In fact, what if they *know* you couldn't have killed him—because he's still alive?"

"What?" Murphy laughed despite himself, but then got upset. What kind of painkiller had they given her at the hospital? "Damnit, Han, are you high?"

Again, she spoke over him. "I know you probably think I've lost it, but Murph, those pictures we took? At the compound? I think the hairless naked guy is Tim Ebersole."

"Sophia," Murphy implored.

"We found a photo of Ebersole," she told him, "taken about twenty years ago, before he grew the ZZ-Top beard. Of course, now we're dealing with a twenty-year age difference, but—"

"Why would he fake his death?" Murph asked.

"*I'm* definitely not high," Sophia continued, "and comparing the men in the two photos? It could be Ebersole. Murph wants to know why he would fake his death," she added, obviously speaking to Hannah.

"Because it would be a total hat trick win for him." Hannah had clearly given this some thought. "He was under investigation for tax evasion," she pointed out. "Not only would that case be dropped, his death would invigorate the Freedom Network financially. I've got to assume they had an insurance policy for him—bingo, instant funds, but on top of that, hundreds of FN members would donate money in his memory. And then there's the whole martyrdom dealio. A good assassination always gets the mob mentality revving. *They killed our leader*—even though two weeks ago they were going *Tim who?* But now the Freedom Network's back in the news, all those fringe groups that were considering splintering off repledge their allegiance, new members join, and a new leader steps in—only most people don't realize it's the same leader with a new name, risen from the ashes."

"Soph, express my total disbelief and ask Hannah how the store tags on the dishes and towels play into her conspiracy theory," Murphy said, waiting while his words were repeated.

"Shut. Up," Hannah said. "Murph, you need to see these photos—it's *him*. And you know what? It does play in. It totally reinforces the idea that Tim *didn't* spend months at that cabin on sabbatical. He was in seclusion, prepping for his impending death, and then waiting for his 'body' to be discovered in a cabin where no one had eaten a meal or taken a shower. God, I wonder who it really was who died. We should ask the FBI to check the Freedom Network's records, see who left the organization—no doubt for personal reasons—back in March."

"This is crazy," Murphy said.

"No, it's not."

"Hannah," Murphy said. "I know you don't want it to have been me, you know, who killed Ebersole. I appreciate your loyalty, and your willingness to reach for another answer—any answer—other than the one that has me climbing that fence and firing that rifle. But the FBI is pretty convinced that the Freedom Network has some kind of proof as to the shooter's identity, and I've got to agree with them." He paused, to give Sophia time to repeat his words to Hannah.

"Murph," Hannah started.

"Sophia, will you ask her to let me finish? Please?"

There was a murmur of voices, then Hannah spoke, her voice tight. "Go ahead."

"I don't want your help," Murphy told her, then realized he had to get specific. "I don't want Hannah's help, I don't want Troubleshooters' help—other than to get Han safely to Arizona as soon as possible. Like now. Like, get into your cars and drive away. I'm coming to Dalton, but I'm only coming there to pick up my gear. I'm outa here, and it'll be much easier—for all of us—if Hannah's not there when I stop by."

The pause was only a brief one, because Sophia was getting faster at repeating his words.

"I'm not going to Arizona," Hannah said. "I'm going back to Sacramento. I've already e-mailed those photos to the FBI. I'm going to tell them the whole truth this time—that we hopped those fences, and that these pictures were taken yesterday morning. I'm going to tell them that we're the reason the Freedom Network sent those ten cars out of the compound—that they were looking for us, and that when they found us at Steve and Paul's, they were shooting to kill, and that I believe it's because of what we saw and not anything we did."

Murphy laughed his despair. "And you think, what? The gang from the Bureau's going to take one look at you and go, *wow, she's completely impartial, so her crazy-ass conspiracy theory* must *be true.* Jesus, Han, it's beyond obvious to anyone with *eyes* that there's something going on between us, and *you* should *know* it's a law enforcement fact that having sex with someone makes you the opposite of impartial. You told me that, yourself, a few years ago. What they're going to think is that you're involved with me—on all levels."

"I *am* involved," she retorted. "And you know what? I'm freaking tired of pretending that I'm not—that I'm not in love with you. God, you've been wrong about a lot of things, Murph, for so many years, but you finally got that one right. I love you. And I'm *not* leaving you to face this alone."

DALTON, CALIFORNIA

Hannah died a million times, watching Sophia for Murphy's response.

The other woman hated this almost as much as she did—caught in the middle, the way she was, of their intimate conversation.

I love you.

Hannah had finally told Murphy that she loved him—in front of an audience.

Nash, thank God, had slipped out of the house. With a damp towel in his hand, pressed against the gash on his head that probably would need stitches to truly stop bleeding, he'd gone to stand in the heat of the morning, with Tess.

Eden was lying on the couch, with her eyes closed. If she wasn't asleep, she was pretending to be.

Sophia—cool and slim and elegant, her blond hair up in a neat twist atop her head—sat across from Hannah at the kitchen table, her hands clasped in front of her, her blue eyes filled with dread as she listened to the words Murphy was saying on the other end of the cell phone that lay on the table between them. Words she was going to have to repeat to Hannah.

"Murphy, please don't make me . . ." Hannah clearly read Sophia's lips.

"It's okay," Hannah told her. "Just tell me what he said. You don't need to edit."

"He said a lot of . . . of . . . crap that he didn't mean," Sophia told her. "And then he said how important your friendship is to him, but that . . ." She closed her eyes and said it. "He doesn't love you. Not the same way." She looked at Hannah through tears that filled her eyes. "He's sorry and . . . I am, too," she added.

"I wasn't expecting him to . . ." Hannah shook her head. "I just wanted him to know and . . . understand why I'm not going to walk away." She stood up. Spoke slightly louder—at least it felt louder. "I'm sorry to make things harder for you, Murph, but if you're hellbent on getting your gear, we're going to wait here for you. I think it would be better if we travel back to Sacramento and speak to the FBI together. So I'm going to go pack some clean clothes and I'll see you when you get here. Oh, and this conversation? It's over."

She flipped shut the phone and looked at Sophia. "Thank you," she told the other woman, and went to gather her things.

SACRAMENTO, CALIFORNIA

"Before you drop me off," Dr. Heissman said, from the passenger seat of Decker's truck, "there is one extremely important topic that we haven't yet discussed."

Deck knew exactly what was coming—he'd actually been surprised it had taken her this long. Still, he tried to head it off. "I would never intentionally harm myself."

"That's not what you said last night."

There was nothing Decker could say in response to that, because she was right, so he said nothing.

"I wish you could see yourself through my eyes," she finally said. "You probably think it's not noticeable but . . . I feel as if I've been watching you unravel. Aside from occasional moments, like the parking lot incident that made Tom call me, or the night you got . . . How did you put it? Ripshit drunk. Or last night. It's been happening relatively slowly. You've been doing it for a while, so I don't doubt it now feels normal to you. But it's not."

He glanced up from the traffic and over at her. "Normal is such a subjective idea. What is normal? The life my parents shared? Or maybe your marriage to your ex-husband—"

"Nice try, but we are *not* going *there*," she told him firmly.

"When I was really young," Decker told her, "I thought my family was normal. I thought everyone's father spent six months of the year at sea. And even after I realized that normal was relative, I still struggled to understand why Emily—my ex-fiancée—got so upset when I went TDY for six weeks. I thought she was ridiculous, she thought I was cold and uncaring, and yet I'm still not over her leaving and taking our dog." He looked at her again. "Is *that* normal? Me missing Ranger more than Emily?"

The doctor laughed, a brief burst of amused air. "You *are* talented at redirection, aren't you?" she said. "And yes, short answer, I think missing a dog, who probably never questioned anything you did and loved you unconditionally, *does* fall into the realm of normal. Let's get back on topic, though. How often do you consider suicide?"

Shit. "Never," Decker said.

"That's not what you said last night," she countered. "Which, by the way, was not the first time you mentioned—"

"*Consider* it," he interrupted. "What you asked was how often I *considered* it and I'm telling you I never seriously do. It has, however, occasionally crossed my mind as an option, but *never* as a viable one. So my answer stands: Never." He was gripping the steering wheel so tightly, his knuckles were white, and he consciously made himself relax.

She sighed, which was never a good sound to hear from a doctor. "Lawrence, you trusted me enough to come to me last night," she said quietly. "I know you probably think you drove all that way to get information from me about Jim Nash and the Agency, but I have to believe that you also knew—deep down—that you were going to tell me the things that you did. And despite what you're telling me now, the words *eat a bullet* came out of your mouth, and I cannot allow myself to believe it is anything less than a gravely consequential cry for help. I'm going to have to talk to Tom."

And there it was. The end of Decker's career with Troubleshooters. They drove for a mile. Two.

He finally broke the silence. "Way to make me *really* suicidal."

She didn't laugh. Instead, she bristled. "That's not funny."

"Hmm, maybe I'm in worse shape than I thought, because I kind of thought it was." He looked at her. "What happened to doctor-patient confidentiality? You gonna tell him I cried like a baby, too?"

"Of course not. And you didn't cry like a . . ." She started over. "You cry like a man, Lawrence. Trust me on that one. It was not new or shocking. You have nothing to be embarrassed about."

"And yet," he said, "I find that I am."

"As far as your . . . kissing me," she said. "That wasn't shocking or new either."

"I'm not embarrassed about that."

Dr. Heissman laughed. "Again, no surprises there. And as far as doctor-patient confidentiality . . ." She went into a long-winded explanation of how threats of suicide were outside of the rules and blah, blah, blah.

Decker tuned her out as he pulled into the parking garage next to the FBI building, and found a spot right next to an ancient Chevy Impala.

"Look," he said, interrupting her as he pulled up the parking brake. "It's time to be honest with you. Everything I said last night was just to get you to talk to me about the Agency. I played you, Doctor."

Apparently he'd finally done something that she *did* find shocking and new. But then the surprise on her face turned to unbridled disbelief. "That's BS."

"Nope," he disagreed. "Just me refusing to be manipulated, and, in turn, manipulating you." He made a *too bad* face. "Sorry."

"Nice try, but I'm sorry, too. I'm still going to have to tell Tom."

Decker nodded and turned off the engine. Hit the unlock button for the doors. "He'll get my report, too." He opened the door.

"Decker, wait."

He turned back to look at her.

"Don't throw it away," she implored him. "You took a big step last night, and I wish I didn't have to tell Tom, but I do. I wouldn't be able to live with myself if you—"

"I wouldn't," he said. "I'm telling you, that was—"

"You're lying. I can tell when you're lying and you're definitely—"

"I *was* lying," he said, "last night. Honey, trust me, I would've convinced you that I'm—" he laughed "—seriously considering a sex change operation if it meant you'd give me the information I need to help Nash."

"Tom Paoletti won't find this funny," she told him grimly.

Decker stopped laughing, too. "You come in here and think you can *save* me?" he asked her. "Get over yourself."

He didn't wait for her. He got out of the truck and headed for the FBI office, to see exactly what evidence they had against Murphy, and to ask his old friend Jules Cassidy what info—if any—the Bureau had on the Agency's Black Op Group.

NORTH OF DALTON, CALIFORNIA

It was impossible to have a private conversation, squeezed into the back of Jay Lopez's Prius with Lindsey and Mark Jenkins. Still, Dave needed to talk to Sophia, so he didn't have much of a choice.

"I know it sounds crazy," she told him over their tenuous cell phone connection, "but these photos that Hannah took are . . . We hacked into an Agency website that has one of the rare on-file photos of Tim Ebersole without his trademark beard, and it absolutely could be him. I've spoken to Jules Cassidy, and he's forwarded the photos on to computer analysis— they're going to compare facial structure from the photos we have, plus analyze a file photo they've got of Ebersole. It sounds as if Cassidy's taking this seriously, although he did point out that photos alone wouldn't help Murphy if he were on trial for Ebersole's murder. However, coming from a trusted source—Hannah—they could be used to open an investigation of a crime—fraud—which is what it would be, if Ebersole did fake his death. The Freedom Network is going to receive five *million* dollars from his life insurance policy. And then there's the question of whose body was found at the crime scene—if it wasn't Ebersole. *Some*one was murdered to perpetrate Ebersole's fraud. Long story short, Cassidy's looking into getting a warrant to go into the Freedom Network compound."

"Which he'd be crazy to use," Dave pointed out. "One word: Waco. The FBI knocks on the compound gate with a warrant, everyone inside cowboys up and we'll have an instant standoff on our hands. What the FBI needs is someone to go in covertly—someone not working for the government—to find Hannah's bald guy and deliver him to the FBI for a DNA test."

"Talk about crazy," Sophia said. "Who in their right mind would willingly go into that compound?"

"Jim Nash would," Dave reminded her. "And Decker. Murphy and Hannah not only would, but did. And you know what? I would, too, if I weren't otherwise engaged."

Dan Gillman turned from his seat in the front to roll his eyes at Dave.

"I would," Dave repeated. "You know nothing about me, asshole."

"Excuse me?" Sophia said.

"Not you," Dave told her. "Just . . . Sorry."

She lowered her voice. "Tess was right about Nash. He was still in Dalton. He got to the cabin before we did—and Hannah nearly killed him. Seriously, it was close."

"Nash is unkillable," Dave said.

"Don't say that, you'll jinx him." She lowered her voice even more. "What did he say to you, yesterday, in the motel parking lot?"

"In the where?" Dave asked, even though he knew exactly what she was talking about. In the middle of his slam-bam-drag-out fight with Tess, Nash had turned and spoken, quietly into Dave's ear. *Picture Sophia, broken and bleeding. What would* you *do to save her . . . ?*

"You were the only one brave enough to attempt to play referee," Sophia told him. "But Nash said something to you, and you just . . . you turned and looked at me . . ."

"He just, um . . ." Dave shifted in his seat.

"Sorry," Lindsey murmured, trying to move closer to Mark.

He shook his head at her. It wasn't her fault that Lopez had gone green and gotten the smallest car in the universe.

"If it's none of my business—" Sophia started.

"No," Dave said. "I'm actually . . . I'm glad you asked. Because I was talking to Dr. Heissman and . . . Well, what Nash said *was* private, yeah, but it reminded me of what I was talking about with Dr. Heissman—that's how this is connected, just so you don't think I've changed the subject . . .

"But see, I've always wanted you to be happy," Dave continued, trying to turn more toward the window, which no doubt sent his voice directly up toward Lopez, who was driving. "More than anything. More than I want *me* to be happy. So for years now, I've just kind of sat on what I feel, which is that I'm in love with you and, um . . ."

There was silence. The socially-deadly kind. Both in the car and on the other end of the phone.

"Wow," Dave said. "I can't believe I actually said that."

The phone at his ear started to ring, and as he pulled it back to look at it, he realized that it was Sophia. Calling him back. Because they'd been disconnected.

Un-fucking-believable.

"Hey," he said weakly. "When did I lose you?"

"You said you were talking to Dr. Heissman," she told him. "It's really not important. But before I lose you again—are you with Lindsey and Jenk? Because I forgot to tell you—Eden Gillman is here at the cabin."

"What?" Dave couldn't believe that. "Is Zanella—"

"No," Sophia said. "She's alone. I think she might've hitchhiked here from San Diego. She won't talk about Izzy or . . . Best I can figure is something went bad after the wedding. Whatever happened, it's entirely possible that Izzy has no idea where she is. If that's the case, he's probably worried."

"I'll have Jenk or Lindsey call him," Dave told her. Lindsey looked at him, and he made the mistake of telling her, "Eden Gillman's in Dalton, at Hannah's cabin."

Danny turned around from his spacious seat in the front, lucky bastard. "Are you kidding me?"

Dave waved him off because Sophia was talking again. "Thanks," she said. "I'll call you as soon as Murphy gets here."

"Soph," Dave said, closing his eyes because no way was he going to try to drop the *I love you* bomb again with Gillman still glaring at him from the front seat.

But Sophia didn't let him get a chance to speak. "We can meet somewhere in the middle and caravan back to Sacramento. Okay?"

"Yeah."

"I really have to go."

"Be careful," Dave said.

"You, too. See you soon."

And with that, Sophia was gone. Dave flipped his phone shut and met Gillman's baleful stare.

"And I thought I was a loser," the SEAL said.

"Danny," Lopez reprimanded him quietly. "Have a heart. That had to have sucked." He glanced in the rearview mirror. "Sorry about that, Dr. Malkoff."

Dave nodded. It had sucked, and was pretty much continuing to suck, too.

"What did you really think?" Gillman said. "That she would say, *oh my God Dave, I love you, too?*" He snorted. "Dream on."

"Dan." This time Mark Jenkins tried to shut him up. He shook his head at his friend.

"So what the hell is Eden doing back in Dalton?" Gillman asked. "And where the fuck is Zanella?"

NEAR FRESNO, CALIFORNIA

Izzy was ten minutes outside of Fresno when his cell phone rang.

He could see from the incoming call's number that it was Jenk, and he almost didn't answer. But he was tired as shit and any conversation at all would help him better aim his truck between the road's often blurry lines.

"Zanella," he answered, because he didn't feel like giving anyone, even Marky-Mark, a cheery *hi*.

"Izzy, where are you, man?"

"That depends," Izzy said.

Jenk laughed his disbelief. "On what?"

"Is Gilligan with you?"

"Cha," Jenk said. "Murphy took Lindsey's car, so we're sardined into Jay's with Dave Malkoff, too. We're about twenty minutes behind Murph, heading back to Dalton, ETA forty-five minutes."

"Don't tell Gillman," Izzy said, "but I'm about ten outside of Fresno, chasing down his crazy sister."

"Fresno?" Jenk said. "Dude, Eden's at Hannah's cabin in Dalton."

Izzy almost swerved off the road. "What the fuck is she doing back in Dalton?"

"We'd thought you'd be able to tell us."

Dalton. "Is she okay?"

"Yeah," Jenk said. "I mean, no one said she wasn't, so I assume . . . She's with Hannah and Sophia. And Nash and Tess."

"Thank God," Izzy said. He had to pull over, he was so overwhelmed with dizzying relief. "Holy shit . . ."

After seeing those clips on that bullshit website, he'd hit the redial button on his kitchen phone to see if Eden had made any calls before she'd left. He'd hung up before the line connected, but the numbers last dialed came up on the screen and . . .

It was a phone number he vaguely recognized, with a Vegas area code, but he knew it wasn't one that he'd dialed recently. Suspicious, he'd checked his cell phone address book and, sure enough, it was the number Eden had given him, all those months ago, for Jerry's cell phone.

Ergo, before taking her bag of clothes and leaving, Eden had called Jerry from his kitchen phone, probably to beg him to pull those unseemly videos from that homemade porn website.

Jerry, wonk that he was, no doubt said something like, "You want me to do that badly enough, you'll meet me in person."

Which put Eden exactly where she didn't want to be—back in Jerry and Richie's fucked up, drug-dealing world.

Trying hard not to lose his cool, Izzy had gone down to the gas station on the corner, and using all of the coins he had floating loose in his truck, had called Jerry's cell from a pay phone, pretending he was looking to buy some weed.

"I need me some of that superfine shit you got for me, you know, last time?" he'd bullshitted the asshole, pretending he'd done business with him many times before, IDing himself as Roger Starrett from Texas, out here on the left coast for business. "I've got wheels, so tell me where, my man, and I'll bring cash, plus a bonus for your trouble. Just make the when ASAP."

Which was when Jerry had let slip the news that he was spending the week in Fresno. But he gave Izzy a street address and told him to call back when he'd arrived outside the house.

Izzy's intention was to show up, kick down the door, find Eden, and get her and Pinkie the hell out of there.

But she hadn't gone to Fresno, thank God again.

"You really have no clue why she went back to Dalton?" Jenk asked him now.

And now Izzy did have a clue. She'd probably gone there because she was resourceful and she'd assumed Hannah wouldn't be using her cabin for a while. She'd gone for some solitude—both to lick her wounds and figure out her next move.

Because Eden had been certain that, upon seeing those video clips, Izzy would kick her out onto the street.

"Jenk, as much as I love you, bro," Izzy said, as he got back on the highway and drove as fast as he dared, which meant pedal to the metal. "This is one problem I definitely can't share. Just . . . If you get to Dalton before me? Tell Eden that you spoke to me, that I didn't tell you anything about what was going down, but that I said . . . Well, just tell her I still be-lieve her, okay? And that I'm going to help her make this go away."

"I'm pretty sure you're going to get there first," Jenk told him.

"Then do me a different huge-large," Izzy told him, "and give Lopez a big wet kiss for me."

"Why?"

"He'll know," Izzy said.

"Can't do it," Jenk said. "He's driving and I'm in the back. But I'll pass along the sentiment."

"Gillman's in the front," Izzy deducted. "Tell him to give—"

"He respectfully declines the do-age of any favors," Jenk reported, which was no doubt a paraphrasing of Gillman's predictable *Fuck you, douchebag.*

Oh, Danny, Danny, Danny. Such animosity. They were family now.

"Seriously, Mark," Izzy told Jenkie. "Thanks for calling me. I was worried about Eden, and . . . Thank you."

"You're welcome," Jenkins said, and hung up, leaving Izzy alone to break the speed limit along an otherwise empty road, thanking God again that Eden was someplace safe.

CHAPTER
TWENTY-TWO

Eden had just gotten up to stretch her legs.

She'd gone out onto the porch, and was feeling a little awkward about being there, since the man named Nash and the woman named Tess were having something of a heated discussion. "I don't care," Tess kept saying, occasionally throwing in an absolute "Yeah, well, I don't believe you!"

But before Eden could slink back into the cabin, an explosion echoed and Tess staggered. Just a little bit.

And for a moment, time seemed to stand completely still. But then Tess looked down at her shirt, at the blossom of red that had appeared just above the waist of her jeans, and staggered again—as Nash grabbed her and started to shout.

He had his gun out as he pulled Tess back toward the cabin.

"Get inside!" He was screaming at Eden, but she couldn't do more than crouch by the porch swing, arms around her belly, in a futile attempt to protect Pinkie as a second gunshot boomed and a second bullet hit the side of the building, as a third crashed and shattered a window.

As a fourth struck Nash and brought him down into the dust at the edge of the porch.

His gun left his hand as he cracked his head against the wooden stairs and he bounced like a ragdoll, lifeless and limp.

It was Tess who was screaming now—"No!" Her entire shirt front was dark with her blood, but, shielding Nash with her own body, she reached to reclaim the handgun she, too, had dropped when Nash went down, but another gunshot cracked, and she screamed again, pulling her hand in to her chest.

A voice rang out, male and with a rich twang that Eden had always associated with good times, with the colors and lights and music of New Orleans: "Nobody moves, nobody returns fire—or the next bullet goes directly into the head of the pregnant girl!"

Hannah looked at Sophia, who'd positioned herself so that she had a clear view of the back door, shotgun from Patrick's case held at ready.

They both crouched underneath the front window, which was maybe not the smartest move strategically. But Hannah needed Sophia's ears.

"I want hands where I can see them," Sophia repeated the words spoken by the man outside. Whoever he was, he was back beyond the tree line, concealed by the brush. And whoever he was, he wasn't alone. Hannah had caught the glint of reflected sunlight off of at least seven different rifle barrels.

Bayou drawl, Sophia had reported. Deep voice. Male.

"You with the baby coming," Sophia relayed, "off the porch. Hands on your head. Good girl."

Hannah's cell phone couldn't get a connection. They'd no doubt taken out the cell tower. And they'd cut the landline and the power lines to the cabin, too.

She'd just noticed that the electricity had gone down, just before Sophia had knocked her to the kitchen floor, and told her that shots were being fired.

If any of them died here today, Hannah knew that Murphy would never recover. And God, it was possibly already too late. Nash's position as he lay in the dust was that of a dead man.

"How many are inside?" Sophia relayed. "He's asking Eden, and threatening—dear God—to cut her baby out of her womb if she doesn't tell him the truth."

"Two," Hannah shouted. "There are two of us inside. Cooperate with them, Eden. Do exactly what they tell you to do."

"She's verifying that there are two of us," Sophia said, watching as

Hannah checked her watch, nodding as she held out her wrist so that Sophia, too, could see the time.

Thirty minutes, and Murphy would arrive. But it was another twenty after that before Dave and the others—three Navy SEALs and a former LAPD detective—got here.

Hannah could stall and hope that Murphy would try to call as he got closer, notice that cell service was down, and approach the cabin as carefully as she herself had done hours ago. But if he didn't, he'd drive right into an ambush.

And then there was the fact that stalling was a potential death sentence for Nash and even Tess, who desperately needed even the kind of rudimentary medical assistance that Hannah, with her police training, could provide.

"Come out with your hands up," Sophia repeated the order from the man who was still hidden in the brush. "One at a time." She looked at Hannah, speaking for herself now. "We don't have a choice."

Hannah nodded. "I'm right behind you," she told the other woman, scrambling over to the computer and disconnecting the camera from the cord, looping the wrist-guard over her left hand.

They *didn't* have a choice. Of course, full surrender—laying down their weapons and exiting the cabin the way they were doing—could result in bullets in all of their heads. Please God, Hannah didn't want to do that to Murphy. Not without at least trying to negotiate.

Although there was no time to do it either slowly or carefully. She had to get directly to the bottom line. "We haven't seen you, we can't identify you," Hannah shouted as she followed Sophia through the cabin door, hands held up so all could see they were empty. "Go back the way you came, and we will not pursue you. I know why you're here, and you're too late. Those pictures I took in the compound, two days ago? I've already e-mailed them to the FBI. They clearly show that Tim Ebersole is still alive—".

"Silence." Sophia looked back at her to say. "Freeze."

And there they stood. Instinctively, they'd each gone to stand on either side of Eden, who had tears running down her face, but still stood, chin high, defiant.

Hannah stole a look over at Tess, who was kneeling in the dust and gravel, trying to stop Nash from bleeding, all but ignoring her own wounds. She met Hannah's eye, and the look on her face was terrible, and Hannah knew that unless he got to a hospital soon, Nash would not survive. But despite being injured herself, Tess was a fighter and as Hannah glanced at her again, she lifted the edge of Nash's coat, showing her that she had access to another weapon.

Oh, God.

Hannah turned to see a man coming out of the cabin—clearly he'd gone in through the back—giving his compatriots an all clear.

And then they came, out of the brush. There were almost two dozen of them, a virtual army, all heavily armed. Most of them had rifles, but some held AK-47s—huge machine guns that could cut a human being in half in less than a heartbeat.

One of the men went directly to Tess, and hit her hard in the head with the butt of his rifle. She slumped over, and the man reached down and took the handgun she'd been hiding, out from under Nash's jacket.

Beside her, both Sophia and Eden dropped to the ground, and for one awful moment, Hannah thought they'd been shot. But then one of the men holding an AK-47 screamed at her—getting right in her face, spittle flying out of the corner of his mouth, "I said, get on the ground, bitch, hands on your head!"

Please God, keep Nash and Tess alive and Murphy safe. Please God, keep Nash and Tess alive and Murphy safe. Hannah closed her eyes as rough hands searched her for weapons, as someone pulled the camera off her wrist, as something pricked her—a needle poke and then searing heat in her leg as, damnit, they'd drugged her, as the world blurred and swirled and then went black.

Murphy's first clue that something was wrong was when he tried to call Sophia, to tell her he was ten minutes from the cabin, but she didn't pick up. He took the shortcut that wasn't really a shortcut unless you knew the roads, and he gunned it around the familiar curves, forcing himself to keep breathing.

What if the Freedom Network had followed Hannah here from Sacramento?

What if they somehow had made the connection between the VW Rabbit with Alaskan plates and this cabin here in Dalton?

What if . . . ?

One thing Murphy knew for sure was that *he* wasn't followed. He'd driven all the way from Sacramento with one eye watching his rearview mirror, yet had seen no one. And there was no way, since he'd taken Lindsey's car, that the Network was tracking him via GPS. *No* way.

He cursed Dave for a bit, for letting Hannah out of his sight. And then he cursed Hannah for being Hannah and evading Dave.

And then he focused on a different *what if*. What if he got there, and Hannah knew that he'd been lying when he'd told her he didn't love her, too?

Oh, God, he loved her—which should have been hard enough to deal with, were he and Hannah isolated and alone in the idyllic quiet of her cabin. He should have been wracked with grief and guilt. How could he move on without feeling as if he were betraying Angelina, or at least Angelina's memory?

But he didn't feel that way. He felt . . . at peace.

Part of it came from the realization that he was no longer the man that Angelina had loved. That Vinh Murphy had turned to ashes, alongside of her.

Part of it came from knowing that, for as long as he lived, he would always love Angelina, and a small part of him would forever mourn the life they didn't get to share.

It was similar to the small part of him that had mourned the loss of Hannah, when he'd let himself be claimed by Angelina. Even on his wedding day, a beautiful, perfect day of joy, he'd looked at Hannah standing alone in the church, and he'd felt a sadness for the loss of a dream he'd once held, a dream he believed would never come true.

Life was about choices, and he'd made his with gladness and—most of the time—hadn't looked back.

But life was also filled with accidents, with randomness, with inexplicable happenstance. With death, and unchosen loss.

For years, he'd railed against fate and God and the unfairness of life, but his tears and his grief and his pain hadn't brought Angelina back.

And here he'd come, full circle—back to Hannah. He always came back to Hannah.

Who loved him. She'd always loved him and she loved him still—this angry, broken, still-healing man he'd become.

And Jesus Christ, all he wanted was to sit somewhere. Quietly. With her beside him. For about two years. And just . . . be.

But no. The same violence and hatred that had taken Angelina from him was back—and this time the fault was completely his. Whether he'd murdered Tim Ebersole or not, he'd gotten Hannah involved. He'd gotten her shot at and nearly killed.

And he would *not* do this again. He would not bury Hannah.

He would not.

His original plan, when he'd first gotten into Lindsey's car, had been a simple one. Get his gear out of the cabin, then wrestle Hannah to the ground to get his hands on that letter he'd written her last spring. As long as she was insisting they have a face-to-face, he might as well make it worthwhile and burn that evidence—as circumstantial as it was. He'd even let her say whatever she wanted to say—hell, she could try to convince him that Tim Ebersole was the freaking tooth fairy—as long as she said it in his car, heading back north, with Tess Bailey and Jim Nash literally riding shotgun.

Yeah, he'd get her to Sacramento, return Lindsey's car, and if, after FBI analysis, the photos Hannah had taken turned out to *not* be Tim Ebersole, he'd go in for psychiatric analysis, pretend the fog lifted, and confess to killing the man.

Alone. Without Hannah's help.

He'd then go into custody where the Freedom Network could hate him as much as they wanted, and Hannah could have her life back.

At least that had been his plan before she'd told him that she loved him.

He then spent some time cursing himself, for writing that note that he'd given her back in Steve and Paul's kitchen. *Don't give up on me . . .* And then he thanked God that he'd written it, because doing so had saved her life.

As he got closer, as he tried again to call, he saw that he, too, no longer had cell service, so maybe the disaster he was imagining was completely in his head. Service was down. It happened.

But he slowed as he made the turn off onto Warson's Gate because there was a car—a blue subcompact with California plates—parked among the brush there at the bottom of the hill.

It was where guests parked, Hannah had told him, when Pat had a party and the driveway was full. It was also possibly where Hannah parked when she was hiding her presence at the cabin.

Too in a hurry to be equally cautious, Murphy continued up the road. The driveway was empty.

There was no sign of anyone—not Tess or Nash or Hannah—and his stomach twisted as he saw that, behind the screen, the front door was hanging open.

And then he saw the blood.

Oh, God, no . . .

In a heartbeat, Murphy was out of the car and over to the stairs. There was a still-red stain of blood there in the dirt, and a trail leading up and into the cabin. "Hannah!" A second trail led around to the side of the structure. "Han!"

"Murph," a voice answered him, a genderless whisper, but it couldn't be Hannah—she couldn't have heard him calling.

Still, Murphy ran around the side of the cabin where—oh, Jesus—Jim Nash sat leaning against the woodshed, covered in blood.

He looked nightmarish, like a dead man still moving, and the world spun and Murphy almost fell down, he was so dizzy, but he heard an echo of Hannah's voice in his head, *I need you here!* and he fought not to go back in time to that driveway in Malibu, to Angelina . . .

"Gotta call for help," Nash told him through lips that should have already breathed their last.

Murphy knelt next to him, half afraid that he was hallucinating, that Nash was dead and he was imagining him speaking, the way he'd been so certain Angelina had whispered *I love you* on that awful, awful night, even after the doctors had told him that most of her brain functions had ceased upon the bullet's impact.

He forced himself to focus now on Nash, whose hands *were* moving. He was trying to splice together the two ends of a cut phone line. It shouldn't have been that hard to do, but he'd been shot, in the head and in the chest. The wound in his head was bleeding into his eyes, and the injury in his chest was making it more and more difficult for the man to breathe.

"Gotta call for help," he told Murphy. "Tess—shot."

Oh, Christ, no, not Tess, too. "Is she inside?" Murphy asked, taking the wires from him. Jesus, they were slick with blood, and again he made himself think of Hannah, not Angelina. Hannah, who was still alive. Please, God, let Hannah still be alive. He had to wipe the wire on his shirt before attempting to make the connection. His hands were shaking—son of a *bitch* . . .

"Truck," Nash told him.

Murph shook his head. "There weren't any trucks in the driveway." But then he saw that Nash was trying to pick something up, beside him on the ground. It was a small handgun—.22 caliber—and Murphy realized that by *truck*, Nash meant that one was approaching, pulling into the driveway with no attempt whatsoever at stealth.

He took the weapon from Nash as everything around him slapped into sharp focus. He held the handgun with hands that could have threaded a needle in one try, as he prayed that someone from the Freedom Network had come back for something they'd forgotten—so he could kill the motherfucker where he stood.

But whoever got out of the truck started shouting. "Eden!"

And Nash reached to put his hand on Murphy's arm, leaving a streak of blood. "Pregnant girl," he said. "Eden. Must be . . . Zanella. SEAL."

"Zanella," Murphy shouted, "back here." Because as big of a pain in the ass that Navy SEALs could sometimes be, they could, at times, come in handy.

Sure enough, the man who came around the side of the cabin was wearing a Naval uniform. Dress whites, with plenty of ribbons. His eyes were wild. "What. The *fuck*?"

"You one of Tommy's SEALs?" Murphy asked as the man—Zanella—got right to work, trying to stop Nash's bleeding, as Murph re-attached the wires.

"Yeah, who the fuck shot Nash and where the fuck is my wife?"

"Took her," Nash gasped. "With Tess and . . . the others."

"Took her where?" Zanella's dress whites were no longer white. "Holy shit, Nash, how could you still be alive?"

Murphy shot Zanella a hard look. Things not to say to a man who was hanging onto consciousness by a thread.

"Sorry," he muttered.

"By the others—you mean, Hannah and Sophia?" Murphy asked the wounded man, trying to focus him on information they could use.

Nash nodded. "Think so. Haven't checked . . . the whole . . . cabin . . ."

This time Murphy exchanged a look with Zanella that was mutual apprehension. The SEAL was thinking the same thing. There could be more wounded or even dead inside.

"When you finish there," Zanella told Murphy quietly, "I'll go and look."

Murph managed a nod. Please God, don't let Hannah be in there, dead . . . "What was your wife doing up here?"

"It's a very long, very fucked up story."

"She's pregnant?" Murphy asked. Jesus, he was back to all thumbs . . .

"Yeah," Zanella said. "Six months."

Great. Two more innocents to be caught in the kill zone.

"Who the fuck did this?" Zanella asked Nash again.

He was still conscious. "Don't know. Just started . . . shooting . . ."

Murphy knew. "The Freedom Network. Had to be. How many of them were there?"

"Didn't see them. I was . . ." Blood flecked Nash's lips as he coughed. "Must've . . . left me . . . for dead."

An understandable mistake. Murphy could now see that the wound on Nash's head wasn't a bullet-hole as he'd first thought. Although truth be told, if anyone could keep moving with an injury that would have instantly killed another human being, it would be James Nash.

The man must've crawled into the cabin to find that the phone line had been cut. Before he'd crawled back out, he'd opened the window, broke through the screen, and thrown the telephone out—so he wouldn't have to crawl all the way back inside to use it after he connected the cut wires. It dangled now, by its cord.

Murphy picked it up, hung it up, then put the handset to his ear.

Dial tone.

But instead of dialing 911, Murphy did one better.

He called Dave.

If there was a God, she was a merciless bitch to bring this kind of violence into Murphy's life again—this time to his front door.

"No one's inside," Izzy reported, as he finished his check of the cabin's interior. He went over to the window, beneath which Murphy was now up to his elbows in Nash's blood, even as he stayed on the phone with Dave.

Good old Dave Malkoff. A medevac helicopter was on its way, and Dave himself had an ETA of just a few more minutes. He was traveling with the rest of the cavalry—Jenk, Lindsey, Lopez, and Gilligan.

Who was no doubt already shitting dobermans, and blaming Izzy for Eden's abduction.

How the fuck had this happened? With both Nash and Tess armed and on guard?

And how the fuck was Murphy still standing? Nash's bloody and torn flesh had taken Izzy back, in a rush, to that fucking awful day that a terrorist had walked into a Kazbekistan hotel lobby and opened fire, killing SEAL Chief O'Leary, and damn near doing the same to Izzy.

Murphy'd lost not a friend but his *wife* in a similarly out-of-the-blue incident, far more recently than that.

Izzy had purposely stepped up and volunteered for the dread-filled task of checking the cabin, praying to the God-bitch that no one deader than Nash was inside, praying that he didn't have to break the news to Murph that his new girlfriend, Hannah, wasn't—as Angelina had been—in need of a body bag. Praying to whomever would listen—merciless or otherwise—that Eden and Pinkie were safe.

Even while knowing that, wherever they were, Eden had to be terrified. She was tough, but goddamn.

And as long as Izzy was praying, he threw in a plea for Jim Nash. The man was alive through sheer ire. Izzy could not imagine being Nash—fighting for every breath while knowing he was about to be flown to the nearest hospital trauma center, willing to walk into the fires of hell for Tess, but unable to do anything more than succumb to anesthesia for surgery that he probably wouldn't survive. Knowing that even if he did wake up, it might be to a world in which the woman he loved was no longer a part.

Kind of the way Vinh Murphy had done, a few years ago.

Murphy now put down the phone. "Dave must be close—I lost the connection."

"There's blood—not a lot—on the floor, beneath a window that's broken, up in front," Izzy reported. "But that's it. It doesn't look like anyone else was shot." He held up the note he'd found, so Murphy could see it. "This was stuck to the kitchen table with a knife. It says, *wait for instructions, do not contact the authorities, and no one else will die.*"

The former Marine looked at Izzy with eyes that were murderous. "Dave had Lindsey on the phone with the FBI—their surveillance team reports that a chopper just landed in the Freedom Network compound outside of Sacramento. They're too far away to get a visual, but they have four human infrared images—all being carried off the chopper and into a building."

Izzy's heart was in his throat. *All* being carried.

But Nash stirred—he wasn't unconscious as Izzy had thought. And to him, that was good news. "Tess is alive," he breathed.

Way in the distance, Izzy could hear the thrumming sound of the approaching medevac helo that Dave had called for. But there wasn't just one helo coming toward them—there were two. Murphy heard them, as well, and he looked at Izzy again. "I've got some extra clothes up in the loft. You better go change into something a little less glow in the dark."

Izzy nodded. Yeah. They would await those instructions that were coming from the Freedom Network fuckers, but they damn well weren't going to follow them.

"Because I said so." Dave got right up in Dan Gillman's face to say, "Because *I* am in charge."

They were words he'd never believe he'd ever utter, but there they were, coming out of his mouth.

"Who died and made you God?" Izzy Zanella was not helping things, especially considering that Dave had helped Lopez and Murphy pull Gillman off of him. Five seconds ago, the two SEALs had been at each others' throats, arguing about whose fault it was that Eden was in danger, but now they were united in their never-gone-through-BUD/S-training disdain of Dave.

He knew he could never out-macho them, so he used the same approach Decker did when he was in command. He got quiet. "No one died," Dave reminded them all, reminded himself, too, even though the idea of Sophia in the hands of the Freedom Network made his skin crawl. "And we're going to keep it that way. As for who made me God? Tom Paoletti made me God, ten minutes ago, over the phone. You got a problem with it? Take it up with him—after we get our people back." He turned to Murphy. "We can forward any calls coming in to the cabin's landline to your cell phone, but if you take their call while we're on the chopper, they're going to hear the sound of the blades."

And they'd deduce, correctly, that Murphy was working with the authorities.

"Here's what I suggest we do," Dave said to Murphy. "We recut the phone line and take the chopper north, set up camp outside of the FN compound, start gathering whatever gear we think we'll need. Meanwhile, someone stays behind here in Dalton. At a predetermined time—three, four hours from now—he or she connects the phone line and forwards any incoming calls to your cell. When the Freedom Network calls, you tell them it took you that many hours to get the phone line up and working."

Murphy looked at him. "Suggest?" he said. "I thought Tommy made you God."

"You don't work for him anymore," Dave pointed out, his steady gaze somber.

Murphy nodded. "It's a good plan," he said.

"Yeah," Izzy interjected. "Except, who stays behind?"

"Not me," Gillman said. "My sister's in there—"

"I'm her husband," Izzy argued.

"I'll stay."

Dave turned, and sure enough, it was Jay Lopez who'd volunteered. It was clear it pained him to stay back, out of the action. But he was a team player.

"Let's do it," Dave said. "Let's move."

SACRAMENTO, CALIFORNIA

The Sacramento FBI office was in an uproar.

"I'm sorry, sir," the harried receptionist earnestly told Decker. "But Mr. Cassidy isn't available for walk-in appointments—"

"Decker!" Jules Cassidy was coming out of an elevator and saw him standing there. Waved him over. "It's okay, Janet." He briefly shook Decker's hand. "You got here fast—last I heard, they were still trying to reach you. Come on back, I'll fill you in."

Decker followed the shorter man down the corridor, aware of Jo Heissman, still in the lobby, watching him. He successfully tamped down the urge to turn back and thumb his nose at her.

"What's the word on Nash?" Cassidy asked, and Decker took several steps in double time to catch up.

"He's still out there, in the dark," Decker said, assuming Dave had filled the FBI agent in on Nash's disappearance. "I haven't heard from him yet, which is why I wanted to ask you about . . ." The Agency, Decker was about to say, but the look Cassidy was giving him was a blend of confusion and disbelief.

"Oh shit, you don't know." The FBI agent grabbed him by the arm and pulled him into a conference room, where two young women sat at a table, in front of several open files. "I need this room," he told them. "Immediately."

"Don't know what?" Decker said as the women gaped at them from their seats.

"Get out!" Cassidy actually clapped his hands at them, and they finally grabbed their files and scurried for the door. "Thank you," he called after them, then shut the door. His face was grim as he turned back to Decker. "You better sit down."

CHAPTER
TWENTY-THREE

Decker was reviewing the FBI files documenting their past eight months of surveillance of the Freedom Network's Sacramento area compound when Dr. Heissman was escorted into the conference room.

"Sit," Decker told her, dismissing the aide who'd brought her, then nodding to the chair opposite him. She sat, but her body language screamed that she'd taken disapproving note of his lack of a *please*.

"If I'm under arrest," she said, "I'd like to be read my rights."

"You're not under arrest."

"Then why was my phone and my handbag confiscated?"

"That was done at my request," Decker said. "I have trust issues. And I know you're smart—you've been hanging around for a while, you've probably figured out what's going on. And you'll also know what the next step has got to be."

"Photos have surfaced that have been identified as Tim Ebersole," she told him. "Despite the ability of technology to alter photographs, these are believed to have been taken two days ago, which means that he wasn't murdered back in March. The FBI is now investigating a probable case of insurance fraud and tax evasion, and a warrant has been issued to search the Freedom Network compound, to find the man in the recently taken photos. Only problem is, even if the warrant allows the FBI to enter the compound without warning and with force, the Freedom Network will resist. They're going to have a full-scale battle on their hands, women and children will die, and it will be the biggest snafu in the Bureau's history, surpassing even Waco and Ruby Ridge. How am I doing?"

Decker nodded. "What you don't know," he told her, "is that about an hour ago the Freedom Network attacked Hannah Whitfield's cabin outside of Dalton, critically—perhaps fatally—injuring James Nash and Tess Bailey, and kidnapping Tess, Sophia, Hannah, and Eden Zanella, the pregnant wife of a Navy SEAL who was helping us try to locate Vinh Murphy."

"I'm so sorry to hear that," she said, and despite the animosity between them, it was obvious that she sincerely meant it.

"Murphy's heading north right now, with a team from Troubleshooters. He's going to stall for time, pretend to negotiate—request proof of life. Meanwhile, I'm going in—"

"To the compound?" she interrupted.

Decker nodded. "—to find Ebersole. The FBI can't do it, but as a civilian with a personal agenda—"

"You're going in *alone*?"

"Nash is a little tied up right now," Decker said tightly. "Considering he's in surgery that he's not expected to survive."

"So your response to the impending death of your friend is to get yourself killed, too?"

"I didn't call you in here to analyze me," Decker said.

"I know you spec ops types think you're supermen—"

"I prefer to think of myself as Captain America," Decker said.

"—but to get in and out of the compound with Tim Ebersole—"

"I didn't say anything about getting out," Decker told her. "I just have to find him. And then I'll see what happens. I do know this—I have to be more ready than he is to die. I think I've probably got that going to my advantage."

"So this *is* a suicide mission," she said quietly.

"Most of them are," Decker told her. "But there's a huge difference between being suicidal and being ready and willing to make the ultimate sacrifice. Despite what you think you know, Doctor, I *don't* want to die on this mission. But if I do, and in doing so I help save the lives of people I love? It'll be a win."

She nodded, her eyes somber, her mouth a tight line. "So if you didn't call me in here to talk you out of—"

"I called you in here to contain you," he told her what she'd already figured out. "Until our people are out and safe, I've requested that you remain right here."

She laughed. "So . . . what? Now you think I work for the Freedom Network?"

"Of course not," he said. "But the jury's still out on whether or not you work for the Agency."

THE MOUNTAINS EAST OF SACRAMENTO, CALIFORNIA

Hannah woke up slowly, painfully, as if swimming for a barely discernable surface in the suffocating silence of muddy water.

Her head was pounding and the light—dim as it was through the windows—hurt her eyes. Something was terribly wrong, and she struggled to remember, to . . .

She sat up with a gasp, still foggy and dull, but aware that she was no longer in Patrick's cabin, in Dalton. Whatever the men who'd attacked them had given her to knock her out was still dragging her down, but she fought it, willing herself back to clarity.

The room she was in was small and empty of all furniture. It seemed to have been designed as a jail cell, or the world's least-hygienic, very-public bathroom with a toilet standing alone in one corner, but no sink, no shower. The walls were of concrete block construction—no drywall to try to kick her way through. There was only one window, with bars covering it, through which daylight still shone. She wasn't alone, thank God—or maybe not thank God, because along with Sophia, Tess, too, had been dumped on the floor beside her.

Tess, but not Jim Nash.

Hannah lay back for a moment, hands against her throbbing head, unable to keep tears from escaping—one from each eye, running down her face and into her useless ears. Please, God, let the only reason Nash wasn't with them be because he was male and they were female. The Freedom Network often segregated according to gender. Even in their dining hall, women sat at different tables from the men.

But okay. As much as she wanted to lie here with her eyes closed, weeping about the injustice of having been shot at, drugged, and kidnapped, it was likely that Tess, who hadn't just been shot at, but shot, still needed first aid.

So Hannah forced her eyes open, wiped her face and sat back up. And as she shifted closer to Tess—God, her ankle hurt like a bitch—Hannah saw a bandage beneath the woman's still-bloody shirt, another on her right hand. Apparently she had received at least cursory medical care from their captors—who'd completely ignored the gash on her head from being struck by that rifle barrel. Her hair was sticky with blood and she had a lump the size of a baseball. Had they drugged her, too, along with knocking her unconscious?

Hannah didn't know, but Tess's breathing seemed steady and a finger to her throat revealed that her pulse was strong.

Sophia stirred as Hannah checked her pulse, too. She roused, gasping with alarm and jerking back, as if she couldn't stand to be touched. But she exhaled her relief as she recognized Hannah. "Where are we?"

Hannah tried the door—solid and solidly locked—before she went to the window and . . . sure enough. She'd been here before—she recognized the dining hall, the children's barracks, the armory, and the rows of cabins and guest cottages. If she remembered correctly from her tour back in the spring . . .

"We're in the schoolhouse in the Freedom Network compound. A section of this building doubles as a brig." She turned back to Sophia. "There's a series of rooms—cells—like this, four of them in a row. I'm going to tap on the walls—I want you to listen, see if Nash taps back, because maybe he's being held in the next room and . . ."

The look on Sophia's face stopped her.

"You know something I don't know," Hannah asked, filled with sudden sharp dread. "Tell me."

"Back at the cabin," Sophia said, misery in her blue eyes, "they gave me a shot of something and . . . Before I went under, I heard someone say *Leave that one, he's dead.*"

Murphy's phone finally rang, and across the tent, Lindsey leaped to her feet.

"You ready for this?" she asked as she turned on the recording equipment.

Murphy nodded.

As Lindsey and everyone else in the tent—Zanella, Jenkins, Gillman and Dave—slipped on headphones so that they could listen in, she reminded him, "They think you're still in Dalton."

Instead, they were so close to the Freedom Network compound—a quarter of a mile away—it was all Murphy could do not to grab a rifle and go over the fence. He knew that Izzy Zanella had been thinking similar thoughts, getting more and more distant and grim as each hour passed.

They'd arrived at an airfield, well east of Sacramento, in record time. Dave had arranged for a pair of trucks to be there, waiting, and they'd driven the rest of the way into the wilderness, to this base camp. It was clear that Dave had been talking to the FBI, and that most of this equipment had come with their blessing. It was also apparent that the Agent-in-Charge believed that the Troubleshooters would have a better chance of rescuing their missing people without official FBI involvement.

They believed that bringing in a hostage negotiator would result in a standoff that would last for months—and would surely result in bloodshed.

So here Murphy and the Troubleshooters were, in one of a group of tents, in a base camp festooned with party balloons and a banner hung from the trees saying *Happy Birthday, Grandpa Baker*. This attempt to hide their true purpose from any stray Freedom Network patrols added that little extra surreal spin to the late afternoon.

But now, finally, the wait was over.

"Remember, let them talk. Let's find out what they want, before we ask for proof of life." Lindsey was wearing her police detective face—an impressive blend of take-no-shit and commanding compassion. She was ready and available for anything he might need.

Man, he'd missed having her as a friend. It was a weird time to be thinking that, as he answered his phone, praying this was, indeed, the Freedom Network calling with their instructions—with their kidnap ransom demands.

"This is Murphy," he said, his voice raspy with his anger. Whoever was on the other end of this phone had shot Jim Nash—who'd gone into cardiac arrest as he'd been carried onto the medevac chopper. They'd managed to revive him—but it had been frighteningly difficult to do so.

And there'd been no word on his condition since he'd been lifted into the air.

"Mr. Murphy. What a pain in the balls you are." The voice on the other end of the phone had a distinct bayou drawl. "No doubt you still think we're responsible for killing Angela."

Jesus Christ, the son of a bitch didn't even get her name right.

"It took you awfully long to get your phone back in order. You better not have contacted the police or the FBI," the man continued.

"I haven't," Murphy lied. "I'm alone." *Is Hannah safe? Is Tess still alive? Let Eden go—she has nothing to do with this. I want to speak to Sophia . . .* He clenched his teeth against all of the things he desperately wanted to demand, and Lindsey nodded her approval, her hand warm on his shoulder.

"Then here's what you're going to do," the man instructed. "You're going to go someplace public—to the Taco Bell or the library there in Dalton. You're going to draw a crowd, you're going to come clean. You're going to confess to killing Reverend Ebersole, you're going to admit that the photos you took were photo-shopped, that they were taken months before the murder, back when your friend Hannah was a guest in the compound, and then you're going to put a gun to your head and pull the trigger and end your worthless life."

Murphy sat in silence as his heart sank, because, shit, their plan was brilliant—and additional proof that Hannah's crazy conspiracy theory was right and Ebersole was still alive. The man on the phone clearly knew that the photos had made their way into the world, and probably even to the FBI, but that Murphy's "confession" would throw doubt onto their authenticity. As well as neatly tie up the Ebersole murder case, with no need for a pesky trial or further investigation. Problem was, Hannah, too, could testify as to the exact date and time those photos had been taken. . . .

He finally spoke. "What, am I supposed to just have *faith* that you'll release my friends? I don't think so."

"You hardly have a choice—"

"You want to bet?" Murphy said. "Here's what *you're* going to do. You're going to give me proof that my friends are alive before this negotiation goes any farther. I want to speak to all of the women you took. I want to have a conversation with *each* of them, so that I know you didn't record their voices and then put a bullet in their heads, the way your acolyte did to Angelina." He enunciated each syllable of her name. "You call me back in fifteen minutes with all four of them still alive, or I will put myself into FBI custody so fast your motherfucking head will spin."

He hung up his phone far less forcefully than he wanted to—he couldn't risk breaking the damn thing.

He met Lindsey's and then Dave's eyes as, across the tent, the entire team removed their headphones.

"Okay," Dave said. "This is not something we didn't expect. They want a trade. You for their hostages."

"They want him *dead*," Izzy pointed out the obvious. "That's not a trade. That's fucked up."

"So we Hollywood it," Gillman chimed in. "Lopez is still in Dalton. We send him into the Taco Bell, with fake blood and a weapon loaded with blanks. He says he's Murphy and—"

"That won't work," Murphy cut him off.

"Actually?" Jenkins said. "It might."

"No." Murphy shook his head. "It won't. Because they have absolutely no intention of letting Hannah and the others go."

Eden's back was killing her, and she honestly couldn't remember the last time she'd felt Pinkie kick, which was starting to freak her out.

But that was nothing compared to the solid case of heebie-jeebies that the Freedom Network drone with the wandering eye was giving her.

It wasn't her left eye, looking off God knows where, that was the problem. It was the questions she'd asked, while sitting beside Eden's bed in this pseudo-hospital room, here in the freaking middle of nowhere. Did heart disease, cancer, or mental illness run in Eden's or the baby's father's family? Had she consumed drugs or alcohol during her pregnancy? Had there been any record of mixed race in her ancestry? Was she a Christian—a real, true Christian, not that ignorant kind who didn't believe in the Bible?

Since leaving her stepfather's dictatorship, Eden hadn't spent a lot of time going to church. Despite that, while living in LA, she'd discovered that there *were* Christians who believed in something other than smiting sinners, repentance, and fearful avoidance of hellfire. If only one sect was real and true, however, she suspected it was the church on Santa Monica Boulevard that flew a rainbow flag and warmly welcomed all through its always-open doors.

Still she'd rejected all religion. She'd lived long enough to know that there was no God—there couldn't possibly be. There were just random acts of violence that, if you were lucky, you avoided or survived.

And Eden was working hard to survive this one. Since she'd also lived long enough to recognize crazy when she saw it, she chose not to mention that her Jewish grandmother had died of breast cancer, which had left her part-Cherokee grandfather battling alcoholism and depression for the rest of his life.

Like everything else she'd told her captives so far, she lied, making it all up as she went along. Meanwhile, she asked questions of her own—in hopes of finding out where they'd taken Sophia, Hannah, and Tess, and while constantly watching and waiting for an opportunity to escape.

Although where she'd go if she did make it out of this building, she had no clue. They'd arrived via a helicopter that had immediately flown away, and although Eden had been busy, pretending to have gone into labor, she'd caught a peek or two through the windows during their descent. All she'd seen for miles in every direction were tree-covered mountains.

"*When* is your due date?"

The crazy lady had put some kind of monitor across Eden's belly, to register the time and strength of the contractions that she'd told her captors she was having—another lie. To her surprise, there was actually something to register. But okay. Back when Eden was twelve, her cousin had gone to the hospital ten different times before her baby was finally born—she'd had a series of practice contractions that she'd mistaken for the real deal.

That was surely what was happening to Eden now.

Which was just as good, since she was sticking to the story she'd told back at the cabin—that Pinkie was due any minute. It had worked to her advantage this far—she'd kept the man with the beard and the let-the-good-times-roll Louisiana accent from injecting her with whatever drug had made both Hannah and Sophia sag. She'd implored him, saying that no matter what kind of grudge he held, he couldn't possibly want to risk the life of an innocent, unborn child. And, to her surprise, he'd actually agreed.

Instead, he'd trussed her up good and tossed her into the back of a cargo van with Tess, Sophia, and Hannah. All of whom were out cold.

"Are you a nurse?" Eden finally asked the walking health questionnaire, hoping there was something—even just Tylenol—that she could take for her painful back.

"No." The woman frowned as she adjusted the belt that went across Eden's stomach. "This is supposed to pick up the heartbeat."

"It's probably broken," Eden said, pushing her hands away. The entire machine looked ancient. "Don't you have an ultrasound? And if you're not a nurse, then who—"

"I'm the baby's mother," the woman told her.

"Excuse me?" Eden said.

"When the doctor gets here, he'll perform a C-section and give the baby to me, so you can be punished with your friends."

"What?" A rush of fear made Eden's back hot with pain. "Oh!"

"That was a big one," the woman reported, checking the machine. "Maybe all he'd do is induce. Assuming that God hasn't already punished you by killing the child."

"There's no heartbeat," Eden said testily, her hands on a stomach that oddly felt bowling ball tight, "because the machine is broken." Come on, Pinkie, kick. But he didn't move. She would have thought that the squeezing from the practice contractions would've woken him up—made him do his usual flips and spins.

The woman took a stethoscope, put in the ear pieces, and pressed the end to Eden's belly.

"Get away from me," Eden said.

"Shhh!"

"No!"

The door to the room opened, and the woman immediately backed off, pulling the stethoscope from her ears as the bearded man came back in. He was followed by three men with machine guns—including Adolf, the guard Eden had befriended, so to speak, in the back of the van.

Although how a boy—and he really was just a boy—could have turned eighteen without realizing how bizarre it was that his parents had named him after a mass-murdering fascist dictator, Eden did not know. Jug-eared and nerdly, he was the kind of boy that girls wouldn't bother to talk to—so she'd quickly remedied that.

She'd further won his sympathy by telling him that her husband—the baby's fictional father—had died while fighting in Iraq.

And she'd let him pitch her the idea of joining the Freedom Network. Thanks to years of being lectured by her stepfather, and by Danny, too, Eden knew how to sit through it not just without pissing off Little Hitler, but by making him believe she was actually listening and engaged.

The van ride to the helicopter hadn't been as long as she'd expected, but she'd had enough time to worm a whispered promise out of him—"I won't let anyone hurt your friends." And sure enough, someone had bandaged Tess's bullet wounds while in the air—at Adolf's pink-cheeked but gutsy insistence.

And when they landed and more guards came to take them off the helicopter, when Sophia, Tess, and Hannah had been taken to a different building than Eden, Adolf had caught her eye, nodded, and then gone with them.

The creepy woman now bowed her head in submission to the bearded man, who announced, "The doctor's been delayed, but I need this one, now, with the others."

This one being Eden.

"Of course, Captain," the woman said, and when she turned to lower the rail on the bed, she whispered to Eden, "Your baby's already dead."

"I'm going to tell Reed yes, that I'll do it," Murphy said, as Dave let his team—which included a pair of pissed-off Navy SEALs—help him brainstorm their next move. "But not in Dalton."

Outside, a group of FBI agents who looked like middle-aged moms appeared to be cooking an open-fire dinner. They were, in reality, standing guard and watching the campsite's perimeter, no doubt ready to offer home-baked cookies to any Freedom Network patrols that might stumble past, to keep their true kickass nature concealed.

Meanwhile, in the tent, Lindsey had taken on the task that Tess Bailey usually performed at the computer. Dave was well aware that sitting still wasn't one of Lindsey's strengths, but someone had to be in computer contact with Jules Cassidy and the FBI.

Neither Dave nor Murphy nor Cassidy himself wanted the FBI to be directly involved with the rescue operation, so they were treading the tightrope of bureaucracy in their communications, even knowing it could well come back and slap them on the asses, should something go horribly wrong.

Cassidy was coming through huge, though, and Lindsey reported that they'd received voice match info from that first phone call. The man with the thick accent who'd spoken to Murphy was Craig Reed, the Freedom Network's security chief and Tim Ebersole's former right-hand man.

Lindsey had rattled off the contents of Reed's file—his unremarkable educational record, a short list of priors, info about his dishonorable discharge from the U.S. Army due to his part in the cover-up of a hate-crime against an American mosque—a deadly fire in which a little boy had been killed, perpetrated by two men under his command. Reed had served time, and met one of Ebersole's fervent disciples in prison. The rest, including his callous public comment about the dead child—*The only thing I know for sure about the boy is that now he'll never have the chance to become a terrorist*—was history.

"I'm going to tell Reed," Murphy continued now, "that I've put out some feelers and that my connections tell me that a special delivery was made to the Freedom Network compound, via chopper, and that I know he's holding Hannah and the others there. So I'm coming to them."

"By the way," Lindsey interjected. "We just got a report from the FBI that the helicopter that flew into the compound left almost immediately after discharging its passengers. They've tracked it back to the Dalton area—the pilot and owner is a card-carrying Freedom Network member. There was no one else on the aircraft when he landed."

"I don't get it," Izzy Zanella said. "I'm Tim Ebersole. I faked my death, but now there's a chance I've been exposed—pun intended. Why didn't I get out of Dodge on that helo? Why aren't I halfway to Mexico by now?"

"Because *Dodge* is the safest place in the world for Ebersole, right now," Dave finally spoke up. "Even with a warrant, everyone knows that the FBI's not going into that compound. Imagine if they tried. Instant and ongoing publicity for the Network. *FBI Holds Freedom Network Members Captive—Day Two Hundred and Twelve.* Can't you just see those headlines?"

He glanced at his watch. They had nine more minutes before the proof of life phone call—assuming that Sophia and the others were all still alive. Which was something he absolutely had to believe, in order to keep from driving one of their trucks right through the fence and single-handedly wiping those murderous lunatics off the face of the earth.

"Can we stay on topic?" Dave's request was as much for himself as the others. He turned back to Murphy. "At the end of this phone call, Reed's going to say, *You've had your proof of life. Do it in Dalton and do it now.*"

"Then you say *fuck no*," Izzy answered for him, with all the certainty and conviction of a twenty-something Navy SEAL. "You tell him that you don't have long to talk, that you need a number so that you can call *him* back—"

Gillman interrupted with his usual belligerence—apparently it wasn't reserved purely for Dave. "Yeah, like he's going to give Murphy—"

"Maybe he will," Izzy spoke over him. "The point is to ask for more than you think you'll get. The Freedom Network's watching their entire future flush down the drain, right here, right now. Taking hostages was a last ditch, hail-Mary move if I've ever seen one. We've got the power. Tell *them* how it's going to go down. And for fuck's sake, buy us enough time for the sun to set so we can get in there and get our people out."

Murphy nodded. "I will," he said. "I'm going to tell Reed it's going to take me five hours to get out to the compound, but once I get there? I'll confess. Right at the gate, in front of their surveillance cameras. *After* I see him let Hannah and the others go."

Lindsey shook her head. "He's never going to agree to that," she said.

"He might." Izzy looked the way Dave felt—as though if he had to sit here talking about this much longer, he was going to jump clear out of his skin.

"If he does," Lindsey was certain, "he's bullshitting us. Think about it. The Freedom Network lets Hannah go, Murphy confesses to everything, including doctoring those photos, and then removes himself—permanently—from all future questioning. But hey, Hannah's still in the mix, willing to testify in court that she was the one who took the pictures—just a few days ago. Not to mention the fact that all four of the hostages were taken at gunpoint, and that Tess was *shot* . . . It'll be obvious that Murphy's confession was made under duress, and suddenly there's a fraud investigation underway and a major delay in getting their five mill. Trust me, they are *not* going to let Hannah go."

"They don't have to *do* it," Dave pointed out. "They just have to say that they will."

Lindsey was still shaking her head. "We have to give Reed a way to think that he can still win—otherwise he's going to dig in his heels and push his *do it now* agenda."

Murphy nodded, clearly on the same page. "A car," he said, and Lindsey nodded. "I'll demand a car. I'll say it's so the women can drive out of the compound and get to safety."

"And he'll agree to it," Lindsey added for those of them who hadn't quite figured it out, "because he can fill the trunk with fertilizer, make a bubba bomb and blow the car to pieces after Murphy's dead. When the FBI comes running to investigate the blast, the Freedom Network can claim the bomb was yours, Murph—that you blew them up, then killed yourself. Reed'll probably wave around the fact that Hannah was on the Freedom Network member roster—like you found out she was some kind of double agent and killed her for betraying you. The others were in the wrong place at the wrong time—collateral damage."

Murphy turned to Dave. "We need to have FBI teams in place, hidden right outside the gate. They need to be able to stop Hannah and get everyone out of the car in case it comes to—"

"It's not going to," Dave said as firmly as he could muster. Apparently it wasn't firmly enough, so he added, "But we'll be ready for everything." He looked at Lindsey.

"I'm on it," she said, "but before I make that call, I want to point out that we need to make sure Reed won't come up with his own counterplan. Kill all or most of the hostages now—dead hostages are always easier to control—and when you approach the gate, somehow lure you inside. Coerce you into signing a written confession, then pop you themselves. Invite the FBI in to clean up the remains of a nasty quadruple murder-suicide."

"Yeah, let's *not* have them do that," Izzy said, his anxiety level visibly ratcheting higher.

"Insist on a second proof of life call," Dave told Murphy what he'd no doubt already figured out for himself. Still, it was worth saying aloud.

"Tell Reed you'll call him when you arrive at the compound," Izzy suggested again. He was on his feet pacing. "And why not ask him—no fuck that—*tell* him to let Eden go. Right now. As a show of good faith. She's an innocent bystander—like Lindsey said, she was in the wrong place at the wrong time. She didn't ask to be there, she's had no training . . . Damn it, it's Angelina all over again."

Murphy stood up, anguish in his eyes. "You think I don't know that?"

"Murph," Dave said quietly. "We're going to get them out."

"I'd do it," Murphy told him through gritted teeth, just as softly. "What they want me to do. I'd gladly die. If I knew for sure that Hannah and the others would be okay . . ."

Dear God.

Meanwhile, Gillman was focused on his sister. "Great, Zanella. That's perfect," he was scoffing. "Bring Eden to their attention. They'll think she's special and they'll kill her first." He threw up his hands. "Why am I arguing? These people are monsters. She's probably already dead."

Izzy turned, anger radiating off of him—aimed at his new brother-in-law. "Don't fucking say that!"

"What we do know for sure," Dave tried to convince Murphy, as Jenkins moved between the two SEALs, "is that we're going in there. We're going to get them out, and they're going to be okay."

"Guys." Jenkins was adamant as he kept Izzy from Gillman. "This isn't helping."

"It's *really* not helping," Izzy said, "when he fucking *says* shit like that!"

"Look at me, Murph," Dave said. "And nod your head. We're gonna be okay. *All* of us."

Murphy met his eyes only briefly, but nodded, as Gillman spat, "This is your fault. Eden would've been safe in Las Vegas—"

"With your nutjob of a stepfather locking her in the bathroom and trying to sell her baby to the highest bidder?" Izzy was beside himself. "If this is anyone's fault it's yours, fuckwad, for leaving her behind and not looking back. And it's déjà vu all over again with your little brother—"

"I send money," Gillman shouted.

"And if you think he sees *any* of it, you're a fucking idiot!"

"Stop it. Right now. I could hear your shouting half a mile down the trail."

Dave turned—they all did—to see Decker standing just inside the flap of the tent.

Lawrence Decker was average height, average build. Heck, Dave himself was taller. But the former SEAL chief had the ability to silence much larger men with a single look—let alone a harsh sentence of reprimand like the one he'd just delivered.

It was definitely silent now in the tent.

As Dave watched, Decker looked at Murphy, met his gaze and nodded.

That was it.

Years without contact, and Deck gave the man four seconds of eye contact and a single head nod before refocusing his glare on Izzy and Gillman.

And Dave knew in that instant that walking into this tent and coming face-to-face with Murphy had to be one of the hardest things Deck—who blamed himself for Angelina's death—had ever done. Although, if Nash didn't awaken from surgery, there were a lot of hardest-ever things rushing toward Decker at warp speed.

Dave alone put voice to what they were all thinking: "Thank God you're here, sir."

But Decker shook his head. "I'm not here," he said. "I'm on a separate assignment and I only stopped in to coordinate, because I don't want to fuck up what you've got planned."

Dave couldn't believe it. He pulled Decker aside, lowered his voice. "You're on a *separate*—"

"Excuse us." Decker pulled Dave even farther from the others, outside of the tent, and a good distance from the still-cooking FBI moms, for that matter.

"I'm going in to find Tim Ebersole," Decker informed Dave.

"That can wait. Sophia's in there," Dave reminded him.

Deck nodded curtly. "And Tess and Hannah and Eden. I'm counting on you to get them out."

"Sir," Dave started.

But Decker cut him off. "There's something else you need to know. Nash didn't make it."

Dave heard the words that Decker had said. He recognized each of them. Knew their meaning. But they just didn't make sense. "He didn't . . ."

So Deck said it far more brutally. "Jimmy's dead."

"Shit," Dave breathed. He forced himself to stand tall—there was a reason Decker had given him this news privately—but inside, he was on his knees, screaming. He clenched his teeth. "Oh, *shit*."

"Don't tell Murphy," Decker ordered. "Or Tess. Let's get everyone to safety first. But if I don't come back out . . ."

"Don't even *think* that!" God damn it, Dave never asked to be team leader, and now he was going to have to tell Tess that the man she loved was *dead*?

"Help Tess with the funeral arrangements," Decker instructed. "And rein Murphy in. I'm afraid he's going to take this hard. If I'm not here when the dust settles, sit on him if you have to, and make sure he understands that this wasn't his fault. Make sure he goes to see Jules Cassidy. He's got some information on a Freedom Network plan to use the insurance money on a series of attacks on government buildings across the country. This evidence that Ebersole's death was fraud will allow the FBI to seize the group's assets—and keep them from getting that insurance payout. This is going to shut them down for good. Cassidy'll help Murph understand the stakes involved. And you can also help him understand that both Nash and I knew exactly what the risks were when we went to work for Troubleshooters."

"Decker," Dave started, but again the other man cut him off.

"You've been a good friend," Decker said. "To both Nash and me." It was then, to Dave's total surprise, that Decker put his arms around him in an awkward embrace. "I'm counting on you, Malkoff. Do me proud."

Jim Nash was dead.

Sophia had heard their captors say it. They'd left him behind because he was no longer a threat.

Oh, God.

Hannah's stomach twisted and the room spun and she had to lean back against the wall. But even then, her legs gave out, and she slid down so that she was sitting on the linoleum floor. Nash was *dead*. And Murphy would not, could not survive. He would be as lost to her as Nash was to Tess, sent hurtling back into the darkness . . .

Only this time? Hannah wouldn't sit idly by. She'd go in after him, if she had to, and drag him back out. Because Murphy wasn't dead, not the way Nash was. He was still alive.

And yes, this was a hard blow, but not even half as hard as what Tess was facing. Dear God, the woman was lying there, unconscious and bliss-fully unaware . . .

Sophia tapped her leg, and Hannah looked up.

"Where's Eden?"

"Oh, my God . . ." She hadn't realized it, hadn't noticed, but the young woman who'd broken into Hannah's cabin for solitude's sake was not with them either.

Had their captors left her behind because she, like Nash, was also dead?

Sophia tapped on the walls, on both sides of the room, but shook her head at Hannah. Apparently there were no answering taps. "Maybe she's still unconscious."

"Why wouldn't they put her in here with us?" Hannah pushed herself back up, onto her feet. "I need you to talk to them," she told Sophia.

Sophia didn't understand. "Talk to . . . Who?"

"Whoever's on the other side of this door." Hannah examined it again, and again it was just as impenetrable, with its hinges on the outside and a very secure looking knob and bolt lock. But she banged on it, rapping as hard as she could with her knuckles. "Hey! *Hey!* Open up! Where's our friend? What have you done with her?"

She looked back at Sophia, who came closer to listen, but shook her head.

Hannah kept knocking. *"Hey!"*

Although, really, what was she going to do, even if the door magically opened? Even if there was only one easily overpowered guard on the other side? Even if she gained possession of his automatic weapon, she'd be in the middle of a locked-down compound, surrounded by an electric fence weighed down by an unconscious, badly wounded woman. She herself could barely walk on her bum ankle—and, oh yeah. She was deaf.

As for Sophia . . . She probably wouldn't weigh in at a hundred pounds unless she was carrying a ten-pound bag of potatoes. Unless she had a superhero cape tucked under her shirt, escape from this hellhole would be next to impossible. And that wasn't even taking into considera-tion the fact that they'd first have to locate and free Eden . . .

Although maybe . . .

"If I drew you a map of the compound," Hannah told Sophia, "and showed you how to get to a part of the fence that isn't electrified, we could create a diversion and *you* could—"

"I'm not leaving you," Sophia told her. "Besides, they're going to come for us. Dave will. Murphy and Decker, too. You *do* know that, right?"

"But that's what they want," Hannah said, as the walls of the small room seemed to close in around her. "The men who killed Nash. They want Murphy to come, so that they can kill him, too. We can't just sit and wait."

But Sophia didn't answer. She turned away, sharply, and Hannah realized that someone was opening their prison cell door.

Chapter
Twenty-four

The first thing Sophia saw when the door opened was Eden.

The second thing she saw was that Eden was in tears.

"What did you do to her?" Hannah demanded, but no one deigned to answer.

The girl was, however, pushed into the room. Sophia caught her, kept her from falling onto the floor. "Are you hurt?" she asked, pushing Eden's hair back so she could see her face.

Eden shook her head. "They said Pinkie's heart's not beating."

Oh, no.

"But they're lying!" Eden insisted. "They want to steal him. There was this lady and she had these freakish false teeth and—"

"Quiet!" A tall man with a beard stood in the doorway. "Get back."

That last was aimed at Hannah, who looked as if she were weighing the odds of her survival if she rushed the door. But there were at least three guards behind the bearded man, all of whom were packing serious heat. So she grudgingly took a step back, and then another. But then, defiant, she held her ground, holding the man's gaze.

Eden squeezed Sophia's hand, and when Sophia glanced at her, she whispered an apology. "I'm sorry—my back . . ." She sharply drew in her breath.

Oh, no. No, no. Fate could not be so unkind as to have Eden go into labor right here and right now. Sophia helped her down, so she could sit on the floor.

Meanwhile, the bearded man was talking to Hannah. "Are you really deaf?" he asked. "Or was that just another of your lies?"

Sophia knew that Hannah had gone into the Freedom Network compound last spring, pretending to apply for a job as a guard, while in fact looking for Murphy, who'd gone missing.

Clearly this man—who was in a position of authority—remembered meeting her.

"Of course, you didn't lie about your home address," he said with a smile that held no warmth. "Thanks so much for providing that for us."

"Let my friends go, Reed," Hannah countered. "They have nothing to do with this."

"They do now," he said. "Besides, you'll all be free to go, if Mr. Murphy does as he's told." He pointed to Tess. "Wake her."

"She's not sleeping, she's unconscious," Hannah retorted. "She's badly injured—she needs a doctor."

"Wake her anyway. Or we'll do it for you."

Sophia knew the difference between a false threat and a real one. So she went to Tess, touched her face, shook her shoulder. But Tess, perhaps mercifully, didn't rouse. "I'm sorry," she told Reed.

"Lucas," Reed barked. "Matt!"

Two of the guards came into the room, one of them with his automatic weapon at his shoulder. "Into the corner!" he shouted, and there was nothing to do but move back from the waving barrel of that gun.

Sophia tried to take Tess back with her, too, and Hannah quickly came to help.

"Leave her!"

"Don't do this!" Sophia said as Lucas or Matt, whichever he was, aimed his gun at her head and forced her and Hannah back.

The other guard handed his weapon to Reed and manhandled Tess up off the floor.

"Stop it!" Hannah was furious, and Sophia knew from the way she was eyeing the weapons that she was considering grabbing for one as the guard dragged Tess to the toilet and shoved her head into the water.

"No!"

"Oh, my God!"

"Stop!" All of them were shouting now and Eden was crying again, as Tess came up gasping and sputtering, as the guard tossed her back onto the floor, as she skidded toward them, as they moved to surround her, to pull her back with them to the illusion of safety, just a few feet farther from the business ends of those weapons.

"God damn you," Hannah snarled at Reed, as one of the guards handed him a telephone receiver. It was a white handset for an old-fashioned landline, attached by a long, curly cord to a phone that must've been on the wall out in the hall.

He held it out to them, gave them another of those odious smiles. "Who wants to talk to Mr. Murphy first?"

There'd been no real doubt in Murphy's mind that the Freedom Network had kidnapped Hannah, Sophia, Tess, and Eden, although one of the functions of a proof of life phone call was to verify that fact.

The hostages were, indeed, being held by the bad people who claimed to have them. Check.

Sophia took the phone first, her voice strong and clear through the telephone connection. "Murph?"

"Are you all right?" Murphy asked, his heart so securely lodged in his throat he could barely speak past it. "Is everyone all right?"

"I'm okay," Sophia reported. "Hannah is, too. Tess is badly hurt—she's been shot and they hit her in the head with a . . . a rifle butt, I think, and . . ." Her voice caught. "I'm afraid they haven't been very gentle with any of us, but even less so with her."

Dave Malkoff looked as if he were going to throw up, and across the tent, Decker was glaring down at his boots.

"Soph, you've got to tell Hannah something for me, okay?" Murphy spoke quickly. "You've got to tell her I was lying, okay? When I said I didn't love her . . ."

"I will," Sophia promised. "Oh, Murphy, I'm so sorry this is happening."

"I can only imagine where her head's at," Murphy said, hoping Sophia was listening carefully. "I know I'm not going to get a chance to tell her this and . . . I'm tired of lying, too. Please tell Hannah I wish I'd, um, spent the night with her—that I'm sorry now that I didn't, and that you should stay put and do whatever Reed tells you to do, all right? Will you remember all that?"

Sophia's voice shook as again she said, "I will."

Izzy got to his feet, as if he could no longer contain himself, and Murphy glanced at him, realizing that Sophia hadn't mentioned Eden.

"Is Eden Zanella with you?" Murph asked.

"Yes, she is," Sophia reported.

"Is she hurt?"

Sophia hesitated, during which time Izzy looked as if he'd been stabbed through the heart.

"I don't know," she finally answered, which wasn't what Izzy—or any of them—particularly wanted to hear. "She's pregnant and *hey*—"

"Time's up," Reed came back on. "You've had your proof of life."

"I want to speak to all of them," Murphy demanded. "Put Eden on."

"You've had enough—"

"How do I know you didn't kill the other three and put a gun to Sophia's head, telling her what to say?" Murphy was not going to take any of Reed's shit. "Put. The girl. On."

And there they stood—they were all on their feet by now, just standing in the tent, headphones on, holding their breath until . . .

"Hello?" The voice over the line was very small—Eden sounded impossibly young. She had to be scared to death.

Izzy pushed a piece of paper in front of Murphy, upon which he'd scribbled the words *Nickname for baby = Pinkie. Fav color = yellow. Fav band = Maroon 5. Inside jokes = Manbearpig, "Mr. Big."*

Inside jokes? Good, that was good. But please God, let Eden's brain be functioning despite what had to be crippling fear . . .

"Eden," Murphy said. "We've never spoken over the phone, so I've got to ask you a question to make sure it's really you. Last time I saw your husband, Izzy told me you've got a nickname for your baby. Is it Manbearpig or Mr. Big?"

Message: Izzy was here with Murphy, providing him with that info.

Eden laughed—a staccato rush of air. "Neither. It's Pinkie," she said, and then burst into tears. "Oh God, please, I need you to tell Izzy—and Danny, too, please tell them that I'm so, *so* sorry . . ."

Message received? Murphy glanced at Izzy, who'd started to pace, clearly terribly upset, but who looked at him and nodded. Yes. She knew.

Across the tent, Dan Gillman had his head in his hands.

"Eden," Murphy said. "Are you injured?"

"I don't know," Eden was clearly struggling to control her tears. "I think maybe something's wrong with Pinkie. I think—"

Murphy closed his eyes, unable to look at Izzy or Dan as, on the other end of that phone line Eden shrieked, clearly manhandled away from the phone. He could hear Hannah and Sophia both shouting, their words indiscernible. Then Craig Reed. "Next."

"You be more careful with them!" Murphy demanded.

"Or you'll do what?" Reed said. "Go to the FBI? Do it and they're dead—and then you'll just kill yourself anyway—the way you always said you would in those pathetic e-mails you used to send."

"You'll be dead, too," Murphy pointed out.

"Unlikely," Reed said. "We've got enough supplies and ammunition in here to last for decades. We're ready for anything anyone can throw at us. Here's the deaf one."

"Listen to me, Vinh." Hannah had no doubt read Reed's lips—*you'll kill yourself anyway*—and her voice shook. "Whatever they want you to do? Don't you do it. Don't you dare. Go to the FBI, damnit—"

The sickening thud of Hannah being hit carried through the phone line, and now it was Murphy who had to keep his head down, his teeth clenched. "Don't *hurt* them!"

"You're the one who's hurting them," Reed said.

"I don't need to talk to Tess," Murphy quickly told him, afraid that if they'd slapped around a pregnant woman they'd have no qualms about doing the same to one who was seriously injured. "But you keep her alive. You keep all of them alive, because I'll do what you want—I'm going to do what you want, but I'm not going to do it without seeing you let them go. You read me? So I'm coming to you. I'm coming right to your front gate, and you're going to give them a car . . ."

Izzy had to go outside, because no fucking way was he going to cry in front of Danny Gillman.

Soph, tell Hannah I was lying, okay? When I said that I didn't love her . . .

What the fuck was wrong with the male of the species that, unless they were being flushed down the crapper, they were flipping unable to pony up to the fact that they had feelings—deep chasms of one-fucking-hundred percent intensely emotional, gooey-gushy, heartfelt feelings.

I love you. Why the fuck was it so hard to say those three little words?

Would it really have killed him to say something to Eden, before leaving for the Navy Base? At the time Izzy believed the senior's phone call could well have been a wheels-up order. It was entirely possible that Izzy had been on the verge of being gone for months.

Would it really have been that impossibly hard to have said to Eden, *You know what? I didn't count on this happening. I'm as surprised as I know you're going to be, but somewhere down the line—and it wasn't while you were giving me head but rather some other moment, when you said something, or you smiled, or you got that look of pure love in your eyes because you were thinking about Pinkie—something inside me was made whole. And I know it's so fucking hokey—you complete me—can I be any more cliché? But I think I'm in love with you, Eed. And I believe you about Richie, so please don't run away. Instead, trust me. Come to me when life flips you a shitburger, baby, and let me help . . .*

Instead, he'd locked it all inside because he was a fucking coward, and now . . .

I think maybe something's wrong with Pinkie . . .

Please God, don't be the monster that we both know you can be. Don't do that to this already-damaged girl . . .

"Izzy."

He glanced back at the tent to see Lindsey standing in the rapidly fading light. "Here's the iPod and headset I'm giving Grandpa Barker for his birthday. Want to give it a listen?"

The two-way radio that she was holding out, with its earpiece and mic, *was* about the size of a Nano. Izzy took it from her. Played along with their ridiculous cover. "You spent the big bucks on Gramps this year, huh?"

"Hey, you only turn eighty once." She stepped closer. Lowered her voice. Transformed from a no-nonsense teammate into his best friend's wife, concern for him on her pretty face. "You okay?"

Izzy nodded, suddenly so overcome that he couldn't speak.

Lindsey, of course, used her super-estrogen powers to read him like a book. "You know, there's a reason police officers are removed from a case when family members are involved. No one's going to have a problem if you don't—"

"No," he managed. Cleared his throat. "I'm good." And damn, that was a stupid expression and a poor choice of words. He was far from good. "I'm going. I want to. But . . ." He lowered his voice even more. "He wants there to be some kind of incident, doesn't he—Reed? He actually *wants* a showdown with the FBI."

Lindsey nodded. "That's the consensus inside, too."

"What does he think, he's going to spark a revolution, that across the country all of the Timothy McVeigh-wannabe-bubba-terrorists are going to turn off Rush Limbaugh, leap off their sofas, and rise up to make Ebersole our new dictator?" He shook his head. "Never gonna happen."

"That's why they call it delusions of grandeur," Lindsey told him. "Get in the tent and gear up. Dave wants to be ready to go any time."

"Murphy wants us to get out of here," Hannah said, after Reed closed the door behind him, locking them securely in, after Sophia gave her all of Murphy's messages.

Tell Hannah I was lying . . . I'm tired of lying, too . . .

Eden shook her head. "But he said to stay put—"

"Murphy was lying when he said that. He was telling us to try to break free," Hannah told the girl as they sat on the floor of the little room. Sophia had Tess's head in her lap, trying to make her more comfortable as she drifted in and out of consciousness. "See, he lied when he said he wanted to sleep with me—"

Eden wasn't convinced. "How do you know he was lying about that?"

"Because she's *been* sleeping with him," Sophia gently explained.

"Oh." Eden actually blushed. "Duh. Sorry."

"He knows Reed isn't going to let us live. He doesn't want us sitting here, waiting for them to kill us," Hannah said again.

"I don't want that either," Eden said.

"He said, *I can only imagine where her head's at,*" Sophia said. "I think he was telling us that he doesn't know exactly where we are."

"Unless that was another of his lies."

"No," Sophia said. "He said that before the listen-closely-because-now-I'm-going-to-lie part."

"Unless it was *all* a lie."

It was clear that Sophia knew what Hannah was thinking. "He loves you," she said. "He wasn't lying about that."

Hannah shook her head, willing herself not to cry. "He said it because he thinks he's going to die." Thinks? Try *knows*. Oh, God . . .

"Or maybe he said it because he means it," Sophia countered.

"He told *me* that Izzy's with him," Eden volunteered. Her eyes filled with tears. "I can't believe he followed me here."

"Murphy, Dave, Izzy, Lindsey, Jenk, Gillman, Lopez," Sophia counted off on her fingers. "And I've got to believe Decker's out there somewhere, too. They're coming for us. Absolutely."

"Seven, maybe eight—against an army who'll be shooting to kill." Hannah hated those odds. "Don't you think that's what Reed wants? For Murphy to come in here . . ."

"Reed definitely wants Murphy dead," Sophia said. "I don't doubt that. And I'm also in Murph's camp. I don't believe for a second that Reed has any intention of letting us go."

Tess stirred, opened her eyes, looked up at them in dread. "Jim," she whispered. "Sophia, where's Jimmy?"

"Shhh," Sophia said soothingly, her hand in Tess's hair. "He's all right. He got away, Tess."

"He got away?" Tess asked, searching for the truth in their eyes, struggling to stay conscious.

Hannah couldn't look at her.

"He went to get help." Sophia lied smoothly, convincingly. "He's going to be all right."

"Thank God," Tess breathed before slipping back into oblivion.

And there they sat—no one spoke for a good long time.

"We need to focus on getting out of here," Hannah finally said.

It was then that Eden shifted uncomfortably, her face contorting in pain. "You okay?" Hannah asked.

The girl nodded. She was tough, but she couldn't hide the sudden paleness of her face. "Oh, crap," she said, her hands on her stomach.

Sophia reached out, touched her. "I'm pretty certain you're having contractions," she said.

Oh, crap, indeed. Hannah looked at the girl. "Please tell me that you didn't lie about your due date."

Eden shook her head, her mouth twisted. "It's too soon. They're just . . . practice contractions."

Yeah, right. Hannah's skepticism must've shown on her face because Eden insisted, "The doctor in Germany . . . figured out the due date . . . from the ultrasound. But oh, sweet Jesus, this . . . *hurts.*"

"Okay," Sophia said, reaching out to take both of Eden's hands. "Look at me, Eden, look at me! Don't hold your breath. Breathe through it. Like this." She demonstrated for the girl—short panting breaths.

"We need to tell the guards to get a doctor," Hannah said, pushing herself to her feet.

"No!" Eden grabbed her leg. She was on the verge of panic. "They want . . . to steal my baby. Don't you dare . . . get anyone! They'll take me away. . . ."

"There are drugs that can prevent premature labor," Hannah told her. "And save your baby."

"Sometimes," Sophia said, looking up so that Hannah could read her lips, "the labor's not premature. Sometimes it's not really labor." And then she added, clearly but no doubt silently, over the top of Eden's head, "Sometimes it's a miscarriage. I'm not sure if you saw this, but when she first came in, she said they couldn't hear the baby's heartbeat."

Oh, God. Hannah hadn't caught that. That was terrible news. And if it were true, if the baby had somehow died, Eden's body would work to expel it. Which, at this point in the pregnancy, would look and feel a lot like labor.

Either way, Eden needed to go to a hospital.

The girl's breathing finally slowed and, damp with perspiration, she relaxed back onto the floor, releasing Sophia's hands.

"Eden," Hannah asked, crouching next to her. One of them had to be the bad cop, and she had to know for sure. "Are you positive you didn't exaggerate your due date, so that Izzy—"

"I didn't." Eden was affronted. "Izzy's not the father anyway, and he knows it. He married me because he felt sorry for me. I told you, I'm not due until September."

"Can you remember the last time you felt the baby kick?" Sophia gently asked.

Tears filled Eden's eyes again and she wrapped her arms around herself, as if holding her baby close. "No. But I've been a little preoccupied," she said defensively. "I know what you're thinking, but they were lying about the heartbeat. The monitor they were using was a million years old, and the stupid lady wasn't even a nurse. I know what they were doing—I've seen enough movies of the week. They induce my labor, they drug me, and I wake up and they tell me they're so sorry but the baby didn't survive, only he did and five years later, the lady with the—" She got a little garbled here. Was that *false teeth* and *funny eye?* "—is teaching him to read from the neo-Nazi Manifesto!"

Sophia glanced at Hannah. "You get all that?"

Hannah nodded. "Most of it." God, she was tired. "Eden, I promise you, right now, that we're not going to let them steal your baby."

Eden nodded, but it was clear she didn't believe Hannah. "The way you promised Tess that Jimmy Nash was going to be all right, when you really have no clue if he's even alive?"

Oh, hell.

"Yeah," Hannah said. "That way. Because promises like that give hope. Hope that after this is over, I'm going to have a chance to read Murphy's lips when he says that he loves me. Hope that I'm going to get my life back. Hope that I can be strong enough to get all of us out of here."

"False hope," Eden said, her lip quivering.

"No such thing," Hannah said. "Hope is always, *always* true and good. Now, if it's okay with you, I have some questions that you can answer that will help us get the *hell* out of here."

Eden nodded, subdued.

"When they brought you here," Hannah asked the girl. "How many guards were in the hall?"

"Two."

"You're sure."

"There were two chairs," Eden said. "Two guards were sitting right outside the door. They stood up when we approached."

"Was there anyone else in the corridor?"

"No, the whole building was empty," Eden said. "It felt kind of like a school on a Saturday."

"How about outside?" Hannah asked. "Any guards posted there?"

"Not at the door we came in. But everyone who was walking around in the compound had a gun," Eden reported. "All the men, that is. The women walked with their heads down."

That was pretty typical of Freedom Network security. Rely on the fence and the fact that all of their men were part of their army, were heavily armed, and were paying attention. Except as was the case with most people, the paying attention part was questionable.

At least it was when Hannah had been in the compound in the spring.

She included Sophia—and Tess, whose eyes were open and who seemed to be following the conversation—in her next question, "Have any of you seen anyone—guards or gunmen or anyone—at the cabin or here—using a cell phone or a Blackberry?"

They shook their heads. "In fact, the call to Murphy," Sophia started.

"Was done on a regular phone line," Hannah finished for her. "Yeah. The Freedom Network is cell phone averse. They think if they use anything other than a landline, the FBI'll be able to listen in more easily. Their communication system here in the compound doesn't access any outside telecommunication networks. It's all hard-wired." She forced a smile. "I found that out when I applied for a security position."

"So, if we take out the phone in the hall," Sophia correctly surmised, "the guards can't call for backup."

"Correct," Hannah said. "They'll have to run to get help."

"Or discharge their weapons," Tess spoke up to remind them. Sophia had to repeat her words for Hannah, who nodded.

Tess was right. Nothing said *come quickly and bring help* like a few shots fired, even if just into the air. "We'll only have one chance to do this," Hannah told them. If they tried to escape and failed, if the guards fired their weapons—even if they didn't hit and wound any of them—Reed would come running. And he'd pile on additional security guards. They'd be thick in that hallway. Which would hinder, not help, any rescue effort that was coming.

"Uhhn," Eden said, as what had to be another contraction started.

Again, Sophia grabbed her hands and coached her through it. It didn't seem quite as intense, but still . . .

"We should start timing them," Hannah said.

"I already have." Sophia looked at her watch. "Those last two were four minutes apart."

That wasn't good. Hannah sat back, leaning her head against the wall, woefully aware that their chances of getting to safety had just been further diminished. It was going to be hard enough carrying Tess, but now . . .

Sophia pushed her hair back from a grimy face that still managed to look angelic. She was clearly thinking along the same lines. "Maybe instead of getting out, we should attempt to barricade ourselves in. If we overpowered the guards and gained possession of even just one weapon . . ."

It was not a bad idea—provided that the cavalry coming to rescue them was truly a cavalry and not just seven people.

Hope, Hannah reminded herself. Far fewer than seven people could hold off an entire army—in fact, one person with one weapon could do it. Provided they held the barrel of that weapon against the right person's head . . .

"Of course, before we overpower the guards," Sophia, ever pragmatic, pointed out, "we've got to get them to open the door."

Which was when Eden surprised them.

She lifted her head up off the floor. "I can do that," she said. "One of the guards—Adolf? He'll open the door for me."

Dave never asked to be team leader.

He never asked for it—never wanted it.

And yet, here he was. Facing one of the most difficult moments of his life as the team that he was forced to lead waited.

And waited.

For cover of darkness.

For reinforcements.

News of Nash's death had spread like wildfire among the spec ops community, and everyone—everyone—was coming to Sacramento to help kick the Freedom Network's ass.

Tom Paoletti was flying back from Hong Kong. Lopez was driving up from Dalton. Dave had gotten a call, too, from Sam Starrett and Troubleshooters XO Alyssa Locke, who were also on their way, ETA approximately ninety minutes. Riding with them was Cosmo Richter, a chief in SEAL Team Sixteen and a longtime friend both of Murphy's and Nash's. He'd brought four other SEALs with him, both officers and enlisted. The Troubleshooters' Florida office—Ric and Annie Alvarado and Davis Jones—had about the same arrival time.

Many of them had never worked with Nash, but it didn't matter.

One of their own had been taken.

And the Freedom Network was going to pay.

Problem was, with the news spreading so fast, it was neither feasible nor fair to keep it from Dave's team.

Which meant, as team leader, Dave had to break it to them. He'd sought out Decker's advice. Do it one on one, one at a time? Or make a group announcement?

Deck just shook his head. "Your call," he'd said, although he'd agreed that the news could no longer keep.

At which point Dave had made a comment about where was Dr. Heissman when he really needed her—which had made Decker make a noise that was vaguely laughter-like as he'd walked away.

Dave finally just pulled Murphy aside, over to a corner of the tent. "Got a sec?"

"Apparently," the former Marine said, "I've got a lot of them, because try as I might, I can't mind control the sun to make it set any faster."

There was no point in delaying the inevitable. "I've got bad news," Dave told his old friend. "Jim Nash died in surgery a few hours ago."

Murphy didn't move. He didn't blink. It was as if he'd stopped breathing. He just stood there—a man who'd already lost so much in his short life, facing yet another loss, this time of an old friend.

"Is Decker going to be all right?" he finally spoke. "I mean, going in there? Obviously, he's not going to be all right."

"Are you?" Dave asked.

Murphy met his gaze, and Dave saw sadness and regret but not the maelstrom of pain he'd feared he'd see in the other man's dark eyes.

"Yeah," Murph said. "Right now? Yeah, I'm all right. I'm not sure what I'm going to be feeling later, but . . ."

He turned away, then turned back, but then shook his head as if he'd changed his mind about what he was going to say.

"What?" Dave asked.

"No," Murphy said, "I was just going to ask if you had a problem with me killing Tim Ebersole while we're in there, but then I realized Decker's going in, specifically to find him. Motherfucker's as good as dead."

"Oh, shit," Dave said. But wait. Surely Cassidy at the FBI knew what he was doing when he'd sent Decker after Ebersole.

Murphy turned away again, but again turned back as if he had more to say. He cleared his throat. "When the time comes, if you want . . . If we all, you know, make it? I'll help you. Tell Tess. Nash didn't die through lack of will to live. I can tell her that. Last thing he did was try to connect a cut phone line so he could call for help. So he could go after her. Because he loved her—more than life."

To his intense mortification, Dave started to cry. For Tess, for Decker, and for himself. *You've been a good friend,* Decker had said. But Dave hadn't been. If he had, he would've intervened, months ago—despite what Nash wanted. If Dave had done that, Jim Nash might not be dead.

Dave turned away, and Murphy, thank God, did, too—pretending not to notice that the mighty team leader needed to blow his runny nose.

Adolf-the-guard wanted his blow job.

Eden didn't put it quite so bluntly, but Hannah and Sophia both understood exactly what she was saying when she tip-toed around the promise she'd made to the young Freedom Network soldier, while they were alone in the back of the van.

Sophia, who'd probably never had sex with anyone she wasn't madly in love with, actually dared to ask, "You didn't . . . already . . . ?"

Eden hadn't answered. She'd just shot her a *no way* look, but then was saved—sort of—as she was gripped by another of those stupid practice contractions that made her feel as if her back was going to implode. The breathing helped, but only a little and she was getting very, very frightened that these weren't practice, but instead they were the real deal.

It was much too soon for that. Two different doctors—one in Germany and one in Las Vegas—had given her a conception date within two days of each other, and a due date that was still three months away. All the books Eden had read had stressed the importance of carrying the baby at least until thirty-seven weeks. If Pinkie were born now, he'd need a special incubator in a special hospital. And even then, he might not survive.

But the thing that frightened Eden most was that, throughout it all, even when she wasn't contracting, Pinkie remained absolutely still.

"Are you ready?" Hannah asked, and Eden wasn't, but she nodded, because she knew she'd never truly be ready for this.

Besides, she was in good company. Hannah had been a cop. Sure, she was deaf now and had a limp, but she was tough as nails. Tess, although barely conscious, was a member of Troubleshooters Incorporated. And Sophia just told Eden that she'd first met Tess while she was fighting terrorists in some country that started with a K and ended with a "stan."

With Eden's help, they were going to set themselves free.

As she went toward the door, she was reminded of just yesterday, when she'd approached the door to Hannah's cabin, to knock on it, exactly this way.

Well, not exactly. *Time for that BJ I promised you* hadn't been part of *that* script.

"Hey," she called softly, as she rapped relatively quietly on the door. It wasn't exactly part of *this* script, either, because if old Adolf truly was out there, he wasn't alone. "Everyone's asleep in here, the toilet's clogged, and I need to, you know. Use it?"

She was hoping that Adolf would take that as the invitation that it was, and come into the room to "fix the plumbing"—wink, wink, nudge, nudge.

At which point Eden and Sophia would jump him—not in the way that he hoped for—and steal his weapon. They would knock him unconscious, as Hannah launched herself out into the hall and took out guard number two . . .

The deadbolt on the door clicked open.

Sophia signaled Hannah who, of course, hadn't heard it.

The door—which opened out—opened only a crack. And there he was. Lovely, horny, hopeful Adolf. Proving that all around the world, men were men were men.

"We're not supposed to unlock the door," he told her.

"It's okay," she whispered back, forcing a smile, even though her back was starting to cramp. Please don't let her have a contraction right now. "Everyone's asleep in here."

"We're going to get in trouble," someone in the hall said.

"Can you come in?" Eden asked, resisting the urge to throw up a little in her mouth as she added, "I want to hear more about the Freedom Network. I think it's so cool that you get to wear that jacket and carry a gun."

"See?" Adolf said to the other guard. "She wants to join the cause."

Except, crap, there were two others out there with him. "Three guards," Eden said for Hannah and Sophia's benefit, inwardly cringing at how totally lame she sounded. "Aren't I the dangerous one."

The other guards peered in at her. "She's a fornicator," the disgruntled one said. "It's wrong for a woman to want it."

"Lock the door, Addy," the other recommended. "You don't know where-all she's been at."

Eden was looking into Adolf's eyes and she saw exactly when his fear of breaking the rules trumped his desire to boldly go where he'd never been before. And before he could slam it shut, she threw herself against the door, pushing it all the way open, knocking into him and the others. "Hannah, now!" she stupidly screamed for a woman who couldn't possibly hear her. "Sophia, help me *now!*"

CHAPTER
TWENTY-FIVE

Three guards.

There were three guards with three guns, and Sophia didn't stand a prayer of wrestling one of those automatic weapons away from any of them, so she did what her father had told her never to do. She kicked a man when he was already down.

As her foot connected with the most tender place of the guard on the floor, Sophia could see Hannah out of the corner of her eye, leaping on top of the man who was still standing, and slamming him against the corridor wall before they both went to the ground. Eden, meanwhile, was entangled with the third guard—whose weapon went skittering across the cheap industrial tile.

But it was Tess who put an end to the fight. Tess, who must've crawled on her hands and knees through the open door, who picked up that weapon and aimed it unerringly at Sophia's kick-ee.

"Everyone freeze!" she said, loudly enough to be heard. "Drop your weapons, hands in the air, right now—*right* now!"

She was sitting on the floor, with a blood-soaked bandage around her middle, hair still damp from her toilet dunking.

But the way she held that weapon was all professional business, and hands went into the air.

Not all of them, though. Hannah grabbed the rifle from the guard she was pummeling, and used it to hit him in the head. He finally slumped, as Sophia took possession of the third gun.

"Give me your jacket and your hat," Hannah ordered the youngest one—it had to be Eden's buddy Adolf. He was crying as he took it off, as Hannah quickly searched him, searched them all, briskly, efficiently. It wouldn't do for any of them to have a handgun to use as an alarm.

"Drag him inside," Hannah ordered, pointing to the man who was down, and then to the cell that they'd recently occupied.

"Lucas was right," Adolf sobbed as he obeyed Hannah's order, grabbing the unconscious guard beneath the arms. He spat at Eden as he pulled the man past her. "Fornicator! I hope your baby dies!"

Eden flinched, but she quickly recovered, flipping him the bird as she pushed the heavy door shut and threw the bolt. "Hey, loser. Fornicate *you*."

Decker went in.

It wasn't quite dark enough yet for the entire team to enter the compound, but a single man, accustomed to slipping through the shadows, could make himself invisible.

He clicked twice into his lip mic—a nearly inaudible message to Lindsey, who was staying behind to man the radio. He'd made it. The equipment the FBI had provided had successfully rerouted the energy flowing through the electric fence, allowing him access without any alarms being tripped in the Freedom Network's security center.

And oh, yeah. It had also kept thousands of volts of electricity from surging through his body and cooking him from the inside out as he'd slipped beneath the fence.

That was always a bonus.

Decker quickly climbed the final fence, then took a deep breath. It was time to clear his mind of everything but his mission.

Tess. Sophia's voice, clear but strained from stress: *She's badly injured.*

Dave. Desperate not to lead, unaware that he'd been quietly leading for years: *Thank God you're here, sir.*

Jim Nash. FBI Agent Jules Cassidy's quiet confirmation: *Nash is dead.*

Jo Heissman: *You're safe with me, Lawrence. You don't have to run away . . .*

There was room for none of them, none of their incessant noise and sorrow and pain inside of his head right now, and Decker wiped them all away.

There was only the night.

And Tim Ebersole, who was finally going to meet the newly sharpened blade of Decker's KA-BAR knife.

Adolf's jacket fit well enough, covering Tess's blood-soaked bandages.

Hannah gave his baseball cap to Sophia, to cover the eye-catching shine of her blond hair.

His weapon she kept for herself, and with it loosely cradled in her arms, heart pumping, Hannah went out the window first, into the not-necessarily-silence of the night.

It was dark and getting darker every second, which was a good thing, as she helped Sophia push and pull Tess and then Eden out of the school building-slash-jail. Way to get your kids to love to learn, Freedom Network. But then again, they didn't want their children to learn. They wanted them to memorize rhetoric and lies.

And there they crouched, Hannah on point, still futilely straining to hear, as Sophia joined her in the shadows.

The compound was only dimly lit, which was good.

But people were out and about, which wasn't. They were going about their lives, moving from their living quarters—tiny individual cottages and cabins and the larger more barracklike dorms—to the dining hall. They were socializing in the pleasant evening air, playing basketball, walking their dogs, chatting with neighbors.

Their plan was for Sophia to stay at Hannah's elbow, acting as her ears, even as she supported Tess. For someone so petite and pretty, the blonde had it going on in the strength-of-will-power department.

As for Eden . . .

They had to find a hiding place sometime in the next two minutes—where she could safely—and as quietly as possible—breathe through her next contraction.

Hannah could see the tree line, distant from this part of the clearing. They were going to have to move from building to building, cottage to cabin. Although maybe heading for the forest wasn't that wise of a plan. It was one of the first places security patrols would search when it was discovered that they were missing.

And it would be discovered—sooner rather than later. There was, no doubt, some kind of check-in procedure in place—a scheduled phone call to the security chief that the guards, now locked in the cell, would miss. Either that, or someone would bring dinner and take one look at the empty hallway . . .

Sophia tapped Hannah and pointed to Eden, whose face was already starting to contort with pain.

It was time.

All of the cottages and cabins had garbage sheds—small wooden structures out back, built to prevent animals from getting into the trash. Hannah knew from her visit here that they were not locked—only latched.

She peeked around the corner, where that basketball game was going on in the school yard. The players were far enough away.

She took a deep breath and Eden's arm and, keeping her pace slow— just another lunatic fringe family out for an evening stroll—stepped out of the shadows.

Alarm sirens started wailing and Murphy leapt to his feet.

Izzy was right behind him. "What the fuck?"

"It's coming from the compound," Mark Jenkins reported, as they both followed Murphy out of the tent. Dave and Gillman were on their heels.

Murph stepped it up even faster, booking it for the Freedom Network fences, as Lindsey's voice rang in his radio headset. "Decker! Sitrep!"

Decker's voice came back, a dry whisper. "I'm secure. Whatever tripped the alarm—it wasn't—"

"Jesus!" Murphy ripped the headset off as high volume feedback came through the earpieces.

His radio wasn't the only one squealing.

"What the fuck?" It seemed to be Izzy's mantra, but it was also the question of the moment.

"Turn down the volume," Dave ordered.

"Mine's down so far it's off," Jenkins said.

Lindsey came running after them. "There's some kind of radio jamming," she reported. "It's coming from the compound, and it's across all channels."

"Fix it," Dave ordered.

"I would if I could," Lindsey told him. "The irony is that if Tess were here, *she'd* probably be able to override—"

"I'm not waiting," Murphy announced, heading for the fences. Izzy was at his side.

"Keep trying," Dave ordered Lindsey. "Call Cassidy. Have him cut all power to the compound. I want these radios working!"

"They definitely have generators," Jenk pointed out as Murphy swung himself up and over the first of the fences, sticking the landing, as if it had been days instead of years since he'd last done anything like this on a regular basis.

Jenkins landed effortlessly beside him, still talking as they slid beneath the impotent wires of the electric fence—thanks to the equipment Decker had installed. "They'll kick on when the power goes out. We can't just flip a switch to get them to go off."

"Then we'll take them out the old-fashioned way," Izzy said as he followed them over the third fence.

"Cut phone lines, too, if you get the chance," Dave ordered as he landed far less gracefully, scrambling in the dirt. "Let's try to even the odds. Stay in visual contact, and remember, there are children in here! Let's do this, let's go!"

They didn't have a choice about hiding places. The alarms went off—no doubt someone had discovered the hostages were missing—and they'd hurriedly squeezed into this shed.

A garbage shed.

Eden released Sophia's hand as the pain slowly subsided.

But the urge to gag at the horrendous smell wasn't going to go away. Not anytime soon.

The shit had really hit the fan.

Sirens were still screeching as all across the compound brighter spotlights were going on, one by one, turning the place into the blinding equivalent of the surface of the sun.

As Eden tried to breathe through her shirt sleeve, Hannah pulled the door of the garbage shed closed, but a ray of light from outside came through a crack between two boards, illuminating the grimness of her face. There wasn't enough room in there for them both to hide and hold their rifles ready for attack, so they'd laid most of the weapons on the floor. Hannah alone held hers, but it pointed straight up, at the shed's plywood ceiling.

Sophia took Eden's hand again, squeezing it in warning, and she realized that a two-man patrol had stopped mere feet from their hiding place. She could see their shadows through another crack in the shed wall.

"They had to come this way," one of them said.

"They probably already made it to the woods," the other complained. "We never get the good assignments."

They turned away.

Thank the Lord, they turned away, except another contraction ripped through Eden, this one even stronger than any of the others had been so far. She clenched her teeth against the pain, trying desperately not to cry out—she *would not* cry out and give them away—but then liquid seemed to pour out of her, down her legs, soaking her dress and hitting the concrete flooring of the shed with an audible rush, and the two men turned back, their weapons raised.

"What in hell was *that?*"

The compound was crawling with Freedom Network security patrols.

The good news, as far as Dave could see, was that the women and children were being ushered into the church for safety.

Now, if only he had an operational radio, so that he could report that information to his team members.

He'd given the order to split up—there was no way they could move covertly as a five-man team, with so many patrols out and about.

Dave and Izzy had gone north, while Murphy, Gillman, and Jenkins had headed south, toward the gate and the most heavily populated part of the compound.

He should have thought to bring a leash for Izzy. The SEAL was moving so fast, Dave was hard-pressed to keep up.

He caught up, however, at the edge of a clearing, where there was nothing but grass—no cover of any kind—all the way to the first cluster of buildings.

"Fuck this, I'm going," Izzy told him.

Dave shook his head. "Give Lindsey a few more seconds . . ."

"One," Izzy counted. "Two . . ."

And like magic, the power went out across the compound, plunging it into darkness.

As Dave hurried after Izzy, he tried turning up his radio—and got that same jarring earful of squealing static.

Which meant that whatever the Freedom Network was using to jam their radio signals had its own power source.

It would take about thirty seconds, after the power went out, for the generators to kick in.

Thirty seconds didn't seem like a very long time, but it was.

Decker didn't have to move faster than a leisurely walk as he left the shadows and went into the church.

He'd spotted his target mere minutes after the alarms began to scream, shawl over his head, large for a woman. But it wasn't his size that gave Ebersole away. It was the way he walked. Even the butchest of women just didn't have that balls-a-swinging, cock-of-the-walk gait.

He didn't have any guards with him—he probably thought his disguise was sufficient—which made it all the more simple.

Decker found him easily in the darkness, introduced himself, got the DNA evidence he needed, and left, all with plenty of time to spare before the lights came back on.

Eden's water had broken, splashing onto the shed floor.

Hannah hadn't heard it—Sophia had had to tap her arm to bring it to her attention—but the two men, outside, with the automatic weapons, apparently had.

They'd turned back, weapons raised and aimed. And Hannah knew that if they fired, the thin wooden boards would do little to protect them.

Power had gone out in the compound, plunging them into darkness, and putting the gunmen even more on edge. They had a hunting-size flashlight, though, which they immediately switched on, shining it directly at the shed. Hannah had to squint against the brightness, and she could just barely make out their faces, see their mouths.

"Open the door!"

"No, you open it!"

"No, shit-for-brains, I'm telling whoever's in there to open the door!"

Sophia tapped Hannah's arm, and she looked up into the other woman's face. Her expression was one of horror as she held out her hand, and Hannah saw that it was covered with blood, and her vision tunneled because, God, if Eden was bleeding like that, she was in terrible trouble.

And then everything moved much too fast.

Somewhere a generator must've kicked in, because the lights came back in the compound. They were much less bright than they had been, but they made it easier for Hannah to see the guards' faces.

"Open the door," one of them shouted again—and Hannah could see from his face, from the wildness of his eyes, that he was moments from squeezing the trigger of his gun.

So she kicked the door open, because there was no choice, but now the guard's eyes were even more wild, and Hannah knew that he'd seen her rifle and he screamed, "Drop your weapon," but she couldn't drop it—it was wedged in, the barrel caught by the frame of the door, and she finally just let go of it and held out her empty hands, but the guards couldn't see who or what was behind her, and she knew from the way he pulled his own weapon more tightly to his shoulder that he was going to fire, and, God, they were dead. She threw herself over, in front of Eden and her baby, as she felt the percussive shock of gunfire.

But the bullets didn't rip into her and through her, her world didn't instantly crash to black, and Hannah turned her head to see the guards discharging their weapons into the sky as they fell back, crumpled onto the ground.

And then—holy God—Dave Malkoff was there, dressed in commando gear, his eyes fierce, holding out his hand to help Hannah and then Sophia up and out of the shed.

"Where's Murphy?" Hannah asked, even though there was no time to watch for his response as she immediately turned to help Sophia pull Tess free, too.

Dave wasn't alone, but he wasn't with Murph. He was with a very tall, very broad man who had to be Izzy Zanella.

"Let's go, let's move it," Hannah said, reaching for Eden. The gunshots fired were going to draw more guards—they had to move fast.

• • •

As a dark-haired woman who had to be Hannah helped Eden out of the shed, Izzy's entire world tilted onto its side.

Eden's skirt was drenched with blood.

"Oh, God, no," he said as he scooped her into his arms. "Eden, baby, talk to me—where are you hit?"

"She wasn't shot, she's in labor," Sophia told him as both she and Hannah armed themselves with weapons from the floor of the shed.

"I've got Tess," Dave announced. "Let's go!"

Hannah and Sophia both took point, as Izzy carried Eden. He moved automatically, those endless hours of training kicking in as his brain tried and failed to process the information he'd been given. Eden wasn't shot. She was in *labor*?

This wasn't labor. Labor sucked, but it wasn't supposed to be this gory, blood-soaked reenactment of *Saw II*.

Was it?

Something had to be seriously wrong.

"Izzy," Eden said as her entire body tensed, as she clung to him. "Can't make noise . . . Help me . . ."

God damn, the reality of what Sophia had told him finally penetrated. Eden was in *labor*, which meant she was having painful contractions—while she was hiding from men who wanted to kill her. And *that* meant she couldn't cry out, no matter how much it hurt.

She pressed her face against Izzy's chest, which was good because that way he didn't have to look into her eyes and let her see just how helpless and frightened he felt. Lunatics with guns he could handle, but this was an enemy he didn't know how to help her fight.

"I'm here, sweetheart," he said, because he didn't know what else to do, short of turning into a helo and flying her to a hospital himself—and last time he'd checked, he hadn't yet become Inspector Gadget. "It's going to be okay. We're going to get you and Pinkie out of here."

She was breathing hard, exhaling in short bursts through clenched teeth, but other than that, she didn't make a sound.

But, shit, there was a patrol—five men—directly ahead of them, who opened fire. Sophia and Hannah responded, and the patrol pancaked, which was good because it was hard to aim and shoot when you were flat on the ground, ducking for cover. But there was nowhere to run—another patrol approached from the right. They were penned in and there was nothing to do but head for the safety of the nearest building.

Which was one of the Freedom Network's guest cottages, a nifty little Hansel and Gretl affair, complete with adorable Thomas Kinkade-esque gingerbread trim. The only thing missing was the heavenly light shining from the windows. This place was dark—which didn't mean no one was inside.

But there was no time to play nice and knock—all Izzy could do was pray that if someone were inside they didn't own a shotgun.

He was first up the steps to the tiny porch, his weapon held in one hand as he cradled Eden to him in the other. He kicked the door open and at first glance the place *was* empty—light from the outside spots dimly streaming in through the small windows—two in the front, two in the back.

He stepped inside, and then to the side, because Grumpy Dave, Hannah, and Sophia were right behind him.

The old-fashioned, quirky charm hadn't made its way past the door. The single square-shaped room was decked out like a low-budget motel—two double beds covered with ass-ugly bedspreads, a small table between them, indoor-outdoor carpeting on the floor, a teeny, afterthought of a bathroom with a slanted ceiling hanging out the back, as if it had been a lean-to addition.

G.D. deposited Tess on one of the beds as Hannah and Sophia moved like a team who'd been working together for years, quickly verifying that the place was indeed sans inhabitants. They closed the door as best they could given the damage Izzy'd done to it, pulled the curtains on the back windows, tried the phone on the bedside table—smart one, Sophia, but the line was dead—as Izzy, as gently as he could, put Eden on that second bed.

Her contraction had ended, thank God, and she looked up at him through eyes that were glazed. "I can't believe you're here."

"What," he said, pushing her hair back from her face, "you think I'd miss Pinkie's first public appearance?"

Eden clutched at Izzy's hand with fingers that were clammy and cold. "It's too soon."

He nodded, trying to keep his fear for her off his face. "He's probably going to be one of those kids who wants to learn to drive when he's six. Smoking and drinking when he's ten—"

That got him a laugh that was more than half protest. "He better not . . ."

"Nah," Izzy said. "We'll keep him in line."

He could see her disbelief. "We?"

"Sure," he said. "I mean, I figure even if you don't want me around in ten years, I'm still going to be part of Pinkie's life, right?"

"If I don't want you around . . . ?" Tears spilled from her eyes. "Didn't you watch that horrible video?"

"I watched it," he told her, and damn, it was hard as hell not to cry, too. "Well, as much as I could stand . . ."

"I'm so sorry," she sobbed.

"I am, too." Izzy pulled her into his arms, holding her tightly. Damnit, she was shaking. "Why didn't you trust me, Eed? You should have *trusted* me." And as the words left his mouth, he realized just how stupid he was. Trust. Like it was something you could get out of a vending machine if your dollar bills were new and crisp enough. Like this girl was going to assume that every life lesson that had been cruelly battered into her should be ignored and discarded now that she was with Izzy.

"We could use your help here, Zanella," Dave called from the front window.

Izzy lowered Eden back onto the bed, taking her face in both of his hands. "I believe you," he told her, willing her to believe him, trying to sear his words into her by looking into her eyes. "I still believe what I said in the car—that you were the victim of a crime. And when we're out of here, when two hundred crazy motherfuckers aren't trying to kill us, we're going to talk more about that, okay?"

She was looking back at him as if he were speaking Chinese, her lips trembling as she strained both not to cry and to understand. "You believe me . . . ?"

"Yeah," he said, then fuck it, he just said it. "I'm kinda in love with you, Eed."

He could tell she still didn't get it, so he sang it to her. "*I don't mind standing every day, out on the corner in the pouring rain . . .*"

It was the romantic words to her favorite song, and now she started to cry all over again. But he knew that she understood, because she kissed him.

She tasted like fear and tears, but mostly she tasted like his sweet, sweet Eden.

"Come on, Zanella," Dave barked, "I need your head in the game."

"I'm going to get you and Pinkie out of here," Izzy promised her as he pulled back.

Across the room, Dave and Hannah were arguing. Something about the fucking signal jammer that kept them from being able to call for a helo extraction.

"I know where it is," Hannah was insisting, as she helped Tess out of the Freedom Network's uniform jacket. "There's a guard tower near the front gate. I could go and—"

"Nobody's going anywhere." Dave made it gospel. "Murphy's still out there. And Jenk and Gillman. Let's sit tight and give them a chance to take it out."

"Danny's here?" Eden asked, but then she grabbed for Izzy's hands and she began panting again. She was having another contraction as— holy fuck!—the bedspread beneath her became soaked with her blood.

"Dave," Izzy said. "I appreciate your faith in Murphy and the guys, but we need to get Eden to a hospital. *Now*."

Sophia came over to check on Eden. He could tell that she, too, was worried by all the blood, but she smiled reassuringly when Eden opened her eyes. "You're doing great with the breathing," she said. "Keep it up."

And a bullet smashed through the window and blasted into the wall, an inch above Izzy's head.

Murphy crawled closer.

The gunfire from the other side of the compound had drawn him north, but he'd hunkered down in the shadows of this building when he saw Dave and the former hostages take cover in a small, free-standing cottage.

Hannah had led the firefight against the patrol that was shooting at them, and Murph had had to stomp—hard—on his instinct to run toward her, to make sure she was okay.

It was clear just from watching her that she *was* okay. She moved quickly, confidently, despite her heavy limp from her bad ankle. Sophia was right behind her.

It was Tess and Eden who were being carried by Dave and Izzy.

As they shut the door behind them, Murph cursed his useless radio for the twelve-thousandth time, even as he worked to convince himself that charging forward and getting trapped in that cottage with Hannah and the others would not help the situation.

It *absolutely* would not help.

Except those motherfuckers were *shooting* at her, and it would only take one bullet to end her life. The world spun, and he forced himself to breathe, to stay hidden in the shadows, to crush the fear that rose in him and tried to choke him.

Dave was with Hannah. Izzy was there, too.

They were safe. For now, they were safe.

But God, he ached to hold on to Hannah, to wrap his arms around her and make sure she really was all right.

Although, *shit*, now a sniper had moved into place and was taking out the cottage windows, one by one. Murph could also hear the sound of running feet, furtive commands given as the Freedom Network security chief made sure that the cottage was more completely surrounded.

It was then that Mark Jenkins materialized beside him.

Both as a Marine and as a Troubleshooters operative, Murphy had often worked with Navy SEALs—and had equally often rolled his eyes at what he thought of as the SEAL PITA factor.

Simply put, SEALs could be huge pains in the ass.

They were arrogant and smug, and most of them had superiority complexes. They were egotistical, conceited, rude, and often crude—which, okay, wasn't all that different from most of the Marines Murph knew.

But to a SEAL, every other member of any other branch of the service was less-than in their disdainful eyes. It was an attitude that tended to piss off the Marines.

Of course, most SEALs also happened to be intelligent, creative, and tremendously skilled operators. And, to be honest, the training they went through to get their SEAL trident pin made boot camp look like a Daisy Scout retreat.

Which was why Murphy was extremely glad Mark Jenkins and Dan Gillman were here with him now.

They believed—completely—that the three of them, with no radio communication and no help from reinforcements that were waiting on the other side of the fence, could rescue their trapped people.

If wasn't part of their vocabulary. Only *when*.

And, yeah, in the few short minutes since they'd slid under the fence,

Jenk had conjured up Freedom Network security patrol jackets, hats, and gear for them all to wear, allowing them to move not quite freely throughout the compound, but certainly more easily.

Gillman had already found the location of both the generator and the radio jamming equipment—in a tower near the front gate. Both were heavily guarded, or he would have already done what Navy SEALs loved doing best—and used some of the C4 he carried in his vest pockets to blow the tower and its contents to Kingdom Come. He was currently searching for another way to get the job done.

But now Jenk was back from a quick surveillance of the south side of the compound—where the Freedom Network had shut off their lights, probably in order to send more power to the spots illuminating the hostage-held cottage.

He smiled at Murphy the way that only a Navy SEAL could smile while in the midst of hundreds of heavily armed men who wouldn't have blinked at shooting them dead.

"You won't believe," Jenk said to Murph, "what I just found . . ."

"Help me," Dave said, and Sophia was instantly there, helping him move the mattress up so that it was blocking one of the front windows, even as Izzy and Hannah moved Tess and Eden down onto the much safer floor.

There were windows in the back, and together they schlepped the second mattress in that direction, too.

They moved quickly—Dave needed to get back to the unblocked front window, to help Izzy hold off an attack. But for a moment, as they were standing close enough to touch, Sophia leaned against him—just for a fraction of a second. It wasn't even a real embrace, and yet his heart immediately flipped in his chest. As if it weren't pounding hard enough already . . .

"I knew you'd come," she told him, faith in her blue eyes.

"Always," he promised, unable to do more than whisper. He cleared the trepidation from his throat, bracing himself for the worst, because he *had* to ask, "Did they hurt you?"

"They weren't exactly gentle with any of us," Sophia told him, "but I know what you're asking and . . . No." She reached up and touched the side of his face, her fingers cool and soft as she brushed something from his cheek.

If there'd been more time, he would have done it. He would have leaned in those extra few inches and kissed her—but as Dave instead moved back to the window, as Sophia went to help Eden, who'd begun to breathe through another contraction, he knew that he was kidding himself.

The only time he would ever dare to kiss Sophia was in his wildest dreams.

"Izzy!" Eden cried out.

"I'm right here, sweetheart," the SEAL called back, his voice rough. "I'm not going anywhere." He looked at Dave, his face grim. "We gotta—"

"I know," Dave said as he scanned the open area in front of the cottage, watching for any sign of movement from the Freedom Network troops that were positioned behind the other buildings. "Our options are limited."

"So's our ammunition," Izzy said. "*That* plus the fact we're surrounded . . ."

They *were* completely surrounded.

They'd found the hostages, but now Dave and Izzy were just as much held hostage with them.

And okay, they were slightly better off in that they had weapons and could keep the Freedom Network at bay for an undetermined amount of time.

No, make that a determined amount of time—because, as Izzy had pointed out, they didn't have an unlimited supply of ammunition. In fact, they had an extremely non-unlimited supply of ammo. As in, they could hold off a direct assault for maybe—maybe—two minutes.

Dave's options were to surrender or to wait for rescue.

And surrender was *not* an option.

They all sat in silence for a moment, then Dave made the mistake of glancing at Sophia again.

Who said, "I'm afraid even to ask about Nash."

Tess was out cold, her eyes closed.

"It's better that you don't," Dave agreed, but as he looked at Sophia again, he knew that *she* now knew they'd lost their friend. The expression on her face broke his heart, and he also knew, in that moment, that she was thinking about Decker.

Damn him.

Who was somewhere here, in the compound.

On an entirely different mission.

"If they stage an assault, do we shoot to kill?" Hannah called out from her position at the back window, clearly thinking the very same thing Dave and Izzy had about their limited ammunition.

Do we shoot to kill? It was one of those decisions that Dave had hoped he'd never have to make—one of the reasons he'd so steadfastly resisted taking on the role of team leader.

But then he thought about Angelina and about Jim Nash, and about the dreadful task that awaited him—even after they were all safely rescued: Telling Tess that Nash was dead. And the decision got a little less difficult to make.

"Affirmative," he answered, truly breaking his team-leader-cherry. He didn't look over at Sophia, even though he knew she was watching him, well aware of what he'd just done.

"What the fuck are they doing out there?" Izzy asked, disbelief in his voice.

"What's happening?" Hannah asked. She saw movement out the back window, but the FN security teams seemed to be retreating. They were scrambling away, not coming closer.

Dave answered her, but he turned only briefly, his intense focus on whatever was out that front window, and Hannah didn't catch his response.

She looked to Sophia, who'd just given Eden a quick pelvic exam. The good news was that she didn't seem about to deliver within the next few minutes. The bad news was that she appeared to be at least partially dilated. At only twenty-four weeks, that news didn't bode well for the baby.

Sophia's calm was admirable as she paused to encourage Eden to breathe through her latest contraction. "They've got a . . ."

What? "I'm sorry," Hannah said. "But it looked as if you just said *rocket?*"

"Launcher," Sophia repeated, nodding.

Hannah scrambled for the front window where, sure enough, Craig Reed had brought in, quite literally, the heavy artillery.

Izzy wasn't known in the Teams for being a particularly excellent marksman, but he was working his mojo now, trying to lay down fire to keep the bubba with the RPG-7 shoulder-fired grenade launcher from taking aim and turning their cottage hiding place into rubble.

"Hold your fire," Dave ordered.

What the fuck? Izzy looked at him.

"You're wasting ammunition," Dave snapped.

"Like we're going to have a use for it when we're fried extra crispy . . . ?"

"Fire!"

The sound of a rocket-propelled grenade being launched was like no other. Izzy drew what had to be his very last breath during its roar, but then he realized what Dave had somehow known, as the world shook but didn't end.

It was the cottage next door that exploded, deafeningly, into flames.

Although the shock waves put even Hannah onto the floor.

"Fire at will," Dave commanded through the ringing in Izzy's ears, plaster dust whitening his hair.

"Eden, you all right?" Izzy shouted, aiming at the corner of the brick building behind which the gunman had taken refuge, no doubt to reload.

"I *hate* these assholes," Eden shouted back.

"That's my girl," he said, loving the feel of his heart still pumping blood through his veins, watching, waiting for any sign of movement.

No doubt about it, Craig Reed was playing show-and-tell with his nifty, illegally-gotten artillery. The next grenade—and these were definitely not your grandfather's old-fashioned, go-boom, throw-yourself-on-top-of-them-and-save-your-buddies grenades—*was* gonna be aimed in their direction.

And sure enough, good ol' boy Reed had gotten himself a megaphone, over which he shouted, "Lay down your weapons and surrender! You have sixty seconds to come out with your hands up!"

Smoke billowed into the sky as the flames from the burning cottage brought both more light and more shadow to the compound.

Flames made shadows jump and dance. It was, for someone Murphy's size, the best cover for covert movement.

So he moved closer. And closer.

Watching as someone in the cottage—probably the SEAL, Zanella—

fired a rifle, keeping the Freedom Network artilleryman from moving back into position with that reloaded RPG-7.

Counting down the seconds.

Watching as Reed gave the order for the man with the grenade launcher to move farther back, out of rifle range.

It was then that Murphy couldn't wait any longer.

He stepped out of the shadows and into the light.

"No!" Hannah saw Murphy first, before Reed or any of the other Freedom Network soldiers saw him.

He walked—serenely—into the flickering light between the cottage and the rocket launcher, both hands in the air.

"Oh, shit," Dave's mouth moved, "Hannah, don't!" He grabbed her and held her back, and she realized that she'd lunged for the door.

But then she also realized that Dave wasn't saying *don't*, but rather, *don't look*—and she knew that Murphy was going to die.

But she couldn't not look, and as she watched him—her lover, her best friend—she saw that he held both of his hands the same way—thumb, pinkie and forefinger held out straight, middle and ring fingers bent. It was the ASL sign for *I love you*—and she knew his message was for her.

But it didn't make it any better.

In fact, it made it worse. He loved her, and yet he was still ready and even willing to give up. To surrender.

To die.

"What's he saying?" she asked, unable to tear her eyes away from the sight of him, standing there, a solo figure lit by flames.

"I'm the one you're looking for," Dave repeated. *"I'm the one you want.* Now Reed: *Give me one good reason I shouldn't kill you where you stand.* Now Murph: *Tell your men to stand down, my people will come out, we'll all walk to the gate, I'll watch them leave* . . . Now Reed: *This is the man who murdered Reverend Ebersole.* He shouted that—to the crowd."

"Oh, God," Hannah said. She wasn't just going to watch Murphy die, she was going to watch him be torn apart by an angry mob.

"Okay," Dave said, "Now Reed's giving the order—*Hold your fire.*"

"That wasn't Reed who said that," Izzy said, straining, too, to get a closer look. "Holy shit, is that Tim Ebersole with Decker?"

• • •

Decker knew that Murphy was out of time. The former Marine was mere seconds from being cut down by hundreds of bullets.

Murphy had miscalculated Reed's motivation. *I'm the one you want.* Not true. Reed had already gotten what he wanted—a botched rescue of a hostage situation that was nanoseconds from escalating into an FBI assault on the Freedom Network compound.

Decker was certain by now that Reed didn't give a flying fuck about Tim Ebersole—other than the insurance money his "death" had provided.

But the two-hundred-strong army of Freedom Network apostles was devoted to the reverend—most of them wore black armbands, in mourning for his death.

And, of course, Ebersole himself was a major fan of his own not-being-dead—*and* of his continuing to not be dead.

Deck smoothly sheathed his knife—there was no longer a need for the threat of silent death—and drew his sidearm. He pushed his frightened prisoner out of the shadows, pulling the shawl from Ebersole's head and face, letting the firelight dance and reflect off his Glock as well.

"Hold your fire," Ebersole called again, his voice no doubt familiar to his devoted followers.

"It's a miracle, saints be praised, I'm not dead." Decker quietly fed the man his lines, which Ebersole repeated in a far more elegant oratorical delivery as Deck met Murphy's eyes, as Murph looked over Deck's shoulder and then back, clearly sending him a pointed message.

Decker nodded. Just once, just slightly. He knew. Jenkins and Gillman were coming.

But seconds ticked by—where the hell were they?—as much of the Freedom Network fell to their knees.

"Tell them to stay back," Decker instructed. "Tell them I've got a gun and if anyone harms Murphy or any of my friends, I *will* kill you . . ."

As soon as the words were out of Ebersole's mouth, Decker knew it had been a mistake. He saw Reed—the only man who not only didn't give that flying fuck if Ebersole survived the next half-second, but probably also the only man who benefited from Decker carrying out his threat—raise his rifle to his shoulder.

"Murphy get down!" Decker bellowed, but it was too late, the bullet hit Murph in the chest, spinning him around.

Ebersole started to scream, and Jesus, now Reed was aiming at him, and Decker felt that bullet hit the man and—shit!—hit him, too, right in the shoulder.

Decker grabbed the preacher beneath the arms and dragged him, toward Murphy, as—about fucking time—Jenkins and Gillman roared up in two of the Freedom Network's armored trucks—with Gillman taking a detour and deftly taking out the RPG-7—good man—by smashing it flat.

Hannah ran out of the cottage.

Murphy had fallen, then gotten back up, then fallen again, and it was possible the entire Freedom Network had opened fire, but she didn't care—she ran toward him.

But then, God, a truck squealed to a stop right next to Murphy, and Jenkins was there shouting, "Get 'em in, get 'em in."

With Decker's help she got Murphy and a wounded, bald-headed Tim Ebersole into the back of the truck.

"Go, go!" she shouted, and Jenkins gunned it.

"Han," Murphy said, struggling to breathe, to sit up.

"Stay still, bwee," she said. "Don't move!"

"They're having trouble getting out the door!" Decker shouted, and Hannah realized that the other truck had tried to pull up close to the cottage door, but the Freedom Network had, indeed, opened fire.

Murphy was shouting something—she could not make him stay still while she searched for a first aid kit—and the truck lurched forward. He grabbed her. "Hang on!"

And then, holy God, Jenkins drove, full speed into the little lean-to bathroom that was sticking out, off the side of the cottage. He just sheared it right off, skidding to a stop just beyond it.

Decker jumped out, and Gillman was there, too—having abandoned the other truck—and together, with Izzy and Dave's help, they loaded Tess and Eden into the back.

Hannah did a quick head count. She knew Decker and probably Dave did, too—they were all there, thank God—as Jenkins ground the gears—

she could feel the truck groaning—and they barreled toward the front entrance.

Murphy grabbed her again—"Hang on!"—and she clung to him. He was alive—please God, keep him alive . . .

Sophia stayed out of the way, hanging on to a grab bar as the truck bounced, speeding toward the front gate, letting Gillman, Izzy, and Dave have access to the back of the truck. They laid down a field of fire that kept the Freedom Network from following too closely.

"Hold on!" Jenkins shouted and Sophia scrambled to help Decker anchor both Tess and Eden as, with a crash, the truck went through the gate.

She felt herself lift into the air, but Decker then had her, too, his leg thrown across her to hold her down.

"You okay?" he shouted, and she nodded. And for a half a second, time seemed to stop as she looked into his eyes. For a half a second, he actually let her in, and she clearly saw his heart—his regret, his grief, all of his anger and pain, and even, yes, his honest affection.

"We're out!" Jenkins shouted from the driver's seat.

And Decker, still holding Sophia's gaze, gave her the funniest half-smile. "Out of the frying pan," he said, so quietly she couldn't even hear him, she just read his lips.

But then he turned away, giving his attention and his medical training to Tess and Eden, and the moment—that weird half-second they'd just shared—was over.

It was then that Sophia looked back, out of the truck, to watch the broken gate receding behind them. It was then that she witnessed an even more amazing miracle.

Behind them, were dozens of FBI agents, SEALs, and Troubleshooters—she saw Tom Paoletti with Sam Starrett and Alyssa Locke, Ric and Annie Alvarado, Jules Cassidy and George Faulkner and Yashi and Cosmo and Jazz Jacquette and Stan Wolchonok and so many more. They rose up from their hiding places in the woods, weapons raised and aimed at the Freedom Network gate. They moved swiftly and surely into the road, blocking anyone who might've even remotely been considering the escaping truck's pursuit.

They were, indeed, out.

. . .

Murphy had pulled Hannah down, onto his lap, holding her tightly as Jenkins had plowed through the gate, but now he pulled her chin toward him and kissed her.

He *kissed* her? She jerked her head back. "You were shot!"

But he shook his head. "No." And he opened his jacket—he was wearing one of those disgusting Freedom Network windbreakers—and he showed her the body armor he'd had on beneath it, the bullet trapped just above his heart.

"Jenkins and Gillman are good," he told her, but beneath her, her leg felt warm and almost wet, and God, when she reached down to touch it, her hand came away bright red with blood.

"Oh, shit," Murphy said, looking down, "Han, were you hit?"

But it wasn't her, it was him. He *had* been shot—in the leg. The bullet must've hit an artery—there was a growing pool of blood beneath his seat. God, this was the kind of wound that killed. Grown men could bleed out in a matter of minutes.

"We need a medic!" Hannah shouted, taking off her shirt and tearing it so she could use it as a tourniquet.

"I'm going to be all right, Han," Murphy tried to tell her, as she tied the fabric around his upper leg. "It's going to be all right."

"It better," she all but snarled at him. "Don't you dare die on me now!"

And then, thank God, thank God, the truck skidded to a stop, and paramedics swarmed aboard. Hannah was pushed back as Murphy and the other wounded were rushed to the medevac choppers that Lindsey and Lopez had made sure were there, waiting for them.

CHAPTER
TWENTY-SIX

Izzy was ready for a happy ending.

Instead, he was pushed aside and left behind as paramedics rushed Eden to the waiting helo.

There wasn't room for him. They had so many wounded—Murphy, Tess, and Decker, and even the extremely not-dead Tim Ebersole, who'd been gut shot.

And maybe that was what pushed him over the edge—the knowledge that Izzy had to wait for the next helicopter because Tim fucking Ebersole had to be rushed into emergency surgery. Because one of the assholes who had nearly killed Eden had been shot by another of the assholes, Izzy couldn't be by his wife's side as Pinkie was born.

But more likely it was the news that he wasn't meant to overhear as one of the medics radioed the waiting hospital from the front cab of an ambulance. Coming at them ASAP was a fifty-year-old male with a gunshot wound in his abdomen, a thirty-something male with a nicked femoral artery, and an eighteen-year-old female suffering a third trimester miscarriage with severe complications . . .

Wait a minute. *Miscarriage?* Izzy grabbed the radioman by the shirt and nearly took him to the ground. "She's in labor, she's having a baby."

The medic looked terrified, as if it wasn't every day he was damn near thrown up against the side of an ambulance like that, until Izzy said, "She's my wife—in that helo. She's having a baby."

"I'm sorry, man," the medic said. "The baby isn't . . ." He shook his head. "We couldn't get a heartbeat. Even with an emergency C-section . . ." He shook his head again.

Izzy stood there, as the world whirled around him.

And then the medic added, clearly trying to be helpful, "The hospital's excellent—she's got a solid chance of surviving this."

But a *chance* of surviving meant there was also a chance Eden would die.

The spinning intensified, but Lopez was suddenly there, next to him, trying to make Izzy sit down. Except, damn it, he didn't want to sit. "I need to get to the hospital."

"We'll get you there," Lopez reassured him. "Man, you're looking kind of pale."

Izzy tried saying it louder. "I need to get to the hospital!"

"Whoa, Zanella, I heard you." Lopez took a step back. "You've got to wait for the next helo, man. It'll be ready to go soon."

But Izzy had more questions for the medic. He followed the man, ignoring Lopez, brushing aside Jenkins and Gillman, who'd come to see what the shouting was about. He caught the medic's arm. "Does she know?"

The man didn't understand. It was possible Izzy had grabbed him a little too hard again, because he was back to looking frightened. Izzy said it again, more slowly this time. "Eden. My wife. Does she know—" the words choked him "—her baby's dead?"

"I don't know," the medic answered.

Izzy was near meltdown. His eyes felt hot and his heart was pounding, and he felt fucking unsteady on his feet as he tried to understand exactly what he was being told. "You're telling me," he said, "that you put her on that fucking helo, without me, without anyone she knows, and she may or may not have been told that her *baby* is *dead*?" He was shouting by the end of that, the force of it actually hurting his throat, and his teammates were there, pulling him back.

"We'll get you to the hospital," Lopez was saying. "We're going to get you to that hospital, man, okay?"

Even Gillman tried to be solicitous. "Maybe it's for the best, Zanella," he said. "You know? Maybe this is a blessing."

And Izzy detonated.

• • •

Dave watched as Decker sat with Tess, waiting for that second medevac helicopter to lift off.

The medics had set up a triage, and had determined that both Decker and Tess's wounds could wait the few minutes necessary for the second chopper to depart.

Tess had roused as Dave had helped Decker carry her off the truck, and of course the first words out of her mouth were, "Is Jimmy all right?"

Decker briefly met Dave's eyes before he looked down at the injured woman and somehow managed to smile. "Yeah. We're going to go to the hospital, get patched up, and then I'll take you to see him, okay?"

Whatever Tess saw on Decker's face and in his eyes seemed to satisfy her, because she closed her own eyes.

Dave stayed close, preparing to take the chopper to the hospital with her, prepared for the dreadful task of being there with the harsh truth when she woke up after being treated, but Decker pulled him aside and quietly said, "I'll stay with her. I'll tell her."

Dave shook his head. "I should be with you. I should . . ."

Decker put his hand on Dave's shoulder. "You never asked to be team leader. You did great, Dave, as you always do, but now it's my turn. I'll take care of Tess."

It was odd, but there was something different about Decker tonight. It was as if the man Dave had admired for so many years had returned. He was there—all of him—instead of being preoccupied and distant. It was almost as if Jim Nash's death had grounded him. Or even . . . brought him peace?

It didn't make sense.

But Dave nodded and cleared his throat to say, "I thought I should be there, too, sir. To, you know. Help you."

"I got it," Decker reassured him.

But Dave didn't get a chance at rebuttal, because over near the ambulances, Izzy Zanella and Danny Gillman were trying to kill each other again. Apparently, the adrenaline rush from battling an army at ten to two-hundred odds just wasn't enough for the two Navy SEALs.

"Fuck you, asshole!" Zanella was shouting as he pounded the heck out of the smaller man. "*Fuck* you! Don't you ever fucking say that again!"

Sophia was sitting nearby with Hannah, who was looking shell-shocked and wearing a Sacramento Fire Department T-shirt that someone had lent her, waiting for the second helicopter to take her to the hospital, where Murphy was about to be rushed into surgery. Both women stood as Dave ran toward the fracas.

Lopez, Jenkins, and even Lindsey had jumped on top of Zanella and Gillman, trying to separate them. But as they pulled Izzy off of Gillman, Dave saw that the bigger man was in tears.

"Eden lost the baby," Sophia moved closer to quietly report to Dave.

"Oh, no." Dave felt sick.

Lindsey joined them, only slightly out of breath. "Danny said something really stupid and . . . Izzy needs to get to the hospital, boss," she told him. "We need to get him on the next chopper, stat."

Dave nodded. "Hannah, too. Will you go see what's the holdup?"

Lindsey nodded and dashed off.

Jenkins had somehow gotten Izzy to sit down, and Lopez had pulled Gillman aside.

"Dude," Dave overheard Lopez say. "Use your brain before you speak. Your sister wanted this baby."

"She's just a baby herself," Gillman argued.

"She's older than your mother was when she had your older sister," Lopez pointed out.

"Yeah, and look at how well *that* turned out," Gillman came back. "I still think—"

"And *I* think you need to keep your opinion to yourself." As Dave watched, Lopez actually shoved Gillman. Hard.

Which was startling. And *that* was stupid. Jay Lopez was a Navy SEAL, which meant he not only knew how to fight, he knew how to kill.

Whatever he then said to Gillman, he said it too softly for Dave to hear. But Gillman managed to look properly chagrined as his teammate walked away.

Lindsey dashed back. "They're ready to go."

And sure enough, Decker was helping the medics load Tess aboard the aircraft. Sophia was there, helping Hannah, then stepping back so that Izzy could board.

They had room for one more, and Dave tapped Sophia.

But she hesitated. "What about you?"

"I'll see you over there," he promised her.

And then they were away.

SACRAMENTO, CALIFORNIA

Pinkie was blue.

As the alleged father, Izzy was allowed to see the baby's body. He was tiny and perfect—except not really. Not on the inside.

When he'd arrived at the hospital, Eden was already in the recovery room. She'd had emergency surgery—a C-section. At least that's what it would have been called if Pinkie had made it to full term.

But he hadn't.

The doctor sat down with Izzy and gave him a speech about holes in the heart and congenital birth defects and blah blah blah. Bottom line was the cold hard fact that Eden's baby had been doomed from the get-go.

The good news—so to speak—was that Pinkie hadn't died because he and Eden had had sex on their wedding night. He hadn't died because she'd been roughly handled by her stepfather or her kidnappers.

He'd died because he had a design flaw.

He'd died, and Eden's body had known it, and had pushed the eject button.

The fact that Pinkie was blue wasn't the only thing Izzy'd noticed about the baby.

Pinkie was also white. That is, he was Caucasian.

And Richie—whom Izzy had seen on that graphic video—had been African-American.

And the truth was? Izzy'd cried almost as much about that—about the fact that Eden had lied to him after all—as he'd cried about that deadly little hole in Pinkie's imperfect little heart.

But he sat in the recovery room, in the chair beside Eden's bed, thinking about that sex video and about the crazy, mixed-up, disaster-filled, soul-damaging life Eden had led, thinking about how skeptical he himself was when it came to trust and love. And he hoped with all of his already-battered heart, as he sat there holding her hand, that she'd have an explanation that would help him understand why she'd felt she had to lie.

. . .

The nurses came running for Hannah, just as she was about to get into the hospital elevator. Murphy was awake.

She ran for his room, ignoring a scolding from a doctor, skidding on a just-washed floor, and scrambling through the open door.

"I'm here," she said. "Bwee, I'm here. I'm all right."

They'd told her that it would probably be another two hours before he regained consciousness from his surgery. *Go get some coffee, get something to eat* . . . She'd made the mistake of thinking Murphy would follow the rules.

"I was wearing a vest," he said, and he was working it, hard, to keep his diction clear so that she could understand him. The painkiller in his system was damn near making his eyes roll back in his head, but he was bound and determined to talk to her.

"A bulletproof vest," Hannah agreed, fighting the tears that sprang to her eyes. When he'd first stepped out in front of all the Freedom Networks' weapons, she'd thought he was resigned to, and even welcoming, his impending death. But he wasn't. He'd actually been wearing body armor. "I know. I saw."

"You . . . really okay?"

He groped for her hand, and she sat beside him, clasping his in both of hers, bringing his fingers to her lips.

"I am." She laughed, but it was more to cover the fact that she had tears running down her face. "You scared the shit out of me, Vinh."

"I din wanna die," he said, losing the battle with the drugs in his system. "Wan' live."

"I know," Hannah told him.

But even as Murphy faded back to sleep, he managed to arrange the fingers of his right hand into the ASL sign that they both knew so well. Pinkie, thumb and forefinger straight, ring and middle finger bent.

I love you.

"I love you, too, bwee," Hannah told him.

She didn't leave his side again.

Tess's surgery had been relatively minor. But Decker had sat with her until she'd gone in, getting his own bullet wound looked at and stitched up while he waited for her to return to the recovery room. Then he'd sat with her yet again until she roused, and again until the nurses all agreed that she was, once more, sleeping soundly, and would stay that way for quite some time.

Only then did Deck leave the hospital, catching a cab over to the FBI building in downtown Sacramento. The place was far more quiet than it had been earlier in the day, only a few people passing him in the hall.

He released the guard standing at the conference room door with a nod, then let himself inside.

Dr. Heissman was awake, sitting at the table, playing a game of solitaire with a deck of cards that someone had given her. She swept the cards into a pile as he put her phone and handbag on the table in front of her.

"You're alive." She gazed up at him, and Decker knew she didn't miss the bulkiness of the bandage on his shoulder, beneath the ill-fitting shirt someone had lent him—he couldn't even remember who.

"I am," he said. "And you're free to go."

But she didn't stand up. "Did you kill him?"

By him, she meant Ebersole. Decker shook his head. "No. He's in custody. At least he will be after he gets out of surgery."

He'd surprised her with that. But then she acknowledged her surprise with a laugh. "I really should've expected that—with your moral compass and all. I just . . . I heard about Jim Nash. And I'm so, so sorry."

And she really was. The compassion and sympathy that Decker saw in her blue eyes was sincere. As was her heartfelt relief that he'd survived. Go figure.

And then she surprised him. By gesturing to a chair across the table from her. "Will you sit?"

He shook his head.

"Coccyx?" she asked.

"No. I've got to get back to the hospital."

"Tess Bailey?" she asked.

Decker nodded. "Yeah."

"She's lucky to have you as . . . a friend," Dr. Heissman said.

Decker didn't respond to that, so she stood up, gathered up her things. "I want you to know that I'll be sending Tom Paoletti a letter of resignation in the morning."

Decker'd expected that. But he couldn't stop himself from needling her. "So what was the reason you gave him? *It's Lawrence Decker's fault . . .*"

"Of course not," she said. "The blame is entirely mine. But I'll be telling him the truth—that the main reason I'm leaving is because I'm unable to continue working with you, as your therapist, because our relationship crossed into inappropriate territory the other night."

And okay. It was now two to one. She'd surprised him again.

"That's not the way I remember it," he said. "You were extremely appropriate."

"I was," she agreed. She walked past him, out of the conference room. "It's not what I *did* that was inappropriate. It was what I *wanted* to do."

Decker followed her down the hall. "That's total bullshit."

"I assure you, it's not. Dave was right—you *are* an alarmingly attractive man. And I know my limitations. So I'm delivering myself from temptation."

"It's *deliver us from* evil, *lead us not into temptation*," he corrected her.

"That, too," she quipped.

He ran to get in front of her, to block her path. "We both know the real reason you're leaving is because James Nash is dead. Because there's no longer a need for you to monitor him for Doug Brendon."

Dr. Heissman crossed her arms. She was obviously tired, but she still radiated plenty of that warrior-goddess attitude. "Back to this again? Let me repeat myself, Mr. Decker. I no longer work for the Agency."

Decker nodded as he held her gaze, as he searched for the truth in her eyes—and didn't find it.

"I hope, for your sake, that's true," he told her quietly. "Nash died because he was off his game, because of the black ops he was forced to perform—against his will—for the Agency. If I find out you were part of that? I'll hunt you down and I'll kill you."

She didn't blink, didn't flinch, didn't move. She just stood there, looking back into his eyes. But she finally nodded. "I don't work for the Agency," she said again, and she turned and went out the door.

This time, Decker let her go.

The hotel bar was still open, and Dave held out a stool for Sophia, before dragging his sorry, tired ass onto the next one over.

"Whoo-hoo," he said. "Isn't this where we celebrate? Mission accomplished? Oh, yeah, except for the body count, which includes a good friend."

"That wasn't your fault," Sophia said quietly.

Yeah, right. Dave closed his eyes and rested his head on his arms, right there on the bar. "Let's get shit-faced drunk."

She laughed. It was, however, very, very sad, very soft laughter.

"I'm serious, Soph," he said, lifting his head to look at her. "This thing with Nash hasn't quite kicked in, and when it does, I'm going to be a mess. And dear God, *Tess* . . . How do you ever recover from something like that?"

He realized what he'd said as the words left his mouth.

Murphy had had to recover. And so had Sophia, whose husband had died as violently as both Angelina and Nash had.

Dave winced as he sat back up. "I'm sorry. That was insensitive."

But she shook her head and answered as if his question had been real, not rhetorical. "If you're me," she said slowly, "you spend a few years in a fantasy world, imagining that you're in love with someone you probably instinctively know will never—can never—return your affection. Which is good, because that makes this place really safe, which is what you need for a while. But then one day you wake up and you think, *Hmm, I'm alive.* And *Maybe I should see what happens if I spend a little time with someone who truly loves me. . . .*"

Dave just looked at her. "I have no clue what you just told me," he finally said. "It sounded important, but . . ." He shook his head.

Sophia smiled, and she was so beautiful, he almost started to cry, because he couldn't help but think of Nash, who would never again see Tess's equally beautiful smile. Of Tess, who wouldn't smile again, for a long, long time. It was so goddamn unfair.

"I heard what you said," Sophia told him, "when you were in the car with Jenk and Lindsey and . . . I pretended that I didn't hear it, because I couldn't . . . It was too much, you know? So I hung up on you and pretended we lost the connection."

Oh, good. "You mean . . ." *I'm in love with you* . . . This was going to be the perfect crappy end to his outrageously crappy day.

"Can I take your order, folks?" And yes, that was the bartender, because what Dave absolutely needed right now was an audience for his humiliation.

He gestured for Sophia to go first, more than half expecting her to make her excuses and go up to her hotel room, reminding himself that, unlike James Nash, at least he wasn't dead.

But Sophia apparently really needed that drink. "I'd like a glass of wine," she told the barkeep, who was a good-looking young man, clearly appreciative of beautiful women. "Do you have Shiraz?"

"Yes, ma'am." He forced himself to stop smiling into her eyes and turned to Dave. "Sir?"

"Shot of whiskey," he said. "Lower shelf, make it burn. Keep 'em coming. Beer chaser." He looked over at the tap. "Alaskan Amber. Start a tab, please—room 515."

"Sir, yes sir." The bartender looked at Sophia and winked. "Looks like you got yourself a real cowboy there, ma'am."

"I do," she said. "Dave saved my life tonight. And I mean that very literally."

"Oh please." Dave rolled his eyes.

"But a friend of ours just died," Sophia told the man, "so if you wouldn't mind adding the word *quickly* to our order . . . ?"

Shazam. Way to magically make their drinks appear. The bartender left the whiskey bottle, too, vanishing down to the other end of the bar, because his need to avoid the people with the dead friend trumped even a woman as pretty as Sophia.

Dave glanced at her as he picked up his shot glass. "Way to go." The whiskey burned all the way down, making his eyes tear—which maybe wasn't such a good idea—as he braced himself for Sophia's gentle letdown.

I'm so glad we're friends was how it would start. Or maybe, *We've been friends for so long . . .*

"Have you ever thought about having children?" she asked as she delicately sipped her wine, as his beer went down much colder than that whiskey had. She smiled at his confusion. "I was just thinking about Eden and . . ." Her smile faded. "A few years ago, I had a miscarriage. I was barely even three months along, and . . . It was awful. I can't imagine what she's feeling tonight."

"I'm sorry," Dave said. Dear God, life could be a real bitch. "You didn't . . . want to try again?"

Sophia shook her head. "I focused on my company. Work became my baby. I was afraid to . . . And then Dimitri . . . You know."

Dave did know. Dimitri had died. "I'm sorry," he said again. It was the refrain of the evening.

"So . . . have you?" she asked. "Thought about it?"

"Having children?" He laughed. Poured himself another shot. "Not really. I mean, yeah, I grew up watching the *Cosby Show* and I always thought *I'd like to be a dad like that,* but . . ." He shrugged. "I'd also like to be a billionaire and an astronaut. Or even better, a billionaire astronaut." He toasted her and tossed back the whiskey.

"I'd like to have children," Sophia said, "and it's important to me that any man I start a relationship with is at least open to the idea."

It was then, as Dave was struggling to breathe again after that whiskey burn, that dawn broke.

Any man I start a relationship with . . .

"I'm open to the idea," Dave whispered, because his vocal cords appeared to have stopped functioning. He took a long slug of his beer, because, damnit, he had something he needed to say. Or maybe he didn't. Maybe this *wasn't* the time to mention that, in a weird way, by Nash's dying, maybe the universe had been set right. Decker was with Tess—as he should have been from the start and . . . Yeah, this was definitely not the moment for that conversation. Sophia had been on that chopper ride to the hospital with Decker and Tess. She'd surely seen what Dave had seen—Decker's protective and tender possessiveness of his dead friend's fiancée.

But it seemed as if, even before that, Sophia had come to the conclusion that Deck was never going to give her what she wanted.

Which, apparently, included children.

She gazed into her wineglass, as if she were embarrassed or even shy. "I've been thinking about it," she told him, "all day. What you said on the phone. And . . . I think I would like, very much, to spend some time with someone who loves me." She then turned and looked at him.

And there he was. Sitting on a stool in some crappy hotel bar, lost in the heaven that was Sophia's eyes.

"That would be me," he told her. "Of course, there's a lot of us in that subset," he felt compelled to point out. "Dan Gillman, for example . . ."

Sophia laughed and slid off her stool. "In that case, I guess I should go find Dan—"

Dave knew she was only teasing, but he caught her arm, reeled her in. "Don't. He's a . . . a child."

"Maybe," Sophia agreed, her hand on the back of his neck, in his hair, making his mouth go dry. "But he'd probably know when to stop talking and kiss me."

And it was then that hell froze over. It was then that it snowed in July. It was then that pigs flew. Because it was then that Sophia leaned over. And kissed Dave.

She *kissed* him, and her mouth was so soft . . .

Dave had always thought that he'd faint—he'd just drop, bang—if that ever happened. But he was wrong.

He didn't faint after all.

CHAPTER TWENTY-SEVEN

Eden didn't say much of anything to anyone.

She ate when the nurses brought the breakfast tray—when she was prompted. She took the medicine that was given her. She obediently watched the videos on taking care of her stitches, on her post-op care.

But she didn't say much. Not to Izzy. And certainly not to Danny when he came to visit.

And wasn't *that* a fun half hour?

Although it did spark a conversation that she'd been avoiding: *What are you going to do now?*

Izzy had been constant, to say the least. He'd stayed with her. He'd held her hand while the doctor explained why Pinkie had died. He was there when they brought the baby in to her and let her hold his tiny little body, and he'd held her tightly afterward, in his arms, as she'd wept.

He'd even cried a little, too.

But then he'd asked her, gently, who the father really was, and she realized what he must've known from the moment he'd seen Pinkie, before she'd regained consciousness after her surgery—that Richie wasn't the baby's father after all.

And she'd said, "I don't know," because she *didn't* know, and she'd grasped at straws: "Maybe someone else was there with Richie, that night . . ." But then she'd stopped, because she knew that Izzy no longer believed her.

She didn't blame him. *She* wouldn't have believed her.

So there wasn't much to say.

Except, *what are you going to do now* had been laid on the table.

Izzy started. "I'm going wheels up in a few days. I already spoke to the senior chief and he tried, but he couldn't get me leave—not right now. Not for a couple of weeks. But Lindsey volunteered to—"

"No," Eden interrupted him. "I don't need a babysitter. And I don't need you to come back early."

Izzy nodded. "Regardless, I've already put in the paperwork. I'll be back in San Diego on thirteen August—at the latest, and I'll have a whole month to—"

"Why bother?" Eden asked. "You shouldn't. You should just—" She exhaled wearily. "I'm not very good company, anyway. We'd just sit around staring at each other. I mean, I can't even have sex for, I don't know, *months*, so . . ."

He was silent, just watching her, a muscle jumping in his jaw.

"Well, I can't," she finally said.

Izzy nodded. "And since that's all I've ever wanted from you . . ." He stood up, a fluid burst of energy, as if he couldn't sit still another moment. "I know you're angry at the entire world, Eden, and since I'm a resident here—"

"I just want to be left alone," she implored him. God, God, don't let her start to cry again . . . "*How* long until we can get a divorce?" Izzy had told her that the health insurance company would look at them funny if they immediately turned around and dissolved their marriage.

He rubbed his forehead now, and she knew he had a headache. She had one, too. "I don't know, Eed. Let's just . . . I'll be back in a few weeks. Stay at the apartment until then, okay? Lindsey'll check in on you, and when I get back, we'll sort everything out."

Sort everything out. As if everything would be hunky-dory in a week or two. As if her heart and soul hadn't been burned to ashes in that horrible little box with Pinkie. As if she'd ever feel like smiling and laughing again.

"Okay," she said now, because it was easier than arguing. Because she knew that she could—and would—leave long before he returned.

Because she'd discovered that there *was* something worse than someone not believing her and ditching her in a Krispy Kreme.

It was Izzy—not believing her, yet still not cutting his losses and walking away.

• • •

Decker's shoes squeaked on the tile in the hospital corridor, as he looked for room 261.

It was kind of obnoxious—the noise that he made—and as he passed room after room, he tried walking on his toes, hoping he wasn't waking anyone.

The doctors had estimated at least another two weeks before release— maybe longer—which meant Decker would be back here tomorrow.

Wearing sneakers.

He stopped in front of 261. The door was closed, so he knocked softly, which was stupid, because Tess was injured. It was highly unlikely she was in there, dancing naked.

"Come in," she called, and Decker went in.

She was out of bed, sitting up, her eyes bright with tears, as if she'd been crying.

He would have thought that—eventually—she'd stop. Apparently not.

"How's he doing?" Deck asked.

"Freaking great—for a dead man." Jim Nash opened his eyes to look at Decker.

"He's awake," Decker said, somewhat inanely, to Tess.

She nodded. "He's pretty groggy."

Nash looked like shit warmed over. His skin was gray and he looked almost small in that hospital bed. He was hooked up to monitors and machines and IV tubes and God knows what-all. And yet he still managed to be a demanding son of a bitch.

"Are we really safe?" he asked. "Is Tess . . . ?"

Decker went over to him and kissed him on the forehead. "She's safe," he reassured his friend. "You're safe, I'm safe. Jules Cassidy helped me get you here. We're very safe."

Thank God for Jules Cassidy. When Decker had told him what he suspected was going on—that Nash was being blackmailed by someone from the Agency—Cassidy hadn't been surprised. Apparently, there was an ongoing, top secret FBI investigation into illegal Agency operations. The high-ranking FBI agent couldn't say too much about it, but when Decker had suggested that Nash not survive his gunshot wound from the recent battle with the Freedom Network, in order to pull him free from the Agency's grasp, Cassidy had nodded.

And he'd gone about making it happen, coming back into that conference room to say quietly to Decker, "Nash is dead." Meaning he'd successfully moved Nash from surgery to this safe location, while providing the necessary paperwork—and even a body—to convince the Agency's leaders that Nash would be taking all of his secrets with him to his grave.

"Does Dave . . . know I'm not dead?" Nash now asked.

Decker shook his head. "No."

"Who knows?"

Decker ticked them off on his fingers. "You, obviously. Me. Tess. Cassidy." That was it.

"Gotta tell Murph," Nash said. It really was a struggle for him to talk. "Don't let this . . . fuck him up . . ."

Decker looked at Tess, who nodded her agreement. "I trust Murphy," she said. "I trust Dave, too—"

"I can't," Decker said. "Tell him. Not without . . ." He cleared his throat. "He's been spending a lot of time with, um, Sophia. We have to draw the line."

Nash nodded. "It's your call."

And there Decker stood, just looking at his friend's legs beneath the hospital blanket. Because God knows it would've been too hard to stand there looking into Nash's eyes.

"You should have come to me," Decker said quietly. "You should have told me what was going on."

Nash laughed. Winced as if laughing hurt. "I just had this . . . exact same conversation . . . with Tess."

"You're going to have to talk to both of us," Decker told him. "About everything. Working for the Agency's Ghost Group . . . ?"

Nash glanced at his fiancée.

She leaned forward. Narrowed her eyes at him. "Did you *really* think I didn't know *some*thing like that was going on?"

Nash held out his hand to her, and she took it. "We're really safe?" he asked Decker again, his voice a whisper. "All of us?"

"We are," Decker promised him. "We're safe." He put his hand on Nash's head, the way he used to do to Ranger, when his dog was too keyed up to fall asleep. He gently covered Nash's eyes, gently forcing them to shut, and, with them closed, his friend finally relaxed into sleep.

Tess was watching him, and Deck met her gaze. "He's safe," he reassured her. "The Agency thinks he's dead. I made sure of it."

"Playing dead didn't work for Tim Ebersole," she pointed out.

"It worked for him for four months," Decker countered. "Hopefully we won't need Nash to stay dead for that long." He headed for the door. "We're going to fix this, Tess. I promise you."

"You need to sleep sometime, too," she called after him.

"I know," he called back. "There's one more thing I've got to do . . ."

Murphy was far more coherent the next time he woke up.

Hannah had curled up next to him on the bed, which was probably breaking all kind of hospital rules, but she was so tired, and she needed to feel him, safe and solid beside her, in order to fall asleep.

He was awake when she finally stirred. He was running his fingers through her hair, and Hannah just lay there for a while, enjoying the gentleness of his touch. She finally looked up at him, and he smiled.

"You need a good hosing down," he said. "I've been introducing you to the nurses as Hannah, who was raised by wolves."

She laughed as she moved off the bed, careful not to jostle him, settling back into a chair that was an olfactory-safe distance away. "Think they'll let me shower down the hall?" she asked. "Because I'm not leaving the hospital. Not even to shower."

"I think they're circulating a petition to make it mandatory," he said, spelling out both petition and mandatory with his fingers.

She shot him an easily recognized sign language message that was American, if not quite ASL, and he laughed. "Me, I've always loved the way you smell."

She nodded. "Right."

"I have," he admitted. "From day one, Han. I've always had a thing for you."

"So you marry my best friend?" she scoffed, but then looked down at her lap, because she knew what was coming, and she wasn't ready for this conversation. "Can we not talk about Angelina? I'm just . . . I want to talk about her but . . . Not today. I mean, I want you to know that I really am okay with being, well, your second choice. She was special. I know that."

A crumpled tissue landed in her lap, and she forced herself to look up at him. He was shaking his head at her.

"You don't want to talk about her," he chided, "except then you go and talk about her."

"I just wanted to say that one thing," Hannah defended herself.

"Don't I get to say one thing?" he countered.

"No," she said. "You don't."

Murphy laughed his disbelief. "Don't make me get out of this bed."

She rolled her eyes. "Okay. *One* thing."

"It was easier," he told her, spelling out the word, "to fall in love with Angelina, than it was to deal with the fact that I've always been in love with you. You remember the day after my father's funeral, when I told you that, you know . . ."

That Angelina had jumped him the night before, while she was out directing traffic after a high school basketball game. Hannah nodded. She remembered that night, very clearly.

"I came this close," Murphy held his thumb and forefinger apart about a half an inch, "to kissing you that night. But I was scared of losing you as a friend. And there was Angelina. And I have to admit, it was nice to be wanted. And then, I fell in love with her because . . . it was so damn easy. Don't get me wrong, I loved her. With all my heart. I still love her, I always will. But . . . I know I've told you this before—I'm not the same man I was back then. I'm different—and I'm more equipped to deal with things that are . . . harder.

"And I know that telling someone you love them in times of duress—" he spelled it out as he continued " —is maybe not the smartest thing in the world to do. Because maybe you only *think* you love me, and if that's true, that's okay, because I've learned, the hard way, that I can live without you. I'm a survivor, Han. I'm going to keep on keeping on, no matter how hard it gets. But I'd like—very much—to live the rest of my life with you. You're the love of my life—this new life that I've chosen."

Hannah waited, but he was finally done. And she had to give him shit—it was that or cry. "That was one thing?"

"I love you, Han," he said.

"I love you, too," she told him, her chest aching with the tears she wouldn't let herself cry. "But Vinh, you didn't choose to live. You got lucky. When you went out into the compound . . ."

"I wouldn't have done it without the body armor," he reminded her.

"Really?"

"Okay," he said, "you're right, I probably would have, but my only other option was to shoot Craig Reed. From where I was hiding, I had a pretty clear shot. But doing that would've definitely gotten me killed."

"You could've stayed hidden."

"No," Murphy said emphatically, "I couldn't. Look, Han, I was buying time, when I did what I did. I knew Jenkins and Gillman were coming with the trucks." He shook his head. "I remember hiding in the compound, and thinking, *I've got a future again.* I don't know exactly when it happened, when I started thinking that it'd be nice to do more than eat and sleep and get through another day. But I'm here. There. Here. And I *definitely* didn't want to die. I didn't bank on Reed trying to start a war with the FBI, though. That was a potentially fatal call. I thank God Decker was there."

Decker, who blamed himself for Angelina's death . . .

Hannah sat there, just looking at Murphy.

"He stopped in while you were sleeping," Murphy said, and at first she didn't understand. But then she did. *Decker* had stopped in. Which meant that Murphy knew about Nash.

"Deck told me Ebersole's still in intensive care," Murphy continued, spelling out ICU. "He's expected to survive. Reed was hogtied and delivered to the FBI by his own people for shooting Ebersole. The entire compound surrendered and Reed, Ebersole, and a bunch of other Freedom Network leaders are gonna go to jail for a long, long time. The FBI's still trying to ID the body that was supposed to be Ebersole's. It's all good."

Not all. "I'm so sorry about Jim Nash," Hannah said, and Murph held out his hand to her.

"Come here."

"Hannah of the wolves," she reminded him.

"I don't care," he said. "Maybe we should write that into our wedding vows. Through richer and poorer, through three days without a shower . . ."

Hannah just sat there, her heart in her throat.

"That was my kind of lame way of asking you to marry me," Murphy said.

She nodded. "I was thinking we could go to Juneau," she told him. "Maybe talk to Pat about getting the boat up and running. There's still plenty of summer left."

Now Murph had tears in his eyes. "Was that your kind of lame way of saying yes?" he asked her.

She nodded again. "Pat's looking to sell it," she said. "The *California Dreamin'*. I could probably swing it with the money from the insurance settlement, but I want to make sure I have enough for these cochlear hearing implants I was checking out, before you came back. They're expensive and there's no guarantee that they'll work, but, I want to give 'em a try."

"Definitely," Murphy said. "Besides, you know, I have . . . that insurance money from, you know . . ."

Angelina.

"She would love it if we used it to buy the boat," Murphy said quietly. "We could run the business, Han. You and me."

"Tourist season's only five months," she pointed out. "We couldn't earn the kind of money we'd make working someplace like Troubleshooters."

But Murphy was already shaking his head. "I'm not going back to that. I left it a long time ago." He held out his hand to her again. "Come. Here."

Hannah pushed herself out of her chair, and it was then, as she sat beside him on the bed that he used his hands to spell out three words.

Nash is alive.

His message was even better than the three words she was expecting, and she gazed at him in stunned surprise. He nodded, his smile wide.

"What—"

"Don't ask," he said. "And don't tell anyone. Just . . . kiss me, Hannah."

Despite the almost unbearable lightness and joy that had flooded her at Murphy's incredible news, she was still reluctant to get too close. "Let me go shower."

He shook his head as he smiled, and pulled her toward him. "Mmmm," he said after kissing her. "Good thing I'm a nature lover."

Hannah laughed her dismay. "I don't really smell *that* bad, do I?"

"You kind of do." But Murphy caught her by the belt and pulled her in to kiss him again. "But you know the way clean's on your wishlist?" he told her, contentment in his dark brown eyes. "I've got just one thing on mine. *You.*"

No doubt about it, life was good.

ABOUT THE AUTHOR

Since her explosion onto the publishing scene more than ten years ago, SUZANNE BROCKMANN has written more than forty books, and is now widely recognized as one of the leading voices in romantic suspense. Her work has earned her repeated appearances on the *USA Today* and *New York Times* bestseller lists, as well as numerous awards, including Romance Writers of America's #1 Favorite Book of the Year (three years running), two RITA Awards, and many *Romantic Times* Reviewer's Choice Awards. Suzanne Brockmann lives west of Boston with her husband, author Ed Gaffney.

ABOUT THE TYPE

This book was set in Electra, a typeface designed for Linotype by W. A. Dwiggins, the renowned type designer (1880-1956). Electra is a fluid typeface, avoiding the contrasts of thick and thin strokes that are prevalent in most modern typefaces.